Fyodor Mikhailovich Dostoevsky (11 November 1821 – 9 February 1881), sometimes transliterated Dostoyevsky, was a Russian novelist, short story writer, essayist, journalist and philosopher. Dostoevsky's literary works explore human psychology in the troubled political, social, and spiritual atmospheres of 19th-century Russia, and engage with a variety of philosophical and religious themes. His most acclaimed works include Crime and Punishment (1866), The Idiot (1869), Demons (1872) and The Brothers Karamazov (1880). Dostoevsky's oeuvre consists of 11 novels, three novellas, 17 short stories and numerous other works. Many literary critics rate him as one of the greatest psychologists in world literature. His 1864 novella Notes from Underground is considered to be one of the first works of existentialist literature. Born in Moscow in 1821, Dostoevsky was introduced to literature at an early age through fairy tales and legends, and through books by Russian and foreign authors. His mother died in 1837 when he was 15, and around the same time, he left school to enter the Nikolayev Military Engineering Institute.(Source: Wikipedia)

Literary works:

(1846) Poor Folk (novella)
(1846) The Double (novella)
(1847) The Landlady (novella)
(1849) Netochka Nezvanova (unfinished)
(1859) Uncle's Dream (novella)
(1859) The Village of Stepanchikovo
(1861) Humiliated and Insulted
(1862) The House of the Dead
(1864) Notes from Underground (novella)
(1866) Crime and Punishment
(1867) The Gambler (novella)
(1869) The Idiot
(1870) The Eternal Husband (novella)
(1872) Demons (also titled: The Possessed, The Devils)
(1875) The Adolescent
(1880) The Brothers Karamazov

DEMONS

FYODOR DOSTOYEVSKY

PRINCE CLASSICS

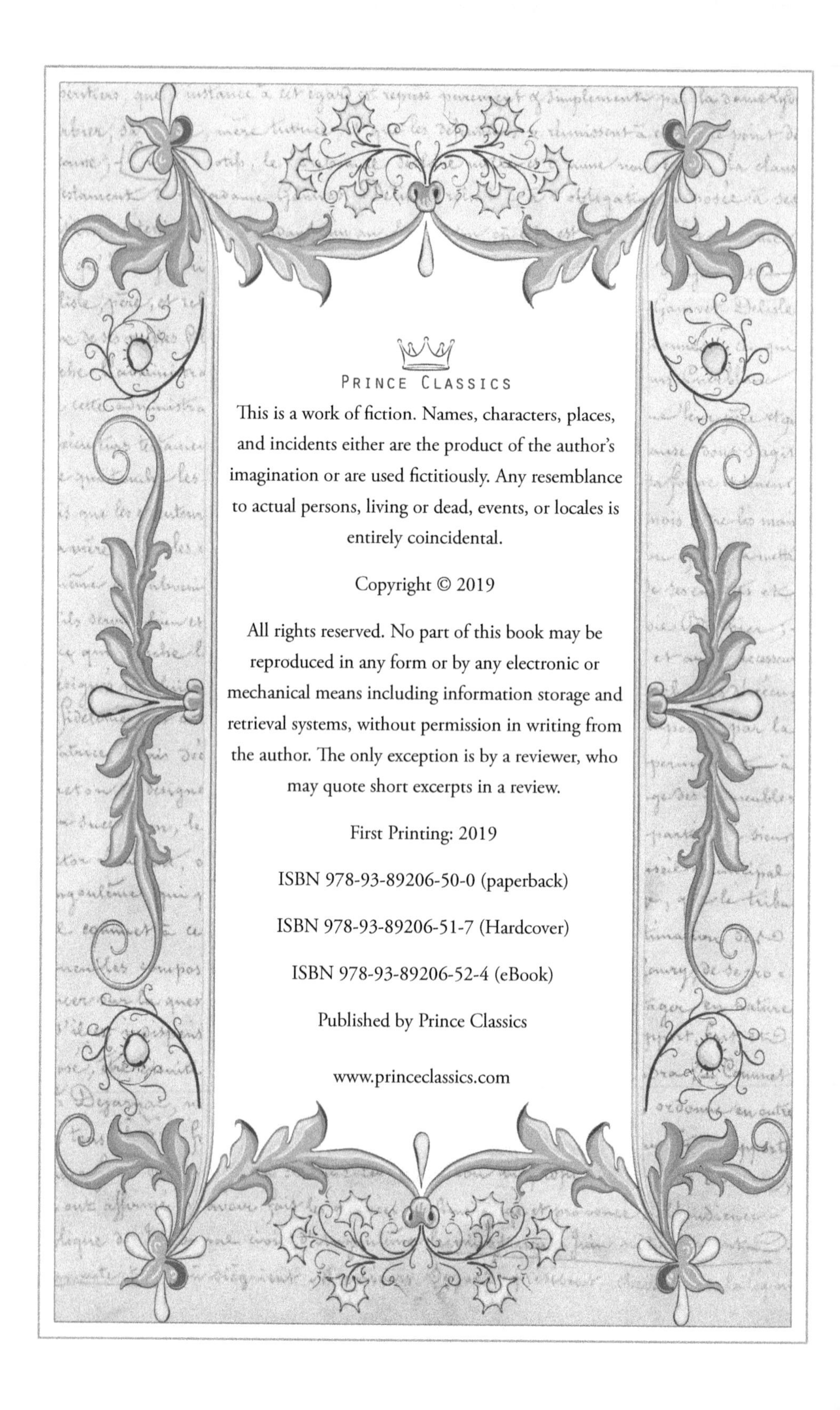

PRINCE CLASSICS

First Printing: 2019

ISBN 978-93-89206-50-0 (paperback)

ISBN 978-93-89206-51-7 (Hardcover)

ISBN 978-93-89206-52-4 (eBook)

Published by Prince Classics

www.princeclassics.com

Contents

DEMONS

"Strike me dead, the track has vanished,
Well, what now? We've lost the way,
Demons have bewitched our horses,
Led us in the wilds astray.
"What a number! Whither drift they?
What's the mournful dirge they sing?
Do they hail a witch's marriage
Or a goblin's burying?"

A. Pushkin.

"And there was one herd of many swine feeding on this mountain; and they besought him that he would suffer them to enter into them. And he suffered them.
"Then went the devils out of the man and entered into the swine; and the herd ran violently down a steep place into the lake and were choked.
"When they that fed them saw what was done, they fled, and went and told it in the city and in the country.
"Then they went out to see what was done; and came to Jesus and found the man, out of whom the devils were departed, sitting at the feet of Jesus, clothed and in his right mind; and they were afraid."

Luke, ch. viii. 32-37.

PART I

CHAPTER I. INTRODUCTORY

turned out afterwards that there had been no "vortex" and even no "circumstances," at least in that connection. I only learned the other day to my intense amazement, though on the most unimpeachable authority, that Stepan Trofimovitch had lived among us in our province not as an "exile" as we were accustomed to believe, and had never even been under police supervision at all. Such is the force of imagination! All his life he sincerely believed that in certain spheres he was a constant cause of apprehension, that every step he took was watched and noted, and that each on ry moral nobility of certain knights at a certain epoch or something of that nature.

Some lofty and exceptionally noble idea was maintained in it, anyway. It was said afterwards that the continuation was hurriedly forbidden and even that the progressive review had to suffer for having printed the first part. That may very well have been so, for what was not possible in those days? Though, in this case, it is more likely that there was nothing of the kind, and that the author himself was too lazy to conclude his essay. He cut short his lectures on the Arabs because, somehow and by someone (probably one of his reactionary enemies) a letter had been seized giving an account of certain circumstances, in consequence of which someone had demanded an explanation from him. I don't know whether the story is true, but it was asserted that at the same time there was discovered in Petersburg a vast, unnatural, and illegal conspiracy of thirty people which almost shook society to its foundations. It was said that they were positively on the point of translating Fourier. As though of design a poem of Stepan Trofimovitch's was seized in Moscow at that very time, though it had been written six years before in Berlin in his earliest youth, and manuscript copies had been passed round a circle consisting of two poetical amateurs and one student. This poem is lying now on my table. No longer ago than last year I received a recent copy in his own handwriting from Stepan Trofimovitch himself, signed by him, and bound in a splendid red leather binding. It is not without poetic merit, however, and even a certain talent. It's strange, but in those days (or to be more exact, in the thirties) people were constantly composing in that style. I find it difficult to describe the subject, for I really do not understand it. It is some sort of an allegory in lyrical-dramatic form, recalling the second part of Faust. The scene opens with a chorus of women, followed by a chorus of men, then a chorus of incorporeal powers of some sort, and at the end of all a chorus of spirits not yet living but very eager to come to life. All these choruses sing about something very indefinite, for the most part about somebody's curse, but with a tinge of the higher humour. But the scene is suddenly changed. There begins a sort of "festival of life" at which even insects sing, a tortoise comes on the scene with certain sacramental Latin words, and even, if I remember aright, a mineral sings about something that is a quite inanimate object. In fact, they all sing continually, or if they converse, it is simply to abuse one another vaguely, but again with a tinge of higher meaning. At last the scene is changed again;

a wilderness appears, and among the rocks there wanders a civilized young man who picks and sucks certain herbs. Asked by a fairy why he sucks these herbs, he answers that, conscious of a superfluity of life in himself, he seeks forgetfulness, and finds it in the juice of these herbs, but that his great desire is to lose his reason at once (a desire possibly superfluous). Then a youth of indescribable beauty rides in on a black steed, and an immense multitude of all nations follow him. The youth represents death, for whom all the peoples are yearning. And finally, in the last scene we are suddenly shown the Tower of Babel, and certain athletes at last finish building it with a song of new hope, and when at length they complete the topmost pinnacle, the lord (of Olympia, let us say) takes flight in a comic fashion, and man, grasping the situation and seizing his place, at once begins a new life with new insight into things. Well, this poem was thought at that time to be dangerous. Last year I proposed to Stepan Trofimovitch to publish it, on the ground of its perfect harmlessness nowadays, but he declined the suggestion with evident dissatisfaction. My view of its complete harmlessness evidently displeased him, and I even ascribe to it a certain coldness on his part, which lasted two whole months.

And what do you think? Suddenly, almost at the time I proposed printing it here, our poem was published abroad in a collection of revolutionary verse, without the knowledge of Stepan Trofimovitch. He was at first alarmed, rushed to the governor, and wrote a noble letter in self-defence to Petersburg. He read it to me twice, but did not send it, not knowing to whom to address it. In fact he was in a state of agitation for a whole month, but I am convinced that in the secret recesses of his heart he was enormously flattered. He almost took the copy of the collection to bed with him, and kept it hidden under his mattress in the daytime; he positively would not allow the women to turn his bed, and although he expected every day a telegram, he held his head high. No telegram came. Then he made friends with me again, which is a proof of the extreme kindness of his gentle and unresentful heart.

II

Of course I don't assert that he had never suffered for his convictions at all, but I am fully convinced that he might have gone on lecturing on his Arabs as long as he liked, if he had only given the necessary explanations. But he was too lofty, and he proceeded with peculiar haste to assure himself that his career was ruined forever "by the vortex of circumstance." And if the whole truth is to be told the real cause of the change in his career was the very delicate proposition which had been made before and was then renewed by Varvara Petrovna Stavrogin, a lady of great wealth, the wife of a lieutenant-general, that he should undertake the education and the whole intellectual development of her only son in the capacity of a superior sort of teacher and friend, to say nothing of a magnificent salary. This proposal had been made to him the first time in Berlin, at the moment when he was first left a widower. His first wife was a frivolous girl from our province, whom he married in his early and unthinking youth, and apparently he had had a great deal of trouble with this young person, charming as she was, owing to the lack of means for her support; and also from other, more delicate, reasons. She died in Paris after three years' separation from him, leaving him a son of five years old; "the fruit of our first, joyous, and unclouded love," were the words the sorrowing father once let fall in my presence.

The child had, from the first, been sent back to Russia, where he was brought up in the charge of distant cousins in some remote region. Stepan Trofimovitch had declined Varvara

Petrovna's proposal on that occasion and had quickly married again, before the year was over, a taciturn Berlin girl, and, what makes it more strange, there was no particular necessity for him to do so. But apart from his marriage there were, it appears, other reasons for his declining the situation. He was tempted by the resounding fame of a professor, celebrated at that time, and he, in his turn, hastened to the lecturer's chair for which he had been preparing himself, to try his eagle wings in flight. But now with singed wings he naturally remembered the proposition which even then had made him hesitate. The sudden death of his second wife, who did not live a year with him, settled the matter decisively. To put it plainly it was all brought about by the passionate sympathy and priceless, so to speak, classic friendship of Varvara Petrovna, if one may use such an expression of friendship. He flung himself into the arms of this friendship, and his position was settled for more than twenty years. I use the expression "flung himself into the arms of," but God forbid that anyone should fly to idle and superfluous conclusions. These embraces must be understood only in the most loftily moral sense. The most refined and delicate tie united these two beings, both so remarkable, forever.

The post of tutor was the more readily accepted too, as the property—a very small one—left to Stepan Trofimovitch by his first wife was close to Skvoreshniki, the Stavrogins' magnificent estate on the outskirts of our provincial town. Besides, in the stillness of his study, far from the immense burden of university work, it was always possible to devote himself to the service of science, and to enrich the literature of his country with erudite studies. These works did not appear. But on the other hand it did appear possible to spend the rest of his life, more than twenty years, "a reproach incarnate," so to speak, to his native country, in the words of a popular poet:

Reproach incarnate thou didst stand Erect before thy Fatherland, O Liberal idealist!

But the person to whom the popular poet referred may perhaps have had the right to adopt that pose for the rest of his life if he had wished to do so, though it must have been tedious. Our Stepan Trofimovitch was, to tell the truth, only an imitator compared with such people; moreover, he had grown weary of standing erect and often lay down for a while. But, to do him justice, the "incarnation of reproach" was preserved even in the recumbent attitude, the more so as that was quite sufficient for the province. You should have seen him at our club when he sat down to cards. His whole figure seemed to exclaim "Cards! Me sit down to whist with you! Is it consistent? Who is responsible for it? Who has shattered my energies and turned them to whist? Ah, perish, Russia!" and he would majestically trump with a heart.

And to tell the truth he dearly loved a game of cards, which led him, especially in later years, into frequent and unpleasant skirmishes with Varvara Petrovna, particularly as he was always losing. But of that later. I will only observe that he was a man of tender conscience (that is, sometimes) and so was often depressed. In the course of his twenty years' friendship with Varvara Petrovna he used regularly, three or four times a year, to sink into a state of "patriotic grief," as it was called among us, or rather really into an attack of spleen, but our estimable Varvara Petrovna preferred the former phrase. Of late years his grief had begun to be not only patriotic, but at times alcoholic too; but Varvara Petrovna's alertness succeeded in keeping him all his life from trivial inclinations. And he needed someone to look after him indeed, for he sometimes behaved very oddly: in the midst of his exalted sorrow he would begin laughing like any simple peasant. There were moments when he began to take a humorous tone even about himself. But there was nothing Varvara Petrovna dreaded so much as a humorous tone. She was a woman of the classic type, a female Mæcenas, invariably guided only by the highest considerations. The influence of this exalted lady over her poor friend for twenty years is a fact of the first importance. I shall need to speak of her more particularly, which I now proceed to do.

III

There are strange friendships. The two friends are always ready to fly at one another, and go on like that all their lives, and yet they cannot separate. Parting, in fact, is utterly impossible. The one who has begun the quarrel and separated will be the first to fall ill and even die, perhaps, if the separation comes off. I know for a positive fact that several times Stepan Trofimovitch has jumped up from the sofa and beaten the wall with his fists after the most intimate and emotional tête-à-tête with Varvara Petrovna.

This proceeding was by no means an empty symbol; indeed, on one occasion, he broke some plaster off the wall. It may be asked how I come to know such delicate details. What if I were myself a witness of it? What if Stepan Trofimovitch himself has, on more than one occasion, sobbed on my shoulder while he described to me in lurid colours all his most secret feelings. (And what was there he did not say at such times!) But what almost always happened after these tearful outbreaks was that next day he was ready to crucify himself for his ingratitude. He would send for me in a hurry or run over to see me simply to assure me that Varvara Petrovna was "an angel of honour and delicacy, while he was very much the opposite." He did not only run to confide in me, but, on more than one occasion, described it all to her in the most eloquent letter, and wrote a full signed confession that no longer ago than the day before he had told an outsider that she kept him out of vanity, that she was envious of his talents and erudition, that she hated him and was only afraid to express her hatred openly, dreading that he would leave her and so damage her literary reputation, that this drove him to self-contempt, and he was resolved to die a violent death, and that he was waiting for the final word from her which would decide everything, and so on and so on in the same style. You can fancy after this what an hysterical pitch the nervous outbreaks of this most innocent of all fifty-year-old infants sometimes reached! I once read one of these letters after some quarrel between them, arising from a trivial matter, but growing venomous as it went on. I was horrified and besought him not to send it.

"I must … more honourable … duty … I shall die if I don't confess everything, everything!" he answered almost in delirium, and he did send the letter.

That was the difference between them, that Varvara Petrovna never would have sent such a letter. It is true that he was passionately fond of writing, he wrote to her though he lived in the same house, and during hysterical interludes he would write two letters a day. I know for a fact that she always read these letters with the greatest attention, even when she received two a day, and after reading them she put them away in a special drawer, sorted and annotated; moreover, she pondered them in her heart. But she kept her friend all day without an answer, met him as though there were nothing the matter, exactly as though nothing special had happened the day before. By degrees she broke him in so completely that at last he did not himself dare to allude to what had happened the day before, and only glanced into her eyes at times. But she never forgot anything, while he sometimes forgot too quickly, and encouraged by her composure he would not infrequently, if friends came in, laugh and make jokes over the champagne the very same day. With what malignancy she must have looked at him at such moments, while he noticed nothing! Perhaps in a week's time, a month's time, or even six months later, chancing to recall some phrase in such a letter, and then the whole letter with all its attendant circumstances, he would suddenly grow hot with shame, and be so upset that he fell ill with one of his attacks of "summer cholera." These attacks of a sort of "summer cholera" were, in some cases, the regular consequence of his nervous agitations and were an interesting peculiarity of his physical constitution.

No doubt Varvara Petrovna did very often hate him. But there was one thing he had not discerned up to the end: that was that he had become for her a son, her creation, even, one may say, her invention; he had become flesh of her flesh, and she kept and supported him not simply from "envy of his talents." And how wounded she must have been by such suppositions! An inexhaustible love for him lay concealed in her heart in the midst of continual hatred, jealousy, and contempt. She would not let a speck of dust fall upon him, coddled him up for twenty-two years, would not have slept for nights together if there were the faintest breath against his reputation as a poet, a learned man, and a public character. She had invented him, and had been the first to believe in her own invention. He was, after a fashion, her day-dream.... But in return she exacted a great deal from him, sometimes even slavishness. It was incredible how long she harboured resentment. I have two anecdotes to tell about that.

IV

On one occasion, just at the time when the first rumours of the emancipation of the serfs were in the air, when all Russia was exulting and making ready for a complete regeneration, Varvara Petrovna was visited by a baron from Petersburg, a man of the highest connections, and very closely associated with the new reform. Varvara Petrovna prized such visits highly, as her connections in higher circles had grown weaker and weaker since the death of her husband, and had at last ceased altogether. The baron spent an hour drinking tea with her. There was no one else present but Stepan Trofimovitch, whom Varvara Petrovna invited and exhibited. The baron had heard something about him before or affected to have done so, but paid little attention to him at tea. Stepan Trofimovitch of course was incapable of making a social blunder, and his manners were most elegant. Though I believe he was by no means of exalted origin, yet it happened that he had from earliest childhood been brought up in a Moscow household—of high rank, and consequently was well bred. He spoke French like a Parisian. Thus the baron was to have seen from the first glance the sort of people with whom Varvara Petrovna surrounded herself, even in provincial seclusion. But things did not fall out like this. When the baron positively asserted the absolute truth of the rumours of the great reform, which were then only just beginning to be heard, Stepan Trofimovitch could not contain himself, and suddenly shouted "Hurrah!" and even made some gesticulation indicative of delight. His ejaculation was not over-loud and quite polite, his delight was even perhaps premeditated, and his gesture purposely studied before the looking-glass half an hour before tea. But something must have been amiss with it, for the baron permitted himself a faint smile, though he, at once, with extraordinary courtesy, put in a phrase concerning the universal and befitting emotion of all Russian hearts in view of the great event. Shortly afterwards he took his leave and at parting did not forget to hold out two fingers to Stepan Trofimovitch. On returning to the drawing-room Varvara Petrovna was at first silent for two or three minutes, and seemed to be looking for something on the table. Then she turned to Stepan Trofimovitch, and with pale face and flashing eyes she hissed in a whisper:

"I shall never forgive you for that!"

Next day she met her friend as though nothing had happened, she never referred to the incident, but thirteen years afterwards, at a tragic moment, she recalled it and reproached him with it, and she turned pale, just as she had done thirteen years before. Only twice in the course of her life did she say to him:

"I shall never forgive you for that!"

The incident with the baron was the second time, but the first incident was so characteristic and had so much influence on the fate of Stepan Trofimovitch that I venture to refer to that too.

It was in 1855, in spring-time, in May, just after the news had reached Skvoreshniki of the death of Lieutenant-General Stavrogin, a frivolous old gentleman who died of a stomach ailment on the way to the Crimea, where he was hastening to join the army on active service. Varvara Petrovna was left a widow and put on deep mourning. She could not, it is true, deplore his death very deeply, since, for the last four years, she had been completely separated from him owing to incompatibility of temper, and was giving him an allowance. (The Lieutenant-General himself had nothing but one hundred and fifty serfs and his pay, besides his position and his connections. All the money and Skvoreshniki belonged to Varvara Petrovna, the only daughter of a very rich contractor.) Yet she was shocked by the suddenness of the news, and retired into complete solitude. Stepan Trofimovitch, of course, was always at her side.

May was in its full beauty. The evenings were exquisite. The wild cherry was in flower. The two friends walked every evening in the garden and used to sit till nightfall in the arbour, and pour out their thoughts and feelings to one another. They had poetic moments. Under the influence of the change in her position, Varvara Petrovna talked more than usual. She, as it were, clung to the heart of her friend, and this continued for several evenings. A strange idea suddenly came over Stepan Trofimovitch: "Was not the inconsolable widow reckoning upon him, and expecting from him, when her mourning was over, the offer of his hand?" A cynical idea, but the very loftiness of a man's nature sometimes increases a disposition to cynical ideas if only from the many-sidedness of his culture. He began to look more deeply into it, and thought it seemed like it. He pondered: "Her fortune is immense, of course, but ..." Varvara Petrovna certainly could not be called a beauty. She was a tall, yellow, bony woman with an extremely long face, suggestive of a horse. Stepan Trofimovitch hesitated more and more, he was tortured by doubts, he positively shed tears of indecision once or twice (he wept not infrequently). In the evenings, that is to say in the arbour, his countenance involuntarily began to express something capricious and ironical, something coquettish and at the same time condescending. This is apt to happen as it were by accident, and the more gentlemanly the man the more noticeable it is. Goodness only knows what one is to think about it, but it's most likely that nothing had begun working in her heart that could have fully justified Stepan Trofimovitch's suspicions. Moreover, she would not have changed her name, Stavrogin, for his name, famous as it was. Perhaps there was nothing in it but the play of femininity on her side; the manifestation of an unconscious feminine yearning so natural in some extremely feminine types. However, I won't answer for it; the depths of the female heart have not been explored to this day. But I must continue.

It is to be supposed that she soon inwardly guessed the significance of her friend's strange expression; she was quick and observant, and he was sometimes extremely guileless. But the evenings went on as before, and their conversations were just as poetic and interesting. And behold on one occasion at nightfall, after the most lively and poetical conversation, they parted affectionately, warmly pressing each other's hands at the steps of the lodge where Stepan Trofimovitch slept. Every summer he used to move into this little lodge which stood adjoining the huge seignorial house of Skvoreshniki, almost in the garden. He had only just gone in, and in restless hesitation taken a cigar, and not having yet lighted it, was standing weary and motionless before the open window, gazing at the light feathery white clouds gliding around the bright moon, when suddenly a faint rustle made him start and turn round. Varvara Petrovna, whom he had left only four minutes earlier, was standing before him again. Her yellow face was almost blue. Her lips were pressed tightly together and twitching at the corners. For ten full seconds she looked him in the eyes in silence with a firm relentless gaze, and suddenly whispered rapidly:

"I shall never forgive you for this!"

When, ten years later, Stepan Trofimovitch, after closing the doors, told me this melancholy tale in a whisper, he vowed that he had been so petrified on the spot that he had not seen or heard how Varvara Petrovna had disappeared. As she never once afterwards alluded to the incident and everything went on as though nothing had happened, he was all his life inclined to the idea that it was all an hallucination, a symptom of illness, the more so as he was actually taken ill that very night and was indisposed for a fortnight, which, by the way, cut short the interviews in the arbour.

But in spite of his vague theory of hallucination he seemed every day, all his life, to be expecting the continuation, and, so to say, the dénouement of this affair. He could not believe that that was the end of it! And if so he must have looked strangely sometimes at his friend.

V

She had herself designed the costume for him which he wore for the rest of his life. It was elegant and characteristic; a long black frock-coat, buttoned almost to the top, but stylishly cut; a soft hat (in summer a straw hat) with a wide brim, a white batiste cravat with a full bow and hanging ends, a cane with a silver knob; his hair flowed on to his shoulders. It was dark brown, and only lately had begun to get a little grey. He was clean-shaven. He was said to have been very handsome in his youth. And, to my mind, he was still an exceptionally impressive figure even in old age. Besides, who can talk of old age at fifty-three? From his special pose as a patriot, however, he did not try to appear younger, but seemed rather to pride himself on the solidity of his age, and, dressed as described, tall and thin with flowing hair, he looked almost like a patriarch, or even more like the portrait of the poet Kukolnik, engraved in the edition of his works published in 1830 or thereabouts. This resemblance was especially striking when he sat in the garden in summertime, on a seat under a bush of flowering lilac, with both hands propped on his cane and an open book beside him, musing poetically over the setting sun. In regard to books I may remark that he came in later years rather to avoid reading. But that was only quite towards the end. The papers and magazines ordered in great profusion by Varvara Petrovna he was continually reading. He never lost interest in the successes of Russian literature either, though he always maintained a dignified attitude with regard to them. He was at one time engrossed in the study of our home and foreign politics, but he soon gave up the undertaking with a gesture of despair. It sometimes happened that he would take De Tocqueville with him into the garden while he had a Paul de Kock in his pocket. But these are trivial matters.

I must observe in parenthesis about the portrait of Kukolnik; the engraving had first come into the hands of Varvara Petrovna when she was a girl in a high-class boarding-school in Moscow. She fell in love with the portrait at once, after the habit of all girls at school who fall in love with anything they come across, as well as with their teachers, especially the drawing and writing masters. What is interesting in this, though, is not the characteristics of girls but the fact that even at fifty Varvara Petrovna kept the engraving among her most intimate and treasured possessions, so that perhaps it was only on this account that she had designed for Stepan Trofimovitch a costume somewhat like the poet's in the engraving. But that, of course, is a trifling matter too.

For the first years or, more accurately, for the first half of the time he spent with Varvara Petrovna, Stepan Trofimovitch was still planning a book and every day seriously prepared to write it. But during the later period, he must have forgotten even what he had done. More and more frequently he used to say to us:

"I seem to be ready for work, my materials are collected, yet the work doesn't get done! Nothing is done!"

And he would bow his head dejectedly. No doubt this was calculated to increase his prestige in our eyes as a martyr to science, but he himself was longing for something else. "They have forgotten me! I'm no use to anyone!" broke from him more than once. This intensified depression took special hold of him towards the end of the fifties. Varvara Petrovna realised at last that it was a serious matter. Besides, she could not endure the idea that her friend was forgotten and useless. To distract him and at the same time to renew his fame she carried him off to Moscow, where she had fashionable acquaintances in the literary and scientific world; but it appeared that Moscow too was unsatisfactory.

It was a peculiar time; something new was beginning, quite unlike the stagnation of the past, something very strange too, though it was felt everywhere, even at Skvoreshniki. Rumours of all sorts reached us. The facts were generally more or less well known, but it was evident that in addition to the facts there were certain ideas accompanying them, and what's more, a great number of them. And this was perplexing. It was impossible to estimate and find out exactly what was the drift of these ideas. Varvara Petrovna was prompted by the feminine composition of her character to a compelling desire to penetrate the secret of them. She took to reading newspapers and magazines, prohibited publications printed abroad and even the revolutionary manifestoes which were just beginning to appear at the time (she was able to procure them all); but this only set her head in a whirl. She fell to writing letters; she got few answers, and they grew more incomprehensible as time went on. Stepan Trofimovitch was solemnly called upon to explain "these ideas" to her once for all, but she remained distinctly dissatisfied with his explanations.

Stepan Trofimovitch's view of the general movement was supercilious in the extreme. In his eyes all it amounted to was that he was forgotten and of no use. At last his name was mentioned, at first in periodicals published abroad as that of an exiled martyr, and immediately afterwards in Petersburg as that of a former star in a celebrated constellation. He was even for some reason compared with Radishtchev. Then someone printed the statement that he was dead and promised an obituary notice of him. Stepan Trofimovitch instantly perked up and assumed an air of immense dignity. All his disdain for his contemporaries evaporated and he began to cherish the dream of joining the movement and showing his powers. Varvara Petrovna's faith in everything instantly revived and she was thrown into a violent ferment. It was decided to go to Petersburg without a moment's delay, to find out everything on the spot, to go into everything personally, and, if possible, to throw themselves heart and soul into the new movement. Among other things she announced that she was prepared to found a magazine of her own, and henceforward to devote her whole life to it. Seeing what it had come to, Stepan Trofimovitch became more condescending than ever, and on the journey began to behave almost patronisingly to Varvara Petrovna—which she at once laid up in her heart against him. She had, however, another very important reason for the trip, which was to renew her connections in higher spheres. It was necessary, as far as she could, to remind the world of her existence, or at any rate to make an attempt to do so. The ostensible object of the journey was to see her only son, who was just finishing his studies at a Petersburg lyceum.

VI

They spent almost the whole winter season in Petersburg. But by Lent everything burst like a rainbow-coloured soap-bubble.

Their dreams were dissipated, and the muddle, far from being cleared up, had become even more revoltingly incomprehensible. To begin with, connections with the higher spheres were not established, or only on a microscopic scale, and by humiliating exertions. In her mortification Varvara Petrovna threw herself heart and soul into the "new ideas," and began giving evening receptions. She invited literary people, and they were brought to her at once in multitudes. Afterwards they came of themselves without invitation, one brought another. Never had she seen such literary men. They were incredibly vain, but quite open in their vanity, as though they were performing a duty by the display of it. Some (but by no means all) of them even turned up intoxicated, seeming, however, to detect in this a peculiar, only recently discovered, merit. They were all strangely proud of something. On every face was written that they had only just discovered some extremely important secret. They abused one another, and took credit to themselves for it. It was rather difficult to find out what they had written exactly, but among them there were critics, novelists, dramatists, satirists, and exposers of abuses. Stepan Trofimovitch penetrated into their very highest circle from which the movement was directed. Incredible heights had to be scaled to reach this group; but they gave him a cordial welcome, though, of course, no one of them had ever heard of him or knew anything about him except that he "represented an idea." His manœuvres among them were so successful that he got them twice to Varvara Petrovna's salon in spite of their Olympian grandeur. These people were very serious and very polite; they behaved nicely; the others were evidently afraid of them; but it was obvious that they had no time to spare. Two or three former literary celebrities who happened to be in Petersburg, and with whom Varvara Petrovna had long maintained a most refined correspondence, came also. But to her surprise these genuine and quite indubitable celebrities were stiller than water, humbler than the grass, and some of them simply hung on to this new rabble, and were shamefully cringing before them. At first Stepan Trofimovitch was a success. People caught at him and began to exhibit him at public literary gatherings. The first time he came on to the platform at some public reading in which he was to take part, he was received with enthusiastic clapping which lasted for five minutes. He recalled this with tears nine years afterwards, though rather from his natural artistic sensibility than from gratitude. "I swear, and I'm ready to bet," he declared (but only to me, and in secret), "that not one of that audience knew anything whatever about me." A noteworthy admission. He must have had a keen intelligence since he was capable of grasping his position so clearly even on the platform, even in such a state of exaltation; it also follows that he had not a keen intelligence if, nine years afterwards, he could not recall it without mortification. He was made to sign two or three collective protests (against what he did not know); he signed them. Varvara Petrovna too was made to protest against some "disgraceful action" and she signed too. The majority of these new people, however, though they visited Varvara Petrovna, felt themselves for some reason called upon to regard her with contempt, and with undisguised irony. Stepan Trofimovitch hinted to me at bitter moments afterwards that it was from that time she had been envious of him. She saw, of course, that she could not get on with these people, yet she received them eagerly, with all the hysterical impatience of her sex, and, what is more, she expected something. At her parties she talked little, although she could talk, but she listened the more. They talked of the abolition of the censorship, and of phonetic spelling, of the substitution of the Latin characters for the Russian alphabet, of someone's having been sent into exile the day before, of some scandal, of the advantage of splitting Russia into nationalities united in a free federation, of the abolition of the army and the navy, of the restoration of Poland as far as the Dnieper, of the peasant reforms, and of the manifestoes, of the abolition of the hereditary principle, of the family, of children, and of priests, of women's rights, of Kraevsky's house, for which no one ever seemed able to forgive Mr. Kraevsky, and so on, and so on. It was evident that in this mob of new people there were many impostors, but undoubtedly there were also many honest and very attractive people, in spite of some surprising characteristics in them. The honest ones were far more difficult to understand than the coarse and dishonest, but it was impossible to tell which was being made a tool of by the other. When Varvara Petrovna announced her idea of founding a magazine, people flocked to her in even larger numbers, but charges of being a capitalist and an exploiter of labour were showered upon her to her face. The rudeness of these accusations was only equalled by their unexpectedness. The aged General Ivan Ivanovitch Drozdov, an old friend and comrade of the late General Stavrogin's, known to us all here as an extremely stubborn and irritable, though very estimable, man (in his own way, of course), who ate a great deal, and was dreadfully afraid of atheism, quarrelled at one of Varvara Petrovna's parties with a distinguished young man. The latter at the first word exclaimed, "You must be a general if you talk like that," meaning that he could find no word of abuse worse than "general."

Ivan Ivanovitch flew into a terrible passion: "Yes, sir, I am a general, and a lieutenant-general, and I have served my Tsar, and you, sir, are a puppy and an infidel!"

An outrageous scene followed. Next day the incident was exposed in print, and they began getting up a collective protest against Varvara Petrovna's disgraceful conduct in not having immediately turned the general out. In an illustrated paper there appeared a malignant caricature in which Varvara Petrovna, Stepan Trofimovitch, and General Drozdov were depicted as three reactionary friends. There were verses attached to this caricature written by a popular poet especially for the occasion. I may observe, for my own part, that many persons of general's rank certainly have an absurd habit of saying, "I have served my Tsar" ... just as though they had not the same Tsar as all the rest of us, their simple fellow-subjects, but had a special Tsar of their own.

It was impossible, of course, to remain any longer in Petersburg, all the more so as Stepan Trofimovitch was overtaken by a complete fiasco. He could not resist talking of the claims of art, and they laughed at him more loudly as time went on. At his last lecture he thought to impress them with patriotic eloquence, hoping to touch their hearts, and reckoning on the respect inspired by his "persecution." He did not attempt to dispute the uselessness and absurdity of the word "fatherland," acknowledged the pernicious influence of religion, but firmly and loudly declared that boots were of less consequence than Pushkin; of much less, indeed. He was hissed so mercilessly that he burst into tears, there and then, on the platform. Varvara Petrovna took him home more dead than alive. "On m'a traité comme un vieux bonnet de coton," he babbled senselessly. She was looking after him all night, giving him laurel-drops and repeating to him till daybreak, "You will still be of use; you will still make your mark; you will be appreciated ... in another place."

Early next morning five literary men called on Varvara Petrovna, three of them complete strangers, whom she had never set eyes on before. With a stern air they informed her that they had looked into the question of her magazine, and had brought her their decision on the subject. Varvara Petrovna had never authorised anyone to look into or decide anything concerning her magazine. Their decision was that, having founded the magazine, she should at once hand it over to them with the capital to run it, on the basis of a co-operative society. She herself was to go back to Skvoreshniki, not forgetting to take with her Stepan Trofimovitch, who was "out of date." From delicacy they agreed to recognise the right of property in her case, and to send her every year a sixth part of the net profits. What was most touching about it was that of these five men, four certainly were not actuated by any mercenary motive, and were simply acting in the interests of the "cause."

"We came away utterly at a loss," Stepan Trofimovitch used to say afterwards. "I couldn't make head or tail of it, and kept muttering, I remember, to the rumble of the train:

'Vyek, and vyek, and Lyov Kambek,

Lyov Kambek and vyek, and vyek.'

and goodness knows what, all the way to Moscow. It was only in Moscow that I came to myself—as though we really might find something different there."

"Oh, my friends!" he would exclaim to us sometimes with fervour, "you cannot imagine what wrath and sadness overcome your whole soul when a great idea, which you have long cherished as holy, is caught up by the ignorant and dragged forth before fools like themselves into the street, and you suddenly meet it in the market unrecognisable, in the mud, absurdly set up, without proportion, without harmony, the plaything of foolish louts! No! In our day it was not so, and it was not this for which we strove. No, no, not this at all. I don't recognise it.... Our day will come again and will turn all the tottering fabric of to-day into a true path. If not, what will happen?..."

VII

Immediately on their return from Petersburg Varvara Petrovna sent her friend abroad to "recruit"; and, indeed, it was necessary for them to part for a time, she felt that. Stepan Trofimovitch was delighted to go.

"There I shall revive!" he exclaimed. "There, at last, I shall set to work!" But in the first of his letters from Berlin he struck his usual note:

"My heart is broken!" he wrote to Varvara Petrovna. "I can forget nothing! Here, in Berlin, everything brings back to me my old past, my first raptures and my first agonies. Where is she? Where are they both? Where are you two angels of whom I was never worthy? Where is my son, my beloved son? And last of all, where am I, where is my old self, strong as steel, firm as a rock, when now some Andreev, our orthodox clown with a beard, peut briser mon existence en deux"—and so on.

As for Stepan Trofimovitch's son, he had only seen him twice in his life, the first time when he was born and the second time lately in Petersburg, where the young man was preparing to enter the university. The boy had been all his life, as we have said already, brought up by his aunts (at Varvara Petrovna's expense) in a remote province, nearly six hundred miles from Skvoreshniki. As for Andreev, he was nothing more or less than our local shopkeeper, a very eccentric fellow, a self-taught archæologist who had a passion for collecting Russian antiquities and sometimes tried to outshine Stepan Trofimovitch in erudition and in the progressiveness of his opinions. This worthy shopkeeper, with a grey beard and silver-rimmed spectacles, still owed Stepan Trofimovitch four hundred roubles for some acres of timber he had bought on the latter's little estate (near Skvoreshniki). Though Varvara Petrovna had liberally provided her friend with funds when she sent him to Berlin, yet Stepan Trofimovitch had, before starting, particularly reckoned on getting that four hundred roubles, probably for his secret expenditure, and was ready to cry when Andreev asked leave to defer payment for a month, which he had a right to do, since he had brought the first installments of the money almost six months in advance to meet Stepan Trofimovitch's special need at the time.

Varvara Petrovna read this first letter greedily, and underlining in pencil the exclamation: "Where are they both?" numbered it and put it away in a drawer. He had, of course, referred to his two deceased wives. The second letter she received from Berlin was in a different strain:

"I am working twelve hours out of the twenty-four." ("Eleven would be enough," muttered Varvara Petrovna.) "I'm rummaging in the libraries, collating, copying, rushing about. I've visited the professors. I have renewed my acquaintance with the delightful Dundasov family. What a charming creature Lizaveta Nikolaevna is even now! She sends you her greetings. Her young husband and three nephews are all in Berlin. I sit up talking till daybreak with the young people and we have almost Athenian evenings, Athenian, I mean, only in their intellectual subtlety and refinement. Everything is in noble style; a great deal of music, Spanish airs, dreams of the regeneration of all humanity, ideas of eternal beauty, of the Sistine Madonna, light interspersed with darkness, but there are spots even on the sun! Oh, my friend, my noble, faithful friend! In heart I am with you and am yours; with you alone, always, en tout pays, even in le pays de Makar et de ses veaux, of which we often used to talk in agitation in Petersburg, do you remember, before we came away. I think of it with a smile. Crossing the frontier I felt myself in safety, a sensation, strange and new, for the first time after so many years"—and so on and so on.

"Come, it's all nonsense!" Varvara Petrovna commented, folding up that letter too. "If he's up till daybreak with his Athenian nights, he isn't at his books for twelve hours a day. Was he drunk when he wrote it? That Dundasov woman dares to send me greetings! But there, let him amuse himself!"

The phrase "dans le pays de Makar et de ses veaux" meant: "wherever Makar may drive his calves." Stepan Trofimovitch sometimes purposely translated Russian proverbs and traditional sayings into French in the most stupid way, though no doubt he was able to understand and translate them better. But he did it from a feeling that it was chic, and thought it witty.

But he did not amuse himself for long. He could not hold out for four months, and was soon flying back to Skvoreshniki. His last letters consisted of nothing but outpourings of the most sentimental love for his absent friend, and were literally wet with tears. There are natures extremely attached to home like lap-dogs. The meeting of the friends was enthusiastic. Within two days everything was as before and even duller than before. "My friend," Stepan Trofimovitch said to me a fortnight after, in dead secret, "I have discovered something awful for me ... something new: je suis un simple dependent, et rien de plus! Mais r-r-rien de plus."

VIII

After this we had a period of stagnation which lasted nine years. The hysterical outbreaks and sobbings on my shoulder that recurred at regular intervals did not in the least mar our prosperity. I wonder that Stepan Trofimovitch did not grow stout during this period. His nose was a little redder, and his manner had gained in urbanity, that was all. By degrees a circle of friends had formed around him, although it was never a very large one. Though Varvara Petrovna had little to do with the circle, yet we all recognised her as our patroness. After the lesson she had received in Petersburg, she settled down in our town for good. In winter she lived in her town house and spent the summer on her estate in the neighbourhood. She had never enjoyed so much consequence and prestige in our provincial society as during the last seven years of this period, that is up to the time of the appointment of our present governor. Our former governor, the mild Ivan Ossipovitch, who will never be forgotten among us, was a near relation of Varvara Petrovna's, and had at one time been under obligations to her. His wife trembled at the very thought of displeasing her, while the homage paid her by provincial society was carried almost to a pitch that suggested idolatry. So Stepan Trofimovitch, too, had a good time. He was a member of the club, lost at cards majestically, and was everywhere treated with respect, though many people regarded him only as a "learned man." Later on, when

Varvara Petrovna allowed him to live in a separate house, we enjoyed greater freedom than before. Twice a week we used to meet at his house. We were a merry party, especially when he was not sparing of the champagne. The wine came from the shop of the same Andreev. The bill was paid twice a year by Varvara Petrovna, and on the day it was paid Stepan Trofimovitch almost invariably suffered from an attack of his "summer cholera."

One of the first members of our circle was Liputin, an elderly provincial official, and a great liberal, who was reputed in the town to be an atheist. He had married for the second time a young and pretty wife with a dowry, and had, besides, three grown-up daughters. He brought up his family in the fear of God, and kept a tight hand over them. He was extremely stingy, and out of his salary had bought himself a house and amassed a fortune. He was an uncomfortable sort of man, and had not been in the service. He was not much respected in the town, and was not received in the best circles. Moreover, he was a scandal-monger, and had more than once had to smart for his back-biting, for which he had been badly punished by an officer, and again by a country gentleman, the respectable head of a family. But we liked his wit, his inquiring mind, his peculiar, malicious liveliness. Varvara Petrovna disliked him, but he always knew how to make up to her.

Nor did she care for Shatov, who became one of our circle during the last years of this period. Shatov had been a student and had been expelled from the university after some disturbance. In his childhood he had been a student of Stepan Trofimovitch's and was by birth a serf of Varvara Petrovna's, the son of a former valet of hers, Pavel Fyodoritch, and was greatly indebted to her bounty. She disliked him for his pride and ingratitude and could never forgive him for not having come straight to her on his expulsion from the university. On the contrary he had not even answered the letter she had expressly sent him at the time, and preferred to be a drudge in the family of a merchant of the new style, with whom he went abroad, looking after his children more in the position of a nurse than of a tutor. He was very eager to travel at the time. The children had a governess too, a lively young Russian lady, who also became one of the household on the eve of their departure, and had been engaged chiefly because she was so cheap. Two months later the merchant turned her out of the house for "free thinking." Shatov took himself off after her and soon afterwards married her in Geneva. They lived together about three weeks, and then parted as free people recognising no bonds, though, no doubt, also through poverty. He wandered about Europe alone for a long time afterwards, living God knows how; he is said to have blacked boots in the street, and to have been a porter in some dockyard. At last, a year before, he had returned to his native place among us and settled with an old aunt, whom he buried a month later. His sister Dasha, who had also been brought up by Varvara Petrovna, was a favourite of hers, and treated with respect and consideration in her house. He saw his sister rarely and was not on intimate terms with her. In our circle he was always sullen, and never talkative; but from time to time, when his convictions were touched upon, he became morbidly irritable and very unrestrained in his language.

"One has to tie Shatov up and then argue with him," Stepan Trofimovitch would sometimes say in joke, but he liked him.

Shatov had radically changed some of his former socialistic convictions abroad and had rushed to the opposite extreme. He was one of those idealistic beings common in Russia, who are suddenly struck by some overmastering idea which seems, as it were, to crush them at once, and sometimes forever. They are never equal to coping with it, but put passionate faith in it, and their whole life passes afterwards, as it were, in the last agonies under the weight of the stone that has fallen upon them and half crushed them. In appearance Shatov was in complete harmony with his convictions: he was short, awkward, had a shock of flaxen hair, broad shoulders, thick lips, very thick overhanging white eyebrows, a wrinkled forehead, and a hostile, obstinately downcast, as it were shamefaced, expression in his eyes. His hair was always in a wild tangle and stood up in a shock which nothing could smooth. He was seven- or eight-and-twenty.

"I no longer wonder that his wife ran away from him," Varvara Petrovna enunciated on one occasion after gazing intently at him. He tried to be neat in his dress, in spite of his extreme poverty. He refrained again from appealing to Varvara Petrovna, and struggled along as best he could, doing various jobs for tradespeople. At one time he served in a shop, at another he was on the point of going as an assistant clerk on a freight steamer, but he fell ill just at the time of sailing. It is hard to imagine what poverty he was capable of enduring without thinking about it at all. After his illness Varvara Petrovna sent him a hundred roubles, anonymously and in secret. He found out the secret, however, and after some reflection took the money and went to Varvara Petrovna to thank her. She received him with warmth, but on this occasion, too, he shamefully disappointed her. He only stayed five minutes, staring blankly at the ground and smiling stupidly in profound silence, and suddenly, at the most interesting point, without listening to what she was saying, he got up, made an uncouth sideways bow, helpless with confusion, caught against the lady's expensive inlaid work-table, upsetting it on the floor and smashing it to atoms, and walked out nearly dead with shame. Liputin blamed him severely afterwards for having accepted the hundred roubles and having even gone to thank Varvara Petrovna for them, instead of having returned the money with contempt, because it had come from his former despotic mistress. He lived in solitude on the outskirts of the town, and did not like any of us to go and see him. He used to turn up invariably at Stepan Trofimovitch's evenings, and borrowed newspapers and books from him.

There was another young man who always came, one Virginsky, a clerk in the service here, who had something in common with Shatov, though on the surface he seemed his complete opposite in every respect. He was a "family man" too. He was a pathetic and very quiet young man though he was thirty; he had considerable education though he was chiefly self-taught. He was poor, married, and in the service, and supported the aunt and sister of his wife. His wife and all the ladies of his family professed the very latest convictions, but in rather a crude form. It was a case of "an idea dragged forth into the street," as Stepan Trofimovitch had expressed it upon a former occasion. They got it all out of books, and at the first hint coming from any of our little progressive corners in Petersburg they were prepared to throw anything overboard, so soon as they were advised to do so. Madame Virginsky practised as a midwife in the town. She had lived a long while in Petersburg as a girl. Virginsky himself was a man of rare single-heartedness, and I have seldom met more honest fervour.

"I will never, never, abandon these bright hopes," he used to say to me with shining eyes. Of these "bright hopes" he always spoke quietly, in a blissful half-whisper, as it were secretly. He was rather tall, but extremely thin and narrow-shouldered, and had extraordinarily lank hair of a reddish hue. All Stepan Trofimovitch's condescending gibes at some of his opinions he accepted mildly, answered him sometimes very seriously, and often nonplussed him. Stepan Trofimovitch treated him very kindly, and indeed he behaved like a father to all of us. "You are all half-hearted chickens," he observed to Virginsky in joke. "All who are like you, though in you, Virginsky, I have not observed that narrow-mindedness I found in Petersburg, chez ces séminaristes. But you're a half-hatched chicken all the same. Shatov would give anything to hatch out, but he's half-hatched too."

"And I?" Liputin inquired.

"You're simply the golden mean which will get on anywhere in its own way." Liputin was offended.

The story was told of Virginsky, and it was unhappily only too true, that before his wife had spent a year in lawful wedlock with him she announced that he was superseded and that she preferred Lebyadkin. This Lebyadkin, a stranger to the town, turned out afterwards to be a very dubious character, and not a retired captain as he represented himself to be. He could do nothing but twist his moustache, drink, and chatter the most inept nonsense that can possibly be imagined. This fellow, who was utterly lacking in delicacy, at once settled in his house, glad to live at another man's expense, ate and slept there and came, in the end, to treating the master of the house with condescension. It was asserted that when Virginsky's wife had announced to him that he was superseded he said to her:

"My dear, hitherto I have only loved you, but now I respect you," but I doubt whether this renunciation, worthy of ancient Rome, was ever really uttered. On the contrary they say that he wept violently. A fortnight after he was superseded, all of them, in a "family party," went one day for a picnic to a wood outside the town to drink tea with their friends. Virginsky was in a feverishly lively mood and took part in the dances. But suddenly, without any preliminary quarrel, he seized the giant Lebyadkin with both hands, by the hair, just as the latter was dancing a can-can solo, pushed him down, and began dragging him along with shrieks, shouts, and tears. The giant was so panic-stricken that he did not attempt to defend himself, and hardly uttered a sound all the time he was being dragged along. But afterwards he resented it with all the heat of an honourable man. Virginsky spent a whole night on his knees begging his wife's forgiveness. But this forgiveness was not granted, as he refused to apologise to Lebyadkin; moreover, he was upbraided for the meanness of his ideas and his foolishness, the latter charge based on the fact that he knelt down in the interview with his wife. The captain soon disappeared and did not reappear in our town till quite lately, when he came with his sister, and with entirely different aims; but of him later. It was no wonder that the poor young husband sought our society and found comfort in it. But he never spoke of his home-life to us. On one occasion only, returning with me from Stepan Trofimovitch's, he made a remote allusion to his position, but clutching my hand at once he cried ardently:

"It's of no consequence. It's only a personal incident. It's no hindrance to the 'cause,' not the slightest!"

Stray guests visited our circle too; a Jew, called Lyamshin, and a Captain Kartusov came. An old gentleman of inquiring mind used to come at one time, but he died. Liputin brought an exiled Polish priest called Slontsevsky, and for a time we received him on principle, but afterwards we didn't keep it up.

IX

At one time it was reported about the town that our little circle was a hotbed of nihilism, profligacy, and godlessness, and the rumour gained more and more strength. And yet we did nothing but indulge in the most harmless, agreeable, typically Russian, light-hearted liberal chatter. "The higher liberalism" and the "higher liberal," that is, a liberal without any definite aim, is only possible in Russia.

Stepan Trofimovitch, like every witty man, needed a listener, and, besides that, he needed the consciousness that he was fulfilling the lofty duty of disseminating ideas. And finally he had to have someone to drink champagne with, and over the wine to exchange light-hearted views of a certain sort, about Russia and the "Russian spirit," about God in general, and the "Russian God" in particular, to repeat for the hundredth time the same Russian scandalous stories that every one knew and every one repeated. We had no distaste for the gossip of the town which often, indeed, led us to the most severe and loftily moral verdicts. We fell into generalising about humanity, made stern reflections on the future of Europe and mankind in general, authoritatively predicted that after Cæsarism France would at once sink into the position of a second-rate power, and were firmly convinced that this might terribly easily and quickly come to pass. We had long ago predicted that the Pope would play the part of a simple archbishop in a united Italy, and were firmly convinced that this thousand-year-old question had, in our age of humanitarianism, industry, and railways, become a trifling matter. But, of course, "Russian higher liberalism" could not look at the question in any other way. Stepan Trofimovitch sometimes talked of art, and very well, though rather abstractly. He sometimes spoke of the friends of his youth—all names noteworthy in the history of Russian progress. He talked of them with emotion and reverence, though sometimes with envy. If we were very much bored, the Jew, Lyamshin (a little post-office clerk), a wonderful performer on the piano, sat down to play, and in the intervals would imitate a pig, a thunderstorm, a confinement with the first cry of the baby, and so on, and so on; it was only for this that he was invited, indeed. If we had drunk a great deal—and that did happen sometimes, though not often—we flew into raptures, and even on one occasion sang the "Marseillaise" in chorus to the accompaniment of Lyamshin, though I don't know how it went off. The great day, the nineteenth of February, we welcomed enthusiastically, and for a long time beforehand drank toasts in its honour. But that was long ago, before the advent of Shatov or Virginsky, when Stepan Trofimovitch was still living in the same house with Varvara Petrovna. For some time before the great day Stepan Trofimovitch fell into the habit of muttering to himself well-known, though rather far-fetched, lines which must have been written by some liberal landowner of the past:

"The peasant with his axe is coming, Something terrible will happen."

Something of that sort, I don't remember the exact words. Varvara Petrovna overheard him on one occasion, and crying, "Nonsense, nonsense!" she went out of the room in a rage. Liputin, who happened to be present, observed malignantly to Stepan Trofimovitch:

"It'll be a pity if their former serfs really do some mischief to messieurs les landowners to celebrate the occasion," and he drew his forefinger round his throat.

"Cher ami," Stepan Trofimovitch observed, "believe me that—this (he repeated the gesture) will never be of any use to our landowners nor to any of us in general. We shall never be capable of organising anything even without our heads, though our heads hinder our understanding more than anything."

I may observe that many people among us anticipated that something extraordinary, such as Liputin predicted, would take place on the day of the emancipation, and those who held this view were the so-called "authorities" on the peasantry and the government. I believe Stepan Trofimovitch shared this idea, so much so that almost on the eve of the great day he began asking Varvara Petrovna's leave to go abroad; in fact he began to be uneasy. But the great day passed, and some time passed after it, and the condescending smile reappeared on Stepan Trofimovitch's lips. In our presence he delivered himself of some noteworthy thoughts on the character of the Russian in general, and the Russian peasant in particular.

"Like hasty people we have been in too great a hurry with our peasants," he said in conclusion of a series of remarkable utterances. "We have made them the fashion, and a whole section of writers have for several years treated them as though they were newly discovered curiosities. We have put laurel-wreaths on lousy heads. The Russian village has given us only 'Kamarinsky' in a thousand years. A remarkable Russian poet who was also something of a wit, seeing the great Rachel on the stage for the first time cried in ecstasy, 'I wouldn't exchange Rachel for a peasant!' I am prepared to go further. I would give all the peasants in Russia for one Rachel. It's high time to look things in the face more soberly, and not to mix up our national rustic pitch with bouquet de l'Impératrice."

Liputin agreed at once, but remarked that one had to perjure oneself and praise the peasant all the same for the sake of being progressive, that even ladies in good society shed tears reading "Poor Anton," and that some of them even wrote from Paris to their bailiffs that they were, henceforward, to treat the peasants as humanely as possible.

It happened, and as ill-luck would have it just after the rumours of the Anton Petrov affair had reached us, that there was some disturbance in our province too, only about ten miles from Skvoreshniki, so that a detachment of soldiers was sent down in a hurry.

This time Stepan Trofimovitch was so much upset that he even frightened us. He cried out at the club that more troops were needed, that they ought to be telegraphed for from another province; he rushed off to the governor to protest that he had no hand in it, begged him not to allow his name on account of old associations to be brought into it, and offered to write about his protest to the proper quarter in Petersburg. Fortunately it all passed over quickly and ended in nothing, but I was surprised at Stepan Trofimovitch at the time.

Three years later, as every one knows, people were beginning to talk of nationalism, and "public opinion" first came upon the scene. Stepan Trofimovitch laughed a great deal.

"My friends," he instructed us, "if our nationalism has 'dawned' as they keep repeating in the papers—it's still at school, at some German 'Peterschule,' sitting over a German book and repeating its everlasting German lesson, and its German teacher will make it go down on its knees when he thinks fit. I think highly of the German teacher. But nothing has happened and nothing of the kind has dawned and everything is going on in the old way, that is, as ordained by God. To my thinking that should be enough for Russia, pour notre Sainte Russie. Besides, all this Slavism and nationalism is too old to be new. Nationalism, if you like, has never existed among us except as a distraction for gentlemen's clubs, and Moscow ones at that. I'm not talking of the days of Igor, of course. And besides it all comes of idleness. Everything in Russia comes of idleness, everything good and fine even. It all springs from the charming, cultured, whimsical idleness of our gentry! I'm ready to repeat it for thirty thousand years. We don't know how to live by our own labour. And as for the fuss they're making now about the 'dawn' of some sort of public opinion, has it so suddenly dropped from heaven without any warning? How is it they don't understand that before we can have an opinion of our own we must have work, our own work, our own initiative in things, our own experience. Nothing is to be gained for nothing. If we work we shall have an opinion of our own. But as we never shall work, our opinions will be formed for us by those who have hitherto done the work instead of us, that is, as always, Europe, the everlasting Germans—our teachers for the last two centuries. Moreover, Russia is too big a tangle for us to unravel alone without the Germans, and without hard work. For the last twenty years I've been sounding the alarm, and the summons to work. I've given up my life to that appeal, and, in my folly I put faith in it. Now I have lost faith in it, but I sound the alarm still, and shall sound it to the tomb. I will pull at the bell-ropes until they toll for my own requiem!"

"Alas! We could do nothing but assent. We applauded our teacher and with what warmth, indeed! And, after all, my friends, don't we still hear to-day, every hour, at every step, the same "charming," "clever," "liberal," old Russian nonsense? Our teacher believed in God.

"I can't understand why they make me out an infidel here," he used to say sometimes. "I believe in God, mais distinguons, I believe in Him as a Being who is conscious of Himself in me only. I cannot believe as my Nastasya (the servant) or like some country gentleman who believes 'to be on the safe side,' or like our dear Shatov—but no, Shatov doesn't come into it. Shatov believes 'on principle,' like a Moscow Slavophil. As for Christianity, for all my genuine respect for it, I'm not a Christian. I am more of an antique pagan, like the great Goethe, or like an ancient Greek. The very fact that Christianity has failed to understand woman is enough, as George Sand has so splendidly shown in one of her great novels. As for the bowings, fasting and all the rest of it, I don't understand what they have to do with me. However busy the informers may be here, I don't care to become a Jesuit. In the year 1847 Byelinsky, who was abroad, sent his famous letter to Gogol, and warmly reproached him for believing in some sort of God. Entre nous soit dit, I can imagine nothing more comic than the moment when Gogol (the Gogol of that period!) read that phrase, and … the whole letter! But dismissing the humorous aspect, and, as I am fundamentally in agreement, I point to them and say—these were men! They knew how to love their people, they knew how to suffer for them, they knew how to sacrifice everything for them, yet they knew how to differ from them when they ought, and did not filch certain ideas from them. Could Byelinsky have sought salvation in Lenten oil, or peas with radish!…" But at this point Shatov interposed.

"Those men of yours never loved the people, they didn't suffer for them, and didn't sacrifice anything for them, though they may have amused themselves by imagining it!" he growled sullenly, looking down, and moving impatiently in his chair.

"They didn't love the people!" yelled Stepan Trofimovitch. "Oh, how they loved Russia!"

"Neither Russia nor the people!" Shatov yelled too, with flashing eyes. "You can't love what you don't know and they had no conception of the Russian people. All of them peered at the Russian people through their fingers, and you do too; Byelinsky especially: from that very letter to Gogol one can see it. Byelinsky, like the Inquisitive Man in Krylov's fable, did not notice the elephant in the museum of curiosities, but concentrated his whole attention on the French Socialist beetles; he did not get beyond them. And yet perhaps he was cleverer than any of you. You've not only overlooked the people, you've taken up an attitude of disgusting contempt for them, if only because you could not imagine any but the French people, the Parisians indeed, and were ashamed that the Russians were not like them. That's the naked truth. And he who has no people has no God. You may be sure that all who cease to understand their own people and lose their connection with them at once lose to the same extent the faith of their fathers, and become atheistic or indifferent. I'm speaking the truth! This is a fact which will be realised. That's why all of you and all of us now are either beastly atheists or careless, dissolute imbeciles, and nothing more. And you too, Stepan Trofimovitch, I don't make an exception of you at all! In fact, it is on your account I am speaking, let me tell you that!"

As a rule, after uttering such monologues (which happened to him pretty frequently) Shatov snatched up his cap and rushed to the door, in the full conviction that everything was now over, and that he had cut short all friendly relations with Stepan Trofimovitch forever. But the latter always succeeded in stopping him in time.

"Hadn't we better make it up, Shatov, after all these endearments," he would say, benignly holding out his hand to him from his arm-chair.

Shatov, clumsy and bashful, disliked sentimentality. Externally he was rough, but inwardly, I believe, he had great delicacy. Although he often went too far, he was the first to suffer for it. Muttering something between his teeth in response to Stepan Trofimovitch's appeal, and shuffling with his feet like a bear, he gave a sudden and unexpected smile, put down his cap, and sat down in the same chair as before, with his eyes stubbornly fixed on the ground. Wine was, of course, brought in, and Stepan Trofimovitch proposed some suitable toast, for instance the memory of some leading man of the past.

CHAPTER II. PRINCE HARRY. MATCHMAKING.

I

THERE WAS ANOTHER being in the world to whom Varvara Petrovna was as much attached as she was to Stepan Trofimovitch, her only son, Nikolay Vsyevolodovitch Stavrogin. It was to undertake his education that Stepan Trofimovitch had been engaged. The boy was at that time eight years old, and his frivolous father, General Stavrogin, was already living apart from Varvara Petrovna, so that the child grew up entirely in his mother's care. To do Stepan Trofimovitch justice, he knew how to win his pupil's heart. The whole secret of this lay in the fact that he was a child himself. I was not there in those days, and he continually felt the want of a real friend. He did not hesitate to make a friend of this little creature as soon as he had grown a little older. It somehow came to pass quite naturally that there seemed to be no discrepancy of age between them. More than once he awaked his ten- or eleven-year-old friend at night, simply to pour out his wounded feelings and weep before him, or to tell him some family secret, without realising that this was an outrageous proceeding. They threw themselves into each other's arms and wept. The boy knew that his mother loved him very much, but I doubt whether he cared much for her. She talked little to him and did not often interfere with him, but he was always morbidly conscious of her intent, searching eyes fixed upon him. Yet the mother confided his whole instruction and moral education to Stepan Trofimovitch. At that time her faith in him was unshaken. One can't help believing that the tutor had rather a bad influence on his pupil's nerves. When at sixteen he was taken to a lyceum he was fragile-looking and pale, strangely quiet and dreamy. (Later on he was distinguished by great physical strength.) One must assume too that the friends went on weeping at night, throwing themselves in each other's arms, though their tears were not always due to domestic difficulties. Stepan Trofimovitch succeeded in reaching the deepest chords in his pupil's heart, and had aroused in him a vague sensation of that eternal, sacred yearning which some elect souls can never give up for cheap gratification when once they have tasted and known it. (There are some connoisseurs who prize this yearning more than the most complete satisfaction of it, if such were possible.) But in any case it was just as well that the pupil and the preceptor were, though none too soon, parted.

For the first two years the lad used to come home from the lyceum for the holidays. While Varvara Petrovna and Stepan Trofimovitch were staying in Petersburg he was sometimes present at the literary evenings at his mother's, he listened and looked on. He spoke little, and was quiet and shy as before. His manner to Stepan Trofimovitch was as affectionately attentive as ever, but there was a shade of reserve in it. He unmistakably avoided distressing, lofty subjects or reminiscences of the past. By his mother's wish he entered the army on completing the school course, and soon received a commission in one of the most brilliant regiments of the Horse Guards. He did not come to show himself to his mother in his uniform, and his letters from Petersburg began to be infrequent. Varvara Petrovna sent him money without stint, though after the emancipation the revenue from her estate was so diminished that at first her income was less than half what it had been before. She had, however, a considerable sum laid by through years of economy. She took great interest in her son's success in the highest Petersburg society. Where she had failed, the wealthy young officer with expectations succeeded. He renewed acquaintances which she had hardly dared to dream of, and was welcomed everywhere with pleasure. But very soon rather strange rumours reached Varvara Petrovna. The young man had suddenly taken to riotous living with a sort of frenzy. Not that he gambled or drank too much; there was only talk of savage recklessness, of running over people in the street with his horses, of brutal conduct to a lady of good society with whom he had a liaison and whom he afterwards publicly insulted. There was a callous nastiness about this affair. It was added, too, that he had developed into a regular bully, insulting people for the mere pleasure of insulting them. Varvara Petrovna was greatly agitated and distressed. Stepan Trofimovitch assured her that this was only the first riotous effervescence of a too richly endowed nature, that the storm would subside and that this was only like the youth of Prince Harry, who caroused with Falstaff, Poins, and Mrs. Quickly, as described by Shakespeare.

This time Varvara Petrovna did not cry out, "Nonsense, nonsense!" as she was very apt to do in later years in response to Stepan Trofimovitch. On the contrary she listened very eagerly, asked him to explain this theory more exactly, took up Shakespeare herself and with great attention read the immortal chronicle. But it did not comfort her, and indeed she did not find the resemblance very striking. With feverish impatience she awaited answers to some of her letters. She had not long to wait for them. The fatal news soon reached her that "Prince Harry" had been involved in two duels almost at once, was entirely to blame for both of them, had killed one of his adversaries on the spot and had maimed the other and was awaiting his trial in consequence. The case ended in his being degraded to the ranks, deprived of the rights of a nobleman, and transferred to an infantry line regiment, and he only escaped worse punishment by special favour.

In 1863 he somehow succeeded in distinguishing himself; he received a cross, was promoted to be a non-commissioned officer, and rose rapidly to the rank of an officer. During this period Varvara Petrovna despatched perhaps hundreds of letters to the capital, full of prayers and supplications. She even stooped to some humiliation in this extremity. After his promotion the young man suddenly resigned his commission, but he did not come back to Skvoreshniki again, and gave up writing to his mother altogether. They learned by roundabout means that he was back in Petersburg, but that he was not to be met in the same society as before; he seemed to be in hiding. They found out that he was living in strange company, associating with the dregs of the population of Petersburg, with slip-shod government clerks, discharged military men, beggars of the higher class, and drunkards of all sorts—that he visited their filthy families, spent days and nights in dark slums and all sorts of low haunts, that he had sunk very low, that he was in rags, and that apparently he liked it. He did not ask his mother for money, he had his own little estate—once the property of his father, General Stavrogin, which yielded at least some revenue, and which, it was reported, he had let to a German from Saxony. At last his mother besought him to come to her, and "Prince Harry" made his appearance in our town. I had never set eyes on him before, but now I got a very distinct impression of him. He was a very handsome young man of five-and-twenty, and I must own I was impressed by him. I had expected to see a dirty ragamuffin, sodden with drink and debauchery. He was on the contrary, the most elegant gentleman I had ever met, extremely well dressed, with an air and manner only to be found in a man accustomed to culture and refinement. I was not the only person surprised. It was a surprise to all the townspeople to whom, of course, young Stavrogin's whole biography was well known in its minutest details, though one could not imagine how they had got hold of them, and, what was still more surprising, half of their stories about him turned out to be true.

All our ladies were wild over the new visitor. They were sharply divided into two parties, one of which adored him while the other half regarded him with a hatred that was almost blood-thirsty: but both were crazy about him. Some of them were particularly fascinated by the idea that he had perhaps a fateful secret hidden in his soul; others were positively delighted at the fact that he was a murderer. It appeared too that he had had a very good education and was indeed a man of considerable culture. No great acquirements were needed, of course, to astonish us. But he could judge also of very interesting everyday affairs, and, what was of the utmost value, he judged of them with remarkable good sense. I must mention as a peculiar fact that almost from the first day we all of us thought him a very sensible fellow. He was not very talkative, he was elegant without exaggeration, surprisingly modest, and at the same time bold and self-reliant, as none of us were. Our dandies gazed at him with envy, and were completely eclipsed by him. His face, too, impressed me. His hair was of a peculiarly intense black, his light-coloured eyes were peculiarly light and calm, his complexion was peculiarly soft and white, the red in his cheeks was too bright and clear, his teeth were like pearls, and his lips like coral—one would have thought that he must be a paragon of beauty, yet at the same time there seemed something repellent about him. It was said that his face suggested a mask; so much was said though, among other things they talked of his extraordinary physical strength. He was rather tall. Varvara Petrovna looked at him with pride, yet with continual uneasiness. He spent about six months among us—listless, quiet, rather morose. He made his appearance in society, and with unfailing propriety performed all the duties demanded by our provincial etiquette. He was related, on his father's side, to the governor, and was received by the latter as a near kinsman. But a few months passed and the wild beast showed his claws.

I may observe by the way, in parenthesis, that Ivan Ossipovitch, our dear mild governor, was rather like an old woman, though he was of good family and highly connected—which explains the fact that he remained so long among us, though he steadily avoided all the duties of his office. From his munificence and hospitality he ought rather to have been a marshal of nobility of the good old days than a governor in such busy times as ours. It was always said in the town that it was not he, but Varvara Petrovna who governed the province. Of course this was said sarcastically; however, it was certainly a falsehood. And, indeed, much wit was wasted on the subject among us. On the contrary, in later years, Varvara Petrovna purposely and consciously withdrew from anything like a position of authority, and, in spite of the extraordinary respect in which she was held by the whole province, voluntarily confined her influence within strict limits set up by herself. Instead of these higher responsibilities she suddenly took up the management of her estate, and, within two or three years, raised the revenue from it almost to what it had yielded in the past. Giving up her former romantic impulses (trips to Petersburg, plans for founding a magazine, and so on) she began to be careful and to save money. She kept even Stepan Trofimovitch at a distance, allowing him to take lodgings in another house (a change for which he had long been worrying her under various pretexts). Little by little Stepan Trofimovitch began to call her a prosaic woman, or more jestingly, "My prosaic friend." I need hardly say he only ventured on such jests in an extremely respectful form, and on rare, and carefully chosen, occasions.

All of us in her intimate circle felt—Stepan Trofimovitch more acutely than any of us—

that her son had come to her almost, as it were, as a new hope, and even as a sort of new aspiration. Her passion for her son dated from the time of his successes in Petersburg society, and grew more intense from the moment that he was degraded in the army. Yet she was evidently afraid of him, and seemed like a slave in his presence. It could be seen that she was afraid of something vague and mysterious which she could not have put into words, and she often stole searching glances at "Nicolas," scrutinising him reflectively … and behold—the wild beast suddenly showed his claws.

II

Suddenly, apropos of nothing, our prince was guilty of incredible outrages upon various persons and, what was most striking these outrages were utterly unheard of, quite inconceivable, unlike anything commonly done, utterly silly and mischievous, quite unprovoked and objectless. One of the most respected of our club members, on our committee of management, Pyotr Pavlovitch Gaganov, an elderly man of high rank in the service, had formed the innocent habit of declaring vehemently on all sorts of occasions: "No, you can't lead me by the nose!" Well, there is no harm in that. But one day at the club, when he brought out this phrase in connection with some heated discussion in the midst of a little group of members (all persons of some consequence) Nikolay Vsyevolodovitch, who was standing on one side, alone and unnoticed, suddenly went up to Pyotr Pavlovitch, took him unexpectedly and firmly with two fingers by the nose, and succeeded in leading him two or three steps across the room. He could have had no grudge against Mr. Gaganov. It might be thought to be a mere schoolboy prank, though, of course, a most unpardonable one. Yet, describing it afterwards, people said that he looked almost dreamy at the very instant of the operation, "as though he had gone out of his mind," but that was recalled and reflected upon long afterwards. In the excitement of the moment all they recalled was the minute after, when he certainly saw it all as it really was, and far from being confused smiled gaily and maliciously "without the slightest regret." There was a terrific outcry; he was surrounded. Nikolay Vsyevolodovitch kept turning round, looking about him, answering nobody, and glancing curiously at the persons exclaiming around him. At last he seemed suddenly, as it were, to sink into thought again—so at least it was reported—frowned, went firmly up to the affronted Pyotr Pavlovitch, and with evident vexation said in a rapid mutter:

"You must forgive me, of course … I really don't know what suddenly came over me … it's silly."

The carelessness of his apology was almost equivalent to a fresh insult. The outcry was greater than ever. Nikolay Vsyevolodovitch shrugged his shoulders and went away. All this was very stupid, to say nothing of its gross indecency—

A calculated and premeditated indecency as it seemed at first sight—and therefore a premeditated and utterly brutal insult to our whole society. So it was taken to be by everyone. We began by promptly and unanimously striking young Stavrogin's name off the list of club members. Then it was decided to send an appeal in the name of the whole club to the governor, begging him at once (without waiting for the case to be formally tried in court) to use "the administrative power entrusted to him" to restrain this dangerous ruffian, "this duelling bully from the capital, and so protect the tranquillity of all the gentry of our town from injurious encroachments." It was added with angry resentment that "a law might be found to control even Mr. Stavrogin." This phrase was prepared by way of a thrust at the governor on account of Varvara Petrovna. They elaborated it with relish. As ill luck would have it, the governor was not in the town at the time. He had gone to a little distance to stand godfather to the child of a very charming lady, recently left a widow in an interesting condition. But it was known that he would soon be back. In the meanwhile they got up a regular ovation for the respected and insulted gentleman; people embraced and kissed him; the whole town called upon him. It was even proposed to give a subscription dinner in his honour, and they only gave up the idea at his earnest request—reflecting possibly at last that the man had, after all, been pulled by the nose and that that was really nothing to congratulate him upon. Yet, how had it happened? How could it have happened? It is remarkable that no one in the whole town put down this savage act to madness. They must have been predisposed to expect such actions from Nikolay Vsyevolodovitch, even when he was sane. For my part I don't know to this day how to explain it, in spite of the event that quickly followed and apparently explained everything, and conciliated every one. I will add also that, four years later, in reply to a discreet question from me about the incident at the club, Nikolay Vsyevolodovitch answered, frowning: "I wasn't quite well at the time." But there is no need to anticipate events.

The general outburst of hatred with which every one fell upon the "ruffian and duelling bully from the capital" also struck me as curious. They insisted on seeing an insolent design and deliberate intention to insult our whole society at once. The truth was no one liked the fellow, but, on the contrary, he had set every one against him—and one wonders how. Up to the last incident he had never quarrelled with anyone, nor insulted anyone, but was as courteous as a gentleman in a fashion-plate, if only the latter were able to speak. I imagine that he was hated for his pride. Even our ladies, who had begun by adoring him, railed against him now, more loudly than the men. Varvara Petrovna was dreadfully overwhelmed. She confessed afterwards to Stepan Trofimovitch that she had had a foreboding of all this long before, that every day for the last six months she had been expecting "just something of that sort," a remarkable admission on the part of his own mother. "It's begun!" she thought to herself with a shudder. The morning after the incident at the club she cautiously but firmly approached the subject with her son, but the poor woman was trembling all over in spite of her firmness. She had not slept all night and even went out early to Stepan Trofimovitch's lodgings to ask his advice, and shed tears there, a thing which she had never been known to do before anyone. She longed for "Nicolas" to say something to her, to deign to give some explanation. Nikolay, who was always so polite and respectful to his mother, listened to her for some time scowling, but very seriously. He suddenly got up without saying a word, kissed her hand and went away. That very evening, as though by design, he perpetrated another scandal. It was of a more harmless and ordinary character than the first. Yet, owing to the state of the public mind, it increased the outcry in the town.

Our friend Liputin turned up and called on Nikolay Vsyevolodovitch immediately after the latter's interview with his mother, and earnestly begged for the honour of his company at a little party he was giving for his wife's birthday that evening. Varvara Petrovna had long watched with a pang at her heart her son's taste for such low company, but she had not dared to speak of it to him. He had made several acquaintances besides Liputin in the third rank of our society, and even in lower depths—he had a propensity for making such friends. He had never been in Liputin's house before, though he had met the man himself. He guessed that Liputin's invitation now was the consequence of the previous day's scandal, and that as a local liberal he was delighted at the scandal, genuinely believing that that was the proper way to treat stewards at the club, and that it was very well done. Nikolay Vsyevolodovitch smiled and promised to come.

A great number of guests had assembled. The company was not very presentable, but very sprightly. Liputin, vain and envious, only entertained visitors twice a year, but on those occasions he did it without stint. The most honoured of the invited guests, Stepan Trofimovitch, was prevented by illness from being present. Tea was handed, and there were refreshments and vodka in plenty. Cards were played at three tables, and while waiting for supper the young people got up a dance. Nikolay Vsyevolodovitch led out Madame Liputin—a very pretty little woman who was dreadfully shy of him—took two turns round the room with her, sat down beside her, drew her into conversation and made her laugh. Noticing at last how pretty she was when she laughed, he suddenly, before all the company, seized her round the waist and kissed her on the lips two or three times with great relish. The poor frightened lady fainted. Nikolay Vsyevolodovitch took his hat and went up to the husband, who stood petrified in the middle of the general excitement. Looking at him he, too, became confused and muttering hurriedly "Don't be angry," went away. Liputin ran after him in the entry, gave him his fur-coat with his own hands, and saw him down the stairs, bowing. But next day a rather amusing sequel followed this comparatively harmless prank—a sequel from which Liputin gained some credit, and of which he took the fullest possible advantage.

At ten o'clock in the morning Liputin's servant Agafya, an easy-mannered, lively, rosy-cheeked peasant woman of thirty, made her appearance at Stavrogin's house, with a message for Nikolay Vsyevolodovitch. She insisted on seeing "his honour himself." He had a very bad headache, but he went out. Varvara Petrovna succeeded in being present when the message was given.

"Sergay Vassilyevitch" (Liputin's name), Agafya rattled off briskly, "bade me first of all give you his respectful greetings and ask after your health, what sort of night your honour spent after yesterday's doings, and how your honour feels now after yesterday's doings?"

Nikolay Vsyevolodovitch smiled.

"Give him my greetings and thank him, and tell your master from me, Agafya, that he's the most sensible man in the town."

"And he told me to answer that," Agafya caught him up still more briskly, "that he knows that without your telling him, and wishes you the same."

"Really! But how could he tell what I should say to you?"

"I can't say in what way he could tell, but when I had set off and had gone right down the street, I heard something, and there he was, running after me without his cap. 'I say, Agafya, if by any chance he says to you, "Tell your master that he has more sense than all the town," you tell him at once, don't forget, "The master himself knows that very well, and wishes you the same."'"

III

At last the interview with the governor took place too. Our dear, mild, Ivan Ossipovitch had only just returned and only just had time to hear the angry complaint from the club. There was no doubt that something must be done, but he was troubled. The hospitable old man seemed also rather afraid of his young kinsman. He made up his mind, however, to induce him to apologise to the club and to his victim in satisfactory form, and, if required, by letter, and then to persuade him to leave us for a time, travelling, for instance, to improve his mind, in Italy, or in fact anywhere abroad. In the waiting-room in which on this occasion he received Nikolay Vsyevolodovitch (who had been at other times privileged as a relation to wander all over the house unchecked), Alyosha Telyatnikov, a clerk of refined manners, who was also a member of the governor's household, was sitting in a corner opening envelopes at a table, and in the next room, at the window nearest to the door, a stout and sturdy colonel, a former friend and colleague of the governor, was sitting alone reading the Golos, paying no attention, of course, to what was taking place in the waiting-room; in fact, he had his back turned. Ivan Ossipovitch approached the subject in a roundabout way, almost in a whisper, but kept getting a little muddled. Nikolay looked anything but cordial, not at all as a relation should. He was pale and sat looking down and continually moving his eyebrows as though trying to control acute pain.

"You have a kind heart and a generous one, Nicolas," the old man put in among other things, "you're a man of great culture, you've grown up in the highest circles, and here too your behaviour has hitherto been a model, which has been a great consolation to your mother, who is so precious to all of us.... And now again everything has appeared in such an unaccountable light, so detrimental to all! I speak as a friend of your family, as an old man who loves you sincerely and a relation, at whose words you cannot take offence.... Tell me, what drives you to such reckless proceedings so contrary to all accepted rules and habits? What can be the meaning of such acts which seem almost like outbreaks of delirium?"

Nikolay listened with vexation and impatience. All at once there was a gleam of something sly and mocking in his eyes.

"I'll tell you what drives me to it," he said sullenly, and looking round him he bent down to Ivan Ossipovitch's ear. The refined Alyosha Telyatnikov moved three steps farther away towards the window, and the colonel coughed over the Golos. Poor Ivan Ossipovitch hurriedly and trustfully inclined his ear; he was exceedingly curious. And then something utterly incredible, though on the other side only too unmistakable, took place. The old man suddenly felt that, instead of telling him some interesting secret, Nikolay had seized the upper part of his ear between his teeth and was nipping it rather hard. He shuddered, and breath failed him.

"Nicolas, this is beyond a joke!" he moaned mechanically in a voice not his own.

Alyosha and the colonel had not yet grasped the situation, besides they couldn't see, and fancied up to the end that the two were whispering together; and yet the old man's desperate face alarmed them. They looked at one another with wide-open eyes, not knowing whether to rush to his assistance as agreed or to wait. Nikolay noticed this perhaps, and bit the harder.

"Nicolas! Nicolas!" his victim moaned again, "come ... you've had your joke, that's enough!"

In another moment the poor governor would certainly have died of terror; but the monster had mercy on him, and let go his ear. The old man's deadly terror lasted for a full minute, and it was followed by a sort of fit. Within half an hour Nikolay was arrested and removed for the time to the guard-room, where he was confined in a special cell, with a special sentinel at the door. This decision was a harsh one, but our mild governor was so angry that he was prepared to take the responsibility even if he had to face Varvara Petrovna. To the general amazement, when this lady arrived at the governor's in haste and in nervous irritation to discuss the matter with him at once, she was refused admittance, whereupon, without getting out of the carriage, she returned home, unable to believe her senses.

And at last everything was explained! At two o'clock in the morning the prisoner, who had till then been calm and had even slept, suddenly became noisy, began furiously beating on the door with his fists,—with unnatural strength wrenched the iron grating off the door, broke the window, and cut his hands all over. When the officer on duty ran with a detachment of men and the keys and ordered the cell to be opened that they might rush in and bind the maniac, it appeared that he was suffering from acute brain fever. He was taken home to his mother.

Everything was explained at once. All our three doctors gave it as their opinion that the patient might well have been in a delirious state for three days before, and that though he might have apparently been in possession of full consciousness and cunning, yet he might have been deprived of common sense and will, which was indeed borne out by the facts. So it turned out that Liputin had guessed the truth sooner than any one. Ivan Ossipovitch, who was a man of delicacy and feeling, was completely abashed. But what was striking was that he, too, had considered Nikolay Vsyevolodovitch capable of any mad action even when in the full possession of his faculties. At the club, too, people were ashamed and wondered how it was they had failed to "see the elephant" and had missed the only explanation of all these marvels: there were, of course, sceptics among them, but they could not long maintain their position.

Nikolay was in bed for more than two months. A famous doctor was summoned from Moscow for a consultation; the whole town called on Varvara Petrovna. She forgave them. When in the spring Nikolay had completely recovered and assented without discussion to his mother's proposal that he should go for a tour to Italy, she begged him further to pay visits of farewell to all the neighbours, and so far as possible to apologise where necessary. Nikolay agreed with great alacrity. It became known at the club that he had had a most delicate explanation with Pyotr Pavlovitch Gaganov, at the house of the latter, who had been completely satisfied with his apology. As he went round to pay these calls Nikolay was very grave and even gloomy. Every one appeared to receive him sympathetically, but everybody seemed embarrassed and glad that he was going to Italy. Ivan Ossipovitch was positively tearful, but was, for some reason, unable to bring himself to embrace him, even at the final leave-taking. It is true that some of us retained the conviction that the scamp had simply been making fun of us, and that the illness was neither here nor there. He went to see Liputin too.

"Tell me," he said, "how could you guess beforehand what I should say about your sense and prime Agafya with an answer to it?"

"Why," laughed Liputin, "it was because I recognised that you were a clever man, and so I foresaw what your answer would be."

"Anyway, it was a remarkable coincidence. But, excuse me, did you consider me a sensible man and not insane when you sent Agafya?"

"For the cleverest and most rational, and I only pretended to believe that you were insane.... And you guessed at once what was in my mind, and sent a testimonial to my wit through Agafya."

"Well, there you're a little mistaken. I really was ... unwell ..." muttered Nikolay Vsyevolodovitch, frowning. "Bah!" he cried, "do you suppose I'm capable of attacking people when I'm in my senses? What object would there be in it?"

Liputin shrank together and didn't know what to answer. Nikolay turned pale or, at least, so it seemed to Liputin.

"You have a very peculiar way of looking at things, anyhow," Nikolay went on, "but as for Agafya, I understand, of course, that you simply sent her to be rude to me."

"I couldn't challenge you to a duel, could I?"

"Oh, no, of course! I seem to have heard that you're not fond of duels...."

"Why borrow from the French?" said Liputin, doubling up again.

"You're for nationalism, then?"

Liputin shrank into himself more than ever.

"Bah, bah! What do I see?" cried Nicolas, noticing a volume of Considérant in the most conspicuous place on the table. "You don't mean to say you're a Fourierist! I'm afraid you must be! And isn't this too borrowing from the French?" he laughed, tapping the book with his finger.

"No, that's not taken from the French," Liputin cried with positive fury, jumping up from his chair. "That is taken from the universal language of humanity, not simply from the French. From the language of the universal social republic and harmony of mankind, let me tell you! Not simply from the French!"

"Foo! hang it all! There's no such language!" laughed Nikolay.

Sometimes a trifle will catch the attention and exclusively absorb it for a time. Most of what I have to tell of young Stavrogin will come later. But I will note now as a curious fact that of all the impressions made on him by his stay in our town, the one most sharply imprinted on his memory was the unsightly and almost abject figure of the little provincial official, the coarse and jealous family despot, the miserly money-lender who picked up the candle-ends and scraps left from dinner, and was at the same time a passionate believer in some visionary future "social harmony," who at night gloated in ecstasies over fantastic pictures of a future phalanstery, in the approaching realisation of which, in Russia, and in our province, he believed as firmly as in his own existence. And that in the very place where he had saved up to buy himself a "little home," where he had married for the second time, getting a dowry with his bride, where perhaps, for a hundred miles round there was not one man, himself included, who was the very least like a future member "of the universal human republic and social harmony."

"God knows how these people come to exist!" Nikolay wondered, recalling sometimes the unlooked-for Fourierist.

IV

Our prince travelled for over three years, so that he was almost forgotten in the town. We learned from Stepan Trofimovitch that he had travelled all over Europe, that he had even been in Egypt and had visited Jerusalem, and then had joined some scientific expedition to Iceland, and he actually did go to Iceland. It was reported too that he had spent one winter attending lectures in a German university. He did not write often to his mother, twice a year, or even less, but Varvara Petrovna was not angry or offended at this. She accepted submissively and without repining the relations that had been established once for all between her son and herself. She fretted for her "Nicolas" and dreamed of him continually. She kept her dreams and lamentations to herself. She seemed to have become less intimate even with Stepan Trofimovitch. She was forming secret projects, and seemed to have become more careful about money than ever. She was more than ever given to saving money and being angry at Stepan Trofimovitch's losses at cards.

At last, in the April of this year, she received a letter from Paris from Praskovya Ivanovna Drozdov, the widow of the general and the friend of Varvara Petrovna's childhood. Praskovya Ivanovna, whom Varvara Petrovna had not seen or corresponded with for eight years, wrote, informing her that Nikolay Vsyevolodovitch had become very intimate with them and a great friend of her only daughter, Liza, and that he was intending to accompany them to Switzerland, to Verney-Montreux, though in the household of Count K. (a very influential personage in Petersburg), who was now staying in Paris. He was received like a son of the family, so that he almost lived at the count's. The letter was brief, and the object of it was perfectly clear, though it contained only a plain statement of the above-mentioned facts without drawing any inferences from them. Varvara Petrovna did not pause long to consider; she made up her mind instantly, made her preparations, and taking with her her protégée, Dasha (Shatov's sister), she set off in the middle of April for Paris, and from there went on to Switzerland. She returned in July, alone, leaving Dasha with the Drozdovs. She brought us the news that the Drozdovs themselves had promised to arrive among us by the end of August.

The Drozdovs, too, were landowners of our province, but the official duties of General Ivan Ivanovitch Drozdov (who had been a friend of Varvara Petrovna's and a colleague of her husband's) had always prevented them from visiting their magnificent estate. On the death of the general, which had taken place the year before, the inconsolable widow had gone abroad with her daughter, partly in order to try the grape-cure which she proposed to carry out at Verney-Montreux during the latter half of the summer. On their return to Russia they intended to settle in our province for good. She had a large house in the town which had stood empty for many years with the windows nailed up. They were wealthy people. Praskovya

Ivanovna had been, in her first marriage, a Madame Tushin, and like her school-friend, Varvara Petrovna, was the daughter of a government contractor of the old school, and she too had been an heiress at her marriage. Tushin, a retired cavalry captain, was also a man of means, and of some ability. At his death he left a snug fortune to his only daughter Liza, a child of seven. Now that Lizaveta Nikolaevna was twenty-two her private fortune might confidently be reckoned at 200,000 roubles, to say nothing of the property—which was bound to come to her at the death of her mother, who had no children by her second marriage. Varvara Petrovna seemed to be very well satisfied with her expedition. In her own opinion she had succeeded in coming to a satisfactory understanding with Praskovya Ivanovna, and immediately on her arrival she confided everything to Stepan Trofimovitch. She was positively effusive with him as she had not been for a very long time.

"Hurrah!" cried Stepan Trofimovitch, and snapped his fingers.

He was in a perfect rapture, especially as he had spent the whole time of his friend's absence in extreme dejection. On setting off she had not even taken leave of him properly, and had said nothing of her plan to "that old woman," dreading, perhaps, that he might chatter about it. She was cross with him at the time on account of a considerable gambling debt which she had suddenly discovered. But before she left Switzerland she had felt that on her return she must make up for it to her forsaken friend, especially as she had treated him very curtly for a long time past. Her abrupt and mysterious departure had made a profound and poignant impression on the timid heart of Stepan Trofimovitch, and to make matters worse he was beset with other difficulties at the same time. He was worried by a very considerable money obligation, which had weighed upon him for a long time and which he could never hope to meet without Varvara Petrovna's assistance. Moreover, in the May of this year, the term of office of our mild and gentle Ivan Ossipovitch came to an end. He was superseded under rather unpleasant circumstances. Then, while Varvara Petrovna was still away, there followed the arrival of our new governor, Andrey Antonovitch von Lembke, and with that a change began at once to be perceptible in the attitude of almost the whole of our provincial society towards Varvara Petrovna, and consequently towards Stepan Trofimovitch. He had already had time anyway to make some disagreeable though valuable observations, and seemed very apprehensive alone without Varvara Petrovna. He had an agitating suspicion that he had already been mentioned to the governor as a dangerous man. He knew for a fact that some of our ladies meant to give up calling on Varvara Petrovna. Of our governor's wife (who was only expected to arrive in the autumn) it was reported that though she was, so it was heard, proud, she was a real aristocrat, and "not like that poor Varvara Petrovna." Everybody seemed to know for a fact, and in the greatest detail, that our governor's wife and Varvara Petrovna had met already in society and had parted enemies, so that the mere mention of Madame von Lembke's name would, it was said, make a painful impression on Varvara Petrovna. The confident and triumphant air of Varvara Petrovna, the contemptuous indifference with which she heard of the opinions of our provincial ladies and the agitation in local society, revived the flagging spirits of Stepan Trofimovitch and cheered him up at once. With peculiar, gleefully-obsequious humour, he was beginning to describe the new governor's arrival.

"You are no doubt aware, excellente amie," he said, jauntily and coquettishly drawling his words, "what is meant by a Russian administrator, speaking generally, and what is meant by a new Russian administrator, that is the newly-baked, newly-established … ces interminables mots Russes! But I don't think you can know in practice what is meant by administrative ardour, and what sort of thing that is."

"Administrative ardour? I don't know what that is."

"Well … Vous savez chez nous … En un mot, set the most insignificant nonentity to sell miserable tickets at a railway station, and the nonentity will at once feel privileged to look down on you like a Jupiter, pour montrer son pouvoir when you go to take a ticket. 'Now then,' he says, 'I shall show you my power' … and in them it comes to a genuine, administrative ardour. En un mot, I've read that some verger in one of our Russian churches abroad—mais c'est très curieux—drove, literally drove a distinguished English family, les dames charmantes, out of the church before the beginning of the Lenten service … vous savez ces chants et le livre de Job … on the simple pretext that 'foreigners are not allowed to loaf about a Russian church, and that they must come at the time fixed.…' And he sent them into fainting fits.… That verger was suffering from an attack of administrative ardour, et il a montré son pouvoir."

"Cut it short if you can, Stepan Trofimovitch."

"Mr. von Lembke is making a tour of the province now. En un mot, this Andrey Antonovitch, though he is a russified German and of the Orthodox persuasion, and even—I will say that for him—a remarkably handsome man of about forty …"

"What makes you think he's a handsome man? He has eyes like a sheep's."

"Precisely so. But in this I yield, of course, to the opinion of our ladies."

"Let's get on, Stepan Trofimovitch, I beg you! By the way, you're wearing a red neck-tie. Is it long since you've taken to it?"

"I've … I've only put it on to-day."

"And do you take your constitutional? Do you go for a four-mile walk every day as the doctor told you to?"

"N-not … always."

"I knew you didn't! I felt sure of that when I was in Switzerland!" she cried irritably. "Now you must go not four but six miles a day! You've grown terribly slack, terribly, terribly! You're not simply getting old, you're getting decrepit.… You shocked me when I first saw you just now, in spite of your red tie, quelle idee rouge! Go on about Von Lembke if you've really something to tell me, and do finish some time, I entreat you, I'm tired."

"En un mot, I only wanted to say that he is one of those administrators who begin to have power at forty, who, till they're forty, have been stagnating in insignificance and then suddenly come to the front through suddenly acquiring a wife, or some other equally desperate means.… That is, he has gone away now … that is, I mean to say, it was at once whispered in both his ears that I am a corrupter of youth, and a hot-bed of provincial atheism.… He began making inquiries at once."

"Is that true?"

"I took steps about it, in fact. When he was 'informed' that you 'ruled the province,' vous savez, he allowed himself to use the expression that 'there shall be nothing of that sort in the future.'"

"Did he say that?"

"That 'there shall be nothing of the sort in future,' and, avec cette morgue.... His wife, Yulia Mihailovna, we shall behold at the end of August, she's coming straight from Petersburg."

"From abroad. We met there."

"Vraiment?"

"In Paris and in Switzerland. She's related to the Drozdovs."

"Related! What an extraordinary coincidence! They say she is ambitious and ... supposed to have great connections."

"Nonsense! Connections indeed! She was an old maid without a farthing till she was five-and-forty. But now she's hooked her Von Lembke, and, of course, her whole object is to push him forward. They're both intriguers."

"And they say she's two years older than he is?"

"Five. Her mother used to wear out her skirts on my doorsteps in Moscow; she used to beg for an invitation to our balls as a favour when my husband was living. And this creature used to sit all night alone in a corner without dancing, with her turquoise fly on her forehead, so that simply from pity I used to have to send her her first partner at two o'clock in the morning. She was five-and-twenty then, and they used to rig her out in short skirts like a little girl. It was improper to have them about at last."

"I seem to see that fly."

"I tell you, as soon as I arrived I was in the thick of an intrigue. You read Madame Drozdov's letter, of course. What could be clearer? What did I find? That fool Praskovya herself—she always was a fool—looked at me as much as to ask why I'd come. You can fancy how surprised I was. I looked round, and there was that Lembke woman at her tricks, and that cousin of hers—old Drozdov's nephew—it was all clear. You may be sure I changed all that in a twinkling, and Praskovya is on my side again, but what an intrigue!"

"In which you came off victor, however. Bismarck!"

"Without being a Bismarck I'm equal to falseness and stupidity wherever I meet it, falseness, and Praskovya's folly. I don't know when I've met such a flabby woman, and what's more her legs are swollen, and she's a good-natured simpleton, too. What can be more foolish than a good-natured simpleton?"

"A spiteful fool, ma bonne amie, a spiteful fool is still more foolish," Stepan Trofimovitch protested magnanimously.

"You're right, perhaps. Do you remember Liza?"

"Charmante enfant!"

"But she's not an enfant now, but a woman, and a woman of character. She's a generous, passionate creature, and what I like about her, she stands up to that confiding fool, her mother. There was almost a row over that cousin."

"Bah, and of course he's no relation of Lizaveta Nikolaevna's at all.... Has he designs on her?"

"You see, he's a young officer, not by any means talkative, modest in fact. I always want to be just. I fancy he is opposed to the intrigue himself, and isn't aiming at anything, and it was only the Von Lembke's tricks. He had a great respect for Nicolas. You understand, it all depends on Liza. But I left her on the best of terms with Nicolas, and he promised he would come to us in November. So it's only the Von Lembke who is intriguing, and Praskovya is a blind woman. She suddenly tells me that all my suspicions are fancy. I told her to her face she was a fool. I am ready to repeat it at the day of judgment. And if it hadn't been for Nicolas begging me to leave it for a time, I wouldn't have come away without unmasking that false woman. She's been trying to ingratiate herself with Count K. through Nicolas. She wants to come between mother and son. But Liza's on our side, and I came to an understanding with Praskovya. Do you know that Karmazinov is a relation of hers?"

"What? A relation of Madame von Lembke?"

"Yes, of hers. Distant."

"Karmazinov, the novelist?"

"Yes, the writer. Why does it surprise you? Of course he considers himself a great man. Stuck-up creature! She's coming here with him. Now she's making a fuss of him out there. She's got a notion of setting up a sort of literary society here. He's coming for a month, he wants to sell his last piece of property here. I very nearly met him in Switzerland, and was very anxious not to. Though I hope he will deign to recognise me. He wrote letters to me in the old days, he has been in my house. I should like you to dress better, Stepan Trofimovitch; you're growing more slovenly every day.... Oh, how you torment me! What are you reading now?"

"I ... I ..."

"I understand. The same as ever, friends and drinking, the club and cards, and the reputation of an atheist. I don't like that reputation, Stepan Trofimovitch; I don't care for you to be called an atheist, particularly now. I didn't care for it in old days, for it's all nothing but empty chatter. It must be said at last."

"Mais, ma chère ..."

"Listen, Stepan Trofimovitch, of course I'm ignorant compared with you on all learned subjects, but as I was travelling here I thought a great deal about you. I've come to one conclusion."

"What conclusion?"

"That you and I are not the wisest people in the world, but that there are people wiser than we are."

"Witty and apt. If there are people wiser than we are, then there are people more right than we are, and we may be mistaken, you mean? Mais, ma bonne amie, granted that I may make a mistake, yet have I not the common, human, eternal, supreme right of freedom of conscience? I have the right not to be bigoted or superstitious if I don't wish to, and for that I shall naturally be hated by certain persons to the end of time. Et puis, comme on trouve toujours plus de moines que de raison, and as I thoroughly agree with that …"

"What, what did you say?"

"I said, on trouve toujours plus de moines que de raison, and as I thoroughly …"

"I'm sure that's not your saying. You must have taken it from somewhere."

"It was Pascal said that."

"Just as I thought … it's not your own. Why don't you ever say anything like that yourself, so shortly and to the point, instead of dragging things out to such a length? That's much better than what you said just now about administrative ardour …"

"Ma foi, chère …" why? In the first place probably because I'm not a Pascal after all, et puis … secondly, we Russians never can say anything in our own language.… We never have said anything hitherto, at any rate.…"

"H'm! That's not true, perhaps. Anyway, you'd better make a note of such phrases, and remember them, you know, in case you have to talk.… Ach, Stephan Trofimovitch. I have come to talk to you seriously, quite seriously."

"Chère, chère amie!"

"Now that all these Von Lembkes and Karmazinovs.… Oh, my goodness, how you have deteriorated!… Oh, my goodness, how you do torment me!… I should have liked these people to feel a respect for you, for they're not worth your little finger—but the way you behave!… What will they see? What shall I have to show them? Instead of nobly standing as an example, keeping up the tradition of the past, you surround yourself with a wretched rabble, you have picked up impossible habits, you've grown feeble, you can't do without wine and cards, you read nothing but Paul de Kock, and write nothing, while all of them write; all your time's wasted in gossip. How can you bring yourself to be friends with a wretched creature like your inseparable Liputin?"

"Why is he mine and inseparable?" Stepan Trofimovitch protested timidly.

"Where is he now?" Varvara Petrovna went on, sharply and sternly.

"He … he has an infinite respect for you, and he's gone to S——k, to receive an inheritance left him by his mother."

"He seems to do nothing but get money. And how's Shatov? Is he just the same?"

"Irascible, mais bon."

"I can't endure your Shatov. He's spiteful and he thinks too much of himself."

"How is Darya Pavlovna?"

"You mean Dasha? What made you think of her?" Varvara Petrovna looked at him inquisitively. "She's quite well. I left her with the Drozdovs. I heard something about your son in Switzerland. Nothing good."

"Oh, c'est un histoire bien bête! Je vous attendais, ma bonne amie, pour vous raconter …"

"Enough, Stepan Trofimovitch. Leave me in peace. I'm worn out. We shall have time to talk to our heart's content, especially of what's unpleasant. You've begun to splutter when you laugh, it's a sign of senility! And what a strange way of laughing you've taken to!… Good Heavens, what a lot of bad habits you've fallen into! Karmazinov won't come and see you! And people are only too glad to make the most of anything as it is.… You've betrayed yourself completely now. Well, come, that's enough, that's enough, I'm tired. You really might have mercy upon one!"

Stepan Trofimovitch "had mercy," but he withdrew in great perturbation.

V

Our friend certainly had fallen into not a few bad habits, especially of late. He had obviously and rapidly deteriorated; and it was true that he had become slovenly. He drank more and had become more tearful and nervous; and had grown too impressionable on the artistic side. His face had acquired a strange facility for changing with extraordinary quickness, from the most solemn expression, for instance, to the most absurd, and even foolish. He could not endure solitude, and was always craving for amusement. One had always to repeat to him some gossip, some local anecdote, and every day a new one. If no one came to see him for a long time he wandered disconsolately about the rooms, walked to the window, puckering up his lips, heaved deep sighs, and almost fell to whimpering at last. He was always full of forebodings, was afraid of something unexpected and inevitable; he had become timorous; he began to pay great attention to his dreams.

He spent all that day and evening in great depression, he sent for me, was very much agitated, talked a long while, gave me a long account of things, but all rather disconnected. Varvara Petrovna had known for a long time that he concealed nothing from me. It seemed to me at last that he was worried about something particular, and was perhaps unable to form a definite idea of it himself. As a rule when we met tête-à-tête and he began making long complaints to me, a bottle was almost always brought in after a little time, and things became much more comfortable. This time there was no wine, and he was evidently struggling all the while against the desire to send for it.

"And why is she always so cross?" he complained every minute, like a child. "Tous les hommes de génie et de progrès en Russie étaient, sont, et seront toujours des gamblers et des drunkards qui boivent in outbreaks … and I'm not such a gambler after all, and I'm not such a drunkard. She reproaches me for not writing anything. Strange idea!… She asks why I lie down? She says I ought to stand, 'an example and reproach.' Mais, entre nous soit dit, what is a man to do who is destined to stand as a 'reproach,' if not to lie down? Does she understand that?"

And at last it became clear to me what was the chief particular trouble which was worrying him so persistently at this time. Many times that evening he went to the looking-glass, and stood a long while before it. At last he turned from the looking-glass to me, and with a sort of strange despair, said: "Mon cher, je suis un broken-down man." Yes, certainly, up to that time, up to that very day there was one thing only of which he had always felt confident in spite of the "new views," and of the "change in Varvara Petrovna's ideas," that was, the conviction that still he had a fascination for her feminine heart, not simply as an exile or a celebrated man of learning, but as a handsome man. For twenty years this soothing and flattering opinion had been rooted in his mind, and perhaps of all his convictions this was the hardest to part with. Had he any presentiment that evening of the colossal ordeal which was preparing for him in the immediate future?

VI

I will now enter upon the description of that almost forgotten incident with which my story properly speaking begins.

At last at the very end of August the Drozdovs returned. Their arrival made a considerable sensation in local society, and took place shortly before their relation, our new governor's wife, made her long-expected appearance. But of all these interesting events I will speak later. For the present I will confine myself to saying that Praskovya Ivanovna brought Varvara Petrovna, who was expecting her so impatiently, a most perplexing problem: Nikolay had parted from them in July, and, meeting Count K. on the Rhine, had set off with him and his family for Petersburg. (N.B.—The Count's three daughters were all of marriageable age.)

"Lizaveta is so proud and obstinate that I could get nothing out of her," Praskovya Ivanovna said in conclusion. "But I saw for myself that something had happened between her and Nikolay Vsyevolodovitch. I don't know the reasons, but I fancy, my dear Varvara Petrovna, that you will have to ask your Darya Pavlovna for them. To my thinking Liza was offended. I'm glad. I can tell you that I've brought you back your favourite at last and handed her over to you; it's a weight off my mind."

These venomous words were uttered with remarkable irritability. It was evident that the "flabby" woman had prepared them and gloated beforehand over the effect they would produce. But Varvara Petrovna was not the woman to be disconcerted by sentimental effects and enigmas. She sternly demanded the most precise and satisfactory explanations. Praskovya Ivanovna immediately lowered her tone and even ended by dissolving into tears and expressions of the warmest friendship. This irritable but sentimental lady, like Stepan Trofimovitch, was forever yearning for true friendship, and her chief complaint against her daughter Lizaveta Nikolaevna was just that "her daughter was not a friend to her."

But from all her explanations and outpourings nothing certain could be gathered but that there actually had been some sort of quarrel between Liza and Nikolay, but of the nature of the quarrel Praskovya Ivanovna was obviously unable to form a definite idea. As for her imputations against Darya Pavlovna, she not only withdrew them completely in the end, but even particularly begged Varvara Petrovna to pay no attention to her words, because "they had been said in irritation." In fact, it had all been left very far from clear—suspicious, indeed. According to her account the quarrel had arisen from Liza's "obstinate and ironical character." "Nikolay Vsyevolodovitch is proud, too, and though he was very much in love, yet he could not endure sarcasm, and began to be sarcastic himself. Soon afterwards we made the acquaintance of a young man, the nephew, I believe, of your 'Professor' and, indeed, the surname's the same."

"The son, not the nephew," Varvara Petrovna corrected her.

Even in the old days Praskovya Ivanovna had been always unable to recall Stepan Trofimovitch's name, and had always called him the "Professor."

"Well, his son, then; so much the better. Of course, it's all the same to me. An ordinary young man, very lively and free in his manners, but nothing special in him. Well, then, Liza herself did wrong, she made friends with the young man with the idea of making Nikolay Vsyevolodovitch jealous. I don't see much harm in that; it's the way of girls, quite usual, even charming in them. Only instead of being jealous Nikolay Vsyevolodovitch made friends with the young man himself, just as though he saw nothing and didn't care. This made Liza furious. The young man soon went away (he was in a great hurry to get somewhere) and Liza took to picking quarrels with Nikolay Vsyevolodovitch at every opportunity. She noticed that he used sometimes to talk to Dasha; and, well, she got in such a frantic state that even my life wasn't worth living, my dear. The doctors have forbidden my being irritated, and I was so sick of their lake they make such a fuss about, it simply gave me toothache, I had such rheumatism. It's stated in print that the Lake of Geneva does give people the toothache. It's a feature of the place. Then Nikolay Vsyevolodovitch suddenly got a letter from the countess and he left us at once. He packed up in one day. They parted in a friendly way, and Liza became very cheerful and frivolous, and laughed a great deal seeing him off; only that was all put on. When he had gone she became very thoughtful, and she gave up speaking of him altogether and wouldn't let me mention his name. And I should advise you, dear Varvara Petrovna, not to approach the subject with Liza, you'll only do harm. But if you hold your tongue she'll begin to talk of it herself, and then you'll learn more. I believe they'll come together again, if only Nikolay Vsyevolodovitch doesn't put off coming, as he promised."

"I'll write to him at once. If that's how it was, there was nothing in the quarrel; all nonsense! And I know Darya too well. It's nonsense!"

"I'm sorry for what I said about Dashenka, I did wrong. Their conversations were quite ordinary and they talked out loud, too. But it all upset me so much at the time, my dear. And Liza, I saw, got on with her again as affectionately as before...."

That very day Varvara Petrovna wrote to Nikolay, and begged him to come, if only one month, earlier than the date he had fixed. But yet she still felt that there was something unexplained and obscure in the matter. She pondered over it all the evening and all night. Praskovya's opinion seemed to her too innocent and sentimental. "Praskovya has always been too sentimental from the old schooldays upwards," she reflected. "Nicolas is not the man to run away from a girl's taunts. There's some other reason for it, if there really has been a breach between them. That officer's here though, they've brought him with them. As a relation he lives in their house. And, as for Darya, Praskovya was in too much haste to apologise. She must have kept something to herself, which she wouldn't tell me."

By the morning Varvara Petrovna had matured a project for putting a stop once for all to one misunderstanding at least; a project amazing in its unexpectedness. What was in her heart when she conceived it? It would be hard to decide and I will not undertake to explain beforehand all the incongruities of which it was made up. I simply confine myself as chronicler to recording events precisely as they happened, and it is not my fault if they seem incredible. Yet I must once more testify that by the morning there was not the least suspicion of Dasha left in Varvara Petrovna's mind, though in reality there never had been any—she had too much confidence in her. Besides, she could not admit the idea that "Nicolas" could be attracted by her Darya. Next morning when Darya Pavlovna was pouring out tea at the table Varvara Petrovna looked for a long while intently at her and, perhaps for the twentieth time since the previous day, repeated to herself: "It's all nonsense!"

All she noticed was that Dasha looked rather tired, and that she was even quieter and more apathetic than she used to be. After their morning tea, according to their invariable custom, they sat down to needlework. Varvara Petrovna demanded from her a full account of her impressions abroad, especially of nature, of the inhabitants, of the towns, the customs, their arts and commerce—of everything she had time to observe. She asked no questions about the Drozdovs or how she had got on with them. Dasha, sitting beside her at the work-table helping her with the embroidery, talked for half an hour in her even, monotonous, but rather weak voice.

"Darya!" Varvara Petrovna interrupted suddenly, "is there nothing special you want to tell me?"

"No, nothing," said Dasha, after a moment's thought, and she glanced at Varvara Petrovna with her light-coloured eyes.

"Nothing on your soul, on your heart, or your conscience?"

"Nothing," Dasha repeated, quietly, but with a sort of sullen firmness.

"I knew there wasn't! Believe me, Darya, I shall never doubt you. Now sit still and listen. In front of me, on that chair. I want to see the whole of you. That's right. Listen, do you want to be married?"

Dasha responded with a long, inquiring, but not greatly astonished look.

"Stay, hold your tongue. In the first place there is a very great difference in age, but of course you know better than anyone what nonsense that is. You're a sensible girl, and there must be no mistakes in your life. Besides, he's still a handsome man … In short, Stepan Trofimovitch, for whom you have always had such a respect. Well?"

Dasha looked at her still more inquiringly, and this time not simply with surprise; she blushed perceptibly.

"Stay, hold your tongue, don't be in a hurry! Though you will have money under my will, yet when I die, what will become of you, even if you have money? You'll be deceived and robbed of your money, you'll be lost in fact. But married to him you're the wife of a distinguished man. Look at him on the other hand. Though I've provided for him, if I die what will become of him? But I could trust him to you. Stay, I've not finished. He's frivolous, shilly-shally, cruel, egoistic, he has low habits. But mind you think highly of him, in the first place because there are many worse. I don't want to get you off my hands by marrying you to a rascal, you don't imagine anything of that sort, do you? And, above all, because I ask you, you'll think highly of him,"—

She broke off suddenly and irritably. "Do you hear? Why won't you say something?"

Dasha still listened and did not speak.

"Stay, wait a little. He's an old woman, but you know, that's all the better for you. Besides, he's a pathetic old woman. He doesn't deserve to be loved by a woman at all, but he deserves to be loved for his helplessness, and you must love him for his helplessness. You understand me, don't you? Do you understand me?"

Dasha nodded her head affirmatively.

"I knew you would. I expected as much of you. He will love you because he ought, he ought; he ought to adore you." Varvara Petrovna almost shrieked with peculiar exasperation. "Besides, he will be in love with you without any ought about it. I know him. And another thing, I shall always be here. You may be sure I shall always be here. He will complain of you, he'll begin to say things against you behind your back, he'll whisper things against you to any stray person he meets, he'll be for ever whining and whining; he'll write you letters from one room to another, two a day, but he won't be able to get on without you all the same, and that's the chief thing. Make him obey you. If you can't make him you'll be a fool. He'll want to hang himself and threaten, to—don't you believe it. It's nothing but nonsense. Don't believe it; but still keep a sharp look-out, you never can tell, and one day he may hang himself. It does happen with people like that. It's not through strength of will but through weakness that people hang themselves, and so never drive him to an extreme, that's the first rule in married life. Remember, too, that he's a poet. Listen, Dasha, there's no greater happiness than self-sacrifice. And besides, you'll be giving me great satisfaction and that's the chief thing. Don't think I've been talking nonsense. I understand what I'm saying. I'm an egoist, you be an egoist, too. Of course I'm not forcing you. It's entirely for you to decide. As you say, so it shall be. Well, what's the good of sitting like this. Speak!"

"I don't mind, Varvara Petrovna, if I really must be married," said Dasha firmly.

"Must? What are you hinting at?" Varvara Petrovna looked sternly and intently at her.

Dasha was silent, picking at her embroidery canvas with her needle.

"Though you're a clever girl, you're talking nonsense; though it is true that I have certainly set my heart on marrying you, yet it's not because it's necessary, but simply because the idea has occurred to me, and only to Stepan Trofimovitch. If it had not been for Stepan Trofimovitch, I should not have thought of marrying you yet, though you are twenty.... Well?"

"I'll do as you wish, Varvara Petrovna."

"Then you consent! Stay, be quiet. Why are you in such a hurry? I haven't finished. In my will I've left you fifteen thousand roubles. I'll give you that at once, on your wedding-day. You will give eight thousand of it to him; that is, not to him but to me. He has a debt of eight thousand. I'll pay it, but he must know that it is done with your money. You'll have seven thousand left in your hands. Never let him touch a farthing of it. Don't pay his debts ever. If once you pay them, you'll never be free of them. Besides, I shall always be here. You shall have twelve hundred roubles a year from me, with extras, fifteen hundred, besides board and lodging, which shall be at my expense, just as he has it now. Only you must set up your own servants. Your yearly allowance shall be paid to you all at once straight into your hands. But be kind, and sometimes give him something, and let his friends come to see him once a week, but if they come more often, turn them out. But I shall be here, too. And if I die, your pension will go on till his death, do you hear, till his death, for it's his pension, not yours. And besides the seven thousand you'll have now, which you ought to keep untouched if you're not foolish, I'll leave you another eight thousand in my will. And you'll get nothing more than that from me, it's right that you should know it. Come, you consent, eh? Will you say something at last?"

"I have told you already, Varvara Petrovna."

"Remember that you're free to decide. As you like, so it shall be."

"Then, may I ask, Varvara Petrovna, has Stepan Trofimovitch said anything yet?"

"No, he hasn't said anything, he doesn't know ... but he will speak directly."

She jumped up at once and threw on a black shawl. Dasha flushed a little again, and watched her with questioning eyes. Varvara Petrovna turned suddenly to her with a face flaming with anger.

"You're a fool!" She swooped down on her like a hawk. "An ungrateful fool! What's in your mind? Can you imagine that I'd compromise you, in any way, in the smallest degree. Why, he shall crawl on his knees to ask you, he must be dying of happiness, that's how it shall be arranged. Why, you know that I'd never let you suffer. Or do you suppose he'll take you for the sake of that eight thousand, and that I'm hurrying off to sell you? You're a fool, a fool! You're all ungrateful fools. Give me my umbrella!"

And she flew off to walk by the wet brick pavements and the wooden planks to Stepan Trofimovitch's.

VII

It was true that she would never have let Dasha suffer; on the contrary, she considered now that she was acting as her benefactress. The most generous and legitimate indignation was glowing in her soul, when, as she put on her shawl, she caught fixed upon her the embarrassed and mistrustful eyes of her protégée. She had genuinely loved the girl from her childhood upwards. Praskovya Ivanovna had with justice called Darya Pavlovna her favourite. Long ago Varvara Petrovna had made up her mind once for all that "Darya's disposition was not like her brother's" (not, that is, like Ivan Shatov's), that she was quiet and gentle, and capable of great self-sacrifice; that she was distinguished by a power of devotion, unusual modesty, rare reasonableness, and, above all, by gratitude. Till that time Dasha had, to all appearances, completely justified her expectations.

"In that life there will be no mistakes," said Varvara Petrovna when the girl was only twelve years old, and as it was characteristic of her to attach herself doggedly and passionately to any dream that fascinated her, any new design, any idea that struck her as noble, she made up her mind at once to educate Dasha as though she were her own daughter. She at once set aside a sum of money for her, and sent for a governess, Miss Criggs, who lived with them until the girl was sixteen, but she was for some reason suddenly dismissed. Teachers came for her from the High School, among them a real Frenchman, who taught Dasha French. He, too, was suddenly dismissed, almost turned out of the house. A poor lady, a widow of good family, taught her to play the piano. Yet her chief tutor was Stepan Trofimovitch.

In reality he first discovered Dasha. He began teaching the quiet child even before Varvara Petrovna had begun to think about her. I repeat again, it was wonderful how children took to him. Lizaveta Nikolaevna Tushin had been taught by him from the age of eight till eleven (Stepan Trofimovitch took no fees, of course, for his lessons, and would not on any account have taken payment from the Drozdovs). But he fell in love with the charming child and used to tell her poems of a sort about the creation of the world, about the earth, and the history of humanity. His lectures about the primitive peoples and primitive man were more interesting than the Arabian Nights. Liza, who was ecstatic over these stories, used to mimic Stepan Trofimovitch very funnily at home. He heard of this and once peeped in on her unawares. Liza, overcome with confusion, flung herself into his arms and shed tears; Stepan Trofimovitch wept too with delight. But Liza soon after went away, and only Dasha was left. When Dasha began to have other teachers, Stepan Trofimovitch gave up his lessons with her, and by degrees left off noticing her. Things went on like this for a long time. Once when she was seventeen he was struck by her prettiness. It happened at Varvara Petrovna's table. He began to talk to the young girl, was much pleased with her answers, and ended by offering to give her a serious and comprehensive course of lessons on the history of Russian literature. Varvara Petrovna approved, and thanked him for his excellent idea, and Dasha was delighted. Stepan Trofimovitch proceeded to make special preparations for the lectures, and at last they began. They began with the most ancient period. The first lecture went off enchantingly. Varvara Petrovna was present. When Stepan Trofimovitch had finished, and as he was going informed his pupil that the next time he would deal with "The Story of the Expedition of Igor," Varvara Petrovna suddenly got up and announced that there would be no more lessons. Stepan Trofimovitch winced, but said nothing, and Dasha flushed crimson. It put a stop to the scheme, however. This had happened just three years before Varvara Petrovna's unexpected fancy.

Poor Stepan Trofimovitch was sitting alone free from all misgivings. Plunged in mournful reveries he had for some time been looking out of the window to see whether any of his friends were coming. But nobody would come. It was drizzling. It was turning cold, he would have to have the stove heated. He sighed. Suddenly a terrible apparition flashed upon his eyes:

Varvara Petrovna in such weather and at such an unexpected hour to see him! And on foot! He was so astounded that he forgot to put on his coat, and received her as he was, in his everlasting pink-wadded dressing-jacket.

"Ma bonne amie!" he cried faintly, to greet her. "You're alone; I'm glad; I can't endure your friends. How you do smoke! Heavens, what an atmosphere! You haven't finished your morning tea and it's nearly twelve o'clock. It's your idea of bliss—disorder! You take pleasure in dirt. What's that torn paper on the floor? Nastasya, Nastasya! What is your Nastasya about? Open the window, the casement, the doors, fling everything wide open. And we'll go into the drawing-room. I've come to you on a matter of importance. And you sweep up, my good woman, for once in your life."

"They make such a muck!" Nastasya whined in a voice of plaintive exasperation.

"Well, you must sweep, sweep it up fifteen times a day! You've a wretched drawing-room" (when they had gone into the drawing-room). "Shut the door properly. She'll be listening. You must have it repapered. Didn't I send a paperhanger to you with patterns? Why didn't you choose one? Sit down, and listen. Do sit down, I beg you. Where are you off to? Where are you off to? Where are you off to?"

"I'll be back directly," Stepan Trofimovitch cried from the next room. "Here I am again."

"Ah,—you've changed your coat." She scanned him mockingly. (He had flung his coat on over the dressing-jacket.) "Well, certainly that's more suited to our subject. Do sit down, I entreat you."

She told him everything at once, abruptly and impressively. She hinted at the eight thousand of which he stood in such terrible need. She told him in detail of the dowry. Stepan Trofimovitch sat trembling, opening his eyes wider and wider. He heard it all, but he could not realise it clearly. He tried to speak, but his voice kept breaking. All he knew was that everything would be as she said, that to protest and refuse to agree would be useless, and that he was a married man irrevocably.

"Mais, ma bonne amie! … for the third time, and at my age … and to such a child." He brought out at last, "Mais, c'est une enfant!"

"A child who is twenty years old, thank God. Please don't roll your eyes, I entreat you, you're not on the stage. You're very clever and learned, but you know nothing at all about life. You will always want a nurse to look after you. I shall die, and what will become of you? She will be a good nurse to you; she's a modest girl, strong-willed, reasonable; besides, I shall be here too, I shan't die directly. She's fond of home, she's an angel of gentleness. This happy thought came to me in Switzerland. Do you understand if I tell you myself that she is an angel of gentleness!" she screamed with sudden fury. "Your house is dirty, she will bring in order, cleanliness. Everything will shine like a mirror. Good gracious, do you expect me to go on my knees to you with such a treasure, to enumerate all the advantages, to court you! Why, you ought to be on your knees.… Oh, you shallow, shallow, faint-hearted man!"

"But … I'm an old man!"

"What do your fifty-three years matter! Fifty is the middle of life, not the end of it. You are a handsome man and you know it yourself. You know, too, what a respect she has for you. If I die, what will become of her? But married to you she'll be at peace, and I shall be at peace. You have renown, a name, a loving heart. You receive a pension which I look upon as an obligation. You will save her perhaps, you will save her! In any case you will be doing her an honour. You will form her for life, you will develop her heart, you will direct her ideas. How many people come to grief nowadays because their ideas are wrongly directed. By that time your book will be ready, and you will at once set people talking about you again."

"I am, in fact," he muttered, at once flattered by Varvara Petrovna's adroit insinuations. "I was just preparing to sit down to my 'Tales from Spanish History.'"

"Well, there you are. It's just come right."

"But … she? Have you spoken to her?"

"Don't worry about her. And there's no need for you to be inquisitive. Of course, you must ask her yourself, entreat her to do you the honour, you understand? But don't be uneasy. I shall be here. Besides, you love her."

Stepan Trofimovitch felt giddy. The walls were going round. There was one terrible idea underlying this to which he could not reconcile himself.

"Excellente amie," his voice quivered suddenly. "I could never have conceived that you would make up your mind to give me in marriage to another … woman."

"You're not a girl, Stepan Trofimovitch. Only girls are given in marriage. You are taking a wife," Varvara Petrovna hissed malignantly.

"Oui, j'ai pris un mot pour un autre. Mais c'est égal." He gazed at her with a hopeless air.

"I see that c'est égal," she muttered contemptuously through her teeth. "Good heavens! Why he's going to faint. Nastasya, Nastasya, water!"

But water was not needed. He came to himself. Varvara Petrovna took up her umbrella.

"I see it's no use talking to you now…."

"Oui, oui, je suis incapable."

"But by to-morrow you'll have rested and thought it over. Stay at home. If anything happens let me know, even if it's at night. Don't write letters, I shan't read them. To-morrow I'll come again at this time alone, for a final answer, and I trust it will be satisfactory. Try to have nobody here and no untidiness, for the place isn't fit to be seen. Nastasya, Nastasya!"

The next day, of course, he consented, and, indeed, he could do nothing else. There was one circumstance …

VIII

Stepan Trofimovitch's estate, as we used to call it (which consisted of fifty souls, reckoning in the old fashion, and bordered on Skvoreshniki), was not really his at all, but his first wife's, and so belonged now to his son Pyotr Stepanovitch Verhovensky. Stepan Trofimovitch was simply his trustee, and so, when the nestling was full-fledged, he had given his father a formal authorisation to manage the estate. This transaction was a profitable one for the young man. He received as much as a thousand roubles a year by way of revenue from the estate, though under the new regime it could not have yielded more than five hundred, and possibly not that. God knows how such an arrangement had arisen. The whole sum, however, was sent the young man by Varvara Petrovna, and Stepan Trofimovitch had nothing to do with a single rouble of it. On the other hand, the whole revenue from the land remained in his pocket, and he had, besides, completely ruined the estate, letting it to a mercenary rogue, and without the knowledge of Varvara Petrovna selling the timber which gave the estate its chief value. He had some time before sold the woods bit by bit. It was worth at least eight thousand, yet he had only received five thousand for it. But he sometimes lost too much at the club, and was afraid to ask Varvara Petrovna for the money. She clenched her teeth when she heard at last of everything. And now, all at once, his son announced that he was coming himself to sell his property for what he could get for it, and commissioned his father to take steps promptly to arrange the sale. It was clear that Stepan Trofimovitch, being a generous and disinterested man, felt ashamed of his treatment of ce cher enfant (whom he had seen for the last time nine years before as a student in Petersburg). The estate might originally have been worth thirteen or fourteen thousand. Now it was doubtful whether anyone would give five for it. No doubt Stepan Trofimovitch was fully entitled by the terms of the trust to sell the wood, and taking into account the incredibly large yearly revenue of a thousand roubles which had been sent punctually for so many years, he could have put up a good defence of his management. But Stepan Trofimovitch was a generous man of exalted impulses. A wonderfully fine inspiration occurred to his mind: when Petrusha returned, to lay on the table before him the maximum price of fifteen thousand roubles without a hint at the sums that had been sent him hitherto, and warmly and with tears to press ce cher fils to his heart, and so to make an end of all accounts between them. He began cautiously and indirectly unfolding this picture before Varvara Petrovna. He hinted that this would add a peculiarly noble note to their friendship … to their "idea." This would set the parents of the last generation—and people of the last generation generally—in such a disinterested and magnanimous light in comparison with the new frivolous and socialistic younger generation. He said a great deal more, but Varvara Petrovna was obstinately silent. At last she informed him airily that she was prepared to buy their estate, and to pay for it the maximum price, that is, six or seven thousand (though four would have been a fair price for it). Of the remaining eight thousand which had vanished with the woods she said not a word.

This conversation took place a month before the match was proposed to him. Stepan Trofimovitch was overwhelmed, and began to ponder. There might in the past have been a hope that his son would not come, after all—an outsider, that is to say, might have hoped so. Stepan Trofimovitch as a father would have indignantly rejected the insinuation that he could entertain such a hope. Anyway queer rumours had hitherto been reaching us about Petrusha. To begin with, on completing his studies at the university six years before, he had hung about in Petersburg without getting work. Suddenly we got the news that he had taken part in issuing some anonymous manifesto and that he was implicated in the affair. Then he suddenly turned up abroad in Switzerland at Geneva—he had escaped, very likely.

"It's surprising to me," Stepan Trofimovitch commented, greatly disconcerted. "Petrusha, c'est une si pauvre tête! He's good, noble-hearted, very sensitive, and I was so delighted with him in Petersburg, comparing him with the young people of to-day. But c'est un pauvre sire, tout de même.... And you know it all comes from that same half-bakedness, that sentimentality. They are fascinated, not by realism, but by the emotional ideal side of socialism, by the religious note in it, so to say, by the poetry of it ... second-hand, of course. And for me, for me, think what it means! I have so many enemies here and more still there, they'll put it down to the father's influence. Good God! Petrusha a revolutionist! What times we live in!"

Very soon, however, Petrusha sent his exact address from Switzerland for money to be sent him as usual; so he could not be exactly an exile. And now, after four years abroad, he was suddenly making his appearance again in his own country, and announced that he would arrive shortly, so there could be no charge against him. What was more, someone seemed to be interested in him and protecting him. He wrote now from the south of Russia, where he was busily engaged in some private but important business. All this was capital, but where was his father to get that other seven or eight thousand, to make up a suitable price for the estate? And what if there should be an outcry, and instead of that imposing picture it should come to a lawsuit? Something told Stepan Trofimovitch that the sensitive Petrusha would not relinquish anything that was to his interest. "Why is it—as I've noticed," Stepan Trofimovitch whispered to me once, "why is it that all these desperate socialists and communists are at the same time such incredible skinflints, so avaricious, so keen over property, and, in fact, the more socialistic, the more extreme they are, the keener they are over property ... why is it? Can that, too, come from sentimentalism?" I don't know whether there is any truth in this observation of Stepan Trofimovitch's. I only know that Petrusha had somehow got wind of the sale of the woods and the rest of it, and that Stepan Trofimovitch was aware of the fact. I happened, too, to read some of Petrusha's letters to his father. He wrote extremely rarely, once a year, or even less often. Only recently, to inform him of his approaching visit, he had sent two letters, one almost immediately after the other. All his letters were short, dry, consisting only of instructions, and as the father and son had, since their meeting in Petersburg, adopted the fashionable "thou" and "thee," Petrusha's letters had a striking resemblance to the missives that used to be sent by landowners of the old school from the town to their serfs whom they had left in charge of their estates. And now suddenly this eight thousand which would solve the difficulty would be wafted to him by Varvara Petrovna's proposition. And at the same time she made him distinctly feel that it never could be wafted to him from anywhere else. Of course Stepan Trofimovitch consented.

He sent for me directly she had gone and shut himself up for the whole day, admitting no one else. He cried, of course, talked well and talked a great deal, contradicted himself continually, made a casual pun, and was much pleased with it. Then he had a slight attack of his "summer cholera"—everything in fact followed the usual course. Then he brought out the portrait of his German bride, now twenty years deceased, and began plaintively appealing to her: "Will you forgive me?" In fact he seemed somehow distracted. Our grief led us to get a little drunk. He soon fell into a sweet sleep, however. Next morning he tied his cravat in masterly fashion, dressed with care, and went frequently to look at himself in the glass. He sprinkled his handkerchief with scent, only a slight dash of it, however, and as soon as he saw Varvara Petrovna out of the window he hurriedly took another handkerchief and hid the scented one under the pillow.

"Excellent!" Varvara Petrovna approved, on receiving his consent. "In the first place you show a fine decision, and secondly you've listened to the voice of reason, to which you generally pay so little heed in your private affairs. There's no need of haste, however," she added, scanning the knot of his white tie, "for the present say nothing, and I will say nothing. It will soon be your birthday; I will come to see you with her. Give us tea in the evening, and please without wine or other refreshments, but I'll arrange it all myself. Invite your friends, but we'll make the list together. You can talk to her the day before, if necessary. And at your party we won't exactly announce it, or make an engagement of any sort, but only hint at it, and let people know without any sort of ceremony. And then the wedding a fortnight later, as far as possible without any fuss.... You two might even go away for a time after the wedding, to Moscow, for instance. I'll go with you, too, perhaps ... The chief thing is, keep quiet till then."

Stepan Trofimovitch was surprised. He tried to falter that he could not do like that, that he must talk it over with his bride. But Varvara Petrovna flew at him in exasperation.

"What for? In the first place it may perhaps come to nothing."

"Come to nothing!" muttered the bridegroom, utterly dumbfoundered.

"Yes. I'll see.... But everything shall be as I've told you, and don't be uneasy. I'll prepare her myself. There's really no need for you. Everything necessary shall be said and done, and there's no need for you to meddle. Why should you? In what character? Don't come and don't write letters. And not a sight or sound of you, I beg. I will be silent too."

She absolutely refused to explain herself, and went away, obviously upset. Stepan Trofimovitch's excessive readiness evidently impressed her. Alas! he was utterly unable to grasp his position, and the question had not yet presented itself to him from certain other points of view. On the contrary a new note was apparent in him, a sort of conquering and jaunty air. He swaggered.

"I do like that!" he exclaimed, standing before me, and flinging wide his arms. "Did you hear? She wants to drive me to refusing at last. Why, I may lose patience, too, and ... refuse! 'Sit still, there's no need for you to go to her.' But after all, why should I be married? Simply because she's taken an absurd fancy into her heart. But I'm a serious man, and I can refuse to submit to the idle whims of a giddy-woman! I have duties to my son and ... and to myself! I'm making a sacrifice. Does she realise that? I have agreed, perhaps, because I am weary of life and nothing matters to me. But she may exasperate me, and then it will matter. I shall resent it and refuse. Et enfin, le ridicule ... what will they say at the club? What will ... what will ... Laputin say? 'Perhaps nothing will come of it'—what a thing to say! That beats everything. That's really ... what is one to say to that?... Je suis un forçat, un Badinguet, un man pushed to the wall...."

And at the same time a sort of capricious complacency, something frivolous and playful, could be seen in the midst of all these plaintive exclamations. In the evening we drank too much again.

CHAPTER III. THE SINS OF OTHERS

I

ABOUT A WEEK had passed, and the position had begun to grow more complicated.

I may mention in passing that I suffered a great deal during that unhappy week, as I scarcely left the side of my affianced friend, in the capacity of his most intimate confidant. What weighed upon him most was the feeling of shame, though we saw no one all that week, and sat indoors alone. But he was even ashamed before me, and so much so that the more he confided to me the more vexed he was with me for it. He was so morbidly apprehensive that he expected that every one knew about it already, the whole town, and was afraid to show himself, not only at the club, but even in his circle of friends. He positively would not go out to take his constitutional till well after dusk, when it was quite dark.

A week passed and he still did not know whether he were betrothed or not, and could not find out for a fact, however much he tried. He had not yet seen his future bride, and did not know whether she was to be his bride or not; did not, in fact, know whether there was anything serious in it at all. Varvara Petrovna, for some reason, resolutely refused to admit him to her presence. In answer to one of his first letters to her (and he wrote a great number of them) she begged him plainly to spare her all communications with him for a time, because she was very busy, and having a great deal of the utmost importance to communicate to him she was waiting for a more free moment to do so, and that she would let him know in time when he could come to see her. She declared she would send back his letters unopened, as they were "simple self-indulgence." I read that letter myself—he showed it me.

Yet all this harshness and indefiniteness were nothing compared with his chief anxiety. That anxiety tormented him to the utmost and without ceasing. He grew thin and dispirited through it. It was something of which he was more ashamed than of anything else, and of which he would not on any account speak, even to me; on the contrary, he lied on occasion, and shuffled before me like a little boy; and at the same time he sent for me himself every day, could not stay two hours without me, needing me as much as air or water.

Such conduct rather wounded my vanity. I need hardly say that I had long ago privately guessed this great secret of his, and saw through it completely. It was my firmest conviction at the time that the revelation of this secret, this chief anxiety of Stepan Trofimovitch's would not have redounded to his credit, and, therefore, as I was still young, I was rather indignant at the coarseness of his feelings and the ugliness of some of his suspicions. In my warmth—and, I must confess, in my weariness of being his confidant—I perhaps blamed him too much. I was so cruel as to try and force him to confess it all to me himself, though I did recognise that it might be difficult to confess some things. He, too, saw through me; that is, he clearly perceived that I saw through him, and that I was angry with him indeed, and he was angry with me too for being angry with him and seeing through him. My irritation was perhaps petty and stupid; but the unrelieved solitude of two friends together is sometimes extremely prejudicial to true friendship. From a certain point of view he had a very true understanding of some aspects of his position, and defined it, indeed, very subtly on those points about which he did not think it necessary to be secret.

"Oh, how different she was then!" he would sometimes say to me about Varvara Petrovna. "How different she was in the old days when we used to talk together.... Do you know that she could talk in those days! Can you believe that she had ideas in those days, original ideas! Now, everything has changed! She says all that's only old-fashioned twaddle. She despises the past.... Now she's like some shopman or cashier, she has grown hard-hearted, and she's always cross...."

"Why is she cross now if you are carrying out her orders?" I answered.

He looked at me subtly.

"Cher ami; if I had not agreed she would have been dreadfully angry, dread-ful-ly! But yet less than now that I have consented."

He was pleased with this saying of his, and we emptied a bottle between us that evening. But that was only for a moment, next day he was worse and more ill-humoured than ever.

But what I was most vexed with him for was that he could not bring himself to call on the Drozdovs, as he should have done on their arrival, to renew the acquaintance of which, so we heard they were themselves desirous, since they kept asking about him. It was a source of daily distress to him. He talked of Lizaveta Nikolaevna with an ecstasy which I was at a loss to understand. No doubt he remembered in her the child whom he had once loved. But besides that, he imagined for some unknown reason that he would at once find in her company a solace for his present misery, and even the solution of his more serious doubts. He expected to meet in Lizaveta Nikolaevna an extraordinary being. And yet he did not go to see her though he meant to do so every day. The worst of it was that I was desperately anxious to be presented to her and to make her acquaintance, and I could look to no one but Stepan Trofimovitch to effect this. I was frequently meeting her, in the street of course, when she was out riding, wearing a riding-habit and mounted on a fine horse, and accompanied by her cousin, so-called, a handsome officer, the nephew of the late General Drozdov—and these meetings made an extraordinary impression on me at the time. My infatuation lasted only a moment, and I very soon afterwards recognised the impossibility of my dreams myself—but though it was a fleeting impression it was a very real one, and so it may well be imagined how indignant I was at the time with my poor friend for keeping so obstinately secluded.

All the members of our circle had been officially informed from the beginning that Stepan Trofimovitch would see nobody for a time, and begged them to leave him quite alone. He insisted on sending round a circular notice to this effect, though I tried to dissuade him. I went round to every one at his request and told everybody that Varvara Petrovna had given "our old man" (as we all used to call Stepan Trofimovitch among ourselves) a special job, to arrange in order some correspondence lasting over many years; that he had shut himself up to do it and I was helping him. Liputin was the only one I did not have time to visit, and I kept putting it off—to tell the real truth I was afraid to go to him. I knew beforehand that he would not believe one word of my story, that he would certainly imagine that there was some secret at the bottom of it, which they were trying to hide from him alone, and as soon as I left him he would set to work to make inquiries and gossip all over the town. While I was picturing all this to myself I happened to run across him in the street. It turned out that he had heard all about it from our friends, whom I had only just informed. But, strange to say, instead of being inquisitive and asking questions about Stepan Trofimovitch, he interrupted me, when I began apologising for not having come to him before, and at once passed to other subjects. It is true that he had a great deal stored up to tell me. He was in a state of great excitement, and was delighted to have got hold of me for a listener. He began talking of the news of the town, of the arrival of the governor's wife, "with new topics of conversation," of an opposition party already formed in the club, of how they were all in a hubbub over the new ideas, and how charmingly this suited him, and so on. He talked for a quarter of an hour and so amusingly that I could not tear myself away. Though I could not endure him, yet I must admit he had the gift of making one listen to him, especially when he was very angry at something. This man was, in my opinion, a regular spy from his very nature. At every moment he knew the very latest gossip and all the trifling incidents of our town, especially the unpleasant ones, and it was surprising to me how he took things to heart that were sometimes absolutely no concern of his. It always seemed to me that the leading feature of his character was envy. When I told Stepan Trofimovitch the same evening of my meeting Liputin that morning and our conversation, the latter to my amazement became greatly agitated, and asked me the wild question: "Does Liputin know or not?"

I began trying to prove that there was no possibility of his finding it out so soon, and that there was nobody from whom he could hear it. But Stepan Trofimovitch was not to be shaken. "Well, you may believe it or not," he concluded unexpectedly at last, "but I'm convinced that he not only knows every detail of 'our' position, but that he knows something else besides, something neither you nor I know yet, and perhaps never shall, or shall only know when it's too late, when there's no turning back!..."

I said nothing, but these words suggested a great deal. For five whole days after that we did not say one word about Liputin; it was clear to me that Stepan Trofimovitch greatly regretted having let his tongue run away with him, and having revealed such suspicions before me.

II

One morning, on the seventh or eighth day after Stepan Trofimovitch had consented to become "engaged," about eleven o'clock, when I was hurrying as usual to my afflicted friend, I had an adventure on the way.

I met Karmazinov, "the great writer," as Liputin called him. I had read Karmazinov from a child. His novels and tales were well known to the past and even to the present generation. I revelled in them; they were the great enjoyment of my childhood and youth. Afterwards I grew rather less enthusiastic over his work. I did not care so much for the novels with a purpose which he had been writing of late as for his first, early works, which were so full of spontaneous poetry, and his latest publications I had not liked at all. Speaking generally, if I may venture to express my opinion on so delicate a subject, all these talented gentlemen of the middling sort who are sometimes in their lifetime accepted almost as geniuses, pass out of memory quite suddenly and without a trace when they die, and what's more, it often happens that even during their lifetime, as soon as a new generation grows up and takes the place of the one in which they have flourished, they are forgotten and neglected by everyone in an incredibly short time. This somehow happens among us quite suddenly, like the shifting of the scenes on the stage. Oh, it's not at all the same as with Pushkin, Gogol, Molière, Voltaire, all those great men who really had a new original word to say! It's true, too, that these talented gentlemen of the middling sort in the decline of their venerable years usually write themselves out in the most pitiful way, though they don't observe the fact themselves. It happens not infrequently that a writer who has been for a long time credited with extraordinary profundity and expected to exercise a great and serious influence on the progress of society, betrays in the end such poverty, such insipidity in his fundamental ideas that no one regrets that he succeeded in writing himself out so soon. But the old grey-beards don't notice this, and are angry. Their vanity sometimes, especially towards the end of their career, reaches proportions that may well provoke wonder. God knows what they begin to take themselves for—for gods at least! People used to say about Karmazinov that his connections with aristocratic society and powerful personages were dearer to him than his own soul, people used to say that on meeting you he would be cordial, that he would fascinate and enchant you with his open-heartedness, especially if you were of use to him in some way, and if you came to him with some preliminary recommendation. But that before any stray prince, any stray countess, anyone that he was afraid of, he would regard it as his sacred duty to forget your existence with the most insulting carelessness, like a chip of wood, like a fly, before you had even time to get out of his sight; he seriously considered this the best and most aristocratic style. In spite of the best of breeding and perfect knowledge of good manners he is, they say, vain to such an hysterical pitch that he cannot conceal his irritability as an author even in those circles of society where little interest is taken in literature. If anyone were to surprise him by being indifferent, he would be morbidly chagrined, and try to revenge himself.

A year before, I had read an article of his in a review, written with an immense affectation of naïve poetry, and psychology too. He described the wreck of some steamer on the English coast, of which he had been the witness, and how he had seen the drowning people saved, and the dead bodies brought ashore. All this rather long and verbose article was written solely with the object of self-display. One seemed to read between the lines: "Concentrate yourselves on me. Behold what I was like at those moments. What are the sea, the storm, the rocks, the splinters of wrecked ships to you? I have described all that sufficiently to you with my mighty pen. Why look at that drowned woman with the dead child in her dead arms? Look rather at me, see how I was unable to bear that sight and turned away from it. Here I stood with my back to it; here I was horrified and could not bring myself to look; I blinked my eyes—isn't that interesting?" When I told Stepan Trofimovitch my opinion of Karmazinov's article he quite agreed with me.

When rumours had reached us of late that Karmazinov was coming to the neighbourhood I was, of course, very eager to see him, and, if possible, to make his acquaintance. I knew that this might be done through Stepan Trofimovitch, they had once been friends. And now I suddenly met him at the cross-roads. I knew him at once. He had been pointed out to me two or three days before when he drove past with the governor's wife. He was a short, stiff-looking old man, though not over fifty-five, with a rather red little face, with thick grey locks of hair clustering under his chimney-pot hat, and curling round his clean little pink ears. His clean little face was not altogether handsome with its thin, long, crafty-looking lips, with its rather fleshy nose, and its sharp, shrewd little eyes. He was dressed somewhat shabbily in a sort of cape such as would be worn in Switzerland or North Italy at that time of year. But, at any rate, all the minor details of his costume, the little studs, and collar, the buttons, the tortoise-shell lorgnette on a narrow black ribbon, the signet-ring, were all such as are worn by persons of the most irreproachable good form. I am certain that in summer he must have worn light prunella shoes with mother-of-pearl buttons at the side. When we met he was standing still at the turning and looking about him, attentively. Noticing that I was looking at him with interest, he asked me in a sugary, though rather shrill voice:

"Allow me to ask, which is my nearest way to Bykovy Street?"

"To Bykovy Street? Oh, that's here, close by," I cried in great excitement. "Straight on along this street and the second turning to the left."

"Very much obliged to you."

A curse on that minute! I fancy I was shy, and looked cringing. He instantly noticed all that, and of course realised it all at once; that is, realised that I knew who he was, that I had read him and revered him from a child, and that I was shy and looked at him cringingly. He smiled, nodded again, and walked on as I had directed him. I don't know why I turned back to follow him; I don't know why I ran for ten paces beside him. He suddenly stood still again.

"And could you tell me where is the nearest cab-stand?" he shouted out to me again.

It was a horrid shout! A horrid voice!

"A cab-stand? The nearest cab-stand is ... by the Cathedral; there are always cabs standing there," and I almost turned to run for a cab for him. I almost believe that that was what he expected me to do. Of course I checked myself at once, and stood still, but he had noticed my movement and was still watching me with the same horrid smile. Then something happened which I shall never forget.

He suddenly dropped a tiny bag, which he was holding in his left hand; though indeed it was not a bag, but rather a little box, or more probably some part of a pocket-book, or to be more accurate a little reticule, rather like an old-fashioned lady's reticule, though I really don't know what it was. I only know that I flew to pick it up.

I am convinced that I did not really pick it up, but my first motion was unmistakable. I could not conceal it, and, like a fool, I turned crimson. The cunning fellow at once got all that could be got out of the circumstance.

"Don't trouble, I'll pick it up," he pronounced charmingly; that is, when he was quite sure that I was not going to pick up the reticule, he picked it up as though forestalling me, nodded once more, and went his way, leaving me to look like a fool. It was as good as though I had picked it up myself. For five minutes I considered myself utterly disgraced forever, but as I reached Stepan Trofimovitch's house I suddenly burst out laughing; the meeting struck me as so amusing that I immediately resolved to entertain Stepan Trofimovitch with an account of it, and even to act the whole scene to him.

III

But this time to my surprise I found an extraordinary change in him. He pounced on me with a sort of avidity, it is true, as soon as I went in, and began listening to me, but with such a distracted air that at first he evidently did not take in my words. But as soon as I pronounced the name of Karmazinov he suddenly flew into a frenzy.

"Don't speak of him! Don't pronounce that name!" he exclaimed, almost in a fury. "Here, look, read it! Read it!"

He opened the drawer and threw on the table three small sheets of paper, covered with a hurried pencil scrawl, all from Varvara Petrovna. The first letter was dated the day before yesterday, the second had come yesterday, and the last that day, an hour before. Their contents were quite trivial, and all referred to Karmazinov and betrayed the vain and fussy uneasiness of Varvara Petrovna and her apprehension that Karmazinov might forget to pay her a visit. Here is the first one dating from two days before. (Probably there had been one also three days before, and possibly another four days before as well.)

"If he deigns to visit you to-day, not a word about me, I beg. Not the faintest hint. Don't speak of me, don't mention me.—V. S."

The letter of the day before:

"If he decides to pay you a visit this morning, I think the most dignified thing would be not to receive him. That's what I think about it; I don't know what you think.—V. S."

To-day's, the last:

"I feel sure that you're in a regular litter and clouds of tobacco smoke. I'm sending you Marya and Fomushka. They'll tidy you up in half an hour. And don't hinder them, but go and sit in the kitchen while they clear up. I'm sending you a Bokhara rug and two china vases. I've long been meaning to make you a present of them, and I'm sending you my Teniers, too, for a time! You can put the vases in the window and hang the Teniers on the right under the portrait of Goethe; it will be more conspicuous there and it's always light there in the morning. If he does turn up at last, receive him with the utmost courtesy but try and talk of trifling matters, of some intellectual subject, and behave as though you had seen each other lately. Not a word about me. Perhaps I may look in on you in the evening.—V. S.

"P.S.—If he does not come to-day he won't come at all."

I read and was amazed that he was in such excitement over such trifles. Looking at him inquiringly, I noticed that he had had time while I was reading to change the everlasting white tie he always wore, for a red one. His hat and stick lay on the table. He was pale, and his hands were positively trembling.

"I don't care a hang about her anxieties," he cried frantically, in response to my inquiring look. "Je m'en fiche! She has the face to be excited about Karmazinov, and she does not answer my letters. Here is my unopened letter which she sent me back yesterday, here on the table under the book, under L'Homme qui rit. What is it to me that she's wearing herself out over Nikolay! Je m'en fiche, et je proclame ma liberté! Au diable le Karmazinov! Au diable la Lembke!

I've hidden the vases in the entry, and the Teniers in the chest of drawers, and I have demanded that she is to see me at once. Do you hear. I've insisted! I've sent her just such a scrap of paper, a pencil scrawl, unsealed, by Nastasya, and I'm waiting. I want Darya Pavlovna to speak to me with her own lips, before the face of Heaven, or at least before you. Vous me seconderez, n'est-ce pas, comme ami et témoin. I don't want to have to blush, to lie, I don't want secrets, I won't have secrets in this matter. Let them confess everything to me openly, frankly, honourably and then … then perhaps I may surprise the whole generation by my magnanimity.… Am I a scoundrel or not, my dear sir?" he concluded suddenly, looking menacingly at me, as though I'd considered him a scoundrel.

I offered him a sip of water; I had never seen him like this before. All the while he was talking he kept running from one end of the room to the other, but he suddenly stood still before me in an extraordinary attitude.

"Can you suppose," he began again with hysterical haughtiness, looking me up and down, "can you imagine that I, Stepan Verhovensky, cannot find in myself the moral strength to take my bag—my beggar's bag—and laying it on my feeble shoulders to go out at the gate and vanish forever, when honour and the great principle of independence demand it! It's not the first time that Stepan Verhovensky has had to repel despotism by moral force, even though it be the despotism of a crazy woman, that is, the most cruel and insulting despotism which can exist on earth, although you have, I fancy, forgotten yourself so much as to laugh at my phrase, my dear sir! Oh, you don't believe that I can find the moral strength in myself to end my life as a tutor in a merchant's family, or to die of hunger in a ditch! Answer me, answer at once; do you believe it, or don't you believe it?"

But I was purposely silent. I even affected to hesitate to wound him by answering in the negative, but to be unable to answer affirmatively. In all this nervous excitement of his there was something which really did offend me, and not personally, oh, no! But … I will explain later on. He positively turned pale.

"Perhaps you are bored with me, G——v (this is my surname), and you would like … not to come and see me at all?" he said in that tone of pale composure which usually precedes some extraordinary outburst. I jumped up in alarm. At that moment Nastasya came in, and, without a word, handed Stepan Trofimovitch a piece of paper, on which something was written in pencil. He glanced at it and flung it to me. On the paper, in Varvara Petrovna's hand three words were written: "Stay at home."

Stepan Trofimovitch snatched up his hat and stick in silence and went quickly out of the room. Mechanically I followed him. Suddenly voices and sounds of rapid footsteps were heard in the passage. He stood still, as though thunder-struck.

"It's Liputin; I am lost!" he whispered, clutching at my arm.

At the same instant Liputin walked into the room.

IV

Why he should be lost owing to Liputin I did not know, and indeed I did not attach much significance to the words; I put it all down to his nerves. His terror, however, was remarkable, and I made up my mind to keep a careful watch on him.

The very appearance of Liputin as he came in assured us that he had on this occasion a special right to come in, in spite of the prohibition. He brought with him an unknown gentleman, who must have been a new arrival in the town. In reply to the senseless stare of my petrified friend, he called out immediately in a loud voice:

"I'm bringing you a visitor, a special one! I make bold to intrude on your solitude. Mr. Kirillov, a very distinguished civil engineer. And what's more he knows your son, the much esteemed Pyotr Stepanovitch, very intimately; and he has a message from him. He's only just arrived."

"The message is your own addition," the visitor observed curtly. "There's no message at all. But I certainly do know Verhovensky. I left him in the X. province, ten days ahead of us."

Stepan Trofimovitch mechanically offered his hand and motioned him to sit down. He looked at me, he looked at Liputin, and then as though suddenly recollecting himself sat down himself, though he still kept his hat and stick in his hands without being aware of it.

"Bah, but you were going out yourself! I was told that you were quite knocked up with work."

"Yes, I'm ill, and you see, I meant to go for a walk, I ..." Stepan Trofimovitch checked himself, quickly flung his hat and stick on the sofa and—turned crimson.

Meantime, I was hurriedly examining the visitor. He was a young man, about twenty-seven, decently dressed, well made, slender and dark, with a pale, rather muddy-coloured face and black lustreless eyes. He seemed rather thoughtful and absent-minded, spoke jerkily and ungrammatically, transposing words in rather a strange way, and getting muddled if he attempted a sentence of any length. Liputin was perfectly aware of Stepan Trofimovitch's alarm, and was obviously pleased at it. He sat down in a wicker chair which he dragged almost into the middle of the room, so as to be at an equal distance between his host and the visitor, who had installed themselves on sofas on opposite sides of the room. His sharp eyes darted inquisitively from one corner of the room to another.

"It's.... a long while since I've seen Petrusha.... You met abroad?" Stepan Trofimovitch managed to mutter to the visitor.

"Both here and abroad."

"Alexey Nilitch has only just returned himself after living four years abroad," put in Liputin. "He has been travelling to perfect himself in his speciality and has come to us because he has good reasons to expect a job on the building of our railway bridge, and he's now waiting for an answer about it. He knows the Drozdovs and Lizaveta Nikolaevna, through Pyotr Stepanovitch."

The engineer sat, as it were, with a ruffled air, and listened with awkward impatience. It seemed to me that he was angry about something.

"He knows Nikolay Vsyevolodovitch too."

"Do you know Nikolay Vsyevolodovitch?" inquired Stepan Trofimovitch.

"I know him too."

"It's … it's a very long time since I've seen Petrusha, and … I feel I have so little right to call myself a father … c'est le mot; I … how did you leave him?"

"Oh, yes, I left him … he comes himself," replied Mr. Kirillov, in haste to be rid of the question again. He certainly was angry.

"He's coming! At last I … you see, it's very long since I've seen Petrusha!" Stepan Trofimovitch could not get away from this phrase. "Now I expect my poor boy to whom … to whom I have been so much to blame! That is, I mean to say, when I left him in Petersburg, I … in short, I looked on him as a nonentity, quelque chose dans ce genre. He was a very nervous boy, you know, emotional, and … very timid. When he said his prayers going to bed he used to bow down to the ground, and make the sign of the cross on his pillow that he might not die in the night…. Je m'en souviens. Enfin, no artistic feeling whatever, not a sign of anything higher, of anything fundamental, no embryo of a future ideal … c'était comme un petit idiot, but I'm afraid I am incoherent; excuse me … you came upon me …"

"You say seriously that he crossed his pillow?" the engineer asked suddenly with marked curiosity.

"Yes, he used to …"

"All right. I just asked. Go on."

Stepan Trofimovitch looked interrogatively at Liputin.

"I'm very grateful to you for your visit. But I must confess I'm … not in a condition … just now … But allow me to ask where you are lodging."

"At Filipov's, in Bogoyavlensky Street."

"Ach, that's where Shatov lives," I observed involuntarily.

"Just so, in the very same house," cried Liputin, "only Shatov lodges above, in the attic, while he's down below, at Captain Lebyadkin's. He knows Shatov too, and he knows Shatov's wife. He was very intimate with her, abroad."

"Comment! Do you really know anything about that unhappy marriage de ce pauvre ami and that woman," cried Stepan Trofimovitch, carried away by sudden feeling. "You are the first man I've met who has known her personally; and if only …"

"What nonsense!" the engineer snapped out, flushing all over. "How you add to things, Liputin! I've not seen Shatov's wife; I've only once seen her in the distance and not at all close…. I know Shatov. Why do you add things of all sorts?"

He turned round sharply on the sofa, clutched his hat, then laid it down again, and settling himself down once more as before, fixed his angry black eyes on Stepan Trofimovitch with a sort of defiance. I was at a loss to understand such strange irritability.

"Excuse me," Stepan Trofimovitch observed impressively. "I understand that it may be a very delicate subject…."

"No sort of delicate subject in it, and indeed it's shameful, and I didn't shout at you that it's nonsense, but at Liputin, because he adds things. Excuse me if you took it to yourself. I know Shatov, but I don't know his wife at all … I don't know her at all!"

"I understand. I understand. And if I insisted, it's only because I'm very fond of our poor friend, notre irascible ami, and have always taken an interest in him…. In my opinion that man changed his former, possibly over-youthful but yet sound ideas, too abruptly. And now he says all sorts of things about notre Sainte Russie to such a degree that I've long explained this upheaval in his whole constitution, I can only call it that, to some violent shock in his family life, and, in fact, to his unsuccessful marriage. I, who know my poor Russia like the fingers on my hand, and have devoted my whole life to the Russian people, I can assure you that he does not know the Russian people, and what's more …"

"I don't know the Russian people at all, either, and I haven't time to study them," the engineer snapped out again, and again he turned sharply on the sofa. Stepan Trofimovitch was pulled up in the middle of his speech.

"He is studying them, he is studying them," interposed Liputin. "He has already begun the study of them, and is writing a very interesting article dealing with the causes of the increase of suicide in Russia, and, generally speaking, the causes that lead to the increase or decrease of suicide in society. He has reached amazing results."

The engineer became dreadfully excited. "You have no right at all," he muttered wrathfully. "I'm not writing an article. I'm not going to do silly things. I asked you confidentially, quite by chance. There's no article at all. I'm not publishing, and you haven't the right …" Liputin was obviously enjoying himself.

"I beg your pardon, perhaps I made a mistake in calling your literary work an article. He is only collecting observations, and the essence of the question, or, so to say, its moral aspect he is not touching at all. And, indeed, he rejects morality itself altogether, and holds with the last new principle of general destruction for the sake of ultimate good. He demands already more than a hundred million heads for the establishment of common sense in Europe; many more than they demanded at the last Peace Congress. Alexey Nilitch goes further than anyone in that sense." The engineer listened with a pale and contemptuous smile. For half a minute every one was silent.

"All this is stupid, Liputin," Mr. Kirillov observed at last, with a certain dignity. "If I by chance had said some things to you, and you caught them up again, as you like. But you have no right, for I never speak to anyone. I scorn to talk…. If one has a conviction then it's clear to me…. But you're doing foolishly. I don't argue about things when everything's settled. I can't bear arguing. I never want to argue…."

"And perhaps you are very wise," Stepan Trofimovitch could not resist saying.

"I apologise to you, but I am not angry with anyone here," the visitor went on, speaking hotly and rapidly. "I have seen few people for four years. For four years I have talked little and have tried to see no one, for my own objects which do not concern anyone else, for four years. Liputin found this out and is laughing. I understand and don't mind. I'm not ready to take offence, only annoyed at his liberty. And if I don't explain my ideas to you," he concluded unexpectedly, scanning us all with resolute eyes, "it's not at all that I'm afraid of your giving information to the government; that's not so; please do not imagine nonsense of that sort."

No one made any reply to these words. We only looked at each other. Even Liputin forgot to snigger.

"Gentlemen, I'm very sorry"—Stepan Trofimovitch got up resolutely from the sofa—"but I feel ill and upset. Excuse me."

"Ach, that's for us to go." Mr. Kirillov started, snatching up his cap. "It's a good thing you told us. I'm so forgetful."

He rose, and with a good-natured air went up to Stepan Trofimovitch, holding out his hand.

"I'm sorry you're not well, and I came."

"I wish you every success among us," answered Stepan Trofimovitch, shaking hands with him heartily and without haste. "I understand that, if as you say you have lived so long abroad, cutting yourself off from people for objects of your own and forgetting Russia, you must inevitably look with wonder on us who are Russians to the backbone, and we must feel the same about you. Mais cela passera. I'm only puzzled at one thing: you want to build our bridge and at the same time you declare that you hold with the principle of universal destruction. They won't let you build our bridge."

"What! What's that you said? Ach, I say!" Kirillov cried, much struck, and he suddenly broke into the most frank and good-humoured laughter. For a moment his face took a quite childlike expression, which I thought suited him particularly. Liputin rubbed his hand with delight at Stepan Trofimovitch's witty remark. I kept wondering to myself why Stepan Trofimovitch was so frightened of Liputin, and why he had cried out "I am lost" when he heard him coming.

V

We were all standing in the doorway. It was the moment when hosts and guests hurriedly exchange the last and most cordial words, and then part to their mutual gratification.

"The reason he's so cross to-day," Liputin dropped all at once, as it were casually, when he was just going out of the room, "is because he had a disturbance to-day with Captain Lebyadkin over his sister. Captain Lebyadkin thrashes that precious sister of his, the mad girl, every day with a whip, a real Cossack whip, every morning and evening. So Alexey Nilitch has positively taken the lodge so as not to be present. Well, good-bye."

"A sister? An invalid? With a whip?" Stepan Trofimovitch cried out, as though he had suddenly been lashed with a whip himself. "What sister? What Lebyadkin?" All his former terror came back in an instant.

"Lebyadkin! Oh, that's the retired captain; he used only to call himself a lieutenant before...."

"Oh, what is his rank to me? What sister? Good heavens!... You say Lebyadkin? But there used to be a Lebyadkin here...."

"That's the very man. 'Our' Lebyadkin, at Virginsky's, you remember?"

"But he was caught with forged papers?"

"Well, now he's come back. He's been here almost three weeks and under the most peculiar circumstances."

"Why, but he's a scoundrel?"

"As though no one could be a scoundrel among us," Liputin grinned suddenly, his knavish little eyes seeming to peer into Stepan Trofimovitch's soul.

"Good heavens! I didn't mean that at all ... though I quite agree with you about that, with you particularly. But what then, what then? What did you mean by that? You certainly meant something by that."

"Why, it's all so trivial.... This captain to all appearances went away from us at that time; not because of the forged papers, but simply to look for his sister, who was in hiding from him somewhere, it seems; well, and now he's brought her and that's the whole story. Why do you seem frightened, Stepan Trofimovitch? I only tell this from his drunken chatter though, he doesn't speak of it himself when he's sober. He's an irritable man, and, so to speak, æsthetic in a military style; only he has bad taste. And this sister is lame as well as mad. She seems to have been seduced by someone, and Mr. Lebyadkin has, it seems, for many years received a yearly grant from the seducer by way of compensation for the wound to his honour, so it would seem at least from his chatter, though I believe it's only drunken talk. It's simply his brag. Besides, that sort of thing is done much cheaper. But that he has a sum of money is perfectly certain. Ten days ago he was walking barefoot, and now I've seen hundreds in his hands. His sister has fits of some sort every day, she shrieks and he 'keeps her in order' with the whip. You must inspire a woman with respect, he says. What I can't understand is how Shatov goes on living above him. Alexey Nilitch has only been three days with them. They were acquainted in Petersburg, and now he's taken the lodge to get away from the disturbance."

"Is this all true?" said Stepan Trofimovitch, addressing the engineer.

"You do gossip a lot, Liputin," the latter muttered wrathfully.

"Mysteries, secrets! Where have all these mysteries and secrets among us sprung from?" Stepan Trofimovitch could not refrain from exclaiming.

The engineer frowned, flushed red, shrugged his shoulders and went out of the room.

"Alexey Nilitch positively snatched the whip out of his hand, broke it and threw it out of the window, and they had a violent quarrel," added Liputin.

"Why are you chattering, Liputin; it's stupid. What for?" Alexey Nilitch turned again instantly.

"Why be so modest and conceal the generous impulses of one's soul; that is, of your soul? I'm not speaking of my own."

"How stupid it is … and quite unnecessary. Lebyadkin's stupid and quite worthless—and no use to the cause, and … utterly mischievous. Why do you keep babbling all sorts of things? I'm going."

"Oh, what a pity!" cried Liputin with a candid smile, "or I'd have amused you with another little story, Stepan Trofimovitch. I came, indeed, on purpose to tell you, though I dare say you've heard it already. Well, till another time, Alexey Nilitch is in such a hurry. Good-bye for the present. The story concerns Varvara Petrovna. She amused me the day before yesterday; she sent for me on purpose. It's simply killing. Good-bye."

But at this Stepan Trofimovitch absolutely would not let him go. He seized him by the shoulders, turned him sharply back into the room, and sat him down in a chair. Liputin was positively scared.

"Why, to be sure," he began, looking warily at Stepan Trofimovitch from his chair, "she suddenly sent for me and asked me 'confidentially' my private opinion, whether Nikolay Vsyevolodovitch is mad or in his right mind. Isn't that astonishing?"

"You're out of your mind!" muttered Stepan Trofimovitch, and suddenly, as though he were beside himself: "Liputin, you know perfectly well that you only came here to tell me something insulting of that sort and … something worse!"

In a flash, I recalled his conjecture that Liputin knew not only more than we did about our affair, but something else which we should never know.

"Upon my word, Stepan Trofimovitch," muttered Liputin, seeming greatly alarmed, "upon my word …"

"Hold your tongue and begin! I beg you, Mr. Kirillov, to come back too, and be present. I earnestly beg you! Sit down, and you, Liputin, begin directly, simply and without any excuses."

"If I had only known it would upset you so much I wouldn't have begun at all. And of course I thought you knew all about it from Varvara Petrovna herself."

"You didn't think that at all. Begin, begin, I tell you."

"Only do me the favour to sit down yourself, or how can I sit here when you are running about before me in such excitement. I can't speak coherently."

Stepan Trofimovitch restrained himself and sank impressively into an easy chair. The engineer stared gloomily at the floor. Liputin looked at them with intense enjoyment,

"How am I to begin?… I'm too overwhelmed.…"

VI

"The day before yesterday a servant was suddenly sent to me: 'You are asked to call at twelve o'clock,' said he. Can you fancy such a thing? I threw aside my work, and precisely at midday yesterday I was ringing at the bell. I was let into the drawing room; I waited a minute—she came in; she made me sit down and sat down herself, opposite. I sat down, and I couldn't believe it; you know how she has always treated me. She began at once without beating about the bush, you know her way. 'You remember,' she said, 'that four years ago when Nikolay Vsyevolodovitch was ill he did some strange things which made all the town wonder till the position was explained. One of those actions concerned you personally. When Nikolay Vsyevolodovitch recovered he went at my request to call on you. I know that he talked to you several times before, too. Tell me openly and candidly what you ... (she faltered a little at this point) what you thought of Nikolay Vsyevolodovitch then ... what was your view of him altogether ... what idea you were able to form of him at that time ... and still have?'

"Here she was completely confused, so that she paused for a whole minute, and suddenly flushed. I was alarmed. She began again—touchingly is not quite the word, it's not applicable to her—but in a very impressive tone:

"'I want you,' she said, 'to understand me clearly and without mistake. I've sent for you now because I look upon you as a keen-sighted and quick-witted man, qualified to make accurate observations.' (What compliments!) 'You'll understand too,' she said, 'that I am a mother appealing to you.... Nikolay Vsyevolodovitch has suffered some calamities and has passed through many changes of fortune in his life. All that,' she said, 'might well have affected the state of his mind. I'm not speaking of madness, of course,' she said, 'that's quite out of the question!' (This was uttered proudly and resolutely.) 'But there might be something strange, something peculiar, some turn of thought, a tendency to some particular way of looking at things.' (Those were her exact words, and I admired, Stepan Trofimovitch, the exactness with which Varvara Petrovna can put things. She's a lady of superior intellect!) 'I have noticed in him, anyway,' she said, 'a perpetual restlessness and a tendency to peculiar impulses. But I am a mother and you are an impartial spectator, and therefore qualified with your intelligence to form a more impartial opinion. I implore you, in fact' (yes, that word, 'implore' was uttered!), 'to tell me the whole truth, without mincing matters. And if you will give me your word never to forget that I have spoken to you in confidence, you may reckon upon my always being ready to seize every opportunity in the future to show my gratitude.' Well, what do you say to that?"

"You have ... so amazed me ..." faltered Stepan Trofimovitch, "that I don't believe you."

"Yes, observe, observe," cried Liputin, as though he had not heard Stepan Trofimovitch, "observe what must be her agitation and uneasiness if she stoops from her grandeur to appeal to a man like me, and even condescends to beg me to keep it secret. What do you call that? Hasn't she received some news of Nikolay Vsyevolodovitch, something unexpected?"

"I don't know ... of news of any sort ... I haven't seen her for some days, but ... but I must say ..." lisped Stepan Trofimovitch, evidently hardly able to think clearly, "but I must say, Liputin, that if it was said to you in confidence, and here you're telling it before every one ..."

"Absolutely in confidence! But God strike me dead if I ... But as for telling it here ... what does it matter? Are we strangers, even Alexey Nilitch?"

"I don't share that attitude. No doubt we three here will keep the secret, but I'm afraid of the fourth, you, and wouldn't trust you in anything...."

"What do you mean by that? Why it's more to my interest than anyone's, seeing I was promised eternal gratitude! What I wanted was to point out in this connection one extremely strange incident, rather to say, psychological than simply strange. Yesterday evening, under the influence of my conversation with Varvara Petrovna—you can fancy yourself what an impression it made on me—I approached Alexey Nilitch with a discreet question: 'You knew Nikolay Vsyevolodovitch abroad,' said I, 'and used to know him before in Petersburg too. What do you think of his mind and his abilities?' said I. He answered laconically, as his way is, that he was a man of subtle intellect and sound judgment. 'And have you never noticed in the course of years,' said I, 'any turn of ideas or peculiar way of looking at things, or any, so to say, insanity?' In fact, I repeated Varvara Petrovna's own question. And would you believe it, Alexey Nilitch suddenly grew thoughtful, and scowled, just as he's doing now. 'Yes,' said he, 'I have sometimes thought there was something strange.' Take note, too, that if anything could have seemed strange even to Alexey Nilitch, it must really have been something, mustn't it?"

"Is that true?" said Stepan Trofimovitch, turning to Alexey Nilitch.

"I should prefer not to speak of it," answered Alexey Nilitch, suddenly raising his head, and looking at him with flashing eyes. "I wish to contest your right to do this, Liputin. You've no right to drag me into this. I did not give my whole opinion at all. Though I knew Nikolay Stavrogin in Petersburg that was long ago, and though I've met him since I know him very little. I beg you to leave me out and … All this is something like scandal."

Liputin threw up his hands with an air of oppressed innocence.

"A scandal-monger! Why not say a spy while you're about it? It's all very well for you, Alexey Nilitch, to criticise when you stand aloof from everything. But you wouldn't believe it, Stepan Trofimovitch—take Captain Lebyadkin, he is stupid enough, one may say … in fact, one's ashamed to say how stupid he is; there is a Russian comparison, to signify the degree of it; and do you know he considers himself injured by Nikolay Vsyevolodovitch, though he is full of admiration for his wit. 'I'm amazed,' said he, 'at that man. He's a subtle serpent.' His own words. And I said to him (still under the influence of my conversation, and after I had spoken to Alexey Nilitch), 'What do you think, captain, is your subtle serpent mad or not?' Would you believe it, it was just as if I'd given him a sudden lash from behind. He simply leapt up from his seat. 'Yes,' said he, ' … yes, only that,' he said, 'cannot affect …' 'Affect what?' He didn't finish. Yes, and then he fell to thinking so bitterly, thinking so much, that his drunkenness dropped off him. We were sitting in Filipov's restaurant. And it wasn't till half an hour later that he suddenly struck the table with his fist. 'Yes,' said he, 'maybe he's mad, but that can't affect it.…' Again he didn't say what it couldn't affect. Of course I'm only giving you an extract of the conversation, but one can understand the sense of it. You may ask whom you like, they all have the same idea in their heads, though it never entered anyone's head before. 'Yes,' they say, 'he's mad; he's very clever, but perhaps he's mad too.'"

Stepan Trofimovitch sat pondering, and thought intently.

"And how does Lebyadkin know?"

"Do you mind inquiring about that of Alexey Nilitch, who has just called me a spy? I'm a spy, yet I don't know, but Alexey Nilitch knows all the ins and outs of it, and holds his tongue."

"I know nothing about it, or hardly anything," answered the engineer with the same irritation. "You make Lebyadkin drunk to find out. You brought me here to find out and to make me say. And so you must be a spy."

"I haven't made him drunk yet, and he's not worth the money either, with all his secrets. They are not worth that to me. I don't know what they are to you. On the contrary, he is scattering the money, though twelve days ago he begged fifteen kopecks of me, and it's he treats me to champagne, not I him. But you've given me an idea, and if there should be occasion I will make him drunk, just to get to the bottom of it and maybe I shall find out ... all your little secrets," Liputin snapped back spitefully.

Stepan Trofimovitch looked in bewilderment at the two disputants. Both were giving themselves away, and what's more, were not standing on ceremony. The thought crossed my mind that Liputin had brought this Alexey Nilitch to us with the simple object of drawing him into a conversation through a third person for purposes of his own—his favourite manœuvre.

"Alexey Nilitch knows Nikolay Vsyevolodovitch quite well," he went on, irritably, "only he conceals it. And as to your question about Captain Lebyadkin, he made his acquaintance before any of us did, six years ago in Petersburg, in that obscure, if one may so express it, epoch in the life of Nikolay Vsyevolodovitch, before he had dreamed of rejoicing our hearts by coming here. Our prince, one must conclude, surrounded himself with rather a queer selection of acquaintances. It was at that time, it seems, that he made acquaintance with this gentleman here."

"Take care, Liputin. I warn you, Nikolay Vsyevolodovitch meant to be here soon himself, and he knows how to defend himself."

"Why warn me? I am the first to cry out that he is a man of the most subtle and refined intelligence, and I quite reassured Varvara Petrovna yesterday on that score. 'It's his character,' I said to her, 'that I can't answer for.' Lebyadkin said the same thing yesterday: 'A lot of harm has come to me from his character,' he said. Stepan Trofimovitch, it's all very well for you to cry out about slander and spying, and at the very time observe that you wring it all out of me, and with such immense curiosity too. Now, Varvara Petrovna went straight to the point yesterday. 'You have had a personal interest in the business,' she said, 'that's why I appeal to you.' I should say so! What need to look for motives when I've swallowed a personal insult from his excellency before the whole society of the place. I should think I have grounds to be interested, not merely for the sake of gossip. He shakes hands with you one day, and next day, for no earthly reason, he returns your hospitality by slapping you on the cheeks in the face of all decent society, if the fancy takes him, out of sheer wantonness. And what's more, the fair sex is everything for them, these butterflies and mettlesome cocks! Grand gentlemen with little wings like the ancient cupids, lady-killing Petchorins! It's all very well for you, Stepan Trofimovitch, a confirmed bachelor, to talk like that, stick up for his excellency and call me a slanderer. But if you married a pretty young wife—as you're still such a fine fellow—then I dare say you'd bolt your door against our prince, and throw up barricades in your house! Why, if only that Mademoiselle Lebyadkin, who is thrashed with a whip, were not mad and bandy-legged, by Jove, I should fancy she was the victim of the passions of our general, and that it was from him that Captain Lebyadkin had suffered 'in his family dignity,' as he expresses it himself. Only perhaps that is inconsistent with his refined taste, though, indeed, even that's no hindrance to him. Every berry is worth picking if only he's in the mood for it. You talk of slander, but I'm not crying this aloud though the whole town is ringing with it; I only listen and assent. That's not prohibited."

"The town's ringing with it? What's the town ringing with?"

"That is, Captain Lebyadkin is shouting for all the town to hear, and isn't that just the same as the market-place ringing with it? How am I to blame? I interest myself in it only among friends, for, after all, I consider myself among friends here." He looked at us with an innocent air. "Something's happened, only consider: they say his excellency has sent three hundred roubles from Switzerland by a most honourable young lady, and, so to say, modest orphan, whom I have the honour of knowing, to be handed over to Captain Lebyadkin. And Lebyadkin, a little later, was told as an absolute fact also by a very honourable and therefore trustworthy person, I won't say whom, that not three hundred but a thousand roubles had been sent!… And so, Lebyadkin keeps crying out 'the young lady has grabbed seven hundred roubles belonging to me,' and he's almost ready to call in the police; he threatens to, anyway, and he's making an uproar all over the town."

"This is vile, vile of you!" cried the engineer, leaping up suddenly from his chair.

"But I say, you are yourself the honourable person who brought word to Lebyadkin from Nikolay Vsyevolodovitch that a thousand roubles were sent, not three hundred. Why, the captain told me so himself when he was drunk."

"It's … it's an unhappy misunderstanding. Some one's made a mistake and it's led to … It's nonsense, and it's base of you."

"But I'm ready to believe that it's nonsense, and I'm distressed at the story, for, take it as you will, a girl of an honourable reputation is implicated first over the seven hundred roubles, and secondly in unmistakable intimacy with Nikolay Vsyevolodovitch. For how much does it mean to his excellency to disgrace a girl of good character, or put to shame another man's wife, like that incident with me? If he comes across a generous-hearted man he'll force him to cover the sins of others under the shelter of his honourable name. That's just what I had to put up with, I'm speaking of myself…."

"Be careful, Liputin." Stepan Trofimovitch got up from his easy chair and turned pale.

"Don't believe it, don't believe it! Somebody has made a mistake and Lebyadkin's drunk …" exclaimed the engineer in indescribable excitement. "It will all be explained, but I can't…. And I think it's low…. And that's enough, enough!"

He ran out of the room.

"What are you about? Why, I'm going with you!" cried Liputin, startled. He jumped up and ran after Alexey Nilitch.

VII

Stepan Trofimovitch stood a moment reflecting, looked at me as though he did not see me, took up his hat and stick and walked quietly out of the room. I followed him again, as before. As we went out of the gate, noticing that I was accompanying him, he said:

"Oh yes, you may serve as a witness … de l'accident. Vous m'accompagnerez, n'est-ce pas?"

"Stepan Trofimovitch, surely you're not going there again? Think what may come of it!"

With a pitiful and distracted smile, a smile of shame and utter despair, and at the same time of a sort of strange ecstasy, he whispered to me, standing still for an instant:

"I can't marry to cover 'another man's sins'!"

These words were just what I was expecting. At last that fatal sentence that he had kept hidden from me was uttered aloud, after a whole week of shuffling and pretence. I was positively enraged.

"And you, Stepan Verhovensky, with your luminous mind, your kind heart, can harbour such a dirty, such a low idea … and could before Liputin came!"

He looked at me, made no answer and walked on in the same direction. I did not want to be left behind. I wanted to give Varvara Petrovna my version. I could have forgiven him if he had simply with his womanish faint-heartedness believed Liputin, but now it was clear that he had thought of it all himself long before, and that Liputin had only confirmed his suspicions and poured oil on the flames. He had not hesitated to suspect the girl from the very first day, before he had any kind of grounds, even Liputin's words, to go upon. Varvara Petrovna's despotic behaviour he had explained to himself as due to her haste to cover up the aristocratic misdoings of her precious "Nicolas" by marrying the girl to an honourable man! I longed for him to be punished for it.

"Oh, Dieu, qui est si grand et si bon! Oh, who will comfort me!" he exclaimed, halting suddenly again, after walking a hundred paces.

"Come straight home and I'll make everything clear to you," I cried, turning him by force towards home.

"It's he! Stepan Trofimovitch, it's you? You?" A fresh, joyous young voice rang out like music behind us.

We had seen nothing, but a lady on horseback suddenly made her appearance beside us—Lizaveta Nikolaevna with her invariable companion. She pulled up her horse.

"Come here, come here quickly!" she called to us, loudly and merrily. "It's twelve years since I've seen him, and I know him, while he.… Do you really not know me?"

Stepan Trofimovitch clasped the hand held out to him and kissed it reverently. He gazed at her as though he were praying and could not utter a word.

"He knows me, and is glad! Mavriky Nikolaevitch, he's delighted to see me! Why is it you haven't been to see us all this fortnight? Auntie tried to persuade me you were ill and must not be disturbed; but I know Auntie tells lies. I kept stamping and swearing at you, but I had made up my mind, quite made up my mind, that you should come to me first, that was why I didn't send to you. Heavens, why he hasn't changed a bit!" She scrutinised him, bending down from the saddle. "He's absurdly unchanged. Oh, yes, he has wrinkles, a lot of wrinkles, round his eyes and on his cheeks some grey hair, but his eyes are just the same. And have I changed? Have I changed? Why don't you say something?"

I remembered at that moment the story that she had been almost ill when she was taken away to Petersburg at eleven years old, and that she had cried during her illness and asked for Stepan Trofimovitch.

"You … I …" he faltered now in a voice breaking with joy. "I was just crying out 'who will comfort me?' and I heard your voice. I look on it as a miracle et je commence à croire."

"En Dieu! En Dieu qui est là-haut et qui est si grand et si bon! You see, I know all your lectures by heart. Mavriky Nikolaevitch, what faith he used to preach to me then, en Dieu qui est si grand et si bon! And do you remember your story of how Columbus discovered America, and they all cried out, 'Land! land!'? My nurse Alyona Frolovna says I was light-headed at night afterwards, and kept crying out 'land! land!' in my sleep. And do you remember how you told me the story of Prince Hamlet? And do you remember how you described to me how the poor emigrants were transported from Europe to America? And it was all untrue; I found out afterwards how they were transited. But what beautiful fibs he used to tell me then, Mavriky Nikolaevitch! They were better than the truth. Why do you look at Mavriky Nikolaevitch like that? He is the best and finest man on the face of the globe and you must like him just as you do me! Il fait tout ce que je veux. But, dear Stepan Trofimovitch, you must be unhappy again, since you cry out in the middle of the street asking who will comfort you. Unhappy, aren't you? Aren't you?"

"Now I'm happy…."

"Aunt is horrid to you?" she went on, without listening. "She's just the same as ever, cross, unjust, and always our precious aunt! And do you remember how you threw yourself into my arms in the garden and I comforted you and cried—don't be afraid of Mavriky Nikolaevitch; he has known all about you, everything, for ever so long; you can weep on his shoulder as long as you like, and he'll stand there as long as you like! … Lift up your hat, take it off altogether for a minute, lift up your head, stand on tiptoe, I want to kiss you on the forehead as I kissed you for the last time when we parted. Do you see that young lady's admiring us out of the window? Come closer, closer! Heavens! How grey he is!"

And bending over in the saddle she kissed him on the forehead.

"Come, now to your home! I know where you live. I'll be with you directly, in a minute. I'll make you the first visit, you stubborn man, and then I must have you for a whole day at home. You can go and make ready for me."

And she galloped off with her cavalier. We returned. Stepan Trofimovitch sat down on the sofa and began to cry.

"Dieu, Dieu." he exclaimed, "enfin une minute de bonheur!"

Not more than ten minutes afterwards she reappeared according to her promise, escorted by her Mavriky Nikolaevitch.

"Vous et le bonheur, vous arrivez en même temps!" He got up to meet her.

"Here's a nosegay for you; I rode just now to Madame Chevalier's, she has flowers all the winter for name-days. Here's Mavriky Nikolaevitch, please make friends. I wanted to bring you a cake instead of a nosegay, but Mavriky Nikolaevitch declares that is not in the Russian spirit."

Mavriky Nikolaevitch was an artillery captain, a tall and handsome man of thirty-three, irreproachably correct in appearance, with an imposing and at first sight almost stern countenance, in spite of his wonderful and delicate kindness which no one could fail to perceive almost the first moment of making his acquaintance. He was taciturn, however, seemed very self-possessed and made no efforts to gain friends. Many of us said later that he was by no means clever; but this was not altogether just.

I won't attempt to describe the beauty of Lizaveta Nikolaevna. The whole town was talking of it, though some of our ladies and young girls indignantly differed on the subject. There were some among them who already detested her, and principally for her pride. The Drozdovs had scarcely begun to pay calls, which mortified them, though the real reason for the delay was Praskovya Ivanovna's invalid state. They detested her in the second place because she was a relative of the governor's wife, and thirdly because she rode out every day on horseback. We had never had young ladies who rode on horseback before; it was only natural that the appearance of Lizaveta Nikolaevna on horseback and her neglect to pay calls was bound to offend local society. Yet every one knew that riding was prescribed her by the doctor's orders, and they talked sarcastically of her illness. She really was ill. What struck me at first sight in her was her abnormal, nervous, incessant restlessness. Alas, the poor girl was very unhappy, and everything was explained later. To-day, recalling the past, I should not say she was such a beauty as she seemed to me then. Perhaps she was really not pretty at all. Tall, slim, but strong and supple, she struck one by the irregularities of the lines of her face. Her eyes were set somewhat like a Kalmuck's, slanting; she was pale and thin in the face with high cheek-bones, but there was something in the face that conquered and fascinated! There was something powerful in the ardent glance of her dark eyes. She always made her appearance "like a conquering heroine, and to spread her conquests." She seemed proud and at times even arrogant. I don't know whether she succeeded in being kind, but I know that she wanted to, and made terrible efforts to force herself to be a little kind. There were, no doubt, many fine impulses and the very best elements in her character, but everything in her seemed perpetually seeking its balance and unable to find it; everything was in chaos, in agitation, in uneasiness. Perhaps the demands she made upon herself were too severe, and she was never able to find in herself the strength to satisfy them.

She sat on the sofa and looked round the room.

"Why do I always begin to feel sad at such moments; explain that mystery, you learned person? I've been thinking all my life that I should be goodness knows how pleased at seeing you and recalling everything, and here I somehow don't feel pleased at all, although I do love you.... Ach, heavens! He has my portrait on the wall! Give it here. I remember it! I remember it!"

An exquisite miniature in water-colour of Liza at twelve years old had been sent nine years before to Stepan Trofimovitch from Petersburg by the Drozdovs. He had kept it hanging on his wall ever since.

"Was I such a pretty child? Can that really have been my face?"

She stood up, and with the portrait in her hand looked in the looking-glass.

"Make haste, take it!" she cried, giving back the portrait. "Don't hang it up now, afterwards. I don't want to look at it."

She sat down on the sofa again. "One life is over and another is begun, then that one is over—a third begins, and so on, endlessly. All the ends are snipped off as it were with scissors. See what stale things I'm telling you. Yet how much truth there is in them!"

She looked at me, smiling; she had glanced at me several times already, but in his excitement Stepan Trofimovitch forgot that he had promised to introduce me.

"And why have you hung my portrait under those daggers? And why have you got so many daggers and sabres?"

He had as a fact hanging on the wall, I don't know why, two crossed daggers and above them a genuine Circassian sabre. As she asked this question she looked so directly at me that I wanted to answer, but hesitated to speak. Stepan Trofimovitch grasped the position at last and introduced me.

"I know, I know," she said, "I'm delighted to meet you. Mother has heard a great deal about you, too. Let me introduce you to Mavriky Nikolaevitch too, he's a splendid person. I had formed a funny notion of you already. You're Stepan Trofimovitch's confidant, aren't you?"

I turned rather red.

"Ach, forgive me, please. I used quite the wrong word: not funny at all, but only ..." She was confused and blushed. "Why be ashamed though at your being a splendid person? Well, it's time we were going, Mavriky Nikolaevitch! Stepan Trofimovitch, you must be with us in half an hour. Mercy, what a lot we shall talk! Now I'm your confidante, and about everything, everything, you understand?"

Stepan Trofimovitch was alarmed at once.

"Oh, Mavriky Nikolaevitch knows everything, don't mind him!"

"What does he know?"

"Why, what do you mean?" she cried in astonishment. "Bah, why it's true then that they're hiding it! I wouldn't believe it! And they're hiding Dasha, too. Aunt wouldn't let me go in to see Dasha to-day. She says she's got a headache."

"But ... but how did you find out?"

"My goodness, like every one else. That needs no cunning!"

"But does every one else ...?"

"Why, of course. Mother, it's true, heard it first through Alyona Frolovna, my nurse; your Nastasya ran round to tell her. You told Nastasya, didn't you? She says you told her yourself."

"I ... I did once speak," Stepan Trofimovitch faltered, crimsoning all over, "but ... I only hinted ... j'étais si nerveux et malade, et puis ..."

She laughed.

"And your confidant didn't happen to be at hand, and Nastasya turned up. Well that was enough! And the whole town's full of her cronies! Come, it doesn't matter, let them know; it's all the better. Make haste and come to us, we dine early.... Oh, I forgot," she added, sitting down again; "listen, what sort of person is Shatov?"

"Shatov? He's the brother of Darya Pavlovna."

"I know he's her brother! What a person you are, really," she interrupted impatiently. "I want to know what he's like; what sort of man he is."

"C'est un pense-creux d'ici. C'est le meilleur et le plus irascible homme du monde."

"I've heard that he's rather queer. But that wasn't what I meant. I've heard that he knows three languages, one of them English, and can do literary work. In that case I've a lot of work for him. I want someone to help me and the sooner the better. Would he take the work or not? He's been recommended to me...."

"Oh, most certainly he will. Et vous ferez un bienfait...."

"I'm not doing it as a bienfait. I need someone to help me."

"I know Shatov pretty well," I said, "and if you will trust me with a message to him I'll go to him this minute."

"Tell him to come to me at twelve o'clock to-morrow morning. Capital! Thank you. Mavriky Nikolaevitch, are you ready?"

They went away. I ran at once, of course, to Shatov.

"Mon ami!" said Stepan Trofimovitch, overtaking me on the steps. "Be sure to be at my lodging at ten or eleven o'clock when I come back. Oh, I've acted very wrongly in my conduct to you and to every one."

VIII

I did not find Shatov at home. I ran round again, two hours later. He was still out. At last, at eight o'clock I went to him again, meaning to leave a note if I did not find him; again I failed to find him. His lodging was shut up, and he lived alone without a servant of any sort. I did think of knocking at Captain Lebyadkin's down below to ask about Shatov; but it was all shut up below, too, and there was no sound or light as though the place were empty. I passed by Lebyadkin's door with curiosity, remembering the stories I had heard that day. Finally, I made up my mind to come very early next morning. To tell the truth I did not put much confidence in the effect of a note. Shatov might take no notice of it; he was so obstinate and shy. Cursing my want of success, I was going out of the gate when all at once I stumbled on Mr. Kirillov. He was going into the house and he recognised me first. As he began questioning me of himself, I told him how things were, and that I had a note.

"Let us go in," said he, "I will do everything."

I remembered that Liputin had told us he had taken the wooden lodge in the yard that morning. In the lodge, which was too large for him, a deaf old woman who waited upon him was living too. The owner of the house had moved into a new house in another street, where he kept a restaurant, and this old woman, a relation of his, I believe, was left behind to look after everything in the old house. The rooms in the lodge were fairly clean, though the wall-papers were dirty. In the one we went into the furniture was of different sorts, picked up here and there, and all utterly worthless. There were two card-tables, a chest of drawers made of elder, a big deal table that must have come from some peasant hut or kitchen, chairs and a sofa with trellis-work back and hard leather cushions. In one corner there was an old-fashioned ikon, in front of which the old woman had lighted a lamp before we came in, and on the walls hung two dingy oil-paintings, one, a portrait of the Tsar Nikolas I, painted apparently between 1820 and 1830; the other the portrait of some bishop. Mr. Kirillov lighted a candle and took out of his trunk, which stood not yet unpacked in a corner, an envelope, sealing-wax, and a glass seal.

"Seal your note and address the envelope."

I would have objected that this was unnecessary, but he insisted. When I had addressed the envelope I took my cap.

"I was thinking you'd have tea," he said. "I have bought tea. Will you?"

I could not refuse. The old woman soon brought in the tea, that is, a very large tea-pot of boiling water, a little tea-pot full of strong tea, two large earthenware cups, coarsely decorated, a fancy loaf, and a whole deep saucer of lump sugar.

"I love tea at night," said he. "I walk much and drink it till daybreak. Abroad tea at night is inconvenient."

"You go to bed at daybreak?"

"Always; for a long while. I eat little; always tea. Liputin's sly, but impatient."

I was surprised at his wanting to talk; I made up my mind to take advantage of the opportunity. "There were unpleasant misunderstandings this morning," I observed.

He scowled.

"That's foolishness; that's great nonsense. All this is nonsense because Lebyadkin is drunk. I did not tell Liputin, but only explained the nonsense, because he got it all wrong. Liputin has a great deal of fantasy, he built up a mountain out of nonsense. I trusted Liputin yesterday."

"And me to-day?" I said, laughing.

"But you see, you knew all about it already this morning; Liputin is weak or impatient, or malicious or … he's envious."

The last word struck me.

"You've mentioned so many adjectives, however, that it would be strange if one didn't describe him."

"Or all at once."

"Yes, and that's what Liputin really is—he's a chaos. He was lying this morning when he said you were writing something, wasn't he?

"Why should he?" he said, scowling again and staring at the floor.

I apologised, and began assuring him that I was not inquisitive. He flushed.

"He told the truth; I am writing. Only that's no matter."

We were silent for a minute. He suddenly smiled with the childlike smile I had noticed that morning.

"He invented that about heads himself out of a book, and told me first himself, and understands badly. But I only seek the causes why men dare not kill themselves; that's all. And it's all no matter."

"How do you mean they don't dare? Are there so few suicides?"

"Very few."

"Do you really think so?"

He made no answer, got up, and began walking to and fro lost in thought.

"What is it restrains people from suicide, do you think?" I asked.

He looked at me absent-mindedly, as though trying to remember what we were talking about.

"I … I don't know much yet.… Two prejudices restrain them, two things; only two, one very little, the other very big."

"What is the little thing?"

"Pain."

"Pain? Can that be of importance at such a moment?"

"Of the greatest. There are two sorts: those who kill themselves either from great sorrow or from spite, or being mad, or no matter what … they do it suddenly. They think little about the pain, but kill themselves suddenly. But some do it from reason—they think a great deal."

"Why, are there people who do it from reason?"

"Very many. If it were not for superstition there would be more, very many, all."

"What, all?"

He did not answer.

"But aren't there means of dying without pain?"

"Imagine"—he stopped before me—"imagine a stone as big as a great house; it hangs and you are under it; if it falls on you, on your head, will it hurt you?"

"A stone as big as a house? Of course it would be fearful."

"I speak not of the fear. Will it hurt?"

"A stone as big as a mountain, weighing millions of tons? Of course it wouldn't hurt."

"But really stand there and while it hangs you will fear very much that it will hurt. The most learned man, the greatest doctor, all, all will be very much frightened. Every one will know that it won't hurt, and every one will be afraid that it will hurt."

"Well, and the second cause, the big one?"

"The other world!"

"You mean punishment?"

"That's no matter. The other world; only the other world."

"Are there no atheists, such as don't believe in the other world at all?"

Again he did not answer.

"You judge from yourself, perhaps."

"Every one cannot judge except from himself," he said, reddening. "There will be full freedom when it will be just the same to live or not to live. That's the goal for all."

"The goal? But perhaps no one will care to live then?"

"No one," he pronounced with decision.

"Man fears death because he loves life. That's how I understand it," I observed, "and that's determined by nature."

"That's abject; and that's where the deception comes in." His eyes flashed. "Life is pain, life is terror, and man is unhappy. Now all is pain and terror. Now man loves life, because he loves pain and terror, and so they have done according. Life is given now for pain and terror, and that's the deception. Now man is not yet what he will be. There will be a new man, happy and proud. For whom it will be the same to live or not to live, he will be the new man. He who will conquer pain and terror will himself be a god. And this God will not be."

"Then this God does exist according to you?"

"He does not exist, but He is. In the stone there is no pain, but in the fear of the stone is the pain. God is the pain of the fear of death. He who will conquer pain and terror will become himself a god. Then there will be a new life, a new man; everything will be new … then they will divide history into two parts: from the gorilla to the annihilation of God, and from the annihilation of God to …"

"To the gorilla?"

"… To the transformation of the earth, and of man physically. Man will be God, and will be transformed physically, and the world will be transformed and things will be transformed and thoughts and all feelings. What do you think: will man be changed physically then?"

"If it will be just the same living or not living, all will kill themselves, and perhaps that's what the change will be?"

"That's no matter. They will kill deception. Every one who wants the supreme freedom must dare to kill himself. He who dares to kill himself has found out the secret of the deception. There is no freedom beyond; that is all, and there is nothing beyond. He who dares kill himself is God. Now every one can do so that there shall be no God and shall be nothing. But no one has once done it yet."

"There have been millions of suicides."

"But always not for that; always with terror and not for that object. Not to kill fear. He who kills himself only to kill fear will become a god at once."

"He won't have time, perhaps," I observed.

"That's no matter," he answered softly, with calm pride, almost disdain. "I'm sorry that you seem to be laughing," he added half a minute later.

"It seems strange to me that you were so irritable this morning and are now so calm, though you speak with warmth."

"This morning? It was funny this morning," he answered with a smile. "I don't like scolding, and I never laugh," he added mournfully.

"Yes, you don't spend your nights very cheerfully over your tea."

I got up and took my cap.

"You think not?" he smiled with some surprise. "Why? No, I … I don't know." He was suddenly confused. "I know not how it is with the others, and I feel that I cannot do as others. Everybody thinks and then at once thinks of something else. I can't think of something else. I think all my life of one thing. God has tormented me all my life," he ended up suddenly with astonishing expansiveness.

"And tell me, if I may ask, why is it you speak Russian not quite correctly? Surely you haven't forgotten it after five years abroad?"

"Don't I speak correctly? I don't know. No, it's not because of abroad. I have talked like that all my life … it's no matter to me."

"Another question, a more delicate one. I quite believe you that you're disinclined to meet people and talk very little. Why have you talked to me now?"

"To you? This morning you sat so nicely and you ... but it's all no matter ... you are like my brother, very much, extremely," he added, flushing. "He has been dead seven years. He was older, very, very much."

"I suppose he had a great influence on your way of thinking?"

"N-no. He said little; he said nothing. I'll give your note."

He saw me to the gate with a lantern, to lock it after me. "Of course he's mad," I decided. In the gateway I met with another encounter.

IX

I had only just lifted my leg over the high barrier across the bottom of the gateway, when suddenly a strong hand clutched at my chest.

"Who's this?" roared a voice, "a friend or an enemy? Own up!"

"He's one of us; one of us!" Liputin's voice squealed near by. "It's Mr. G——v, a young man of classical education, in touch with the highest society."

"I love him if he's in society, clas-si ... that means he's high-ly ed-u-cated. The retired Captain Ignat Lebyadkin, at the service of the world and his friends ... if they're true ones, if they're true ones, the scoundrels."

Captain Lebyadkin, a stout, fleshy man over six feet in height, with curly hair and a red face, was so extremely drunk that he could scarcely stand up before me, and articulated with difficulty. I had seen him before, however, in the distance.

"And this one!" he roared again, noticing Kirillov, who was still standing with the lantern; he raised his fist, but let it fall again at once.

"I forgive you for your learning! Ignat Lebyadkin—high-ly ed-u-cated....

'A bomb of love with stinging smart

Exploded in Ignaty's heart.

In anguish dire I weep again

The arm that at Sevastopol

I lost in bitter pain!'

Not that I ever was at Sevastopol, or ever lost my arm, but you know what rhyme is." He pushed up to me with his ugly, tipsy face.

"He is in a hurry, he is going home!" Liputin tried to persuade him. "He'll tell Lizaveta Nikolaevna to-morrow."

"Lizaveta!" he yelled again. "Stay, don't go! A variation:

'Among the Amazons a star,

Upon her steed she flashes by,

And smiles upon me from afar,

The child of aris-to-cra-cy!'

To a Starry Amazon.

You know that's a hymn. It's a hymn, if you're not an ass! The duffers, they don't understand! Stay!"

He caught hold of my coat, though I pulled myself away with all my might.

"Tell her I'm a knight and the soul of honour, and as for that Dasha ... I'd pick her up and chuck her out.... She's only a serf, she daren't ..."

At this point he fell down, for I pulled myself violently out of his hands and ran into the street. Liputin clung on to me.

"Alexey Nilitch will pick him up. Do you know what I've just found out from him?" he babbled in desperate haste. "Did you hear his verses? He's sealed those verses to the 'Starry Amazon' in an envelope and is going to send them to-morrow to Lizaveta Nikolaevna, signed with his name in full. What a fellow!"

"I bet you suggested it to him yourself."

"You'll lose your bet," laughed Liputin. "He's in love, in love like a cat, and do you know it began with hatred. He hated Lizaveta Nikolaevna at first so much, for riding on horseback that he almost swore aloud at her in the street. Yes, he did abuse her! Only the day before yesterday he swore at her when she rode by—luckily she didn't hear. And, suddenly, to-day—poetry! Do you know he means to risk a proposal? Seriously! Seriously!"

"I wonder at you, Liputin; whenever there's anything nasty going on you're always on the spot taking a leading part in it," I said angrily.

"You're going rather far, Mr. G——v. Isn't your poor little heart quaking, perhaps, in terror of a rival?"

"Wha-at!" I cried, standing still.

"Well, now to punish you I won't say anything more, and wouldn't you like to know though? Take this alone, that that lout is not a simple captain now but a landowner of our province, and rather an important one, too, for Nikolay Vsyevolodovitch sold him all his estate the other day, formerly of two hundred serfs; and as God's above, I'm not lying. I've only just heard it, but it was from a most reliable source. And now you can ferret it out for yourself; I'll say nothing more; good-bye."

X

Stepan Trofimovitch was awaiting me with hysterical impatience. It was an hour since he had returned. I found him in a state resembling intoxication; for the first five minutes at least I thought he was drunk. Alas, the visit to the Drozdovs had been the finishing-stroke.

"Mon ami! I have completely lost the thread … Lise … I love and respect that angel as before; just as before; but it seems to me they both asked me simply to find out something from me, that is more simply to get something out of me, and then to get rid of me.... That's how it is."

"You ought to be ashamed!" I couldn't help exclaiming.

"My friend, now I am utterly alone. Enfin, c'est ridicule. Would you believe it, the place is positively packed with mysteries there too. They simply flew at me about those ears and noses, and some mysteries in Petersburg too. You know they hadn't heard till they came about the tricks Nicolas played here four years ago. 'You were here, you saw it, is it true that he is mad?' Where they got the idea I can't make out. Why is it that Praskovya is so anxious Nicolas should be mad? The woman will have it so, she will. Ce Maurice, or what's his name, Mavriky Nikolaevitch, brave homme tout de même … but can it be for his sake, and after she wrote herself from Paris to cette pauvre amie?… Enfin, this Praskovya, as cette chère amie calls her, is a type. She's Gogol's Madame Box, of immortal memory, only she's a spiteful Madame Box, a malignant Box, and in an immensely exaggerated form."

"That's making her out a regular packing-case if it's an exaggerated form."

"Well, perhaps it's the opposite; it's all the same, only don't interrupt me, for I'm all in a whirl. They are all at loggerheads, except Lise, she keeps on with her 'Auntie, auntie!' but Lise's sly, and there's something behind it too. Secrets. She has quarrelled with the old lady. Cette pauvre auntie tyrannises over every one it's true, and then there's the governor's wife, and the rudeness of local society, and Karmazinov's 'rudeness'; and then this idea of madness, ce Lipoutine, ce que je ne comprends pas … and … and they say she's been putting vinegar on her head, and here are we with our complaints and letters.... Oh, how I have tormented her and at such a time! Je suis un ingrat! Only imagine, I come back and find a letter from her; read it, read it! Oh, how ungrateful it was of me!"

He gave me a letter he had just received from Varvara Petrovna. She seemed to have repented of her "stay at home." The letter was amiable but decided in tone, and brief. She invited Stepan Trofimovitch to come to her the day after to-morrow, which was Sunday, at twelve o'clock, and advised him to bring one of his friends with him. (My name was mentioned in parenthesis). She promised on her side to invite Shatov, as the brother of Darya Pavlovna. "You can obtain a final answer from her: will that be enough for you? Is this the formality you were so anxious for?"

"Observe that irritable phrase about formality. Poor thing, poor thing, the friend of my whole life! I confess the sudden determination of my whole future almost crushed me.... I confess I still had hopes, but now tout est dit. I know now that all is over. C'est terrible! Oh, that that Sunday would never come and everything would go on in the old way. You would have gone on coming and I'd have gone on here...."

"You've been upset by all those nasty things Liputin said, those slanders."

"My dear, you have touched on another sore spot with your friendly finger. Such friendly fingers are generally merciless and sometimes unreasonable; pardon, you may not believe it, but I'd almost forgotten all that, all that nastiness, not that I forgot it, indeed, but in my foolishness I tried all the while I was with Lise to be happy and persuaded myself I was happy. But now ... Oh, now I'm thinking of that generous, humane woman, so long-suffering with my contemptible failings—not that she's been altogether long-suffering, but what have I been with my horrid, worthless character! I'm a capricious child, with all the egoism of a child and none of the innocence. For the last twenty years she's been looking after me like a nurse, cette pauvre auntie, as Lise so charmingly calls her.... And now, after twenty years, the child clamours to be married, sending letter after letter, while her head's in a vinegar-compress and ... now he's got it—on Sunday I shall be a married man, that's no joke.... And why did I keep insisting myself, what did I write those letters for? Oh, I forgot. Lise idolizes Darya Pavlovna, she says so anyway; she says of her 'c'est un ange, only rather a reserved one.' They both advised me, even Praskovya. ... Praskovya didn't advise me though. Oh, what venom lies concealed in that 'Box'! And Lise didn't exactly advise me: 'What do you want to get married for,' she said, 'your intellectual pleasures ought to be enough for you.' She laughed. I forgive her for laughing, for there's an ache in her own heart. You can't get on without a woman though, they said to me. The infirmities of age are coming upon you, and she will tuck you up, or whatever it is.... Ma foi, I've been thinking myself all this time I've been sitting with you that Providence was sending her to me in the decline of my stormy years and that she would tuck me up, or whatever they call it ... enfin, she'll be handy for the housekeeping. See what a litter there is, look how everything's lying about. I said it must be cleared up this morning, and look at the book on the floor! La pauvre amie was always angry at the untidiness here. ... Ah, now I shall no longer hear her voice! Vingt ans! And it seems they've had anonymous letters. Only fancy, it's said that Nicolas has sold Lebyadkin his property. C'est un monstre; et enfin what is Lebyadkin? Lise listens, and listens, ooh, how she listens! I forgave her laughing. I saw her face as she listened, and ce Maurice ... I shouldn't care to be in his shoes now, brave homme tout de même, but rather shy; but never mind him...."

He paused. He was tired and upset, and sat with drooping head, staring at the floor with his tired eyes. I took advantage of the interval to tell him of my visit to Filipov's house, and curtly and dryly expressed my opinion that Lebyadkin's sister (whom I had never seen) really might have been somehow victimised by Nicolas at some time during that mysterious period of his life, as Liputin had called it, and that it was very possible that Lebyadkin received sums of money from Nicolas for some reason, but that was all. As for the scandal about Darya Pavlovna, that was all nonsense, all that brute Liputin's misrepresentations, that this was anyway what Alexey Nilitch warmly maintained, and we had no grounds for disbelieving him. Stepan Trofimovitch listened to my assurances with an absent air, as though they did not concern him. I mentioned by the way my conversation with Kirillov, and added that he might be mad.

"He's not mad, but one of those shallow-minded people," he mumbled listlessly. "Ces gens-là supposent la nature et la societé humaine autres que Dieu ne les a faites et qu'elles ne sont réellement. People try to make up to them, but Stepan Verhovensky does not, anyway. I saw them that time in Petersburg avec cette chère amie (oh, how I used to wound her then), and I wasn't afraid of their abuse or even of their praise. I'm not afraid now either. Mais parlons d'autre chose.... I believe I have done dreadful things. Only fancy, I sent a letter yesterday to Darya Pavlovna and ... how I curse myself for it!"

"What did you write about?"

"Oh, my friend, believe me, it was all done in a noble spirit. I let her know that I had written to Nicolas five days before, also in a noble spirit."

"I understand now!" I cried with heat. "And what right had you to couple their names like that?"

"But, mon cher, don't crush me completely, don't shout at me; as it is I'm utterly squashed like ... a black-beetle. And, after all, I thought it was all so honourable. Suppose that something really happened ... en Suisse ... or was beginning. I was bound to question their hearts beforehand that I ... enfin, that I might not constrain their hearts, and be a stumbling-block in their paths. I acted simply from honourable feeling."

"Oh, heavens! What a stupid thing you've done!" I cried involuntarily.

"Yes, yes," he assented with positive eagerness. "You have never said anything more just, c'était bête, mais que faire? Tout est dit. I shall marry her just the same even if it be to cover 'another's sins.' So there was no object in writing, was there?"

"You're at that idea again!"

"Oh, you won't frighten me with your shouts now. You see a different Stepan Verhovensky before you now. The man I was is buried. Enfin, tout est dit. And why do you cry out? Simply because you're not getting married, and you won't have to wear a certain decoration on your head. Does that shock you again? My poor friend, you don't know woman, while I have done nothing but study her. 'If you want to conquer the world, conquer yourself'—the one good thing that another romantic like you, my bride's brother, Shatov, has succeeded in saying. I would gladly borrow from him his phrase. Well, here I am ready to conquer myself, and I'm getting married. And what am I conquering by way of the whole world? Oh, my friend, marriage is the moral death of every proud soul, of all independence. Married life will corrupt me, it will sap my energy, my courage in the service of the cause. Children will come, probably not my own either—certainly not my own: a wise man is not afraid to face the truth. Liputin proposed this morning putting up barricades to keep out Nicolas; Liputin's a fool. A woman would deceive the all-seeing eye itself. Le bon Dieu knew what He was in for when He was creating woman, but I'm sure that she meddled in it herself and forced Him to create her such as she is ... and with such attributes: for who would have incurred so much trouble for nothing? I know Nastasya may be angry with me for free-thinking, but ... enfin, tout est dit."

He wouldn't have been himself if he could have dispensed with the cheap gibing free-thought which was in vogue in his day. Now, at any rate, he comforted himself with a gibe, but not for long.

"Oh, if that day after to-morrow, that Sunday, might never come!" he exclaimed suddenly, this time in utter despair. "Why could not this one week be without a Sunday—si le miracle existe? What would it be to Providence to blot out one Sunday from the calendar? If only to prove His power to the atheists et que tout soit dit! Oh, how I loved her! Twenty years, these twenty years, and she has never understood me!"

"But of whom are you talking? Even I don't understand you!" I asked, wondering.

"Vingt ans! And she has not once understood me; oh, it's cruel! And can she really believe that I am marrying from fear, from poverty? Oh, the shame of it! Oh, Auntie, Auntie, I do it for you!... Oh, let her know, that Auntie, that she is the one woman I have adored for twenty years! She must learn this, it must be so, if not they will need force to drag me under ce qu'on appelle le wedding-crown."

It was the first time I had heard this confession, and so vigorously uttered. I won't conceal the fact that I was terribly tempted to laugh. I was wrong.

"He is the only one left me now, the only one, my one hope!" he cried suddenly, clasping his hands as though struck by a new idea. "Only he, my poor boy, can save me now, and, oh, why doesn't he come! Oh, my son, oh, my Petrusha.... And though I do not deserve the name of father, but rather that of tiger, yet ... Laissez-moi, mon ami, I'll lie down a little, to collect my ideas. I am so tired, so tired. And I think it's time you were in bed. Voyez vous, it's twelve o'clock...."

CHAPTER IV. THE CRIPPLE

I

SHATOV WAS NOT PERVERSE but acted on my note, and called at midday on Lizaveta Nikolaevna. We went in almost together; I was also going to make my first call. They were all, that is Liza, her mother, and Mavriky Nikolaevitch, sitting in the big drawing-room, arguing. The mother was asking Liza to play some waltz on the piano, and as soon as Liza began to play the piece asked for, declared it was not the right one. Mavriky Nikolaevitch in the simplicity of his heart took Liza's part, maintaining that it was the right waltz. The elder lady was so angry that she began to cry. She was ill and walked with difficulty. Her legs were swollen, and for the last few days she had been continually fractious, quarrelling with every one, though she always stood rather in awe of Liza. They were pleased to see us. Liza flushed with pleasure, and saying "merci" to me, on Shatov's account of course, went to meet him, looking at him with interest.

Shatov stopped awkwardly in the doorway. Thanking him for coming she led him up to her mother.

"This is Mr. Shatov, of whom I have told you, and this is Mr. G——v, a great friend of mine and of Stepan Trofimovitch's. Mavriky Nikolaevitch made his acquaintance yesterday, too."

"And which is the professor?"

"There's no professor at all, maman."

"But there is. You said yourself that there'd be a professor. It's this one, probably." She disdainfully indicated Shatov.

"I didn't tell you that there'd be a professor. Mr. G——v is in the service, and Mr. Shatov is a former student."

"A student or professor, they all come from the university just the same. You only want to argue. But the Swiss one had moustaches and a beard."

"It's the son of Stepan Trofimovitch that maman always calls the professor," said Liza, and she took Shatov away to the sofa at the other end of the drawing-room.

"When her legs swell, she's always like this, you understand she's ill," she whispered to Shatov, still with the same marked curiosity, scrutinising him, especially his shock of hair.

"Are you an officer?" the old lady inquired of me. Liza had mercilessly abandoned me to her.

"N-no.—I'm in the service...."

"Mr. G——v is a great friend of Stepan Trofimovitch's," Liza chimed in immediately.

"Are you in Stepan Trofimovitch's service? Yes, and he's a professor, too, isn't he?"

"Ah, maman, you must dream at night of professors," cried Liza with annoyance.

"I see too many when I'm awake. But you always will contradict your mother. Were you here four years ago when Nikolay Vsyevolodovitch was in the neighbourhood?"

I answered that I was.

"And there was some Englishman with you?"

"No, there was not."

Liza laughed.

"Well, you see there was no Englishman, so it must have been idle gossip. And Varvara Petrovna and Stepan Trofimovitch both tell lies. And they all tell lies."

"Auntie and Stepan Trofimovitch yesterday thought there was a resemblance between Nikolay Vsyevolodovitch and Prince Harry in Shakespeare's Henry IV, and in answer to that maman says that there was no Englishman here," Liza explained to us.

"If Harry wasn't here, there was no Englishman. It was no one else but Nikolay Vsyevolodovitch at his tricks."

"I assure you that maman's doing it on purpose," Liza thought necessary to explain to Shatov. "She's really heard of Shakespeare. I read her the first act of Othello myself. But she's in great pain now. Maman, listen, it's striking twelve, it's time you took your medicine."

"The doctor's come," a maid-servant announced at the door.

The old lady got up and began calling her dog: "Zemirka, Zemirka, you come with me at least."

Zemirka, a horrid little old dog, instead of obeying, crept under the sofa where Liza was sitting.

"Don't you want to? Then I don't want you. Good-bye, my good sir, I don't know your name or your father's," she said, addressing me.

"Anton Lavrentyevitch ..."

"Well, it doesn't matter, with me it goes in at one ear and out of the other. Don't you come with me, Mavriky Nikolaevitch, it was Zemirka I called. Thank God I can still walk without help and to-morrow I shall go for a drive."

She walked angrily out of the drawing-room.

"Anton Lavrentyevitch, will you talk meanwhile to Mavriky Nikolaevitch; I assure you you'll both be gainers by getting to know one another better," said Liza, and she gave a friendly smile to Mavriky Nikolaevitch, who beamed all over as she looked at him. There was no help for it, I remained to talk to Mavriky Nikolaevitch.

II

Lizaveta Nikolaevna's business with Shatov turned out, to my surprise, to be really only concerned with literature. I had imagined, I don't know why, that she had asked him to come with some other object. We, Mavriky Nikolaevitch and I that is, seeing that they were talking aloud and not trying to hide anything from us, began to listen, and at last they asked our advice. It turned out that Lizaveta Nikolaevna was thinking of bringing out a book which she thought would be of use, but being quite inexperienced she needed someone to help her. The earnestness with which she began to explain her plan to Shatov quite surprised me.

"She must be one of the new people," I thought. "She has not been to Switzerland for nothing."

Shatov listened with attention, his eyes fixed on the ground, showing not the slightest surprise that a giddy young lady in society should take up work that seemed so out of keeping with her.

Her literary scheme was as follows. Numbers of papers and journals are published in the capitals and the provinces of Russia, and every day a number of events are reported in them. The year passes, the newspapers are everywhere folded up and put away in cupboards, or are torn up and become litter, or are used for making parcels or wrapping things. Numbers of these facts make an impression and are remembered by the public, but in the course of years they are forgotten. Many people would like to look them up, but it is a labour for them to embark upon this sea of paper, often knowing nothing of the day or place or even year in which the incident occurred. Yet if all the facts for a whole year were brought together into one book, on a definite plan, and with a definite object, under headings with references, arranged according to months and days, such a compilation might reflect the characteristics of Russian life for the whole year, even though the facts published are only a small fraction of the events that take place.

"Instead of a number of newspapers there would be a few fat books, that's all," observed Shatov.

But Lizaveta Nikolaevna clung to her idea, in spite of the difficulty of carrying it out and her inability to describe it. "It ought to be one book, and not even a very thick one," she maintained. But even if it were thick it would be clear, for the great point would be the plan and the character of the presentation of facts. Of course not all would be collected and reprinted. The decrees and acts of government, local regulations, laws—all such facts, however important, might be altogether omitted from the proposed publication. They could leave out a great deal and confine themselves to a selection of events more or less characteristic of the moral life of the people, of the personal character of the Russian people at the present moment. Of course everything might be put in: strange incidents, fires, public subscriptions, anything good or bad, every speech or word, perhaps even floodings of the rivers, perhaps even some government decrees, but only such things to be selected as are characteristic of the period; everything would be put in with a certain view, a special significance and intention, with an idea which would illuminate the facts looked at in the aggregate, as a whole. And finally the book ought to be interesting even for light reading, apart from its value as a work of reference. It would be, so to say, a presentation of the spiritual, moral, inner life of Russia for a whole year.

"We want everyone to buy it, we want it to be a book that will be found on every table," Liza declared. "I understand that all lies in the plan, and that's why I apply to you," she concluded. She grew very warm over it, and although her explanation was obscure and incomplete, Shatov began to understand.

"So it would amount to something with a political tendency, a selection of facts with a special tendency," he muttered, still not raising his head.

"Not at all, we must not select with a particular bias, and we ought not to have any political tendency in it. Nothing but impartiality—that will be the only tendency."

"But a tendency would be no harm," said Shatov, with a slight movement, "and one can hardly avoid it if there is any selection at all. The very selection of facts will suggest how they are to be understood. Your idea is not a bad one."

"Then such a book is possible?" cried Liza delightedly.

"We must look into it and consider. It's an immense undertaking. One can't work it out on the spur of the moment. We need experience. And when we do publish the book I doubt whether we shall find out how to do it. Possibly after many trials; but the thought is alluring. It's a useful idea."

He raised his eyes at last, and they were positively sparkling with pleasure, he was so interested.

"Was it your own idea?" he asked Liza, in a friendly and, as it were, bashful way.

"The idea's no trouble, you know, it's the plan is the trouble," Liza smiled. "I understand very little. I am not very clever, and I only pursue what is clear to me, myself. . . ."

"Pursue?"

"Perhaps that's not the right word?" Liza inquired quickly.

"The word is all right; I meant nothing."

"I thought while I was abroad that even I might be of some use. I have money of my own lying idle. Why shouldn't I—even I—work for the common cause? Besides, the idea somehow occurred to me all at once of itself. I didn't invent it at all, and was delighted with it. But I saw at once that I couldn't get on without someone to help, because I am not competent to do anything of myself. My helper, of course, would be the co-editor of the book. We would go halves. You would give the plan and the work. Mine would be the original idea and the means for publishing it. Would the book pay its expenses, do you think?"

"If we hit on a good plan the book will go."

"I warn you that I am not doing it for profit; but I am very anxious that the book should circulate and should be very proud of making a profit."

"Well, but how do I come in?"

"Why, I invite you to be my fellow-worker, to go halves. You will think out the plan."

"How do you know that I am capable of thinking out the plan?"

"People have talked about you to me, and here I've heard … I know that you are very clever and … are working for the cause … and think a great deal. Pyotr Stepanovitch Verhovensky spoke about you in Switzerland," she added hurriedly. "He's a very clever man, isn't he?"

Shatov stole a fleeting, momentary glance at her, but dropped his eyes again.

"Nikolay Vsyevolodovitch told me a great deal about you, too."

Shatov suddenly turned red.

"But here are the newspapers." Liza hurriedly picked up from a chair a bundle of newspapers that lay tied up ready. "I've tried to mark the facts here for selection, to sort them, and I have put the papers together … you will see."

Shatov took the bundle.

"Take them home and look at them. Where do you live?"

"In Bogoyavlensky Street, Filipov's house."

"I know. I think it's there, too, I've been told, a captain lives, beside you, Mr. Lebyadkin," said Liza in the same hurried manner.

Shatov sat for a full minute with the bundle in his outstretched hand, making no answer and staring at the floor.

"You'd better find someone else for these jobs. I shouldn't suit you at all," he brought out at last, dropping his voice in an awfully strange way, almost to a whisper.

Liza flushed crimson.

"What jobs are you speaking of? Mavriky Nikolaevitch," she cried, "please bring that letter here."

I too followed Mavriky Nikolaevitch to the table.

"Look at this," she turned suddenly to me, unfolding the letter in great excitement. "Have you ever seen anything like it. Please read it aloud. I want Mr. Shatov to hear it too."

With no little astonishment I read aloud the following missive:

"To the Perfection, Miss Tushin.

"Gracious Lady

"Lizaveta Nikolaevna!

"Oh, she's a sweet queen,

Lizaveta Tushin!

When on side-saddle she gallops by,

And in the breeze her fair tresses fly!

Or when with her mother in church she bows low

And on devout faces a red flush doth flow!

Then for the joys of lawful wedlock I aspire,

And follow her and her mother with tears of desire.

"Composed by an unlearned man in the midst of a discussion.

"Gracious Lady!

"I pity myself above all men that I did not lose my arm at Sevastopol, not having been there at all, but served all the campaign delivering paltry provisions, which I look on as a degradation. You are a goddess of antiquity, and I am nothing, but have had a glimpse of infinity. Look on it as a poem and no more, for, after all, poetry is nonsense and justifies what would be considered impudence in prose. Can the sun be angry with the infusoria if the latter composes verses to her from the drop of water, where there is a multitude of them if you look through the microscope? Even the club for promoting humanity to the larger animals in tip-top society in Petersburg, which rightly feels compassion for dogs and horses, despises the brief infusoria making no reference to it whatever, because it is not big enough. I'm not big enough either. The idea of marriage might seem droll, but soon I shall have property worth two hundred souls through a misanthropist whom you ought to despise. I can tell a lot and I can undertake to produce documents that would mean Siberia. Don't despise my proposal. A letter from an infusoria is of course in verse.

"Captain Lebyadkin your most humble friend.

And he has time no end."

"That was written by a man in a drunken condition, a worthless fellow," I cried indignantly. "I know him."

"That letter I received yesterday," Liza began to explain, flushing and speaking hurriedly. "I saw myself, at once, that it came from some foolish creature, and I haven't yet shown it to maman, for fear of upsetting her more. But if he is going to keep on like that, I don't know how to act. Mavriky Nikolaevitch wants to go out and forbid him to do it. As I have looked upon you as a colleague," she turned to Shatov, "and as you live there, I wanted to question you so as to judge what more is to be expected of him."

"He's a drunkard and a worthless fellow," Shatov muttered with apparent reluctance.

"Is he always so stupid?"

"No, he's not stupid at all when he's not drunk."

"I used to know a general who wrote verses exactly like that," I observed, laughing.

"One can see from the letter that he is clever enough for his own purposes," Mavriky Nikolaevitch, who had till then been silent, put in unexpectedly.

"He lives with some sister?" Liza queried.

"Yes, with his sister."

"They say he tyrannises over her, is that true?"

Shatov looked at Liza again, scowled, and muttering, "What business is it of mine?" moved towards the door.

"Ah, stay!" cried Liza, in a flutter. "Where are you going? We have so much still to talk over...."

"What is there to talk over? I'll let you know to-morrow."

"Why, the most important thing of all—the printing-press! Do believe me that I am not in jest, that I really want to work in good earnest!" Liza assured him in growing agitation. "If we decide to publish it, where is it to be printed? You know it's a most important question, for we shan't go to Moscow for it, and the printing-press here is out of the question for such a publication. I made up my mind long ago to set up a printing-press of my own, in your name perhaps—and I know maman will allow it so long as it is in your name...."

"How do you know that I could be a printer?" Shatov asked sullenly.

"Why, Pyotr Stepanovitch told me of you in Switzerland, and referred me to you as one who knows the business and able to set up a printing-press. He even meant to give me a note to you from himself, but I forgot it."

Shatov's face changed, as I recollect now. He stood for a few seconds longer, then went out of the room.

Liza was angry.

"Does he always go out like that?" she asked, turning to me.

I was just shrugging my shoulders when Shatov suddenly came back, went straight up to the table and put down the roll of papers he had taken.

"I'm not going to be your helper, I haven't the time…."

"Why? Why? I think you are angry!" Liza asked him in a grieved and imploring voice.

The sound of her voice seemed to strike him; for some moments he looked at her intently, as though trying to penetrate to her very soul.

"No matter," he muttered, softly, "I don't want to…."

And he went away altogether.

Liza was completely overwhelmed, quite disproportionately in fact, so it seemed to me.

"Wonderfully queer man," Mavriky Nikolaevitch observed aloud.

III

He certainly was queer, but in all this there was a very great deal not clear to me. There was something underlying it all. I simply did not believe in this publication; then that stupid letter, in which there was an offer, only too barefaced, to give information and produce "documents," though they were all silent about that, and talked of something quite different; finally that printing-press and Shatov's sudden exit, just because they spoke of a printing-press. All this led me to imagine that something had happened before I came in of which I knew nothing; and, consequently, that it was no business of mine and that I was in the way. And, indeed, it was time to take leave, I had stayed long enough for the first call. I went up to say good-bye to Lizaveta Nikolaevna.

She seemed to have forgotten that I was in the room, and was still standing in the same place by the table with her head bowed, plunged in thought, gazing fixedly at one spot on the carpet.

"Ah, you, too, are going, good-bye," she murmured in an ordinary friendly tone. "Give my greetings to Stepan Trofimovitch, and persuade him to come and see me as soon as he can. Mavriky Nikolaevitch, Anton Lavrentyevitch is going. Excuse maman's not being able to come out and say good-bye to you…."

I went out and had reached the bottom of the stairs when a footman suddenly overtook me at the street door.

"My lady begs you to come back…."

"The mistress, or Lizaveta Nikolaevna?"

"The young lady."

I found Liza not in the big room where we had been sitting, but in the reception-room next to it. The door between it and the drawing-room, where Mavriky Nikolaevitch was left alone, was closed.

Liza smiled to me but was pale. She was standing in the middle of the room in evident indecision, visibly struggling with herself; but she suddenly took me by the hand, and led me quickly to the window.

"I want to see her at once," she whispered, bending upon me a burning, passionate, impatient glance, which would not admit a hint of opposition. "I must see her with my own eyes, and I beg you to help me."

She was in a perfect frenzy, and—in despair.

"Who is it you want to see, Lizaveta Nikolaevna?" I inquired in dismay.

"That Lebyadkin's sister, that lame girl.... Is it true that she's lame?"

I was astounded.

"I have never seen her, but I've heard that she's lame. I heard it yesterday," I said with hurried readiness, and also in a whisper.

"I must see her, absolutely. Could you arrange it to-day?"

I felt dreadfully sorry for her.

"That's utterly impossible, and, besides, I should not know at all how to set about it," I began persuading her. "I'll go to Shatov...."

"If you don't arrange it by to-morrow I'll go to her by myself, alone, for Mavriky Nikolaevitch has refused. I rest all my hopes on you and I've no one else; I spoke stupidly to Shatov.... I'm sure that you are perfectly honest and perhaps ready to do anything for me, only arrange it."

I felt a passionate desire to help her in every way.

"This is what I'll do," I said, after a moment's thought. "I'll go myself to-day and will see her for sure, for sure. I will manage so as to see her. I give you my word of honour. Only let me confide in Shatov."

"Tell him that I do desire it, and that I can't wait any longer, but that I wasn't deceiving him just now. He went away perhaps because he's very honest and he didn't like my seeming to deceive him. I wasn't deceiving him, I really do want to edit books and found a printing-press...."

"He is honest, very honest," I assented warmly.

"If it's not arranged by to-morrow, though, I shall go myself whatever happens, and even if every one were to know."

"I can't be with you before three o'clock to-morrow," I observed, after a moment's deliberation.

"At three o'clock then. Then it was true what I imagined yesterday at Stepan Trofimovitch's, that you—are rather devoted to me?" she said with a smile, hurriedly pressing my hand to say good-bye, and hurrying back to the forsaken Mavriky Nikolaevitch.

I went out weighed down by my promise, and unable to understand what had happened. I had seen a woman in real despair, not hesitating to compromise herself by confiding in a man she hardly knew. Her womanly smile at a moment so terrible for her and her hint that she had noticed my feelings the day before sent a pang to my heart; but I felt sorry for her, very sorry—that was all! Her secrets became at once something sacred for me, and if anyone had begun to reveal them to me now, I think I should have covered my ears, and should have refused to hear anything more. I only had a presentiment of something ... yet I was utterly at a loss to see how I could do anything. What's more I did not even yet understand exactly what I had to arrange; an interview, but what sort of an interview? And how could I bring them together? My only hope was Shatov, though I could be sure that he wouldn't help me in any way. But all the same, I hurried to him.

IV

I did not find him at home till past seven o'clock that evening. To my surprise he had visitors with him—Alexey Nilitch, and another gentleman I hardly knew, one Shigalov, the brother of Virginsky's wife.

This gentleman must, I think, have been staying about two months in the town; I don't know where he came from. I had only heard that he had written some sort of article in a progressive Petersburg magazine. Virginsky had introduced me casually to him in the street. I had never in my life seen in a man's face so much despondency, gloom, and moroseness. He looked as though he were expecting the destruction of the world, and not at some indefinite time in accordance with prophecies, which might never be fulfilled, but quite definitely, as though it were to be the day after to-morrow at twenty-five minutes past ten. We hardly said a word to one another on that occasion, but had simply shaken hands like two conspirators. I was most struck by his ears, which were of unnatural size, long, broad, and thick, sticking out in a peculiar way. His gestures were slow and awkward.

If Liputin had imagined that a phalanstery might be established in our province, this gentleman certainly knew the day and the hour when it would be founded. He made a sinister impression on me. I was the more surprised at finding him here, as Shatov was not fond of visitors.

I could hear from the stairs that they were talking very loud, all three at once, and I fancy they were disputing; but as soon as I went in, they all ceased speaking. They were arguing, standing up, but now they all suddenly sat down, so that I had to sit down too. There was a stupid silence that was not broken for fully three minutes. Though Shigalov knew me, he affected not to know me, probably not from hostile feelings, but for no particular reason. Alexey Nilitch and I bowed to one another in silence, and for some reason did not shake hands. Shigalov began at last looking at me sternly and frowningly, with the most naïve assurance that I should immediately get up and go away. At last Shatov got up from his chair and the others jumped up at once. They went out without saying good-bye. Shigalov only said in the doorway to Shatov, who was seeing him out:

"Remember that you are bound to give an explanation."

"Hang your explanation, and who the devil am I bound to?" said Shatov. He showed them out and fastened the door with the latch.

"Snipes!" he said, looking at me, with a sort of wry smile.

His face looked angry, and it seemed strange to me that he spoke first. When I had been to see him before (which was not often) it had usually happened that he sat scowling in a corner, answered ill-humouredly and only completely thawed and began to talk with pleasure after a considerable time. Even so, when he was saying good-bye he always scowled, and let one out as though he were getting rid of a personal enemy.

"I had tea yesterday with that Alexey Nilitch," I observed. "I think he's mad on atheism."

"Russian atheism has never gone further than making a joke," growled Shatov, putting up a new candle in place of an end that had burnt out.

"No, this one doesn't seem to me a joker, I think he doesn't know how to talk, let alone trying to make jokes."

"Men made of paper! It all comes from flunkeyism of thought," Shatov observed calmly, sitting down on a chair in the corner, and pressing the palms of both hands on his knees.

"There's hatred in it, too," he went on, after a minute's pause. "They'd be the first to be terribly unhappy if Russia could be suddenly reformed, even to suit their own ideas, and became extraordinarily prosperous and happy. They'd have no one to hate then, no one to curse, nothing to find fault with. There is nothing in it but an immense animal hatred for Russia which has eaten into their organism.... And it isn't a case of tears unseen by the world under cover of a smile! There has never been a falser word said in Russia than about those unseen tears," he cried, almost with fury.

"Goodness only knows what you're saying," I laughed.

"Oh, you're a 'moderate liberal,'" said Shatov, smiling too. "Do you know," he went on suddenly, "I may have been talking nonsense about the 'flunkeyism of thought.' You will say to me no doubt directly, 'it's you who are the son of a flunkey, but I'm not a flunkey.'"

"I wasn't dreaming of such a thing.... What are you saying!"

"You need not apologise. I'm not afraid of you. Once I was only the son of a flunkey, but now I've become a flunkey myself, like you. Our Russian liberal is a flunkey before everything, and is only looking for someone whose boots he can clean."

"What boots? What allegory is this?"

"Allegory, indeed! You are laughing, I see.... Stepan Trofimovitch said truly that I lie under a stone, crushed but not killed, and do nothing but wriggle. It was a good comparison of his."

"Stepan Trofimovitch declares that you are mad over the Germans," I laughed. "We've borrowed something from them anyway."

"We took twenty kopecks, but we gave up a hundred roubles of our own."

We were silent a minute.

"He got that sore lying in America."

"Who? What sore?"

"I mean Kirillov. I spent four months with him lying on the floor of a hut."

"Why, have you been in America?" I asked, surprised. "You never told me about it."

"What is there to tell? The year before last we spent our last farthing, three of us, going to America in an emigrant steamer, to test the life of the American workman on ourselves, and to verify by personal experiment the state of a man in the hardest social conditions. That was our object in going there."

"Good Lord!" I laughed. "You'd much better have gone somewhere in our province at harvest-time if you wanted to 'make a personal experiment' instead of bolting to America."

"We hired ourselves out as workmen to an exploiter; there were six of us Russians working for him—students, even landowners coming from their estates, some officers, too, and all with the same grand object. Well, so we worked, sweated, wore ourselves out; Kirillov and I were exhausted at last; fell ill—went away—we couldn't stand it. Our employer cheated us when he paid us off; instead of thirty dollars, as he had agreed, he paid me eight and Kirillov fifteen; he beat us, too, more than once. So then we were left without work, Kirillov and I, and we spent four months lying on the floor in that little town. He thought of one thing and I thought of another."

"You don't mean to say your employer beat you? In America? How you must have sworn at him!"

"Not a bit of it. On the contrary, Kirillov and I made up our minds from the first that we Russians were like little children beside the Americans, and that one must be born in America, or at least live for many years with Americans to be on a level with them. And do you know, if we were asked a dollar for a thing worth a farthing, we used to pay it with pleasure, in fact with enthusiasm. We approved of everything: spiritualism, lynch-law, revolvers, tramps. Once when we were travelling a fellow slipped his hand into my pocket, took my brush, and began brushing his hair with it. Kirillov and I only looked at one another, and made up our minds that that was the right thing and that we liked it very much. . . ."

"The strange thing is that with us all this is not only in the brain but is carried out in practice," I observed.

"Men made of paper," Shatov repeated.

"But to cross the ocean in an emigrant steamer, though, to go to an unknown country, even to make a personal experiment and all that—by Jove . . . there really is a large-hearted staunchness about it. . . . But how did you get out of it?"

"I wrote to a man in Europe and he sent me a hundred roubles."

As Shatov talked he looked doggedly at the ground as he always did, even when he was excited. At this point he suddenly raised his head.

"Do you want to know the man's name?"

"Who was it?"

"Nikolay Stavrogin."

He got up suddenly, turned to his limewood writing-table and began searching for something on it. There was a vague, though well-authenticated rumour among us that Shatov's wife had at one time had a liaison with Nikolay Stavrogin, in Paris, and just about two years ago, that is when Shatov was in America. It is true that this was long after his wife had left him in Geneva.

"If so, what possesses him now to bring his name forward and to lay stress on it?" I thought.

"I haven't paid him back yet," he said, turning suddenly to me again, and looking at me intently he sat down in the same place as before in the corner, and asked abruptly, in quite a different voice:

"You have come no doubt with some object. What do you want?"

I told him everything immediately, in its exact historical order, and added that though I had time to think it over coolly after the first excitement was over, I was more puzzled than ever. I saw that it meant something very important to Lizaveta Nikolaevna. I was extremely anxious to help her, but the trouble was that I didn't know how to keep the promise I had made her, and didn't even quite understand now what I had promised her. Then I assured him impressively once more that she had not meant to deceive him, and had had no thought of doing so; that there had been some misunderstanding, and that she had been very much hurt by the extraordinary way in which he had gone off that morning.

He listened very attentively.

"Perhaps I was stupid this morning, as I usually am.... Well, if she didn't understand why I went away like that ... so much the better for her."

He got up, went to the door, opened it, and began listening on the stairs.

"Do you want to see that person yourself?"

"That's just what I wanted, but how is it to be done?" I cried, delighted.

"Let's simply go down while she's alone. When he comes in he'll beat her horribly if he finds out we've been there. I often go in on the sly. I went for him this morning when he began beating her again."

"What do you mean?"

"I dragged him off her by the hair. He tried to beat me, but I frightened him, and so it ended. I'm afraid he'll come back drunk, and won't forget it—he'll give her a bad beating because of it."

We went downstairs at once.

The Lebyadkins' door was shut but not locked, and we were able to go in. Their lodging consisted of two nasty little rooms, with smoke-begrimed walls on which the filthy wall-paper literally hung in tatters. It had been used for some years as an eating-house, until Filipov, the tavern-keeper, moved to another house. The other rooms below what had been the eating-house were now shut up, and these two were all the Lebyadkins had. The furniture consisted of plain benches and deal tables, except for an old arm-chair that had lost its arms. In the second room there was the bedstead that belonged to Mlle. Lebyadkin standing in the corner, covered with a chintz quilt; the captain himself went to bed anywhere on the floor, often without undressing. Everything was in disorder, wet and filthy; a huge soaking rag lay in the middle of the floor in the first room, and a battered old shoe lay beside it in the wet. It was evident that no one looked after anything here. The stove was not heated, food was not cooked; they had not even a samovar as Shatov told me. The captain had come to the town with his sister utterly destitute, and had, as Liputin said, at first actually gone from house to house begging. But having unexpectedly received some money, he had taken to drinking at once, and had become so besotted that he was incapable of looking after things.

Mlle. Lebyadkin, whom I was so anxious to see, was sitting quietly at a deal kitchen table on a bench in the corner of the inner room, not making a sound. When we opened the door she did not call out to us or even move from her place. Shatov said that the door into the passage would not lock and it had once stood wide open all night. By the dim light of a thin candle in an iron candlestick, I made out a woman of about thirty, perhaps, sickly and emaciated, wearing an old dress of dark cotton material, with her long neck uncovered, her scanty dark hair twisted into a knot on the nape of her neck, no larger than the fist of a two-year-old child. She looked at us rather cheerfully. Besides the candlestick, she had on the table in front of her a little peasant looking-glass, an old pack of cards, a tattered book of songs, and a white roll of German bread from which one or two bites had been taken. It was noticeable that Mlle. Lebyadkin used powder and rouge, and painted her lips. She also blackened her eyebrows, which were fine, long, and black enough without that. Three long wrinkles stood sharply conspicuous across her high, narrow forehead in spite of the powder on it. I already knew that she was lame, but on this occasion she did not attempt to get up or walk. At some time, perhaps in early youth, that wasted face may have been pretty; but her soft, gentle grey eyes were remarkable even now. There was something dreamy and sincere in her gentle, almost joyful, expression. This gentle serene joy, which was reflected also in her smile, astonished me after all I had heard of the Cossack whip and her brother's violence. Strange to say, instead of the oppressive repulsion and almost dread one usually feels in the presence of these creatures afflicted by God, I felt it almost pleasant to look at her from the first moment, and my heart was filled afterwards with pity in which there was no trace of aversion.

"This is how she sits literally for days together, utterly alone, without moving; she tries her fortune with the cards, or looks in the looking-glass," said Shatov, pointing her out to me from the doorway. "He doesn't feed her, you know. The old woman in the lodge brings her something sometimes out of charity; how can they leave her all alone like this with a candle!"

To my surprise Shatov spoke aloud, just as though she were not in the room.

"Good day, Shatushka!" Mlle. Lebyadkin said genially.

"I've brought you a visitor, Marya Timofyevna," said Shatov.

"The visitor is very welcome. I don't know who it is you've brought, I don't seem to remember him." She scrutinised me intently from behind the candle, and turned again at once to Shatov (and she took no more notice of me for the rest of the conversation, as though I had not been near her).

"Are you tired of walking up and down alone in your garret?" she laughed, displaying two rows of magnificent teeth.

"I was tired of it, and I wanted to come and see you."

Shatov moved a bench up to the table, sat down on it and made me sit beside him.

"I'm always glad to have a talk, though you're a funny person, Shatushka, just like a monk. When did you comb your hair last? Let me do it for you." And she pulled a little comb out of her pocket. "I don't believe you've touched it since I combed it last."

"Well, I haven't got a comb," said Shatov, laughing too.

"Really? Then I'll give you mine; only remind me, not this one but another."

With a most serious expression she set to work to comb his hair. She even parted it on one side; drew back a little, looked to see whether it was right and put the comb back in her pocket.

"Do you know what, Shatushka?" She shook her head. "You may be a very sensible man but you're dull. It's strange for me to look at all of you. I don't understand how it is people are dull. Sadness is not dullness. I'm happy."

"And are you happy when your brother's here?"

"You mean Lebyadkin? He's my footman. And I don't care whether he's here or not. I call to him: 'Lebyadkin, bring the water!' or 'Lebyadkin, bring my shoes!' and he runs. Sometimes one does wrong and can't help laughing at him."

"That's just how it is," said Shatov, addressing me aloud without ceremony. "She treats him just like a footman. I've heard her myself calling to him, 'Lebyadkin, give me some water!' And she laughed as she said it. The only difference is that he doesn't fetch the water but beats her for it; but she isn't a bit afraid of him. She has some sort of nervous fits, almost every day, and they are destroying her memory so that afterwards she forgets everything that's just happened, and is always in a muddle over time. You imagine she remembers how you came in; perhaps she does remember, but no doubt she has changed everything to please herself, and she takes us now for different people from what we are, though she knows I'm 'Shatushka.' It doesn't matter my speaking aloud, she soon leaves off listening to people who talk to her, and plunges into dreams. Yes, plunges. She's an extraordinary person for dreaming; she'll sit for eight hours, for whole days together in the same place. You see there's a roll lying there, perhaps she's only taken one bite at it since the morning, and she'll finish it to-morrow. Now she's begun trying her fortune on cards...."

"I keep trying my fortune, Shatushka, but it doesn't come out right," Marya Timofyevna put in suddenly, catching the last word, and without looking at it she put out her left hand for the roll (she had heard something about the roll too very likely). She got hold of the roll at last and after keeping it for some time in her left hand, while her attention was distracted by the conversation which sprang up again, she put it back again on the table unconsciously without having taken a bite of it.

"It always comes out the same, a journey, a wicked man, somebody's treachery, a death-bed, a letter, unexpected news. I think it's all nonsense. Shatushka, what do you think? If people can tell lies why shouldn't a card?" She suddenly threw the cards together again. "I said the same thing to Mother Praskovya, she's a very venerable woman, she used to run to my cell to tell her fortune on the cards, without letting the Mother Superior know. Yes, and she wasn't the only one who came to me. They sigh, and shake their heads at me, they talk it over while I laugh. 'Where are you going to get a letter from, Mother Praskovya,' I say, 'when you haven't had one for twelve years?' Her daughter had been taken away to Turkey by her husband, and for twelve years there had been no sight nor sound of her. Only I was sitting the next evening at tea with the Mother Superior (she was a princess by birth), there was some lady there too, a visitor, a great dreamer, and a little monk from Athos was sitting there too, a rather absurd man to my thinking. What do you think, Shatushka, that monk from Athos had brought Mother Praskovya a letter from her daughter in Turkey, that morning—so much for the knave of diamonds—unexpected news! We were drinking our tea, and the monk from Athos said to the Mother Superior, 'Blessed Mother Superior, God has blessed your convent above all things in that you preserve so great a treasure in its precincts,' said he. 'What treasure is that?' asked the Mother Superior. 'The Mother Lizaveta, the Blessed.' This Lizaveta the Blessed was enshrined in the nunnery wall, in a cage seven feet long and five feet high, and she had been sitting there for seventeen years in nothing but a hempen shift, summer and winter, and she always kept pecking at the hempen cloth with a straw or a twig of some sort, and she never said a word, and never combed her hair, or washed, for seventeen years. In the winter they used to put a sheepskin in for her, and every day a piece of bread and a jug of water. The pilgrims gaze at her, sigh and exclaim, and make offerings of money. 'A treasure you've pitched on,' answered the Mother Superior—(she was angry, she disliked Lizaveta dreadfully)—'Lizaveta only sits there out of spite, out of pure obstinacy, it is nothing but hypocrisy.' I didn't like this; I was thinking at the time of shutting myself up too. 'I think,' said I, 'that God and nature are just the same thing.' They all cried out with one voice at me, 'Well, now!' The Mother Superior laughed, whispered something to the lady and called me up, petted me, and the lady gave me a pink ribbon. Would you like me to show it to you? And the monk began to admonish me. But he talked so kindly, so humbly, and so wisely, I suppose. I sat and listened. 'Do you understand?' he asked. 'No,' I said, 'I don't understand a word, but leave me quite alone.' Ever since then they've left me in peace, Shatushka. And at that time an old woman who was living in the convent doing penance for prophesying the future, whispered to me as she was coming out of church, 'What is the mother of God? What do you think?' 'The great mother,' I answer, 'the hope of the human race.' 'Yes,' she answered, 'the mother of God is the great mother—the damp earth, and therein lies great joy for men. And every earthly woe and every earthly tear is a joy for us; and when you water the earth with your tears a foot deep, you will rejoice at everything at once, and your sorrow will be no more, such is the prophecy.' That word sank into my heart at the time. Since then when I bow down to the ground at my prayers, I've taken to kissing the earth. I kiss it and weep. And let me tell you, Shatushka, there's no harm in those tears; and even if one has no grief, one's tears flow from joy. The tears flow of themselves, that's the truth. I used to go out to the shores of the lake; on one side was our convent and on the other the pointed mountain, they called it the Peak. I used to go up that mountain, facing the east, fall down to the ground, and weep and weep, and I don't know how long I wept, and I don't remember or know anything about it. I would get up, and turn back when the sun was setting, it was so big, and splendid and glorious—do you like looking at the sun, Shatushka? It's beautiful but sad. I would turn to the east again, and the shadow, the shadow of our mountain was flying like an arrow over our lake, long, long and narrow, stretching a mile beyond, right up to the island on the lake and cutting that rocky island right in two, and as it cut it in two, the sun would set altogether and suddenly all would be darkness. And then I used to be quite miserable, suddenly I used to remember, I'm afraid of the dark, Shatushka. And what I wept for most was my baby...."

"Why, had you one?" And Shatov, who had been listening attentively all the time, nudged me with his elbow.

"Why, of course. A little rosy baby with tiny little nails, and my only grief is I can't remember whether it was a boy or a girl. Sometimes I remember it was a boy, and sometimes it was a girl. And when he was born, I wrapped him in cambric and lace, and put pink ribbons on him, strewed him with flowers, got him ready, said prayers over him. I took him away un-christened and carried him through the forest, and I was afraid of the forest, and I was frightened, and what I weep for most is that I had a baby and I never had a husband."

"Perhaps you had one?" Shatov queried cautiously.

"You're absurd, Shatushka, with your reflections. I had, perhaps I had, but what's the use of my having had one, if it's just the same as though I hadn't. There's an easy riddle for you. Guess it!" she laughed.

"Where did you take your baby?"

"I took it to the pond," she said with a sigh.

Shatov nudged me again.

"And what if you never had a baby and all this is only a wild dream?"

"You ask me a hard question, Shatushka," she answered dreamily, without a trace of surprise at such a question. "I can't tell you anything about that, perhaps I hadn't; I think that's only your curiosity. I shan't leave off crying for him anyway, I couldn't have dreamt it." And big tears glittered in her eyes. "Shatushka, Shatushka, is it true that your wife ran away from you?"

She suddenly put both hands on his shoulders, and looked at him pityingly. "Don't be angry, I feel sick myself. Do you know, Shatushka, I've had a dream: he came to me again, he beckoned me, called me. 'My little puss,' he cried to me, 'little puss, come to me!' And I was more delighted at that 'little puss' than anything; he loves me, I thought."

"Perhaps he will come in reality," Shatov muttered in an undertone.

"No, Shatushka, that's a dream.... He can't come in reality. You know the song:

'A new fine house I do not crave,

This tiny cell's enough for me;

There will I dwell my soul to save

And ever pray to God for thee.'

Ach, Shatushka, Shatushka, my dear, why do you never ask me about anything?"

"Why, you won't tell. That's why I don't ask."

"I won't tell, I won't tell," she answered quickly. "You may kill me, I won't tell. You may burn me, I won't tell. And whatever I had to bear I'd never tell, people won't find out!"

"There, you see. Every one has something of their own," Shatov said, still more softly, his head drooping lower and lower.

"But if you were to ask perhaps I should tell, perhaps I should!" she repeated ecstatically. "Why don't you ask? Ask, ask me nicely, Shatushka, perhaps I shall tell you. Entreat me, Shatushka, so that I shall consent of myself. Shatushka, Shatushka!"

But Shatushka was silent. There was complete silence lasting a minute. Tears slowly trickled down her painted cheeks. She sat forgetting her two hands on Shatov's shoulders, but no longer looking at him.

"Ach, what is it to do with me, and it's a sin." Shatov suddenly got up from the bench.

"Get up!" He angrily pulled the bench from under me and put it back where it stood before.

"He'll be coming, so we must mind he doesn't guess. It's time we were off."

"Ach, you're talking of my footman," Marya Timofyevna laughed suddenly. "You're afraid of him. Well, good-bye, dear visitors, but listen for one minute, I've something to tell you. That Nilitch came here with Filipov, the landlord, a red beard, and my fellow had flown at me just then, so the landlord caught hold of him and pulled him about the room while he shouted 'It's not my fault, I'm suffering for another man's sin!' So would you believe it, we all burst out laughing...."

"Ach, Timofyevna, why it was I, not the red beard, it was I pulled him away from you by his hair, this morning; the landlord came the day before yesterday to make a row; you've mixed it up."

"Stay, I really have mixed it up. Perhaps it was you. Why dispute about trifles? What does it matter to him who it is gives him a beating?" She laughed.

"Come along!" Shatov pulled me. "The gate's creaking, he'll find us and beat her."

And before we had time to run out on to the stairs we heard a drunken shout and a shower of oaths at the gate.

Shatov let me into his room and locked the door.

"You'll have to stay a minute if you don't want a scene. He's squealing like a little pig, he must have stumbled over the gate again. He falls flat every time."

We didn't get off without a scene, however.

VI

Shatov stood at the closed door of his room and listened; suddenly he sprang back.

"He's coming here, I knew he would," he whispered furiously. "Now there'll be no getting rid of him till midnight."

Several violent thumps of a fist on the door followed.

"Shatov, Shatov, open!" yelled the captain. "Shatov, friend!

'I have come, to thee to tell thee

That the sun doth r-r-rise apace,

That the forest glows and tr-r-rembles

In ... the fire of ... his ... embrace.

Tell thee I have waked, God damn thee,

Wakened under the birch-twigs.... '

("As it might be under the birch-rods, ha ha!")

'Every little bird ... is ... thirsty,

Says I'm going to ... have a drink,

But I don't ... know what to drink.... '

"Damn his stupid curiosity! Shatov, do you understand how good it is to be alive!"

"Don't answer!" Shatov whispered to me again.

"Open the door! Do you understand that there's something higher than brawling ... in mankind; there are moments of an hon-hon-honourable man.... Shatov, I'm good; I'll forgive you.... Shatov, damn the manifestoes, eh?"

Silence.

"Do you understand, you ass, that I'm in love, that I've bought a dress-coat, look, the garb of love, fifteen roubles; a captain's love calls for the niceties of style.... Open the door!" he roared savagely all of a sudden, and he began furiously banging with his fists again.

"Go to hell!" Shatov roared suddenly.

"S-s-slave! Bond-slave, and your sister's a slave, a bondswoman … a th … th … ief!"

"And you sold your sister."

"That's a lie! I put up with the libel though. I could with one word … do you understand what she is?"

"What?" Shatov at once drew near the door inquisitively.

"But will you understand?"

"Yes, I shall understand, tell me what?"

"I'm not afraid to say! I'm never afraid to say anything in public!…"

"You not afraid? A likely story," said Shatov, taunting him, and nodding to me to listen.

"Me afraid?"

"Yes, I think you are."

"Me afraid?"

"Well then, tell away if you're not afraid of your master's whip.… You're a coward, though you are a captain!"

"I … I … she's … she's …" faltered Lebyadkin in a voice shaking with excitement.

"Well?" Shatov put his ear to the door.

A silence followed, lasting at least half a minute.

"Sc-ou-oundrel!" came from the other side of the door at last, and the captain hurriedly beat a retreat downstairs, puffing like a samovar, stumbling on every step.

"Yes, he's a sly one, and won't give himself away even when he's drunk."

Shatov moved away from the door.

"What's it all about?" I asked.

Shatov waved aside the question, opened the door and began listening on the stairs again. He listened a long while, and even stealthily descended a few steps. At last he came back.

"There's nothing to be heard; he isn't beating her; he must have flopped down at once to go to sleep. It's time for you to go."

"Listen, Shatov, what am I to gather from all this?"

"Oh, gather what you like!" he answered in a weary and disgusted voice, and he sat down to his writing-table.

I went away. An improbable idea was growing stronger and stronger in my mind. I thought of the next day with distress.…

VII

This "next day," the very Sunday which was to decide Stepan Trofimovitch's fate irrevocably, was one of the most memorable days in my chronicle. It was a day of surprises, a day that solved past riddles and suggested new ones, a day of startling revelations, and still more hopeless perplexity. In the morning, as the reader is already aware, I had by Varvara Petrovna's particular request to accompany my friend on his visit to her, and at three o'clock in the afternoon I had to be with Lizaveta Nikolaevna in order to tell her—I did not know what—and to assist her—I did not know how. And meanwhile it all ended as no one could have expected. In a word, it was a day of wonderful coincidences.

To begin with, when Stepan Trofimovitch and I arrived at Varvara Petrovna's at twelve o'clock punctually, the time she had fixed, we did not find her at home; she had not yet come back from church. My poor friend was so disposed, or, more accurately speaking, so indisposed that this circumstance crushed him at once; he sank almost helpless into an arm-chair in the drawing-room. I suggested a glass of water; but in spite of his pallor and the trembling of his hands, he refused it with dignity. His get-up for the occasion was, by the way, extremely recherché: a shirt of batiste and embroidered, almost fit for a ball, a white tie, a new hat in his hand, new straw-coloured gloves, and even a suspicion of scent. We had hardly sat down when Shatov was shown in by the butler, obviously also by official invitation. Stepan Trofimovitch was rising to shake hands with him, but Shatov, after looking attentively at us both, turned away into a corner, and sat down there without even nodding to us. Stepan Trofimovitch looked at me in dismay again.

We sat like this for some minutes longer in complete silence. Stepan Trofimovitch suddenly began whispering something to me very quickly, but I could not catch it; and indeed, he was so agitated himself that he broke off without finishing. The butler came in once more, ostensibly to set something straight on the table, more probably to take a look at us.

Shatov suddenly addressed him with a loud question:

"Alexey Yegorytch, do you know whether Darya Pavlovna has gone with her?"

"Varvara Petrovna was pleased to drive to the cathedral alone, and Darya Pavlovna was pleased to remain in her room upstairs, being indisposed," Alexey Yegorytch announced formally and reprovingly.

My poor friend again stole a hurried and agitated glance at me, so that at last I turned away from him. Suddenly a carriage rumbled at the entrance, and some commotion at a distance in the house made us aware of the lady's return. We all leapt up from our easy chairs, but again a surprise awaited us; we heard the noise of many footsteps, so our hostess must have returned not alone, and this certainly was rather strange, since she had fixed that time herself. Finally, we heard some one come in with strange rapidity as though running, in a way that Varvara Petrovna could not have come in. And, all at once she almost flew into the room, panting and extremely agitated. After her a little later and much more quickly Lizaveta Nikolaevna came in, and with her, hand in hand, Marya Timofyevna Lebyadkin! If I had seen this in my dreams, even then I should not have believed it.

To explain their utterly unexpected appearance, I must go back an hour and describe more in detail an extraordinary adventure which had befallen Varvara Petrovna in church.

In the first place almost the whole town, that is, of course, all of the upper stratum of society, were assembled in the cathedral. It was known that the governor's wife was to make her appearance there for the first time since her arrival amongst us. I must mention that there were already rumours that she was a free-thinker, and a follower of "the new principles." All the ladies were also aware that she would be dressed with magnificence and extraordinary elegance. And so the costumes of our ladies were elaborate and gorgeous for the occasion.

Only Varvara Petrovna was modestly dressed in black as she always was, and had been for the last four years. She had taken her usual place in church in the first row on the left, and a footman in livery had put down a velvet cushion for her to kneel on; everything in fact, had been as usual. But it was noticed, too, that all through the service she prayed with extreme fervour. It was even asserted afterwards when people recalled it, that she had had tears in her eyes. The service was over at last, and our chief priest, Father Pavel, came out to deliver a solemn sermon. We liked his sermons and thought very highly of them. We used even to try to persuade him to print them, but he never could make up his mind to. On this occasion the sermon was a particularly long one.

And behold, during the sermon a lady drove up to the church in an old fashioned hired droshky, that is, one in which the lady could only sit sideways, holding on to the driver's sash, shaking at every jolt like a blade of grass in the breeze. Such droshkys are still to be seen in our town. Stopping at the corner of the cathedral—for there were a number of carriages, and mounted police too, at the gates—the lady sprang out of the droshky and handed the driver four kopecks in silver.

"Isn't it enough, Vanya?" she cried, seeing his grimace. "It's all I've got," she added plaintively.

"Well, there, bless you. I took you without fixing the price," said the driver with a hopeless gesture, and looking at her he added as though reflecting:

"And it would be a sin to take advantage of you too."

Then, thrusting his leather purse into his bosom, he touched up his horse and drove off, followed by the jeers of the drivers standing near. Jeers, and wonder too, followed the lady as she made her way to the cathedral gates, between the carriages and the footmen waiting for their masters to come out. And indeed, there certainly was something extraordinary and surprising to every one in such a person's suddenly appearing in the street among people. She was painfully thin and she limped, she was heavily powdered and rouged; her long neck was quite bare, she had neither kerchief nor pelisse; she had nothing on but an old dark dress in spite of the cold and windy, though bright, September day. She was bareheaded, and her hair was twisted up into a tiny knot, and on the right side of it was stuck an artificial rose, such as are used to dedicate cherubs sold in Palm week. I had noticed just such a one with a wreath of paper roses in a corner under the ikons when I was at Marya Timofyevna's the day before. To put a finishing-touch to it, though the lady walked with modestly downcast eyes there was a sly and merry smile on her face. If she had lingered a moment longer, she would perhaps not have been allowed to enter the cathedral. But she succeeded in slipping by, and entering the building, gradually pressed forward.

Though it was half-way through the sermon, and the dense crowd that filled the cathedral was listening to it with absorbed and silent attention, yet several pairs of eyes glanced with curiosity and amazement at the new-comer. She sank on to the floor, bowed her painted face down to it, lay there a long time, unmistakably weeping; but raising her head again and getting up from her knees, she soon recovered, and was diverted. Gaily and with evident and intense enjoyment she let her eyes rove over the faces, and over the walls of the cathedral. She looked with particular curiosity at some of the ladies, even standing on tip-toe to look at them, and even laughed once or twice, giggling strangely. But the sermon was over, and they brought out the cross. The governor's wife was the first to go up to the cross, but she stopped short two steps from it, evidently wishing to make way for Varvara Petrovna, who, on her side, moved towards it quite directly as though she noticed no one in front of her. There was an obvious and, in its way, clever malice implied in this extraordinary act of deference on the part of the governor's wife; every one felt this; Varvara Petrovna must have felt it too; but she went on as before, apparently noticing no one, and with the same unfaltering air of dignity kissed the cross, and at once turned to leave the cathedral. A footman in livery cleared the way for her, though every one stepped back spontaneously to let her pass. But just as she was going out, in the porch the closely packed mass of people blocked the way for a moment. Varvara Petrovna stood still, and suddenly a strange, extraordinary creature, the woman with the paper rose on her head, squeezed through the people, and fell on her knees before her. Varvara Petrovna, who was not easily disconcerted, especially in public, looked at her sternly and with dignity.

I hasten to observe here, as briefly as possible, that though Varvara Petrovna had become, it was said, excessively careful and even stingy, yet sometimes she was not sparing of money, especially for benevolent objects. She was a member of a charitable society in the capital. In the last famine year she had sent five hundred roubles to the chief committee for the relief of the sufferers, and people talked of it in the town. Moreover, just before the appointment of the new governor, she had been on the very point of founding a local committee of ladies to assist the poorest mothers in the town and in the province. She was severely censured among us for ambition; but Varvara Petrovna's well-known strenuousness and, at the same time, her persistence nearly triumphed over all obstacles. The society was almost formed, and the original idea embraced a wider and wider scope in the enthusiastic mind of the foundress. She was already dreaming of founding a similar society in Moscow, and the gradual expansion of its influence over all the provinces of Russia. And now, with the sudden change of governor, everything was at a standstill; and the new governor's wife had, it was said, already uttered in society some biting, and, what was worse, apt and sensible remarks about the impracticability of the fundamental idea of such a committee, which was, with additions of course, repeated to Varvara Petrovna. God alone knows the secrets of men's hearts; but I imagine that Varvara Petrovna stood still now at the very cathedral gates positively with a certain pleasure, knowing that the governor's wife and, after her, all the congregation, would have to pass by immediately, and "let her see for herself how little I care what she thinks, and what pointed things she says about the vanity of my benevolence. So much for all of you!"

"What is it my dear? What are you asking?" said Varvara Petrovna, looking more attentively at the kneeling woman before her, who gazed at her with a fearfully panic-stricken, shame-faced, but almost reverent expression, and suddenly broke into the same strange giggle.

"What does she want? Who is she?"

Varvara Petrovna bent an imperious and inquiring gaze on all around her. Every one was silent.

"You are unhappy? You are in need of help?"

"I am in need.... I have come ..." faltered the "unhappy" creature, in a voice broken with emotion. "I have come only to kiss your hand...."

Again she giggled. With the childish look with which little children caress someone, begging for a favour, she stretched forward to seize Varvara Petrovna's hand, but, as though panic-stricken, drew her hands back.

"Is that all you have come for?" said Varvara Petrovna, with a compassionate smile; but at once she drew her mother-of-pearl purse out of her pocket, took out a ten-rouble note and gave it to the unknown. The latter took it. Varvara Petrovna was much interested and evidently did not look upon her as an ordinary low-class beggar.

"I say, she gave her ten roubles!" someone said in the crowd.

"Let me kiss your hand," faltered the unknown, holding tight in the fingers of her left hand the corner of the ten-rouble note, which fluttered in the draught. Varvara Petrovna frowned slightly, and with a serious, almost severe, face held out her hand. The cripple kissed it with reverence. Her grateful eyes shone with positive ecstasy. At that moment the governor's wife came up, and a whole crowd of ladies and high officials flocked after her. The governor's wife was forced to stand still for a moment in the crush; many people stopped.

"You are trembling. Are you cold?" Varvara Petrovna observed suddenly, and flinging off her pelisse which a footman caught in mid-air, she took from her own shoulders a very expensive black shawl, and with her own hands wrapped it round the bare neck of the still kneeling woman.

"But get up, get up from your knees I beg you!"

The woman got up.

"Where do you live? Is it possible no one knows where she lives?" Varvara Petrovna glanced round impatiently again. But the crowd was different now: she saw only the faces of acquaintances, people in society, surveying the scene, some with severe astonishment, others with sly curiosity and at the same time guileless eagerness for a sensation, while others positively laughed.

"I believe her name's Lebyadkin," a good-natured person volunteered at last in answer to Varvara Petrovna. It was our respectable and respected merchant Andreev, a man in spectacles with a grey beard, wearing Russian dress and holding a high round hat in his hands. "They live in the Filipovs' house in Bogoyavlensky Street."

"Lebyadkin? Filipovs' house? I have heard something.... Thank you, Nikon Semyonitch.

But who is this Lebyadkin?"

"He calls himself a captain, a man, it must be said, not over careful in his behaviour. And no doubt this is his sister. She must have escaped from under control," Nikon Semyonitch went on, dropping his voice, and glancing significantly at Varvara Petrovna.

"I understand. Thank you, Nikon Semyonitch. Your name is Mlle. Lebyadkin?"

"No, my name's not Lebyadkin."

"Then perhaps your brother's name is Lebyadkin?"

"My brother's name is Lebyadkin."

"This is what I'll do, I'll take you with me now, my dear, and you shall be driven from me to your family. Would you like to go with me?"

"Ach, I should!" cried Mlle. Lebyadkin, clasping her hands.

"Auntie, auntie, take me with you too!" the voice of Lizaveta Nikolaevna cried suddenly.

I must observe that Lizaveta Nikolaevna had come to the cathedral with the governor's wife, while Praskovya Ivanovna had by the doctor's orders gone for a drive in her carriage, taking Mavriky Nikolaevitch to entertain her. Liza suddenly left the governor's wife and ran up to Varvara Petrovna.

"My dear, you know I'm always glad to have you, but what will your mother say?" Varvara Petrovna began majestically, but she became suddenly confused, noticing Liza's extraordinary agitation.

"Auntie, auntie, I must come with you!" Liza implored, kissing Varvara Petrovna.

"Mais qu'avez vous donc, Lise?" the governor's wife asked with expressive wonder.

"Ah, forgive me, darling, chère cousine, I'm going to auntie's."

Liza turned in passing to her unpleasantly surprised chère cousine, and kissed her twice.

"And tell maman to follow me to auntie's directly; maman meant, fully meant to come and see you, she said so this morning herself, I forgot to tell you," Liza pattered on. "I beg your pardon, don't be angry, Julie, chère ... cousine.... Auntie, I'm ready!"

"If you don't take me with you, auntie, I'll run after your carriage, screaming," she whispered rapidly and despairingly in Varvara Petrovna's ear; it was lucky that no one heard. Varvara Petrovna positively staggered back, and bent her penetrating gaze on the mad girl. That gaze settled everything. She made up her mind to take Liza with her.

"We must put an end to this!" broke from her lips. "Very well, I'll take you with pleasure, Liza," she added aloud, "if Yulia Mihailovna is willing to let you come, of course." With a candid air and straightforward dignity she addressed the governor's wife directly.

"Oh, certainly, I don't want to deprive her of such a pleasure especially as I am myself

. . ." Yulia Mihailovna lisped with amazing affability—"I myself . . . know well what a fantastic, wilful little head it is!" Yulia Mihailovna gave a charming smile.

"I thank you extremely," said Varvara Petrovna, with a courteous and dignified bow.

"And I am the more gratified," Yulia Mihailovna went on, lisping almost rapturously, flushing all over with agreeable excitement, "that, apart from the pleasure of being with you Liza should be carried away by such an excellent, I may say lofty, feeling . . . of compassion . . ." (she glanced at the "unhappy creature") "and . . . and at the very portal of the temple. . . ."

"Such a feeling does you honour," Varvara Petrovna approved magnificently. Yulia Mihailovna impulsively held out her hand and Varvara Petrovna with perfect readiness touched it with her fingers. The general effect was excellent, the faces of some of those present beamed with pleasure, some bland and insinuating smiles were to be seen.

In short it was made manifest to every one in the town that it was not Yulia Mihailovna who had up till now neglected Varvara Petrovna in not calling upon her, but on the contrary that Varvara Petrovna had "kept Yulia Mihailovna within bounds at a distance, while the latter would have hastened to pay her a visit, going on foot perhaps if necessary, had she been fully assured that Varvara Petrovna would not turn her away." And Varvara Petrovna's prestige was enormously increased.

"Get in, my dear." Varvara Petrovna motioned Mlle. Lebyadkin towards the carriage which had driven up.

The "unhappy creature" hurried gleefully to the carriage door, and there the footman lifted her in.

"What! You're lame!" cried Varvara Petrovna, seeming quite alarmed, and she turned pale. (Every one noticed it at the time, but did not understand it.)

The carriage rolled away. Varvara Petrovna's house was very near the cathedral. Liza told me afterwards that Miss Lebyadkin laughed hysterically for the three minutes that the drive lasted, while Varvara Petrovna sat "as though in a mesmeric sleep." Liza's own expression.

CHAPTER V. THE SUBTLE SERPENT

I

VARVARA PETROVNA rang the bell and threw herself into an easy chair by the window.

"Sit here, my dear." She motioned Marya Timofyevna to a seat in the middle of the room, by a large round table. "Stepan Trofimovitch, what is the meaning of this? See, see, look at this woman, what is the meaning of it?"

"I … I …" faltered Stepan Trofimovitch.

But a footman came in.

"A cup of coffee at once, we must have it as quickly as possible! Keep the horses!"

"Mais, chère et excellente amie, dans quelle inquiétude …" Stepan Trofimovitch exclaimed in a dying voice.

"Ach! French! French! I can see at once that it's the highest society," cried Marya Timofyevna, clapping her hands, ecstatically preparing herself to listen to a conversation in French. Varvara Petrovna stared at her almost in dismay.

We all sat in silence, waiting to see how it would end. Shatov did not lift up his head, and Stepan Trofimovitch was overwhelmed with confusion as though it were all his fault; the perspiration stood out on his temples. I glanced at Liza (she was sitting in the corner almost beside Shatov). Her eyes darted keenly from Varvara Petrovna to the cripple and back again; her lips were drawn into a smile, but not a pleasant one. Varvara Petrovna saw that smile. Meanwhile Marya Timofyevna was absolutely transported. With evident enjoyment and without a trace of embarrassment she stared at Varvara Petrovna's beautiful drawing-room—the furniture, the carpets, the pictures on the walls, the old-fashioned painted ceiling, the great bronze crucifix in the corner, the china lamp, the albums, the objects on the table.

"And you're here, too, Shatushka!" she cried suddenly. "Only fancy, I saw you a long time ago, but I thought it couldn't be you! How could you come here!" And she laughed gaily.

"You know this woman?" said Varvara Petrovna, turning to him at once.

"I know her," muttered Shatov. He seemed about to move from his chair, but remained sitting.

"What do you know of her? Make haste, please!"

"Oh, well …" he stammered with an incongruous smile. "You see for yourself.…"

"What do I see? Come now, say something!"

"She lives in the same house as I do … with her brother … an officer."

"Well?"

Shatov stammered again.

"It's not worth talking about ..." he muttered, and relapsed into determined silence. He positively flushed with determination.

"Of course one can expect nothing else from you," said Varvara Petrovna indignantly. It was clear to her now that they all knew something and, at the same time, that they were all scared, that they were evading her questions, and anxious to keep something from her.

The footman came in and brought her, on a little silver tray, the cup of coffee she had so specially ordered, but at a sign from her moved with it at once towards Marya Timofyevna.

"You were very cold just now, my dear; make haste and drink it and get warm."

"Merci."

Marya Timofyevna took the cup and at once went off into a giggle at having said merci to the footman. But meeting Varvara Petrovna's reproving eyes, she was overcome with shyness and put the cup on the table.

"Auntie, surely you're not angry?" she faltered with a sort of flippant playfulness.

"Wh-a-a-t?" Varvara Petrovna started, and drew herself up in her chair. "I'm not your aunt. What are you thinking of?"

Marya Timofyevna, not expecting such an angry outburst, began trembling all over in little convulsive shudders, as though she were in a fit, and sank back in her chair.

"I ... I ... thought that was the proper way," she faltered, gazing open-eyed at Varvara Petrovna. "Liza called you that."

"What Liza?"

"Why, this young lady here," said Marya Timofyevna, pointing with her finger.

"So she's Liza already?"

"You called her that yourself just now," said Marya Timofyevna growing a little bolder. "And I dreamed of a beauty like that," she added, laughing, as it were accidentally.

Varvara Petrovna reflected, and grew calmer, she even smiled faintly at Marya Timofyevna's last words; the latter, catching her smile, got up from her chair, and limping, went timidly towards her.

"Take it. I forgot to give it back. Don't be angry with my rudeness."

She took from her shoulders the black shawl that Varvara Petrovna had wrapped round her.

"Put it on again at once, and you can keep it always. Go and sit down, drink your coffee, and please don't be afraid of me, my dear, don't worry yourself. I am beginning to understand you."

"Chère amie ..." Stepan Trofimovitch ventured again.

"Ach, Stepan Trofimovitch, it's bewildering enough without you. You might at least spare me.... Please ring that bell there, near you, to the maid's room."

A silence followed. Her eyes strayed irritably and suspiciously over all our faces. Agasha, her favourite maid, came in.

"Bring me my check shawl, the one I bought in Geneva. What's Darya Pavlovna doing?"

"She's not very well, madam."

"Go and ask her to come here. Say that I want her particularly, even if she's not well."

At that instant there was again, as before, an unusual noise of steps and voices in the next room, and suddenly Praskovya Ivanovna, panting and "distracted," appeared in the doorway. She was leaning on the arm of Mavriky Nikolaevitch.

"Ach, heavens, I could scarcely drag myself here. Liza, you mad girl, how you treat your mother!" she squeaked, concentrating in that squeak, as weak and irritable people are wont to do, all her accumulated irritability. "Varvara Petrovna, I've come for my daughter!"

Varvara Petrovna looked at her from under her brows, half rose to meet her, and scarcely concealing her vexation brought out: "Good morning, Praskovya Ivanovna, please be seated, I knew you would come!"

II

There could be nothing surprising to Praskovya Ivanovna in such a reception. Varvara Petrovna had from childhood upwards treated her old school friend tyrannically, and under a show of friendship almost contemptuously. And this was an exceptional occasion too. During the last few days there had almost been a complete rupture between the two households, as I have mentioned incidentally already. The reason of this rupture was still a mystery to Varvara Petrovna, which made it all the more offensive; but the chief cause of offence was that Praskovya Ivanovna had succeeded in taking up an extraordinarily supercilious attitude towards Varvara Petrovna. Varvara Petrovna was wounded of course, and meanwhile some strange rumours had reached her which also irritated her extremely, especially by their vagueness. Varvara Petrovna was of a direct and proudly frank character, somewhat slap-dash in her methods, indeed, if the expression is permissible. There was nothing she detested so much as secret and mysterious insinuations, she always preferred war in the open. Anyway, the two ladies had not met for five days. The last visit had been paid by Varvara Petrovna, who had come back from "that Drozdov woman" offended and perplexed. I can say with certainty that Praskovya Ivanovna had come on this occasion with the naïve conviction that Varvara Petrovna would, for some reason, be sure to stand in awe of her. This was evident from the very expression of her face. Evidently too, Varvara Petrovna was always possessed by a demon of haughty pride whenever she had the least ground for suspecting that she was for some reason supposed to be humiliated. Like many weak people, who for a long time allow themselves to be insulted without resenting it, Praskovya Ivanovna showed an extraordinary violence in her attack at the first favourable opportunity. It is true that she was not well, and always became more irritable in illness. I must add finally, that our presence in the drawing-room could hardly be much check to the two ladies who had been friends from childhood, if a quarrel had broken out between them. We were looked upon as friends of the family, and almost as their subjects. I made that reflection with some alarm at the time. Stepan Trofimovitch, who had not sat down since the entrance of Varvara Petrovna, sank helplessly into an arm-chair on hearing Praskovya Ivanovna's squeal, and tried to catch my eye with a look of despair. Shatov turned sharply in his chair, and growled something to himself. I believe he meant to get up and go away. Liza rose from her chair but sank back again at once without even paying befitting attention to her mother's squeal—not from "waywardness," but obviously because she was entirely absorbed by some other overwhelming impression. She was looking absent-mindedly into the air, no longer noticing even Marya Timofyevna.

III

"Ach, here!" Praskovya Ivanovna indicated an easy chair near the table and sank heavily into it with the assistance of Mavriky Nikolaevitch. "I wouldn't have sat down in your house, my lady, if it weren't for my legs," she added in a breaking voice.

Varvara Petrovna raised her head a little, and with an expression of suffering pressed the fingers of her right hand to her right temple, evidently in acute pain (tic douloureux).

"Why so, Praskovya Ivanovna; why wouldn't you sit down in my house? I possessed your late husband's sincere friendship all his life; and you and I used to play with our dolls at school together as girls."

Praskovya Ivanovna waved her hands.

"I knew that was coming! You always begin about the school when you want to reproach me—that's your way. But to my thinking that's only fine talk. I can't stand the school you're always talking about."

"You've come in rather a bad temper, I'm afraid; how are your legs? Here they're bringing you some coffee, please have some, drink it and don't be cross."

"Varvara Petrovna, you treat me as though I were a child. I won't have any coffee, so there!"

And she pettishly waved away the footman who was bringing her coffee. (All the others refused coffee too except Mavriky Nikolaevitch and me. Stepan Trofimovitch took it, but put it aside on the table. Though Marya Timofyevna was very eager to have another cup and even put out her hand to take it, on second thoughts she refused it ceremoniously, and was obviously pleased with herself for doing so.)

Varvara Petrovna gave a wry smile.

"I'll tell you what it is, Praskovya Ivanovna, my friend, you must have taken some fancy into your head again, and that's why you've come. You've simply lived on fancies all your life. You flew into a fury at the mere mention of our school; but do you remember how you came and persuaded all the class that a hussar called Shablykin had proposed to you, and how Mme. Lefebure proved on the spot you were lying. Yet you weren't lying, you were simply imagining it all to amuse yourself. Come, tell me, what is it now? What are you fancying now; what is it vexes you?"

"And you fell in love with the priest who used to teach us scripture at school—so much for you, since you've such a spiteful memory. Ha ha ha!"

She laughed viciously and went off into a fit of coughing.

"Ah, you've not forgotten the priest then ..." said Varvara Petrovna, looking at her vindictively.

Her face turned green. Praskovya Ivanovna suddenly assumed a dignified air.

"I'm in no laughing mood now, madam. Why have you drawn my daughter into your scandals in the face of the whole town? That's what I've come about."

"My scandals?" Varvara Petrovna drew herself up menacingly.

"Maman, I entreat you too, to restrain yourself," Lizaveta Nikolaevna brought out suddenly.

"What's that you say?" The maman was on the point of breaking into a squeal again, but catching her daughter's flashing eye, she subsided suddenly.

"How could you talk about scandal, maman?" cried Liza, flushing red. "I came of my own accord with Yulia Mihailovna's permission, because I wanted to learn this unhappy woman's story and to be of use to her."

"This unhappy woman's story!" Praskovya Ivanovna drawled with a spiteful laugh. "Is it your place to mix yourself up with such 'stories.' Ach, enough of your tyrannising!" She turned furiously to Varvara Petrovna. "I don't know whether it's true or not, they say you keep the whole town in order, but it seems your turn has come at last."

Varvara Petrovna sat straight as an arrow ready to fly from the bow. For ten seconds she looked sternly and immovably at Praskovya Ivanovna.

"Well, Praskovya, you must thank God that all here present are our friends," she said at last with ominous composure. "You've said a great deal better unsaid."

"But I'm not so much afraid of what the world will say, my lady, as some people. It's you who, under a show of pride, are trembling at what people will say. And as for all here being your friends, it's better for you than if strangers had been listening."

"Have you grown wiser during this last week?"

"It's not that I've grown wiser, but simply that the truth has come out this week."

"What truth has come out this week? Listen, Praskovya Ivanovna, don't irritate me. Explain to me this minute, I beg you as a favour, what truth has come out and what do you mean by that?"

"Why there it is, sitting before you!" and Praskovya Ivanovna suddenly pointed at Marya Timofyevna with that desperate determination which takes no heed of consequences, if only it can make an impression at the moment. Marya Timofyevna, who had watched her all the time with light-hearted curiosity, laughed exultingly at the sight of the wrathful guest's finger pointed impetuously at her, and wriggled gleefully in her easy chair.

"God Almighty have mercy on us, they've all gone crazy!" exclaimed Varvara Petrovna, and turning pale she sank back in her chair.

She turned so pale that it caused some commotion. Stepan Trofimovitch was the first to rush up to her. I drew near also; even Liza got up from her seat, though she did not come forward. But the most alarmed of all was Praskovya Ivanovna herself. She uttered a scream, got up as far as she could and almost wailed in a lachrymose voice:

"Varvara Petrovna, dear, forgive me for my wicked foolishness! Give her some water, somebody."

"Don't whimper, please, Praskovya Ivanovna, and leave me alone, gentlemen, please, I don't want any water!" Varvara Petrovna pronounced in a firm though low voice, with blanched lips.

"Varvara Petrovna, my dear," Praskovya Ivanovna went on, a little reassured, "though I am to blame for my reckless words, what's upset me more than anything are these anonymous letters that some low creatures keep bombarding me with; they might write to you, since it concerns you, but I've a daughter!"

Varvara Petrovna looked at her in silence, with wide-open eyes, listening with wonder. At that moment a side-door in the corner opened noiselessly, and Darya Pavlovna made her appearance. She stood still and looked round. She was struck by our perturbation. Probably she did not at first distinguish Marya Timofyevna, of whose presence she had not been informed. Stepan Trofimovitch was the first to notice her; he made a rapid movement, turned red, and for some reason proclaimed in a loud voice: "Darya Pavlovna!" so that all eyes turned on the new-comer.

"Oh, is this your Darya Pavlovna!" cried Marya Timofyevna. "Well, Shatushka, your sister's not like you. How can my fellow call such a charmer the serf-wench Dasha?"

Meanwhile Darya Pavlovna had gone up to Varvara Petrovna, but struck by Marya Timofyevna's exclamation she turned quickly and stopped just before her chair, looking at the imbecile with a long fixed gaze.

"Sit down, Dasha," Varvara Petrovna brought out with terrifying composure. "Nearer, that's right. You can see this woman, sitting down. Do you know her?"

"I have never seen her," Dasha answered quietly, and after a pause, she added at once:

"She must be the invalid sister of Captain Lebyadkin."

"And it's the first time I've set eyes on you, my love, though I've been interested and wanted to know you a long time, for I see how well-bred you are in every movement you make," Marya Timofyevna cried enthusiastically. "And though my footman swears at you, can such a well-educated charming person as you really have stolen money from him? For you are sweet, sweet, sweet, I tell you that from myself!" she concluded, enthusiastically waving her hand.

"Can you make anything of it?" Varvara Petrovna asked with proud dignity.

"I understand it...."

"Have you heard about the money?"

"No doubt it's the money that I undertook at Nikolay Vsyevolodovitch's request to hand over to her brother, Captain Lebyadkin."

A silence followed.

"Did Nikolay Vsyevolodovitch himself ask you to do so?"

"He was very anxious to send that money, three hundred roubles, to Mr. Lebyadkin. And as he didn't know his address, but only knew that he was to be in our town, he charged me to give it to Mr. Lebyadkin if he came."

"What is the money ... lost? What was this woman speaking about just now?"

"That I don't know. I've heard before that Mr. Lebyadkin says I didn't give him all the money, but I don't understand his words. There were three hundred roubles and I sent him three hundred roubles."

Darya Pavlovna had almost completely regained her composure. And it was difficult, I may mention, as a rule, to astonish the girl or ruffle her calm for long—whatever she might be feeling. She brought out all her answers now without haste, replied immediately to every question with accuracy, quietly, smoothly, and without a trace of the sudden emotion she had shown at first, or the slightest embarrassment which might have suggested a consciousness of guilt. Varvara Petrovna's eyes were fastened upon her all the time she was speaking. Varvara Petrovna thought for a minute:

"If," she pronounced at last firmly, evidently addressing all present, though she only looked at Dasha, "if Nikolay Vsyevolodovitch did not appeal even to me but asked you to do this for him, he must have had his reasons for doing so. I don't consider I have any right to inquire into them, if they are kept secret from me. But the very fact of your having taken part in the matter reassures me on that score, be sure of that, Darya, in any case. But you see, my dear, you may, through ignorance of the world, have quite innocently done something imprudent; and you did so when you undertook to have dealings with a low character. The rumours spread by this rascal show what a mistake you made. But I will find out about him, and as it is my task to protect you, I shall know how to defend you. But now all this must be put a stop to."

"The best thing to do," said Marya Timofyevna, popping up from her chair, "is to send him to the footmen's room when he comes. Let him sit on the benches there and play cards with them while we sit here and drink coffee. We might send him a cup of coffee too, but I have a great contempt for him."

And she wagged her head expressively.

"We must put a stop to this," Varvara Petrovna repeated, listening attentively to Marya Timofyevna. "Ring, Stepan Trofimovitch, I beg you."

Stepan Trofimovitch rang, and suddenly stepped forward, all excitement.

"If ... if ..." he faltered feverishly, flushing, breaking off and stuttering, "if I too have heard the most revolting story, or rather slander, it was with utter indignation ... enfin c'est un homme perdu, et quelque chose comme un forçat evadé...."

He broke down and could not go on. Varvara Petrovna, screwing up her eyes, looked him up and down.

The ceremonious butler Alexey Yegorytch came in.

"The carriage," Varvara Petrovna ordered. "And you, Alexey Yegorytch, get ready to escort Miss Lebyadkin home; she will give you the address herself."

"Mr. Lebyadkin has been waiting for her for some time downstairs, and has been begging me to announce him."

"That's impossible, Varvara Petrovna!" and Mavriky Nikolaevitch, who had sat all the time in unbroken silence, suddenly came forward in alarm. "If I may speak, he is not a man who can be admitted into society. He ... he ... he's an impossible person, Varvara Petrovna!"

"Wait a moment," said Varvara Petrovna to Alexey Yegorytch, and he disappeared at once.

"C'est un homme malhonnête et je crois même que c'est un forçat evadé ou quelque chose dans ce genre," Stepan Trofimovitch muttered again, and again he flushed red and broke off.

"Liza, it's time we were going," announced Praskovya Ivanovna disdainfully, getting up from her seat. She seemed sorry that in her alarm she had called herself a fool. While Darya Pavlovna was speaking, she listened, pressing her lips superciliously. But what struck me most was the expression of Lizaveta Nikolaevna from the moment Darya Pavlovna had come in. There was a gleam of hatred and hardly disguised contempt in her eyes.

"Wait one minute, Praskovya Ivanovna, I beg you." Varvara Petrovna detained her, still with the same exaggerated composure. "Kindly sit down. I intend to speak out, and your legs are bad. That's right, thank you. I lost my temper just now and uttered some impatient words. Be so good as to forgive me. I behaved foolishly and I'm the first to regret it, because I like fairness in everything. Losing your temper too, of course, you spoke of certain anonymous letters. Every anonymous communication is deserving of contempt, just because it's not signed. If you think differently I'm sorry for you. In any case, if I were in your place, I would not pry into such dirty corners, I would not soil my hands with it. But you have soiled yours. However, since you have begun on the subject yourself, I must tell you that six days ago I too received a clownish anonymous letter. In it some rascal informs me that Nikolay Vsyevolodovitch has gone out of his mind, and that I have reason to fear some lame woman, who 'is destined to play a great part in my life.' I remember the expression. Reflecting and being aware that Nikolay Vsyevolodovitch has very numerous enemies, I promptly sent for a man living here, one of his secret enemies, and the most vindictive and contemptible of them, and from my conversation with him I gathered what was the despicable source of the anonymous letter. If you too, my poor Praskovya Ivanovna, have been worried by similar letters on my account, and as you say 'bombarded' with them, I am, of course, the first to regret having been the innocent cause of it. That's all I wanted to tell you by way of explanation. I'm very sorry to see that you are so tired and so upset. Besides, I have quite made up my mind to see that suspicious personage of whom Mavriky Nikolaevitch said just now, a little inappropriately, that it was impossible to receive him. Liza in particular need have nothing to do with it. Come to me, Liza, my dear, let me kiss you again."

Liza crossed the room and stood in silence before Varvara Petrovna. The latter kissed her, took her hands, and, holding her at arm's-length, looked at her with feeling, then made the sign of the cross over her and kissed her again.

"Well, good-bye, Liza" (there was almost the sound of tears in Varvara Petrovna's voice), "believe that I shall never cease to love you whatever fate has in store for you. God be with you. I have always blessed His Holy Will. . . ."

She would have added something more, but restrained herself and broke off. Liza was walking back to her place, still in the same silence, as it were plunged in thought, but she suddenly stopped before her mother.

"I am not going yet, mother. I'll stay a little longer at auntie's," she brought out in a low voice, but there was a note of iron determination in those quiet words.

"My goodness! What now?" wailed Praskovya Ivanovna, clasping her hands helplessly. But Liza did not answer, and seemed indeed not to hear her; she sat down in the same corner and fell to gazing into space again as before.

There was a look of pride and triumph in Varvara Petrovna's face.

"Mavriky Nikolaevitch, I have a great favour to ask of you. Be so kind as to go and take a look at that person downstairs, and if there is any possibility of admitting him, bring him up here."

Mavriky Nikolaevitch bowed and went out. A moment later he brought in Mr. Lebyadkin.

IV

I have said something of this gentleman's outward appearance. He was a tall, curly-haired, thick-set fellow about forty with a purplish, rather bloated and flabby face, with cheeks that quivered at every movement of his head, with little bloodshot eyes that were sometimes rather crafty, with moustaches and side-whiskers, and with an incipient double chin, fleshy and rather unpleasant-looking. But what was most striking about him was the fact that he appeared now wearing a dress-coat and clean linen.

"There are people on whom clean linen is almost unseemly," as Liputin had once said when Stepan Trofimovitch reproached him in jest for being untidy. The captain had perfectly new black gloves too, of which he held the right one in his hand, while the left, tightly stretched and unbuttoned, covered part of the huge fleshy fist in which he held a brand-new, glossy round hat, probably worn for the first time that day. It appeared therefore that "the garb of love," of which he had shouted to Shatov the day before, really did exist. All this, that is, the dress-coat and clean linen, had been procured by Liputin's advice with some mysterious object in view (as I found out later). There was no doubt that his coming now (in a hired carriage) was at the instigation and with the assistance of someone else; it would never have dawned on him, nor could he by himself have succeeded in dressing, getting ready and making up his mind in three-quarters of an hour, even if the scene in the porch of the cathedral had reached his ears at once. He was not drunk, but was in the dull, heavy, dazed condition of a man suddenly awakened after many days of drinking. It seemed as though he would be drunk again if one were to put one's hands on his shoulders and rock him to and fro once or twice. He was hurrying into the drawing-room but stumbled over a rug near the doorway. Marya Timofyevna was helpless with laughter. He looked savagely at her and suddenly took a few rapid steps towards Varvara Petrovna.

"I have come, madam ..." he blared out like a trumpet-blast.

"Be so good, sir, as to take a seat there, on that chair," said Varvara Petrovna, drawing herself up. "I shall hear you as well from there, and it will be more convenient for me to look at you from here."

The captain stopped short, looking blankly before him. He turned, however, and sat down on the seat indicated close to the door. An extreme lack of self-confidence and at the same time insolence, and a sort of incessant irritability, were apparent in the expression of his face. He was horribly scared, that was evident, but his self-conceit was wounded, and it might be surmised that his mortified vanity might on occasion lead him to any effrontery, in spite of his cowardice. He was evidently uneasy at every movement of his clumsy person. We all know that when such gentlemen are brought by some marvellous chance into society, they find their worst ordeal in their own hands, and the impossibility of disposing them becomingly, of which they are conscious at every moment. The captain sat rigid in his chair, with his hat and gloves in his hands and his eyes fixed with a senseless stare on the stern face of Varvara Petrovna. He would have liked, perhaps, to have looked about more freely, but he could not bring himself to do so yet. Marya Timofyevna, apparently thinking his appearance very funny, laughed again, but he did not stir. Varvara Petrovna ruthlessly kept him in this position for a long time, a whole minute, staring at him without mercy.

"In the first place allow me to learn your name from yourself," Varvara Petrovna pronounced in measured and impressive tones.

"Captain Lebyadkin," thundered the captain. "I have come, madam ..." He made a movement again.

"Allow me!" Varvara Petrovna checked him again. "Is this unfortunate person who interests me so much really your sister?"

"My sister, madam, who has escaped from control, for she is in a certain condition...."

He suddenly faltered and turned crimson. "Don't misunderstand me, madam," he said, terribly confused. "Her own brother's not going to throw mud at her ... in a certain condition doesn't mean in such a condition ... in the sense of an injured reputation ... in the last stage ..." he suddenly broke off.

"Sir!" said Varvara Petrovna, raising her head.

"In this condition!" he concluded suddenly, tapping the middle of his forehead with his finger.

A pause followed.

"And has she suffered in this way for long?" asked Varvara Petrovna, with a slight drawl.

"Madam, I have come to thank you for the generosity you showed in the porch, in a Russian, brotherly way."

"Brotherly?"

"I mean, not brotherly, but simply in the sense that I am my sister's brother; and believe me, madam," he went on more hurriedly, turning crimson again, "I am not so uneducated as I may appear at first sight in your drawing-room. My sister and I are nothing, madam, compared with the luxury we observe here. Having enemies who slander us, besides. But on the question of reputation Lebyadkin is proud, madam ... and ... and ... and I've come to repay with thanks.... Here is money, madam!"

At this point he pulled out a pocket-book, drew out of it a bundle of notes, and began turning them over with trembling fingers in a perfect fury of impatience. It was evident that he was in haste to explain something, and indeed it was quite necessary to do so. But probably feeling himself that his fluster with the money made him look even more foolish, he lost the last traces of self-possession. The money refused to be counted. His fingers fumbled helplessly, and to complete his shame a green note escaped from the pocket-book, and fluttered in zigzags on to the carpet.

"Twenty roubles, madam." He leapt up suddenly with the roll of notes in his hand, his face perspiring with discomfort. Noticing the note which had dropped on the floor, he was bending down to pick it up, but for some reason overcome by shame, he dismissed it with a wave.

"For your servants, madam; for the footman who picks it up. Let them remember my sister!"

"I cannot allow that," Varvara Petrovna brought out hurriedly, even with some alarm.

"In that case ..."

He bent down, picked it up, flushing crimson, and suddenly going up to Varvara Petrovna held out the notes he had counted.

"What's this?" she cried, really alarmed at last, and positively shrinking back in her chair.

Mavriky Nikolaevitch, Stepan Trofimovitch, and I all stepped forward.

"Don't be alarmed, don't be alarmed; I'm not mad, by God, I'm not mad," the captain kept asseverating excitedly.

"Yes, sir, you're out of your senses."

"Madam, she's not at all as you suppose. I am an insignificant link. Oh, madam, wealthy are your mansions, but poor is the dwelling of Marya Anonyma, my sister, whose maiden name was Lebyadkin, but whom we'll call Anonyma for the time, only for the time, madam, for God Himself will not suffer it forever. Madam, you gave her ten roubles and she took it, because it was from you, madam! Do you hear, madam? From no one else in the world would this Marya Anonyma take it, or her grandfather, the officer killed in the Caucasus before the very eyes of Yermolov, would turn in his grave. But from you, madam, from you she will take anything. But with one hand she takes it, and with the other she holds out to you twenty roubles by way of subscription to one of the benevolent committees in Petersburg and Moscow, of which you are a member … for you published yourself, madam, in the Moscow News, that you are ready to receive subscriptions in our town, and that any one may subscribe.…"

The captain suddenly broke off; he breathed hard as though after some difficult achievement. All he said about the benevolent society had probably been prepared beforehand, perhaps under Liputin's supervision. He perspired more than ever; drops literally trickled down his temples. Varvara Petrovna looked searchingly at him.

"The subscription list," she said severely, "is always downstairs in charge of my porter. There you can enter your subscriptions if you wish to. And so I beg you to put your notes away and not to wave them in the air. That's right. I beg you also to go back to your seat. That's right. I am very sorry, sir, that I made a mistake about your sister, and gave her something as though she were poor when she is so rich. There's only one thing I don't understand, why she can only take from me, and no one else. You so insisted upon that that I should like a full explanation."

"Madam, that is a secret that may be buried only in the grave!" answered the captain.

"Why?" Varvara Petrovna asked, not quite so firmly.

"Madam, madam …"

He relapsed into gloomy silence, looking on the floor, laying his right hand on his heart. Varvara Petrovna waited, not taking her eyes off him.

"Madam!" he roared suddenly. "Will you allow me to ask you one question? Only one, but frankly, directly, like a Russian, from the heart?"

"Kindly do so."

"Have you ever suffered madam, in your life?"

"You simply mean to say that you have been or are being ill-treated by someone."

"Madam, madam!" He jumped up again, probably unconscious of doing so, and struck himself on the breast. "Here in this bosom so much has accumulated, so much that God

Himself will be amazed when it is revealed at the Day of Judgment."

"H'm! A strong expression!"

"Madam, I speak perhaps irritably…."

"Don't be uneasy. I know myself when to stop you."

"May I ask you another question, madam?"

"Ask another question."

"Can one die simply from the generosity of one's feelings?"

"I don't know, as I've never asked myself such a question."

"You don't know! You've never asked yourself such a question," he said with pathetic irony. "Well, if that's it, if that's it …

"Be still, despairing heart!"

And he struck himself furiously on the chest. He was by now walking about the room again.

It is typical of such people to be utterly incapable of keeping their desires to themselves; they have, on the contrary, an irresistible impulse to display them in all their unseemliness as soon as they arise. When such a gentleman gets into a circle in which he is not at home he usually begins timidly,—but you have only to give him an inch and he will at once rush into impertinence. The captain was already excited. He walked about waving his arms and not listening to questions, talked about himself very, very quickly, so that sometimes his tongue would not obey him, and without finishing one phrase he passed to another. It is true he was probably not quite sober. Moreover, Lizaveta Nikolaevna was sitting there too, and though he did not once glance at her, her presence seemed to over-excite him terribly; that, however, is only my supposition. There must have been some reason which led Varvara Petrovna to resolve to listen to such a man in spite of her repugnance. Praskovya Ivanovna was simply shaking with terror, though, I believe she really did not quite understand what it was about. Stepan Trofimovitch was trembling too, but that was, on the contrary, because he was disposed to understand everything, and exaggerate it. Mavriky Nikolaevitch stood in the attitude of one ready to defend all present; Liza was pale, and she gazed fixedly with wide-open eyes at the wild captain. Shatov sat in the same position as before, but, what was strangest of all, Marya Timofyevna had not only ceased laughing, but had become terribly sad. She leaned her right elbow on the table, and with a prolonged, mournful gaze watched her brother declaiming. Darya Pavlovna alone seemed to me calm.

"All that is nonsensical allegory," said Varvara Petrovna, getting angry at last. "You haven't answered my question, why? I insist on an answer."

"I haven't answered, why? You insist on an answer, why?" repeated the captain, winking. "That little word 'why' has run through all the universe from the first day of creation, and all nature cries every minute to it's Creator, 'why?' And for seven thousand years it has had no answer, and must Captain Lebyadkin alone answer? And is that justice, madam?"

"That's all nonsense and not to the point!" cried Varvara Petrovna, getting angry and losing patience. "That's allegory; besides, you express yourself too sensationally, sir, which I consider impertinence."

"Madam," the captain went on, not hearing, "I should have liked perhaps to be called Ernest, yet I am forced to bear the vulgar name Ignat—why is that do you suppose? I should have liked to be called Prince de Monbart, yet I am only Lebyadkin, derived from a swan.* Why is that? I am a poet, madam, a poet in soul, and might be getting a thousand roubles at a time from a publisher, yet I am forced to live in a pig pail. Why? Why, madam? To my mind Russia is a freak of nature and nothing else."

* *From lebyed, a swan.*

"Can you really say nothing more definite?"

"I can read you the poem, 'The Cockroach,' madam."

"Wha-a-t?"

"Madam, I'm not mad yet! I shall be mad, no doubt I shall be, but I'm not so yet. Madam, a friend of mine—a most honourable man—has written a Krylov's fable, called 'The Cockroach.' May I read it?"

"You want to read some fable of Krylov's?"

"No, it's not a fable of Krylov's I want to read. It's my fable, my own composition. Believe me, madam, without offence I'm not so uneducated and depraved as not to understand that Russia can boast of a great fable-writer, Krylov, to whom the Minister of Education has raised a monument in the Summer Gardens for the diversion of the young. Here, madam, you ask me why? The answer is at the end of this fable, in letters of fire."

"Read your fable."

"Lived a cockroach in the world

Such was his condition,

In a glass he chanced to fall

Full of fly-perdition."

"Heavens! What does it mean?" cried Varvara Petrovna.

"That's when flies get into a glass in the summer-time," the captain explained hurriedly with the irritable impatience of an author interrupted in reading. "Then it is perdition to the flies, any fool can understand. Don't interrupt, don't interrupt. You'll see, you'll see...." He kept waving his arms.

"But he squeezed against the flies,

They woke up and cursed him,

Raised to Jove their angry cries;

'The glass is full to bursting!'

In the middle of the din

Came along Nikifor,

Fine old man, and looking in ...

I haven't quite finished it. But no matter, I'll tell it in words," the captain rattled on. "Nikifor takes the glass, and in spite of their outcry empties away the whole stew, flies, and beetles and all, into the pig pail, which ought to have been done long ago. But observe, madam, observe, the cockroach doesn't complain. That's the answer to your question, why?" he cried triumphantly. "'The cockroach does not complain.' As for Nikifor he typifies nature," he added, speaking rapidly and walking complacently about the room.

Varvara Petrovna was terribly angry.

"And allow me to ask you about that money said to have been received from Nikolay Vsyevolodovitch, and not to have been given to you, about which you dared to accuse a person belonging to my household."

"It's a slander!" roared Lebyadkin, flinging up his right hand tragically.

"No, it's not a slander."

"Madam, there are circumstances that force one to endure family disgrace rather than proclaim the truth aloud. Lebyadkin will not blab, madam!"

He seemed dazed; he was carried away; he felt his importance; he certainly had some fancy in his mind. By now he wanted to insult some one, to do something nasty to show his power.

"Ring, please, Stepan Trofimovitch," Varvara Petrovna asked him.

"Lebyadkin's cunning, madam," he said, winking with his evil smile; "he's cunning, but he too has a weak spot, he too at times is in the portals of passions, and these portals are the old military hussars' bottle, celebrated by Denis Davydov. So when he is in those portals, madam, he may happen to send a letter in verse, a most magnificent letter—but which afterwards he would have wished to take back, with the tears of all his life; for the feeling of the beautiful is destroyed. But the bird has flown, you won't catch it by the tail. In those portals now, madam, Lebyadkin may have spoken about an honourable young lady, in the honourable indignation of a soul revolted by wrongs, and his slanderers have taken advantage of it. But Lebyadkin is cunning, madam! And in vain a malignant wolf sits over him every minute, filling his glass and waiting for the end. Lebyadkin won't blab. And at the bottom of the bottle he always finds instead Lebyadkin's cunning. But enough, oh, enough, madam! Your splendid halls might belong to the noblest in the land, but the cockroach will not complain. Observe that, observe that he does not complain, and recognise his noble spirit!"

At that instant a bell rang downstairs from the porter's room, and almost at the same moment Alexey Yegorytch appeared in response to Stepan Trofimovitch's ring, which he had somewhat delayed answering. The correct old servant was unusually excited.

"Nikolay Vsyevolodovitch has graciously arrived this moment and is coming here," he pronounced, in reply to Varvara Petrovna's questioning glance. I particularly remember her at that moment; at first she turned pale, but suddenly her eyes flashed. She drew herself up in her chair with an air of extraordinary determination. Every one was astounded indeed. The utterly unexpected arrival of Nikolay Vsyevolodovitch, who was not expected for another month, was not only strange from its unexpectedness but from its fateful coincidence with the present moment. Even the captain remained standing like a post in the middle of the room with his mouth wide open, staring at the door with a fearfully stupid expression.

And, behold, from the next room—a very large and long apartment—came the sound of swiftly approaching footsteps, little, exceedingly rapid steps; someone seemed to be running, and that someone suddenly flew into the drawing-room, not Nikolay Vsyevolodovitch, but a young man who was a complete stranger to all.

V

I will permit myself to halt here to sketch in a few hurried strokes this person who had so suddenly arrived on the scene.

He was a young man of twenty-seven or thereabouts, a little above the medium height, with rather long, lank, flaxen hair, and with faintly defined, irregular moustache and beard. He was dressed neatly, and in the fashion, though not like a dandy. At the first glance he looked round-shouldered and awkward, but yet he was not round-shouldered, and his manner was easy. He seemed a queer fish, and yet later on we all thought his manners good, and his conversation always to the point.

No one would have said that he was ugly, and yet no one would have liked his face. His head was elongated at the back, and looked flattened at the sides, so that his face seemed pointed, his forehead was high and narrow, but his features were small; his eyes were keen, his nose was small and sharp, his lips were long and thin. The expression of his face suggested ill-health, but this was misleading. He had a wrinkle on each cheek which gave him the look of a man who had just recovered from a serious illness. Yet he was perfectly well and strong, and had never been ill.

He walked and moved very hurriedly, yet never seemed in a hurry to be off. It seemed as though nothing could disconcert him; in every circumstance and in every sort of society he remained the same. He had a great deal of conceit, but was utterly unaware of it himself.

He talked quickly, hurriedly, but at the same time with assurance, and was never at a loss for a word. In spite of his hurried manner his ideas were in perfect order, distinct and definite—and this was particularly striking. His articulation was wonderfully clear. His words pattered out like smooth, big grains, always well chosen, and at your service. At first this attracted one, but afterwards it became repulsive, just because of this over-distinct articulation, this string of ever-ready words. One somehow began to imagine that he must have a tongue of special shape, somehow exceptionally long and thin, extremely red with a very sharp everlastingly active little tip.

Well, this was the young man who darted now into the drawing-room, and really, I believe to this day, that he began to talk in the next room, and came in speaking. He was standing before Varvara Petrovna in a trice.

"... Only fancy, Varvara Petrovna," he pattered on, "I came in expecting to find he'd been here for the last quarter of an hour; he arrived an hour and a half ago; we met at Kirillov's: he set off half an hour ago meaning to come straight here, and told me to come here too, a quarter of an hour later...."

"But who? Who told you to come here?" Varvara Petrovna inquired.

"Why, Nikolay Vsyevolodovitch! Surely this isn't the first you've heard of it! But his luggage must have been here a long while, anyway. How is it you weren't told? Then I'm the first to bring the news. One might send out to look for him; he's sure to be here himself directly though. And I fancy, at the moment that just fits in with some of his expectations, and is far as I can judge, at least, some of his calculations."

At this point he turned his eyes about the room and fixed them with special attention on the captain.

"Ach, Lizaveta Nikolaevna, how glad I am to meet you at the very first step, delighted to shake hands with you." He flew up to Liza, who was smiling gaily, to take her proffered hand, "and I observe that my honoured friend Praskovya Ivanovna has not forgotten her 'professor,' and actually isn't cross with him, as she always used to be in Switzerland. But how are your legs, here, Praskovya Ivanovna, and were the Swiss doctors right when at the consultation they prescribed your native air? What? Fomentations? That ought to do good. But how sorry I was, Varvara Petrovna" (he turned rapidly to her) "that I didn't arrive in time to meet you abroad, and offer my respects to you in person; I had so much to tell you too. I did send word to my old man here, but I fancy that he did as he always does ..."

"Petrusha!" cried Stepan Trofimovitch, instantly roused from his stupefaction. He clasped his hands and flew to his son. "Pierre, mon enfant! Why, I didn't know you!" He pressed him in his arms and the tears rolled down his cheeks.

"Come, be quiet, be quiet, no flourishes, that's enough, that's enough, please," Petrusha muttered hurriedly, trying to extricate himself from his embrace.

"I've always sinned against you, always!"

"Well, that's enough. We can talk of that later. I knew you'd carry on. Come, be a little more sober, please."

"But it's ten years since I've seen you."

"The less reason for demonstrations."

"Mon enfant!..."

"Come, I believe in your affection, I believe in it, take your arms away. You see, you're disturbing other people.... Ah, here's Nikolay Vsyevolodovitch; keep quiet, please."

Nikolay Vsyevolodovitch was already in the room; he came in very quietly and stood still for an instant in the doorway, quietly scrutinising the company.

I was struck by the first sight of him just as I had been four years before, when I saw him for the first time. I had not forgotten him in the least. But I think there are some countenances which always seem to exhibit something new which one has not noticed before, every time one meets them, though one may have seen them a hundred times already. Apparently he was exactly the same as he had been four years before. He was as elegant, as dignified, he moved with the same air of consequence as before, indeed he looked almost as young. His faint smile had just the same official graciousness and complacency. His eyes had the same stern, thoughtful and, as it were, preoccupied look. In fact, it seemed as though we had only parted the day before. But one thing struck me. In old days, though he had been considered handsome, his face was "like a mask," as some of our sharp-tongued ladies had expressed it. Now—now, I don't know why he impressed me at once as absolutely, incontestably beautiful, so that no one could have said that his face was like a mask. Wasn't it perhaps that he was a little paler and seemed rather thinner than before? Or was there, perhaps, the light of some new idea in his eyes?

"Nikolay Vsyevolodovitch!" cried Varvara Petrovna, drawing herself up but not rising from her chair. "Stop a minute!" She checked his advance with a peremptory gesture.

But to explain the awful question which immediately followed that gesture and exclamation—a question which I should have imagined to be impossible even in Varvara Petrovna, I must ask the reader to remember what that lady's temperament had always been, and the extraordinary impulsiveness she showed at some critical moments. I beg him to consider also, that in spite of the exceptional strength of her spirit and the very considerable amount of common sense and practical, so to say business, tact she possessed, there were moments in her life in which she abandoned herself altogether, entirely and, if it's permissible to say so, absolutely without restraint. I beg him to take into consideration also that the present moment might really be for her one of those in which all the essence of life, of all the past and all the present, perhaps, too, all the future, is concentrated, as it were, focused. I must briefly recall, too, the anonymous letter of which she had spoken to Praskovya Ivanovna with so much irritation, though I think she said nothing of the latter part of it. Yet it perhaps contained the explanation of the possibility of the terrible question with which she suddenly addressed her son.

"Nikolay Vsyevolodovitch," she repeated, rapping out her words in a resolute voice in which there was a ring of menacing challenge, "I beg you to tell me at once, without moving from that place; is it true that this unhappy cripple—here she is, here, look at her—is it true that she is ... your lawful wife?"

I remember that moment only too well; he did not wink an eyelash but looked intently at his mother. Not the faintest change in his face followed. At last he smiled, a sort of indulgent smile, and without answering a word went quietly up to his mother, took her hand, raised it respectfully to his lips and kissed it. And so great was his invariable and irresistible ascendancy over his mother that even now she could not bring herself to pull away her hand. She only gazed at him, her whole figure one concentrated question, seeming to betray that she could not bear the suspense another moment.

But he was still silent. When he had kissed her hand, he scanned the whole room once more, and moving, as before, without haste went towards Marya Timofyevna. It is very difficult to describe people's countenances at certain moments. I remember, for instance, that Marya Timofyevna, breathless with fear, rose to her feet to meet him and clasped her hands before her, as though beseeching him. And at the same time I remember the frantic ecstasy which almost distorted her face—an ecstasy almost too great for any human being to bear. Perhaps both were there, both the terror and the ecstasy. But I remember moving quickly towards her (I was standing not far off), for I fancied she was going to faint.

"You should not be here," Nikolay Vsyevolodovitch said to her in a caressing and melodious voice; and there was the light of an extraordinary tenderness in his eyes. He stood before her in the most respectful attitude, and every gesture showed sincere respect for her. The poor girl faltered impulsively in a half-whisper.

"But may I … kneel down … to you now?"

"No, you can't do that."

He smiled at her magnificently, so that she too laughed joyfully at once. In the same melodious voice, coaxing her tenderly as though she were a child, he went on gravely.

"Only think that you are a girl, and that though I'm your devoted friend I'm an outsider, not your husband, nor your father, nor your betrothed. Give me your arm and let us go; I will take you to the carriage, and if you will let me I will see you all the way home."

She listened, and bent her head as though meditating.

"Let's go," she said with a sigh, giving him her hand.

But at that point a slight mischance befell her. She must have turned carelessly, resting on her lame leg, which was shorter than the other. She fell sideways into the chair, and if the chair had not been there would have fallen on to the floor. He instantly seized and supported her, and holding her arm firmly in his, led her carefully and sympathetically to the door. She was evidently mortified at having fallen; she was overwhelmed, blushed, and was terribly abashed. Looking dumbly on the ground, limping painfully, she hobbled after him, almost hanging on his arm. So they went out. Liza, I saw, suddenly jumped up from her chair for some reason as they were going out, and she followed them with intent eyes till they reached the door. Then she sat down again in silence, but there was a nervous twitching in her face, as though she had touched a viper.

While this scene was taking place between Nikolay Vsyevolodovitch and Marya Timofyevna every one was speechless with amazement; one could have heard a fly; but as soon as they had gone out, every one began suddenly talking.

VI

It was very little of it talk, however; it was mostly exclamation. I've forgotten a little the order in which things happened, for a scene of confusion followed. Stepan Trofimovitch uttered some exclamation in French, clasping his hands, but Varvara Petrovna had no thought for him. Even Mavriky Nikolaevitch muttered some rapid, jerky comment. But Pyotr Stepanovitch was the most excited of all. He was trying desperately with bold gesticulations to persuade Varvara Petrovna of something, but it was a long time before I could make out what it was. He appealed to Praskovya Ivanovna, and Lizaveta Nikolaevna too, even, in his excitement, addressed a passing shout to his father—in fact he seemed all over the room at once. Varvara Petrovna, flushing all over, sprang up from her seat and cried to Praskovya Ivanovna:

"Did you hear what he said to her here just now, did you hear it?"

But the latter was incapable of replying. She could only mutter something and wave her hand. The poor woman had troubles of her own to think about. She kept turning her head towards Liza and was watching her with unaccountable terror, but she didn't even dare to think of getting up and going away until her daughter should get up. In the meantime the captain wanted to slip away. That I noticed. There was no doubt that he had been in a great panic from the instant that Nikolay Vsyevolodovitch had made his appearance; but Pyotr Stepanovitch took him by the arm and would not let him go.

"It is necessary, quite necessary," he pattered on to Varvara Petrovna, still trying to persuade her. He stood facing her, as she was sitting down again in her easy chair, and, I remember, was listening to him eagerly; he had succeeded in securing her attention.

"It is necessary. You can see for yourself, Varvara Petrovna, that there is a misunderstanding here, and much that is strange on the surface, and yet the thing's as clear as daylight, and as simple as my finger. I quite understand that no one has authorised me to tell the story, and I dare say I look ridiculous putting myself forward. But in the first place, Nikolay Vsyevolodovitch attaches no sort of significance to the matter himself, and, besides, there are incidents of which it is difficult for a man to make up his mind to give an explanation himself. And so it's absolutely necessary that it should be undertaken by a third person, for whom it's easier to put some delicate points into words. Believe me, Varvara Petrovna, that Nikolay Vsyevolodovitch is not at all to blame for not immediately answering your question just now with a full explanation, it's all a trivial affair. I've known him since his Petersburg days. Besides, the whole story only does honour to Nikolay Vsyevolodovitch, if one must make use of that vague word 'honour.'"

"You mean to say that you were a witness of some incident which gave rise ... to this misunderstanding?" asked Varvara Petrovna.

"I witnessed it, and took part in it," Pyotr Stepanovitch hastened to declare.

"If you'll give me your word that this will not wound Nikolay Vsyevolodovitch's delicacy in regard to his feeling for me, from whom he ne-e-ver conceals anything ... and if you are convinced also that your doing this will be agreeable to him ..."

"Certainly it will be agreeable, and for that reason I consider it a particularly agreeable duty. I am convinced that he would beg me to do it himself."

The intrusive desire of this gentleman, who seemed to have dropped on us from heaven to tell stories about other people's affairs, was rather strange and inconsistent with ordinary usage.

But he had caught Varvara Petrovna by touching on too painful a spot. I did not know the man's character at that time, and still less his designs.

"I am listening," Varvara Petrovna announced with a reserved and cautious manner. She was rather painfully aware of her condescension.

"It's a short story; in fact if you like it's not a story at all," he rattled on, "though a novelist might work it up into a novel in an idle hour. It's rather an interesting little incident, Praskovya Ivanovna, and I am sure that Lizaveta Nikolaevna will be interested to hear it, because there are a great many things in it that are odd if not wonderful. Five years ago, in Petersburg, Nikolay Vsyevolodovitch made the acquaintance of this gentleman, this very Mr. Lebyadkin who's standing here with his mouth open, anxious, I think, to slip away at once. Excuse me, Varvara Petrovna. I don't advise you to make your escape though, you discharged clerk in the former commissariat department; you see, I remember you very well. Nikolay Vsyevolodovitch and I know very well what you've been up to here, and, don't forget, you'll have to answer for it. I ask your pardon once more, Varvara Petrovna. In those days Nikolay Vsyevolodovitch used to call this gentleman his Falstaff; that must be," he explained suddenly, "some old burlesque character, at whom every one laughs, and who is willing to let every one laugh at him, if only they'll pay him for it. Nikolay Vsyevolodovitch was leading at that time in Petersburg a life, so to say, of mockery. I can't find another word to describe it, because he is not a man who falls into disillusionment, and he disdained to be occupied with work at that time. I'm only speaking of that period, Varvara Petrovna. Lebyadkin had a sister, the woman who was sitting here just now. The brother and sister hadn't a corner* of their own, but were always quartering themselves on different people. He used to hang about the arcades in the Gostiny Dvor, always wearing his old uniform, and would stop the more respectable-looking passers-by, and everything he got from them he'd spend in drink. His sister lived like the birds of heaven. She'd help people in their 'corners,' and do jobs for them on occasion. It was a regular Bedlam. I'll pass over the description of this life in 'corners,' a life to which Nikolay Vsyevolodovitch had taken,"

** In the poorer quarters of Russian towns a single room is often*

let out to several families, each of which occupies a "corner."

"at that time, from eccentricity. I'm only talking of that period, Varvara Petrovna; as for 'eccentricity,' that's his own expression. He does not conceal much from me. Mlle. Lebyadkin, who was thrown in the way of meeting Nikolay Vsyevolodovitch very often, at one time, was fascinated by his appearance. He was, so to say, a diamond set in the dirty background of her life. I am a poor hand at describing feelings, so I'll pass them over; but some of that dirty lot took to jeering at her once, and it made her sad. They always had laughed at her, but she did not seem to notice it before. She wasn't quite right in her head even then, but very different from what she is now. There's reason to believe that in her childhood she received something like an education through the kindness of a benevolent lady. Nikolay Vsyevolodovitch had never taken the slightest notice of her. He used to spend his time chiefly in playing preference with a greasy old pack of cards for stakes of a quarter-farthing with clerks. But once, when she was being ill-treated, he went up (without inquiring into the cause) and seized one of the clerks by the collar and flung him out of a second-floor window. It was not a case of chivalrous indignation at the sight of injured innocence; the whole operation took place in the midst of roars of laughter, and the one who laughed loudest was Nikolay Vsyevolodovitch himself. As it all ended without harm, they were reconciled and began drinking punch. But the injured innocent herself did not forget it. Of course it ended in her becoming completely crazy. I repeat I'm a poor hand at describing feelings. But a delusion was the chief feature in this case. And Nikolay Vsyevolodovitch aggravated that delusion as though he did it on purpose. Instead of laughing at her he began all at once treating Mlle. Lebyadkin with sudden respect. Kirillov, who was there (a very original man, Varvara Petrovna, and very abrupt, you'll see him perhaps one day, for he's here now), well, this Kirillov who, as a rule, is perfectly silent, suddenly got hot, and said to Nikolay Vsyevolodovitch, I remember, that he treated the girl as though she were a marquise, and that that was doing for her altogether. I must add that Nikolay Vsyevolodovitch had rather a respect for this Kirillov. What do you suppose was the answer he gave him: 'You imagine, Mr. Kirillov, that I am laughing at her. Get rid of that idea, I really do respect her, for she's better than any of us.' And, do you know, he said it in such a serious tone. Meanwhile, he hadn't really said a word to her for two or three months, except 'good morning' and 'good-bye.' I remember, for I was there, that she came at last to the point of looking on him almost as her betrothed who dared not 'elope with her,' simply because he had many enemies and family difficulties, or something of the sort. There was a great deal of laughter about it. It ended in Nikolay Vsyevolodovitch's making provision for her when he had to come here, and I believe he arranged to pay a considerable sum, three hundred roubles a year, if not more, as a pension for her. In short it was all a caprice, a fancy of a man prematurely weary on his side, perhaps—it may even have been, as Kirillov says, a new experiment of a blasé man, with the object of finding out what you can bring a crazy cripple to." (You picked out on purpose, he said, the lowest creature, a cripple, forever covered with disgrace and blows, knowing, too, that this creature was dying of comic love for you, and set to work to mystify her completely on purpose, simply to see what would come of it.) "Though, how is a man so particularly to blame for the fancies of a crazy woman, to whom he had hardly uttered two sentences the whole time. There are things, Varvara Petrovna, of which it is not only impossible to speak sensibly, but it's even nonsensical to begin speaking of them at all. Well, eccentricity then, let it stand at that. Anyway, there's nothing worse to be said than that; and yet now they've made this scandal out of it.... I am to some extent aware, Varvara Petrovna, of what is happening here."

The speaker suddenly broke off and was turning to Lebyadkin. But Varvara Petrovna checked him. She was in a state of extreme exaltation.

"Have you finished?" she asked.

"Not yet; to complete my story I should have to ask this gentleman one or two questions if you'll allow me ... you'll see the point in a minute, Varvara Petrovna."

"Enough, afterwards, leave it for the moment I beg you. Oh, I was quite right to let you speak!"

"And note this, Varvara Petrovna," Pyotr Stepanovitch said hastily. "Could Nikolay Vsyevolodovitch have explained all this just now in answer to your question, which was perhaps too peremptory?"

"Oh, yes, it was."

"And wasn't I right in saying that in some cases it's much easier for a third person to explain things than for the person interested?"

"Yes, yes ... but in one thing you were mistaken, and, I see with regret, are still mistaken."

"Really, what's that?"

"You see.... But won't you sit down, Pyotr Stepanovitch?"

"Oh, as you please. I am tired indeed. Thank you." He instantly moved up an easy chair and turned it so that he had Varvara Petrovna on one side and Praskovya Ivanovna at the table on the other, while he faced Lebyadkin, from whom he did not take his eyes for one minute.

"You are mistaken in calling this eccentricity...."

"Oh, if it's only that...."

"No, no, no, wait a little," said Varvara Petrovna, who was obviously about to say a good deal and to speak with enthusiasm. As soon as Pyotr Stepanovitch noticed it, he was all attention.

"No, it was something higher than eccentricity, and I assure you, something sacred even! A proud man who has suffered humiliation early in life and reached the stage of 'mockery' as you so subtly called it—Prince Harry, in fact, to use the capital nickname Stepan Trofimovitch gave him then, which would have been perfectly correct if it were not that he is more like Hamlet, to my thinking at least."

"Et vous avez raison," Stepan Trofimovitch pronounced, impressively and with feeling.

"Thank you, Stepan Trofimovitch. I thank you particularly too for your unvarying faith in Nicolas, in the loftiness of his soul and of his destiny. That faith you have even strengthened in me when I was losing heart."

"Chère, chère." Stepan Trofimovitch was stepping forward, when he checked himself, reflecting that it was dangerous to interrupt.

"And if Nicolas had always had at his side" (Varvara Petrovna almost shouted) "a gentle Horatio, great in his humility—another excellent expression of yours, Stepan Trofimovitch—he might long ago have been saved from the sad and 'sudden demon of irony,' which has tormented him all his life. ('The demon of irony' was a wonderful expression of yours again, Stepan Trofimovitch.) But Nicolas has never had an Horatio or an Ophelia. He had no one but his mother, and what can a mother do alone, and in such circumstances? Do you know, Pyotr Stepanovitch, it's perfectly comprehensible to me now that a being like Nicolas could be found even in such filthy haunts as you have described. I can so clearly picture now that 'mockery' of life. (A wonderfully subtle expression of yours!) That insatiable thirst of contrast, that gloomy background against which he stands out like a diamond, to use your comparison again, Pyotr Stepanovitch. And then he meets there a creature ill-treated by every one, crippled, half insane, and at the same time perhaps filled with noble feelings."

"H'm.... Yes, perhaps."

"And after that you don't understand that he's not laughing at her like every one. Oh, you people! You can't understand his defending her from insult, treating her with respect 'like a marquise' (this Kirillov must have an exceptionally deep understanding of men, though he didn't understand Nicolas). It was just this contrast, if you like, that led to the trouble. If the unhappy creature had been in different surroundings, perhaps she would never have been brought to entertain such a frantic delusion. Only a woman can understand it, Pyotr Stepanovitch, only a woman. How sorry I am that you ... not that you're not a woman, but that you can't be one just for the moment so as to understand."

"You mean in the sense that the worse things are the better it is. I understand, I understand, Varvara Petrovna. It's rather as it is in religion; the harder life is for a man or the more crushed and poor the people are, the more obstinately they dream of compensation in heaven; and if a hundred thousand priests are at work at it too, inflaming their delusion, and speculating on it, then ... I understand you, Varvara Petrovna, I assure you."

"That's not quite it; but tell me, ought Nicolas to have laughed at her and have treated her as the other clerks, in order to extinguish the delusion in this unhappy organism." (Why Varvara Petrovna used the word organism I couldn't understand.) "Can you really refuse to recognise the lofty compassion, the noble tremor of the whole organism with which Nicolas answered Kirillov: 'I do not laugh at her.' A noble, sacred answer!"

"Sublime," muttered Stepan Trofimovitch.

"And observe, too, that he is by no means so rich as you suppose. The money is mine and not his, and he would take next to nothing from me then."

"I understand, I understand all that, Varvara Petrovna," said Pyotr Stepanovitch, with a movement of some impatience.

"Oh, it's my character! I recognise myself in Nicolas. I recognise that youthfulness, that liability to violent, tempestuous impulses. And if we ever come to be friends, Pyotr Stepanovitch, and, for my part, I sincerely hope we may, especially as I am so deeply indebted to you, then, perhaps you'll understand...."

"Oh, I assure you, I hope for it too," Pyotr Stepanovitch muttered jerkily.

"You'll understand then the impulse which leads one in the blindness of generous feeling to take up a man who is unworthy of one in every respect, a man who utterly fails to understand one, who is ready to torture one at every opportunity and, in contradiction to everything, to exalt such a man into a sort of ideal, into a dream. To concentrate in him all one's hopes, to bow down before him; to love him all one's life, absolutely without knowing why—perhaps just because he was unworthy of it.... Oh, how I've suffered all my life, Pyotr Stepanovitch!"

Stepan Trofimovitch, with a look of suffering on his face, began trying to catch my eye, but I turned away in time.

"… And only lately, only lately—oh, how unjust I've been to Nicolas! … You would not believe how they have been worrying me on all sides, all, all, enemies, and rascals, and friends, friends perhaps more than enemies. When the first contemptible anonymous letter was sent to me, Pyotr Stepanovitch, you'll hardly believe it, but I had not strength enough to treat all this wickedness with contempt.… I shall never, never forgive myself for my weakness."

"I had heard something of anonymous letters here already," said Pyotr Stepanovitch, growing suddenly more lively, "and I'll find out the writers of them, you may be sure."

"But you can't imagine the intrigues that have been got up here. They have even been pestering our poor Praskovya Ivanovna, and what reason can they have for worrying her? I was quite unfair to you to-day perhaps, my dear Praskovya Ivanovna," she added in a generous impulse of kindliness, though not without a certain triumphant irony.

"Don't say any more, my dear," the other lady muttered reluctantly. "To my thinking we'd better make an end of all this; too much has been said."

And again she looked timidly towards Liza, but the latter was looking at Pyotr Stepanovitch.

"And I intend now to adopt this poor unhappy creature, this insane woman who has lost everything and kept only her heart," Varvara Petrovna exclaimed suddenly. "It's a sacred duty I intend to carry out. I take her under my protection from this day."

"And that will be a very good thing in one way," Pyotr Stepanovitch cried, growing quite eager again. "Excuse me, I did not finish just now. It's just the care of her I want to speak of. Would you believe it, that as soon as Nikolay Vsyevolodovitch had gone (I'm beginning from where I left off, Varvara Petrovna), this gentleman here, this Mr. Lebyadkin, instantly imagined he had the right to dispose of the whole pension that was provided for his sister. And he did dispose of it. I don't know exactly how it had been arranged by Nikolay Vsyevolodovitch at that time. But a year later, when he learned from abroad what had happened, he was obliged to make other arrangements. Again, I don't know the details; he'll tell you them himself. I only know that the interesting young person was placed somewhere in a remote nunnery, in very comfortable surroundings, but under friendly superintendence—you understand? But what do you think Mr. Lebyadkin made up his mind to do? He exerted himself to the utmost, to begin with, to find where his source of income, that is his sister, was hidden. Only lately he attained his object, took her from the nunnery, asserting some claim to her, and brought her straight here. Here he doesn't feed her properly, beats her, and bullies her. As soon as by some means he gets a considerable sum from Nikolay Vsyevolodovitch, he does nothing but get drunk, and instead of gratitude ends by impudently defying Nikolay Vsyevolodovitch, making senseless demands, threatening him with proceedings if the pension is not paid straight into his hands. So he takes what is a voluntary gift from Nikolay Vsyevolodovitch as a tax—can you imagine it? Mr. Lebyadkin, is that all true that I have said just now?"

The captain, who had till that moment stood in silence looking down, took two rapid steps forward and turned crimson.

"Pyotr Stepanovitch, you've treated me cruelly," he brought out abruptly.

"Why cruelly? How? But allow us to discuss the question of cruelty or gentleness later on. Now answer my first question; is it true all that I have said or not? If you consider it's false you are at liberty to give your own version at once."

"I ... you know yourself, Pyotr Stepanovitch," the captain muttered, but he could not go on and relapsed into silence. It must be observed that Pyotr Stepanovitch was sitting in an easy chair with one leg crossed over the other, while the captain stood before him in the most respectful attitude.

Lebyadkin's hesitation seemed to annoy Pyotr Stepanovitch; a spasm of anger distorted his face.

"Then you have a statement you want to make?" he said, looking subtly at the captain. "Kindly speak. We're waiting for you."

"You know yourself Pyotr Stepanovitch, that I can't say anything."

"No, I don't know it. It's the first time I've heard it. Why can't you speak?"

The captain was silent, with his eyes on the ground.

"Allow me to go, Pyotr Stepanovitch," he brought out resolutely.

"No, not till you answer my question: is it all true that I've said?"

"It is true," Lebyadkin brought out in a hollow voice, looking at his tormentor. Drops of perspiration stood out on his forehead.

"Is it all true?"

"It's all true."

"Have you nothing to add or to observe? If you think that we've been unjust, say so; protest, state your grievance aloud."

"No, I think nothing."

"Did you threaten Nikolay Vsyevolodovitch lately?"

"It was ... it was more drink than anything, Pyotr Stepanovitch." He suddenly raised his head. "If family honour and undeserved disgrace cry out among men then—then is a man to blame?" he roared suddenly, forgetting himself as before.

"Are you sober now, Mr. Lebyadkin?"

Pyotr Stepanovitch looked at him penetratingly.

"I am ... sober."

"What do you mean by family honour and undeserved disgrace?"

"I didn't mean anybody, anybody at all. I meant myself," the captain said, collapsing again.

"You seem to be very much offended by what I've said about you and your conduct? You are very irritable, Mr. Lebyadkin. But let me tell you I've hardly begun yet what I've got to say about your conduct, in its real sense. I'll begin to discuss your conduct in its real sense. I shall begin, that may very well happen, but so far I've not begun, in a real sense."

Lebyadkin started and stared wildly at Pyotr Stepanovitch.

"Pyotr Stepanovitch, I am just beginning to wake up."

"H'm! And it's I who have waked you up?"

"Yes, it's you who have waked me, Pyotr Stepanovitch; and I've been asleep for the last four years with a storm-cloud hanging over me. May I withdraw at last, Pyotr Stepanovitch?"

"Now you may, unless Varvara Petrovna thinks it necessary ..."

But the latter dismissed him with a wave of her hand.

The captain bowed, took two steps towards the door, stopped suddenly, laid his hand on his heart, tried to say something, did not say it, and was moving quickly away. But in the doorway he came face to face with Nikolay Vsyevolodovitch; the latter stood aside. The captain shrank into himself, as it were, before him, and stood as though frozen to the spot, his eyes fixed upon him like a rabbit before a boa-constrictor. After a little pause Nikolay Vsyevolodovitch waved him aside with a slight motion of his hand, and walked into the drawing-room.

VII

He was cheerful and serene. Perhaps something very pleasant had happened to him, of which we knew nothing as yet; but he seemed particularly contented.

"Do you forgive me, Nicolas?" Varvara Petrovna hastened to say, and got up suddenly to meet him.

But Nicolas positively laughed.

"Just as I thought," he said, good-humouredly and jestingly. "I see you know all about it already. When I had gone from here I reflected in the carriage that I ought at least to have told you the story instead of going off like that. But when I remembered that Pyotr Stepanovitch was still here, I thought no more of it."

As he spoke he took a cursory look round.

"Pyotr Stepanovitch told us an old Petersburg episode in the life of a queer fellow," Varvara Petrovna rejoined enthusiastically—"a mad and capricious fellow, though always lofty in his feelings, always chivalrous and noble...."

"Chivalrous? You don't mean to say it's come to that," laughed Nicolas. "However, I'm very grateful to Pyotr Stepanovitch for being in such a hurry this time." He exchanged a rapid glance with the latter. "You must know, maman, that Pyotr Stepanovitch is the universal peacemaker; that's his part in life, his weakness, his hobby, and I particularly recommend him to you from that point of view. I can guess what a yarn he's been spinning. He's a great hand at spinning them; he has a perfect record-office in his head. He's such a realist, you know, that he can't tell a lie, and prefers truthfulness to effect … except, of course, in special cases when effect is more important than truth." (As he said this he was still looking about him.) "So, you see clearly, maman, that it's not for you to ask my forgiveness, and if there's any craziness about this affair it's my fault, and it proves that, when all's said and done, I really am mad.… I must keep up my character here.…"

Then he tenderly embraced his mother.

"In any case the subject has been fully discussed and is done with," he added, and there was a rather dry and resolute note in his voice. Varvara Petrovna understood that note, but her exaltation was not damped, quite the contrary.

"I didn't expect you for another month, Nicolas!"

"I will explain everything to you, maman, of course, but now …"

And he went towards Praskovya Ivanovna.

But she scarcely turned her head towards him, though she had been completely overwhelmed by his first appearance. Now she had fresh anxieties to think of; at the moment the captain had stumbled upon Nikolay Vsyevolodovitch as he was going out, Liza had suddenly begun laughing—at first quietly and intermittently, but her laughter grew more and more violent, louder and more conspicuous. She flushed crimson, in striking contrast with her gloomy expression just before.

While Nikolay Vsyevolodovitch was talking to Varvara Petrovna, she had twice beckoned to Mavriky Nikolaevitch as though she wanted to whisper something to him; but as soon as the young man bent down to her, she instantly burst into laughter; so that it seemed as though it was at poor Mavriky Nikolaevitch that she was laughing. She evidently tried to control herself, however, and put her handkerchief to her lips. Nikolay Vsyevolodovitch turned to greet her with a most innocent and open-hearted air.

"Please excuse me," she responded, speaking quickly. "You … you've seen Mavriky Nikolaevitch of course.… My goodness, how inexcusably tall you are, Mavriky Nikolaevitch!"

And laughter again, Mavriky Nikolaevitch was tall, but by no means inexcusably so.

"Have … you been here long?" she muttered, restraining herself again, genuinely embarrassed though her eyes were shining.

"More than two hours," answered Nicolas, looking at her intently. I may remark that he was exceptionally reserved and courteous, but that apart from his courtesy his expression was utterly indifferent, even listless.

"And where are you going to stay?"

"Here."

Varvara Petrovna, too, was watching Liza, but she was suddenly struck by an idea.

"Where have you been all this time, Nicolas, more than two hours?" she said, going up to him. "The train comes in at ten o'clock."

"I first took Pyotr Stepanovitch to Kirillov's. I came across Pyotr Stepanovitch at Matveyev (three stations away), and we travelled together."

"I had been waiting at Matveyev since sunrise," put in Pyotr Stepanovitch. "The last carriages of our train ran off the rails in the night, and we nearly had our legs broken."

"Your legs broken!" cried Liza. "Maman, maman, you and I meant to go to Matveyev last week, we should have broken our legs too!"

"Heaven have mercy on us!" cried Praskovya Ivanovna, crossing herself.

"Maman, maman, dear maman, you mustn't be frightened if I break both my legs. It may so easily happen to me; you say yourself that I ride so recklessly every day. Mavriky Nikolaevitch, will you go about with me when I'm lame?" She began giggling again. "If it does happen I won't let anyone take me about but you, you can reckon on that.... Well, suppose I break only one leg. Come, be polite, say you'll think it a pleasure."

"A pleasure to be crippled?" said Mavriky Nikolaevitch, frowning gravely.

"But then you'll lead me about, only you and no one else."

"Even then it'll be you leading me about, Lizaveta Nikolaevna," murmured Mavriky Nikolaevitch, even more gravely.

"Why, he's trying to make a joke!" cried Liza, almost in dismay. "Mavriky Nikolaevitch, don't you ever dare take to that! But what an egoist you are! I am certain that, to your credit, you're slandering yourself. It will be quite the contrary; from morning till night you'll assure me that I have become more charming for having lost my leg. There's one insurmountable difficulty—you're so fearfully tall, and when I've lost my leg I shall be so very tiny. How will you be able to take me on your arm; we shall look a strange couple!"

And she laughed hysterically. Her jests and insinuations were feeble, but she was not capable of considering the effect she was producing.

"Hysterics!" Pyotr Stepanovitch whispered to me. "A glass of water, make haste!"

He was right. A minute later every one was fussing about, water was brought. Liza embraced her mother, kissed her warmly, wept on her shoulder, then drawing back and looking her in the face she fell to laughing again. The mother too began whimpering. Varvara Petrovna made haste to carry them both off to her own rooms, going out by the same door by which Darya Pavlovna had come to us. But they were not away long, not more than four minutes.

I am trying to remember now every detail of these last moments of that memorable morning. I remember that when we were left without the ladies (except Darya Pavlovna, who had not moved from her seat), Nikolay Vsyevolodovitch made the round, greeting us all except Shatov, who still sat in his corner, his head more bowed than ever. Stepan Trofimovitch was beginning something very witty to Nikolay Vsyevolodovitch, but the latter turned away hurriedly to Darya Pavlovna. But before he reached her, Pyotr Stepanovitch caught him and drew him away, almost violently, towards the window, where he whispered something quickly to him, apparently something very important to judge by the expression of his face and the gestures that accompanied the whisper. Nikolay Vsyevolodovitch listened inattentively and listlessly with his official smile, and at last even impatiently, and seemed all the time on the point of breaking away. He moved away from the window just as the ladies came back. Varvara Petrovna made Liza sit down in the same seat as before, declaring that she must wait and rest another ten minutes; and that the fresh air would perhaps be too much for her nerves at once. She was looking after Liza with great devotion, and sat down beside her. Pyotr Stepanovitch, now disengaged, skipped up to them at once, and broke into a rapid and lively flow of conversation. At that point Nikolay Vsyevolodovitch at last went up to Darya Pavlovna with his leisurely step. Dasha began stirring uneasily at his approach, and jumped up quickly in evident embarrassment, flushing all over her face.

"I believe one may congratulate you ... or is it too soon?" he brought out with a peculiar line in his face.

Dasha made him some answer, but it was difficult to catch it.

"Forgive my indiscretion," he added, raising his voice, "but you know I was expressly informed. Did you know about it?"

"Yes, I know that you were expressly informed."

"But I hope I have not done any harm by my congratulations," he laughed. "And if Stepan Trofimovitch ..."

"What, what's the congratulation about?" Pyotr Stepanovitch suddenly skipped up to them. "What are you being congratulated about, Darya Pavlovna? Bah! Surely that's not it? Your blush proves I've guessed right. And indeed, what else does one congratulate our charming and virtuous young ladies on? And what congratulations make them blush most readily? Well, accept mine too, then, if I've guessed right! And pay up. Do you remember when we were in Switzerland you bet you'd never be married.... Oh, yes, apropos of Switzerland—what am I thinking about? Only fancy, that's half what I came about, and I was almost forgetting it. Tell me," he turned quickly to Stepan Trofimovitch, "when are you going to Switzerland?"

"I ... to Switzerland?" Stepan Trofimovitch replied, wondering and confused.

"What? Aren't you going? Why you're getting married, too, you wrote?"

"Pierre!" cried Stepan Trofimovitch.

"Well, why Pierre?... You see, if that'll please you, I've flown here to announce that I'm not at all against it, since you were set on having my opinion as quickly as possible; and if, indeed," he pattered on, "you want to 'be saved,' as you wrote, beseeching my help in the same letter, I am at your service again. Is it true that he is going to be married, Varvara Petrovna?" He turned quickly to her. "I hope I'm not being indiscreet; he writes himself that the whole town knows it and every one's congratulating him, so that, to avoid it he only goes out at night. I've got his letters in my pocket. But would you believe it, Varvara Petrovna, I can't make head or tail of it? Just tell me one thing, Stepan Trofimovitch, are you to be congratulated or are you to be 'saved'? You wouldn't believe it; in one line he's despairing and in the next he's most joyful. To begin with he begs my forgiveness; well, of course, that's their way … though it must be said; fancy, the man's only seen me twice in his life and then by accident. And suddenly now, when he's going to be married for the third time, he imagines that this is a breach of some sort of parental duty to me, and entreats me a thousand miles away not to be angry and to allow him to. Please don't be hurt, Stepan Trofimovitch. It's characteristic of your generation, I take a broad view of it, and don't blame you. And let's admit it does you honour and all the rest. But the point is again that I don't see the point of it. There's something about some sort of 'sins in Switzerland.' 'I'm getting married,' he says, 'for my sins or on account of the 'sins' of another,' or whatever it is—'sins' anyway. 'The girl,' says he, 'is a pearl and a diamond,' and, well, of course, he's 'unworthy of her'; it's their way of talking; but on account of some sins or circumstances 'he is obliged to lead her to the altar, and go to Switzerland, and therefore abandon everything and fly to save me.' Do you understand anything of all that? However … however, I notice from the expression of your faces"—(he turned about with the letter in his hand looking with an innocent smile into the faces of the company)—"that, as usual, I seem to have put my foot in it through my stupid way of being open, or, as Nikolay Vsyevolodovitch says, 'being in a hurry.' I thought, of course, that we were all friends here, that is, your friends, Stepan Trofimovitch, your friends. I am really a stranger, and I see … and I see that you all know something, and that just that something I don't know." He still went on looking about him.

"So Stepan Trofimovitch wrote to you that he was getting married for the 'sins of another committed in Switzerland,' and that you were to fly here 'to save him,' in those very words?" said Varvara Petrovna, addressing him suddenly. Her face was yellow and distorted, and her lips were twitching.

"Well, you see, if there's anything I've not understood," said Pyotr Stepanovitch, as though in alarm, talking more quickly than ever, "it's his fault, of course, for writing like that. Here's the letter. You know, Varvara Petrovna, his letters are endless and incessant, and, you know, for the last two or three months there has been letter upon letter, till, I must own, at last I sometimes didn't read them through. Forgive me, Stepan Trofimovitch, for my foolish confession, but you must admit, please, that, though you addressed them to me, you wrote them more for posterity, so that you really can't mind.… Come, come, don't be offended; we're friends, anyway. But this letter, Varvara Petrovna, this letter, I did read through. These 'sins'—these 'sins of another'—are probably some little sins of our own, and I don't mind betting very innocent ones, though they have suddenly made us take a fancy to work up a terrible story, with a glamour of the heroic about it; and it's just for the sake of that glamour we've got it up. You see there's something a little lame about our accounts—it must be confessed, in the end. We've a great weakness for cards, you know.… But this is unnecessary, quite unnecessary, I'm sorry, I chatter too much. But upon my word, Varvara Petrovna, he gave me a fright, and I really was half prepared to save him. He really made me feel ashamed. Did he expect me to hold a knife to his throat, or what? Am I such a merciless creditor? He writes something here of a dowry.… But are you really going to get married, Stepan Trofimovitch? That would be just like you, to say a lot for the sake of talking. Ach, Varvara Petrovna, I'm sure you must be blaming me now, and just for my way of talking too.…"

"On the contrary, on the contrary, I see that you are driven out of all patience, and, no doubt you have had good reason," Varvara Petrovna answered spitefully. She had listened with spiteful enjoyment to all the "candid outbursts" of Pyotr Stepanovitch, who was obviously playing a part (what part I did not know then, but it was unmistakable, and over-acted indeed).

"On the contrary," she went on, "I'm only too grateful to you for speaking; but for you I might not have known of it. My eyes are opened for the first time for twenty years. Nikolay Vsyevolodovitch, you said just now that you had been expressly informed; surely Stepan Trofimovitch hasn't written to you in the same style?"

"I did get a very harmless and ... and ... very generous letter from him...."

"You hesitate, you pick out your words. That's enough! Stepan Trofimovitch, I request a great favour from you." She suddenly turned to him with flashing eyes. "Kindly leave us at once, and never set foot in my house again."

I must beg the reader to remember her recent "exaltation," which had not yet passed. It's true that Stepan Trofimovitch was terribly to blame! But what was a complete surprise to me then was the wonderful dignity of his bearing under his son's "accusation," which he had never thought of interrupting, and before Varvara Petrovna's "denunciation." How did he come by such spirit? I only found out one thing, that he had certainly been deeply wounded at his first meeting with Petrusha, by the way he had embraced him. It was a deep and genuine grief; at least in his eyes and to his heart. He had another grief at the same time, that is the poignant consciousness of having acted contemptibly. He admitted this to me afterwards with perfect openness. And you know real genuine sorrow will sometimes make even a phenomenally frivolous, unstable man solid and stoical; for a short time at any rate; what's more, even fools are by genuine sorrow turned into wise men, also only for a short time of course; it is characteristic of sorrow. And if so, what might not happen with a man like Stepan Trofimovitch? It worked a complete transformation—though also only for a time, of course.

He bowed with dignity to Varvara Petrovna without uttering a word (there was nothing else left for him to do, indeed). He was on the point of going out without a word, but could not refrain from approaching Darya Pavlovna. She seemed to foresee that he would do so, for she began speaking of her own accord herself, in utter dismay, as though in haste to anticipate him.

"Please, Stepan Trofimovitch, for God's sake, don't say anything," she began, speaking with haste and excitement, with a look of pain in her face, hurriedly stretching out her hands to him. "Be sure that I still respect you as much ... and think just as highly of you, and ... think well of me too, Stepan Trofimovitch, that will mean a great deal to me, a great deal...."

Stepan Trofimovitch made her a very, very low bow.

"It's for you to decide, Darya Pavlovna; you know that you are perfectly free in the whole matter! You have been, and you are now, and you always will be," Varvara Petrovna concluded impressively.

"Bah! Now I understand it all!" cried Pyotr Stepanovitch, slapping himself on the forehead. "But ... but what a position I am put in by all this! Darya Pavlovna, please forgive me!... What do you call your treatment of me, eh?" he said, addressing his father.

"Pierre, you might speak to me differently, mightn't you, my boy," Stepan Trofimovitch observed quite quietly.

"Don't cry out, please," said Pierre, with a wave of his hand. "Believe me, it's all your sick old nerves, and crying out will do no good at all. You'd better tell me instead, why didn't you warn me since you might have supposed I should speak out at the first chance?"

Stepan Trofimovitch looked searchingly at him.

"Pierre, you who know so much of what goes on here, can you really have known nothing of this business and have heard nothing about it?"

"What? What a set! So it's not enough to be a child in your old age, you must be a spiteful child too! Varvara Petrovna, did you hear what he said?"

There was a general outcry; but then suddenly an incident took place which no one could have anticipated.

VIII

First of all I must mention that, for the last two or three minutes Lizaveta Nikolaevna had seemed to be possessed by a new impulse; she was whispering something hurriedly to her mother, and to Mavriky Nikolaevitch, who bent down to listen. Her face was agitated, but at the same time it had a look of resolution. At last she got up from her seat in evident haste to go away, and hurried her mother whom Mavriky Nikolaevitch began helping up from her low chair. But it seemed they were not destined to get away without seeing everything to the end.

Shatov, who had been forgotten by every one in his corner (not far from Lizaveta Nikolaevna), and who did not seem to know himself why he went on sitting there, got up from his chair, and walked, without haste, with resolute steps right across the room to Nikolay Vsyevolodovitch, looking him straight in the face. The latter noticed him approaching at some distance, and faintly smiled, but when Shatov was close to him he left off smiling.

When Shatov stood still facing him with his eyes fixed on him, and without uttering a word, every one suddenly noticed it and there was a general hush; Pyotr Stepanovitch was the last to cease speaking. Liza and her mother were standing in the middle of the room. So passed five seconds; the look of haughty astonishment was followed by one of anger on Nikolay Vsyevolodovitch's face; he scowled....

And suddenly Shatov swung his long, heavy arm, and with all his might struck him a blow in the face. Nikolay Vsyevolodovitch staggered violently.

Shatov struck the blow in a peculiar way, not at all after the conventional fashion (if one may use such an expression). It was not a slap with the palm of his hand, but a blow with the whole fist, and it was a big, heavy, bony fist covered with red hairs and freckles. If the blow had struck the nose, it would have broken it. But it hit him on the cheek, and struck the left corner of the lip and the upper teeth, from which blood streamed at once.

I believe there was a sudden scream, perhaps Varvara Petrovna screamed—that I don't remember, because there was a dead hush again; the whole scene did not last more than ten seconds, however.

Yet a very great deal happened in those seconds.

I must remind the reader again that Nikolay Vsyevolodovitch's was one of those natures that know nothing of fear. At a duel he could face the pistol of his opponent with indifference, and could take aim and kill with brutal coolness. If anyone had slapped him in the face, I should have expected him not to challenge his assailant to a duel, but to murder him on the spot. He was just one of those characters, and would have killed the man, knowing very well what he was doing, and without losing his self-control. I fancy, indeed, that he never was liable to those fits of blind rage which deprive a man of all power of reflection. Even when overcome with intense anger, as he sometimes was, he was always able to retain complete self-control, and therefore to realise that he would certainly be sent to penal servitude for murdering a man not in a duel; nevertheless, he'd have killed any one who insulted him, and without the faintest hesitation.

I have been studying Nikolay Vsyevolodovitch of late, and through special circumstances I know a great many facts about him now, at the time I write. I should compare him, perhaps, with some gentlemen of the past of whom legendary traditions are still perceived among us. We are told, for instance, about the Decabrist L—n, that he was always seeking for danger, that he revelled in the sensation, and that it had become a craving of his nature; that in his youth he had rushed into duels for nothing; that in Siberia he used to go to kill bears with nothing but a knife; that in the Siberian forests he liked to meet with runaway convicts, who are, I may observe in passing, more formidable than bears. There is no doubt that these legendary gentlemen were capable of a feeling of fear, and even to an extreme degree, perhaps, or they would have been a great deal quieter, and a sense of danger would never have become a physical craving with them. But the conquest of fear was what fascinated them. The continual ecstasy of vanquishing and the consciousness that no one could vanquish them was what attracted them. The same L—n struggled with hunger for some time before he was sent into exile, and toiled to earn his daily bread simply because he did not care to comply with the requests of his rich father, which he considered unjust. So his conception of struggle was many-sided, and he did not prize stoicism and strength of character only in duels and bear-fights.

But many years have passed since those times, and the nervous, exhausted, complex character of the men of to-day is incompatible with the craving for those direct and unmixed sensations which were so sought after by some restlessly active gentlemen of the good old days. Nikolay Vsyevolodovitch would, perhaps, have looked down on L—n, and have called him a boastful cock-a-hoop coward; it's true he wouldn't have expressed himself aloud. Stavrogin would have shot his opponent in a duel, and would have faced a bear if necessary, and would have defended himself from a brigand in the forest as successfully and as fearlessly as L—n, but it would be without the slightest thrill of enjoyment, languidly, listlessly, even with ennui and entirely from unpleasant necessity. In anger, of course, there has been a progress compared with L—n, even compared with Lermontov. There was perhaps more malignant anger in Nikolay Vsyevolodovitch than in both put together, but it was a calm, cold, if one may so say, reasonable anger, and therefore the most revolting and most terrible possible. I repeat again, I considered him then, and I still consider him (now that everything is over), a man who, if he received a slap in the face, or any equivalent insult, would be certain to kill his assailant at once, on the spot, without challenging him.

Yet, in the present case, what happened was something different and amazing.

He had scarcely regained his balance after being almost knocked over in this humiliating way, and the horrible, as it were, sodden, thud of the blow in the face had scarcely died away in the room when he seized Shatov by the shoulders with both hands, but at once, almost at the same instant, pulled both hands away and clasped them behind his back. He did not speak, but looked at Shatov, and turned as white as his shirt. But, strange to say, the light in his eyes seemed to die out. Ten seconds later his eyes looked cold, and I'm sure I'm not lying—calm. Only he was terribly pale. Of course I don't know what was passing within the man, I saw only his exterior. It seems to me that if a man should snatch up a bar of red-hot iron and hold it tight in his hand to test his fortitude, and after struggling for ten seconds with insufferable pain end by overcoming it, such a man would, I fancy, go through something like what Nikolay Vsyevolodovitch was enduring during those ten seconds.

Shatov was the first to drop his eyes, and evidently because he was unable to go on facing him; then he turned slowly and walked out of the room, but with a very different step. He withdrew quietly, with peculiar awkwardness, with his shoulders hunched, his head hanging as though he were inwardly pondering something. I believe he was whispering something. He made his way to the door carefully, without stumbling against anything or knocking anything over; he opened the door a very little way, and squeezed through almost sideways. As he went out his shock of hair standing on end at the back of his head was particularly noticeable.

Then first of all one fearful scream was heard. I saw Lizaveta Nikolaevna seize her mother by the shoulder and Mavriky Nikolaevitch by the arm and make two or three violent efforts to draw them out of the room. But she suddenly uttered a shriek, and fell full length on the floor, fainting. I can hear the thud of her head on the carpet to this day.

PART II

CHAPTER I. NIGHT

I

EIGHT DAYS HAD PASSED. Now that it is all over and I am writing a record of it, we know all about it; but at the time we knew nothing, and it was natural that many things should seem strange to us: Stepan Trofimovitch and I, anyway, shut ourselves up for the first part of the time, and looked on with dismay from a distance. I did, indeed, go about here and there, and, as before, brought him various items of news, without which he could not exist.

I need hardly say that there were rumours of the most varied kind going about the town in regard to the blow that Stavrogin had received, Lizaveta Nikolaevna's fainting fit, and all that happened on that Sunday. But what we wondered was, through whom the story had got about so quickly and so accurately. Not one of the persons present had any need to give away the secret of what had happened, or interest to serve by doing so.

The servants had not been present. Lebyadkin was the only one who might have chattered, not so much from spite, for he had gone out in great alarm (and fear of an enemy destroys spite against him), but simply from incontinence of speech. But Lebyadkin and his sister had disappeared next day, and nothing could be heard of them. There was no trace of them at Filipov's house, they had moved, no one knew where, and seemed to have vanished. Shatov, of whom I wanted to inquire about Marya Timofyevna, would not open his door, and I believe sat locked up in his room for the whole of those eight days, even discontinuing his work in the town. He would not see me. I went to see him on Tuesday and knocked at his door. I got no answer, but being convinced by unmistakable evidence that he was at home, I knocked a second time. Then, jumping up, apparently from his bed, he strode to the door and shouted at the top of his voice:

"Shatov is not at home!"

With that I went away.

Stepan Trofimovitch and I, not without dismay at the boldness of the supposition, though we tried to encourage one another, reached at last a conclusion: we made up our mind that the only person who could be responsible for spreading these rumours was Pyotr Stepanovitch, though he himself not long after assured his father that he had found the story on every one's lips, especially at the club, and that the governor and his wife were familiar with every detail of it. What is even more remarkable is that the next day, Monday evening, I met Liputin, and he knew every word that had been passed, so that he must have heard it first-hand. Many of the ladies (and some of the leading ones) were very inquisitive about the "mysterious cripple," as they called Marya Timofyevna. There were some, indeed, who were anxious to see her and make her acquaintance, so the intervention of the persons who had been in such haste to conceal the Lebyadkins was timely. But Lizaveta Nikolaevna's fainting certainly took the foremost place in the story, and "all society" was interested, if only because it directly concerned Yulia Mihailovna, as the kinswoman and patroness of the young lady. And what was there they didn't say! What increased the gossip was the mysterious position of affairs; both houses were obstinately closed; Lizaveta Nikolaevna, so they said, was in bed with brain fever. The same thing was asserted of Nikolay Vsyevolodovitch, with the revolting addition of a tooth knocked out and a swollen face. It was even whispered in corners that there would soon be murder among us, that Stavrogin was not the man to put up with such an insult, and that he would kill Shatov, but with the secrecy of a Corsican vendetta. People liked this idea, but the majority of our young people listened with contempt, and with an air of the most nonchalant indifference, which was, of course, assumed. The old hostility to Nikolay Vsyevolodovitch in the town was in general strikingly manifest. Even sober-minded people were eager to throw blame on him though they could not have said for what. It was whispered that he had ruined Lizaveta Nikolaevna's reputation, and that there had been an intrigue between them in Switzerland. Cautious people, of course, restrained themselves, but all listened with relish. There were other things said, though not in public, but in private, on rare occasions and almost in secret, extremely strange things, to which I only refer to warn my readers of them with a view to the later events of my story. Some people, with knitted brows, said, God knows on what foundation, that Nikolay Vsyevolodovitch had some special business in our province, that he had, through Count K., been brought into touch with exalted circles in Petersburg, that he was even, perhaps, in government service, and might almost be said to have been furnished with some sort of commission from someone. When very sober-minded and sensible people smiled at this rumour, observing very reasonably that a man always mixed up with scandals, and who was beginning his career among us with a swollen face did not look like a government official, they were told in a whisper that he was employed not in the official, but, so to say, the confidential service, and that in such cases it was essential to be as little like an official as possible. This remark produced a sensation; we knew that the Zemstvo of our province was the object of marked attention in the capital. I repeat, these were only flitting rumours that disappeared for a time when Nikolay Vsyevolodovitch first came among us. But I may observe that many of the rumours were partly due to a few brief but malicious words, vaguely and disconnectedly dropped at the club by a gentleman who had lately returned from Petersburg. This was a retired captain in the guards, Artemy Pavlovitch Gaganov. He was a very large landowner in our province and district, a man used to the society of Petersburg, and a son of the late Pavel Pavlovitch Gaganov, the venerable old man with whom Nikolay Vsyevolodovitch had, over four years before, had the extraordinarily coarse and sudden encounter which I have described already in the beginning of my story.

It immediately became known to every one that Yulia Mihailovna had made a special call on Varvara Petrovna, and had been informed at the entrance: "Her honour was too unwell to see visitors." It was known, too, that Yulia Mihailovna sent a message two days later to inquire after Varvara Petrovna's health. At last she began "defending" Varvara Petrovna everywhere, of course only in the loftiest sense, that is, in the vaguest possible way. She listened coldly and sternly to the hurried remarks made at first about the scene on Sunday, so that during the later days they were not renewed in her presence. So that the belief gained ground everywhere that

Yulia Mihailovna knew not only the whole of the mysterious story but all its secret significance to the smallest detail, and not as an outsider, but as one taking part in it. I may observe, by the way, that she was already gradually beginning to gain that exalted influence among us for which she was so eager and which she was certainly struggling to win, and was already beginning to see herself "surrounded by a circle." A section of society recognised her practical sense and tact … but of that later. Her patronage partly explained Pyotr Stepanovitch's rapid success in our society—a success with which Stepan Trofimovitch was particularly impressed at the time.

We possibly exaggerated it. To begin with, Pyotr Stepanovitch seemed to make acquaintance almost instantly with the whole town within the first four days of his arrival. He only arrived on Sunday; and on Tuesday I saw him in a carriage with Artemy Pavlovitch Gaganov, a man who was proud, irritable, and supercilious, in spite of his good breeding, and who was not easy to get on with. At the governor's, too, Pyotr Stepanovitch met with a warm welcome, so much so that he was at once on an intimate footing, like a young friend, treated, so to say, affectionately. He dined with Yulia Mihailovna almost every day. He had made her acquaintance in Switzerland, but there was certainly something curious about the rapidity of his success in the governor's house. In any case he was reputed, whether truly or not, to have been at one time a revolutionist abroad, he had had something to do with some publications and some congresses abroad, "which one can prove from the newspapers," to quote the malicious remark of Alyosha Telyatnikov, who had also been once a young friend affectionately treated in the house of the late governor, but was now, alas, a clerk on the retired list. But the fact was unmistakable: the former revolutionist, far from being hindered from returning to his beloved Fatherland, seemed almost to have been encouraged to do so, so perhaps there was nothing in it. Liputin whispered to me once that there were rumours that Pyotr Stepanovitch had once professed himself penitent, and on his return had been pardoned on mentioning certain names and so, perhaps, had succeeded in expiating his offence, by promising to be of use to the government in the future. I repeated these malignant phrases to Stepan Trofimovitch, and although the latter was in such a state that he was hardly capable of reflection, he pondered profoundly. It turned out later that Pyotr Stepanovitch had come to us with a very influential letter of recommendation, that he had, at any rate, brought one to the governor's wife from a very important old lady in Petersburg, whose husband was one of the most distinguished old dignitaries in the capital. This old lady, who was Yulia Mihailovna's godmother, mentioned in her letter that Count K. knew Pyotr Stepanovitch very well through Nikolay Vsyevolodovitch, made much of him, and thought him "a very excellent young man in spite of his former errors." Yulia Mihailovna set the greatest value on her relations with the "higher spheres," which were few and maintained with difficulty, and was, no doubt, pleased to get the old lady's letter, but still there was something peculiar about it. She even forced her husband upon a familiar footing with Pyotr Stepanovitch, so much so that Mr. von Lembke complained of it … but of that, too, later. I may mention, too, that the great author was also favourably disposed to Pyotr Stepanovitch, and at once invited him to go and see him. Such alacrity on the part of a man so puffed up with conceit stung Stepan Trofimovitch more painfully than anything; but I put a different interpretation on it. In inviting a nihilist to see him, Mr. Karmazinov, no doubt, had in view his relations with the progressives of the younger generation in both capitals. The great author trembled nervously before the revolutionary youth of Russia, and imagining, in his ignorance, that the future lay in their hands, fawned upon them in a despicable way, chiefly because they paid no attention to him whatever.

II

Pyotr Stepanovitch ran round to see his father twice, but unfortunately, I was absent on both occasions. He visited him for the first time only on Wednesday, that is, not till the fourth day after their first meeting, and then only on business. Their difficulties over the property were settled, by the way, without fuss or publicity. Varvara Petrovna took it all on herself, and paid all that was owing, taking over the land, of course, and only informed Stepan Trofimovitch that it was all settled and her butler, Alexey Yegorytch, was, by her authorisation, bringing him something to sign. This Stepan Trofimovitch did, in silence, with extreme dignity. Apropos of his dignity, I may mention that I hardly recognised my old friend during those days. He behaved as he had never done before; became amazingly taciturn and had not even written one letter to Varvara Petrovna since Sunday, which seemed to me almost a miracle. What's more, he had become quite calm. He had fastened upon a final and decisive idea which gave him tranquillity. That was evident. He had hit upon this idea, and sat still, expecting something. At first, however, he was ill, especially on Monday. He had an attack of his summer cholera. He could not remain all that time without news either; but as soon as I departed from the statement of facts, and began discussing the case in itself, and formulated any theory, he at once gesticulated to me to stop. But both his interviews with his son had a distressing effect on him, though they did not shake his determination. After each interview he spent the whole day lying on the sofa with a handkerchief soaked in vinegar on his head. But he continued to remain calm in the deepest sense.

Sometimes, however, he did not hinder my speaking. Sometimes, too, it seemed to me that the mysterious determination he had taken seemed to be failing him and he appeared to be struggling with a new, seductive stream of ideas. That was only at moments, but I made a note of it. I suspected that he was longing to assert himself again, to come forth from his seclusion, to show fight, to struggle to the last.

"Cher, I could crush them!" broke from him on Thursday evening after his second interview with Pyotr Stepanovitch, when he lay stretched on the sofa with his head wrapped in a towel.

Till that moment he had not uttered one word all day.

"Fils, fils, cher," and so on, "I agree all those expressions are nonsense, kitchen talk, and so be it. I see it for myself. I never gave him food or drink, I sent him a tiny baby from Berlin to X province by post, and all that, I admit it.... 'You gave me neither food nor drink, and sent me by post,' he says, 'and what's more you've robbed me here.'"

"'But you unhappy boy,' I cried to him, 'my heart has been aching for you all my life; though I did send you by post.' Il rit."

"But I admit it. I admit it, granted it was by post," he concluded, almost in delirium.

"Passons," he began again, five minutes later. "I don't understand Turgenev. That Bazarov of his is a fictitious figure, it does not exist anywhere. The fellows themselves were the first to disown him as unlike anyone. That Bazarov is a sort of indistinct mixture of Nozdryov and Byron, c'est le mot. Look at them attentively: they caper about and squeal with joy like puppies in the sun. They are happy, they are victorious! What is there of Byron in them!... and with that, such ordinariness! What a low-bred, irritable vanity! What an abject craving to faire du bruit autour de son nom, without noticing that son nom.... Oh, it's a caricature! 'Surely,' I cried to him, 'you don't want to offer yourself just as you are as a substitute for Christ?' Il rit. Il rit beaucoup. Il rit trop. He has a strange smile. His mother had not a smile like that. Il rit toujours."

Silence followed again.

"They are cunning; they were acting in collusion on Sunday," he blurted out suddenly....

"Oh, not a doubt of it," I cried, pricking up my ears. "It was a got-up thing and it was too transparent, and so badly acted."

"I don't mean that. Do you know that it was all too transparent on purpose, that those ... who had to, might understand it. Do you understand that?"

"I don't understand."

"Tant mieux; passons. I am very irritable to-day."

"But why have you been arguing with him, Stepan Trofimovitch?" I asked him reproachfully.

"Je voulais convertir—you'll laugh of course—cette pauvre auntie, elle entendra de belles choses! Oh, my dear boy, would you believe it. I felt like a patriot. I always recognised that I was a Russian, however ... a genuine Russian must be like you and me. Il y a là dedans quelque chose d'aveugle et de louche."

"Not a doubt of it," I assented.

"My dear, the real truth always sounds improbable, do you know that? To make truth sound probable you must always mix in some falsehood with it. Men have always done so. Perhaps there's something in it that passes our understanding. What do you think: is there something we don't understand in that triumphant squeal? I should like to think there was. I should like to think so."

I did not speak. He, too, was silent for a long time. "They say that French cleverness ..." he babbled suddenly, as though in a fever ... "that's false, it always has been. Why libel French cleverness? It's simply Russian indolence, our degrading impotence to produce ideas, our revolting parasitism in the rank of nations. Ils sont tout simplement des paresseux, and not French cleverness. Oh, the Russians ought to be extirpated for the good of humanity, like noxious parasites! We've been striving for something utterly, utterly different. I can make nothing of it. I have given up understanding. 'Do you understand,' I cried to him, 'that if you have the guillotine in the foreground of your programme and are so enthusiastic about it too, it's simply because nothing's easier than cutting off heads, and nothing's harder than to have an idea. Vous êtes des paresseux! Votre drapeau est un guenille, une impuissance. It's those carts, or, what was it?… the rumble of the carts carrying bread to humanity being more important than the Sistine Madonna, or, what's the saying?… une bêtise dans ce genre. Don't you understand, don't you understand,' I said to him, 'that unhappiness is just as necessary to man as happiness.' Il rit. 'All you do is to make a bon mot,' he said, 'with your limbs snug on a velvet sofa.' … (He used a coarser expression.) And this habit of addressing a father so familiarly is very nice when father and son are on good terms, but what do you think of it when they are abusing one another?"

We were silent again for a minute.

"Cher," he concluded at last, getting up quickly, "do you know this is bound to end in something?"

"Of course," said I.

"Vous ne comprenez pas. Passons. But … usually in our world things come to nothing, but this will end in something; it's bound to, it's bound to!"

He got up, and walked across the room in violent emotion, and coming back to the sofa sank on to it exhausted.

On Friday morning, Pyotr Stepanovitch went off somewhere in the neighbourhood, and remained away till Monday. I heard of his departure from Liputin, and in the course of conversation I learned that the Lebyadkins, brother and sister, had moved to the riverside quarter. "I moved them," he added, and, dropping the Lebyadkins, he suddenly announced to me that Lizaveta Nikolaevna was going to marry Mavriky Nikolaevitch, that, although it had not been announced, the engagement was a settled thing. Next day I met Lizaveta Nikolaevna out riding with Mavriky Nikolaevitch; she was out for the first time after her illness. She beamed at me from the distance, laughed, and nodded in a very friendly way. I told all this to Stepan Trofimovitch; he paid no attention, except to the news about the Lebyadkins.

And now, having described our enigmatic position throughout those eight days during which we knew nothing, I will pass on to the description of the succeeding incidents of my chronicle, writing, so to say, with full knowledge, and describing things as they became known afterwards, and are clearly seen to-day. I will begin with the eighth day after that Sunday, that is, the Monday evening—for in reality a "new scandal" began with that evening.

III

It was seven o'clock in the evening. Nikolay Vsyevolodovitch was sitting alone in his study—the room he had been fond of in old days. It was lofty, carpeted with rugs, and contained somewhat heavy old-fashioned furniture. He was sitting on the sofa in the corner, dressed as though to go out, though he did not seem to be intending to do so. On the table before him stood a lamp with a shade. The sides and corners of the big room were left in shadow. His eyes looked dreamy and concentrated, not altogether tranquil; his face looked tired and had grown a little thinner. He really was ill with a swollen face; but the story of a tooth having been knocked out was an exaggeration. One had been loosened, but it had grown into its place again: he had had a cut on the inner side of the upper lip, but that, too, had healed. The swelling on his face had lasted all the week simply because the invalid would not have a doctor, and instead of having the swelling lanced had waited for it to go down. He would not hear of a doctor, and would scarcely allow even his mother to come near him, and then only for a moment, once a day, and only at dusk, after it was dark and before lights had been brought in. He did not receive Pyotr Stepanovitch either, though the latter ran round to Varvara Petrovna's two or three times a day so long as he remained in the town. And now, at last, returning on the Monday morning after his three days' absence, Pyotr Stepanovitch made a circuit of the town, and, after dining at Yulia Mihailovna's, came at last in the evening to Varvara Petrovna, who was impatiently expecting him. The interdict had been removed, Nikolay Vsyevolodovitch was "at home." Varvara Petrovna herself led the visitor to the door of the study; she had long looked forward to their meeting, and Pyotr Stepanovitch had promised to run to her and repeat what passed. She knocked timidly at Nikolay Vsyevolodovitch's door, and getting no answer ventured to open the door a couple of inches.

"Nicolas, may I bring Pyotr Stepanovitch in to see you?" she asked, in a soft and restrained voice, trying to make out her son's face behind the lamp.

"You can—you can, of course you can," Pyotr Stepanovitch himself cried out, loudly and gaily. He opened the door with his hand and went in.

Nikolay Vsyevolodovitch had not heard the knock at the door, and only caught his mother's timid question, and had not had time to answer it. Before him, at that moment, there lay a letter he had just read over, which he was pondering deeply. He started, hearing Pyotr Stepanovitch's sudden outburst, and hurriedly put the letter under a paper-weight, but did not quite succeed; a corner of the letter and almost the whole envelope showed.

"I called out on purpose that you might be prepared," Pyotr Stepanovitch said hurriedly, with surprising naïveté, running up to the table, and instantly staring at the corner of the letter, which peeped out from beneath the paper-weight.

"And no doubt you had time to see how I hid the letter I had just received, under the paper-weight," said Nikolay Vsyevolodovitch calmly, without moving from his place.

"A letter? Bless you and your letters, what are they to do with me?" cried the visitor. "But ... what does matter ..." he whispered again, turning to the door, which was by now closed, and nodding his head in that direction.

"She never listens," Nikolay Vsyevolodovitch observed coldly.

"What if she did overhear?" cried Pyotr Stepanovitch, raising his voice cheerfully, and settling down in an arm-chair. "I've nothing against that, only I've come here now to speak to you alone. Well, at last I've succeeded in getting at you. First of all, how are you? I see you're getting on splendidly. To-morrow you'll show yourself again—eh?"

"Perhaps."

"Set their minds at rest. Set mine at rest at last." He gesticulated violently with a jocose and amiable air. "If only you knew what nonsense I've had to talk to them. You know, though." He laughed.

"I don't know everything. I only heard from my mother that you've been ... very active."

"Oh, well, I've said nothing definite," Pyotr Stepanovitch flared up at once, as though defending himself from an awful attack. "I simply trotted out Shatov's wife; you know, that is, the rumours of your liaison in Paris, which accounted, of course, for what happened on Sunday. You're not angry?"

"I'm sure you've done your best."

"Oh, that's just what I was afraid of. Though what does that mean, 'done your best'? That's a reproach, isn't it? You always go straight for things, though.... What I was most afraid of, as I came here, was that you wouldn't go straight for the point."

"I don't want to go straight for anything," said Nikolay Vsyevolodovitch with some irritation. But he laughed at once.

"I didn't mean that, I didn't mean that, don't make a mistake," cried Pyotr Stepanovitch, waving his hands, rattling his words out like peas, and at once relieved at his companion's irritability. "I'm not going to worry you with our business, especially in your present position. I've only come about Sunday's affair, and only to arrange the most necessary steps, because, you see, it's impossible. I've come with the frankest explanations which I stand in more need of than you—so much for your vanity, but at the same time it's true. I've come to be open with you from this time forward."

"Then you have not been open with me before?"

"You know that yourself. I've been cunning with you many times ... you smile; I'm very glad of that smile as a prelude to our explanation. I provoked that smile on purpose by using the word 'cunning,' so that you might get cross directly at my daring to think I could be cunning, so that I might have a chance of explaining myself at once. You see, you see how open I have become now! Well, do you care to listen?"

In the expression of Nikolay Vsyevolodovitch's face, which was contemptuously composed, and even ironical, in spite of his visitor's obvious desire to irritate him by the insolence of his premeditated and intentionally coarse naïvetés, there was, at last, a look of rather uneasy curiosity.

"Listen," said Pyotr Stepanovitch, wriggling more than ever, "when I set off to come here, I mean here in the large sense, to this town, ten days ago, I made up my mind, of course, to assume a character. It would have been best to have done without anything, to have kept one's own character, wouldn't it? There is no better dodge than one's own character, because no one believes in it. I meant, I must own, to assume the part of a fool, because it is easier to be a fool than to act one's own character; but as a fool is after all something extreme, and anything extreme excites curiosity, I ended by sticking to my own character. And what is my own character? The golden mean: neither wise nor foolish, rather stupid, and dropped from the moon, as sensible people say here, isn't that it?"

"Perhaps it is," said Nikolay Vsyevolodovitch, with a faint smile.

"Ah, you agree—I'm very glad; I knew beforehand that it was your own opinion.... You needn't trouble, I am not annoyed, and I didn't describe myself in that way to get a flattering contradiction from you—no, you're not stupid, you're clever.... Ah! you're smiling again!... I've blundered once more. You would not have said 'you're clever,' granted; I'll let it pass anyway. Passons, as papa says, and, in parenthesis, don't be vexed with my verbosity. By the way, I always say a lot, that is, use a great many words and talk very fast, and I never speak well. And why do I use so many words, and why do I never speak well? Because I don't know how to speak. People who can speak well, speak briefly. So that I am stupid, am I not? But as this gift of stupidity is natural to me, why shouldn't I make skilful use of it? And I do make use of it. It's true that as I came here, I did think, at first, of being silent. But you know silence is a great talent, and therefore incongruous for me, and secondly silence would be risky, anyway. So I made up my mind finally that it would be best to talk, but to talk stupidly—that is, to talk and talk and talk—to be in a tremendous hurry to explain things, and in the end to get muddled in my own explanations, so that my listener would walk away without hearing the end, with a shrug, or, better still, with a curse. You succeed straight off in persuading them of your simplicity, in boring them and in being incomprehensible—three advantages all at once! Do you suppose anybody will suspect you of mysterious designs after that? Why, every one of them would take it as a personal affront if anyone were to say I had secret designs. And I sometimes amuse them too, and that's priceless. Why, they're ready to forgive me everything now, just because the clever fellow who used to publish manifestoes out there turns out to be stupider than themselves—that's so, isn't it? From your smile I see you approve."

Nikolay Vsyevolodovitch was not smiling at all, however.

On the contrary, he was listening with a frown and some impatience.

"Eh? What? I believe you said 'no matter.'"

Pyotr Stepanovitch rattled on. (Nikolay Vsyevolodovitch had said nothing at all.) "Of course, of course. I assure you I'm not here to compromise you by my company, by claiming you as my comrade. But do you know you're horribly captious to-day; I ran in to you with a light and open heart, and you seem to be laying up every word I say against me. I assure you I'm not going to begin about anything shocking to-day, I give you my word, and I agree beforehand to all your conditions."

Nikolay Vsyevolodovitch was obstinately silent.

"Eh? What? Did you say something? I see, I see that I've made a blunder again, it seems; you've not suggested conditions and you're not going to; I believe you, I believe you; well, you can set your mind at rest; I know, of course, that it's not worth while for me to suggest them, is it? I'll answer for you beforehand, and—just from stupidity, of course; stupidity again.... You're laughing? Eh? What?"

"Nothing," Nikolay Vsyevolodovitch laughed at last. "I just remembered that I really did call you stupid, but you weren't there then, so they must have repeated it.... I would ask you to make haste and come to the point."

"Why, but I am at the point! I am talking about Sunday," babbled Pyotr Stepanovitch. "Why, what was I on Sunday? What would you call it? Just fussy, mediocre stupidity, and in the stupidest way I took possession of the conversation by force. But they forgave me everything, first because I dropped from the moon, that seems to be settled here, now, by every one; and, secondly, because I told them a pretty little story, and got you all out of a scrape, didn't they, didn't they?"

"That is, you told your story so as to leave them in doubt and suggest some compact and collusion between us, when there was no collusion and I'd not asked you to do anything."

"Just so, just so!" Pyotr Stepanovitch caught him up, apparently delighted. "That's just what I did do, for I wanted you to see that I implied it; I exerted myself chiefly for your sake, for I caught you and wanted to compromise you, above all I wanted to find out how far you're afraid."

"It would be interesting to know why you are so open now?"

"Don't be angry, don't be angry, don't glare at me.... You're not, though. You wonder why I am so open? Why, just because it's all changed now; of course, it's over, buried under the sand. I've suddenly changed my ideas about you. The old way is closed; now I shall never compromise you in the old way, it will be in a new way now."

"You've changed your tactics?"

"There are no tactics. Now it's for you to decide in everything, that is, if you want to, say yes, and if you want to, say no. There you have my new tactics. And I won't say a word about our cause till you bid me yourself. You laugh? Laugh away. I'm laughing myself. But I'm in earnest now, in earnest, in earnest, though a man who is in such a hurry is stupid, isn't he? Never mind, I may be stupid, but I'm in earnest, in earnest."

He really was speaking in earnest in quite a different tone, and with a peculiar excitement, so that Nikolay Vsyevolodovitch looked at him with curiosity.

"You say you've changed your ideas about me?" he asked.

"I changed my ideas about you at the moment when you drew your hands back after Shatov's attack, and, that's enough, that's enough, no questions, please, I'll say nothing more now."

He jumped up, waving his hands as though waving off questions. But as there were no questions, and he had no reason to go away, he sank into an arm-chair again, somewhat reassured.

"By the way, in parenthesis," he rattled on at once, "some people here are babbling that you'll kill him, and taking bets about it, so that Lembke positively thought of setting the police on, but Yulia Mihailovna forbade it.... But enough about that, quite enough, I only spoke of it to let you know. By the way, I moved the Lebyadkins the same day, you know; did you get my note with their address?"

"I received it at the time."

"I didn't do that by way of 'stupidity.' I did it genuinely, to serve you. If it was stupid, anyway, it was done in good faith."

"Oh, all right, perhaps it was necessary...." said Nikolay Vsyevolodovitch dreamily, "only don't write any more letters to me, I beg you."

"Impossible to avoid it. It was only one."

"So Liputin knows?"

"Impossible to help it: but Liputin, you know yourself, dare not ... By the way, you ought to meet our fellows, that is, the fellows not our fellows, or you'll be finding fault again. Don't disturb yourself, not just now, but sometime. Just now it's raining. I'll let them know, they'll meet together, and we'll go in the evening. They're waiting, with their mouths open like young crows in a nest, to see what present we've brought them. They're a hot-headed lot. They've brought out leaflets, they're on the point of quarrelling. Virginsky is a universal humanity man, Liputin is a Fourierist with a marked inclination for police work; a man, I assure you, who is precious from one point of view, though he requires strict supervision in all others; and, last of all, that fellow with the long ears, he'll read an account of his own system. And do you know, they're offended at my treating them casually, and throwing cold water over them, but we certainly must meet."

"You've made me out some sort of chief?" Nikolay Vsyevolodovitch dropped as carelessly as possible.

Pyotr Stepanovitch looked quickly at him.

"By the way," he interposed, in haste to change the subject, as though he had not heard. "I've been here two or three times, you know, to see her excellency, Varvara Petrovna, and I have been obliged to say a great deal too."

"So I imagine."

"No, don't imagine, I've simply told her that you won't kill him, well, and other sweet things. And only fancy; the very next day she knew I'd moved Marya Timofyevna beyond the river. Was it you told her?"

"I never dreamed of it!"

"I knew it wasn't you. Who else could it be? It's interesting."

"Liputin, of course."

"N-no, not Liputin," muttered Pyotr Stepanovitch, frowning; "I'll find out who. It's more like Shatov.... That's nonsense though. Let's leave that! Though it's awfully important.... By the way, I kept expecting that your mother would suddenly burst out with the great question.... Ach! yes, she was horribly glum at first, but suddenly, when I came to-day, she was beaming all over, what does that mean?"

"It's because I promised her to-day that within five days I'll be engaged to Lizaveta Nikolaevna," Nikolay Vsyevolodovitch said with surprising openness.

"Oh!... Yes, of course," faltered Pyotr Stepanovitch, seeming disconcerted. "There are rumours of her engagement, you know. It's true, too. But you're right, she'd run from under the wedding crown, you've only to call to her. You're not angry at my saying so?"

"No, I'm not angry."

"I notice it's awfully hard to make you angry to-day, and I begin to be afraid of you. I'm awfully curious to know how you'll appear to-morrow. I expect you've got a lot of things ready. You're not angry at my saying so?"

Nikolay Vsyevolodovitch made no answer at all, which completed Pyotr Stepanovitch's irritation.

"By the way, did you say that in earnest to your mother, about Lizaveta Nikolaevna?" he asked.

Nikolay Vsyevolodovitch looked coldly at him.

"Oh, I understand, it was only to soothe her, of course."

"And if it were in earnest?" Nikolay Vsyevolodovitch asked firmly.

"Oh, God bless you then, as they say in such cases. It won't hinder the cause (you see, I don't say 'our,' you don't like the word 'our') and I … well, I … am at your service, as you know."

"You think so?"

"I think nothing—nothing," Pyotr Stepanovitch hurriedly declared, laughing, "because I know you consider what you're about beforehand for yourself, and everything with you has been thought out. I only mean that I am seriously at your service, always and everywhere, and in every sort of circumstance, every sort really, do you understand that?"

Nikolay Vsyevolodovitch yawned.

"I've bored you," Pyotr Stepanovitch cried, jumping up suddenly, and snatching his perfectly new round hat as though he were going away. He remained and went on talking, however, though he stood up, sometimes pacing about the room and tapping himself on the knee with his hat at exciting parts of the conversation.

"I meant to amuse you with stories of the Lembkes, too," he cried gaily.

"Afterwards, perhaps, not now. But how is Yulia Mihailovna?"

"What conventional manners all of you have! Her health is no more to you than the health of the grey cat, yet you ask after it. I approve of that. She's quite well, and her respect for you amounts to a superstition, her immense anticipations of you amount to a superstition. She does not say a word about what happened on Sunday, and is convinced that you will overcome everything yourself by merely making your appearance. Upon my word! She fancies you can do anything. You're an enigmatic and romantic figure now, more than ever you were—extremely advantageous position. It is incredible how eager every one is to see you. They were pretty hot when I went away, but now it is more so than ever. Thanks again for your letter. They are all afraid of Count K. Do you know they look upon you as a spy? I keep that up, you're not angry?"

"It does not matter."

"It does not matter; it's essential in the long run. They have their ways of doing things here. I encourage it, of course; Yulia Mihailovna, in the first place, Gaganov too.... You laugh? But you know I have my policy; I babble away and suddenly I say something clever just as they are on the look-out for it. They crowd round me and I humbug away again. They've all given me up in despair by now: 'he's got brains but he's dropped from the moon.' Lembke invites me to enter the service so that I may be reformed. You know I treat him mockingly, that is, I compromise him and he simply stares. Yulia Mihailovna encourages it. Oh, by the way, Gaganov is in an awful rage with you. He said the nastiest things about you yesterday at Duhovo. I told him the whole truth on the spot, that is, of course, not the whole truth. I spent the whole day at Duhovo. It's a splendid estate, a fine house."

"Then is he at Duhovo now?" Nikolay Vsyevolodovitch broke in suddenly, making a sudden start forward and almost leaping up from his seat.

"No, he drove me here this morning, we returned together," said Pyotr Stepanovitch, appearing not to notice Stavrogin's momentary excitement. "What's this? I dropped a book." He bent down to pick up the "keepsake" he had knocked down. "'The Women of Balzac,' with illustrations." He opened it suddenly. "I haven't read it. Lembke writes novels too."

"Yes?" queried Nikolay Vsyevolodovitch, as though beginning to be interested.

"In Russian, on the sly, of course, Yulia Mihailovna knows and allows it. He's henpecked, but with good manners; it's their system. Such strict form—such self-restraint! Something of the sort would be the thing for us."

"You approve of government methods?"

"I should rather think so! It's the one thing that's natural and practicable in Russia.... I won't ... I won't," he cried out suddenly, "I'm not referring to that—not a word on delicate subjects. Good-bye, though, you look rather green."

"I'm feverish."

"I can well believe it; you should go to bed. By the way, there are Skoptsi here in the neighbourhood—they're curious people ... of that later, though. Ah, here's another anecdote. There's an infantry regiment here in the district. I was drinking last Friday evening with the officers. We've three friends among them, vous comprenez? They were discussing atheism and I need hardly say they made short work of God. They were squealing with delight. By the way, Shatov declares that if there's to be a rising in Russia we must begin with atheism. Maybe it's true. One grizzled old stager of a captain sat mum, not saying a word. All at once he stands up in the middle of the room and says aloud, as though speaking to himself: 'If there's no God, how can I be a captain then?' He took up his cap and went out, flinging up his hands."

"He expressed a rather sensible idea," said Nikolay Vsyevolodovitch, yawning for the third time.

"Yes? I didn't understand it; I meant to ask you about it. Well what else have I to tell you? The Shpigulin factory's interesting; as you know, there are five hundred workmen in it, it's a hotbed of cholera, it's not been cleaned for fifteen years and the factory hands are swindled. The owners are millionaires. I assure you that some among the hands have an idea of the Internationale. What, you smile? You'll see—only give me ever so little time! I've asked you to fix the time already and now I ask you again and then.... But I beg your pardon, I won't, I won't speak of that, don't frown. There!" He turned back suddenly. "I quite forgot the chief thing. I was told just now that our box had come from Petersburg."

"You mean ..." Nikolay Vsyevolodovitch looked at him, not understanding.

"Your box, your things, coats, trousers, and linen have come. Is it true?"

"Yes ... they said something about it this morning."

"Ach, then can't I open it at once!..."

"Ask Alexey."

"Well, to-morrow, then, will to-morrow do? You see my new jacket, dress-coat and three pairs of trousers are with your things, from Sharmer's, by your recommendation, do you remember?"

"I hear you're going in for being a gentleman here," said Nikolay Vsyevolodovitch with a smile. "Is it true you're going to take lessons at the riding school?"

Pyotr Stepanovitch smiled a wry smile. "I say," he said suddenly, with excessive haste in a voice that quivered and faltered, "I say, Nikolay Vsyevolodovitch, let's drop personalities once for all. Of course, you can despise me as much as you like if it amuses you—but we'd better dispense with personalities for a time, hadn't we?"

"All right," Nikolay Vsyevolodovitch assented.

Pyotr Stepanovitch grinned, tapped his knee with his hat, shifted from one leg to the other, and recovered his former expression.

"Some people here positively look upon me as your rival with Lizaveta Nikolaevna, so I must think of my appearance, mustn't I," he laughed. "Who was it told you that though? H'm. It's just eight o'clock; well I must be off. I promised to look in on Varvara Petrovna, but I shall make my escape. And you go to bed and you'll be stronger to-morrow. It's raining and dark, but I've a cab, it's not over safe in the streets here at night.... Ach, by the way, there's a run-away convict from Siberia, Fedka, wandering about the town and the neighbourhood. Only fancy, he used to be a serf of mine, and my papa sent him for a soldier fifteen years ago and took the money for him. He's a very remarkable person."

"You have been talking to him?" Nikolay Vsyevolodovitch scanned him.

"I have. He lets me know where he is. He's ready for anything, anything, for money of course, but he has convictions, too, of a sort, of course. Oh yes, by the way, again, if you meant anything of that plan, you remember, about Lizaveta Nikolaevna, I tell you once again, I too am a fellow ready for anything of any kind you like, and absolutely at your service.... Hullo! are you reaching for your stick. Oh no ... only fancy ... I thought you were looking for your stick."

Nikolay Vsyevolodovitch was looking for nothing and said nothing.

But he had risen to his feet very suddenly with a strange look in his face.

"If you want any help about Mr. Gaganov either," Pyotr Stepanovitch blurted out suddenly, this time looking straight at the paper-weight, "of course I can arrange it all, and I'm certain you won't be able to manage without me."

He went out suddenly without waiting for an answer, but thrust his head in at the door once more. "I mention that," he gabbled hurriedly, "because Shatov had no right either, you know, to risk his life last Sunday when he attacked you, had he? I should be glad if you would make a note of that." He disappeared again without waiting for an answer.

IV

Perhaps he imagined, as he made his exit, that as soon as he was left alone, Nikolay Vsyevolodovitch would begin beating on the wall with his fists, and no doubt he would have been glad to see this, if that had been possible. But, if so, he was greatly mistaken. Nikolay Vsyevolodovitch was still calm. He remained standing for two minutes in the same position by the table, apparently plunged in thought, but soon a cold and listless smile came on to his lips. He slowly sat down again in the same place in the corner of the sofa, and shut his eyes as though from weariness. The corner of the letter was still peeping from under the paperweight, but he didn't even move to cover it.

He soon sank into complete forgetfulness.

When Pyotr Stepanovitch went out without coming to see her, as he had promised, Varvara Petrovna, who had been worn out by anxiety during these days, could not control herself, and ventured to visit her son herself, though it was not her regular time. She was still haunted by the idea that he would tell her something conclusive. She knocked at the door gently as before, and again receiving no answer, she opened the door. Seeing that Nikolay Vsyevolodovitch was sitting strangely motionless, she cautiously advanced to the sofa with a throbbing heart. She seemed struck by the fact that he could fall asleep so quickly and that he could sleep sitting like that, so erect and motionless, so that his breathing even was scarcely perceptible. His face was pale and forbidding, but it looked, as it were, numb and rigid. His brows were somewhat contracted and frowning. He positively had the look of a lifeless wax figure. She stood over him for about three minutes, almost holding her breath, and suddenly she was seized with terror. She withdrew on tiptoe, stopped at the door, hurriedly made the sign of the cross over him, and retreated unobserved, with a new oppression and a new anguish at her heart.

He slept a long while, more than an hour, and still in the same rigid pose: not a muscle of his face twitched, there was not the faintest movement in his whole body, and his brows were still contracted in the same forbidding frown. If Varvara Petrovna had remained another three minutes she could not have endured the stifling sensation that this motionless lethargy roused in her, and would have waked him. But he suddenly opened his eyes, and sat for ten minutes as immovable as before, staring persistently and curiously, as though at some object in the corner which had struck him, although there was nothing new or striking in the room.

Suddenly there rang out the low deep note of the clock on the wall.

With some uneasiness he turned to look at it, but almost at the same moment the other door opened, and the butler, Alexey Yegorytch came in. He had in one hand a greatcoat, a scarf, and a hat, and in the other a silver tray with a note on it.

"Half-past nine," he announced softly, and laying the other things on a chair, he held out the tray with the note—a scrap of paper unsealed and scribbled in pencil. Glancing through it, Nikolay Vsyevolodovitch took a pencil from the table, added a few words, and put the note back on the tray.

"Take it back as soon as I have gone out, and now dress me," he said, getting up from the sofa.

Noticing that he had on a light velvet jacket, he thought a minute, and told the man to bring him a cloth coat, which he wore on more ceremonious occasions. At last, when he was dressed and had put on his hat, he locked the door by which his mother had come into the room, took the letter from under the paperweight, and without saying a word went out into the corridor, followed by Alexey Yegorytch. From the corridor they went down the narrow stone steps of the back stairs to a passage which opened straight into the garden. In the corner stood a lantern and a big umbrella.

"Owing to the excessive rain the mud in the streets is beyond anything," Alexey Yegorytch announced, making a final effort to deter his master from the expedition. But opening his umbrella the latter went without a word into the damp and sodden garden, which was dark as a cellar. The wind was roaring and tossing the bare tree-tops. The little sandy paths were wet and slippery. Alexey Yegorytch walked along as he was, bareheaded, in his swallow-tail coat, lighting up the path for about three steps before them with the lantern.

"Won't it be noticed?" Nikolay Vsyevolodovitch asked suddenly.

"Not from the windows. Besides I have seen to all that already," the old servant answered in quiet and measured tones.

"Has my mother retired?"

"Her excellency locked herself in at nine o'clock as she has done the last few days, and there is no possibility of her knowing anything. At what hour am I to expect your honour?"

"At one or half-past, not later than two."

"Yes, sir."

Crossing the garden by the winding paths that they both knew by heart, they reached the stone wall, and there in the farthest corner found a little door, which led out into a narrow and deserted lane, and was always kept locked. It appeared that Alexey Yegorytch had the key in his hand.

"Won't the door creak?" Nikolay Vsyevolodovitch inquired again.

But Alexey Yegorytch informed him that it had been oiled yesterday "as well as to-day." He was by now wet through. Unlocking the door he gave the key to Nikolay Vsyevolodovitch.

"If it should be your pleasure to be taking a distant walk, I would warn your honour that I am not confident of the folk here, especially in the back lanes, and especially beyond the river," he could not resist warning him again. He was an old servant, who had been like a nurse to Nikolay Vsyevolodovitch, and at one time used to dandle him in his arms; he was a grave and severe man who was fond of listening to religious discourse and reading books of devotion.

"Don't be uneasy, Alexey Yegorytch."

"May God's blessing rest on you, sir, but only in your righteous undertakings."

"What?" said Nikolay Vsyevolodovitch, stopping short in the lane.

Alexey Yegorytch resolutely repeated his words. He had never before ventured to express himself in such language in his master's presence.

Nikolay Vsyevolodovitch locked the door, put the key in his pocket, and crossed the lane, sinking five or six inches into the mud at every step. He came out at last into a long deserted street. He knew the town like the five fingers of his hand, but Bogoyavlensky Street was a long way off. It was past ten when he stopped at last before the locked gates of the dark old house that belonged to Filipov. The ground floor had stood empty since the Lebyadkins had left it, and the windows were boarded up, but there was a light burning in Shatov's room on the second floor. As there was no bell he began banging on the gate with his hand. A window was opened and Shatov peeped out into the street. It was terribly dark, and difficult to make out anything. Shatov was peering out for some time, about a minute.

"Is that you?" he asked suddenly.

"Yes," replied the uninvited guest.

Shatov slammed the window, went downstairs and opened the gate. Nikolay Vsyevolodovitch stepped over the high sill, and without a word passed by him straight into Kirillov's lodge.

V

There everything was unlocked and all the doors stood open. The passage and the first two rooms were dark, but there was a light shining in the last, in which Kirillov lived and drank tea, and laughter and strange cries came from it. Nikolay Vsyevolodovitch went towards the light, but stood still in the doorway without going in. There was tea on the table. In the middle of the room stood the old woman who was a relation of the landlord. She was bareheaded and was dressed in a petticoat and a hare-skin jacket, and her stockingless feet were thrust into slippers. In her arms she had an eighteen-months-old baby, with nothing on but its little shirt; with bare legs, flushed cheeks, and ruffled white hair. It had only just been taken out of the cradle. It seemed to have just been crying; there were still tears in its eyes. But at that instant it was stretching out its little arms, clapping its hands, and laughing with a sob as little children do. Kirillov was bouncing a big red india-rubber ball on the floor before it. The ball bounced up to the ceiling, and back to the floor, the baby shrieked "Baw! baw!" Kirillov caught the "baw", and gave it to it. The baby threw it itself with its awkward little hands, and Kirillov ran to pick it up again.

At last the "baw" rolled under the cupboard. "Baw! baw!" cried the child. Kirillov lay down on the floor, trying to reach the ball with his hand under the cupboard. Nikolay Vsyevolodovitch went into the room. The baby caught sight of him, nestled against the old woman, and went off into a prolonged infantile wail. The woman immediately carried it out of the room.

"Stavrogin?" said Kirillov, beginning to get up from the floor with the ball in his hand, and showing no surprise at the unexpected visit. "Will you have tea?"

He rose to his feet.

"I should be very glad of it, if it's hot," said Nikolay Vsyevolodovitch; "I'm wet through."

"It's hot, nearly boiling in fact," Kirillov declared delighted. "Sit down. You're muddy, but that's nothing; I'll mop up the floor later."

Nikolay Vsyevolodovitch sat down and emptied the cup he handed him almost at a gulp.

"Some more?" asked Kirillov.

"No, thank you."

Kirillov, who had not sat down till then, seated himself facing him, and inquired:

"Why have you come?"

"On business. Here, read this letter from Gaganov; do you remember, I talked to you about him in Petersburg."

Kirillov took the letter, read it, laid it on the table and looked at him expectantly.

"As you know, I met this Gaganov for the first time in my life a month ago, in Petersburg," Nikolay Vsyevolodovitch began to explain. "We came across each other two or three times in company with other people. Without making my acquaintance and without addressing me, he managed to be very insolent to me. I told you so at the time; but now for something you don't know. As he was leaving Petersburg before I did, he sent me a letter, not like this one, yet impertinent in the highest degree, and what was queer about it was that it contained no sort of explanation of why it was written. I answered him at once, also by letter, and said, quite frankly, that he was probably angry with me on account of the incident with his father four years ago in the club here, and that I for my part was prepared to make him every possible apology, seeing that my action was unintentional and was the result of illness. I begged him to consider and accept my apologies. He went away without answering, and now here I find him in a regular fury. Several things he has said about me in public have been repeated to me, absolutely abusive, and making astounding charges against me. Finally, to-day, I get this letter, a letter such as no one has ever had before, I should think, containing such expressions as 'the punch you got in your ugly face.' I came in the hope that you would not refuse to be my second."

"You said no one has ever had such a letter," observed Kirillov, "they may be sent in a rage. Such letters have been written more than once. Pushkin wrote to Hekern. All right, I'll come. Tell me how."

Nikolay Vsyevolodovitch explained that he wanted it to be to-morrow, and that he must begin by renewing his offers of apology, and even with the promise of another letter of apology, but on condition that Gaganov, on his side, should promise to send no more letters. The letter he had received he would regard as unwritten.

"Too much concession; he won't agree," said Kirillov.

"I've come first of all to find out whether you would consent to be the bearer of such terms."

"I'll take them. It's your affair. But he won't agree."

"I know he won't agree."

"He wants to fight. Say how you'll fight."

"The point is that I want the thing settled to-morrow. By nine o'clock in the morning you must be at his house. He'll listen, and won't agree, but will put you in communication with his second—let us say about eleven. You will arrange things with him, and let us all be on the spot by one or two o'clock. Please try to arrange that. The weapons, of course, will be pistols. And I particularly beg you to arrange to fix the barriers at ten paces apart; then you put each of us ten paces from the barrier, and at a given signal we approach. Each must go right up to his barrier, but you may fire before, on the way. I believe that's all."

"Ten paces between the barriers is very near," observed Kirillov.

"Well, twelve then, but not more. You understand that he wants to fight in earnest. Do you know how to load a pistol?"

"I do. I've got pistols. I'll give my word that you've never fired them. His second will give his word about his. There'll be two pairs of pistols, and we'll toss up, his or ours?"

"Excellent."

"Would you like to look at the pistols?"

"Very well."

Kirillov squatted on his heels before the trunk in the corner, which he had never yet unpacked, though things had been pulled out of it as required. He pulled out from the bottom a palm-wood box lined with red velvet, and from it took out a pair of smart and very expensive pistols.

"I've got everything, powder, bullets, cartridges. I've a revolver besides, wait."

He stooped down to the trunk again and took out a six-chambered American revolver.

"You've got weapons enough, and very good ones."

"Very, extremely."

Kirillov, who was poor, almost destitute, though he never noticed his poverty, was evidently proud of showing precious weapons, which he had certainly obtained with great sacrifice.

"You still have the same intentions?" Stavrogin asked after a moment's silence, and with a certain wariness.

"Yes," answered Kirillov shortly, guessing at once from his voice what he was asking about, and he began taking the weapons from the table.

"When?" Nikolay Vsyevolodovitch inquired still more cautiously, after a pause.

In the meantime Kirillov had put both the boxes back in his trunk, and sat down in his place again.

"That doesn't depend on me, as you know—when they tell me," he muttered, as though disliking the question; but at the same time with evident readiness to answer any other question. He kept his black, lustreless eyes fixed continually on Stavrogin with a calm but warm and kindly expression in them.

"I understand shooting oneself, of course," Nikolay Vsyevolodovitch began suddenly, frowning a little, after a dreamy silence that lasted three minutes. "I sometimes have thought of it myself, and then there always came a new idea: if one did something wicked, or, worse still, something shameful, that is, disgraceful, only very shameful and … ridiculous, such as people would remember for a thousand years and hold in scorn for a thousand years, and suddenly the thought comes: 'one blow in the temple and there would be nothing more.' One wouldn't care then for men and that they would hold one in scorn for a thousand years, would one?"

"You call that a new idea?" said Kirillov, after a moment's thought.

"I … didn't call it so, but when I thought it I felt it as a new idea."

"You 'felt the idea'?" observed Kirillov. "That's good. There are lots of ideas that are always there and yet suddenly become new. That's true. I see a great deal now as though it were for the first time."

"Suppose you had lived in the moon," Stavrogin interrupted, not listening, but pursuing his own thought, "and suppose there you had done all these nasty and ridiculous things.… You know from here for certain that they will laugh at you and hold you in scorn for a thousand years as long as the moon lasts. But now you are here, and looking at the moon from here. You don't care here for anything you've done there, and that the people there will hold you in scorn for a thousand years, do you?"

"I don't know," answered Kirillov. "I've not been in the moon," he added, without any irony, simply to state the fact.

"Whose baby was that just now?"

"The old woman's mother-in-law was here—no, daughter-in-law, it's all the same. Three days. She's lying ill with the baby, it cries a lot at night, it's the stomach. The mother sleeps, but the old woman picks it up; I play ball with it. The ball's from Hamburg. I bought it in Hamburg to throw it and catch it, it strengthens the spine. It's a girl."

"Are you fond of children?"

"I am," answered Kirillov, though rather indifferently.

"Then you're fond of life?"

"Yes, I'm fond of life! What of it?"

"Though you've made up your mind to shoot yourself."

"What of it? Why connect it? Life's one thing and that's another. Life exists, but death doesn't at all."

"You've begun to believe in a future eternal life?"

"No, not in a future eternal life, but in eternal life here. There are moments, you reach moments, and time suddenly stands still, and it will become eternal."

"You hope to reach such a moment?"

"Yes."

"That'll scarcely be possible in our time," Nikolay Vsyevolodovitch responded slowly and, as it were, dreamily; the two spoke without the slightest irony. "In the Apocalypse the angel swears that there will be no more time."

"I know. That's very true; distinct and exact. When all mankind attains happiness then there will be no more time, for there'll be no need of it, a very true thought."

"Where will they put it?"

"Nowhere. Time's not an object but an idea. It will be extinguished in the mind."

"The old commonplaces of philosophy, the same from the beginning of time," Stavrogin muttered with a kind of disdainful compassion.

"Always the same, always the same, from the beginning of time and never any other," Kirillov said with sparkling eyes, as though there were almost a triumph in that idea.

"You seem to be very happy, Kirillov."

"Yes, very happy," he answered, as though making the most ordinary reply.

"But you were distressed so lately, angry with Liputin."

"H'm … I'm not scolding now. I didn't know then that I was happy. Have you seen a leaf, a leaf from a tree?"

"Yes."

"I saw a yellow one lately, a little green. It was decayed at the edges. It was blown by the wind. When I was ten years old I used to shut my eyes in the winter on purpose and fancy a green leaf, bright, with veins on it, and the sun shining. I used to open my eyes and not believe them, because it was very nice, and I used to shut them again."

"What's that? An allegory?"

"N-no … why? I'm not speaking of an allegory, but of a leaf, only a leaf. The leaf is good. Everything's good."

"Everything?"

"Everything. Man is unhappy because he doesn't know he's happy. It's only that. That's all, that's all! If anyone finds out he'll become happy at once, that minute. That mother-in-law will die; but the baby will remain. It's all good. I discovered it all of a sudden."

"And if anyone dies of hunger, and if anyone insults and outrages the little girl, is that good?"

"Yes! And if anyone blows his brains out for the baby, that's good too. And if anyone doesn't, that's good too. It's all good, all. It's good for all those who know that it's all good. If they knew that it was good for them, it would be good for them, but as long as they don't know it's good for them, it will be bad for them. That's the whole idea, the whole of it."

"When did you find out you were so happy?"

"Last week, on Tuesday, no, Wednesday, for it was Wednesday by that time, in the night."

"By what reasoning?"

"I don't remember; I was walking about the room; never mind. I stopped my clock. It was thirty-seven minutes past two."

"As an emblem of the fact that there will be no more time?"

Kirillov was silent.

"They're bad because they don't know they're good. When they find out, they won't outrage a little girl. They'll find out that they're good and they'll all become good, every one of them."

"Here you've found it out, so have you become good then?"

"I am good."

"That I agree with, though," Stavrogin muttered, frowning.

"He who teaches that all are good will end the world."

"He who taught it was crucified."

"He will come, and his name will be the man-god."

"The god-man?"

"The man-god. That's the difference."

"Surely it wasn't you lighted the lamp under the ikon?"

"Yes, it was I lighted it."

"Did you do it believing?"

"The old woman likes to have the lamp and she hadn't time to do it to-day," muttered Kirillov.

"You don't say prayers yourself?"

"I pray to everything. You see the spider crawling on the wall, I look at it and thank it for crawling."

His eyes glowed again. He kept looking straight at Stavrogin with firm and unflinching expression. Stavrogin frowned and watched him disdainfully, but there was no mockery in his eyes.

"I'll bet that when I come next time you'll be believing in God too," he said, getting up and taking his hat.

"Why?" said Kirillov, getting up too.

"If you were to find out that you believe in God, then you'd believe in Him; but since you don't know that you believe in Him, then you don't believe in Him," laughed Nikolay Vsyevolodovitch.

"That's not right," Kirillov pondered, "you've distorted the idea. It's a flippant joke. Remember what you have meant in my life, Stavrogin."

"Good-bye, Kirillov."

"Come at night; when will you?"

"Why, haven't you forgotten about to-morrow?"

"Ach, I'd forgotten. Don't be uneasy. I won't oversleep. At nine o'clock. I know how to wake up when I want to. I go to bed saying 'seven o'clock,' and I wake up at seven o'clock, 'ten o'clock,' and I wake up at ten o'clock."

"You have remarkable powers," said Nikolay Vsyevolodovitch, looking at his pale face.

"I'll come and open the gate."

"Don't trouble, Shatov will open it for me."

"Ah, Shatov. Very well, good-bye."

VI

The door of the empty house in which Shatov was lodging was not closed; but, making his way into the passage, Stavrogin found himself in utter darkness, and began feeling with his hand for the stairs to the upper story. Suddenly a door opened upstairs and a light appeared. Shatov did not come out himself, but simply opened his door. When Nikolay Vsyevolodovitch was standing in the doorway of the room, he saw Shatov standing at the table in the corner, waiting expectantly.

"Will you receive me on business?" he queried from the doorway.

"Come in and sit down," answered Shatov. "Shut the door; stay, I'll shut it."

He locked the door, returned to the table, and sat down, facing Nikolay Vsyevolodovitch. He had grown thinner during that week, and now he seemed in a fever.

"You've been worrying me to death," he said, looking down, in a soft half-whisper. "Why didn't you come?"

"You were so sure I should come then?"

"Yes, stay, I have been delirious … perhaps I'm delirious now.… Stay a moment."

He got up and seized something that was lying on the uppermost of his three bookshelves. It was a revolver.

"One night, in delirium, I fancied that you were coming to kill me, and early next morning I spent my last farthing on buying a revolver from that good-for-nothing fellow Lyamshin; I did not mean to let you do it. Then I came to myself again … I've neither powder nor shot; it has been lying there on the shelf till now; wait a minute.…"

He got up and was opening the casement.

"Don't throw it away, why should you?" Nikolay Vsyevolodovitch checked him. "It's worth something. Besides, tomorrow people will begin saying that there are revolvers lying about under Shatov's window. Put it back, that's right; sit down. Tell me, why do you seem to be penitent for having thought I should come to kill you? I have not come now to be reconciled, but to talk of something necessary. Enlighten me to begin with. You didn't give me that blow because of my connection with your wife?"

"You know I didn't, yourself," said Shatov, looking down again.

"And not because you believed the stupid gossip about Darya Pavlovna?"

"No, no, of course not! It's nonsense! My sister told me from the very first …" Shatov said, harshly and impatiently, and even with a slight stamp of his foot.

"Then I guessed right and you too guessed right," Nikolay Vsyevolodovitch went on in a tranquil voice. "You are right. Marya Timofyevna Lebyadkin is my lawful wife, married to me four and a half years ago in Petersburg. I suppose the blow was on her account?"

Shatov, utterly astounded, listened in silence.

"I guessed, but did not believe it," he muttered at last, looking strangely at Stavrogin.

"And you struck me?"

Shatov flushed and muttered almost incoherently:

"Because of your fall … your lie. I didn't go up to you to punish you … I didn't know when I went up to you that I should strike you … I did it because you meant so much to me in my life … I …"

"I understand, I understand, spare your words. I am sorry you are feverish. I've come about a most urgent matter."

"I have been expecting you too long." Shatov seemed to be quivering all over, and he got up from his seat. "Say what you have to say … I'll speak too … later."

He sat down.

"What I have come about is nothing of that kind," began Nikolay Vsyevolodovitch, scrutinising him with curiosity. "Owing to certain circumstances I was forced this very day to choose such an hour to come and tell you that they may murder you."

Shatov looked wildly at him.

"I know that I may be in some danger," he said in measured tones, "but how can you have come to know of it?"

"Because I belong to them as you do, and am a member of their society, just as you are."

"You … you are a member of the society?"

"I see from your eyes that you were prepared for anything from me rather than that," said Nikolay Vsyevolodovitch, with a faint smile. "But, excuse me, you knew then that there would be an attempt on your life?"

"Nothing of the sort. And I don't think so now, in spite of your words, though … though there's no being sure of anything with these fools!" he cried suddenly in a fury, striking the table with his fist. "I'm not afraid of them! I've broken with them. That fellow's run here four times to tell me it was possible … but"—he looked at Stavrogin—"what do you know about it, exactly?"

"Don't be uneasy; I am not deceiving you," Nikolay Vsyevolodovitch went on, rather coldly, with the air of a man who is only fulfilling a duty. "You question me as to what I know. I know that you entered that society abroad, two years ago, at the time of the old organisation, just before you went to America, and I believe, just after our last conversation, about which you wrote so much to me in your letter from America. By the way, I must apologise for not having answered you by letter, but confined myself to …"

"To sending the money; wait a bit," Shatov interrupted, hurriedly pulling out a drawer in the table and taking from under some papers a rainbow-coloured note. "Here, take it, the hundred roubles you sent me; but for you I should have perished out there. I should have been a long time paying it back if it had not been for your mother. She made me a present of that note nine months ago, because I was so badly off after my illness. But, go on, please...."

He was breathless.

"In America you changed your views, and when you came back you wanted to resign. They gave you no answer, but charged you to take over a printing press here in Russia from someone, and to keep it till you handed it over to someone who would come from them for it. I don't know the details exactly, but I fancy that's the position in outline. You undertook it in the hope, or on the condition, that it would be the last task they would require of you, and that then they would release you altogether. Whether that is so or not, I learnt it, not from them, but quite by chance. But now for what I fancy you don't know; these gentry have no intention of parting with you."

"That's absurd!" cried Shatov. "I've told them honestly that I've cut myself off from them in everything. That is my right, the right to freedom of conscience and of thought.... I won't put up with it! There's no power which could ..."

"I say, don't shout," Nikolay Vsyevolodovitch said earnestly, checking him. "That Verhovensky is such a fellow that he may be listening to us now in your passage, perhaps, with his own ears or someone else's. Even that drunkard, Lebyadkin, was probably bound to keep an eye on you, and you on him, too, I dare say? You'd better tell me, has Verhovensky accepted your arguments now, or not?"

"He has. He has said that it can be done and that I have the right...."

"Well then, he's deceiving you. I know that even Kirillov, who scarcely belongs to them at all, has given them information about you. And they have lots of agents, even people who don't know that they're serving the society. They've always kept a watch on you. One of the things Pyotr Verhovensky came here for was to settle your business once for all, and he is fully authorised to do so, that is at the first good opportunity, to get rid of you, as a man who knows too much and might give them away. I repeat that this is certain, and allow me to add that they are, for some reason, convinced that you are a spy, and that if you haven't informed against them yet, you will. Is that true?"

Shatov made a wry face at hearing such a question asked in such a matter-of fact tone.

"If I were a spy, whom could I inform?" he said angrily, not giving a direct answer. "No, leave me alone, let me go to the devil!" he cried suddenly, catching again at his original idea, which agitated him violently. Apparently it affected him more deeply than the news of his own danger. "You, you, Stavrogin, how could you mix yourself up with such shameful, stupid, second-hand absurdity? You a member of the society? What an exploit for Stavrogin!" he cried suddenly, in despair.

He clasped his hands, as though nothing could be a bitterer and more inconsolable grief to him than such a discovery.

"Excuse me," said Nikolay Vsyevolodovitch, extremely surprised, "but you seem to look upon me as a sort of sun, and on yourself as an insect in comparison. I noticed that even from your letter in America."

"You ... you know.... Oh, let us drop me altogether," Shatov broke off suddenly, "and if you can explain anything about yourself explain it.... Answer my question!" he repeated feverishly.

"With pleasure. You ask how I could get into such a den? After what I have told you, I'm bound to be frank with you to some extent on the subject. You see, strictly speaking, I don't belong to the society at all, and I never have belonged to it, and I've much more right than you to leave them, because I never joined them. In fact, from the very beginning I told them that I was not one of them, and that if I've happened to help them it has simply been by accident as a man of leisure. I took some part in reorganising the society, on the new plan, but that was all. But now they've changed their views, and have made up their minds that it would be dangerous to let me go, and I believe I'm sentenced to death too."

"Oh, they do nothing but sentence to death, and all by means of sealed documents, signed by three men and a half. And you think they've any power!"

"You're partly right there and partly not," Stavrogin answered with the same indifference, almost listlessness. "There's no doubt that there's a great deal that's fanciful about it, as there always is in such cases: a handful magnifies its size and significance. To my thinking, if you will have it, the only one is Pyotr Verhovensky, and it's simply good-nature on his part to consider himself only an agent of the society. But the fundamental idea is no stupider than others of the sort. They are connected with the Internationale. They have succeeded in establishing agents in Russia, they have even hit on a rather original method, though it's only theoretical, of course. As for their intentions here, the movements of our Russian organisation are something so obscure and almost always unexpected that really they might try anything among us. Note that Verhovensky is an obstinate man."

"He's a bug, an ignoramus, a buffoon, who understands nothing in Russia!" cried Shatov spitefully.

"You know him very little. It's quite true that none of them understand much about Russia, but not much less than you and I do. Besides, Verhovensky is an enthusiast."

"Verhovensky an enthusiast?"

"Oh, yes. There is a point when he ceases to be a buffoon and becomes a madman. I beg you to remember your own expression: 'Do you know how powerful a single man may be?' Please don't laugh about it, he's quite capable of pulling a trigger. They are convinced that I am a spy too. As they don't know how to do things themselves, they're awfully fond of accusing people of being spies."

"But you're not afraid, are you?"

"N—no. I'm not very much afraid.... But your case is quite different. I warned you that you might anyway keep it in mind. To my thinking there's no reason to be offended in being threatened with danger by fools; their brains don't affect the question. They've raised their hand against better men than you or me. It's a quarter past eleven, though." He looked at his watch and got up from his chair. "I wanted to ask you one quite irrelevant question."

"For God's sake!" cried Shatov, rising impulsively from his seat.

"I beg your pardon?" Nikolay Vsyevolodovitch looked at him inquiringly.

"Ask it, ask your question for God's sake," Shatov repeated in indescribable excitement, "but on condition that I ask you a question too. I beseech you to allow me … I can't … ask your question!"

Stavrogin waited a moment and then began. "I've heard that you have some influence on Marya Timofyevna, and that she was fond of seeing you and hearing you talk. Is that so?"

"Yes … she used to listen …" said Shatov, confused.

"Within a day or two I intend to make a public announcement of our marriage here in the town."

"Is that possible?" Shatov whispered, almost with horror.

"I don't quite understand you. There's no sort of difficulty about it, witnesses to the marriage are here. Everything took place in Petersburg, perfectly legally and smoothly, and if it has not been made known till now, it is simply because the witnesses, Kirillov, Pyotr Verhovensky, and Lebyadkin (whom I now have the pleasure of claiming as a brother-in-law) promised to hold their tongues."

"I don't mean that … You speak so calmly … but good! Listen! You weren't forced into that marriage, were you?"

"No, no one forced me into it." Nikolay Vsyevolodovitch smiled at Shatov's importunate haste.

"And what's that talk she keeps up about her baby?" Shatov interposed disconnectedly, with feverish haste.

"She talks about her baby? Bah! I didn't know. It's the first time I've heard of it. She never had a baby and couldn't have had: Marya Timofyevna is a virgin."

"Ah! That's just what I thought! Listen!"

"What's the matter with you, Shatov?"

Shatov hid his face in his hands, turned away, but suddenly clutched Stavrogin by the shoulders.

"Do you know why, do you know why, anyway," he shouted, "why you did all this, and why you are resolved on such a punishment now!"

"Your question is clever and malignant, but I mean to surprise you too; I fancy I do know why I got married then, and why I am resolved on such a punishment now, as you express it."

"Let's leave that ... of that later. Put it off. Let's talk of the chief thing, the chief thing. I've been waiting two years for you."

"Yes?"

"I've waited too long for you. I've been thinking of you incessantly. You are the only man who could move ... I wrote to you about it from America."

"I remember your long letter very well."

"Too long to be read? No doubt; six sheets of notepaper. Don't speak! Don't speak! Tell me, can you spare me another ten minutes?... But now, this minute ... I have waited for you too long."

"Certainly, half an hour if you like, but not more, if that will suit you."

"And on condition, too," Shatov put in wrathfully, "that you take a different tone. Do you hear? I demand when I ought to entreat. Do you understand what it means to demand when one ought to entreat?"

"I understand that in that way you lift yourself above all ordinary considerations for the sake of loftier aims," said Nikolay Vsyevolodovitch with a faint smile. "I see with regret, too, that you're feverish."

"I beg you to treat me with respect, I insist on it!" shouted Shatov, "not my personality—I don't care a hang for that, but something else, just for this once. While I am talking ... we are two beings, and have come together in infinity ... for the last time in the world. Drop your tone, and speak like a human being! Speak, if only for once in your life with the voice of a man. I say it not for my sake but for yours. Do you understand that you ought to forgive me that blow in the face if only because I gave you the opportunity of realising your immense power.... Again you smile your disdainful, worldly smile! Oh, when will you understand me! Have done with being a snob! Understand that I insist on that. I insist on it, else I won't speak, I'm not going to for anything!"

His excitement was approaching frenzy. Nikolay Vsyevolodovitch frowned and seemed to become more on his guard.

"Since I have remained another half-hour with you when time is so precious," he pronounced earnestly and impressively, "you may rest assured that I mean to listen to you at least with interest ... and I am convinced that I shall hear from you much that is new."

He sat down on a chair.

"Sit down!" cried Shatov, and he sat down himself.

"Please remember," Stavrogin interposed once more, "that I was about to ask a real favour of you concerning Marya Timofyevna, of great importance for her, anyway...."

"What?" Shatov frowned suddenly with the air of a man who has just been interrupted at the most important moment, and who gazes at you unable to grasp the question.

"And you did not let me finish," Nikolay Vsyevolodovitch went on with a smile.

"Oh, nonsense, afterwards!" Shatov waved his hand disdainfully, grasping, at last, what he wanted, and passed at once to his principal theme.

VII

"Do you know," he began, with flashing eyes, almost menacingly, bending right forward in his chair, raising the forefinger of his right hand above him (obviously unaware that he was doing so), "do you know who are the only 'god-bearing' people on earth, destined to regenerate and save the world in the name of a new God, and to whom are given the keys of life and of the new world … Do you know which is that people and what is its name?"

"From your manner I am forced to conclude, and I think I may as well do so at once, that it is the Russian people."

"And you can laugh, oh, what a race!" Shatov burst out.

"Calm yourself, I beg of you; on the contrary, I was expecting something of the sort from you."

"You expected something of the sort? And don't you know those words yourself?"

"I know them very well. I see only too well what you're driving at. All your phrases, even the expression 'god-bearing people' is only a sequel to our talk two years ago, abroad, not long before you went to America.… At least, as far as I can recall it now."

"It's your phrase altogether, not mine. Your own, not simply the sequel of our conversation. 'Our' conversation it was not at all. It was a teacher uttering weighty words, and a pupil who was raised from the dead. I was that pupil and you were the teacher."

"But, if you remember, it was just after my words you joined their society, and only afterwards went away to America."

"Yes, and I wrote to you from America about that. I wrote to you about everything. Yes, I could not at once tear my bleeding heart from what I had grown into from childhood, on which had been lavished all the raptures of my hopes and all the tears of my hatred.… It is difficult to change gods. I did not believe you then, because I did not want to believe, I plunged for the last time into that sewer.… But the seed remained and grew up. Seriously, tell me seriously, didn't you read all my letter from America, perhaps you didn't read it at all?"

"I read three pages of it. The two first and the last. And I glanced through the middle as well. But I was always meaning …"

"Ah, never mind, drop it! Damn it!" cried Shatov, waving his hand. "If you've renounced those words about the people now, how could you have uttered them then?… That's what crushes me now."

"I wasn't joking with you then; in persuading you I was perhaps more concerned with myself than with you," Stavrogin pronounced enigmatically.

"You weren't joking! In America I was lying for three months on straw beside a hapless creature, and I learnt from him that at the very time when you were sowing the seed of God and the Fatherland in my heart, at that very time, perhaps during those very days, you were infecting the heart of that hapless creature, that maniac Kirillov, with poison … you confirmed false malignant ideas in him, and brought him to the verge of insanity.… Go, look at him now, he is your creation … you've seen him though."

"In the first place, I must observe that Kirillov himself told me that he is happy and that he's good. Your supposition that all this was going on at the same time is almost correct. But what of it? I repeat, I was not deceiving either of you."

"Are you an atheist? An atheist now?"

"Yes."

"And then?"

"Just as I was then."

"I wasn't asking you to treat me with respect when I began the conversation. With your intellect you might have understood that," Shatov muttered indignantly.

"I didn't get up at your first word, I didn't close the conversation, I didn't go away from you, but have been sitting here ever since submissively answering your questions and … cries, so it seems I have not been lacking in respect to you yet."

Shatov interrupted, waving his hand.

"Do you remember your expression that 'an atheist can't be a Russian,' that 'an atheist at once ceases to be a Russian'? Do you remember saying that?"

"Did I?" Nikolay Vsyevolodovitch questioned him back.

"You ask? You've forgotten? And yet that was one of the truest statements of the leading peculiarity of the Russian soul, which you divined. You can't have forgotten it! I will remind you of something else: you said then that 'a man who was not orthodox could not be Russian.'"

"I imagine that's a Slavophil idea."

"The Slavophils of to-day disown it. Nowadays, people have grown cleverer. But you went further: you believed that Roman Catholicism was not Christianity; you asserted that Rome proclaimed Christ subject to the third temptation of the devil. Announcing to all the world that Christ without an earthly kingdom cannot hold his ground upon earth, Catholicism by so doing proclaimed Antichrist and ruined the whole Western world. You pointed out that if France is in agonies now it's simply the fault of Catholicism, for she has rejected the iniquitous God of Rome and has not found a new one. That's what you could say then! I remember our conversations."

"If I believed, no doubt I should repeat it even now. I wasn't lying when I spoke as though I had faith," Nikolay Vsyevolodovitch pronounced very earnestly. "But I must tell you, this repetition of my ideas in the past makes a very disagreeable impression on me. Can't you leave off?"

"If you believe it?" repeated Shatov, paying not the slightest attention to this request. "But didn't you tell me that if it were mathematically proved to you that the truth excludes Christ, you'd prefer to stick to Christ rather than to the truth? Did you say that? Did you?"

"But allow me too at last to ask a question," said Nikolay Vsyevolodovitch, raising his voice. "What is the object of this irritable and ... malicious cross-examination?"

"This examination will be over for all eternity, and you will never hear it mentioned again."

"You keep insisting that we are outside the limits of time and space."

"Hold your tongue!" Shatov cried suddenly. "I am stupid and awkward, but let my name perish in ignominy! Let me repeat your leading idea.... Oh, only a dozen lines, only the conclusion."

"Repeat it, if it's only the conclusion...." Stavrogin made a movement to look at his watch, but restrained himself and did not look.

Shatov bent forward in his chair again and again held up his finger for a moment.

"Not a single nation," he went on, as though reading it line by line, still gazing menacingly at Stavrogin, "not a single nation has ever been founded on principles of science or reason. There has never been an example of it, except for a brief moment, through folly. Socialism is from its very nature bound to be atheism, seeing that it has from the very first proclaimed that it is an atheistic organisation of society, and that it intends to establish itself exclusively on the elements of science and reason. Science and reason have, from the beginning of time, played a secondary and subordinate part in the life of nations; so it will be till the end of time. Nations are built up and moved by another force which sways and dominates them, the origin of which is unknown and inexplicable: that force is the force of an insatiable desire to go on to the end, though at the same time it denies that end. It is the force of the persistent assertion of one's own existence, and a denial of death. It's the spirit of life, as the Scriptures call it, 'the river of living water,' the drying up of which is threatened in the Apocalypse. It's the æsthetic principle, as the philosophers call it, the ethical principle with which they identify it, 'the seeking for God,' as I call it more simply. The object of every national movement, in every people and at every period of its existence is only the seeking for its god, who must be its own god, and the faith in Him as the only true one. God is the synthetic personality of the whole people, taken from its beginning to its end. It has never happened that all, or even many, peoples have had one common god, but each has always had its own. It's a sign of the decay of nations when they begin to have gods in common. When gods begin to be common to several nations the gods are dying and the faith in them, together with the nations themselves. The stronger a people the more individual their God. There never has been a nation without a religion, that is, without an idea of good and evil. Every people has its own conception of good and evil, and its own good and evil. When the same conceptions of good and evil become prevalent in several nations, then these nations are dying, and then the very distinction between good and evil is beginning to disappear. Reason has never had the power to define good and evil, or even to distinguish between good and evil, even approximately; on the contrary, it has always mixed them up in a disgraceful and pitiful way; science has even given the solution by the fist. This is particularly characteristic of the half-truths of science, the most terrible scourge of humanity, unknown till this century, and worse than plague, famine, or war. A half-truth is a despot … such as has never been in the world before. A despot that has its priests and its slaves, a despot to whom all do homage with love and superstition hitherto inconceivable, before which science itself trembles and cringes in a shameful way. These are your own words, Stavrogin, all except that about the half-truth; that's my own because I am myself a case of half-knowledge, and that's why I hate it particularly. I haven't altered anything of your ideas or even of your words, not a syllable."

"I don't agree that you've not altered anything," Stavrogin observed cautiously. "You accepted them with ardour, and in your ardour have transformed them unconsciously. The very fact that you reduce God to a simple attribute of nationality …"

He suddenly began watching Shatov with intense and peculiar attention, not so much his words as himself.

"I reduce God to the attribute of nationality?" cried Shatov. "On the contrary, I raise the people to God. And has it ever been otherwise? The people is the body of God. Every people is only a people so long as it has its own god and excludes all other gods on earth irreconcilably; so long as it believes that by its god it will conquer and drive out of the world all other gods. Such, from the beginning of time, has been the belief of all great nations, all, anyway, who have been specially remarkable, all who have been leaders of humanity. There is no going against facts. The Jews lived only to await the coming of the true God and left the world the true God. The Greeks deified nature and bequeathed the world their religion, that is, philosophy and art. Rome deified the people in the State, and bequeathed the idea of the State to the nations. France throughout her long history was only the incarnation and development of the Roman god, and if they have at last flung their Roman god into the abyss and plunged into atheism, which, for the time being, they call socialism, it is solely because socialism is, anyway, healthier than Roman Catholicism. If a great people does not believe that the truth is only to be found in itself alone (in itself alone and in it exclusively); if it does not believe that it alone is fit and destined to raise up and save all the rest by its truth, it would at once sink into being ethnographical material, and not a great people. A really great people can never accept a secondary part in the history of Humanity, nor even one of the first, but will have the first part. A nation which loses this belief ceases to be a nation. But there is only one truth, and therefore only a single one out of the nations can have the true God, even though other nations may have great gods of their own. Only one nation is 'god-bearing,' that's the Russian people, and … and … and can you think me such a fool, Stavrogin," he yelled frantically all at once, "that I can't distinguish whether my words at this moment are the rotten old commonplaces that have been ground out in all the Slavophil mills in Moscow, or a perfectly new saying, the last word, the sole word of renewal and resurrection, and … and what do I care for your laughter at this minute! What do I care that you utterly, utterly fail to understand me, not a word, not a sound! Oh, how I despise your haughty laughter and your look at this minute!"

He jumped up from his seat; there was positively foam on his lips.

"On the contrary Shatov, on the contrary," Stavrogin began with extraordinary earnestness and self-control, still keeping his seat, "on the contrary, your fervent words have revived many extremely powerful recollections in me. In your words I recognise my own mood two years ago, and now I will not tell you, as I did just now, that you have exaggerated my ideas. I believe, indeed, that they were even more exceptional, even more independent, and I assure you for the third time that I should be very glad to confirm all that you've said just now, every syllable of it, but ..."

"But you want a hare?"

"Wh-a-t?"

"Your own nasty expression," Shatov laughed spitefully, sitting down again. "To cook your hare you must first catch it, to believe in God you must first have a god. You used to say that in Petersburg, I'm told, like Nozdryov, who tried to catch a hare by his hind legs."

"No, what he did was to boast he'd caught him. By the way, allow me to trouble you with a question though, for indeed I think I have the right to one now. Tell me, have you caught your hare?"

"Don't dare to ask me in such words! Ask differently, quite differently." Shatov suddenly began trembling all over.

"Certainly I'll ask differently." Nikolay Vsyevolodovitch looked coldly at him. "I only wanted to know, do you believe in God, yourself?"

"I believe in Russia.... I believe in her orthodoxy.... I believe in the body of Christ.... I believe that the new advent will take place in Russia.... I believe ..." Shatov muttered frantically.

"And in God? In God?"

"I ... I will believe in God."

Not one muscle moved in Stavrogin's face. Shatov looked passionately and defiantly at him, as though he would have scorched him with his eyes.

"I haven't told you that I don't believe," he cried at last. "I will only have you know that I am a luckless, tedious book, and nothing more so far, so far.... But confound me! We're discussing you not me.... I'm a man of no talent, and can only give my blood, nothing more, like every man without talent; never mind my blood either! I'm talking about you. I've been waiting here two years for you.... Here I've been dancing about in my nakedness before you for the last half-hour. You, only you can raise that flag!..."

He broke off, and sat as though in despair, with his elbows on the table and his head in his hands.

"I merely mention it as something queer," Stavrogin interrupted suddenly. "Every one for some inexplicable reason keeps foisting a flag upon me. Pyotr Verhovensky, too, is convinced that I might 'raise his flag,' that's how his words were repeated to me, anyway. He has taken it into his head that I'm capable of playing the part of Stenka Razin for them, 'from my extraordinary aptitude for crime,' his saying too."

"What?" cried Shatov, "'from your extraordinary aptitude for crime'?"

"Just so."

"H'm! And is it true?" he asked, with an angry smile. "Is it true that when you were in Petersburg you belonged to a secret society for practising beastly sensuality? Is it true that you could give lessons to the Marquis de Sade? Is it true that you decoyed and corrupted children? Speak, don't dare to lie," he cried, beside himself. "Nikolay Stavrogin cannot lie to Shatov, who struck him in the face. Tell me everything, and if it's true I'll kill you, here, on the spot!"

"I did talk like that, but it was not I who outraged children," Stavrogin brought out, after a silence that lasted too long. He turned pale and his eyes gleamed.

"But you talked like that," Shatov went on imperiously, keeping his flashing eyes fastened upon him. "Is it true that you declared that you saw no distinction in beauty between some brutal obscene action and any great exploit, even the sacrifice of life for the good of humanity? Is it true that you have found identical beauty, equal enjoyment, in both extremes?"

"It's impossible to answer like this.... I won't answer," muttered Stavrogin, who might well have got up and gone away, but who did not get up and go away.

"I don't know either why evil is hateful and good is beautiful, but I know why the sense of that distinction is effaced and lost in people like the Stavrogins," Shatov persisted, trembling all over. "Do you know why you made that base and shameful marriage? Simply because the shame and senselessness of it reached the pitch of genius! Oh, you are not one of those who linger on the brink. You fly head foremost. You married from a passion for martyrdom, from a craving for remorse, through moral sensuality. It was a laceration of the nerves ... Defiance of common sense was too tempting. Stavrogin and a wretched, half-witted, crippled beggar! When you bit the governor's ear did you feel sensual pleasure? Did you? You idle, loafing, little snob. Did you?"

"You're a psychologist," said Stavrogin, turning paler and paler, "though you're partly mistaken as to the reasons of my marriage. But who can have given you all this information?" he asked, smiling, with an effort. "Was it Kirillov? But he had nothing to do with it."

"You turn pale."

"But what is it you want?" Nikolay Vsyevolodovitch asked, raising his voice at last. "I've been sitting under your lash for the last half-hour, and you might at least let me go civilly. Unless you really have some reasonable object in treating me like this."

"Reasonable object?"

"Of course, you're in duty bound, anyway, to let me know your object. I've been expecting you to do so all the time, but you've shown me nothing so far but frenzied spite. I beg you to open the gate for me."

He got up from the chair. Shatov rushed frantically after him. "Kiss the earth, water it with your tears, pray for forgiveness," he cried, clutching him by the shoulder.

"I didn't kill you ... that morning, though ... I drew back my hands ..." Stavrogin brought out almost with anguish, keeping his eyes on the ground.

"Speak out! Speak out! You came to warn me of danger. You have let me speak. You mean to-morrow to announce your marriage publicly.... Do you suppose I don't see from your face that some new menacing idea is dominating you?... Stavrogin, why am I condemned to believe in you through all eternity? Could I speak like this to anyone else? I have modesty, but I am not ashamed of my nakedness because it's Stavrogin I am speaking to. I was not afraid of caricaturing a grand idea by handling it because Stavrogin was listening to me.... Shan't I kiss your footprints when you've gone? I can't tear you out of my heart, Nikolay Stavrogin!"

"I'm sorry I can't feel affection for you, Shatov," Stavrogin replied coldly.

"I know you can't, and I know you are not lying. Listen. I can set it all right. I can 'catch your hare' for you."

Stavrogin did not speak.

"You're an atheist because you're a snob, a snob of the snobs. You've lost the distinction between good and evil because you've lost touch with your own people. A new generation is coming, straight from the heart of the people, and you will know nothing of it, neither you nor the Verhovenskys, father or son; nor I, for I'm a snob too—I, the son of your serf and lackey, Pashka.... Listen. Attain to God by work; it all lies in that; or disappear like rotten mildew. Attain to Him by work."

"God by work? What sort of work?"

"Peasants' work. Go, give up all your wealth.... Ah! you laugh, you're afraid of some trick?"

But Stavrogin was not laughing.

"You suppose that one may attain to God by work, and by peasants' work," he repeated, reflecting as though he had really come across something new and serious which was worth considering. "By the way," he passed suddenly to a new idea, "you reminded me just now. Do you know that I'm not rich at all, that I've nothing to give up? I'm scarcely in a position even to provide for Marya Timofyevna's future.... Another thing: I came to ask you if it would be possible for you to remain near Marya Timofyevna in the future, as you are the only person who has some influence over her poor brain. I say this so as to be prepared for anything."

"All right, all right. You're speaking of Marya Timofyevna," said Shatov, waving one hand, while he held a candle in the other. "All right. Afterwards, of course.... Listen. Go to Tikhon."

"To whom?"

"To Tikhon, who used to be a bishop. He lives retired now, on account of illness, here in the town, in the Bogorodsky monastery."

"What do you mean?"

"Nothing. People go and see him. You go. What is it to you? What is it to you?"

"It's the first time I've heard of him, and … I've never seen anything of that sort of people. Thank you, I'll go."

"This way."

Shatov lighted him down the stairs. "Go along." He flung open the gate into the street.

"I shan't come to you any more, Shatov," said Stavrogin quietly as he stepped through the gateway.

The darkness and the rain continued as before.

CHAPTER II. NIGHT (continued)

I

HE WALKED THE LENGTH of Bogoyavlensky Street. At last the road began to go downhill; his feet slipped in the mud and suddenly there lay open before him a wide, misty, as it were empty expanse—the river. The houses were replaced by hovels; the street was lost in a multitude of irregular little alleys.

Nikolay Vsyevolodovitch was a long while making his way between the fences, keeping close to the river bank, but finding his way confidently, and scarcely giving it a thought indeed. He was absorbed in something quite different, and looked round with surprise when suddenly, waking up from a profound reverie, he found himself almost in the middle of one long, wet, floating bridge.

There was not a soul to be seen, so that it seemed strange to him when suddenly, almost at his elbow, he heard a deferentially familiar, but rather pleasant, voice, with a suave intonation, such as is affected by our over-refined tradespeople or befrizzled young shop assistants.

"Will you kindly allow me, sir, to share your umbrella?"

There actually was a figure that crept under his umbrella, or tried to appear to do so. The tramp was walking beside him, almost "feeling his elbow," as the soldiers say. Slackening his pace, Nikolay Vsyevolodovitch bent down to look more closely, as far as he could, in the darkness. It was a short man, and seemed like an artisan who had been drinking; he was shabbily and scantily dressed; a cloth cap, soaked by the rain and with the brim half torn off, perched on his shaggy, curly head. He looked a thin, vigorous, swarthy man with dark hair; his eyes were large and must have been black, with a hard glitter and a yellow tinge in them, like a gipsy's; that could be divined even in the darkness. He was about forty, and was not drunk.

"Do you know me?" asked Nikolay Vsyevolodovitch. "Mr. Stavrogin, Nikolay Vsyevolodovitch. You were pointed out to me at the station, when the train stopped last Sunday, though I had heard enough of you beforehand."

"From Pyotr Stepanovitch? Are you … Fedka the convict?"

"I was christened Fyodor Fyodorovitch. My mother is living to this day in these parts; she's an old woman, and grows more and more bent every day. She prays to God for me, day and night, so that she doesn't waste her old age lying on the stove."

"You escaped from prison?"

"I've had a change of luck. I gave up books and bells and church-going because I'd a life sentence, so that I had a very long time to finish my term."

"What are you doing here?"

"Well, I do what I can. My uncle, too, died last week in prison here. He was there for false coin, so I threw two dozen stones at the dogs by way of memorial. That's all I've been doing so far. Moreover Pyotr Stepanovitch gives me hopes of a passport, and a merchant's one, too, to go all over Russia, so I'm waiting on his kindness. 'Because,' says he, 'my papa lost you at cards at the English club, and I,' says he, 'find that inhumanity unjust.' You might have the kindness to give me three roubles, sir, for a glass to warm myself."

"So you've been spying on me. I don't like that. By whose orders?"

"As to orders, it's nothing of the sort; it's simply that I knew of your benevolence, which is known to all the world. All we get, as you know, is an armful of hay, or a prod with a fork. Last Friday I filled myself as full of pie as Martin did of soap; since then I didn't eat one day, and the day after I fasted, and on the third I'd nothing again. I've had my fill of water from the river. I'm breeding fish in my belly.... So won't your honour give me something? I've a sweetheart expecting me not far from here, but I daren't show myself to her without money."

"What did Pyotr Stepanovitch promise you from me?"

"He didn't exactly promise anything, but only said that I might be of use to your honour if my luck turns out good, but how exactly he didn't explain; for Pyotr Stepanovitch wants to see if I have the patience of a Cossack, and feels no sort of confidence in me."

"Why?"

"Pyotr Stepanovitch is an astronomer, and has learnt all God's planets, but even he may be criticised. I stand before you, sir, as before God, because I have heard so much about you. Pyotr Stepanovitch is one thing, but you, sir, maybe, are something else. When he's said of a man he's a scoundrel, he knows nothing more about him except that he's a scoundrel. Or if he's said he's a fool, then that man has no calling with him except that of fool. But I may be a fool Tuesday and Wednesday, and on Thursday wiser than he. Here now he knows about me that I'm awfully sick to get a passport, for there's no getting on in Russia without papers—so he thinks that he's snared my soul. I tell you, sir, life's a very easy business for Pyotr Stepanovitch, for he fancies a man to be this and that, and goes on as though he really was. And, what's more, he's beastly stingy. It's his notion that, apart from him, I daren't trouble you, but I stand before you, sir, as before God. This is the fourth night I've been waiting for your honour on this bridge, to show that I can find my own way on the quiet, without him. I'd better bow to a boot, thinks I, than to a peasant's shoe."

"And who told you that I was going to cross the bridge at night?"

"Well, that, I'll own, came out by chance, most through Captain Lebyadkin's foolishness, because he can't keep anything to himself.... So that three roubles from your honour would pay me for the weary time I've had these three days and nights. And the clothes I've had soaked, I feel that too much to speak of it."

"I'm going to the left; you'll go to the right. Here's the end of the bridge. Listen, Fyodor; I like people to understand what I say, once for all. I won't give you a farthing. Don't meet me in future on the bridge or anywhere. I've no need of you, and never shall have, and if you don't obey, I'll tie you and take you to the police. March!"

"Eh-heh! Fling me something for my company, anyhow. I've cheered you on your way."

"Be off!"

"But do you know the way here? There are all sorts of turnings.... I could guide you; for this town is for all the world as though the devil carried it in his basket and dropped it in bits here and there."

"I'll tie you up!" said Nikolay Vsyevolodovitch, turning upon him menacingly.

"Perhaps you'll change your mind, sir; it's easy to ill-treat the helpless."

"Well, I see you can rely on yourself!"

"I rely upon you, sir, and not very much on myself...."

"I've no need of you at all. I've told you so already."

"But I have need, that's how it is! I shall wait for you on the way back. There's nothing for it."

"I give you my word of honour if I meet you I'll tie you up."

"Well, I'll get a belt ready for you to tie me with. A lucky journey to you, sir. You kept the helpless snug under your umbrella. For that alone I'll be grateful to you to my dying day." He fell behind. Nikolay Vsyevolodovitch walked on to his destination, feeling disturbed. This man who had dropped from the sky was absolutely convinced that he was indispensable to him, Stavrogin, and was in insolent haste to tell him so. He was being treated unceremoniously all round. But it was possible, too, that the tramp had not been altogether lying, and had tried to force his services upon him on his own initiative, without Pyotr Stepanovitch's knowledge, and that would be more curious still.

II

The house which Nikolay Vsyevolodovitch had reached stood alone in a deserted lane between fences, beyond which market gardens stretched, at the very end of the town. It was a very solitary little wooden house, which was only just built and not yet weather-boarded. In one of the little windows the shutters were not yet closed, and there was a candle standing on the window-ledge, evidently as a signal to the late guest who was expected that night. Thirty paces away Stavrogin made out on the doorstep the figure of a tall man, evidently the master of the house, who had come out to stare impatiently up the road. He heard his voice, too, impatient and, as it were, timid.

"Is that you? You?"

"Yes," responded Nikolay Vsyevolodovitch, but not till he had mounted the steps and was folding up his umbrella.

"At last, sir." Captain Lebyadkin, for it was he, ran fussily to and fro. "Let me take your umbrella, please. It's very wet; I'll open it on the floor here, in the corner. Please walk in. Please walk in."

The door was open from the passage into a room that was lighted by two candles.

"If it had not been for your promise that you would certainly come, I should have given up expecting you."

"A quarter to one," said Nikolay Vsyevolodovitch, looking at his watch, as he went into the room.

"And in this rain; and such an interesting distance. I've no clock ... and there are nothing but market-gardens round me ... so that you fall behind the times. Not that I murmur exactly; for I dare not, I dare not, but only because I've been devoured with impatience all the week ... to have things settled at last."

"How so?"

"To hear my fate, Nikolay Vsyevolodovitch. Please sit down."

He bowed, pointing to a seat by the table, before the sofa.

Nikolay Vsyevolodovitch looked round. The room was tiny and low-pitched. The furniture consisted only of the most essential articles, plain wooden chairs and a sofa, also newly made without covering or cushions. There were two tables of limewood; one by the sofa, and the other in the corner was covered with a table-cloth, laid with things over which a clean table-napkin had been thrown. And, indeed, the whole room was obviously kept extremely clean.

Captain Lebyadkin had not been drunk for eight days. His face looked bloated and yellow. His eyes looked uneasy, inquisitive, and obviously bewildered. It was only too evident that he did not know what tone he could adopt, and what line it would be most advantageous for him to take.

"Here," he indicated his surroundings, "I live like Zossima. Sobriety, solitude, and poverty—the vow of the knights of old."

"You imagine that the knights of old took such vows?"

"Perhaps I'm mistaken. Alas! I have no culture. I've ruined all. Believe me, Nikolay Vsyevolodovitch, here first I have recovered from shameful propensities—not a glass nor a drop! I have a home, and for six days past I have experienced a conscience at ease. Even the walls smell of resin and remind me of nature. And what have I been; what was I?

'At night without a bed I wander

And my tongue put out by day ...'

to use the words of a poet of genius. But you're wet through.... Wouldn't you like some tea?"

"Don't trouble."

"The samovar has been boiling since eight o'clock, but it went out at last like everything in this world. The sun, too, they say, will go out in its turn. But if you like I'll get up the samovar. Agafya is not asleep."

"Tell me, Marya Timofyevna ..."

"She's here, here," Lebyadkin replied at once, in a whisper. "Would you like to have a look at her?" He pointed to the closed door to the next room.

"She's not asleep?"

"Oh, no, no. How could she be? On the contrary, she's been expecting you all the evening, and as soon as she heard you were coming she began making her toilet."

He was just twisting his mouth into a jocose smile, but he instantly checked himself.

"How is she, on the whole?" asked Nikolay Vsyevolodovitch, frowning.

"On the whole? You know that yourself, sir." He shrugged his shoulders commiseratingly. "But just now ... just now she's telling her fortune with cards...."

"Very good. Later on. First of all I must finish with you."

Nikolay Vsyevolodovitch settled himself in a chair. The captain did not venture to sit down on the sofa, but at once moved up another chair for himself, and bent forward to listen, in a tremor of expectation.

"What have you got there under the table-cloth?" asked Nikolay Vsyevolodovitch, suddenly noticing it.

"That?" said Lebyadkin, turning towards it also. "That's from your generosity, by way of house-warming, so to say; considering also the length of the walk, and your natural fatigue," he sniggered ingratiatingly. Then he got up on tiptoe, and respectfully and carefully lifted the table-cloth from the table in the corner. Under it was seen a slight meal: ham, veal, sardines, cheese, a little green decanter, and a long bottle of Bordeaux. Everything had been laid neatly, expertly, and almost daintily.

"Was that your effort?"

"Yes, sir. Ever since yesterday I've done my best, and all to do you honour.... Marya Timofyevna doesn't trouble herself, as you know, on that score. And what's more its all from your liberality, your own providing, as you're the master of the house and not I, and I'm only, so to say, your agent. All the same, all the same, Nikolay Vsyevolodovitch, all the same, in spirit, I'm independent! Don't take away from me this last possession!" he finished up pathetically.

"H'm! You might sit down again."

"Gra-a-teful, grateful, and independent." He sat down. "Ah, Nikolay Vsyevolodovitch, so much has been fermenting in this heart that I have not known how to wait for your coming. Now you will decide my fate, and ... that unhappy creature's, and then ... shall I pour out all I feel to you as I used to in old days, four years ago? You deigned to listen to me then, you read my verses.... They might call me your Falstaff from Shakespeare in those days, but you meant so much in my life! I have great terrors now, and it's only to you I look for counsel and light. Pyotr Stepanovitch is treating me abominably!"

Nikolay Vsyevolodovitch listened with interest, and looked at him attentively. It was evident that though Captain Lebyadkin had left off drinking he was far from being in a harmonious state of mind. Drunkards of many years' standing, like Lebyadkin, often show traces of incoherence, of mental cloudiness, of something, as it were, damaged, and crazy, though they may deceive, cheat, and swindle, almost as well as anybody if occasion arises.

"I see that you haven't changed a bit in these four years and more, captain," said Nikolay Vsyevolodovitch, somewhat more amiably. "It seems, in fact, as though the second half of a man's life is usually made up of nothing but the habits he has accumulated during the first half."

"Grand words! You solve the riddle of life!" said the captain, half cunningly, half in genuine and unfeigned admiration, for he was a great lover of words. "Of all your sayings, Nikolay Vsyevolodovitch, I remember one thing above all; you were in Petersburg when you said it: 'One must really be a great man to be able to make a stand even against common sense.' That was it."

"Yes, and a fool as well."

"A fool as well, maybe. But you've been scattering clever sayings all your life, while they.... Imagine Liputin, imagine Pyotr Stepanovitch saying anything like that! Oh, how cruelly Pyotr Stepanovitch has treated me!"

"But how about yourself, captain? What can you say of your behaviour?"

"Drunkenness, and the multitude of my enemies. But now that's all over, all over, and I have new skin, like a snake. Do you know, Nikolay Vsyevolodovitch, I am making my will; in fact, I've made it already?"

"That's interesting. What are you leaving, and to whom?"

"To my fatherland, to humanity, and to the students. Nikolay Vsyevolodovitch, I read in the paper the biography of an American. He left all his vast fortune to factories and to the exact sciences, and his skeleton to the students of the academy there, and his skin to be made into a drum, so that the American national hymn might be beaten upon it day and night. Alas! we are pigmies in mind compared with the soaring thought of the States of North America. Russia is the play of nature but not of mind. If I were to try leaving my skin for a drum, for instance, to the Akmolinsky infantry regiment, in which I had the honour of beginning my service, on condition of beating the Russian national hymn upon it every day, in face of the regiment, they'd take it for liberalism and prohibit my skin ... and so I confine myself to the students. I want to leave my skeleton to the academy, but on the condition though, on the condition that a label should be stuck on the forehead forever and ever, with the words: 'A repentant free-thinker.' There now!"

The captain spoke excitedly, and genuinely believed, of course, that there was something fine in the American will, but he was cunning too, and very anxious to entertain Nikolay Vsyevolodovitch, with whom he had played the part of a buffoon for a long time in the past. But the latter did not even smile, on the contrary, he asked, as it were, suspiciously:

"So you intend to publish your will in your lifetime and get rewarded for it?"

"And what if I do, Nikolay Vsyevolodovitch? What if I do?" said Lebyadkin, watching him carefully. "What sort of luck have I had? I've given up writing poetry, and at one time even you were amused by my verses, Nikolay Vsyevolodovitch. Do you remember our reading them over a bottle? But it's all over with my pen. I've written only one poem, like Gogol's 'The Last Story.' Do you remember he proclaimed to Russia that it broke spontaneously from his bosom? It's the same with me; I've sung my last and it's over."

"What sort of poem?"

"'In case she were to break her leg.'"

"Wha-a-t?"

That was all the captain was waiting for. He had an unbounded admiration for his own poems, but, through a certain cunning duplicity, he was pleased, too, that Nikolay Vsyevolodovitch always made merry over his poems, and sometimes laughed at them immoderately. In this way he killed two birds with one stone, satisfying at once his poetical aspirations and his desire to be of service; but now he had a third special and very ticklish object in view. Bringing his verses on the scene, the captain thought to exculpate himself on one point about which, for some reason, he always felt himself most apprehensive, and most guilty.

"'In case of her breaking her leg.' That is, of her riding on horseback. It's a fantasy, Nikolay Vsyevolodovitch, a wild fancy, but the fancy of a poet. One day I was struck by meeting a lady on horseback, and asked myself the vital question, 'What would happen then?' That is, in case of accident. All her followers turn away, all her suitors are gone. A pretty kettle of fish. Only the poet remains faithful, with his heart shattered in his breast, Nikolay Vsyevolodovitch. Even a louse may be in love, and is not forbidden by law. And yet the lady was offended by the letter and the verses. I'm told that even you were angry. Were you? I wouldn't believe in anything so grievous. Whom could I harm simply by imagination? Besides, I swear on my honour, Liputin kept saying, 'Send it, send it,' every man, however humble, has a right to send a letter! And so I sent it."

"You offered yourself as a suitor, I understand."

"Enemies, enemies, enemies!"

"Repeat the verses," said Nikolay Vsyevolodovitch sternly.

"Ravings, ravings, more than anything."

However, he drew himself up, stretched out his hand, and began:

"With broken limbs my beauteous queen

Is twice as charming as before,

And, deep in love as I have been,

To-day I love her even more."

"Come, that's enough," said Nikolay Vsyevolodovitch, with a wave of his hand.

"I dream of Petersburg," cried Lebyadkin, passing quickly to another subject, as though there had been no mention of verses. "I dream of regeneration.... Benefactor! May I reckon that you won't refuse the means for the journey? I've been waiting for you all the week as my sunshine."

"I'll do nothing of the sort. I've scarcely any money left. And why should I give you money?"

Nikolay Vsyevolodovitch seemed suddenly angry. Dryly and briefly he recapitulated all the captain's misdeeds; his drunkenness, his lying, his squandering of the money meant for Marya Timofyevna, his having taken her from the nunnery, his insolent letters threatening to publish the secret, the way he had behaved about Darya Pavlovna, and so on, and so on. The captain heaved, gesticulated, began to reply, but every time Nikolay Vsyevolodovitch stopped him peremptorily.

"And listen," he observed at last, "you keep writing about 'family disgrace.' What disgrace is it to you that your sister is the lawful wife of a Stavrogin?"

"But marriage in secret, Nikolay Vsyevolodovitch—a fatal secret. I receive money from you, and I'm suddenly asked the question, 'What's that money for?' My hands are tied; I cannot answer to the detriment of my sister, to the detriment of the family honour."

The captain raised his voice. He liked that subject and reckoned boldly upon it. Alas! he did not realise what a blow was in store for him.

Calmly and exactly, as though he were speaking of the most everyday arrangement, Nikolay Vsyevolodovitch informed him that in a few days, perhaps even to-morrow or the day after, he intended to make his marriage known everywhere, "to the police as well as to local society." And so the question of family honour would be settled once for all, and with it the question of subsidy. The captain's eyes were ready to drop out of his head; he positively could not take it in. It had to be explained to him.

"But she is ... crazy."

"I shall make suitable arrangements."

"But ... how about your mother?"

"Well, she must do as she likes."

"But will you take your wife to your house?"

"Perhaps so. But that is absolutely nothing to do with you and no concern of yours."

"No concern of mine!" cried the captain. "What about me then?"

"Well, certainly you won't come into my house."

"But, you know, I'm a relation."

"One does one's best to escape from such relations. Why should I go on giving you money then? Judge for yourself."

"Nikolay Vsyevolodovitch, Nikolay Vsyevolodovitch, this is impossible. You will think better of it, perhaps? You don't want to lay hands upon.... What will people think? What will the world say?"

"Much I care for your world. I married your sister when the fancy took me, after a drunken dinner, for a bet, and now I'll make it public ... since that amuses me now."

He said this with a peculiar irritability, so that Lebyadkin began with horror to believe him.

"But me, me? What about me? I'm what matters most!... Perhaps you're joking, Nikolay Vsyevolodovitch?"

"No, I'm not joking."

"As you will, Nikolay Vsyevolodovitch, but I don't believe you.... Then I'll take proceedings."

"You're fearfully stupid, captain."

"Maybe, but this is all that's left me," said the captain, losing his head completely. "In old days we used to get free quarters, anyway, for the work she did in the 'corners.' But what will happen now if you throw me over altogether?"

"But you want to go to Petersburg to try a new career. By the way, is it true what I hear, that you mean to go and give information, in the hope of obtaining a pardon, by betraying all the others?"

The captain stood gaping with wide-open eyes, and made no answer.

"Listen, captain," Stavrogin began suddenly, with great earnestness, bending down to the table. Until then he had been talking, as it were, ambiguously, so that Lebyadkin, who had wide experience in playing the part of buffoon, was up to the last moment a trifle uncertain whether his patron were really angry or simply putting it on; whether he really had the wild intention of making his marriage public, or whether he were only playing. Now Nikolay Vsyevolodovitch's stern expression was so convincing that a shiver ran down the captain's back.

"Listen, and tell the truth, Lebyadkin. Have you betrayed anything yet, or not? Have you succeeded in doing anything really? Have you sent a letter to somebody in your foolishness?"

"No, I haven't ... and I haven't thought of doing it," said the captain, looking fixedly at him.

"That's a lie, that you haven't thought of doing it. That's what you're asking to go to Petersburg for. If you haven't written, have you blabbed to anybody here? Speak the truth. I've heard something."

“When I was drunk, to Liputin. Liputin’s a traitor. I opened my heart to him,” whispered the poor captain.

“That’s all very well, but there’s no need to be an ass. If you had an idea you should have kept it to yourself. Sensible people hold their tongues nowadays; they don’t go chattering.”

“Nikolay Vsyevolodovitch!” said the captain, quaking. “You’ve had nothing to do with it yourself; it’s not you I’ve ...”

“Yes. You wouldn’t have ventured to kill the goose that laid your golden eggs.”

“Judge for yourself, Nikolay Vsyevolodovitch, judge for yourself,” and, in despair, with tears, the captain began hurriedly relating the story of his life for the last four years. It was the most stupid story of a fool, drawn into matters that did not concern him, and in his drunkenness and debauchery unable, till the last minute, to grasp their importance. He said that before he left Petersburg ‘he had been drawn in, at first simply through friendship, like a regular student, although he wasn’t a student,’ and knowing nothing about it, ‘without being guilty of anything,’ he had scattered various papers on staircases, left them by dozens at doors, on bell-handles, had thrust them in as though they were newspapers, taken them to the theatre, put them in people’s hats, and slipped them into pockets. Afterwards he had taken money from them, ‘for what means had I?’ He had distributed all sorts of rubbish through the districts of two provinces. “Oh, Nikolay Vsyevolodovitch!” he exclaimed, “what revolted me most was that this was utterly opposed to civic, and still more to patriotic laws. They suddenly printed that men were to go out with pitchforks, and to remember that those who went out poor in the morning might go home rich at night. Only think of it! It made me shudder, and yet I distributed it. Or suddenly five or six lines addressed to the whole of Russia, apropos of nothing, ‘Make haste and lock up the churches, abolish God, do away with marriage, destroy the right of inheritance, take up your knives,’ that’s all, and God knows what it means. I tell you, I almost got caught with this five-line leaflet. The officers in the regiment gave me a thrashing, but, bless them for it, let me go. And last year I was almost caught when I passed off French counterfeit notes for fifty roubles on Korovayev, but, thank God, Korovayev fell into the pond when he was drunk, and was drowned in the nick of time, and they didn’t succeed in tracking me. Here, at Virginsky’s, I proclaimed the freedom of the communistic life. In June I was distributing manifestoes again in X district. They say they will make me do it again.... Pyotr Stepanovitch suddenly gave me to understand that I must obey; he’s been threatening me a long time. How he treated me that Sunday! Nikolay Vsyevolodovitch, I am a slave, I am a worm, but not a God, which is where I differ from Derzhavin.* But I’ve no income, no income!”

* *The reference is to a poem of Derzhavin’s.*

Nikolay Vsyevolodovitch heard it all with curiosity.

“A great deal of that I had heard nothing of,” he said. “Of course, anything may have happened to you.... Listen,” he said, after a minute’s thought. “If you like, you can tell them, you know whom, that Liputin was lying, and that you were only pretending to give information to frighten me, supposing that I, too, was compromised, and that you might get more money out of me that way.... Do you understand?”

"Dear Nikolay Vsyevolodovitch, is it possible that there's such a danger hanging over me? I've been longing for you to come, to ask you."

Nikolay Vsyevolodovitch laughed.

"They certainly wouldn't let you go to Petersburg, even if I were to give you money for the journey.... But it's time for me to see Marya Timofyevna." And he got up from his chair.

"Nikolay Vsyevolodovitch, but how about Marya Timofyevna?"

"Why, as I told you."

"Can it be true?"

"You still don't believe it?"

"Will you really cast me off like an old worn-out shoe?"

"I'll see," laughed Nikolay Vsyevolodovitch. "Come, let me go."

"Wouldn't you like me to stand on the steps ... for fear I might by chance overhear something ... for the rooms are small?"

"That's as well. Stand on the steps. Take my umbrella."

"Your umbrella.... Am I worth it?" said the captain over-sweetly.

"Anyone is worthy of an umbrella."

"At one stroke you define the minimum of human rights...."

But he was by now muttering mechanically. He was too much crushed by what he had learned, and was completely thrown out of his reckoning. And yet almost as soon as he had gone out on to the steps and had put up the umbrella, there his shallow and cunning brain caught again the ever-present, comforting idea that he was being cheated and deceived, and if so they were afraid of him, and there was no need for him to be afraid.

"If they're lying and deceiving me, what's at the bottom of it?" was the thought that gnawed at his mind. The public announcement of the marriage seemed to him absurd. "It's true that with such a wonder-worker anything may come to pass; he lives to do harm. But what if he's afraid himself, since the insult of Sunday, and afraid as he's never been before? And so he's in a hurry to declare that he'll announce it himself, from fear that I should announce it. Eh, don't blunder, Lebyadkin! And why does he come on the sly, at night, if he means to make it public himself? And if he's afraid, it means that he's afraid now, at this moment, for these few days.... Eh, don't make a mistake, Lebyadkin!

"He scares me with Pyotr Stepanovitch. Oy, I'm frightened, I'm frightened! Yes, this is what's so frightening! And what induced me to blab to Liputin. Goodness knows what these devils are up to. I never can make head or tail of it. Now they are all astir again as they were five years ago. To whom could I give information, indeed? 'Haven't I written to anyone in my foolishness?' H'm! So then I might write as though through foolishness? Isn't he giving me a hint? 'You're going to Petersburg on purpose.' The sly rogue. I've scarcely dreamed of it, and he guesses my dreams. As though he were putting me up to going himself. It's one or the other of two games he's up to. Either he's afraid because he's been up to some pranks himself ... or he's not afraid for himself, but is simply egging me on to give them all away! Ach, it's terrible, Lebyadkin! Ach, you must not make a blunder!"

He was so absorbed in thought that he forgot to listen. It was not easy to hear either. The door was a solid one, and they were talking in a very low voice. Nothing reached the captain but indistinct sounds. He positively spat in disgust, and went out again, lost in thought, to whistle on the steps.

III

Marya Timofyevna's room was twice as large as the one occupied by the captain, and furnished in the same rough style; but the table in front of the sofa was covered with a gay-coloured table-cloth, and on it a lamp was burning. There was a handsome carpet on the floor. The bed was screened off by a green curtain, which ran the length of the room, and besides the sofa there stood by the table a large, soft easy chair, in which Marya Timofyevna never sat, however. In the corner there was an ikon as there had been in her old room, and a little lamp was burning before it, and on the table were all her indispensable properties. The pack of cards, the little looking-glass, the song-book, even a milk loaf. Besides these there were two books with coloured pictures—one, extracts from a popular book of travels, published for juvenile reading, the other a collection of very light, edifying tales, for the most part about the days of chivalry, intended for Christmas presents or school reading. She had, too, an album of photographs of various sorts.

Marya Timofyevna was, of course, expecting the visitor, as the captain had announced. But when Nikolay Vsyevolodovitch went in, she was asleep, half reclining on the sofa, propped on a woolwork cushion. Her visitor closed the door after him noiselessly, and, standing still, scrutinised the sleeping figure.

The captain had been romancing when he told Nikolay Vsyevolodovitch she had been dressing herself up. She was wearing the same dark dress as on Sunday at Varvara Petrovna's. Her hair was done up in the same little close knot at the back of her head; her long thin neck was exposed in the same way. The black shawl Varvara Petrovna had given her lay carefully folded on the sofa. She was coarsely rouged and powdered as before. Nikolay Vsyevolodovitch did not stand there more than a minute. She suddenly waked up, as though she were conscious of his eyes fixed upon her; she opened her eyes, and quickly drew herself up. But something strange must have happened to her visitor: he remained standing at the same place by the door. With a fixed and searching glance he looked mutely and persistently into her face. Perhaps that look was too grim, perhaps there was an expression of aversion in it, even a malignant enjoyment of her fright—if it were not a fancy left by her dreams; but suddenly, after almost a moment of expectation, the poor woman's face wore a look of absolute terror; it twitched convulsively; she lifted her trembling hands and suddenly burst into tears, exactly like a frightened child; in another moment she would have screamed. But Nikolay Vsyevolodovitch pulled himself together; his face changed in one instant, and he went up to the table with the most cordial and amiable smile.

"I'm sorry, Marya Timofyevna, I frightened you coming in suddenly when you were asleep," he said, holding out his hand to her.

The sound of his caressing words produced their effect. Her fear vanished, although she still looked at him with dismay, evidently trying to understand something. She held out her hands timorously also. At last a shy smile rose to her lips.

"How do you do, prince?" she whispered, looking at him strangely.

"You must have had a bad dream," he went on, with a still more friendly and cordial smile.

"But how do you know that I was dreaming about that?" And again she began trembling, and started back, putting up her hand as though to protect herself, on the point of crying again. "Calm yourself. That's enough. What are you afraid of? Surely you know me?" said Nikolay Vsyevolodovitch, trying to soothe her; but it was long before he could succeed. She gazed at him dumbly with the same look of agonising perplexity, with a painful idea in her poor brain, and she still seemed to be trying to reach some conclusion. At one moment she dropped her eyes, then suddenly scrutinised him in a rapid comprehensive glance. At last, though not reassured, she seemed to come to a conclusion.

"Sit down beside me, please, that I may look at you thoroughly later on," she brought out with more firmness, evidently with a new object. "But don't be uneasy, I won't look at you now. I'll look down. Don't you look at me either till I ask you to. Sit down," she added, with positive impatience.

A new sensation was obviously growing stronger and stronger in her.

Nikolay Vsyevolodovitch sat down and waited. Rather a long silence followed.

"H'm! It all seems so strange to me," she suddenly muttered almost disdainfully. "Of course I was depressed by bad dreams, but why have I dreamt of you looking like that?"

"Come, let's have done with dreams," he said impatiently, turning to her in spite of her prohibition, and perhaps the same expression gleamed for a moment in his eyes again. He saw that she several times wanted, very much in fact, to look at him again, but that she obstinately controlled herself and kept her eyes cast down.

"Listen, prince," she raised her voice suddenly, "listen prince...."

"Why do you turn away? Why don't you look at me? What's the object of this farce?" he cried, losing patience.

But she seemed not to hear him.

"Listen, prince," she repeated for the third time in a resolute voice, with a disagreeable, fussy expression. "When you told me in the carriage that our marriage was going to be made public, I was alarmed at there being an end to the mystery. Now I don't know. I've been thinking it all over, and I see clearly that I'm not fit for it at all. I know how to dress, and I could receive guests, perhaps. There's nothing much in asking people to have a cup of tea, especially when there are footmen. But what will people say though? I saw a great deal that Sunday morning in that house. That pretty young lady looked at me all the time, especially after you came in. It was you came in, wasn't it? Her mother's simply an absurd worldly old woman. My Lebyadkin distinguished himself too. I kept looking at the ceiling to keep from laughing; the ceiling there is finely painted. His mother ought to be an abbess. I'm afraid of her, though she did give me a black shawl. Of course, they must all have come to strange conclusions about me. I wasn't vexed, but I sat there, thinking what relation am I to them? Of course, from a countess one doesn't expect any but spiritual qualities; for the domestic ones she's got plenty of footmen; and also a little worldly coquetry, so as to be able to entertain foreign travellers. But yet that Sunday they did look upon me as hopeless. Only Dasha's an angel. I'm awfully afraid they may wound him by some careless allusion to me."

"Don't be afraid, and don't be uneasy," said Nikolay Vsyevolodovitch, making a wry face.

"However, that doesn't matter to me, if he is a little ashamed of me, for there will always be more pity than shame, though it differs with people, of course. He knows, to be sure, that I ought rather to pity them than they me."

"You seem to be very much offended with them, Marya Timofyevna?"

"I? Oh, no," she smiled with simple-hearted mirth. "Not at all. I looked at you all, then. You were all angry, you were all quarrelling. They meet together, and they don't know how to laugh from their hearts. So much wealth and so little gaiety. It all disgusts me. Though I feel for no one now except myself."

"I've heard that you've had a hard life with your brother without me?"

"Who told you that? It's nonsense. It's much worse now. Now my dreams are not good, and my dreams are bad, because you've come. What have you come for, I'd like to know. Tell me please?"

"Wouldn't you like to go back into the nunnery?"

"I knew they'd suggest the nunnery again. Your nunnery is a fine marvel for me! And why should I go to it? What should I go for now? I'm all alone in the world now. It's too late for me to begin a third life."

"You seem very angry about something. Surely you're not afraid that I've left off loving you?"

"I'm not troubling about you at all. I'm afraid that I may leave off loving somebody."

She laughed contemptuously.

"I must have done him some great wrong," she added suddenly, as it were to herself, "only I don't know what I've done wrong; that's always what troubles me. Always, always, for the last five years. I've been afraid day and night that I've done him some wrong. I've prayed and prayed and always thought of the great wrong I'd done him. And now it turns out it was true."

"What's turned out?"

"I'm only afraid whether there's something on his side," she went on, not answering his question, not hearing it in fact. "And then, again, he couldn't get on with such horrid people. The countess would have liked to eat me, though she did make me sit in the carriage beside her. They're all in the plot. Surely he's not betrayed me?" (Her chin and lips were twitching.) "Tell me, have you read about Grishka Otrepyev, how he was cursed in seven cathedrals?"

Nikolay Vsyevolodovitch did not speak.

"But I'll turn round now and look at you." She seemed to decide suddenly. "You turn to me, too, and look at me, but more attentively. I want to make sure for the last time."

"I've been looking at you for a long time."

"H'm!" said Marya Timofyevna, looking at him intently. "You've grown much fatter."

She wanted to say something more, but suddenly, for the third time, the same terror instantly distorted her face, and again she drew back, putting her hand up before her.

"What's the matter with you?" cried Nikolay Vsyevolodovitch, almost enraged.

But her panic lasted only one instant, her face worked with a sort of strange smile, suspicious and unpleasant.

"I beg you, prince, get up and come in," she brought out suddenly, in a firm, emphatic voice.

"Come in? Where am I to come in?"

"I've been fancying for five years how he would come in. Get up and go out of the door into the other room. I'll sit as though I weren't expecting anything, and I'll take up a book, and suddenly you'll come in after five years' travelling. I want to see what it will be like."

Nikolay Vsyevolodovitch ground his teeth, and muttered something to himself.

"Enough," he said, striking the table with his open hand. "I beg you to listen to me, Marya Timofyevna. Do me the favour to concentrate all your attention if you can. You're not altogether mad, you know!" he broke out impatiently. "Tomorrow I shall make our marriage public. You never will live in a palace, get that out of your head. Do you want to live with me for the rest of your life, only very far away from here? In the mountains in Switzerland, there's a place there.... Don't be afraid. I'll never abandon you or put you in a madhouse. I shall have money enough to live without asking anyone's help. You shall have a servant, you shall do no work at all. Everything you want that's possible shall be got for you. You shall pray, go where you like, and do what you like. I won't touch you. I won't go away from the place myself at all. If you like, I won't speak to you all my life, or if you like, you can tell me your stories every evening as you used to do in Petersburg in the corners. I'll read aloud to you if you like. But it must be all your life in the same place, and that place is a gloomy one. Will you? Are you ready? You won't regret it, torment me with tears and curses, will you?"

She listened with extreme curiosity, and for a long time she was silent, thinking.

"It all seems incredible to me," she said at last, ironically and disdainfully. "I might live for forty years in those mountains," she laughed.

"What of it? Let's live forty years then ..." said Nikolay Vsyevolodovitch, scowling.

"H'm! I won't come for anything."

"Not even with me?"

"And what are you that I should go with you? I'm to sit on a mountain beside him for forty years on end—a pretty story! And upon my word, how long-suffering people have become nowadays! No, it cannot be that a falcon has become an owl. My prince is not like that!" she said, raising her head proudly and triumphantly.

Light seemed to dawn upon him.

"What makes you call me a prince, and ... for whom do you take me?" he asked quickly.

"Why, aren't you the prince?"

"I never have been one."

"So yourself, yourself, you tell me straight to my face that you're not the prince?"

"I tell you I never have been."

"Good Lord!" she cried, clasping her hands. "I was ready to expect anything from his enemies, but such insolence, never! Is he alive?" she shrieked in a frenzy, turning upon Nikolay Vsyevolodovitch. "Have you killed him? Confess!"

"Whom do you take me for?" he cried, jumping up from his chair with a distorted face; but it was not easy now to frighten her. She was triumphant.

"Who can tell who you are and where you've sprung from? Only my heart, my heart had misgivings all these five years, of all the intrigues. And I've been sitting here wondering what blind owl was making up to me? No, my dear, you're a poor actor, worse than Lebyadkin even. Give my humble greetings to the countess and tell her to send someone better than you. Has she hired you, tell me? Have they given you a place in her kitchen out of charity? I see through your deception. I understand you all, every one of you."

He seized her firmly above the elbow; she laughed in his face.

"You're like him, very like, perhaps you're a relation—you're a sly lot! Only mine is a bright falcon and a prince, and you're an owl, and a shopman! Mine will bow down to God if it pleases him, and won't if it doesn't. And Shatushka (he's my dear, my darling!) slapped you on the cheeks, my Lebyadkin told me. And what were you afraid of then, when you came in? Who had frightened you then? When I saw your mean face after I'd fallen down and you picked me up—it was like a worm crawling into my heart. It's not he, I thought, not he! My falcon would never have been ashamed of me before a fashionable young lady. Oh heavens! That alone kept me happy for those five years that my falcon was living somewhere beyond the mountains, soaring, gazing at the sun.... Tell me, you impostor, have you got much by it? Did you need a big bribe to consent? I wouldn't have given you a farthing. Ha ha ha! Ha ha!..."

"Ugh, idiot!" snarled Nikolay Vsyevolodovitch, still holding her tight by the arm.

"Go away, impostor!" she shouted peremptorily. "I'm the wife of my prince; I'm not afraid of your knife!"

"Knife!"

"Yes, knife, you've a knife in your pocket. You thought I was asleep but I saw it. When you came in just now you took out your knife!"

"What are you saying, unhappy creature? What dreams you have!" he exclaimed, pushing her away from him with all his might, so that her head and shoulders fell painfully against the sofa. He was rushing away; but she at once flew to overtake him, limping and hopping, and though Lebyadkin, panic-stricken, held her back with all his might, she succeeded in shouting after him into the darkness, shrieking and laughing:

"A curse on you, Grishka Otrepyev!"

IV

"A knife, a knife," he repeated with uncontrollable anger, striding along through the mud and puddles, without picking his way. It is true that at moments he had a terrible desire to laugh aloud frantically; but for some reason he controlled himself and restrained his laughter. He recovered himself only on the bridge, on the spot where Fedka had met him that evening. He found the man lying in wait for him again. Seeing Nikolay Vsyevolodovitch he took off his cap, grinned gaily, and began babbling briskly and merrily about something. At first Nikolay Vsyevolodovitch walked on without stopping, and for some time did not even listen to the tramp who was pestering him again. He was suddenly struck by the thought that he had entirely forgotten him, and had forgotten him at the very moment when he himself was repeating, "A knife, a knife." He seized the tramp by the collar and gave vent to his pent-up rage by flinging him violently against the bridge. For one instant the man thought of fighting, but almost at once realising that compared with his adversary, who had fallen upon him unawares, he was no better than a wisp of straw, he subsided and was silent, without offering any resistance. Crouching on the ground with his elbows crooked behind his back, the wily tramp calmly waited for what would happen next, apparently quite incredulous of danger. He was right in his reckoning. Nikolay Vsyevolodovitch had already with his left hand taken off his thick scarf to tie his prisoner's arms, but suddenly, for some reason, he abandoned him, and shoved him away. The man instantly sprang on to his feet, turned round, and a short, broad boot-knife suddenly gleamed in his hand.

"Away with that knife; put it away, at once!" Nikolay Vsyevolodovitch commanded with an impatient gesture, and the knife vanished as instantaneously as it had appeared.

Without speaking again or turning round, Nikolay Vsyevolodovitch went on his way. But the persistent vagabond did not leave him even now, though now, it is true, he did not chatter, and even respectfully kept his distance, a full step behind.

They crossed the bridge like this and came out on to the river bank, turning this time to the left, again into a long deserted back street, which led to the centre of the town by a shorter way than going through Bogoyavlensky Street.

"Is it true, as they say, that you robbed a church in the district the other day?" Nikolay Vsyevolodovitch asked suddenly.

"I went in to say my prayers in the first place," the tramp answered, sedately and respectfully as though nothing had happened; more than sedately, in fact, almost with dignity. There was no trace of his former "friendly" familiarity. All that was to be seen was a serious, business-like man, who had indeed been gratuitously insulted, but who was capable of overlooking an insult.

"But when the Lord led me there," he went on, "ech, I thought what a heavenly abundance! It was all owing to my helpless state, as in our way of life there's no doing without assistance. And, now, God be my witness, sir, it was my own loss. The Lord punished me for my sins, and what with the censer and the deacon's halter, I only got twelve roubles altogether. The chin setting of St. Nikolay of pure silver went for next to nothing. They said it was plated."

"You killed the watchman?"

"That is, I cleared the place out together with that watchman, but afterwards, next morning, by the river, we fell to quarrelling which should carry the sack. I sinned, I did lighten his load for him."

"Well, you can rob and murder again."

"That's the very advice Pyotr Stepanovitch gives me, in the very same words, for he's uncommonly mean and hard-hearted about helping a fellow-creature. And what's more, he hasn't a ha'p'orth of belief in the Heavenly Creator, who made us out of earthly clay; but he says it's all the work of nature even to the last beast. He doesn't understand either that with our way of life it's impossible for us to get along without friendly assistance. If you begin to talk to him he looks like a sheep at the water; it makes one wonder. Would you believe, at Captain Lebyadkin's, out yonder, whom your honour's just been visiting, when he was living at Filipov's, before you came, the door stood open all night long. He'd be drunk and sleeping like the dead, and his money dropping out of his pockets all over the floor. I've chanced to see it with my own eyes, for in our way of life it's impossible to live without assistance...."

"How do you mean with your own eyes? Did you go in at night then?"

"Maybe I did go in, but no one knows of it."

"Why didn't you kill him?"

"Reckoning it out, I steadied myself. For once having learned for sure that I can always get one hundred and fifty roubles, why should I go so far when I can get fifteen hundred roubles, if I only bide my time. For Captain Lebyadkin (I've heard him with my own ears) had great hopes of you when he was drunk; and there isn't a tavern here—not the lowest pot-house—where he hasn't talked about it when he was in that state. So that hearing it from many lips, I began, too, to rest all my hopes on your excellency. I speak to you, sir, as to my father, or my own brother; for Pyotr Stepanovitch will never learn that from me, and not a soul in the world. So won't your excellency spare me three roubles in your kindness? You might set my mind at rest, so that I might know the real truth; for we can't get on without assistance."

Nikolay Vsyevolodovitch laughed aloud, and taking out his purse, in which he had as much as fifty roubles, in small notes, threw him one note out of the bundle, then a second, a third, a fourth. Fedka flew to catch them in the air. The notes dropped into the mud, and he snatched them up crying, "Ech! ech!" Nikolay Vsyevolodovitch finished by flinging the whole bundle at him, and, still laughing, went on down the street, this time alone. The tramp remained crawling on his knees in the mud, looking for the notes which were blown about by the wind and soaking in the puddles, and for an hour after his spasmodic cries of "Ech! ech!" were still to be heard in the darkness.

CHAPTER III. THE DUEL

I

THE NEXT DAY, at two o'clock in the afternoon, the duel took place as arranged. Things were hastened forward by Gaganov's obstinate desire to fight at all costs. He did not understand his adversary's conduct, and was in a fury. For a whole month he had been insulting him with impunity, and had so far been unable to make him lose patience. What he wanted was a challenge on the part of Nikolay Vsyevolodovitch, as he had not himself any direct pretext for challenging him. His secret motive for it, that is, his almost morbid hatred of Stavrogin for the insult to his family four years before, he was for some reason ashamed to confess. And indeed he regarded this himself as an impossible pretext for a challenge, especially in view of the humble apology offered by Nikolay Stavrogin twice already. He privately made up his mind that Stavrogin was a shameless coward; and could not understand how he could have accepted Shatov's blow. So he made up his mind at last to send him the extraordinarily rude letter that had finally roused Nikolay Vsyevolodovitch himself to propose a meeting. Having dispatched this letter the day before, he awaited a challenge with feverish impatience, and while morbidly reckoning the chances at one moment with hope and at the next with despair, he got ready for any emergency by securing a second, to wit, Mavriky Nikolaevitch Drozdov, who was a friend of his, an old schoolfellow, a man for whom he had a great respect. So when Kirillov came next morning at nine o'clock with his message he found things in readiness. All the apologies and unheard-of condescension of Nikolay Vsyevolodovitch were at once, at the first word, rejected with extraordinary exasperation. Mavriky Nikolaevitch, who had only been made acquainted with the position of affairs the evening before, opened his mouth with surprise at such incredible concessions, and would have urged a reconciliation, but seeing that Gaganov, guessing his intention, was almost trembling in his chair, refrained, and said nothing. If it had not been for the promise given to his old schoolfellow he would have retired immediately; he only remained in the hope of being some help on the scene of action. Kirillov repeated the challenge. All the conditions of the encounter made by Stavrogin were accepted on the spot, without the faintest objection. Only one addition was made, and that a ferocious one. If the first shots had no decisive effect, they were to fire again, and if the second encounter were inconclusive, it was to be followed by a third. Kirillov frowned, objected to the third encounter, but gaining nothing by his efforts agreed on the condition, however, that three should be the limit, and that "a fourth encounter was out of the question." This was conceded. Accordingly at two o'clock in the afternoon the meeting took place at Brykov, that is, in a little copse in the outskirts of the town, lying between Skvoreshniki and the Shpigulin factory. The rain of the previous night was over, but it was damp, grey, and windy. Low, ragged, dingy clouds moved rapidly across the cold sky. The tree-tops roared with a deep droning sound, and creaked on their roots; it was a melancholy morning.

Mavriky Nikolaevitch and Gaganov arrived on the spot in a smart char-à-banc with a pair of horses driven by the latter. They were accompanied by a groom. Nikolay Vsyevolodovitch and Kirillov arrived almost at the same instant. They were not driving, they were on horseback, and were also followed by a mounted servant. Kirillov, who had never mounted a horse before, sat up boldly, erect in the saddle, grasping in his right hand the heavy box of pistols which he would not entrust to the servant. In his inexperience he was continually with his left hand tugging at the reins, which made the horse toss his head and show an inclination to rear. This, however, seemed to cause his rider no uneasiness. Gaganov, who was morbidly suspicious and always ready to be deeply offended, considered their coming on horseback as a fresh insult to himself, inasmuch as it showed that his opponents were too confident of success, since they had not even thought it necessary to have a carriage in case of being wounded and disabled. He got out of his char-à-banc, yellow with anger, and felt that his hands were trembling, as he told Mavriky Nikolaevitch. He made no response at all to Nikolay Vsyevolodovitch's bow, and turned away. The seconds cast lots. The lot fell on Kirillov's pistols. They measured out the barrier and placed the combatants. The servants with the carriage and horses were moved back three hundred paces. The weapons were loaded and handed to the combatants.

I'm sorry that I have to tell my story more quickly and have no time for descriptions. But I can't refrain from some comments. Mavriky Nikolaevitch was melancholy and preoccupied. Kirillov, on the other hand, was perfectly calm and unconcerned, very exact over the details of the duties he had undertaken, but without the slightest fussiness or even curiosity as to the issue of the fateful contest that was so near at hand. Nikolay Vsyevolodovitch was paler than usual. He was rather lightly dressed in an overcoat and a white beaver hat. He seemed very tired, he frowned from time to time, and seemed to feel it superfluous to conceal his ill-humour. But Gaganov was at this moment more worthy of mention than anyone, so that it is quite impossible not to say a few words about him in particular.

II

I have hitherto not had occasion to describe his appearance. He was a tall man of thirty-three, and well fed, as the common folk express it, almost fat, with lank flaxen hair, and with features which might be called handsome. He had retired from the service with the rank of colonel, and if he had served till he reached the rank of general he would have been even more impressive in that position, and would very likely have become an excellent fighting general.

I must add, as characteristic of the man, that the chief cause of his leaving the army was the thought of the family disgrace which had haunted him so painfully since the insult paid to his father by Nikolay Vsyevolodovitch four years before at the club. He conscientiously considered it dishonourable to remain in the service, and was inwardly persuaded that he was contaminating the regiment and his companions, although they knew nothing of the incident. It's true that he had once before been disposed to leave the army long before the insult to his father, and on quite other grounds, but he had hesitated. Strange as it is to write, the original design, or rather desire, to leave the army was due to the proclamation of the 19th of February of the emancipation of the serfs. Gaganov, who was one of the richest landowners in the province, and who had not lost very much by the emancipation, and was, moreover, quite capable of understanding the humanity of the reform and its economic advantages, suddenly felt himself personally insulted by the proclamation. It was something unconscious, a feeling; but was all the stronger for being unrecognised. He could not bring himself, however, to take any decisive step till his father's death. But he began to be well known for his "gentlemanly" ideas to many persons of high position in Petersburg, with whom he strenuously kept up connections. He was secretive and self-contained. Another characteristic: he belonged to that strange section of the nobility, still surviving in Russia, who set an extreme value on their pure and ancient lineage, and take it too seriously. At the same time he could not endure Russian history, and, indeed, looked upon Russian customs in general as more or less piggish. Even in his childhood, in the special military school for the sons of particularly wealthy and distinguished families in which he had the privilege of being educated, from first to last certain poetic notions were deeply rooted in his mind. He loved castles, chivalry; all the theatrical part of it. He was ready to cry with shame that in the days of the Moscow Tsars the sovereign had the right to inflict corporal punishment on the Russian boyars, and blushed at the contrast. This stiff and extremely severe man, who had a remarkable knowledge of military science and performed his duties admirably, was at heart a dreamer. It was said that he could speak at meetings and had the gift of language, but at no time during the thirty-three years of his life had he spoken. Even in the distinguished circles in Petersburg, in which he had moved of late, he behaved with extraordinary haughtiness. His meeting in Petersburg with Nikolay Vsyevolodovitch, who had just returned from abroad, almost sent him out of his mind. At the present moment, standing at the barrier, he was terribly uneasy. He kept imagining that the duel would somehow not come off; the least delay threw him into a tremor. There was an expression of anguish in his face when Kirillov, instead of giving the signal for them to fire, began suddenly speaking, only for form, indeed, as he himself explained aloud.

"Simply as a formality, now that you have the pistols in your hands, and I must give the signal, I ask you for the last time, will you not be reconciled? It's the duty of a second."

As though to spite him, Mavriky Nikolaevitch, who had till then kept silence, although he had been reproaching himself all day for his compliance and acquiescence, suddenly caught up Kirillov's thought and began to speak:

"I entirely agree with Mr. Kirillov's words.... This idea that reconciliation is impossible at the barrier is a prejudice, only suitable for Frenchmen. Besides, with your leave, I don't understand what the offence is. I've been wanting to say so for a long time ... because every apology is offered, isn't it?"

He flushed all over. He had rarely spoken so much, and with such excitement.

"I repeat again my offer to make every possible apology," Nikolay Vsyevolodovitch interposed hurriedly.

"This is impossible," shouted Gaganov furiously, addressing Mavriky Nikolaevitch, and stamping with rage. "Explain to this man," he pointed with his pistol at Nikolay Vsyevolodovitch, "if you're my second and not my enemy, Mavriky Nikolaevitch, that such overtures only aggravate the insult. He feels it impossible to be insulted by me!... He feels it no disgrace to walk away from me at the barrier! What does he take me for, after that, do you think?... And you, you, my second, too! You're simply irritating me that I may miss."

He stamped again. There were flecks of foam on his lips.

"Negotiations are over. I beg you to listen to the signal!" Kirillov shouted at the top of his voice. "One! Two! Three!"

At the word "Three" the combatants took aim at one another. Gaganov at once raised his pistol, and at the fifth or sixth step he fired. For a second he stood still, and, making sure that he had missed, advanced to the barrier. Nikolay Vsyevolodovitch advanced too, raising his pistol, but somehow holding it very high, and fired, almost without taking aim. Then he took out his handkerchief and bound it round the little finger of his right hand. Only then they saw that Gaganov had not missed him completely, but the bullet had only grazed the fleshy part of his finger without touching the bone; it was only a slight scratch. Kirillov at once announced that the duel would go on, unless the combatants were satisfied.

"I declare," said Gaganov hoarsely (his throat felt parched), again addressing Mavriky Nikolaevitch, "that this man," again he pointed in Stavrogin's direction, "fired in the air on purpose ... intentionally.... This is an insult again.... He wants to make the duel impossible!"

"I have the right to fire as I like so long as I keep the rules," Nikolay Vsyevolodovitch asserted resolutely.

"No, he hasn't! Explain it to him! Explain it!" cried Gaganov.

"I'm in complete agreement with Nikolay Vsyevolodovitch," proclaimed Kirillov.

"Why does he spare me?" Gaganov raged, not hearing him. "I despise his mercy.... I spit on it.... I ..."

"I give you my word that I did not intend to insult you," cried Nikolay Vsyevolodovitch impatiently. "I shot high because I don't want to kill anyone else, either you or anyone else. It's nothing to do with you personally. It's true that I don't consider myself insulted, and I'm sorry that angers you. But I don't allow any one to interfere with my rights."

"If he's so afraid of bloodshed, ask him why he challenged me," yelled Gaganov, still addressing Mavriky Nikolaevitch.

"How could he help challenging you?" said Kirillov, intervening. "You wouldn't listen to anything. How was one to get rid of you?"

"I'll only mention one thing," observed Mavriky Nikolaevitch, pondering the matter with painful effort. "If a combatant declares beforehand that he will fire in the air the duel certainly cannot go on ... for obvious and ... delicate reasons."

"I haven't declared that I'll fire in the air every time," cried Stavrogin, losing all patience. "You don't know what's in my mind or how I intend to fire again.... I'm not restricting the duel at all."

"In that case the encounter can go on," said Mavriky Nikolaevitch to Gaganov.

"Gentlemen, take your places," Kirillov commanded. Again they advanced, again Gaganov missed and Stavrogin fired into the air. There might have been a dispute as to his firing into the air. Nikolay Vsyevolodovitch might have flatly declared that he'd fired properly, if he had not admitted that he had missed intentionally. He did not aim straight at the sky or at the trees, but seemed to aim at his adversary, though as he pointed the pistol the bullet flew a yard above his hat. The second time the shot was even lower, even less like an intentional miss. Nothing would have convinced Gaganov now.

"Again!" he muttered, grinding his teeth. "No matter! I've been challenged and I'll make use of my rights. I'll fire a third time … whatever happens."

"You have full right to do so," Kirillov rapped out. Mavriky Nikolaevitch said nothing. The opponents were placed a third time, the signal was given. This time Gaganov went right up to the barrier, and began from there taking aim, at a distance of twelve paces. His hand was trembling too much to take good aim. Stavrogin stood with his pistol lowered and awaited his shot without moving.

"Too long; you've been aiming too long!" Kirillov shouted impetuously. "Fire! Fire!"

But the shot rang out, and this time Stavrogin's white beaver hat flew off. The aim had been fairly correct. The crown of the hat was pierced very low down; a quarter of an inch lower and all would have been over. Kirillov picked up the hat and handed it to Nikolay Vsyevolodovitch.

"Fire; don't detain your adversary!" cried Mavriky Nikolaevitch in extreme agitation, seeing that Stavrogin seemed to have forgotten to fire, and was examining the hat with Kirillov. Stavrogin started, looked at Gaganov, turned round and this time, without the slightest regard for punctilio, fired to one side, into the copse. The duel was over. Gaganov stood as though overwhelmed. Mavriky Nikolaevitch went up and began saying something to him, but he did not seem to understand. Kirillov took off his hat as he went away, and nodded to Mavriky Nikolaevitch. But Stavrogin forgot his former politeness. When he had shot into the copse he did not even turn towards the barrier. He handed his pistol to Kirillov and hastened towards the horses. His face looked angry; he did not speak. Kirillov, too, was silent. They got on their horses and set off at a gallop.

III

"Why don't you speak?" he called impatiently to Kirillov, when they were not far from home.

"What do you want?" replied the latter, almost slipping off his horse, which was rearing.

Stavrogin restrained himself.

"I didn't mean to insult that … fool, and I've insulted him again," he said quietly.

"Yes, you've insulted him again," Kirillov jerked out, "and besides, he's not a fool."

"I've done all I can, anyway."

"No."

"What ought I to have done?"

"Not have challenged him."

"Accept another blow in the face?"

"Yes, accept another."

"I can't understand anything now," said Stavrogin wrathfully. "Why does every one expect of me something not expected from anyone else? Why am I to put up with what no one else puts up with, and undertake burdens no one else can bear?"

"I thought you were seeking a burden yourself."

"I seek a burden?"

"Yes."

"You've … seen that?"

"Yes."

"Is it so noticeable?"

"Yes."

There was silence for a moment. Stavrogin had a very preoccupied face. He was almost impressed.

"I didn't aim because I didn't want to kill anyone. There was nothing more in it, I assure you," he said hurriedly, and with agitation, as though justifying himself.

"You ought not to have offended him."

"What ought I to have done then?"

"You ought to have killed him."

"Are you sorry I didn't kill him?"

"I'm not sorry for anything. I thought you really meant to kill him. You don't know what you're seeking."

"I seek a burden," laughed Stavrogin.

"If you didn't want blood yourself, why did you give him a chance to kill you?"

"If I hadn't challenged him, he'd have killed me simply, without a duel."

"That's not your affair. Perhaps he wouldn't have killed you."

"Only have beaten me?"

"That's not your business. Bear your burden. Or else there's no merit."

"Hang your merit. I don't seek anyone's approbation."

"I thought you were seeking it," Kirillov commented with terrible unconcern.

They rode into the courtyard of the house.

"Do you care to come in?" said Nikolay Vsyevolodovitch.

"No; I'm going home. Good-bye."

He got off the horse and took his box of pistols under his arm.

"Anyway, you're not angry with me?" said Stavrogin, holding out his hand to him.

"Not in the least," said Kirillov, turning round to shake hands with him. "If my burden's light it's because it's from nature; perhaps your burden's heavier because that's your nature. There's no need to be much ashamed; only a little."

"I know I'm a worthless character, and I don't pretend to be a strong one."

"You'd better not; you're not a strong person. Come and have tea."

Nikolay Vsyevolodovitch went into the house, greatly perturbed.

IV

He learned at once from Alexey Yegorytch that Varvara Petrovna had been very glad to hear that Nikolay Vsyevolodovitch had gone out for a ride—the first time he had left the house after eight days' illness. She had ordered the carriage, and had driven out alone for a breath of fresh air "according to the habit of the past, as she had forgotten for the last eight days what it meant to breathe fresh air."

"Alone, or with Darya Pavlovna?" Nikolay Vsyevolodovitch interrupted the old man with a rapid question, and he scowled when he heard that Darya Pavlovna "had declined to go abroad on account of indisposition and was in her rooms."

"Listen, old man," he said, as though suddenly making up his mind. "Keep watch over her all to-day, and if you notice her coming to me, stop her at once, and tell her that I can't see her for a few days at least ... that I ask her not to come myself.... I'll let her know myself, when the time comes. Do you hear?"

"I'll tell her, sir," said Alexey Yegorytch, with distress in his voice, dropping his eyes.

"Not till you see clearly she's meaning to come and see me of herself, though."

"Don't be afraid, sir, there shall be no mistake. Your interviews have all passed through me, hitherto. You've always turned to me for help."

"I know. Not till she comes of herself, anyway. Bring me some tea, if you can, at once."

The old man had hardly gone out, when almost at the same instant the door reopened, and Darya Pavlovna appeared in the doorway. Her eyes were tranquil, though her face was pale.

"Where have you come from?" exclaimed Stavrogin.

"I was standing there, and waiting for him to go out, to come in to you. I heard the order you gave him, and when he came out just now I hid round the corner, on the right, and he didn't notice me."

"I've long meant to break off with you, Dasha ... for a while ... for the present. I couldn't see you last night, in spite of your note. I meant to write to you myself, but I don't know how to write," he added with vexation, almost as though with disgust.

"I thought myself that we must break it off. Varvara Petrovna is too suspicious of our relations."

"Well, let her be."

"She mustn't be worried. So now we part till the end comes."

"You still insist on expecting the end?"

"Yes, I'm sure of it."

"But nothing in the world ever has an end."

"This will have an end. Then call me. I'll come. Now, good-bye."

"And what sort of end will it be?" smiled Nikolay Vsyevolodovitch.

"You're not wounded, and ... have not shed blood?" she asked, not answering his question.

"It was stupid. I didn't kill anyone. Don't be uneasy. However, you'll hear all about it to-day from every one. I'm not quite well."

"I'm going. The announcement of the marriage won't be to-day?" she added irresolutely.

"It won't be to-day, and it won't be to-morrow. I can't say about the day after to-morrow. Perhaps we shall all be dead, and so much the better. Leave me alone, leave me alone, do."

"You won't ruin that other ... mad girl?"

"I won't ruin either of the mad creatures. It seems to be the sane I'm ruining. I'm so vile and loathsome, Dasha, that I might really send for you, 'at the latter end,' as you say. And in spite of your sanity you'll come. Why will you be your own ruin?"

"I know that at the end I shall be the only one left you, and ... I'm waiting for that."

"And what if I don't send for you after all, but run away from you?"

"That can't be. You will send for me."

"There's a great deal of contempt for me in that."

"You know that there's not only contempt."

"Then there is contempt, anyway?"

"I used the wrong word. God is my witness, it's my greatest wish that you may never have need of me."

"One phrase is as good as another. I should also have wished not to have ruined you."

"You can never, anyhow, be my ruin; and you know that yourself, better than anyone," Darya Pavlovna said, rapidly and resolutely. "If I don't come to you I shall be a sister of mercy, a nurse, shall wait upon the sick, or go selling the gospel. I've made up my mind to that. I cannot be anyone's wife. I can't live in a house like this, either. That's not what I want.... You know all that."

"No, I never could tell what you want. It seems to me that you're interested in me, as some veteran nurses get specially interested in some particular invalid in comparison with the others, or still more, like some pious old women who frequent funerals and find one corpse more attractive than another. Why do you look at me so strangely?"

"Are you very ill?" she asked sympathetically, looking at him in a peculiar way. "Good heavens! And this man wants to do without me!"

"Listen, Dasha, now I'm always seeing phantoms. One devil offered me yesterday, on the bridge, to murder Lebyadkin and Marya Timofyevna, to settle the marriage difficulty, and to cover up all traces. He asked me to give him three roubles on account, but gave me to understand that the whole operation wouldn't cost less than fifteen hundred. Wasn't he a calculating devil! A regular shopkeeper. Ha ha!"

"But you're fully convinced that it was an hallucination?"

"Oh, no; not a bit an hallucination! It was simply Fedka the convict, the robber who escaped from prison. But that's not the point. What do you suppose I did! I gave him all I had, everything in my purse, and now he's sure I've given him that on account!"

"You met him at night, and he made such a suggestion? Surely you must see that you're being caught in their nets on every side!"

"Well, let them be. But you've got some question at the tip of your tongue, you know. I see it by your eyes," he added with a resentful and irritable smile.

Dasha was frightened.

"I've no question at all, and no doubt whatever; you'd better be quiet!" she cried in dismay, as though waving off his question.

"Then you're convinced that I won't go to Fedka's little shop?"

"Oh, God!" she cried, clasping her hands. "Why do you torture me like this?"

"Oh, forgive me my stupid joke. I must be picking up bad manners from them. Do you know, ever since last night I feel awfully inclined to laugh, to go on laughing continually forever so long. It's as though I must explode with laughter. It's like an illness.... Oh! my mother's coming in. I always know by the rumble when her carriage has stopped at the entrance."

Dasha seized his hand.

"God save you from your demon, and ... call me, call me quickly!"

"Oh! a fine demon! It's simply a little nasty, scrofulous imp, with a cold in his head, one of the unsuccessful ones. But you have something you don't dare to say again, Dasha?"

She looked at him with pain and reproach, and turned towards the door.

"Listen," he called after her, with a malignant and distorted smile. "If ... Yes, if, in one word, if … you understand, even if I did go to that little shop, and if I called you after that—would you come then?"

She went out, hiding her face in her hands, and neither turning nor answering.

"She will come even after the shop," he whispered, thinking a moment, and an expression of scornful disdain came into his face. "A nurse! H'm!… but perhaps that's what I want."

CHAPTER IV. ALL IN EXPECTATION

I

The impression made on the whole neighbourhood by the story of the duel, which was rapidly noised abroad, was particularly remarkable from the unanimity with which every one hastened to take up the cudgels for Nikolay Vsyevolodovitch. Many of his former enemies declared themselves his friends. The chief reason for this change of front in public opinion was chiefly due to one person, who had hitherto not expressed her opinion, but who now very distinctly uttered a few words, which at once gave the event a significance exceedingly interesting to the vast majority. This was how it happened. On the day after the duel, all the town was assembled at the Marshal of Nobility's in honour of his wife's nameday. Yulia Mihailovna was present, or, rather, presided, accompanied by Lizaveta Nikolaevna, radiant with beauty and peculiar gaiety, which struck many of our ladies at once as particularly suspicious at this time. And I may mention, by the way, her engagement to Mavriky Nikolaevitch was by now an established fact. To a playful question from a retired general of much consequence, of whom we shall have more to say later, Lizaveta Nikolaevna frankly replied that evening that she was engaged. And only imagine, not one of our ladies would believe in her engagement. They all persisted in assuming a romance of some sort, some fatal family secret, something that had happened in Switzerland, and for some reason imagined that Yulia Mihailovna must have had some hand in it. It was difficult to understand why these rumours, or rather fancies, persisted so obstinately, and why Yulia Mihailovna was so positively connected with it. As soon as she came in, all turned to her with strange looks, brimful of expectation. It must be observed that owing to the freshness of the event, and certain circumstances accompanying it, at the party people talked of it with some circumspection, in undertones. Besides, nothing yet was known of the line taken by the authorities. As far as was known, neither of the combatants had been troubled by the police. Every one knew, for instance, that Gaganov had set off home early in the morning to Duhovo, without being hindered. Meanwhile, of course, all were eager for someone to be the first to speak of it aloud, and so to open the door to the general impatience. They rested their hopes on the general above-mentioned, and they were not disappointed.

This general, a landowner, though not a wealthy one, was one of the most imposing members of our club, and a man of an absolutely unique turn of mind. He flirted in the old-fashioned way with the young ladies, and was particularly fond, in large assemblies, of speaking aloud with all the weightiness of a general, on subjects to which others were alluding in discreet whispers. This was, so to say, his special rôle in local society. He drawled, too, and spoke with peculiar suavity, probably having picked up the habit from Russians travelling abroad, or from those wealthy landowners of former days who had suffered most from the emancipation. Stepan Trofimovitch had observed that the more completely a landowner was ruined, the more suavely he lisped and drawled his words. He did, as a fact, lisp and drawl himself, but was not aware of it in himself.

The general spoke like a person of authority. He was, besides, a distant relation of Gaganov's, though he was on bad terms with him, and even engaged in litigation with him. He had, moreover, in the past, fought two duels himself, and had even been degraded to the ranks and sent to the Caucasus on account of one of them. Some mention was made of Varvara Petrovna's having driven out that day and the day before, after being kept indoors "by illness," though the allusion was not to her, but to the marvellous matching of her four grey horses of the Stavrogins' own breeding. The general suddenly observed that he had met "young Stavrogin" that day, on horseback.... Every one was instantly silent. The general munched his lips, and suddenly proclaimed, twisting in his fingers his presentation gold snuff-box.

"I'm sorry I wasn't here some years ago ... I mean when I was at Carlsbad ... H'm! I'm very much interested in that young man about whom I heard so many rumours at that time. H'm! And, I say, is it true that he's mad? Some one told me so then. Suddenly I'm told that he has been insulted by some student here, in the presence of his cousins, and he slipped under the table to get away from him. And yesterday I heard from Stepan Vysotsky that Stavrogin had been fighting with Gaganov. And simply with the gallant object of offering himself as a target to an infuriated man, just to get rid of him. H'm! Quite in the style of the guards of the twenties. Is there any house where he visits here?"

The general paused as though expecting an answer. A way had been opened for the public impatience to express itself.

"What could be simpler?" cried Yulia Mihailovna, raising her voice, irritated that all present had turned their eyes upon her, as though at a word of command. "Can one wonder that Stavrogin fought Gaganov and took no notice of the student? He couldn't challenge a man who used to be his serf!"

A noteworthy saying! A clear and simple notion, yet it had entered nobody's head till that moment. It was a saying that had extraordinary consequences. All scandal and gossip, all the petty tittle-tattle was thrown into the background, another significance had been detected. A new character was revealed whom all had misjudged; a character, almost ideally severe in his standards. Mortally insulted by a student, that is, an educated man, no longer a serf, he despised the affront because his assailant had once been his serf. Society had gossiped and slandered him; shallow-minded people had looked with contempt on a man who had been struck in the face. He had despised a public opinion, which had not risen to the level of the highest standards, though it discussed them.

"And, meantime, you and I, Ivan Alexandrovitch, sit and discuss the correct standards," one old club member observed to another, with a warm and generous glow of self-reproach.

"Yes, Pyotr Mihailovitch, yes," the other chimed in with zest, "talk of the younger generation!"

"It's not a question of the younger generation," observed a third, putting in his spoke, "it's nothing to do with the younger generation; he's a star, not one of the younger generation; that's the way to look at it."

"And it's just that sort we need; they're rare people." The chief point in all this was that the "new man," besides showing himself an unmistakable nobleman, was the wealthiest landowner in the province, and was, therefore, bound to be a leading man who could be of assistance. I've already alluded in passing to the attitude of the landowners of our province.

People were enthusiastic:

“He didn’t merely refrain from challenging the student. He put his hands behind him, note that particularly, your excellency,” somebody pointed out.

“And he didn’t haul him up before the new law-courts, either,” added another.

“In spite of the fact that for a personal insult to a nobleman he’d have got fifteen roubles damages! He he he!”

“No, I’ll tell you a secret about the new courts,” cried a third, in a frenzy of excitement, “if anyone’s caught robbing or swindling and convicted, he’d better run home while there’s yet time, and murder his mother. He’ll be acquitted of everything at once, and ladies will wave their batiste handkerchiefs from the platform. It’s the absolute truth!”

“It’s the truth. It’s the truth!”

The inevitable anecdotes followed: Nikolay Vsyevolodovitch’s friendly relations with Count K. were recalled. Count K.’s stern and independent attitude to recent reforms was well known, as well as his remarkable public activity, though that had somewhat fallen off of late. And now, suddenly, every one was positive that Nikolay Vsyevolodovitch was betrothed to one of the count’s daughters, though nothing had given grounds for such a supposition. And as for some wonderful adventures in Switzerland with Lizaveta Nikolaevna, even the ladies quite dropped all reference to it. I must mention, by the way, that the Drozdovs had by this time succeeded in paying all the visits they had omitted at first. Every one now confidently considered Lizaveta Nikolaevna a most ordinary girl, who paraded her delicate nerves. Her fainting on the day of Nikolay Vsyevolodovitch’s arrival was explained now as due to her terror at the student’s outrageous behaviour. They even increased the prosaicness of that to which before they had striven to give such a fantastic colour. As for a lame woman who had been talked of, she was forgotten completely. They were ashamed to remember her.

“And if there had been a hundred lame girls—we’ve all been young once!”

Nikolay Vsyevolodovitch’s respectfulness to his mother was enlarged upon. Various virtues were discovered in him. People talked with approbation of the learning he had acquired in the four years he had spent in German universities. Gaganov’s conduct was declared utterly tactless: “not knowing friend from foe.” Yulia Mihailovna’s keen insight was unhesitatingly admitted.

So by the time Nikolay Vsyevolodovitch made his appearance among them he was received by every one with naïve solemnity. In all eyes fastened upon him could be read eager anticipation. Nikolay Vsyevolodovitch at once wrapped himself in the most austere silence, which, of course, gratified every one much more than if he had talked till doomsday. In a word, he was a success, he was the fashion. If once one has figured in provincial society, there’s no retreating into the background. Nikolay Vsyevolodovitch began to fulfil all his social duties in the province punctiliously as before. He was not found cheerful company: “a man who has seen suffering; a man not like other people; he has something to be melancholy about.” Even the pride and disdainful aloofness for which he had been so detested four years before was now liked and respected.

Varvara Petrovna was triumphant. I don't know whether she grieved much over the shattering of her dreams concerning Lizaveta Nikolaevna. Family pride, of course, helped her to get over it. One thing was strange: Varvara Petrovna was suddenly convinced that Nikolay Vsyevolodovitch really had "made his choice" at Count K.'s. And what was strangest of all, she was led to believe it by rumours which reached her on no better authority than other people. She was afraid to ask Nikolay Vsyevolodovitch a direct question. Two or three times, however, she could not refrain from slyly and good-humouredly reproaching him for not being open with her. Nikolay Vsyevolodovitch smiled and remained silent. The silence was taken as a sign of assent. And yet, all the time she never forgot the cripple. The thought of her lay like a stone on her heart, a nightmare, she was tortured by strange misgivings and surmises, and all this at the same time as she dreamed of Count K.'s daughters. But of this we shall speak later. Varvara Petrovna began again, of course, to be treated with extreme deference and respect in society, but she took little advantage of it and went out rarely.

She did, however, pay a visit of ceremony to the governor's wife. Of course, no one had been more charmed and delighted by Yulia Mihailovna's words spoken at the marshal's soirée than she. They lifted a load of care off her heart, and had at once relieved much of the distress she had been suffering since that luckless Sunday.

"I misunderstood that woman," she declared, and with her characteristic impulsiveness she frankly told Yulia Mihailovna that she had come to thank her. Yulia Mihailovna was flattered, but she behaved with dignity. She was beginning about this time to be very conscious of her own importance, too much so, in fact. She announced, for example, in the course of conversation, that she had never heard of Stepan Trofimovitch as a leading man or a savant.

"I know young Verhovensky, of course, and make much of him. He's imprudent, but then he's young; he's thoroughly well-informed, though. He's not an out-of-date, old-fashioned critic, anyway." Varvara Petrovna hastened to observe that Stepan Trofimovitch had never been a critic, but had, on the contrary, spent all his life in her house. He was renowned through circumstances of his early career, "only too well known to the whole world," and of late for his researches in Spanish history. Now he intended to write also on the position of modern German universities, and, she believed, something about the Dresden Madonna too. In short, Varvara Petrovna refused to surrender Stepan Trofimovitch to the tender mercies of Yulia Mihailovna.

"The Dresden Madonna? You mean the Sistine Madonna? Chère Varvara Petrovna, I spent two hours sitting before that picture and came away utterly disillusioned. I could make nothing of it and was in complete amazement. Karmazinov, too, says it's hard to understand it. They all see nothing in it now, Russians and English alike. All its fame is just the talk of the last generation."

"Fashions are changed then?"

"What I think is that one mustn't despise our younger generation either. They cry out that they're communists, but what I say is that we must appreciate them and mustn't be hard on them. I read everything now—the papers, communism, the natural sciences—I get everything because, after all, one must know where one's living and with whom one has to do. One mustn't spend one's whole life on the heights of one's own fancy. I've come to the conclusion, and adopted it as a principle, that one must be kind to the young people and so keep them from the brink. Believe me, Varvara Petrovna, that none but we who make up good society can by our kindness and good influence keep them from the abyss towards which they are brought by the intolerance of all these old men. I am glad though to learn from you about Stepan Trofimovitch. You suggest an idea to me: he may be useful at our literary matinée, you know I'm arranging for a whole day of festivities, a subscription entertainment for the benefit of the poor governesses of our province. They are scattered about Russia; in our district alone we can reckon up six of them. Besides that, there are two girls in the telegraph office, two are being trained in the academy, the rest would like to be but have not the means. The Russian woman's fate is a terrible one, Varvara Petrovna! It's out of that they're making the university question now, and there's even been a meeting of the Imperial Council about it. In this strange Russia of ours one can do anything one likes; and that, again, is why it's only by the kindness and the direct warm sympathy of all the better classes that we can direct this great common cause in the true path. Oh, heavens, have we many noble personalities among us! There are some, of course, but they are scattered far and wide. Let us unite and we shall be stronger. In one word, I shall first have a literary matinée, then a light luncheon, then an interval, and in the evening a ball. We meant to begin the evening by living pictures, but it would involve a great deal of expense, and so, to please the public, there will be one or two quadrilles in masks and fancy dresses, representing well-known literary schools. This humorous idea was suggested by Karmazinov. He has been a great help to me. Do you know he's going to read us the last thing he's written, which no one has seen yet. He is laying down the pen, and will write no more. This last essay is his farewell to the public. It's a charming little thing called 'Merci.' The title is French; he thinks that more amusing and even subtler. I do, too. In fact I advised it. I think Stepan Trofimovitch might read us something too, if it were quite short and … not so very learned. I believe Pyotr Stepanovitch and some one else too will read something. Pyotr Stepanovitch shall run round to you and tell you the programme. Better still, let me bring it to you myself."

"Allow me to put my name down in your subscription list too. I'll tell Stepan Trofimovitch and will beg him to consent."

Varvara Petrovna returned home completely fascinated. She was ready to stand up for Yulia Mihailovna through thick and thin, and for some reason was already quite put out with Stepan Trofimovitch, while he, poor man, sat at home, all unconscious.

"I'm in love with her. I can't understand how I could be so mistaken in that woman," she said to Nikolay Vsyevolodovitch and Pyotr Stepanovitch, who dropped in that evening.

"But you must make peace with the old man all the same," Pyotr Stepanovitch submitted. "He's in despair. You've quite sent him to Coventry. Yesterday he met your carriage and bowed, and you turned away. We'll trot him out, you know; I'm reckoning on him for something, and he may still be useful."

"Oh, he'll read something."

"I don't mean only that. And I was meaning to drop in on him to-day. So shall I tell him?"

"If you like. I don't know, though, how you'll arrange it," she said irresolutely. "I was meaning to have a talk with him myself, and wanted to fix the time and place."

She frowned.

"Oh, it's not worth while fixing a time. I'll simply give him the message."

"Very well, do. Add that I certainly will fix a time to see him though. Be sure to say that too."

Pyotr Stepanovitch ran off, grinning. He was, in fact, to the best of my recollection, particularly spiteful all this time, and ventured upon extremely impatient sallies with almost every one. Strange to say, every one, somehow, forgave him. It was generally accepted that he was not to be looked at from the ordinary standpoint. I may remark that he took up an extremely resentful attitude about Nikolay Vsyevolodovitch's duel. It took him unawares. He turned positively green when he was told of it. Perhaps his vanity was wounded: he only heard of it next day when every one knew of it.

"You had no right to fight, you know," he whispered to Stavrogin, five days later, when he chanced to meet him at the club. It was remarkable that they had not once met during those five days, though Pyotr Stepanovitch had dropped in at Varvara Petrovna's almost every day.

Nikolay Vsyevolodovitch looked at him in silence with an absent-minded air, as though not understanding what was the matter, and he went on without stopping. He was crossing the big hall of the club on his way to the refreshment room.

"You've been to see Shatov too.... You mean to make it known about Marya Timofyevna," Pyotr Stepanovitch muttered, running after him, and, as though not thinking of what he was doing he clutched at his shoulder.

Nikolay Vsyevolodovitch shook his hand off and turned round quickly to him with a menacing scowl. Pyotr Stepanovitch looked at him with a strange, prolonged smile. It all lasted only one moment. Nikolay Vsyevolodovitch walked on.

II

He went to the "old man" straight from Varvara Petrovna's, and he was in such haste simply from spite, that he might revenge himself for an insult of which I had no idea at that time. The fact is that at their last interview on the Thursday of the previous week, Stepan Trofimovitch, though the dispute was one of his own beginning, had ended by turning Pyotr Stepanovitch out with his stick. He concealed the incident from me at the time. But now, as soon as Pyotr Stepanovitch ran in with his everlasting grin, which was so naïvely condescending, and his unpleasantly inquisitive eyes peering into every corner, Stepan Trofimovitch at once made a signal aside to me, not to leave the room. This was how their real relations came to be exposed before me, for on this occasion I heard their whole conversation.

Stepan Trofimovitch was sitting stretched out on a lounge. He had grown thin and sallow since that Thursday. Pyotr Stepanovitch seated himself beside him with a most familiar air, unceremoniously tucking his legs up under him, and taking up more room on the lounge than deference to his father should have allowed. Stepan Trofimovitch moved aside, in silence, and with dignity.

On the table lay an open book. It was the novel, "What's to be done?" Alas, I must confess one strange weakness in my friend; the fantasy that he ought to come forth from his solitude and fight a last battle was getting more and more hold upon his deluded imagination. I guessed that he had got the novel and was studying it solely in order that when the inevitable conflict with the "shriekers" came about he might know their methods and arguments beforehand, from their very "catechism," and in that way be prepared to confute them all triumphantly, before her eyes. Oh, how that book tortured him! He sometimes flung it aside in despair, and leaping up, paced about the room almost in a frenzy.

"I agree that the author's fundamental idea is a true one," he said to me feverishly, "but that only makes it more awful. It's just our idea, exactly ours; we first sowed the seed, nurtured it, prepared the way, and, indeed, what could they say new, after us? But, heavens! How it's all expressed, distorted, mutilated!" he exclaimed, tapping the book with his fingers. "Were these the conclusions we were striving for? Who can understand the original idea in this?"

"Improving your mind?" sniggered Pyotr Stepanovitch, taking the book from the table and reading the title. "It's high time. I'll bring you better, if you like."

Stepan Trofimovitch again preserved a dignified silence. I was sitting on a sofa in the corner.

Pyotr Stepanovitch quickly explained the reason of his coming. Of course, Stepan Trofimovitch was absolutely staggered, and he listened in alarm, which was mixed with extreme indignation.

"And that Yulia Mihailovna counts on my coming to read for her!"

"Well, they're by no means in such need of you. On the contrary, it's by way of an attention to you, so as to make up to Varvara Petrovna. But, of course, you won't dare to refuse, and I expect you want to yourself," he added with a grin. "You old fogies are all so devilishly ambitious. But, I say though, you must look out that it's not too boring. What have you got? Spanish history, or what is it? You'd better let me look at it three days beforehand, or else you'll put us to sleep perhaps."

The hurried and too barefaced coarseness of these thrusts was obviously premeditated. He affected to behave as though it were impossible to talk to Stepan Trofimovitch in different and more delicate language. Stepan Trofimovitch resolutely persisted in ignoring his insults, but what his son told him made a more and more overwhelming impression upon him.

"And she, she herself sent me this message through you?" he asked, turning pale.

"Well, you see, she means to fix a time and place for a mutual explanation, the relics of your sentimentalising. You've been coquetting with her for twenty years and have trained her to the most ridiculous habits. But don't trouble yourself, it's quite different now. She keeps saying herself that she's only beginning now to 'have her eyes opened.' I told her in so many words that all this friendship of yours is nothing but a mutual pouring forth of sloppiness. She told me lots, my boy. Foo! what a flunkey's place you've been filling all this time. I positively blushed for you."

"I filling a flunkey's place?" cried Stepan Trofimovitch, unable to restrain himself.

"Worse, you've been a parasite, that is, a voluntary flunkey too lazy to work, while you've an appetite for money. She, too, understands all that now. It's awful the things she's been telling me about you, anyway. I did laugh, my boy, over your letters to her; shameful and disgusting. But you're all so depraved, so depraved! There's always something depraving in charity—you're a good example of it!"

"She showed you my letters!"

"All; though, of course, one couldn't read them all. Foo, what a lot of paper you've covered! I believe there are more than two thousand letters there. And do you know, old chap, I believe there was one moment when she'd have been ready to marry you. You let slip your chance in the silliest way. Of course, I'm speaking from your point of view, though, anyway, it would have been better than now when you've almost been married to 'cover another man's sins,' like a buffoon, for a jest, for money."

"For money! She, she says it was for money!" Stepan Trofimovitch wailed in anguish.

"What else, then? But, of course, I stood up for you. That's your only line of defence, you know. She sees for herself that you needed money like every one else, and that from that point of view maybe you were right. I proved to her as clear as twice two makes four that it was a mutual bargain. She was a capitalist and you were a sentimental buffoon in her service. She's not angry about the money, though you have milked her like a goat. She's only in a rage at having believed in you for twenty years, at your having so taken her in over these noble sentiments, and made her tell lies for so long. She never will admit that she told lies of herself, but you'll catch it the more for that. I can't make out how it was you didn't see that you'd have to have a day of reckoning. For after all you had some sense. I advised her yesterday to put you in an almshouse, a genteel one, don't disturb yourself; there'll be nothing humiliating; I believe that's what she'll do. Do you remember your last letter to me, three weeks ago?"

"Can you have shown her that?" cried Stepan Trofimovitch, leaping up in horror.

"Rather! First thing. The one in which you told me she was exploiting you, envious of your talent; oh, yes, and that about 'other men's sins.' You have got a conceit though, my boy! How I did laugh. As a rule your letters are very tedious. You write a horrible style. I often don't read them at all, and I've one lying about to this day, unopened. I'll send it to you to-morrow. But that one, that last letter of yours was the tiptop of perfection! How I did laugh! Oh, how I laughed!"

"Monster, monster!" wailed Stepan Trofimovitch.

"Foo, damn it all, there's no talking to you. I say, you're getting huffy again as you were last Thursday."

Stepan Trofimovitch drew himself up, menacingly.

"How dare you speak to me in such language?"

"What language? It's simple and clear."

"Tell me, you monster, are you my son or not?"

"You know that best. To be sure all fathers are disposed to be blind in such cases."

"Silence! Silence!" cried Stepan Trofimovitch, shaking all over.

"You see you're screaming and swearing at me as you did last Thursday. You tried to lift your stick against me, but you know, I found that document. I was rummaging all the evening in my trunk from curiosity. It's true there's nothing definite, you can take that comfort. It's only a letter of my mother's to that Pole. But to judge from her character ..."

"Another word and I'll box your ears."

"What a set of people!" said Pyotr Stepanovitch, suddenly addressing himself to me. "You see, this is how we've been ever since last Thursday. I'm glad you're here this time, anyway, and can judge between us. To begin with, a fact: he reproaches me for speaking like this of my mother, but didn't he egg me on to it? In Petersburg before I left the High School, didn't he wake me twice in the night, to embrace me, and cry like a woman, and what do you suppose he talked to me about at night? Why, the same modest anecdotes about my mother! It was from him I first heard them."

"Oh, I meant that in a higher sense! Oh, you didn't understand me! You understood nothing, nothing."

"But, anyway, it was meaner in you than in me, meaner, acknowledge that. You see, it's nothing to me if you like. I'm speaking from your point of view. Don't worry about my point of view. I don't blame my mother; if it's you, then it's you, if it's a Pole, then it's a Pole, it's all the same to me. I'm not to blame because you and she managed so stupidly in Berlin. As though you could have managed things better. Aren't you an absurd set, after that? And does it matter to you whether I'm your son or not? Listen," he went on, turning to me again, "he's never spent a penny on me all his life; till I was sixteen he didn't know me at all; afterwards he robbed me here, and now he cries out that his heart has been aching over me all his life, and carries on before me like an actor. I'm not Varvara Petrovna, mind you."

He got up and took his hat.

"I curse you henceforth!"

Stepan Trofimovitch, as pale as death, stretched out his hand above him.

"Ach, what folly a man will descend to!" cried Pyotr Stepanovitch, actually surprised. "Well, good-bye, old fellow, I shall never come and see you again. Send me the article beforehand, don't forget, and try and let it be free from nonsense. Facts, facts, facts. And above all, let it be short. Good-bye."

III

Outside influences, too, had come into play in the matter, however. Pyotr Stepanovitch certainly had some designs on his parent. In my opinion he calculated upon reducing the old man to despair, and so to driving him to some open scandal of a certain sort. This was to serve some remote and quite other object of his own, of which I shall speak hereafter. All sorts of plans and calculations of this kind were swarming in masses in his mind at that time, and almost all, of course, of a fantastic character. He had designs on another victim besides Stepan Trofimovitch. In fact, as appeared afterwards, his victims were not few in number, but this one he reckoned upon particularly, and it was Mr. von Lembke himself.

Andrey Antonovitch von Lembke belonged to that race, so favoured by nature, which is reckoned by hundreds of thousands at the Russian census, and is perhaps unconscious that it forms throughout its whole mass a strictly organised union. And this union, of course, is not planned and premeditated, but exists spontaneously in the whole race, without words or agreements as a moral obligation consisting in mutual support given by all members of the race to one another, at all times and places, and under all circumstances. Andrey Antonovitch had the honour of being educated in one of those more exalted Russian educational institutions which are filled with the youth from families well provided with wealth or connections. Almost immediately on finishing their studies the pupils were appointed to rather important posts in one of the government departments. Andrey Antonovitch had one uncle a colonel of engineers, and another a baker. But he managed to get into this aristocratic school, and met many of his fellow-countrymen in a similar position. He was a good-humoured companion, was rather stupid at his studies, but always popular. And when many of his companions in the upper forms—chiefly Russians—had already learnt to discuss the loftiest modern questions, and looked as though they were only waiting to leave school to settle the affairs of the universe, Andrey Antonovitch was still absorbed in the most innocent schoolboy interests. He amused them all, it is true, by his pranks, which were of a very simple character, at the most a little coarse, but he made it his object to be funny. At one time he would blow his nose in a wonderful way when the professor addressed a question to him, thereby making his schoolfellows and the professor laugh. Another time, in the dormitory, he would act some indecent living picture, to the general applause, or he would play the overture to "Fra Diavolo" with his nose rather skilfully. He was distinguished, too, by intentional untidiness, thinking this, for some reason, witty. In his very last year at school he began writing Russian poetry.

Of his native language he had only an ungrammatical knowledge, like many of his race in Russia. This turn for versifying drew him to a gloomy and depressed schoolfellow, the son of a poor Russian general, who was considered in the school to be a great future light in literature. The latter patronised him. But it happened that three years after leaving school this melancholy schoolfellow, who had flung up his official career for the sake of Russian literature, and was consequently going about in torn boots, with his teeth chattering with cold, wearing a light summer overcoat in the late autumn, met, one day on the Anitchin bridge, his former protégé, "Lembka," as he always used to be called at school. And, what do you suppose? He did not at first recognise him, and stood still in surprise. Before him stood an irreproachably dressed young man with wonderfully well-kept whiskers of a reddish hue, with pince-nez, with patent-leather boots, and the freshest of gloves, in a full overcoat from Sharmer's, and with a portfolio under his arm. Lembke was cordial to his old schoolfellow, gave him his address, and begged him to come and see him some evening. It appeared, too, that he was by now not "Lembka" but "Von Lembke." The schoolfellow came to see him, however, simply from malice perhaps. On the staircase, which was covered with red felt and was rather ugly and by no means smart, he was met and questioned by the house-porter. A bell rang loudly upstairs. But instead of the wealth which the visitor expected, he found Lembke in a very little side-room, which had a dark and dilapidated appearance, partitioned into two by a large dark green curtain, and furnished with very old though comfortable furniture, with dark green blinds on high narrow windows. Von Lembke lodged in the house of a very distant relation, a general who was his patron. He met his visitor cordially, was serious and exquisitely polite. They talked of literature, too, but kept within the bounds of decorum. A manservant in a white tie brought them some weak tea and little dry, round biscuits. The schoolfellow, from spite, asked for some seltzer water. It was given him, but after some delays, and Lembke was somewhat embarrassed at having to summon the footman a second time and give him orders. But of himself he asked his visitor whether he would like some supper, and was obviously relieved when he refused and went away. In short, Lembke was making his career, and was living in dependence on his fellow-countryman, the influential general.

He was at that time sighing for the general's fifth daughter, and it seemed to him that his feeling was reciprocated. But Amalia was none the less married in due time to an elderly factory-owner, a German, and an old comrade of the general's. Andrey Antonovitch did not shed many tears, but made a paper theatre. The curtain drew up, the actors came in, and gesticulated with their arms. There were spectators in the boxes, the orchestra moved their bows across their fiddles by machinery, the conductor waved his baton, and in the stalls officers and dandies clapped their hands. It was all made of cardboard, it was all thought out and executed by Lembke himself. He spent six months over this theatre. The general arranged a friendly party on purpose. The theatre was exhibited, all the general's five daughters, including the newly married Amalia with her factory-owner, numerous fraus and frauleins with their men folk, attentively examined and admired the theatre, after which they danced. Lembke was much gratified and was quickly consoled.

The years passed by and his career was secured. He always obtained good posts and always under chiefs of his own race; and he worked his way up at last to a very fine position for a man of his age. He had, for a long time, been wishing to marry and looking about him carefully. Without the knowledge of his superiors he had sent a novel to the editor of a magazine, but it had not been accepted. On the other hand, he cut out a complete toy railway, and again his creation was most successful. Passengers came on to the platform with bags and portmanteaux, with dogs and children, and got into the carriages. The guards and porters moved away, the bell was rung, the signal was given, and the train started off. He was a whole year busy over this clever contrivance. But he had to get married all the same. The circle of his acquaintance was fairly wide, chiefly in the world of his compatriots, but his duties brought him into Russian spheres also, of course. Finally, when he was in his thirty-ninth year, he came in for a legacy. His uncle the baker died, and left him thirteen thousand roubles in his will. The one thing needful was a suitable post. In spite of the rather elevated style of his surroundings in the service, Mr. von Lembke was a very modest man. He would have been perfectly satisfied with some independent little government post, with the right to as much government timber as he liked, or something snug of that sort, and he would have been content all his life long. But now, instead of the Minna or Ernestine he had expected, Yulia Mihailovna suddenly appeared on the scene. His career was instantly raised to a more elevated plane. The modest and precise man felt that he too was capable of ambition.

Yulia Mihailovna had a fortune of two hundred serfs, to reckon in the old style, and she had besides powerful friends. On the other hand Lembke was handsome, and she was already over forty. It is remarkable that he fell genuinely in love with her by degrees as he became more used to being betrothed to her. On the morning of his wedding day he sent her a poem. She liked all this very much, even the poem; it's no joke to be forty. He was very quickly raised to a certain grade and received a certain order of distinction, and then was appointed governor of our province.

Before coming to us Yulia Mihailovna worked hard at moulding her husband. In her opinion he was not without abilities, he knew how to make an entrance and to appear to advantage, he understood how to listen and be silent with profundity, had acquired a quite distinguished deportment, could make a speech, indeed had even some odds and ends of thought, and had caught the necessary gloss of modern liberalism. What worried her, however, was that he was not very open to new ideas, and after the long, everlasting plodding for a career, was unmistakably beginning to feel the need of repose. She tried to infect him with her own ambition, and he suddenly began making a toy church: the pastor came out to preach the sermon, the congregation listened with their hands before them, one lady was drying her tears with her handkerchief, one old gentleman was blowing his nose; finally the organ pealed forth. It had been ordered from Switzerland, and made expressly in spite of all expense. Yulia Mihailovna, in positive alarm, carried off the whole structure as soon as she knew about it, and locked it up in a box in her own room. To make up for it she allowed him to write a novel on condition of its being kept secret. From that time she began to reckon only upon herself. Unhappily there was a good deal of shallowness and lack of judgment in her attitude. Destiny had kept her too long an old maid. Now one idea after another fluttered through her ambitious and rather over-excited brain. She cherished designs, she positively desired to rule the province, dreamed of becoming at once the centre of a circle, adopted political sympathies. Von Lembke was actually a little alarmed, though, with his official tact, he quickly divined that he had no need at all to be uneasy about the government of the province itself. The first two or three months passed indeed very satisfactorily. But now Pyotr Stepanovitch had turned up, and something queer began to happen.

The fact was that young Verhovensky, from the first step, had displayed a flagrant lack of respect for Andrey Antonovitch, and had assumed a strange right to dictate to him; while Yulia Mihailovna, who had always till then been so jealous of her husband's dignity, absolutely refused to notice it; or, at any rate, attached no consequence to it. The young man became a favourite, ate, drank, and almost slept in the house. Von Lembke tried to defend himself, called him "young man" before other people, and slapped him patronisingly on the shoulder, but made no impression. Pyotr Stepanovitch always seemed to be laughing in his face even when he appeared on the surface to be talking seriously to him, and he would say the most startling things to him before company. Returning home one day he found the young man had installed himself in his study and was asleep on the sofa there, uninvited. He explained that he had come in, and finding no one at home had "had a good sleep."

Von Lembke was offended and again complained to his wife. Laughing at his irritability she observed tartly that he evidently did not know how to keep up his own dignity; and that with her, anyway, "the boy" had never permitted himself any undue familiarity, "he was naïve and fresh indeed, though not regardful of the conventions of society." Von Lembke sulked. This time she made peace between them. Pyotr Stepanovitch did not go so far as to apologise, but got out of it with a coarse jest, which might at another time have been taken for a fresh offence, but was accepted on this occasion as a token of repentance. The weak spot in Andrey Antonovitch's position was that he had blundered in the first instance by divulging the secret of his novel to him. Imagining him to be an ardent young man of poetic feeling and having long dreamed of securing a listener, he had, during the early days of their acquaintance, on one occasion read aloud two chapters to him. The young man had listened without disguising his boredom, had rudely yawned, had vouchsafed no word of praise; but on leaving had asked for the manuscript that he might form an opinion of it at his leisure, and Andrey Antonovitch had given it him. He had not returned the manuscript since, though he dropped in every day, and had turned off all inquiries with a laugh. Afterwards he declared that he had lost it in the street. At the time Yulia Mihailovna was terribly angry with her husband when she heard of it.

"Perhaps you told him about the church too?" she burst out almost in dismay.

Von Lembke unmistakably began to brood, and brooding was bad for him, and had been forbidden by the doctors. Apart from the fact that there were signs of trouble in the province, of which we will speak later, he had private reasons for brooding, his heart was wounded, not merely his official dignity. When Andrey Antonovitch had entered upon married life, he had never conceived the possibility of conjugal strife, or dissension in the future. It was inconsistent with the dreams he had cherished all his life of his Minna or Ernestine. He felt that he was unequal to enduring domestic storms. Yulia Mihailovna had an open explanation with him at last.

"You can't be angry at this," she said, "if only because you've still as much sense as he has, and are immeasurably higher in the social scale. The boy still preserves many traces of his old free-thinking habits; I believe it's simply mischief; but one can do nothing suddenly, in a hurry; you must do things by degrees. We must make much of our young people; I treat them with affection and hold them back from the brink."

"But he says such dreadful things," Von Lembke objected. "I can't behave tolerantly when he maintains in my presence and before other people that the government purposely drenches the people with vodka in order to brutalise them, and so keep them from revolution. Fancy my position when I'm forced to listen to that before every one."

As he said this, Von Lembke recalled a conversation he had recently had with Pyotr Stepanovitch. With the innocent object of displaying his Liberal tendencies he had shown him his own private collection of every possible kind of manifesto, Russian and foreign, which he had carefully collected since the year 1859, not simply from a love of collecting but from a laudable interest in them. Pyotr Stepanovitch, seeing his object, expressed the opinion that there was more sense in one line of some manifestoes than in a whole government department, "not even excluding yours, maybe."

Lembke winced.

"But this is premature among us, premature," he pronounced almost imploringly, pointing to the manifestoes.

"No, it's not premature; you see you're afraid, so it's not premature."

"But here, for instance, is an incitement to destroy churches."

"And why not? You're a sensible man, and of course you don't believe in it yourself, but you know perfectly well that you need religion to brutalise the people. Truth is honester than falsehood...."

"I agree, I agree, I quite agree with you, but it is premature, premature in this country ..." said Von Lembke, frowning.

"And how can you be an official of the government after that, when you agree to demolishing churches, and marching on Petersburg armed with staves, and make it all simply a question of date?"

Lembke was greatly put out at being so crudely caught.

"It's not so, not so at all," he cried, carried away and more and more mortified in his amour-propre. "You're young, and know nothing of our aims, and that's why you're mistaken. You see, my dear Pyotr Stepanovitch, you call us officials of the government, don't you? Independent officials, don't you? But let me ask you, how are we acting? Ours is the responsibility, but in the long run we serve the cause of progress just as you do. We only hold together what you are unsettling, and what, but for us, would go to pieces in all directions. We are not your enemies, not a bit of it. We say to you, go forward, progress, you may even unsettle things, that is, things that are antiquated and in need of reform. But we will keep you, when need be, within necessary limits, and so save you from yourselves, for without us you would set Russia tottering, robbing her of all external decency, while our task is to preserve external decency. Understand that we are mutually essential to one another. In England the Whigs and Tories are in the same way mutually essential to one another. Well, you're Whigs and we're Tories. That's how I look at it."

Andrey Antonovitch rose to positive eloquence. He had been fond of talking in a Liberal and intellectual style even in Petersburg, and the great thing here was that there was no one to play the spy on him.

Pyotr Stepanovitch was silent, and maintained an unusually grave air. This excited the orator more than ever.

"Do you know that I, the 'person responsible for the province,'" he went on, walking about the study, "do you know I have so many duties I can't perform one of them, and, on the other hand, I can say just as truly that there's nothing for me to do here. The whole secret of it is, that everything depends upon the views of the government. Suppose the government were ever to found a republic, from policy, or to pacify public excitement, and at the same time to increase the power of the governors, then we governors would swallow up the republic; and not the republic only. Anything you like we'll swallow up. I, at least, feel that I am ready. In one word, if the government dictates to me by telegram, activité dévorante, I'll supply activité dévorante. I've told them here straight in their faces: 'Dear sirs, to maintain the equilibrium and to develop all the provincial institutions one thing is essential; the increase of the power of the governor.' You see it's necessary that all these institutions, the zemstvos, the law-courts, should have a two-fold existence, that is, on the one hand, it's necessary they should exist (I agree that it is necessary), on the other hand, it's necessary that they shouldn't. It's all according to the views of the government. If the mood takes them so that institutions seem suddenly necessary, I shall have them at once in readiness. The necessity passes and no one will find them under my rule. That's what I understand by activité dévorante, and you can't have it without an increase of the governor's power. We're talking tête-à-tête. You know I've already laid before the government in Petersburg the necessity of a special sentinel before the governor's house. I'm awaiting an answer."

"You ought to have two," Pyotr Stepanovitch commented.

"Why two?" said Von Lembke, stopping short before him.

"One's not enough to create respect for you. You certainly ought to have two."

Andrey Antonovitch made a wry face.

"You ... there's no limit to the liberties you take, Pyotr Stepanovitch. You take advantage of my good-nature, you say cutting things, and play the part of a bourru bienfaisant...."

"Well, that's as you please," muttered Pyotr Stepanovitch; "anyway you pave the way for us and prepare for our success."

"Now, who are 'we,' and what success?" said Von Lembke, staring at him in surprise. But he got no answer.

Yulia Mihailovna, receiving a report of the conversation, was greatly displeased.

"But I can't exercise my official authority upon your favourite," Andrey Antonovitch protested in self-defence, "especially when we're tête-à-tête.... I may say too much ... in the goodness of my heart."

"From too much goodness of heart. I didn't know you'd got a collection of manifestoes. Be so good as to show them to me."

"But ... he asked to have them for one day."

"And you've let him have them, again!" cried Yulia Mihailovna getting angry. "How tactless!"

"I'll send someone to him at once to get them."

"He won't give them up."

"I'll insist on it," cried Von Lembke, boiling over, and he jumped up from his seat. "Who's he that we should be so afraid of him, and who am I that I shouldn't dare to do any thing?"

"Sit down and calm yourself," said Yulia Mihailovna, checking him. "I will answer your first question. He came to me with the highest recommendations. He's talented, and sometimes says extremely clever things. Karmazinov tells me that he has connections almost everywhere, and extraordinary influence over the younger generation in Petersburg and Moscow. And if through him I can attract them all and group them round myself, I shall be saving them from perdition by guiding them into a new outlet for their ambitions. He's devoted to me with his whole heart and is guided by me in everything."

"But while they're being petted … the devil knows what they may not do. Of course, it's an idea …" said Von Lembke, vaguely defending himself, "but … but here I've heard that manifestoes of some sort have been found in X district."

"But there was a rumour of that in the summer—manifestoes, false bank-notes, and all the rest of it, but they haven't found one of them so far. Who told you?"

"I heard it from Von Blum."

"Ah, don't talk to me of your Blum. Don't ever dare mention him again!"

Yulia Mihailovna flew into a rage, and for a moment could not speak. Von Blum was a clerk in the governor's office whom she particularly hated. Of that later.

"Please don't worry yourself about Verhovensky," she said in conclusion. "If he had taken part in any mischief he wouldn't talk as he does to you, and every one else here. Talkers are not dangerous, and I will even go so far as to say that if anything were to happen I should be the first to hear of it through him. He's quite fanatically devoted to me."

I will observe, anticipating events that, had it not been for Yulia Mihailovna's obstinacy and self-conceit, probably nothing of all the mischief these wretched people succeeded in bringing about amongst us would have happened. She was responsible for a great deal.

CHAPTER V. ON THE EVE OF THE FETE

I

The date of the fête which Yulia Mihailovna was getting up for the benefit of the governesses of our province had been several times fixed and put off. She had invariably bustling round her Pyotr Stepanovitch and a little clerk, Lyamshin, who used at one time to visit Stepan Trofimovitch, and had suddenly found favour in the governor's house for the way he played the piano and now was of use running errands. Liputin was there a good deal too, and Yulia Mihailovna destined him to be the editor of a new independent provincial paper. There were also several ladies, married and single, and lastly, even Karmazinov who, though he could not be said to bustle, announced aloud with a complacent air that he would agreeably astonish every one when the literary quadrille began. An extraordinary multitude of donors and subscribers had turned up, all the select society of the town; but even the unselect were admitted, if only they produced the cash. Yulia Mihailovna observed that sometimes it was a positive duty to allow the mixing of classes, "for otherwise who is to enlighten them?"

A private drawing-room committee was formed, at which it was decided that the fête was to be of a democratic character. The enormous list of subscriptions tempted them to lavish expenditure. They wanted to do something on a marvellous scale—that's why it was put off. They were still undecided where the ball was to take place, whether in the immense house belonging to the marshal's wife, which she was willing to give up to them for the day, or at Varvara Petrovna's mansion at Skvoreshniki. It was rather a distance to Skvoreshniki, but many of the committee were of opinion that it would be "freer" there. Varvara Petrovna would dearly have liked it to have been in her house. It's difficult to understand why this proud woman seemed almost making up to Yulia Mihailovna. Probably what pleased her was that the latter in her turn seemed almost fawning upon Nikolay Vsyevolodovitch and was more gracious to him than to anyone. I repeat again that Pyotr Stepanovitch was always, in continual whispers, strengthening in the governor's household an idea he had insinuated there already, that Nikolay Vsyevolodovitch was a man who had very mysterious connections with very mysterious circles, and that he had certainly come here with some commission from them.

People here seemed in a strange state of mind at the time. Among the ladies especially a sort of frivolity was conspicuous, and it could not be said to be a gradual growth. Certain very free-and-easy notions seemed to be in the air. There was a sort of dissipated gaiety and levity, and I can't say it was always quite pleasant. A lax way of thinking was the fashion. Afterwards when it was all over, people blamed Yulia Mihailovna, her circle, her attitude. But it can hardly have been altogether due to Yulia Mihailovna. On the contrary; at first many people vied with one another in praising the new governor's wife for her success in bringing local society together, and for making things more lively. Several scandalous incidents took place, for which Yulia Mihailovna was in no way responsible, but at the time people were amused and did nothing but laugh, and there was no one to check them. A rather large group of people, it is true, held themselves aloof, and had views of their own on the course of events. But even these made no complaint at the time; they smiled, in fact.

I remember that a fairly large circle came into existence, as it were, spontaneously, the centre of which perhaps was really to be found in Yulia Mihailovna's drawing-room. In this intimate circle which surrounded her, among the younger members of it, of course, it was considered admissible to play all sorts of pranks, sometimes rather free-and-easy ones, and, in fact, such conduct became a principle among them. In this circle there were even some very charming ladies. The young people arranged picnics, and even parties, and sometimes went about the town in a regular cavalcade, in carriages and on horseback. They sought out adventures, even got them up themselves, simply for the sake of having an amusing story to tell. They treated our town as though it were a sort of Glupov. People called them the jeerers or sneerers, because they did not stick at anything. It happened, for instance, that the wife of a local lieutenant, a little brunette, very young though she looked worn out from her husband's ill-treatment, at an evening party thoughtlessly sat down to play whist for high stakes in the fervent hope of winning enough to buy herself a mantle, and instead of winning, lost fifteen roubles. Being afraid of her husband, and having no means of paying, she plucked up the courage of former days and ventured on the sly to ask for a loan, on the spot, at the party, from the son of our mayor, a very nasty youth, precociously vicious. The latter not only refused it, but went laughing aloud to tell her husband. The lieutenant, who certainly was poor, with nothing but his salary, took his wife home and avenged himself upon her to his heart's content in spite of her shrieks, wails, and entreaties on her knees for forgiveness. This revolting story excited nothing but mirth all over the town, and though the poor wife did not belong to Yulia Mihailovna's circle, one of the ladies of the "cavalcade," an eccentric and adventurous character who happened to know her, drove round, and simply carried her off to her own house. Here she was at once taken up by our madcaps, made much of, loaded with presents, and kept for four days without being sent back to her husband. She stayed at the adventurous lady's all day long, drove about with her and all the sportive company in expeditions about the town, and took part in dances and merry-making. They kept egging her on to haul her husband before the court and to make a scandal. They declared that they would all support her and would come and bear witness. The husband kept quiet, not daring to oppose them. The poor thing realised at last that she had got into a hopeless position and, more dead than alive with fright, on the fourth day she ran off in the dusk from her protectors to her lieutenant. It's not definitely known what took place between husband and wife, but two shutters of the low-pitched little house in which the lieutenant lodged were not opened for a fortnight. Yulia Mihailovna was angry with the mischief-makers when she heard about it all, and was greatly displeased with the conduct of the adventurous lady, though the latter had presented the lieutenant's wife to her on the day she carried her off. However, this was soon forgotten.

Another time a petty clerk, a respectable head of a family, married his daughter, a beautiful girl of seventeen, known to every one in the town, to another petty clerk, a young man who came from a different district. But suddenly it was learned that the young husband had treated the beauty very roughly on the wedding night, chastising her for what he regarded as a stain on his honour. Lyamshin, who was almost a witness of the affair, because he got drunk at the wedding and so stayed the night, as soon as day dawned, ran round with the diverting intelligence.

Instantly a party of a dozen was made up, all of them on horseback, some on hired Cossack horses, Pyotr Stepanovitch, for instance, and Liputin, who, in spite of his grey hairs, took part in almost every scandalous adventure of our reckless youngsters. When the young couple appeared in the street in a droshky with a pair of horses to make the calls which are obligatory in our town on the day after a wedding, in spite of anything that may happen, the whole cavalcade, with merry laughter, surrounded the droshky and followed them about the town all the morning. They did not, it's true, go into the house, but waited for them outside, on horseback. They refrained from marked insult to the bride or bridegroom, but still they caused a scandal. The whole town began talking of it. Every one laughed, of course. But at this Von Lembke was angry, and again had a lively scene with Yulia Mihailovna. She, too, was extremely angry, and formed the intention of turning the scapegraces out of her house. But next day she forgave them all after persuasions from Pyotr Stepanovitch and some words from Karmazinov, who considered the affair rather amusing.

"It's in harmony with the traditions of the place," he said. "Anyway it's characteristic and ... bold; and look, every one's laughing, you're the only person indignant."

But there were pranks of a certain character that were absolutely past endurance.

A respectable woman of the artisan class, who went about selling gospels, came into the town. People talked about her, because some interesting references to these gospel women had just appeared in the Petersburg papers. Again the same buffoon, Lyamshin, with the help of a divinity student, who was taking a holiday while waiting for a post in the school, succeeded, on the pretence of buying books from the gospel woman, in thrusting into her bag a whole bundle of indecent and obscene photographs from abroad, sacrificed expressly for the purpose, as we learned afterwards, by a highly respectable old gentleman (I will omit his name) with an order on his breast, who, to use his own words, loved "a healthy laugh and a merry jest." When the poor woman went to take out the holy books in the bazaar, the photographs were scattered about the place. There were roars of laughter and murmurs of indignation. A crowd collected, began abusing her, and would have come to blows if the police had not arrived in the nick of time. The gospel woman was taken to the lock-up, and only in the evening, thanks to the efforts of Mavriky Nikolaevitch, who had learned with indignation the secret details of this loathsome affair, she was released and escorted out of the town. At this point Yulia Mihailovna would certainly have forbidden Lyamshin her house, but that very evening the whole circle brought him to her with the intelligence that he had just composed a new piece for the piano, and persuaded her at least to hear it. The piece turned out to be really amusing, and bore the comic title of "The Franco-Prussian War." It began with the menacing strains of the "Marseillaise":

"Qu'un sang impur abreuve nos sillons."

There is heard the pompous challenge, the intoxication of future victories. But suddenly mingling with the masterly variations on the national hymn, somewhere from some corner quite close, on one side come the vulgar strains of "Mein lieber Augustin." The "Marseillaise" goes on unconscious of them. The "Marseillaise" is at the climax of its intoxication with its own grandeur; but Augustin gains strength; Augustin grows more and more insolent, and suddenly the melody of Augustin begins to blend with the melody of the "Marseillaise." The latter begins, as it were, to get angry; becoming aware of Augustin at last she tries to fling him off, to brush him aside like a tiresome insignificant fly. But "Mein lieber Augustin" holds his ground firmly, he is cheerful and self-confident, he is gleeful and impudent, and the "Marseillaise" seems suddenly to become terribly stupid. She can no longer conceal her anger and mortification; it is a wail of indignation, tears, and curses, with hands outstretched to Providence.

"Pas un pouce de notre terrain; pas une de nos forteresses."

But she is forced to sing in time with "Mein lieber Augustin." Her melody passes in a sort of foolish way into Augustin; she yields and dies away. And only by snatches there is heard again:

"Qu'un sang impur ..."

But at once it passes very offensively into the vulgar waltz. She submits altogether. It is Jules Favre sobbing on Bismarck's bosom and surrendering every thing.... But at this point Augustin too grows fierce; hoarse sounds are heard; there is a suggestion of countless gallons of beer, of a frenzy of self-glorification, demands for millions, for fine cigars, champagne, and hostages. Augustin passes into a wild yell.... "The Franco-Prussian War" is over. Our circle applauded, Yulia Mihailovna smiled, and said, "Now, how is one to turn him out?" Peace was made. The rascal really had talent. Stepan Trofimovitch assured me on one occasion that the very highest artistic talents may exist in the most abominable blackguards, and that the one thing does not interfere with the other. There was a rumour afterwards that Lyamshin had stolen this burlesque from a talented and modest young man of his acquaintance, whose name remained unknown. But this is beside the mark. This worthless fellow who had hung about Stepan Trofimovitch for years, who used at his evening parties, when invited, to mimic Jews of various types, a deaf peasant woman making her confession, or the birth of a child, now at Yulia Mihailovna's caricatured Stepan Trofimovitch himself in a killing way, under the title of "A Liberal of the Forties." Everybody shook with laughter, so that in the end it was quite impossible to turn him out: he had become too necessary a person. Besides he fawned upon Pyotr Stepanovitch in a slavish way, and he, in his turn, had obtained by this time a strange and unaccountable influence over Yulia Mihailovna.

I wouldn't have talked about this scoundrel, and, indeed, he would not be worth dwelling upon, but there was another revolting story, so people declare, in which he had a hand, and this story I cannot omit from my record.

One morning the news of a hideous and revolting sacrilege was all over the town. At the entrance to our immense marketplace there stands the ancient church of Our Lady's Nativity, which was a remarkable antiquity in our ancient town. At the gates of the precincts there is a large ikon of the Mother of God fixed behind a grating in the wall. And behold, one night the ikon had been robbed, the glass of the case was broken, the grating was smashed and several stones and pearls (I don't know whether they were very precious ones) had been removed from the crown and the setting. But what was worse, besides the theft a senseless, scoffing sacrilege had been perpetrated. Behind the broken glass of the ikon they found in the morning, so it was said, a live mouse. Now, four months since, it has been established beyond doubt that the crime was committed by the convict Fedka, but for some reason it is added that Lyamshin took part in it. At the time no one spoke of Lyamshin or had any suspicion of him. But now every one says it was he who put the mouse there. I remember all our responsible officials were rather staggered. A crowd thronged round the scene of the crime from early morning. There was a crowd continually before it, not a very huge one, but always about a hundred people, some coming and some going. As they approached they crossed themselves and bowed down to the ikon. They began to give offerings, and a church dish made its appearance, and with the dish a monk. But it was only about three o'clock in the afternoon it occurred to the authorities that it was possible to prohibit the crowds standing about, and to command them when they had prayed, bowed down and left their offerings, to pass on. Upon Von Lembke this unfortunate incident made the gloomiest impression. As I was told, Yulia Mihailovna said afterwards it was from this ill-omened morning that she first noticed in her husband that strange depression which persisted in him until he left our province on account of illness two months ago, and, I believe, haunts him still in Switzerland, where he has gone for a rest after his brief career amongst us.

I remember at one o'clock in the afternoon I crossed the marketplace; the crowd was silent and their faces solemn and gloomy. A merchant, fat and sallow, drove up, got out of his carriage, made a bow to the ground, kissed the ikon, offered a rouble, sighing, got back into his carriage and drove off. Another carriage drove up with two ladies accompanied by two of our scapegraces. The young people (one of whom was not quite young) got out of their carriage too, and squeezed their way up to the ikon, pushing people aside rather carelessly. Neither of the young men took off his hat, and one of them put a pince-nez on his nose. In the crowd there was a murmur, vague but unfriendly. The dandy with the pince-nez took out of his purse, which was stuffed full of bank-notes, a copper farthing and flung it into the dish. Both laughed, and, talking loudly, went back to their carriage. At that moment Lizaveta Nikolaevna galloped up, escorted by Mavriky Nikolaevitch. She jumped off her horse, flung the reins to her companion, who, at her bidding, remained on his horse, and approached the ikon at the very moment when the farthing had been flung down. A flush of indignation suffused her cheeks; she took off her round hat and her gloves, fell straight on her knees before the ikon on the muddy pavement, and reverently bowed down three times to the earth. Then she took out her purse, but as it appeared she had only a few small coins in it she instantly took off her diamond ear-rings and put them in the dish.

"May I? May I? For the adornment of the setting?" she asked the monk.

"It is permitted," replied the latter, "every gift is good." The crowd was silent, expressing neither dissent nor approval.

Liza got on her horse again, in her muddy riding-habit, and galloped away.

II

Two days after the incident I have described I met her in a numerous company, who were driving out on some expedition in three coaches, surrounded by others on horseback. She beckoned to me, stopped her carriage, and pressingly urged me to join their party. A place was found for me in the carriage, and she laughingly introduced me to her companions, gorgeously attired ladies, and explained to me that they were all going on a very interesting expedition. She was laughing, and seemed somewhat excessively happy. Just lately she had been very lively, even playful, in fact.

The expedition was certainly an eccentric one. They were all going to a house the other side of the river, to the merchant Sevastyanov's. In the lodge of this merchant's house our saint and prophet, Semyon Yakovlevitch, who was famous not only amongst us but in the surrounding provinces and even in Petersburg and Moscow, had been living for the last ten years, in retirement, ease, and comfort. Every one went to see him, especially visitors to the neighbourhood, extracting from him some crazy utterance, bowing down to him, and leaving an offering. These offerings were sometimes considerable, and if Semyon Yakovlevitch did not himself assign them to some other purpose were piously sent to some church or more often to the monastery of Our Lady. A monk from the monastery was always in waiting upon Semyon Yakovlevitch with this object.

All were in expectation of great amusement. No one of the party had seen Semyon Yakovlevitch before, except Lyamshin, who declared that the saint had given orders that he should be driven out with a broom, and had with his own hand flung two big baked potatoes after him. Among the party I noticed Pyotr Stepanovitch, again riding a hired Cossack horse, on which he sat extremely badly, and Nikolay Vsyevolodovitch, also on horseback. The latter did not always hold aloof from social diversions, and on such occasions always wore an air of gaiety, although, as always, he spoke little and seldom. When our party had crossed the bridge and reached the hotel of the town, someone suddenly announced that in one of the rooms of the hotel they had just found a traveller who had shot himself, and were expecting the police. At once the suggestion was made that they should go and look at the suicide. The idea met with approval: our ladies had never seen a suicide. I remember one of them said aloud on the occasion, "Everything's so boring, one can't be squeamish over one's amusements, as long as they're interesting." Only a few of them remained outside. The others went in a body into the dirty corridor, and amongst the others I saw, to my amazement, Lizaveta Nikolaevna. The door of the room was open, and they did not, of course, dare to prevent our going in to look at the suicide. He was quite a young lad, not more than nineteen. He must have been very good-looking, with thick fair hair, with a regular oval face, and a fine, pure forehead. The body was already stiff, and his white young face looked like marble. On the table lay a note, in his handwriting, to the effect that no one was to blame for his death, that he had killed himself because he had "squandered" four hundred roubles. The word "squandered" was used in the letter; in the four lines of his letter there were three mistakes in spelling. A stout country gentleman, evidently a neighbour, who had been staying in the hotel on some business of his own, was particularly distressed about it. From his words it appeared that the boy had been sent by his family, that is, a widowed mother, sisters, and aunts, from the country to the town in order that, under the supervision of a female relation in the town, he might purchase and take home with him various articles for the trousseau of his eldest sister, who was going to be married. The family had, with sighs of apprehension, entrusted him with the four hundred roubles, the savings of ten years, and had sent him on his way with exhortations, prayers, and signs of the cross. The boy had till then been well-behaved and trustworthy. Arriving three days before at the town, he had not gone to his relations, had put up at the hotel, and gone straight to the club in the hope of finding in some back room a "travelling banker," or at least some game of cards for money. But that evening there was no "banker" there or gambling going on. Going back to the hotel about midnight he asked for champagne, Havana cigars, and ordered a supper of six or seven dishes. But the champagne made him drunk, and the cigar made him sick, so that he did not touch the food when it was brought to him, and went to bed almost unconscious. Waking next morning as fresh as an apple, he went at once to the gipsies' camp, which was in a suburb beyond the river, and of which he had heard the day before at the club. He did not reappear at the hotel for two days. At last, at five o'clock in the afternoon of the previous day, he had returned drunk, had at once gone to bed, and had slept till ten o'clock in the evening. On waking up he had asked for a cutlet, a bottle of Chateau d'Yquem, and some grapes, paper, and ink, and his bill. No one noticed anything special about him; he was quiet, gentle, and friendly. He must have shot himself at about midnight, though it was strange that no one had heard the shot, and they only raised the alarm at midday, when, after knocking in vain, they had broken in the door. The bottle of Chateau d'Yquem was half empty, there was half a plateful of grapes left too. The shot had been fired from a little three-chambered revolver, straight into the heart. Very little blood had flowed. The revolver had dropped from his hand on to the carpet. The boy himself was half lying in a corner of the sofa. Death must have been instantaneous. There was no trace of the anguish of death in the face; the expression was serene, almost happy, as though there were no cares in his life. All our party stared at him with greedy curiosity. In every misfortune of one's neighbour there is always something cheering for an onlooker—whoever he may be. Our ladies gazed in silence, their companions distinguished themselves by their wit and their superb equanimity. One observed that his was the best way out of it, and that the boy could not have hit upon anything more sensible; another observed that he had had a good time if only for a moment. A third suddenly blurted out the inquiry why people had begun hanging and shooting themselves among us of late, as though they had suddenly lost their roots, as though the ground were giving way under every one's feet. People looked coldly at this raisonneur. Then Lyamshin, who prided himself on playing the fool, took a bunch of grapes from the plate; another, laughing, followed his example, and a third stretched out his hand for the Chateau d'Yquem. But the head of police arriving checked him, and even ordered that the room should be cleared. As every one had seen all they wanted they went out without disputing, though Lyamshin began pestering the police captain about something. The general merrymaking, laughter, and playful talk were twice as lively on the latter half of the way.

We arrived at Semyon Yakovlevitch's just at one o'clock. The gate of the rather large house stood unfastened, and the approach to the lodge was open. We learnt at once that Semyon Yakovlevitch was dining, but was receiving guests. The whole crowd of us went in. The room in which the saint dined and received visitors had three windows, and was fairly large. It was divided into two equal parts by a wooden lattice-work partition, which ran from wall to wall, and was three or four feet high. Ordinary visitors remained on the outside of this partition, but lucky ones were by the saint's invitation admitted through the partition doors into his half of the room. And if so disposed he made them sit down on the sofa or on his old leather chairs. He himself invariably sat in an old-fashioned shabby Voltaire arm-chair. He was a rather big, bloated-looking, yellow-faced man of five and fifty, with a bald head and scanty flaxen hair. He wore no beard; his right cheek was swollen, and his mouth seemed somehow twisted awry. He had a large wart on the left side of his nose; narrow eyes, and a calm, stolid, sleepy expression. He was dressed in European style, in a black coat, but had no waistcoat or tie. A rather coarse, but white shirt, peeped out below his coat. There was something the matter with his feet, I believe, and he kept them in slippers. I've heard that he had at one time been a clerk, and received a rank in the service. He had just finished some fish soup, and was beginning his second dish of potatoes in their skins, eaten with salt. He never ate anything else, but he drank a great deal of tea, of which he was very fond. Three servants provided by the merchant were running to and fro about him. One of them was in a swallow-tail, the second looked like a workman, and the third like a verger. There was also a very lively boy of sixteen. Besides the servants there was present, holding a jug, a reverend, grey-headed monk, who was a little too fat. On one of the tables a huge samovar was boiling, and a tray with almost two dozen glasses was standing near it. On another table opposite offerings had been placed: some loaves and also some pounds of sugar, two pounds of tea, a pair of embroidered slippers, a foulard handkerchief, a length of cloth, a piece of linen, and so on. Money offerings almost all went into the monk's jug. The room was full of people, at least a dozen visitors, of whom two were sitting with Semyon Yakovlevitch on the other side of the partition. One was a grey-headed old pilgrim of the peasant class, and the other a little, dried-up monk, who sat demurely, with his eyes cast down. The other visitors were all standing on the near side of the partition, and were mostly, too, of the peasant class, except one elderly and poverty-stricken lady, one landowner, and a stout merchant, who had come from the district town, a man with a big beard, dressed in the Russian style, though he was known to be worth a hundred thousand.

All were waiting for their chance, not daring to speak of themselves. Four were on their knees, but the one who attracted most attention was the landowner, a stout man of forty-five, kneeling right at the partition, more conspicuous than any one, waiting reverently for a propitious word or look from Semyon Yakovlevitch. He had been there for about an hour already, but the saint still did not notice him.

Our ladies crowded right up to the partition, whispering gaily and laughingly together. They pushed aside or got in front of all the other visitors, even those on their knees, except the landowner, who remained obstinately in his prominent position even holding on to the partition. Merry and greedily inquisitive eyes were turned upon Semyon Yakovlevitch, as well as lorgnettes, pince-nez, and even opera-glasses. Lyamshin, at any rate, looked through an opera-glass. Semyon Yakovlevitch calmly and lazily scanned all with his little eyes.

"Milovzors! Milovzors!" he deigned to pronounce, in a hoarse bass, and slightly staccato.

All our party laughed: "What's the meaning of 'Milovzors'?" But Semyon Yakovlevitch relapsed into silence, and finished his potatoes. Presently he wiped his lips with his napkin, and they handed him tea.

As a rule, he did not take tea alone, but poured out some for his visitors, but by no means for all, usually pointing himself to those he wished to honour. And his choice always surprised people by its unexpectedness. Passing by the wealthy and the high-placed, he sometimes pitched upon a peasant or some decrepit old woman. Another time he would pass over the beggars to honour some fat wealthy merchant. Tea was served differently, too, to different people, sugar was put into some of the glasses and handed separately with others, while some got it without any sugar at all. This time the favoured one was the monk sitting by him, who had sugar put in; and the old pilgrim, to whom it was given without any sugar. The fat monk with the jug, from the monastery, for some reason had none handed to him at all, though up till then he had had his glass every day.

"Semyon Yakovlevitch, do say something to me. I've been longing to make your acquaintance for ever so long," carolled the gorgeously dressed lady from our carriage, screwing up her eyes and smiling. She was the lady who had observed that one must not be squeamish about one's amusements, so long as they were interesting. Semyon Yakovlevitch did not even look at her. The kneeling landowner uttered a deep, sonorous sigh, like the sound of a big pair of bellows.

"With sugar in it!" said Semyon Yakovlevitch suddenly, pointing to the wealthy merchant. The latter moved forward and stood beside the kneeling gentleman.

"Some more sugar for him!" ordered Semyon Yakovlevitch, after the glass had already been poured out. They put some more in. "More, more, for him!" More was put in a third time, and again a fourth. The merchant began submissively drinking his syrup.

"Heavens!" whispered the people, crossing themselves. The kneeling gentleman again heaved a deep, sonorous sigh.

"Father! Semyon Yakovlevitch!" The voice of the poor lady rang out all at once plaintively, though so sharply that it was startling. Our party had shoved her back to the wall. "A whole hour, dear father, I've been waiting for grace. Speak to me. Consider my case in my helplessness."

"Ask her," said Semyon Yakovlevitch to the verger, who went to the partition.

"Have you done what Semyon Yakovlevitch bade you last time?" he asked the widow in a soft and measured voice.

"Done it! Father Semyon Yakovlevitch. How can one do it with them?" wailed the widow. "They're cannibals; they're lodging a complaint against me, in the court; they threaten to take it to the senate. That's how they treat their own mother!"

"Give her!" Semyon Yakovlevitch pointed to a sugar-loaf. The boy skipped up, seized the sugar-loaf and dragged it to the widow.

"Ach, father; great is your merciful kindness. What am I to do with so much?" wailed the widow.

"More, more," said Semyon Yakovlevitch lavishly.

They dragged her another sugar-loaf. "More, more!" the saint commanded. They took her a third, and finally a fourth. The widow was surrounded with sugar on all sides. The monk from the monastery sighed; all this might have gone to the monastery that day as it had done on former occasions.

"What am I to do with so much," the widow sighed obsequiously. "It's enough to make one person sick!... Is it some sort of a prophecy, father?"

"Be sure it's by way of a prophecy," said someone in the crowd.

"Another pound for her, another!" Semyon Yakovlevitch persisted.

There was a whole sugar-loaf still on the table, but the saint ordered a pound to be given, and they gave her a pound.

"Lord have mercy on us!" gasped the people, crossing themselves. "It's surely a prophecy."

"Sweeten your heart for the future with mercy and loving kindness, and then come to make complaints against your own children; bone of your bone. That's what we must take this emblem to mean," the stout monk from the monastery, who had had no tea given to him, said softly but self-complacently, taking upon himself the rôle of interpreter in an access of wounded vanity.

"What are you saying, father?" cried the widow, suddenly infuriated. "Why, they dragged me into the fire with a rope round me when the Verhishins' house was burnt, and they locked up a dead cat in my chest. They are ready to do any villainy...."

"Away with her! Away with her!" Semyon Yakovlevitch said suddenly, waving his hands.

The verger and the boy dashed through the partition. The verger took the widow by the arm, and without resisting she trailed to the door, keeping her eyes fixed on the loaves of sugar that had been bestowed on her, which the boy dragged after her.

"One to be taken away. Take it away," Semyon Yakovlevitch commanded to the servant like a workman, who remained with him. The latter rushed after the retreating woman, and the three servants returned somewhat later bringing back one loaf of sugar which had been presented to the widow and now taken away from her. She carried off three, however.

"Semyon Yakovlevitch," said a voice at the door. "I dreamt of a bird, a jackdaw; it flew out of the water and flew into the fire. What does the dream mean?"

"Frost," Semyon Yakovlevitch pronounced.

"Semyon Yakovlevitch, why don't you answer me all this time? I've been interested in you ever so long," the lady of our party began again.

"Ask him!" said Semyon Yakovlevitch, not heeding her, but pointing to the kneeling gentleman.

The monk from the monastery to whom the order was given moved sedately to the kneeling figure.

"How have you sinned? And was not some command laid upon you?"

"Not to fight; not to give the rein to my hands," answered the kneeling gentleman hoarsely.

"Have you obeyed?" asked the monk.

"I cannot obey. My own strength gets the better of me."

"Away with him, away with him! With a broom, with a broom!" cried Semyon Yakovlevitch, waving his hands. The gentleman rushed out of the room without waiting for this penalty.

"He's left a gold piece where he knelt," observed the monk, picking up a half-imperial.

"For him!" said the saint, pointing to the rich merchant. The latter dared not refuse it, and took it.

"Gold to gold," the monk from the monastery could not refrain from saying.

"And give him some with sugar in it," said the saint, pointing to Mavriky Nikolaevitch. The servant poured out the tea and took it by mistake to the dandy with the pince-nez.

"The long one, the long one!" Semyon Yakovlevitch corrected him.

Mavriky Nikolaevitch took the glass, made a military half-bow, and began drinking it. I don't know why, but all our party burst into peals of laughter.

"Mavriky Nikolaevitch," cried Liza, addressing him suddenly. "That kneeling gentleman has gone away. You kneel down in his place."

Mavriky Nikolaevitch looked at her in amazement.

"I beg you to. You'll do me the greatest favour. Listen, Mavriky Nikolaevitch," she went on, speaking in an emphatic, obstinate, excited, and rapid voice. "You must kneel down; I must see you kneel down. If you won't, don't come near me. I insist, I insist!"

I don't know what she meant by it; but she insisted upon it relentlessly, as though she were in a fit. Mavriky Nikolaevitch, as we shall see later, set down these capricious impulses, which had been particularly frequent of late, to outbreaks of blind hatred for him, not due to spite, for, on the contrary, she esteemed him, loved him, and respected him, and he knew that himself—but from a peculiar unconscious hatred which at times she could not control.

In silence he gave his cup to an old woman standing behind him, opened the door of the partition, and, without being invited, stepped into Semyon Yakovlevitch's private apartment, and knelt down in the middle of the room in sight of all. I imagine that he was deeply shocked in his candid and delicate heart by Liza's coarse and mocking freak before the whole company. Perhaps he imagined that she would feel ashamed of herself, seeing his humiliation, on which she had so insisted. Of course no one but he would have dreamt of bringing a woman to reason by so naïve and risky a proceeding. He remained kneeling with his imperturbable gravity—long, tall, awkward, and ridiculous. But our party did not laugh. The unexpectedness of the action produced a painful shock. Every one looked at Liza.

"Anoint, anoint!" muttered Semyon Yakovlevitch.

Liza suddenly turned white, cried out, and rushed through the partition. Then a rapid and hysterical scene followed. She began pulling Mavriky Nikolaevitch up with all her might, tugging at his elbows with both hands.

"Get up! Get up!" she screamed, as though she were crazy. "Get up at once, at once. How dare you?"

Mavriky Nikolaevitch got up from his knees. She clutched his arms above the elbow and looked intently into his face. There was terror in her expression.

"Milovzors! Milovzors!" Semyon Yakovlevitch repeated again.

She dragged Mavriky Nikolaevitch back to the other part of the room at last. There was some commotion in all our company. The lady from our carriage, probably intending to relieve the situation, loudly and shrilly asked the saint for the third time, with an affected smile:

"Well, Semyon Yakovlevitch, won't you utter some saying for me? I've been reckoning so much on you."

"Out with the ——, out with the ——," said Semyon Yakovlevitch, suddenly addressing her, with an extremely indecent word. The words were uttered savagely, and with horrifying distinctness. Our ladies shrieked, and rushed headlong away, while the gentlemen escorting them burst into Homeric laughter. So ended our visit to Semyon Yakovlevitch.

At this point, however, there took place, I am told, an extremely enigmatic incident, and, I must own, it was chiefly on account of it that I have described this expedition so minutely.

I am told that when all flocked out, Liza, supported by Mavriky Nikolaevitch, was jostled against Nikolay Vsyevolodovitch in the crush in the doorway. I must mention that since that Sunday morning when she fainted they had not approached each other, nor exchanged a word, though they had met more than once. I saw them brought together in the doorway. I fancied they both stood still for an instant, and looked, as it were, strangely at one another, but I may not have seen rightly in the crowd. It is asserted, on the contrary, and quite seriously, that Liza, glancing at Nikolay Vsyevolodovitch, quickly raised her hand to the level of his face, and would certainly have struck him if he had not drawn back in time. Perhaps she was displeased with the expression of his face, or the way he smiled, particularly just after such an episode with Mavriky Nikolaevitch. I must admit I saw nothing myself, but all the others declared they had, though they certainly could not all have seen it in such a crush, though perhaps some may have. But I did not believe it at the time. I remember, however, that Nikolay Vsyevolodovitch was rather pale all the way home.

III

Almost at the same time, and certainly on the same day, the interview at last took place between Stepan Trofimovitch and Varvara Petrovna. She had long had this meeting in her mind, and had sent word about it to her former friend, but for some reason she had kept putting it off till then. It took place at Skvoreshniki; Varvara Petrovna arrived at her country house all in a bustle; it had been definitely decided the evening before that the fête was to take place at the marshal's, but Varvara Petrovna's rapid brain at once grasped that no one could prevent her from afterwards giving her own special entertainment at Skvoreshniki, and again assembling the whole town. Then every one could see for themselves whose house was best, and in which more taste was displayed in receiving guests and giving a ball. Altogether she was hardly to be recognised. She seemed completely transformed, and instead of the unapproachable "noble lady" (Stepan Trofimovitch's expression) seemed changed into the most commonplace, whimsical society woman. But perhaps this may only have been on the surface.

When she reached the empty house she had gone through all the rooms, accompanied by her faithful old butler, Alexey Yegorytch, and by Fomushka, a man who had seen much of life and was a specialist in decoration. They began to consult and deliberate: what furniture was to be brought from the town house, what things, what pictures, where they were to be put, how the conservatories and flowers could be put to the best use, where to put new curtains, where to have the refreshment rooms, whether one or two, and so on and so on. And, behold, in the midst of this exciting bustle she suddenly took it into her head to send for Stepan Trofimovitch.

The latter had long before received notice of this interview and was prepared for it, and he had every day been expecting just such a sudden summons. As he got into the carriage he crossed himself: his fate was being decided. He found his friend in the big drawing-room on the little sofa in the recess, before a little marble table with a pencil and paper in her hands. Fomushka, with a yard measure, was measuring the height of the galleries and the windows, while Varvara Petrovna herself was writing down the numbers and making notes on the margin. She nodded in Stepan Trofimovitch's direction without breaking off from what she was doing, and when the latter muttered some sort of greeting, she hurriedly gave him her hand, and without looking at him motioned him to a seat beside her.

"I sat waiting for five minutes, 'mastering my heart,'" he told me afterwards. "I saw before me not the woman whom I had known for twenty years. An absolute conviction that all was over gave me a strength which astounded even her. I swear that she was surprised at my stoicism in that last hour."

Varvara Petrovna suddenly put down her pencil on the table and turned quickly to Stepan Trofimovitch.

"Stepan Trofimovitch, we have to talk of business. I'm sure you have prepared all your fervent words and various phrases, but we'd better go straight to the point, hadn't we?"

She had been in too great a hurry to show the tone she meant to take. And what might not come next?

"Wait, be quiet; let me speak. Afterwards you shall, though really I don't know what you can answer me," she said in a rapid patter. "The twelve hundred roubles of your pension I consider a sacred obligation to pay you as long as you live. Though why a sacred obligation, simply a contract; that would be a great deal more real, wouldn't it? If you like, we'll write it out. Special arrangements have been made in case of my death. But you are receiving from me at present lodging, servants, and your maintenance in addition. Reckoning that in money it would amount to fifteen hundred roubles, wouldn't it? I will add another three hundred roubles, making three thousand roubles in all. Will that be enough a year for you? I think that's not too little? In any extreme emergency I would add something more. And so, take your money, send me back my servants, and live by yourself where you like in Petersburg, in Moscow, abroad, or here, only not with me. Do you hear?"

"Only lately those lips dictated to me as imperatively and as suddenly very different demands," said Stepan Trofimovitch slowly and with sorrowful distinctness. "I submitted … and danced the Cossack dance to please you. Oui, la comparaison peut être permise. C'était comme un petit Cosaque du Don qui sautait sur sa propre tombe. Now …"

"Stop, Stepan Trofimovitch, you are horribly long-winded. You didn't dance, but came to see me in a new tie, new linen, gloves, scented and pomatumed. I assure you that you were very anxious to get married yourself; it was written on your face, and I assure you a most unseemly expression it was. If I did not mention it to you at the time, it was simply out of delicacy. But you wished it, you wanted to be married, in spite of the abominable things you wrote about me and your betrothed. Now it's very different. And what has the Cosaque du Don to do with it, and what tomb do you mean? I don't understand the comparison. On the contrary, you have only to live. Live as long as you can. I shall be delighted."

"In an almshouse?"

"In an almshouse? People don't go into almshouses with three thousand roubles a year. Ah, I remember," she laughed. "Pyotr Stepanovitch did joke about an almshouse once. Bah, there certainly is a special almshouse, which is worth considering. It's for persons who are highly respectable; there are colonels there, and there's positively one general who wants to get into it. If you went into it with all your money, you would find peace, comfort, servants to wait on you. There you could occupy yourself with study, and could always make up a party for cards."

"Passons."

"Passons?" Varvara Petrovna winced. "But, if so, that's all. You've been informed that we shall live henceforward entirely apart."

"And that's all?" he said. "All that's left of twenty years? Our last farewell?"

"You're awfully fond of these exclamations, Stepan Trofimovitch. It's not at all the fashion. Nowadays people talk roughly but simply. You keep harping on our twenty years! Twenty years of mutual vanity, and nothing more. Every letter you've written me was written not for me but for posterity. You're a stylist, and not a friend, and friendship is only a splendid word. In reality—a mutual exchange of sloppiness...."

"Good heavens! How many sayings not your own! Lessons learned by heart! They've already put their uniform on you too. You, too, are rejoicing; you, too, are basking in the sunshine. Chère, chère, for what a mess of pottage you have sold them your freedom!"

"I'm not a parrot, to repeat other people's phrases!" cried Varvara Petrovna, boiling over. "You may be sure I have stored up many sayings of my own. What have you been doing for me all these twenty years? You refused me even the books I ordered for you, though, except for the binder, they would have remained uncut. What did you give me to read when I asked you during those first years to be my guide? Always Kapfig, and nothing but Kapfig. You were jealous of my culture even, and took measures. And all the while every one's laughing at you. I must confess I always considered you only as a critic. You are a literary critic and nothing more. When on the way to Petersburg I told you that I meant to found a journal and to devote my whole life to it, you looked at me ironically at once, and suddenly became horribly supercilious."

"That was not that, not that.... we were afraid then of persecution...."

"It was just that. And you couldn't have been afraid of persecution in Petersburg at that time. Do you remember that in February, too, when the news of the emancipation came, you ran to me in a panic, and demanded that I should at once give you a written statement that the proposed magazine had nothing to do with you; that the young people had been coming to see me and not you; that you were only a tutor who lived in the house, only because he had not yet received his salary. Isn't that so? Do remember that? You have distinguished yourself all your life, Stepan Trofimovitch."

"That was only a moment of weakness, a moment when we were alone," he exclaimed mournfully. "But is it possible, is it possible, to break off everything for the sake of such petty impressions? Can it be that nothing more has been left between us after those long years?"

"You are horribly calculating; you keep trying to leave me in your debt. When you came back from abroad you looked down upon me and wouldn't let me utter a word, but when I came back myself and talked to you afterwards of my impressions of the Madonna, you wouldn't hear me, you began smiling condescendingly into your cravat, as though I were incapable of the same feelings as you."

"It was not so. It was probably not so. J'ai oublié!"

"No; it was so," she answered, "and, what's more, you've nothing to pride yourself on. That's all nonsense, and one of your fancies. Now, there's no one, absolutely no one, in ecstasies over the Madonna; no one wastes time over it except old men who are hopelessly out of date. That's established."

"Established, is it?"

"It's of no use whatever. This jug's of use because one can pour water into it. This pencil's of use because you can write anything with it. But that woman's face is inferior to any face in nature. Try drawing an apple, and put a real apple beside it. Which would you take? You wouldn't make a mistake, I'm sure. This is what all our theories amount to, now that the first light of free investigation has dawned upon them."

"Indeed, indeed."

"You laugh ironically. And what used you to say to me about charity? Yet the enjoyment derived from charity is a haughty and immoral enjoyment. The rich man's enjoyment in his wealth, his power, and in the comparison of his importance with the poor. Charity corrupts giver and taker alike; and, what's more, does not attain its object, as it only increases poverty. Fathers who don't want to work crowd round the charitable like gamblers round the gambling-table, hoping for gain, while the pitiful farthings that are flung them are a hundred times too little. Have you given away much in your life? Less than a rouble, if you try and think. Try to remember when last you gave away anything; it'll be two years ago, maybe four. You make an outcry and only hinder things. Charity ought to be forbidden by law, even in the present state of society. In the new regime there will be no poor at all."

"Oh, what an eruption of borrowed phrases! So it's come to the new regime already? Unhappy woman, God help you!"

"Yes; it has, Stepan Trofimovitch. You carefully concealed all these new ideas from me, though every one's familiar with them nowadays. And you did it simply out of jealousy, so as to have power over me. So that now even that Yulia is a hundred miles ahead of me. But now my eyes have been opened. I have defended you, Stepan Trofimovitch, all I could, but there is no one who does not blame you."

"Enough!" said he, getting up from his seat. "Enough! And what can I wish you now, unless it's repentance?"

"Sit still a minute, Stepan Trofimovitch. I have another question to ask you. You've been told of the invitation to read at the literary matinée. It was arranged through me. Tell me what you're going to read?"

"Why, about that very Queen of Queens, that ideal of humanity, the Sistine Madonna, who to your thinking is inferior to a glass or a pencil."

"So you're not taking something historical?'" said Varvara Petrovna in mournful surprise. "But they won't listen to you. You've got that Madonna on your brain. You seem bent on putting every one to sleep! Let me assure you, Stepan Trofimovitch, I am speaking entirely in your own interest. It would be a different matter if you would take some short but interesting story of mediæval court life from Spanish history, or, better still, some anecdote, and pad it out with other anecdotes and witty phrases of your own. There were magnificent courts then; ladies, you know, poisonings. Karmazinov says it would be strange if you couldn't read something interesting from Spanish history."

"Karmazinov—that fool who has written himself out—looking for a subject for me!"

"Karmazinov, that almost imperial intellect. You are too free in your language, Stepan Trofimovitch."

"Your Karmazinov is a spiteful old woman whose day is over. Chère, chère, how long have you been so enslaved by them? Oh God!"

"I can't endure him even now for the airs he gives himself. But I do justice to his intellect. I repeat, I have done my best to defend you as far as I could. And why do you insist on being absurd and tedious? On the contrary, come on to the platform with a dignified smile as the representative of the last generation, and tell them two or three anecdotes in your witty way, as only you can tell things sometimes. Though you may be an old man now, though you may belong to a past age, though you may have dropped behind them, in fact, yet you'll recognise it yourself, with a smile, in your preface, and all will see that you're an amiable, good-natured, witty relic ... in brief, a man of the old savour, and so far advanced as to be capable of appreciating at their value all the absurdities of certain ideas which you have hitherto followed. Come, as a favour to me, I beg you."

"Chère, enough. Don't ask me. I can't. I shall speak of the Madonna, but I shall raise a storm that will either crush them all or shatter me alone."

"It will certainly be you alone, Stepan Trofimovitch."

"Such is my fate. I will speak of the contemptible slave, of the stinking, depraved flunkey who will first climb a ladder with scissors in his hands, and slash to pieces the divine image of the great ideal, in the name of equality, envy, and ... digestion. Let my curse thunder out upon them, and then—then ..."

"The madhouse?"

"Perhaps. But in any case, whether I shall be left vanquished or victorious, that very evening I shall take my bag, my beggar's bag. I shall leave all my goods and chattels, all your presents, all your pensions and promises of future benefits, and go forth on foot to end my life a tutor in a merchant's family or to die somewhere of hunger in a ditch. I have said it. Alea jacta est." He got up again.

"I've been convinced for years," said Varvara Petrovna, getting up with flashing eyes, "that your only object in life is to put me and my house to shame by your calumnies! What do you mean by being a tutor in a merchant's family or dying in a ditch? It's spite, calumny, and nothing more."

"You have always despised me. But I will end like a knight, faithful to my lady. Your good opinion has always been dearer to me than anything. From this moment I will take nothing, but will worship you disinterestedly."

"How stupid that is!"

"You have never respected me. I may have had a mass of weaknesses. Yes, I have sponged on you. I speak the language of nihilism, but sponging has never been the guiding motive of my action. It has happened so of itself. I don't know how.... I always imagined there was something higher than meat and drink between us, and—I've never, never been a scoundrel! And so, to take the open road, to set things right. I set off late, late autumn out of doors, the mist lies over the fields, the hoarfrost of old age covers the road before me, and the wind howls about the approaching grave.... But so forward, forward, on my new way

'Filled with purest love and fervour,

Faith which my sweet dream did yield.'

Oh, my dreams. Farewell. Twenty years. Alea jacta est!"

His face was wet with a sudden gush of tears. He took his hat.

"I don't understand Latin," said Varvara Petrovna, doing her best to control herself.

Who knows, perhaps, she too felt like crying. But caprice and indignation once more got the upper hand.

"I know only one thing, that all this is childish nonsense. You will never be capable of carrying out your threats, which are a mass of egoism. You will set off nowhere, to no merchant; you'll end very peaceably on my hands, taking your pension, and receiving your utterly impossible friends on Tuesdays. Good-bye, Stepan Trofimovitch."

"Alea jacta est!" He made her a deep bow, and returned home, almost dead with emotion.

CHAPTER VI. PYOTR STEPANOVITCH IS BUSY

I

The date of the fête was definitely fixed, and Von Lembke became more and more depressed. He was full of strange and sinister forebodings, and this made Yulia Mihailovna seriously uneasy. Indeed, things were not altogether satisfactory. Our mild governor had left the affairs of the province a little out of gear; at the moment we were threatened with cholera; serious outbreaks of cattle plague had appeared in several places; fires were prevalent that summer in towns and villages; whilst among the peasantry foolish rumours of incendiarism grew stronger and stronger. Cases of robbery were twice as numerous as usual. But all this, of course, would have been perfectly ordinary had there been no other and more weighty reasons to disturb the equanimity of Andrey Antonovitch, who had till then been in good spirits.

What struck Yulia Mihailovna most of all was that he became more silent and, strange to say, more secretive every day. Yet it was hard to imagine what he had to hide. It is true that he rarely opposed her and as a rule followed her lead without question. At her instigation, for instance, two or three regulations of a risky and hardly legal character were introduced with the object of strengthening the authority of the governor. There were several ominous instances of transgressions being condoned with the same end in view; persons who deserved to be sent to prison and Siberia were, solely because she insisted, recommended for promotion. Certain complaints and inquiries were deliberately and systematically ignored. All this came out later on. Not only did Lembke sign everything, but he did not even go into the question of the share taken by his wife in the execution of his duties. On the other hand, he began at times to be restive about "the most trifling matters," to the surprise of Yulia Mihailovna. No doubt he felt the need to make up for the days of suppression by brief moments of mutiny. Unluckily, Yulia Mihailovna was unable, for all her insight, to understand this honourable punctiliousness in an honourable character. Alas, she had no thought to spare for that, and that was the source of many misunderstandings.

There are some things of which it is not suitable for me to write, and indeed I am not in a position to do so. It is not my business to discuss the blunders of administration either, and I prefer to leave out this administrative aspect of the subject altogether. In the chronicle I have begun I've set before myself a different task. Moreover a great deal will be brought to light by the Commission of Inquiry which has just been appointed for our province; it's only a matter of waiting a little. Certain explanations, however, cannot be omitted.

But to return to Yulia Mihailovna. The poor lady (I feel very sorry for her) might have attained all that attracted and allured her (renown and so on) without any such violent and eccentric actions as she resolved upon at the very first step. But either from an exaggerated passion for the romantic or from the frequently blighted hopes of her youth, she felt suddenly, at the change of her fortunes, that she had become one of the specially elect, almost God's anointed, "over whom there gleamed a burning tongue of fire," and this tongue of flame was the root of the mischief, for, after all, it is not like a chignon, which will fit any woman's head. But there is nothing of which it is more difficult to convince a woman than of this;

on the contrary, anyone who cares to encourage the delusion in her will always be sure to meet with success. And people vied with one another in encouraging the delusion in Yulia Mihailovna. The poor woman became at once the sport of conflicting influences, while fully persuaded of her own originality. Many clever people feathered their nests and took advantage of her simplicity during the brief period of her rule in the province. And what a jumble there was under this assumption of independence! She was fascinated at the same time by the aristocratic element and the system of big landed properties and the increase of the governor's power, and the democratic element, and the new reforms and discipline, and free-thinking and stray Socialistic notions, and the correct tone of the aristocratic salon and the free-and-easy, almost pot-house, manners of the young people that surrounded her. She dreamed of "giving happiness" and reconciling the irreconcilable, or, rather, of uniting all and everything in the adoration of her own person. She had favourites too; she was particularly fond of Pyotr Stepanovitch, who had recourse at times to the grossest flattery in dealing with her. But she was attracted by him for another reason, an amazing one, and most characteristic of the poor lady: she was always hoping that he would reveal to her a regular conspiracy against the government. Difficult as it is to imagine such a thing, it really was the case. She fancied for some reason that there must be a nihilist plot concealed in the province. By his silence at one time and his hints at another Pyotr Stepanovitch did much to strengthen this strange idea in her. She imagined that he was in communication with every revolutionary element in Russia but at the same time passionately devoted to her. To discover the plot, to receive the gratitude of the government, to enter on a brilliant career, to influence the young "by kindness," and to restrain them from extremes—all these dreams existed side by side in her fantastic brain. She had saved Pyotr Stepanovitch, she had conquered him (of this she was for some reason firmly convinced); she would save others. None, none of them should perish, she should save them all; she would pick them out; she would send in the right report of them; she would act in the interests of the loftiest justice, and perhaps posterity and Russian liberalism would bless her name; yet the conspiracy would be discovered. Every advantage at once.

Still it was essential that Andrey Antonovitch should be in rather better spirits before the festival. He must be cheered up and reassured. For this purpose she sent Pyotr Stepanovitch to him in the hope that he would relieve his depression by some means of consolation best known to himself, perhaps by giving him some information, so to speak, first hand. She put implicit faith in his dexterity.

It was some time since Pyotr Stepanovitch had been in Mr. von Lembke's study. He popped in on him just when the sufferer was in a most stubborn mood.

II

A combination of circumstances had arisen which Mr. von Lembke was quite unable to deal with. In the very district where Pyotr Stepanovitch had been having a festive time a sub-lieutenant had been called up to be censured by his immediate superior, and the reproof was given in the presence of the whole company. The sub-lieutenant was a young man fresh from Petersburg, always silent and morose, of dignified appearance though small, stout, and rosy-cheeked. He resented the reprimand and suddenly, with a startling shriek that astonished the whole company, he charged at his superior officer with his head bent down like a wild beast's, struck him, and bit him on the shoulder with all his might; they had difficulty in getting him off. There was no doubt that he had gone out of his mind; anyway, it became known that of late he had been observed performing incredibly strange actions. He had, for instance, flung two ikons belonging to his landlady out of his lodgings and smashed up one of them with an axe; in his own room he had, on three stands resembling lecterns, laid out the works of Vogt, Moleschott, and Buchner, and before each lectern he used to burn a church wax-candle. From the number of books found in his rooms, it could be gathered that he was a well-read man. If he had had fifty thousand francs he would perhaps have sailed to the island of Marquisas like the "cadet" to whom Herzen alludes with such sprightly humour in one of his writings. When he was seized, whole bundles of the most desperate manifestoes were found in his pockets and his lodgings.

Manifestoes are a trivial matter too, and to my thinking not worth troubling about. We have seen plenty of them. Besides, they were not new manifestoes; they were, it was said later, just the same as had been circulated in the X province, and Liputin, who had travelled in that district and the neighbouring province six weeks previously, declared that he had seen exactly the same leaflets there then. But what struck Andrey Antonovitch most was that the overseer of Shpigulin's factory had brought the police just at the same time two or three packets of exactly the same leaflets as had been found on the lieutenant. The bundles, which had been dropped in the factory in the night, had not been opened, and none of the factory-hands had had time to read one of them. The incident was a trivial one, but it set Andrey Antonovitch pondering deeply. The position presented itself to him in an unpleasantly complicated light.

In this factory the famous "Shpigulin scandal" was just then brewing, which made so much talk among us and got into the Petersburg and Moscow papers with all sorts of variations. Three weeks previously one of the hands had fallen ill and died of Asiatic cholera; then several others were stricken down. The whole town was in a panic, for the cholera was coming nearer and nearer and had reached the neighbouring province. I may observe that satisfactory sanitary measures had been, so far as possible, taken to meet the unexpected guest. But the factory belonging to the Shpigulins, who were millionaires and well-connected people, had somehow been overlooked. And there was a sudden outcry from every one that this factory was the hot-bed of infection, that the factory itself, and especially the quarters inhabited by the workpeople, were so inveterately filthy that even if cholera had not been in the neighbourhood there might well have been an outbreak there. Steps were immediately taken, of course, and Andrey Antonovitch vigorously insisted on their being carried out without delay within three weeks. The factory was cleansed, but the Shpigulins, for some unknown reason, closed it. One of the Shpigulin brothers always lived in Petersburg and the other went away to Moscow when the order was given for cleansing the factory. The overseer proceeded to pay off the workpeople and, as it appeared, cheated them shamelessly. The hands began to complain among themselves, asking to be paid fairly, and foolishly went to the police, though without much disturbance, for they were not so very much excited. It was just at this moment that the manifestoes were brought to Andrey Antonovitch by the overseer.

Pyotr Stepanovitch popped into the study unannounced, like an intimate friend and one of the family; besides, he had a message from Yulia Mihailovna. Seeing him, Lembke frowned grimly and stood still at the table without welcoming him. Till that moment he had been pacing up and down the study and had been discussing something tête-à-tête with his clerk Blum, a very clumsy and surly German whom he had brought with him from Petersburg, in spite of the violent opposition of Yulia Mihailovna. On Pyotr Stepanovitch's entrance the clerk had moved to the door, but had not gone out. Pyotr Stepanovitch even fancied that he exchanged significant glances with his chief.

"Aha, I've caught you at last, you secretive monarch of the town!" Pyotr Stepanovitch cried out laughing, and laid his hand over the manifesto on the table. "This increases your collection, eh?"

Andrey Antonovitch flushed crimson; his face seemed to twitch.

"Leave off, leave off at once!" he cried, trembling with rage. "And don't you dare … sir …"

"What's the matter with you? You seem to be angry!"

"Allow me to inform you, sir, that I've no intention of putting up with your sans façon henceforward, and I beg you to remember …"

"Why, damn it all, he is in earnest!"

"Hold your tongue, hold your tongue"—Von Lembke stamped on the carpet—"and don't dare …"

God knows what it might have come to. Alas, there was one circumstance involved in the matter of which neither Pyotr Stepanovitch nor even Yulia Mihailovna herself had any idea. The luckless Andrey Antonovitch had been so greatly upset during the last few days that he had begun to be secretly jealous of his wife and Pyotr Stepanovitch. In solitude, especially at night, he spent some very disagreeable moments.

"Well, I imagined that if a man reads you his novel two days running till after midnight and wants to hear your opinion of it, he has of his own act discarded official relations, anyway.… Yulia Mihailovna treats me as a friend; there's no making you out," Pyotr Stepanovitch brought out, with a certain dignity indeed. "Here is your novel, by the way." He laid on the table a large heavy manuscript rolled up in blue paper.

Lembke turned red and looked embarrassed.

"Where did you find it?" he asked discreetly, with a rush of joy which he was unable to suppress, though he did his utmost to conceal it.

"Only fancy, done up like this, it rolled under the chest of drawers. I must have thrown it down carelessly on the chest when I went out. It was only found the day before yesterday, when the floor was scrubbed. You did set me a task, though!"

Lembke dropped his eyes sternly.

"I haven't slept for the last two nights, thanks to you. It was found the day before yesterday, but I kept it, and have been reading it ever since. I've no time in the day, so I've read it at night. Well, I don't like it; it's not my way of looking at things. But that's no matter; I've never set up for being a critic, but I couldn't tear myself away from it, my dear man, though I didn't like it! The fourth and fifth chapters are … they really are … damn it all, they are beyond words! And what a lot of humour you've packed into it; it made me laugh! How you can make fun of things sans que cela paraisse! As for the ninth and tenth chapters, it's all about love; that's not my line, but it's effective though. I was nearly blubbering over Egrenev's letter, though you've shown him up so cleverly.… You know, it's touching, though at the same time you want to show the false side of him, as it were, don't you? Have I guessed right? But I could simply beat you for the ending. For what are you setting up? Why, the same old idol of domestic happiness, begetting children and making money; 'they were married and lived happy ever afterwards'—come, it's too much! You will enchant your readers, for even I couldn't put the book down; but that makes it all the worse! The reading public is as stupid as ever, but it's the duty of sensible people to wake them up, while you … But that's enough. Good-bye. Don't be cross another time; I came in to you because I had a couple of words to say to you, but you are so unaccountable …"

Andrey Antonovitch meantime took his novel and locked it up in an oak bookcase, seizing the opportunity to wink to Blum to disappear. The latter withdrew with a long, mournful face.

"I am not unaccountable, I am simply … nothing but annoyances," he muttered, frowning but without anger, and sitting down to the table. "Sit down and say what you have to say. It's a long time since I've seen you, Pyotr Stepanovitch, only don't burst upon me in the future with such manners … sometimes, when one has business, it's …"

"My manners are always the same.…"

"I know, and I believe that you mean nothing by it, but sometimes one is worried.… Sit down."

Pyotr Stepanovitch immediately lolled back on the sofa and drew his legs under him.

III

"What sort of worries? Surely not these trifles?" He nodded towards the manifesto. "I can bring you as many of them as you like; I made their acquaintance in X province."

"You mean at the time you were staying there?"

"Of course, it was not in my absence. I remember there was a hatchet printed at the top of it. Allow me." (He took up the manifesto.) "Yes, there's the hatchet here too; that's it, the very same."

"Yes, here's a hatchet. You see, a hatchet."

"Well, is it the hatchet that scares you?"

"No, it's not … and I am not scared; but this business … it is a business; there are circumstances."

"What sort? That it's come from the factory? He he! But do you know, at that factory the workpeople will soon be writing manifestoes for themselves."

"What do you mean?" Von Lembke stared at him severely.

"What I say. You've only to look at them. You are too soft, Andrey Antonovitch; you write novels. But this has to be handled in the good old way."

"What do you mean by the good old way? What do you mean by advising me? The factory has been cleaned; I gave the order and they've cleaned it."

"And the workmen are in rebellion. They ought to be flogged, every one of them; that would be the end of it."

"In rebellion? That's nonsense; I gave the order and they've cleaned it."

"Ech, you are soft, Andrey Antonovitch!"

"In the first place, I am not so soft as you think, and in the second place ..." Von Lembke was piqued again. He had exerted himself to keep up the conversation with the young man from curiosity, wondering if he would tell him anything new.

"Ha ha, an old acquaintance again," Pyotr Stepanovitch interrupted, pouncing on another document that lay under a paper-weight, something like a manifesto, obviously printed abroad and in verse. "Oh, come, I know this one by heart, 'A Noble Personality.' Let me have a look at it—yes, 'A Noble Personality' it is. I made acquaintance with that personality abroad. Where did you unearth it?"

"You say you've seen it abroad?" Von Lembke said eagerly.

"I should think so, four months ago, or may be five."

"You seem to have seen a great deal abroad." Von Lembke looked at him subtly.

Pyotr Stepanovitch, not heeding him, unfolded the document and read the poem aloud:

"A NOBLE PERSONALITY

"He was not of rank exalted,

He was not of noble birth,

He was bred among the people

In the breast of Mother Earth.

But the malice of the nobles

And the Tsar's revengeful wrath

Drove him forth to grief and torture

On the martyr's chosen path.

He set out to teach the people

Freedom, love, equality,

To exhort them to resistance;

But to flee the penalty

Of the prison, whip and gallows,

To a foreign land he went.

While the people waited hoping

From Smolensk to far Tashkent,

Waited eager for his coming

To rebel against their fate,

To arise and crush the Tsardom

And the nobles' vicious hate,

To share all the wealth in common,

And the antiquated thrall

Of the church, the home and marriage

To abolish once for all."

"You got it from that officer, I suppose, eh?" asked Pyotr Stepanovitch.

"Why, do you know that officer, then, too?"

"I should think so. I had a gay time with him there for two days; he was bound to go out of his mind."

"Perhaps he did not go out of his mind."

"You think he didn't because he began to bite?"

"But, excuse me, if you saw those verses abroad and then, it appears, at that officer's …"

"What, puzzling, is it? You are putting me through an examination, Andrey Antonovitch, I see. You see," he began suddenly with extraordinary dignity, "as to what I saw abroad I have already given explanations, and my explanations were found satisfactory, otherwise I should not have been gratifying this town with my presence. I consider that the question as regards me has been settled, and I am not obliged to give any further account of myself, not because I am an informer, but because I could not help acting as I did. The people who wrote to Yulia Mihailovna about me knew what they were talking about, and they said I was an honest man.… But that's neither here nor there; I've come to see you about a serious matter, and it's as well you've sent your chimney-sweep away. It's a matter of importance to me, Andrey Antonovitch. I shall have a very great favour to ask of you."

"A favour? H'm … by all means; I am waiting and, I confess, with curiosity. And I must add, Pyotr Stepanovitch, that you surprise me not a little."

Von Lembke was in some agitation. Pyotr Stepanovitch crossed his legs.

"In Petersburg," he began, "I talked freely of most things, but there were things—this, for instance" (he tapped the "Noble Personality" with his finger) "about which I held my tongue—in the first place, because it wasn't worth talking about, and secondly, because I only answered questions. I don't care to put myself forward in such matters; in that I see the distinction between a rogue and an honest man forced by circumstances. Well, in short, we'll dismiss that. But now … now that these fools … now that this has come to the surface and is in your hands, and I see that you'll find out all about it—for you are a man with eyes and one can't tell beforehand what you'll do—and these fools are still going on, I … I … well, the fact is, I've come to ask you to save one man, a fool too, most likely mad, for the sake of his youth, his misfortunes, in the name of your humanity.… You can't be so humane only in the novels you manufacture!" he said, breaking off with coarse sarcasm and impatience.

In fact, he was seen to be a straightforward man, awkward and impolitic from excess of humane feeling and perhaps from excessive sensitiveness—above all, a man of limited intelligence, as Von Lembke saw at once with extraordinary subtlety. He had indeed long suspected it, especially when during the previous week he had, sitting alone in his study at night, secretly cursed him with all his heart for the inexplicable way in which he had gained Yulia Mihailovna's good graces.

"For whom are you interceding, and what does all this mean?" he inquired majestically, trying to conceal his curiosity.

"It … it's … damn it! It's not my fault that I trust you! Is it my fault that I look upon you as a most honourable and, above all, a sensible man … capable, that is, of understanding … damn …"

The poor fellow evidently could not master his emotion.

"You must understand at last," he went on, "you must understand that in pronouncing his name I am betraying him to you—I am betraying him, am I not? I am, am I not?"

"But how am I to guess if you don't make up your mind to speak out?"

"That's just it; you always cut the ground from under one's feet with your logic, damn it.… Well, here goes … this 'noble personality,' this 'student' … is Shatov … that's all."

"Shatov? How do you mean it's Shatov?"

"Shatov is the 'student' who is mentioned in this. He lives here, he was once a serf, the man who gave that slap.…"

"I know, I know." Lembke screwed up his eyes. "But excuse me, what is he accused of? Precisely and, above all, what is your petition?"

"I beg you to save him, do you understand? I used to know him eight years ago, I might almost say I was his friend," cried Pyotr Stepanovitch, completely carried away. "But I am not bound to give you an account of my past life," he added, with a gesture of dismissal. "All this is of no consequence; it's the case of three men and a half, and with those that are abroad you can't make up a dozen. But what I am building upon is your humanity and your intelligence.

You will understand and you will put the matter in its true light, as the foolish dream of a man driven crazy … by misfortunes, by continued misfortunes, and not as some impossible political plot or God knows what!"

He was almost gasping for breath.

"H'm. I see that he is responsible for the manifestoes with the axe," Lembke concluded almost majestically. "Excuse me, though, if he were the only person concerned, how could he have distributed it both here and in other districts and in the X province … and, above all, where did he get them?"

"But I tell you that at the utmost there are not more than five people in it—a dozen perhaps. How can I tell?"

"You don't know?"

"How should I know?—damn it all."

"Why, you knew that Shatov was one of the conspirators."

"Ech!" Pyotr Stepanovitch waved his hand as though to keep off the overwhelming penetration of the inquirer. "Well, listen. I'll tell you the whole truth: of the manifestoes I know nothing—that is, absolutely nothing. Damn it all, don't you know what nothing means?… That sub-lieutenant, to be sure, and somebody else and someone else here … and Shatov perhaps and someone else too—well, that's the lot of them … a wretched lot…. But I've come to intercede for Shatov. He must be saved, for this poem is his, his own composition, and it was through him it was published abroad; that I know for a fact, but of the manifestoes I really know nothing."

"If the poem is his work, no doubt the manifestoes are too. But what data have you for suspecting Mr. Shatov?"

Pyotr Stepanovitch, with the air of a man driven out of all patience, pulled a pocket-book out of his pocket and took a note out of it.

"Here are the facts," he cried, flinging it on the table.

Lembke unfolded it; it turned out to be a note written six months before from here to some address abroad. It was a brief note, only two lines:

"I can't print 'A Noble Personality' here, and in fact I can do nothing; print it abroad.

"Iv. Shatov."

Lembke looked intently at Pyotr Stepanovitch. Varvara Petrovna had been right in saying that he had at times the expression of a sheep.

"You see, it's like this," Pyotr Stepanovitch burst out. "He wrote this poem here six months ago, but he couldn't get it printed here, in a secret printing press, and so he asks to have it printed abroad…. That seems clear."

"Yes, that's clear, but to whom did he write? That's not clear yet," Lembke observed with the most subtle irony.

"Why, Kirillov, of course; the letter was written to Kirillov abroad.... Surely you knew that? What's so annoying is that perhaps you are only putting it on before me, and most likely you knew all about this poem and everything long ago! How did it come to be on your table? It found its way there somehow! Why are you torturing me, if so?"

He feverishly mopped his forehead with his handkerchief.

"I know something, perhaps." Lembke parried dexterously. "But who is this Kirillov?"

"An engineer who has lately come to the town. He was Stavrogin's second, a maniac, a madman; your sub-lieutenant may really only be suffering from temporary delirium, but Kirillov is a thoroughgoing madman—thoroughgoing, that I guarantee. Ah, Andrey Antonovitch, if the government only knew what sort of people these conspirators all are, they wouldn't have the heart to lay a finger on them. Every single one of them ought to be in an asylum; I had a good look at them in Switzerland and at the congresses."

"From which they direct the movement here?"

"Why, who directs it? Three men and a half. It makes one sick to think of them. And what sort of movement is there here? Manifestoes! And what recruits have they made? Sub-lieutenants in brain fever and two or three students! You are a sensible man: answer this question. Why don't people of consequence join their ranks? Why are they all students and half-baked boys of twenty-two? And not many of those. I dare say there are thousands of bloodhounds on their track, but have they tracked out many of them? Seven! I tell you it makes one sick."

Lembke listened with attention but with an expression that seemed to say, "You don't feed nightingales on fairy-tales."

"Excuse me, though. You asserted that the letter was sent abroad, but there's no address on it; how do you come to know that it was addressed to Mr. Kirillov and abroad too and ... and ... that it really was written by Mr. Shatov?"

"Why, fetch some specimen of Shatov's writing and compare it. You must have some signature of his in your office. As for its being addressed to Kirillov, it was Kirillov himself showed it me at the time."

"Then you were yourself ..."

"Of course I was, myself. They showed me lots of things out there. And as for this poem, they say it was written by Herzen to Shatov when he was still wandering abroad, in memory of their meeting, so they say, by way of praise and recommendation—damn it all ... and Shatov circulates it among the young people as much as to say, 'This was Herzen's opinion of me.'"

"Ha ha!" cried Lembke, feeling he had got to the bottom of it at last. "That's just what I was wondering: one can understand the manifesto, but what's the object of the poem?"

"Of course you'd see it. Goodness knows why I've been babbling to you. Listen. Spare Shatov for me and the rest may go to the devil—even Kirillov, who is in hiding now, shut up in

Filipov's house, where Shatov lodges too. They don't like me because I've turned round … but promise me Shatov and I'll dish them all up for you. I shall be of use, Andrey Antonovitch! I reckon nine or ten men make up the whole wretched lot. I am keeping an eye on them myself, on my own account. We know of three already: Shatov, Kirillov, and that sub-lieutenant. The others I am only watching carefully … though I am pretty sharp-sighted too. It's the same over again as it was in the X province: two students, a schoolboy, two noblemen of twenty, a teacher, and a half-pay major of sixty, crazy with drink, have been caught with manifestoes; that was all—you can take my word for it, that was all; it was quite a surprise that that was all. But I must have six days. I have reckoned it out—six days, not less. If you want to arrive at any result, don't disturb them for six days and I can kill all the birds with one stone for you; but if you flutter them before, the birds will fly away. But spare me Shatov. I speak for Shatov.… The best plan would be to fetch him here secretly, in a friendly way, to your study and question him without disguising the facts.… I have no doubt he'll throw himself at your feet and burst into tears! He is a highly strung and unfortunate fellow; his wife is carrying on with Stavrogin. Be kind to him and he will tell you everything, but I must have six days.… And, above all, above all, not a word to Yulia Mihailovna. It's a secret. May it be a secret?"

"What?" cried Lembke, opening wide his eyes. "Do you mean to say you said nothing of this to Yulia Mihailovna?"

"To her? Heaven forbid! Ech, Andrey Antonovitch! You see, I value her friendship and I have the highest respect for her … and all the rest of it … but I couldn't make such a blunder. I don't contradict her, for, as you know yourself, it's dangerous to contradict her. I may have dropped a word to her, for I know she likes that, but to suppose that I mentioned names to her as I have to you or anything of that sort! My good sir! Why am I appealing to you? Because you are a man, anyway, a serious person with old-fashioned firmness and experience in the service. You've seen life. You must know by heart every detail of such affairs, I expect, from what you've seen in Petersburg. But if I were to mention those two names, for instance, to her, she'd stir up such a hubbub.… You know, she would like to astonish Petersburg. No, she's too hot-headed, she really is."

"Yes, she has something of that fougue," Andrey Antonovitch muttered with some satisfaction, though at the same time he resented this unmannerly fellow's daring to express himself rather freely about Yulia Mihailovna. But Pyotr Stepanovitch probably imagined that he had not gone far enough and that he must exert himself further to flatter Lembke and make a complete conquest of him.

"Fougue is just it," he assented. "She may be a woman of genius, a literary woman, but she would scare our sparrows. She wouldn't be able to keep quiet for six hours, let alone six days. Ech, Andrey Antonovitch, don't attempt to tie a woman down for six days! You do admit that I have some experience—in this sort of thing, I mean; I know something about it, and you know that I may very well know something about it. I am not asking for six days for fun but with an object."

"I have heard …" (Lembke hesitated to utter his thought) "I have heard that on your return from abroad you made some expression … as it were of repentance, in the proper quarter?"

"Well, that's as it may be."

"And, of course, I don't want to go into it.... But it has seemed to me all along that you've talked in quite a different style—about the Christian faith, for instance, about social institutions, about the government even...."

"I've said lots of things, no doubt, I am saying them still; but such ideas mustn't be applied as those fools do it, that's the point. What's the good of biting his superior's shoulder! You agreed with me yourself, only you said it was premature."

"I didn't mean that when I agreed and said it was premature."

"You weigh every word you utter, though. He he! You are a careful man!" Pyotr Stepanovitch observed gaily all of a sudden. "Listen, old friend. I had to get to know you; that's why I talked in my own style. You are not the only one I get to know like that. Maybe I needed to find out your character."

"What's my character to you?"

"How can I tell what it may be to me?" He laughed again. "You see, my dear and highly respected Andrey Antonovitch, you are cunning, but it's not come to that yet and it certainly never will come to it, you understand? Perhaps you do understand. Though I did make an explanation in the proper quarter when I came back from abroad, and I really don't know why a man of certain convictions should not be able to work for the advancement of his sincere convictions ... but nobody there has yet instructed me to investigate your character and I've not undertaken any such job from them. Consider: I need not have given those two names to you. I might have gone straight there; that is where I made my first explanations. And if I'd been acting with a view to financial profit or my own interest in any way, it would have been a bad speculation on my part, for now they'll be grateful to you and not to me at headquarters. I've done it solely for Shatov's sake," Pyotr Stepanovitch added generously, "for Shatov's sake, because of our old friendship.... But when you take up your pen to write to headquarters, you may put in a word for me, if you like.... I'll make no objection, he he! Adieu, though; I've stayed too long and there was no need to gossip so much!" he added with some amiability, and he got up from the sofa.

"On the contrary, I am very glad that the position has been defined, so to speak." Von Lembke too got up and he too looked pleasant, obviously affected by the last words. "I accept your services and acknowledge my obligation, and you may be sure that anything I can do by way of reporting your zeal ..."

"Six days—the great thing is to put it off for six days, and that you shouldn't stir for those six days, that's what I want."

"So be it."

"Of course, I don't tie your hands and shouldn't venture to. You are bound to keep watch, only don't flutter the nest too soon; I rely on your sense and experience for that. But I should think you've plenty of bloodhounds and trackers of your own in reserve, ha ha!" Pyotr Stepanovitch blurted out with the gaiety and irresponsibility of youth.

"Not quite so." Lembke parried amiably. "Young people are apt to suppose that there is a great deal in the background.... But, by the way, allow me one little word: if this Kirillov was Stavrogin's second, then Mr. Stavrogin too ..."

"What about Stavrogin?"

"I mean, if they are such friends?"

"Oh, no, no, no! There you are quite out of it, though you are cunning. You really surprise me. I thought that you had some information about it.... H'm ... Stavrogin—it's quite the opposite, quite.... Avis au lecteur."

"Do you mean it? And can it be so?" Lembke articulated mistrustfully. "Yulia Mihailovna told me that from what she heard from Petersburg he is a man acting on some sort of instructions, so to speak...."

"I know nothing about it; I know nothing, absolutely nothing. Adieu. Avis au lecteur!" Abruptly and obviously Pyotr Stepanovitch declined to discuss it.

He hurried to the door.

"Stay, Pyotr Stepanovitch, stay," cried Lembke. "One other tiny matter and I won't detain you."

He drew an envelope out of a table drawer.

"Here is a little specimen of the same kind of thing, and I let you see it to show how completely I trust you. Here, and tell me your opinion."

In the envelope was a letter, a strange anonymous letter addressed to Lembke and only received by him the day before. With intense vexation Pyotr Stepanovitch read as follows:

"Your excellency,—For such you are by rank. Herewith I make known that there is an attempt to be made on the life of personages of general's rank and on the Fatherland. For it's working up straight for that. I myself have been disseminating unceasingly for a number of years. There's infidelity too. There's a rebellion being got up and there are some thousands of manifestoes, and for every one of them there will be a hundred running with their tongues out, unless they've been taken away beforehand by the police. For they've been promised a mighty lot of benefits, and the simple people are foolish, and there's vodka too. The people will attack one after another, taking them to be guilty, and, fearing both sides, I repent of what I had no share in, my circumstances being what they are. If you want information to save the Fatherland, and also the Church and the ikons, I am the only one that can do it. But only on condition that I get a pardon from the Secret Police by telegram at once, me alone, but the rest may answer for it. Put a candle every evening at seven o'clock in the porter's window for a signal. Seeing it, I shall believe and come to kiss the merciful hand from Petersburg. But on condition there's a pension for me, for else how am I to live? You won't regret it for it will mean a star for you. You must go secretly or they'll wring your neck. Your excellency's desperate servant falls at your feet.

"Repentant free-thinker incognito."

Von Lembke explained that the letter had made its appearance in the porter's room when it was left empty the day before.

"So what do you think?" Pyotr Stepanovitch asked almost rudely.

"I think it's an anonymous skit by way of a hoax."

"Most likely it is. There's no taking you in."

"What makes me think that is that it's so stupid."

"Have you received such documents here before?"

"Once or twice, anonymous letters."

"Oh, of course they wouldn't be signed. In a different style? In different handwritings?"

"Yes."

"And were they buffoonery like this one?"

"Yes, and you know … very disgusting."

"Well, if you had them before, it must be the same thing now."

"Especially because it's so stupid. Because these people are educated and wouldn't write so stupidly."

"Of course, of course."

"But what if this is someone who really wants to turn informer?"

"It's not very likely," Pyotr Stepanovitch rapped out dryly. "What does he mean by a telegram from the Secret Police and a pension? It's obviously a hoax."

"Yes, yes," Lembke admitted, abashed.

"I tell you what: you leave this with me. I can certainly find out for you before I track out the others."

"Take it," Lembke assented, though with some hesitation.

"Have you shown it to anyone?"

"Is it likely! No."

"Not to Yulia Mihailovna?"

"Oh, Heaven forbid! And for God's sake don't you show it her!" Lembke cried in alarm. "She'll be so upset … and will be dreadfully angry with me."

"Yes, you'll be the first to catch it; she'd say you brought it on yourself if people write like that to you. I know what women's logic is. Well, good-bye. I dare say I shall bring you the writer in a couple of days or so. Above all, our compact!"

IV

Though Pyotr Stepanovitch was perhaps far from being a stupid man, Fedka the convict had said of him truly "that he would make up a man himself and go on living with him too." He came away from Lembke fully persuaded that for the next six days, anyway, he had put his mind at rest, and this interval was absolutely necessary for his own purposes. But it was a false idea and founded entirely on the fact that he had made up for himself once for all an Andrey Antonovitch who was a perfect simpleton.

Like every morbidly suspicious man, Andrey Antonovitch was always exceedingly and joyfully trustful the moment he got on to sure ground. The new turn of affairs struck him at first in a rather favourable light in spite of some fresh and troublesome complications. Anyway, his former doubts fell to the ground. Besides, he had been so tired for the last few days, so exhausted and helpless, that his soul involuntarily yearned for rest. But alas! he was again uneasy. The long time he had spent in Petersburg had left ineradicable traces in his heart. The official and even the secret history of the "younger generation" was fairly familiar to him—he was a curious man and used to collect manifestoes—but he could never understand a word of it. Now he felt like a man lost in a forest. Every instinct told him that there was something in Pyotr Stepanovitch's words utterly incongruous, anomalous, and grotesque, "though there's no telling what may not happen with this 'younger generation,' and the devil only knows what's going on among them," he mused, lost in perplexity.

And at this moment, to make matters worse, Blum poked his head in. He had been waiting not far off through the whole of Pyotr Stepanovitch's visit. This Blum was actually a distant relation of Andrey Antonovitch, though the relationship had always been carefully and timorously concealed. I must apologise to the reader for devoting a few words here to this insignificant person. Blum was one of that strange class of "unfortunate" Germans who are unfortunate not through lack of ability but through some inexplicable ill luck. "Unfortunate" Germans are not a myth, but really do exist even in Russia, and are of a special type. Andrey Antonovitch had always had a quite touching sympathy for him, and wherever he could, as he rose himself in the service, had promoted him to subordinate positions under him; but Blum had never been successful. Either the post was abolished after he had been appointed to it, or a new chief took charge of the department; once he was almost arrested by mistake with other people. He was precise, but he was gloomy to excess and to his own detriment. He was tall and had red hair; he stooped and was depressed and even sentimental; and in spite of his being humbled by his life, he was obstinate and persistent as an ox, though always at the wrong moment. For Andrey Antonovitch he, as well as his wife and numerous family, had cherished for many years a reverent devotion. Except Andrey Antonovitch no one had ever liked him. Yulia Mihailovna would have discarded him from the first, but could not overcome her husband's obstinacy. It was the cause of their first conjugal quarrel. It had happened soon after their marriage, in the early days of their honeymoon, when she was confronted with Blum, who, together with the humiliating secret of his relationship, had been until then carefully concealed from her. Andrey Antonovitch besought her with clasped hands, told her pathetically all the story of Blum and their friendship from childhood, but Yulia Mihailovna considered herself disgraced forever, and even had recourse to fainting. Von Lembke would not budge an inch, and declared that he would not give up Blum or part from him for anything in the world, so that she was surprised at last and was obliged to put up with Blum. It was settled, however, that the relationship should be concealed even more carefully than before if possible, and that even Blum's Christian name and patronymic should be changed, because he too was for some reason called Andrey Antonovitch. Blum knew no one in the town except the German chemist, had not called on anyone, and led, as he always did, a lonely and niggardly existence. He had long been aware of Andrey Antonovitch's literary peccadilloes. He was generally summoned to listen to secret tête-à-tête readings of his novel; he would sit like a post for six hours at a stretch, perspiring and straining his utmost to keep awake and smile. On reaching home he would groan with his long-legged and lanky wife over their benefactor's unhappy weakness for Russian literature.

Andrey Antonovitch looked with anguish at Blum.

"I beg you to leave me alone, Blum," he began with agitated haste, obviously anxious to avoid any renewal of the previous conversation which had been interrupted by Pyotr Stepanovitch.

"And yet this may be arranged in the most delicate way and with no publicity; you have full power." Blum respectfully but obstinately insisted on some point, stooping forward and coming nearer and nearer by small steps to Andrey Antonovitch.

"Blum, you are so devoted to me and so anxious to serve me that I am always in a panic when I look at you."

"You always say witty things, and sleep in peace satisfied with what you've said, but that's how you damage yourself."

"Blum, I have just convinced myself that it's quite a mistake, quite a mistake."

"Not from the words of that false, vicious young man whom you suspect yourself? He has won you by his flattering praise of your talent for literature."

"Blum, you understand nothing about it; your project is absurd, I tell you. We shall find nothing and there will be a fearful upset and laughter too, and then Yulia Mihailovna ..."

"We shall certainly find everything we are looking for." Blum advanced firmly towards him, laying his right hand on his heart. "We will make a search suddenly early in the morning, carefully showing every consideration for the person himself and strictly observing all the prescribed forms of the law. The young men, Lyamshin and Telyatnikov, assert positively that we shall find all we want. They were constant visitors there. Nobody is favourably disposed to Mr. Verhovensky. Madame Stavrogin has openly refused him her graces, and every honest man, if only there is such a one in this coarse town, is persuaded that a hotbed of infidelity and social doctrines has always been concealed there. He keeps all the forbidden books, Ryliev's 'Reflections,' all Herzen's works.... I have an approximate catalogue, in case of need."

"Oh heavens! Every one has these books; how simple you are, my poor Blum."

"And many manifestoes," Blum went on without heeding the observation. "We shall end by certainly coming upon traces of the real manifestoes here. That young Verhovensky I feel very suspicious of."

"But you are mixing up the father and the son. They are not on good terms. The son openly laughs at his father."

"That's only a mask."

"Blum, you've sworn to torment me! Think! he is a conspicuous figure here, after all. He's been a professor, he is a well-known man. He'll make such an uproar and there will be such gibes all over the town, and we shall make a mess of it all.... And only think how Yulia Mihailovna will take it." Blum pressed forward and did not listen. "He was only a lecturer, only a lecturer, and of a low rank when he retired." He smote himself on the chest. "He has no marks of distinction. He was discharged from the service on suspicion of plots against the government. He has been under secret supervision, and undoubtedly still is so. And in view of the disorders that have come to light now, you are undoubtedly bound in duty. You are losing your chance of distinction by letting slip the real criminal."

"Yulia Mihailovna! Get away, Blum," Von Lembke cried suddenly, hearing the voice of his spouse in the next room. Blum started but did not give in.

"Allow me, allow me," he persisted, pressing both hands still more tightly on his chest.

"Get away!" hissed Andrey Antonovitch. "Do what you like ... afterwards. Oh, my God!"

The curtain was raised and Yulia Mihailovna made her appearance. She stood still majestically at the sight of Blum, casting a haughty and offended glance at him, as though the very presence of this man was an affront to her. Blum respectfully made her a deep bow without speaking and, doubled up with veneration, moved towards the door on tiptoe with his arms held a little away from him.

Either because he really took Andrey Antonovitch's last hysterical outbreak as a direct permission to act as he was asking, or whether he strained a point in this case for the direct advantage of his benefactor, because he was too confident that success would crown his efforts; anyway, as we shall see later on, this conversation of the governor with his subordinate led to a very surprising event which amused many people, became public property, moved Yulia Mihailovna to fierce anger, utterly disconcerting Andrey Antonovitch and reducing him at the crucial moment to a state of deplorable indecision.

V

It was a busy day for Pyotr Stepanovitch. From Von Lembke he hastened to Bogoyavlensky Street, but as he went along Bykovy Street, past the house where Karmazinov was staying, he suddenly stopped, grinned, and went into the house. The servant told him that he was expected, which interested him, as he had said nothing beforehand of his coming.

But the great writer really had been expecting him, not only that day but the day before and the day before that. Three days before he had handed him his manuscript Merci (which he had meant to read at the literary matinée at Yulia Mihailovna's fête). He had done this out of amiability, fully convinced that he was agreeably flattering the young man's vanity by letting him read the great work beforehand. Pyotr Stepanovitch had noticed long before that this vainglorious, spoiled gentleman, who was so offensively unapproachable for all but the elect, this writer "with the intellect of a statesman," was simply trying to curry favour with him, even with avidity. I believe the young man guessed at last that Karmazinov considered him, if not the leader of the whole secret revolutionary movement in Russia, at least one of those most deeply initiated into the secrets of the Russian revolution who had an incontestable influence on the younger generation. The state of mind of "the cleverest man in Russia" interested Pyotr Stepanovitch, but hitherto he had, for certain reasons, avoided explaining himself.

The great writer was staying in the house belonging to his sister, who was the wife of a kammerherr and had an estate in the neighbourhood. Both she and her husband had the deepest reverence for their illustrious relation, but to their profound regret both of them happened to be in Moscow at the time of his visit, so that the honour of receiving him fell to the lot of an old lady, a poor relation of the kammerherr's, who had for years lived in the family and looked after the housekeeping. All the household had moved about on tiptoe since Karmazinov's arrival. The old lady sent news to Moscow almost every day, how he had slept, what he had deigned to eat, and had once sent a telegram to announce that after a dinner-party at the mayor's he was obliged to take a spoonful of a well-known medicine. She rarely plucked up courage to enter his room, though he behaved courteously to her, but dryly, and only talked to her of what was necessary.

When Pyotr Stepanovitch came in, he was eating his morning cutlet with half a glass of red wine. Pyotr Stepanovitch had been to see him before and always found him eating this cutlet, which he finished in his presence without ever offering him anything. After the cutlet a little cup of coffee was served. The footman who brought in the dishes wore a swallow-tail coat, noiseless boots, and gloves.

"Ha ha!" Karmazinov got up from the sofa, wiping his mouth with a table-napkin, and came forward to kiss him with an air of unmixed delight—after the characteristic fashion of Russians if they are very illustrious. But Pyotr Stepanovitch knew by experience that, though Karmazinov made a show of kissing him, he really only proffered his cheek, and so this time he did the same: the cheeks met. Karmazinov did not show that he noticed it, sat down on the sofa, and affably offered Pyotr Stepanovitch an easy chair facing him, in which the latter stretched himself at once.

"You don't … wouldn't like some lunch?" inquired Karmazinov, abandoning his usual habit but with an air, of course, which would prompt a polite refusal. Pyotr Stepanovitch at once expressed a desire for lunch. A shade of offended surprise darkened the face of his host, but only for an instant; he nervously rang for the servant and, in spite of all his breeding, raised his voice scornfully as he gave orders for a second lunch to be served.

"What will you have, cutlet or coffee?" he asked once more.

"A cutlet and coffee, and tell him to bring some more wine, I am hungry," answered Pyotr Stepanovitch, calmly scrutinising his host's attire. Mr. Karmazinov was wearing a sort of indoor wadded jacket with pearl buttons, but it was too short, which was far from becoming to his rather comfortable stomach and the solid curves of his hips. But tastes differ. Over his knees he had a checkered woollen plaid reaching to the floor, though it was warm in the room.

"Are you unwell?" commented Pyotr Stepanovitch.

"No, not unwell, but I am afraid of being so in this climate," answered the writer in his squeaky voice, though he uttered each word with a soft cadence and agreeable gentlemanly lisp. "I've been expecting you since yesterday."

"Why? I didn't say I'd come."

"No, but you have my manuscript. Have you … read it?"

"Manuscript? Which one?"

Karmazinov was terribly surprised.

"But you've brought it with you, haven't you?" He was so disturbed that he even left off eating and looked at Pyotr Stepanovitch with a face of dismay.

"Ah, that Bonjour you mean…."

"Merci."

"Oh, all right. I'd quite forgotten it and hadn't read it; I haven't had time. I really don't know, it's not in my pockets … it must be on my table. Don't be uneasy, it will be found."

"No, I'd better send to your rooms at once. It might be lost; besides, it might be stolen."

"Oh, who'd want it! But why are you so alarmed? Why, Yulia Mihailovna told me you always have several copies made—one kept at a notary's abroad, another in Petersburg, a third in Moscow, and then you send some to a bank, I believe."

"But Moscow might be burnt again and my manuscript with it. No, I'd better send at once."

"Stay, here it is!" Pyotr Stepanovitch pulled a roll of note-paper out of a pocket at the back of his coat. "It's a little crumpled. Only fancy, it's been lying there with my pocket-handkerchief ever since I took it from you; I forgot it."

Karmazinov greedily snatched the manuscript, carefully examined it, counted the pages, and laid it respectfully beside him on a special table, for the time, in such a way that he would not lose sight of it for an instant.

"You don't read very much, it seems?" he hissed, unable to restrain himself.

"No, not very much."

"And nothing in the way of Russian literature?"

"In the way of Russian literature? Let me see, I have read something…. 'On the Way' or 'Away!' or 'At the Parting of the Ways'—something of the sort; I don't remember. It's a long time since I read it, five years ago. I've no time."

A silence followed.

"When I came I assured every one that you were a very intelligent man, and now I believe every one here is wild over you."

"Thank you," Pyotr Stepanovitch answered calmly.

Lunch was brought in. Pyotr Stepanovitch pounced on the cutlet with extraordinary appetite, had eaten it in a trice, tossed off the wine and swallowed his coffee.

"This boor," thought Karmazinov, looking at him askance as he munched the last morsel and drained the last drops—"this boor probably understood the biting taunt in my words ... and no doubt he has read the manuscript with eagerness; he is simply lying with some object. But possibly he is not lying and is only genuinely stupid. I like a genius to be rather stupid. Mayn't he be a sort of genius among them? Devil take the fellow!"

He got up from the sofa and began pacing from one end of the room to the other for the sake of exercise, as he always did after lunch.

"Leaving here soon?" asked Pyotr Stepanovitch from his easy chair, lighting a cigarette.

"I really came to sell an estate and I am in the hands of my bailiff."

"You left, I believe, because they expected an epidemic out there after the war?"

"N-no, not entirely for that reason," Mr. Karmazinov went on, uttering his phrases with an affable intonation, and each time he turned round in pacing the corner there was a faint but jaunty quiver of his right leg. "I certainly intend to live as long as I can." He laughed, not without venom. "There is something in our Russian nobility that makes them wear out very quickly, from every point of view. But I wish to wear out as late as possible, and now I am going abroad for good; there the climate is better, the houses are of stone, and everything stronger. Europe will last my time, I think. What do you think?"

"How can I tell?"

"H'm. If the Babylon out there really does fall, and great will be the fall thereof (about which I quite agree with you, yet I think it will last my time), there's nothing to fall here in Russia, comparatively speaking. There won't be stones to fall, everything will crumble into dirt. Holy Russia has less power of resistance than anything in the world. The Russian peasantry is still held together somehow by the Russian God; but according to the latest accounts the Russian God is not to be relied upon, and scarcely survived the emancipation; it certainly gave Him a severe shock. And now, what with railways, what with you ... I've no faith in the Russian God."

"And how about the European one?"

"I don't believe in any. I've been slandered to the youth of Russia. I've always sympathised with every movement among them. I was shown the manifestoes here. Every one looks at them with perplexity because they are frightened at the way things are put in them, but every one is convinced of their power even if they don't admit it to themselves. Everybody has been rolling downhill, and every one has known for ages that they have nothing to clutch at. I am persuaded of the success of this mysterious propaganda, if only because Russia is now pre-eminently the place in all the world where anything you like may happen without any opposition. I understand only too well why wealthy Russians all flock abroad, and more and more so every year. It's simply instinct. If the ship is sinking, the rats are the first to leave it. Holy Russia is a country of wood, of poverty … and of danger, the country of ambitious beggars in its upper classes, while the immense majority live in poky little huts. She will be glad of any way of escape; you have only to present it to her. It's only the government that still means to resist, but it brandishes its cudgel in the dark and hits its own men. Everything here is doomed and awaiting the end. Russia as she is has no future. I have become a German and I am proud of it."

"But you began about the manifestoes. Tell me everything; how do you look at them?"

"Every one is afraid of them, so they must be influential. They openly unmask what is false and prove that there is nothing to lay hold of among us, and nothing to lean upon. They speak aloud while all is silent. What is most effective about them (in spite of their style) is the incredible boldness with which they look the truth straight in the face. To look facts straight in the face is only possible to Russians of this generation. No, in Europe they are not yet so bold; it is a realm of stone, there-there is still something to lean upon. So far as I see and am able to judge, the whole essence of the Russian revolutionary idea lies in the negation of honour. I like its being so boldly and fearlessly expressed. No, in Europe they wouldn't understand it yet, but that's just what we shall clutch at. For a Russian a sense of honour is only a superfluous burden, and it always has been a burden through all his history. The open 'right to dishonour' will attract him more than anything. I belong to the older generation and, I must confess, still cling to honour, but only from habit. It is only that I prefer the old forms, granted it's from timidity; you see one must live somehow what's left of one's life."

He suddenly stopped.

"I am talking," he thought, "while he holds his tongue and watches me. He has come to make me ask him a direct question. And I shall ask him."

"Yulia Mihailovna asked me by some stratagem to find out from you what the surprise is that you are preparing for the ball to-morrow," Pyotr Stepanovitch asked suddenly.

"Yes, there really will be a surprise and I certainly shall astonish …" said Karmazinov with increased dignity. "But I won't tell you what the secret is."

Pyotr Stepanovitch did not insist.

"There is a young man here called Shatov," observed the great writer. "Would you believe it, I haven't seen him."

"A very nice person. What about him?"

"Oh, nothing. He talks about something. Isn't he the person who gave Stavrogin that slap in the face?"

"Yes."

"And what's your opinion of Stavrogin?"

"I don't know; he is such a flirt."

Karmazinov detested Stavrogin because it was the latter's habit not to take any notice of him.

"That flirt," he said, chuckling, "if what is advocated in your manifestoes ever comes to pass, will be the first to be hanged."

"Perhaps before," Pyotr Stepanovitch said suddenly.

"Quite right too," Karmazinov assented, not laughing, and with pronounced gravity.

"You have said so once before, and, do you know, I repeated it to him."

"What, you surely didn't repeat it?" Karmazinov laughed again.

"He said that if he were to be hanged it would be enough for you to be flogged, not simply as a complement but to hurt, as they flog the peasants."

Pyotr Stepanovitch took his hat and got up from his seat. Karmazinov held out both hands to him at parting.

"And what if all that you are … plotting for is destined to come to pass …" he piped suddenly, in a honeyed voice with a peculiar intonation, still holding his hands in his. "How soon could it come about?"

"How could I tell?" Pyotr Stepanovitch answered rather roughly. They looked intently into each other's eyes.

"At a guess? Approximately?" Karmazinov piped still more sweetly.

"You'll have time to sell your estate and time to clear out too," Pyotr Stepanovitch muttered still more roughly. They looked at one another even more intently.

There was a minute of silence.

"It will begin early next May and will be over by October," Pyotr Stepanovitch said suddenly.

"I thank you sincerely," Karmazinov pronounced in a voice saturated with feeling, pressing his hands.

"You will have time to get out of the ship, you rat," Pyotr Stepanovitch was thinking as he went out into the street. "Well, if that 'imperial intellect' inquires so confidently of the day and the hour and thanks me so respectfully for the information I have given, we mustn't doubt of ourselves. [He grinned.] H'm! But he really isn't stupid … and he is simply a rat escaping; men like that don't tell tales!"

He ran to Filipov's house in Bogoyavlensky Street.

VI

Pyotr Stepanovitch went first to Kirillov's. He found him, as usual, alone, and at the moment practising gymnastics, that is, standing with his legs apart, brandishing his arms above his head in a peculiar way. On the floor lay a ball. The tea stood cold on the table, not cleared since breakfast. Pyotr Stepanovitch stood for a minute on the threshold.

"You are very anxious about your health, it seems," he said in a loud and cheerful tone, going into the room. "What a jolly ball, though; foo, how it bounces! Is that for gymnastics too?"

Kirillov put on his coat.

"Yes, that's for the good of my health too," he muttered dryly. "Sit down."

"I'm only here for a minute. Still, I'll sit down. Health is all very well, but I've come to remind you of our agreement. The appointed time is approaching … in a certain sense," he concluded awkwardly.

"What agreement?"

"How can you ask?" Pyotr Stepanovitch was startled and even dismayed.

"It's not an agreement and not an obligation. I have not bound myself in any way; it's a mistake on your part."

"I say, what's this you're doing?" Pyotr Stepanovitch jumped up.

"What I choose."

"What do you choose?"

"The same as before."

"How am I to understand that? Does that mean that you are in the same mind?"

"Yes. Only there's no agreement and never has been, and I have not bound myself in any way. I could do as I like and I can still do as I like."

Kirillov explained himself curtly and contemptuously.

"I agree, I agree; be as free as you like if you don't change your mind." Pyotr Stepanovitch sat down again with a satisfied air. "You are angry over a word. You've become very irritable of late; that's why I've avoided coming to see you. I was quite sure, though, you would be loyal."

"I dislike you very much, but you can be perfectly sure—though I don't regard it as loyalty and disloyalty."

"But do you know" (Pyotr Stepanovitch was startled again) "we must talk things over thoroughly again so as not to get in a muddle. The business needs accuracy, and you keep giving me such shocks. Will you let me speak?"

"Speak," snapped Kirillov, looking away.

"You made up your mind long ago to take your life … I mean, you had the idea in your mind. Is that the right expression? Is there any mistake about that?"

"I have the same idea still."

"Excellent. Take note that no one has forced it on you."

"Rather not; what nonsense you talk."

"I dare say I express it very stupidly. Of course, it would be very stupid to force anybody to it. I'll go on. You were a member of the society before its organisation was changed, and confessed it to one of the members."

"I didn't confess it, I simply said so."

"Quite so. And it would be absurd to confess such a thing. What a confession! You simply said so. Excellent."

"No, it's not excellent, for you are being tedious. I am not obliged to give you any account of myself and you can't understand my ideas. I want to put an end to my life, because that's my idea, because I don't want to be afraid of death, because … because there's no need for you to know. What do you want? Would you like tea? It's cold. Let me get you another glass."

Pyotr Stepanovitch actually had taken up the teapot and was looking for an empty glass. Kirillov went to the cupboard and brought a clean glass.

"I've just had lunch at Karmazinov's," observed his visitor, "then I listened to him talking, and perspired and got into a sweat again running here. I am fearfully thirsty."

"Drink. Cold tea is good."

Kirillov sat down on his chair again and again fixed his eyes on the farthest corner.

"The idea had arisen in the society," he went on in the same voice, "that I might be of use if I killed myself, and that when you get up some bit of mischief here, and they are looking for the guilty, I might suddenly shoot myself and leave a letter saying I did it all, so that you might escape suspicion for another year."

"For a few days, anyway; one day is precious."

"Good. So for that reason they asked me, if I would, to wait. I said I'd wait till the society fixed the day, because it makes no difference to me."

"Yes, but remember that you bound yourself not to make up your last letter without me and that in Russia you would be at my … well, at my disposition, that is for that purpose only. I need hardly say, in everything else, of course, you are free," Pyotr Stepanovitch added almost amiably.

"I didn't bind myself, I agreed, because it makes no difference to me."

"Good, good. I have no intention of wounding your vanity, but …"

"It's not a question of vanity."

"But remember that a hundred and twenty thalers were collected for your journey, so you've taken money."

"Not at all." Kirillov fired up. "The money was not on that condition. One doesn't take money for that."

"People sometimes do."

"That's a lie. I sent a letter from Petersburg, and in Petersburg I paid you a hundred and twenty thalers; I put it in your hand … and it has been sent off there, unless you've kept it for yourself."

"All right, all right, I don't dispute anything; it has been sent off. All that matters is that you are still in the same mind."

"Exactly the same. When you come and tell me it's time, I'll carry it all out. Will it be very soon?"

"Not very many days.… But remember, we'll make up the letter together, the same night."

"The same day if you like. You say I must take the responsibility for the manifestoes on myself?"

"And something else too."

"I am not going to make myself out responsible for everything."

"What won't you be responsible for?" said Pyotr Stepanovitch again.

"What I don't choose; that's enough. I don't want to talk about it any more."

Pyotr Stepanovitch controlled himself and changed the subject.

"To speak of something else," he began, "will you be with us this evening? It's Virginsky's name-day; that's the pretext for our meeting."

"I don't want to."

"Do me a favour. Do come. You must. We must impress them by our number and our looks. You have a face … well, in one word, you have a fateful face."

"You think so?" laughed Kirillov. "Very well, I'll come, but not for the sake of my face. What time is it?"

"Oh, quite early, half-past six. And, you know, you can go in, sit down, and not speak to any one, however many there may be there. Only, I say, don't forget to bring pencil and paper with you."

"What's that for?"

"Why, it makes no difference to you, and it's my special request. You'll only have to sit still, speaking to no one, listen, and sometimes seem to make a note. You can draw something, if you like."

"What nonsense! What for?"

"Why, since it makes no difference to you! You keep saying that it's just the same to you."

"No, what for?"

"Why, because that member of the society, the inspector, has stopped at Moscow and I told some of them here that possibly the inspector may turn up to-night; and they'll think that you are the inspector. And as you've been here three weeks already, they'll be still more surprised."

"Stage tricks. You haven't got an inspector in Moscow."

"Well, suppose I haven't—damn him!—what business is that of yours and what bother will it be to you? You are a member of the society yourself."

"Tell them I am the inspector; I'll sit still and hold my tongue, but I won't have the pencil and paper."

"But why?"

"I don't want to."

Pyotr Stepanovitch was really angry; he turned positively green, but again he controlled himself. He got up and took his hat.

"Is that fellow with you?" he brought out suddenly, in a low voice.

"Yes."

"That's good. I'll soon get him away. Don't be uneasy."

"I am not uneasy. He is only here at night. The old woman is in the hospital, her daughter-in-law is dead. I've been alone for the last two days. I've shown him the place in the paling where you can take a board out; he gets through, no one sees."

"I'll take him away soon."

"He says he has got plenty of places to stay the night in."

"That's rot; they are looking for him, but here he wouldn't be noticed. Do you ever get into talk with him?"

"Yes, at night. He abuses you tremendously. I've been reading the 'Apocalypse' to him at night, and we have tea. He listened eagerly, very eagerly, the whole night."

"Hang it all, you'll convert him to Christianity!"

"He is a Christian as it is. Don't be uneasy, he'll do the murder. Whom do you want to murder?"

"No, I don't want him for that, I want him for something different.... And does Shatov know about Fedka?"

"I don't talk to Shatov, and I don't see him."

"Is he angry?"

"No, we are not angry, only we shun one another. We lay too long side by side in America."

"I am going to him directly."

"As you like."

"Stavrogin and I may come and see you from there, about ten o'clock."

"Do."

"I want to talk to him about something important.... I say, make me a present of your ball; what do you want with it now? I want it for gymnastics too. I'll pay you for it if you like."

"You can take it without."

Pyotr Stepanovitch put the ball in the back pocket of his coat.

"But I'll give you nothing against Stavrogin," Kirillov muttered after his guest, as he saw him out. The latter looked at him in amazement but did not answer.

Kirillov's last words perplexed Pyotr Stepanovitch extremely; he had not time yet to discover their meaning, but even while he was on the stairs of Shatov's lodging he tried to remove all trace of annoyance and to assume an amiable expression. Shatov was at home and rather unwell. He was lying on his bed, though dressed.

"What bad luck!" Pyotr Stepanovitch cried out in the doorway. "Are you really ill?"

The amiable expression of his face suddenly vanished; there was a gleam of spite in his eyes.

"Not at all." Shatov jumped up nervously. "I am not ill at all ... a little headache ..."

He was disconcerted; the sudden appearance of such a visitor positively alarmed him.

"You mustn't be ill for the job I've come about," Pyotr Stepanovitch began quickly and, as it were, peremptorily. "Allow me to sit down." (He sat down.) "And you sit down again on your bedstead; that's right. There will be a party of our fellows at Virginsky's to-night on the pretext of his birthday; it will have no political character, however—we've seen to that. I am coming with Nikolay Stavrogin. I would not, of course, have dragged you there, knowing your way of thinking at present ... simply to save your being worried, not because we think you would betray us. But as things have turned out, you will have to go. You'll meet there the very people with whom we shall finally settle how you are to leave the society and to whom you are to hand over what is in your keeping. We'll do it without being noticed; I'll take you aside into a corner; there'll be a lot of people and there's no need for every one to know. I must confess I've had to keep my tongue wagging on your behalf; but now I believe they've agreed, on condition you hand over the printing press and all the papers, of course. Then you can go where you please."

Shatov listened, frowning and resentful. The nervous alarm of a moment before had entirely left him.

"I don't acknowledge any sort of obligation to give an account to the devil knows whom," he declared definitely. "No one has the authority to set me free."

"Not quite so. A great deal has been entrusted to you. You hadn't the right to break off simply. Besides, you made no clear statement about it, so that you put them in an ambiguous position."

"I stated my position clearly by letter as soon as I arrived here."

"No, it wasn't clear," Pyotr Stepanovitch retorted calmly. "I sent you 'A Noble Personality' to be printed here, and meaning the copies to be kept here till they were wanted; and the two manifestoes as well. You returned them with an ambiguous letter which explained nothing."

"I refused definitely to print them."

"Well, not definitely. You wrote that you couldn't, but you didn't explain for what reason. 'I can't' doesn't mean 'I don't want to.' It might be supposed that you were simply unable through circumstances. That was how they took it, and considered that you still meant to keep up your connection with the society, so that they might have entrusted something to you again and so have compromised themselves. They say here that you simply meant to deceive them, so that you might betray them when you got hold of something important. I have defended you to the best of my powers, and have shown your brief note as evidence in your favour. But I had to admit on rereading those two lines that they were misleading and not conclusive."

"You kept that note so carefully then?"

"My keeping it means nothing; I've got it still."

"Well, I don't care, damn it!" Shatov cried furiously. "Your fools may consider that I've betrayed them if they like—what is it to me? I should like to see what you can do to me?"

"Your name would be noted, and at the first success of the revolution you would be hanged."

"That's when you get the upper hand and dominate Russia?"

"You needn't laugh. I tell you again, I stood up for you. Anyway, I advise you to turn up to-day. Why waste words through false pride? Isn't it better to part friends? In any case you'll have to give up the printing press and the old type and papers—that's what we must talk about."

"I'll come," Shatov muttered, looking down thoughtfully.

Pyotr Stepanovitch glanced askance at him from his place.

"Will Stavrogin be there?" Shatov asked suddenly, raising his head.

"He is certain to be."

"Ha ha!"

Again they were silent for a minute. Shatov grinned disdainfully and irritably.

"And that contemptible 'Noble Personality' of yours, that I wouldn't print here. Has it been printed?" he asked.

"Yes."

"To make the schoolboys believe that Herzen himself had written it in your album?"

"Yes, Herzen himself."

Again they were silent for three minutes. At last Shatov got up from the bed.

"Go out of my room; I don't care to sit with you."

"I'm going," Pyotr Stepanovitch brought out with positive alacrity, getting up at once. "Only one word: Kirillov is quite alone in the lodge now, isn't he, without a servant?"

"Quite alone. Get along; I can't stand being in the same room with you."

"Well, you are a pleasant customer now!" Pyotr Stepanovitch reflected gaily as he went out into the street, "and you will be pleasant this evening too, and that just suits me; nothing better could be wished, nothing better could be wished! The Russian God Himself seems helping me."

VII

He had probably been very busy that day on all sorts of errands and probably with success, which was reflected in the self-satisfied expression of his face when at six o'clock that evening he turned up at Stavrogin's. But he was not at once admitted: Stavrogin had just locked himself in the study with Mavriky Nikolaevitch. This news instantly made Pyotr Stepanovitch anxious. He seated himself close to the study door to wait for the visitor to go away. He could hear the conversation but could not catch the words. The visit did not last long; soon he heard a noise, the sound of an extremely loud and abrupt voice, then the door opened and Mavriky Nikolaevitch came out with a very pale face. He did not notice Pyotr Stepanovitch, and quickly passed by. Pyotr Stepanovitch instantly ran into the study.

I cannot omit a detailed account of the very brief interview that had taken place between the two "rivals"—an interview which might well have seemed impossible under the circumstances, but which had yet taken place.

This is how it had come about. Nikolay Vsyevolodovitch had been enjoying an after-dinner nap on the couch in his study when Alexey Yegorytch had announced the unexpected visitor. Hearing the name, he had positively leapt up, unwilling to believe it. But soon a smile gleamed on his lips—a smile of haughty triumph and at the same time of a blank, incredulous wonder. The visitor, Mavriky Nikolaevitch, seemed struck by the expression of that smile as he came in; anyway, he stood still in the middle of the room as though uncertain whether to come further in or to turn back. Stavrogin succeeded at once in transforming the expression of his face, and with an air of grave surprise took a step towards him. The visitor did not take his outstretched hand, but awkwardly moved a chair and, not uttering a word, sat down without waiting for his host to do so. Nikolay Vsyevolodovitch sat down on the sofa facing him obliquely and, looking at Mavriky Nikolaevitch, waited in silence.

"If you can, marry Lizaveta Nikolaevna," Mavriky Nikolaevitch brought out suddenly at last, and what was most curious, it was impossible to tell from his tone whether it was an entreaty, a recommendation, a surrender, or a command.

Stavrogin still remained silent, but the visitor had evidently said all he had come to say and gazed at him persistently, waiting for an answer.

"If I am not mistaken (but it's quite certain), Lizaveta Nikolaevna is already betrothed to you," Stavrogin said at last.

"Promised and betrothed," Mavriky Nikolaevitch assented firmly and clearly.

"You have ... quarrelled? Excuse me, Mavriky Nikolaevitch."

"No, she 'loves and respects me'; those are her words. Her words are more precious than anything."

"Of that there can be no doubt."

"But let me tell you, if she were standing in the church at her wedding and you were to call her, she'd give up me and every one and go to you."

"From the wedding?"

"Yes, and after the wedding."

"Aren't you making a mistake?"

"No. Under her persistent, sincere, and intense hatred for you love is flashing out at every moment ... and madness ... the sincerest infinite love and ... madness! On the contrary, behind the love she feels for me, which is sincere too, every moment there are flashes of hatred ... the most intense hatred! I could never have fancied all these transitions ... before."

"But I wonder, though, how could you come here and dispose of the hand of Lizaveta Nikolaevna? Have you the right to do so? Has she authorised you?"

Mavriky Nikolaevitch frowned and for a minute he looked down.

"That's all words on your part," he brought out suddenly, "words of revenge and triumph; I am sure you can read between the lines, and is this the time for petty vanity? Haven't you satisfaction enough? Must I really dot my i's and go into it all? Very well, I will dot my i's, if you are so anxious for my humiliation. I have no right, it's impossible for me to be authorised; Lizaveta Nikolaevna knows nothing about it and her betrothed has finally lost his senses and is only fit for a madhouse, and, to crown everything, has come to tell you so himself. You are the only man in the world who can make her happy, and I am the one to make her unhappy.

You are trying to get her, you are pursuing her, but—I don't know why—you won't marry her. If it's because of a lovers' quarrel abroad and I must be sacrificed to end it, sacrifice me. She is too unhappy and I can't endure it. My words are not a sanction, not a prescription, and so it's no slur on your pride. If you care to take my place at the altar, you can do it without any sanction from me, and there is no ground for me to come to you with a mad proposal, especially as our marriage is utterly impossible after the step I am taking now. I cannot lead her to the altar feeling myself an abject wretch. What I am doing here and my handing her over to you, perhaps her bitterest foe, is to my mind something so abject that I shall never get over it."

"Will you shoot yourself on our wedding day?"

"No, much later. Why stain her bridal dress with my blood? Perhaps I shall not shoot myself at all, either now or later."

"I suppose you want to comfort me by saying that?"

"You? What would the blood of one more mean to you?" He turned pale and his eyes gleamed. A minute of silence followed.

"Excuse me for the questions I've asked you," Stavrogin began again; "some of them I had no business to ask you, but one of them I think I have every right to put to you. Tell me, what facts have led you to form a conclusion as to my feelings for Lizaveta Nikolaevna? I mean to a conviction of a degree of feeling on my part as would justify your coming here … and risking such a proposal."

"What?" Mavriky Nikolaevitch positively started. "Haven't you been trying to win her? Aren't you trying to win her, and don't you want to win her?"

"Generally speaking, I can't speak of my feeling for this woman or that to a third person or to anyone except the woman herself. You must excuse it, it's a constitutional peculiarity. But to make up for it, I'll tell you the truth about everything else; I am married, and it's impossible for me either to marry or to try 'to win' anyone."

Mavriky Nikolaevitch was so astounded that he started back in his chair and for some time stared fixedly into Stavrogin's face.

"Only fancy, I never thought of that," he muttered. "You said then, that morning, that you were not married … and so I believed you were not married."

He turned terribly pale; suddenly he brought his fist down on the table with all his might.

"If after that confession you don't leave Lizaveta Nikolaevna alone, if you make her unhappy, I'll kill you with my stick like a dog in a ditch!"

He jumped up and walked quickly out of the room. Pyotr Stepanovitch, running in, found his host in a most unexpected frame of mind.

"Ah, that's you!" Stavrogin laughed loudly; his laughter seemed to be provoked simply by the appearance of Pyotr Stepanovitch as he ran in with such impulsive curiosity.

"Were you listening at the door? Wait a bit. What have you come about? I promised you something, didn't I? Ah, bah! I remember, to meet 'our fellows.' Let us go. I am delighted. You couldn't have thought of anything more appropriate." He snatched up his hat and they both went at once out of the house.

"Are you laughing beforehand at the prospect of seeing 'our fellows'?" chirped gaily Pyotr Stepanovitch, dodging round him with obsequious alacrity, at one moment trying to walk beside his companion on the narrow brick pavement and at the next running right into the mud of the road; for Stavrogin walked in the middle of the pavement without observing that he left no room for anyone else.

"I am not laughing at all," he answered loudly and gaily; "on the contrary, I am sure that you have the most serious set of people there."

"'Surly dullards,' as you once deigned to express it."

"Nothing is more amusing sometimes than a surly dullard."

"Ah, you mean Mavriky Nikolaevitch? I am convinced he came to give up his betrothed to you, eh? I egged him on to do it, indirectly, would you believe it? And if he doesn't give her up, we'll take her, anyway, won't we—eh?"

Pyotr Stepanovitch knew no doubt that he was running some risk in venturing on such sallies, but when he was excited he preferred to risk anything rather than to remain in uncertainty. Stavrogin only laughed.

"You still reckon you'll help me?" he asked.

"If you call me. But you know there's one way, and the best one."

"Do I know your way?"

"Oh no, that's a secret for the time. Only remember, a secret has its price."

"I know what it costs," Stavrogin muttered to himself, but he restrained himself and was silent.

"What it costs? What did you say?" Pyotr Stepanovitch was startled.

"I said, 'Damn you and your secret!' You'd better be telling me who will be there. I know that we are going to a name-day party, but who will be there?"

"Oh, all sorts! Even Kirillov."

"All members of circles?"

"Hang it all, you are in a hurry! There's not one circle formed yet."

"How did you manage to distribute so many manifestoes then?"

"Where we are going only four are members of the circle. The others on probation are spying on one another with jealous eagerness, and bring reports to me. They are a trustworthy set. It's all material which we must organise, and then we must clear out. But you wrote the rules yourself, there's no need to explain."

"Are things going badly then? Is there a hitch?"

"Going? Couldn't be better. It will amuse you: the first thing which has a tremendous effect is giving them titles. Nothing has more influence than a title. I invent ranks and duties on purpose; I have secretaries, secret spies, treasurers, presidents, registrars, their assistants—they like it awfully, it's taken capitally. Then, the next force is sentimentalism, of course. You know, amongst us socialism spreads principally through sentimentalism. But the trouble is these lieutenants who bite; sometimes you put your foot in it. Then come the out-and-out rogues; well, they are a good sort, if you like, and sometimes very useful; but they waste a lot of one's time, they want incessant looking after. And the most important force of all—the cement that holds everything together—is their being ashamed of having an opinion of their own. That is a force! And whose work is it, whose precious achievement is it, that not one idea of their own is left in their heads! They think originality a disgrace."

"If so, why do you take so much trouble?"

"Why, if people lie simply gaping at every one, how can you resist annexing them? Can you seriously refuse to believe in the possibility of success? Yes, you have the faith, but one wants will. It's just with people like this that success is possible. I tell you I could make them go through fire; one has only to din it into them that they are not advanced enough. The fools reproach me that I have taken in every one here over the central committee and 'the innumerable branches.' You once blamed me for it yourself, but where's the deception? You and I are the central committee and there will be as many branches as we like."

"And always the same sort of rabble!"

"Raw material. Even they will be of use."

"And you are still reckoning on me?"

"You are the chief, you are the head; I shall only be a subordinate, your secretary. We shall take to our barque, you know; the oars are of maple, the sails are of silk, at the helm sits a fair maiden, Lizaveta Nikolaevna … hang it, how does it go in the ballad?"

"He is stuck," laughed Stavrogin. "No, I'd better give you my version. There you reckon on your fingers the forces that make up the circles. All that business of titles and sentimentalism is a very good cement, but there is something better; persuade four members of the circle to do for a fifth on the pretence that he is a traitor, and you'll tie them all together with the blood they've shed as though it were a knot. They'll be your slaves, they won't dare to rebel or call you to account. Ha ha ha!"

"But you … you shall pay for those words," Pyotr Stepanovitch thought to himself, "and this very evening, in fact. You go too far."

This or something like this must have been Pyotr Stepanovitch's reflection. They were approaching Virginsky's house.

"You've represented me, no doubt, as a member from abroad, an inspector in connection with the Internationale?" Stavrogin asked suddenly.

"No, not an inspector; you won't be an inspector; but you are one of the original members from abroad, who knows the most important secrets—that's your rôle. You are going to speak, of course?"

"What's put that idea into your head?"

"Now you are bound to speak."

Stavrogin positively stood still in the middle of the street in surprise, not far from a street lamp. Pyotr Stepanovitch faced his scrutiny calmly and defiantly. Stavrogin cursed and went on.

"And are you going to speak?" he suddenly asked Pyotr Stepanovitch.

"No, I am going to listen to you."

"Damn you, you really are giving me an idea!"

"What idea?" Pyotr Stepanovitch asked quickly.

"Perhaps I will speak there, but afterwards I will give you a hiding—and a sound one too, you know."

"By the way, I told Karmazinov this morning that you said he ought to be thrashed, and not simply as a form but to hurt, as they flog peasants."

"But I never said such a thing; ha ha!"

"No matter. Se non è vero ..."

"Well, thanks. I am truly obliged."

"And another thing. Do you know, Karmazinov says that the essence of our creed is the negation of honour, and that by the open advocacy of a right to be dishonourable a Russian can be won over more easily than by anything."

"An excellent saying! Golden words!" cried Stavrogin. "He's hit the mark there! The right to dishonour—why, they'd all flock to us for that, not one would stay behind! And listen, Verhovensky, you are not one of the higher police, are you?"

"Anyone who has a question like that in his mind doesn't utter it."

"I understand, but we are by ourselves."

"No, so far I am not one of the higher police. Enough, here we are. Compose your features, Stavrogin; I always do mine when I go in. A gloomy expression, that's all, nothing more is wanted; it's a very simple business."

CHAPTER VII. A MEETING

I

VIRGINSKY LIVED IN HIS OWN house, or rather his wife's, in Muravyin Street. It was a wooden house of one story, and there were no lodgers in it. On the pretext of Virginsky's-name-day party, about fifteen guests were assembled; but the entertainment was not in the least like an ordinary provincial name-day party. From the very beginning of their married life the husband and wife had agreed once for all that it was utterly stupid to invite friends to celebrate name-days, and that "there is nothing to rejoice about in fact." In a few years they had succeeded in completely cutting themselves off from all society. Though he was a man of some ability, and by no means very poor, he somehow seemed to every one an eccentric fellow who was fond of solitude, and, what's more, "stuck up in conversation." Madame Virginsky was a midwife by profession—and by that very fact was on the lowest rung of the social ladder, lower even than the priest's wife in spite of her husband's rank as an officer. But she was conspicuously lacking in the humility befitting her position. And after her very stupid and unpardonably open liaison on principle with Captain Lebyadkin, a notorious rogue, even the most indulgent of our ladies turned away from her with marked contempt. But Madame Virginsky accepted all this as though it were what she wanted. It is remarkable that those very ladies applied to Arina Prohorovna (that is, Madame Virginsky) when they were in an interesting condition, rather than to any one of the other three accoucheuses of the town. She was sent for even by country families living in the neighbourhood, so great was the belief in her knowledge, luck, and skill in critical cases. It ended in her practising only among the wealthiest ladies; she was greedy of money. Feeling her power to the full, she ended by not putting herself out for anyone. Possibly on purpose, indeed, in her practice in the best houses she used to scare nervous patients by the most incredible and nihilistic disregard of good manners, or by jeering at "everything holy," at the very time when "everything holy" might have come in most useful. Our town doctor, Rozanov—he too was an accoucheur—asserted most positively that on one occasion when a patient in labour was crying out and calling on the name of the Almighty, a free-thinking sally from Arina Prohorovna, fired off like a pistol-shot, had so terrifying an effect on the patient that it greatly accelerated her delivery.

But though she was a nihilist, Madame Virginsky did not, when occasion arose, disdain social or even old-fashioned superstitions and customs if they could be of any advantage to herself. She would never, for instance, have stayed away from a baby's christening, and always put on a green silk dress with a train and adorned her chignon with curls and ringlets for such events, though at other times she positively revelled in slovenliness. And though during the ceremony she always maintained "the most insolent air," so that she put the clergy to confusion, yet when it was over she invariably handed champagne to the guests (it was for that that she came and dressed up), and it was no use trying to take the glass without a contribution to her "porridge bowl."

The guests who assembled that evening at Virginsky's (mostly men) had a casual and exceptional air. There was no supper nor cards. In the middle of the large drawing-room, which was papered with extremely old blue paper, two tables had been put together and covered with a large though not quite clean table-cloth, and on them two samovars were boiling. The end of the table was taken up by a huge tray with twenty-five glasses on it and a basket with ordinary French bread cut into a number of slices, as one sees it in genteel boarding-schools for boys or girls. The tea was poured out by a maiden lady of thirty, Arina Prohorovna's sister, a silent and malevolent creature, with flaxen hair and no eyebrows, who shared her sister's progressive ideas and was an object of terror to Virginsky himself in domestic life. There were only three ladies in the room: the lady of the house, her eyebrowless sister, and Virginsky's sister, a girl who had just arrived from Petersburg. Arina Prohorovna, a good-looking and buxom woman of seven-and-twenty, rather dishevelled, in an everyday greenish woollen dress, was sitting scanning the guests with her bold eyes, and her look seemed in haste to say, "You see I am not in the least afraid of anything." Miss Virginsky, a rosy-cheeked student and a nihilist, who was also good-looking, short, plump and round as a little ball, had settled herself beside Arina Prohorovna, almost in her travelling clothes. She held a roll of paper in her hand, and scrutinised the guests with impatient and roving eyes. Virginsky himself was rather unwell that evening, but he came in and sat in an easy chair by the tea-table. All the guests were sitting down too, and the orderly way in which they were ranged on chairs suggested a meeting. Evidently all were expecting something and were filling up the interval with loud but irrelevant conversation. When Stavrogin and Verhovensky appeared there was a sudden hush.

But I must be allowed to give a few explanations to make things clear.

I believe that all these people had come together in the agreeable expectation of hearing something particularly interesting, and had notice of it beforehand. They were the flower of the reddest Radicalism of our ancient town, and had been carefully picked out by Virginsky for this "meeting." I may remark, too, that some of them (though not very many) had never visited him before. Of course most of the guests had no clear idea why they had been summoned. It was true that at that time all took Pyotr Stepanovitch for a fully authorised emissary from abroad; this idea had somehow taken root among them at once and naturally flattered them. And yet among the citizens assembled ostensibly to keep a name-day, there were some who had been approached with definite proposals. Pyotr Verhovensky had succeeded in getting together a "quintet" amongst us like the one he had already formed in Moscow and, as appeared later, in our province among the officers. It was said that he had another in X province. This quintet of the elect were sitting now at the general table, and very skilfully succeeded in giving themselves the air of being quite ordinary people, so that no one could have known them. They were—since it is no longer a secret—first Liputin, then Virginsky himself, then Shigalov (a gentleman with long ears, the brother of Madame Virginsky), Lyamshin, and lastly a strange person called Tolkatchenko, a man of forty, who was famed for his vast knowledge of the people, especially of thieves and robbers. He used to frequent the taverns on purpose (though not only with the object of studying the people), and plumed himself on his shabby clothes, tarred boots, and crafty wink and a flourish of peasant phrases. Lyamshin had once or twice brought him to Stepan Trofimovitch's gatherings, where, however, he did not make a great sensation. He used to make his appearance in the town from time to time, chiefly when he was out of a job; he was employed on the railway.

Every one of these fine champions had formed this first group in the fervent conviction that their quintet was only one of hundreds and thousands of similar groups scattered all over

Russia, and that they all depended on some immense central but secret power, which in its turn was intimately connected with the revolutionary movement all over Europe. But I regret to say that even at that time there was beginning to be dissension among them. Though they had ever since the spring been expecting Pyotr Verhovensky, whose coming had been heralded first by Tolkatchenko and then by the arrival of Shigalov, though they had expected extraordinary miracles from him, and though they had responded to his first summons without the slightest criticism, yet they had no sooner formed the quintet than they all somehow seemed to feel insulted; and I really believe it was owing to the promptitude with which they consented to join. They had joined, of course, from a not ignoble feeling of shame, for fear people might say afterwards that they had not dared to join; still they felt Pyotr Verhovensky ought to have appreciated their heroism and have rewarded it by telling them some really important bits of news at least. But Verhovensky was not at all inclined to satisfy their legitimate curiosity, and told them nothing but what was necessary; he treated them in general with great sternness and even rather casually. This was positively irritating, and Comrade Shigalov was already egging the others on to insist on his "explaining himself," though, of course, not at Virginsky's, where so many outsiders were present.

I have an idea that the above-mentioned members of the first quintet were disposed to suspect that among the guests of Virginsky's that evening some were members of other groups, unknown to them, belonging to the same secret organisation and founded in the town by the same Verhovensky; so that in fact all present were suspecting one another, and posed in various ways to one another, which gave the whole party a very perplexing and even romantic air. Yet there were persons present who were beyond all suspicion. For instance, a major in the service, a near relation of Virginsky, a perfectly innocent person who had not been invited but had come of himself for the name-day celebration, so that it was impossible not to receive him. But Virginsky was quite unperturbed, as the major was "incapable of betraying them"; for in spite of his stupidity he had all his life been fond of dropping in wherever extreme Radicals met; he did not sympathise with their ideas himself, but was very fond of listening to them. What's more, he had even been compromised indeed. It had happened in his youth that whole bundles of manifestoes and of numbers of The Bell had passed through his hands, and although he had been afraid even to open them, yet he would have considered it absolutely contemptible to refuse to distribute them—and there are such people in Russia even to this day.

The rest of the guests were either types of honourable amour-propre crushed and embittered, or types of the generous impulsiveness of ardent youth. There were two or three teachers, of whom one, a lame man of forty-five, a master in the high school, was a very malicious and strikingly vain person; and two or three officers. Of the latter, one very young artillery officer who had only just come from a military training school, a silent lad who had not yet made friends with anyone, turned up now at Virginsky's with a pencil in his hand, and, scarcely taking any part in the conversation, continually made notes in his notebook. Everybody saw this, but every one pretended not to. There was, too, an idle divinity student who had helped Lyamshin to put indecent photographs into the gospel-woman's pack. He was a solid youth with a free-and-easy though mistrustful manner, with an unchangeably satirical smile, together with a calm air of triumphant faith in his own perfection. There was also present, I don't know why, the mayor's son, that unpleasant and prematurely exhausted youth to whom I have referred already in telling the story of the lieutenant's little wife. He was silent the whole evening. Finally there was a very enthusiastic and tousle-headed schoolboy of eighteen, who sat with the gloomy air of a young man whose dignity has been wounded, evidently distressed by his eighteen years. This infant was already the head of an independent group of conspirators which had been formed in the highest class of the gymnasium, as it came out afterwards to the surprise of every one.

I haven't mentioned Shatov. He was there at the farthest corner of the table, his chair pushed back a little out of the row. He gazed at the ground, was gloomily silent, refused tea and bread, and did not for one instant let his cap go out of his hand, as though to show that he was not a visitor, but had come on business, and when he liked would get up and go away. Kirillov was not far from him. He, too, was very silent, but he did not look at the ground; on the contrary, he scrutinised intently every speaker with his fixed, lustreless eyes, and listened to everything without the slightest emotion or surprise. Some of the visitors who had never seen him before stole thoughtful glances at him. I can't say whether Madame Virginsky knew anything about the existence of the quintet. I imagine she knew everything and from her husband. The girl-student, of course, took no part in anything; but she had an anxiety of her own: she intended to stay only a day or two and then to go on farther and farther from one university town to another "to show active sympathy with the sufferings of poor students and to rouse them to protest." She was taking with her some hundreds of copies of a lithographed appeal, I believe of her own composition. It is remarkable that the schoolboy conceived an almost murderous hatred for her from the first moment, though he saw her for the first time in his life; and she felt the same for him. The major was her uncle, and met her to-day for the first time after ten years. When Stavrogin and Verhovensky came in, her cheeks were as red as cranberries: she had just quarrelled with her uncle over his views on the woman question.

II

With conspicuous nonchalance Verhovensky lounged in the chair at the upper end of the table, almost without greeting anyone. His expression was disdainful and even haughty. Stavrogin bowed politely, but in spite of the fact that they were all only waiting for them, everybody, as though acting on instruction, appeared scarcely to notice them. The lady of the house turned severely to Stavrogin as soon as he was seated.

"Stavrogin, will you have tea?"

"Please," he answered.

"Tea for Stavrogin," she commanded her sister at the samovar. "And you, will you?" (This was to Verhovensky.)

"Of course. What a question to ask a visitor! And give me cream too; you always give one such filthy stuff by way of tea, and with a name-day party in the house!"

"What, you believe in keeping name-days too!" the girl-student laughed suddenly. "We were just talking of that."

"That's stale," muttered the schoolboy at the other end of the table.

"What's stale? To disregard conventions, even the most innocent is not stale; on the contrary, to the disgrace of every one, so far it's a novelty," the girl-student answered instantly, darting forward on her chair. "Besides, there are no innocent conventions," she added with intensity.

"I only meant," cried the schoolboy with tremendous excitement, "to say that though conventions of course are stale and must be eradicated, yet about name-days everybody knows that they are stupid and very stale to waste precious time upon, which has been wasted already all over the world, so that it would be as well to sharpen one's wits on something more useful. . . ."

"You drag it out so, one can't understand what you mean," shouted the girl.

"I think that every one has a right to express an opinion as well as every one else, and if I want to express my opinion like anybody else . . ."

"No one is attacking your right to give an opinion," the lady of the house herself cut in sharply. "You were only asked not to ramble because no one can make out what you mean."

"But allow me to remark that you are not treating me with respect. If I couldn't fully express my thought, it's not from want of thought but from too much thought," the schoolboy muttered, almost in despair, losing his thread completely.

"If you don't know how to talk, you'd better keep quiet," blurted out the girl.

The schoolboy positively jumped from his chair.

"I only wanted to state," he shouted, crimson with shame and afraid to look about him, "that you only wanted to show off your cleverness because Mr. Stavrogin came in—so there!"

"That's a nasty and immoral idea and shows the worthlessness of your development. I beg you not to address me again," the girl rattled off.

"Stavrogin," began the lady of the house, "they've been discussing the rights of the family before you came—this officer here"—she nodded towards her relation, the major—"and, of course, I am not going to worry you with such stale nonsense, which has been dealt with long ago. But how have the rights and duties of the family come about in the superstitious form in which they exist at present? That's the question. What's your opinion?"

"What do you mean by 'come about'?" Stavrogin asked in his turn.

"We know, for instance, that the superstition about God came from thunder and lightning." The girl-student rushed into the fray again, staring at Stavrogin with her eyes almost jumping out of her head. "It's well known that primitive man, scared by thunder and lightning, made a god of the unseen enemy, feeling their weakness before it. But how did the superstition of the family arise? How did the family itself arise?"

"That's not quite the same thing. . . ." Madame Virginsky tried to check her.

"I think the answer to this question wouldn't be quite discreet," answered Stavrogin.

"How so?" said the girl-student, craning forward suddenly. But there was an audible titter in the group of teachers, which was at once caught up at the other end by Lyamshin and the schoolboy and followed by a hoarse chuckle from the major.

"You ought to write vaudevilles," Madame Virginsky observed to Stavrogin.

"It does you no credit, I don't know what your name is," the girl rapped out with positive indignation.

"And don't you be too forward," boomed the major. "You are a young lady and you ought to behave modestly, and you keep jumping about as though you were sitting on a needle."

"Kindly hold your tongue and don't address me familiarly with your nasty comparisons. I've never seen you before and I don't recognise the relationship."

"But I am your uncle; I used to carry you about when you were a baby!"

"I don't care what babies you used to carry about. I didn't ask you to carry me. It must have been a pleasure to you to do so, you rude officer. And allow me to observe, don't dare to address me so familiarly, unless it's as a fellow-citizen. I forbid you to do it, once for all."

"There, they are all like that!" cried the major, banging the table with his fist and addressing Stavrogin, who was sitting opposite. "But, allow me, I am fond of Liberalism and modern ideas, and I am fond of listening to clever conversation; masculine conversation, though, I warn you. But to listen to these women, these nightly windmills—no, that makes me ache all over! Don't wriggle about!" he shouted to the girl, who was leaping up from her chair. "No, it's my turn to speak, I've been insulted."

"You can't say anything yourself, and only hinder other people talking," the lady of the house grumbled indignantly.

"No, I will have my say," said the major hotly, addressing Stavrogin. "I reckon on you, Mr. Stavrogin, as a fresh person who has only just come on the scene, though I haven't the honour of knowing you. Without men they'll perish like flies—that's what I think. All their woman question is only lack of originality. I assure you that all this woman question has been invented for them by men in foolishness and to their own hurt. I only thank God I am not married. There's not the slightest variety in them, they can't even invent a simple pattern; they have to get men to invent them for them! Here I used to carry her in my arms, used to dance the mazurka with her when she was ten years old; to-day she's come, naturally I fly to embrace her, and at the second word she tells me there's no God. She might have waited a little, she was in too great a hurry! Clever people don't believe, I dare say; but that's from their cleverness. But you, chicken, what do you know about God, I said to her. 'Some student taught you, and if he'd taught you to light the lamp before the ikons you would have lighted it.'"

"You keep telling lies, you are a very spiteful person. I proved to you just now the untenability of your position," the girl answered contemptuously, as though disdaining further explanations with such a man. "I told you just now that we've all been taught in the Catechism if you honour your father and your parents you will live long and have wealth. That's in the Ten Commandments. If God thought it necessary to offer rewards for love, your God must be immoral. That's how I proved it to you. It wasn't the second word, and it was because you asserted your rights. It's not my fault if you are stupid and don't understand even now. You are offended and you are spiteful—and that's what explains all your generation."

"You're a goose!" said the major.

"And you are a fool!"

"You can call me names!"

"Excuse me, Kapiton Maximitch, you told me yourself you don't believe in God," Liputin piped from the other end of the table.

"What if I did say so—that's a different matter. I believe, perhaps, only not altogether. Even if I don't believe altogether, still I don't say God ought to be shot. I used to think about God before I left the hussars. From all the poems you would think that hussars do nothing but carouse and drink. Yes, I did drink, maybe, but would you believe it, I used to jump out of bed at night and stood crossing myself before the images with nothing but my socks on, praying to God to give me faith; for even then I couldn't be at peace as to whether there was a God or not. It used to fret me so! In the morning, of course, one would amuse oneself and one's faith would seem to be lost again; and in fact I've noticed that faith always seems to be less in the daytime."

"Haven't you any cards?" asked Verhovensky, with a mighty yawn, addressing Madame Virginsky.

"I sympathise with your question, I sympathise entirely," the girl-student broke in hotly, flushed with indignation at the major's words.

"We are wasting precious time listening to silly talk," snapped out the lady of the house, and she looked reprovingly at her husband.

The girl pulled herself together.

"I wanted to make a statement to the meeting concerning the sufferings of the students and their protest, but as time is being wasted in immoral conversation ..."

"There's no such thing as moral or immoral," the schoolboy brought out, unable to restrain himself as soon as the girl began.

"I knew that, Mr. Schoolboy, long before you were taught it."

"And I maintain," he answered savagely, "that you are a child come from Petersburg to enlighten us all, though we know for ourselves the commandment 'honour thy father and thy mother,' which you could not repeat correctly; and the fact that it's immoral every one in Russia knows from Byelinsky."

"Are we ever to have an end of this?" Madame Virginsky said resolutely to her husband. As the hostess, she blushed for the ineptitude of the conversation, especially as she noticed smiles and even astonishment among the guests who had been invited for the first time.

"Gentlemen," said Virginsky, suddenly lifting up his voice, "if anyone wishes to say anything more nearly connected with our business, or has any statement to make, I call upon him to do so without wasting time."

"I'll venture to ask one question," said the lame teacher suavely. He had been sitting particularly decorously and had not spoken till then. "I should like to know, are we some sort of meeting, or are we simply a gathering of ordinary mortals paying a visit? I ask simply for the sake of order and so as not to remain in ignorance."

This "sly" question made an impression. People looked at each other, every one expecting someone else to answer, and suddenly all, as though at a word of command, turned their eyes to Verhovensky and Stavrogin.

"I suggest our voting on the answer to the question whether we are a meeting or not," said Madame Virginsky.

"I entirely agree with the suggestion," Liputin chimed in, "though the question is rather vague."

"I agree too."

"And so do I," cried voices. "I too think it would make our proceedings more in order," confirmed Virginsky.

"To the vote then," said his wife. "Lyamshin, please sit down to the piano; you can give your vote from there when the voting begins."

"Again!" cried Lyamshin. "I've strummed enough for you."

"I beg you most particularly, sit down and play. Don't you care to do anything for the cause?"

"But I assure you, Arina Prohorovna, nobody is eavesdropping. It's only your fancy. Besides, the windows are high, and people would not understand if they did hear."

"We don't understand ourselves," someone muttered. "But I tell you one must always be on one's guard. I mean in case there should be spies," she explained to Verhovensky. "Let them hear from the street that we have music and a name-day party."

"Hang it all!" Lyamshin swore, and sitting down to the piano, began strumming a valse, banging on the keys almost with his fists, at random.

"I propose that those who want it to be a meeting should put up their right hands," Madame Virginsky proposed.

Some put them up, others did not. Some held them up and then put them down again and then held them up again. "Foo! I don't understand it at all," one officer shouted. "I don't either," cried the other.

"Oh, I understand," cried a third. "If it's yes, you hold your hand up."

"But what does 'yes' mean?"

"Means a meeting."

"No, it means not a meeting."

"I voted for a meeting," cried the schoolboy to Madame Virginsky.

"Then why didn't you hold up your hand?"

"I was looking at you. You didn't hold up yours, so I didn't hold up mine."

"How stupid! I didn't hold up my hand because I proposed it. Gentlemen, now I propose the contrary. Those who want a meeting, sit still and do nothing; those who don't, hold up their right hands."

"Those who don't want it?" inquired the schoolboy. "Are you doing it on purpose?" cried Madame Virginsky wrathfully.

"No. Excuse me, those who want it, or those who don't want it? For one must know that definitely," cried two or three voices.

"Those who don't want it—those who don't want it."

"Yes, but what is one to do, hold up one's hand or not hold it up if one doesn't want it?" cried an officer.

"Ech, we are not accustomed to constitutional methods yet!" remarked the major.

"Mr. Lyamshin, excuse me, but you are thumping so that no one can hear anything," observed the lame teacher.

"But, upon my word, Arina Prohorovna, nobody is listening, really!" cried Lyamshin, jumping up. "I won't play! I've come to you as a visitor, not as a drummer!"

"Gentlemen," Virginsky went on, "answer verbally, are we a meeting or not?"

"We are! We are!" was heard on all sides. "If so, there's no need to vote, that's enough. Are you satisfied, gentlemen? Is there any need to put it to the vote?"

"No need—no need, we understand."

"Perhaps someone doesn't want it to be a meeting?"

"No, no; we all want it."

"But what does 'meeting' mean?" cried a voice. No one answered.

"We must choose a chairman," people cried from different parts of the room.

"Our host, of course, our host!"

"Gentlemen, if so," Virginsky, the chosen chairman, began, "I propose my original motion. If anyone wants to say anything more relevant to the subject, or has some statement to make, let him bring it forward without loss of time."

There was a general silence. The eyes of all were turned again on Verhovensky and Stavrogin.

"Verhovensky, have you no statement to make?" Madame Virginsky asked him directly.

"Nothing whatever," he answered, yawning and stretching on his chair. "But I should like a glass of brandy."

"Stavrogin, don't you want to?"

"Thank you, I don't drink."

"I mean don't you want to speak, not don't you want brandy."

"To speak, what about? No, I don't want to."

"They'll bring you some brandy," she answered Verhovensky.

The girl-student got up. She had darted up several times already.

"I have come to make a statement about the sufferings of poor students and the means of rousing them to protest."

But she broke off. At the other end of the table a rival had risen, and all eyes turned to him. Shigalov, the man with the long ears, slowly rose from his seat with a gloomy and sullen air and mournfully laid on the table a thick notebook filled with extremely small handwriting. He remained standing in silence. Many people looked at the notebook in consternation, but Liputin, Virginsky, and the lame teacher seemed pleased.

"I ask leave to address the meeting," Shigalov pronounced sullenly but resolutely.

"You have leave." Virginsky gave his sanction.

The orator sat down, was silent for half a minute, and pronounced in a solemn voice,

"Gentlemen!"

"Here's the brandy," the sister who had been pouring out tea and had gone to fetch brandy rapped out, contemptuously and disdainfully putting the bottle before Verhovensky, together with the wineglass which she brought in her fingers without a tray or a plate.

The interrupted orator made a dignified pause.

"Never mind, go on, I am not listening," cried Verhovensky, pouring himself out a glass.

"Gentlemen, asking your attention and, as you will see later, soliciting your aid in a matter of the first importance," Shigalov began again, "I must make some prefatory remarks."

"Arina Prohorovna, haven't you some scissors?" Pyotr Stepanovitch asked suddenly.

"What do you want scissors for?" she asked, with wide-open eyes.

"I've forgotten to cut my nails; I've been meaning to for the last three days," he observed, scrutinising his long and dirty nails with unruffled composure.

Arina Prohorovna crimsoned, but Miss Virginsky seemed pleased.

"I believe I saw them just now on the window." She got up from the table, went and found the scissors, and at once brought them. Pyotr Stepanovitch did not even look at her, took the scissors, and set to work with them. Arina Prohorovna grasped that these were realistic manners, and was ashamed of her sensitiveness. People looked at one another in silence. The lame teacher looked vindictively and enviously at Verhovensky. Shigalov went on.

"Dedicating my energies to the study of the social organisation which is in the future to replace the present condition of things, I've come to the conviction that all makers of social systems from ancient times up to the present year, 187-, have been dreamers, tellers of fairy-tales, fools who contradicted themselves, who understood nothing of natural science and the strange animal called man. Plato, Rousseau, Fourier, columns of aluminium, are only fit for sparrows and not for human society. But, now that we are all at last preparing to act, a new form of social organisation is essential. In order to avoid further uncertainty, I propose my own system of world-organisation. Here it is." He tapped the notebook. "I wanted to expound my views to the meeting in the most concise form possible, but I see that I should need to add a great many verbal explanations, and so the whole exposition would occupy at least ten evenings, one for each of my chapters." (There was the sound of laughter.) "I must add, besides, that my system is not yet complete." (Laughter again.) "I am perplexed by my own data and my conclusion is a direct contradiction of the original idea with which I start. Starting from unlimited freedom, I arrive at unlimited despotism. I will add, however, that there can be no solution of the social problem but mine."

The laughter grew louder and louder, but it came chiefly from the younger and less initiated visitors. There was an expression of some annoyance on the faces of Madame Virginsky, Liputin, and the lame teacher.

"If you've been unsuccessful in making your system consistent, and have been reduced to despair yourself, what could we do with it?" one officer observed warily.

"You are right, Mr. Officer"—Shigalov turned sharply to him—"especially in using the word despair. Yes, I am reduced to despair. Nevertheless, nothing can take the place of the system set forth in my book, and there is no other way out of it; no one can invent anything else. And so I hasten without loss of time to invite the whole society to listen for ten evenings to my book and then give their opinions of it. If the members are unwilling to listen to me, let us break up from the start—the men to take up service under government, the women to their cooking; for if you reject my solution you'll find no other, none whatever! If they let the opportunity slip, it will simply be their loss, for they will be bound to come back to it again."

There was a stir in the company. "Is he mad, or what?" voices asked.

"So the whole point lies in Shigalov's despair," Lyamshin commented, "and the essential question is whether he must despair or not?"

"Shigalov's being on the brink of despair is a personal question," declared the schoolboy.

"I propose we put it to the vote how far Shigalov's despair affects the common cause, and at the same time whether it's worth while listening to him or not," an officer suggested gaily.

"That's not right." The lame teacher put in his spoke at last. As a rule he spoke with a rather mocking smile, so that it was difficult to make out whether he was in earnest or joking. "That's not right, gentlemen. Mr. Shigalov is too much devoted to his task and is also too modest. I know his book. He suggests as a final solution of the question the division of mankind into two unequal parts. One-tenth enjoys absolute liberty and unbounded power over the other nine-tenths. The others have to give up all individuality and become, so to speak, a herd, and, through boundless submission, will by a series of regenerations attain primæval innocence, something like the Garden of Eden. They'll have to work, however. The measures proposed by the author for depriving nine-tenths of mankind of their freedom and transforming them into a herd through the education of whole generations are very remarkable, founded on the facts of nature and highly logical. One may not agree with some of the deductions, but it would be difficult to doubt the intelligence and knowledge of the author. It's a pity that the time required—ten evenings—is impossible to arrange for, or we might hear a great deal that's interesting."

"Can you be in earnest?" Madame Virginsky addressed the lame gentleman with a shade of positive uneasiness in her voice, "when that man doesn't know what to do with people and so turns nine-tenths of them into slaves? I've suspected him for a long time."

"You say that of your own brother?" asked the lame man.

"Relationship? Are you laughing at me?"

"And besides, to work for aristocrats and to obey them as though they were gods is contemptible!" observed the girl-student fiercely.

"What I propose is not contemptible; it's paradise, an earthly paradise, and there can be no other on earth," Shigalov pronounced authoritatively.

"For my part," said Lyamshin, "if I didn't know what to do with nine-tenths of mankind, I'd take them and blow them up into the air instead of putting them in paradise. I'd only leave a handful of educated people, who would live happily ever afterwards on scientific principles."

"No one but a buffoon can talk like that!" cried the girl, flaring up.

"He is a buffoon, but he is of use," Madame Virginsky whispered to her.

"And possibly that would be the best solution of the problem," said Shigalov, turning hotly to Lyamshin. "You certainly don't know what a profound thing you've succeeded in saying, my merry friend. But as it's hardly possible to carry out your idea, we must confine ourselves to an earthly paradise, since that's what they call it."

"This is pretty thorough rot," broke, as though involuntarily, from Verhovensky. Without even raising his eyes, however, he went on cutting his nails with perfect nonchalance.

"Why is it rot?" The lame man took it up instantly, as though he had been lying in wait for his first words to catch at them. "Why is it rot? Mr. Shigalov is somewhat fanatical in his love for humanity, but remember that Fourier, still more Cabet and even Proudhon himself, advocated a number of the most despotic and even fantastic measures. Mr. Shigalov is perhaps far more sober in his suggestions than they are. I assure you that when one reads his book it's almost impossible not to agree with some things. He is perhaps less far from realism than anyone and his earthly paradise is almost the real one—if it ever existed—for the loss of which man is always sighing."

"I knew I was in for something," Verhovensky muttered again.

"Allow me," said the lame man, getting more and more excited. "Conversations and arguments about the future organisation of society are almost an actual necessity for all thinking people nowadays. Herzen was occupied with nothing else all his life. Byelinsky, as I know on very good authority, used to spend whole evenings with his friends debating and settling beforehand even the minutest, so to speak, domestic, details of the social organisation of the future."

"Some people go crazy over it," the major observed suddenly.

"We are more likely to arrive at something by talking, anyway, than by sitting silent and posing as dictators," Liputin hissed, as though at last venturing to begin the attack.

"I didn't mean Shigalov when I said it was rot," Verhovensky mumbled. "You see, gentlemen,"—he raised his eyes a trifle—"to my mind all these books, Fourier, Cabet, all this talk about the right to work, and Shigalov's theories—are all like novels of which one can write a hundred thousand—an æsthetic entertainment. I can understand that in this little town you are bored, so you rush to ink and paper."

"Excuse me," said the lame man, wriggling on his chair, "though we are provincials and of course objects of commiseration on that ground, yet we know that so far nothing has happened in the world new enough to be worth our weeping at having missed it. It is suggested to us in various pamphlets made abroad and secretly distributed that we should unite and form groups with the sole object of bringing about universal destruction. It's urged that, however much you tinker with the world, you can't make a good job of it, but that by cutting off a hundred million heads and so lightening one's burden, one can jump over the ditch more safely. A fine idea, no doubt, but quite as impracticable as Shigalov's theories, which you referred to just now so contemptuously."

"Well, but I haven't come here for discussion." Verhovensky let drop this significant phrase, and, as though quite unaware of his blunder, drew the candle nearer to him that he might see better.

"It's a pity, a great pity, that you haven't come for discussion, and it's a great pity that you are so taken up just now with your toilet."

"What's my toilet to you?"

"To remove a hundred million heads is as difficult as to transform the world by propaganda. Possibly more difficult, especially in Russia," Liputin ventured again.

"It's Russia they rest their hopes on now," said an officer.

"We've heard they are resting their hopes on it," interposed the lame man. "We know that a mysterious finger is pointing to our delightful country as the land most fitted to accomplish the great task. But there's this: by the gradual solution of the problem by propaganda I shall gain something, anyway—I shall have some pleasant talk, at least, and shall even get some recognition from government for my services to the cause of society. But in the second way, by the rapid method of cutting off a hundred million heads, what benefit shall I get personally? If you began advocating that, your tongue might be cut out."

"Yours certainly would be," observed Verhovensky.

"You see. And as under the most favourable circumstances you would not get through such a massacre in less than fifty or at the best thirty years—for they are not sheep, you know, and perhaps they would not let themselves be slaughtered—wouldn't it be better to pack one's bundle and migrate to some quiet island beyond calm seas and there close one's eyes tranquilly? Believe me"—he tapped the table significantly with his finger—"you will only promote emigration by such propaganda and nothing else!"

He finished evidently triumphant. He was one of the intellects of the province. Liputin smiled slyly, Virginsky listened rather dejectedly, the others followed the discussion with great attention, especially the ladies and officers. They all realised that the advocate of the hundred million heads theory had been driven into a corner, and waited to see what would come of it.

"That was a good saying of yours, though," Verhovensky mumbled more carelessly than ever, in fact with an air of positive boredom. "Emigration is a good idea. But all the same, if in spite of all the obvious disadvantages you foresee, more and more come forward every day ready to fight for the common cause, it will be able to do without you. It's a new religion, my good friend, coming to take the place of the old one. That's why so many fighters come forward, and it's a big movement. You'd better emigrate! And, you know, I should advise Dresden, not 'the calm islands.' To begin with, it's a town that has never been visited by an epidemic, and as you are a man of culture, no doubt you are afraid of death. Another thing, it's near the Russian frontier, so you can more easily receive your income from your beloved Fatherland. Thirdly, it contains what are called treasures of art, and you are a man of æsthetic tastes, formerly a teacher of literature, I believe. And, finally, it has a miniature Switzerland of its own—to provide you with poetic inspiration, for no doubt you write verse. In fact it's a treasure in a nutshell!" There was a general movement, especially among the officers. In another instant, they would have all begun talking at once. But the lame man rose irritably to the bait.

"No, perhaps I am not going to give up the common cause. You must understand that ..."

"What, would you join the quintet if I proposed it to you?" Verhovensky boomed suddenly, and he laid down the scissors.

Every one seemed startled. The mysterious man had revealed himself too freely. He had even spoken openly of the "quintet."

"Every one feels himself to be an honest man and will not shirk his part in the common cause"—the lame man tried to wriggle out of it—"but ..."

"No, this is not a question which allows of a but," Verhovensky interrupted harshly and peremptorily. "I tell you, gentlemen, I must have a direct answer. I quite understand that, having come here and having called you together myself, I am bound to give you explanations" (again an unexpected revelation), "but I can give you none till I know what is your attitude to the subject. To cut the matter short—for we can't go on talking for another thirty years as people have done for the last thirty—I ask you which you prefer: the slow way, which consists in the composition of socialistic romances and the academic ordering of the destinies of humanity a thousand years hence, while despotism will swallow the savoury morsels which would almost fly into your mouths of themselves if you'd take a little trouble; or do you, whatever it may imply, prefer a quicker way which will at last untie your hands, and will let humanity make its own social organisation in freedom and in action, not on paper? They shout 'a hundred million heads'; that may be only a metaphor; but why be afraid of it if, with the slow day-dream on paper, despotism in the course of some hundred years will devour not a hundred but five hundred million heads? Take note too that an incurable invalid will not be cured whatever prescriptions are written for him on paper. On the contrary, if there is delay, he will grow so corrupt that he will infect us too and contaminate all the fresh forces which one might still reckon upon now, so that we shall all at last come to grief together. I thoroughly agree that it's extremely agreeable to chatter liberally and eloquently, but action is a little trying.... However, I am no hand at talking; I came here with communications, and so I beg all the honourable company not to vote, but simply and directly to state which you prefer: walking at a snail's pace in the marsh, or putting on full steam to get across it?"

"I am certainly for crossing at full steam!" cried the schoolboy in an ecstasy.

"So am I," Lyamshin chimed in.

"There can be no doubt about the choice," muttered an officer, followed by another, then by someone else. What struck them all most was that Verhovensky had come "with communications" and had himself just promised to speak.

"Gentlemen, I see that almost all decide for the policy of the manifestoes," he said, looking round at the company.

"All, all!" cried the majority of voices.

"I confess I am rather in favour of a more humane policy," said the major, "but as all are on the other side, I go with all the rest."

"It appears, then, that even you are not opposed to it," said Verhovensky, addressing the lame man.

"I am not exactly ..." said the latter, turning rather red, "but if I do agree with the rest now, it's simply not to break up—"

"You are all like that! Ready to argue for six months to practise your Liberal eloquence and in the end you vote the same as the rest! Gentlemen, consider though, is it true that you are all ready?"

(Ready for what? The question was vague, but very alluring.)

"All are, of course!" voices were heard. But all were looking at one another.

"But afterwards perhaps you will resent having agreed so quickly? That's almost always the way with you."

The company was excited in various ways, greatly excited. The lame man flew at him.

"Allow me to observe, however, that answers to such questions are conditional. Even if we have given our decision, you must note that questions put in such a strange way ..."

"In what strange way?"

"In a way such questions are not asked."

"Teach me how, please. But do you know, I felt sure you'd be the first to take offence."

"You've extracted from us an answer as to our readiness for immediate action; but what right had you to do so? By what authority do you ask such questions?"

"You should have thought of asking that question sooner! Why did you answer? You agree and then you go back on it!"

"But to my mind the irresponsibility of your principal question suggests to me that you have no authority, no right, and only asked from personal curiosity."

"What do you mean? What do you mean?" cried Verhovensky, apparently beginning to be much alarmed.

"Why, that the initiation of new members into anything you like is done, anyway, tête-à-tête and not in the company of twenty people one doesn't know!" blurted out the lame man. He had said all that was in his mind because he was too irritated to restrain himself. Verhovensky turned to the general company with a capitally simulated look of alarm.

"Gentlemen, I deem it my duty to declare that all this is folly, and that our conversation has gone too far. I have so far initiated no one, and no one has the right to say of me that I initiate members. We were simply discussing our opinions. That's so, isn't it? But whether that's so or not, you alarm me very much." He turned to the lame man again. "I had no idea that it was unsafe here to speak of such practically innocent matters except tête-à-tête. Are you afraid of informers? Can there possibly be an informer among us here?"

The excitement became tremendous; all began talking.

"Gentlemen, if that is so," Verhovensky went on, "I have compromised myself more than anyone, and so I will ask you to answer one question, if you care to, of course. You are all perfectly free."

"What question? What question?" every one clamoured.

"A question that will make it clear whether we are to remain together, or take up our hats and go our several ways without speaking."

"The question! The question!"

"If any one of us knew of a proposed political murder, would he, in view of all the consequences, go to give information, or would he stay at home and await events? Opinions may differ on this point. The answer to the question will tell us clearly whether we are to separate, or to remain together and for far longer than this one evening. Let me appeal to you first." He turned to the lame man.

"Why to me first?"

"Because you began it all. Be so good as not to prevaricate; it won't help you to be cunning. But please yourself, it's for you to decide."

"Excuse me, but such a question is positively insulting."

"No, can't you be more exact than that?"

"I've never been an agent of the Secret Police," replied the latter, wriggling more than ever.

"Be so good as to be more definite, don't keep us waiting."

The lame man was so furious that he left off answering. Without a word he glared wrathfully from under his spectacles at his tormentor.

"Yes or no? Would you inform or not?" cried Verhovensky.

"Of course I wouldn't," the lame man shouted twice as loudly.

"And no one would, of course not!" cried many voices.

"Allow me to appeal to you, Mr. Major. Would you inform or not?" Verhovensky went on. "And note that I appeal to you on purpose."

"I won't inform."

"But if you knew that someone meant to rob and murder someone else, an ordinary mortal, then you would inform and give warning?"

"Yes, of course; but that's a private affair, while the other would be a political treachery. I've never been an agent of the Secret Police."

"And no one here has," voices cried again. "It's an unnecessary question. Every one will make the same answer. There are no informers here."

"What is that gentleman getting up for?" cried the girl-student.

"That's Shatov. What are you getting up for?" cried the lady of the house.

Shatov did, in fact, stand up. He was holding his cap in his hand and looking at Verhovensky. Apparently he wanted to say something to him, but was hesitating. His face was pale and wrathful, but he controlled himself. He did not say one word, but in silence walked towards the door.

"Shatov, this won't make things better for you!" Verhovensky called after him enigmatically.

"But it will for you, since you are a spy and a scoundrel!" Shatov shouted to him from the door, and he went out.

Shouts and exclamations again.

"That's what comes of a test," cried a voice.

"It's been of use," cried another.

"Hasn't it been of use too late?" observed a third.

"Who invited him? Who let him in? Who is he? Who is Shatov? Will he inform, or won't he?" There was a shower of questions.

"If he were an informer he would have kept up appearances instead of cursing it all and going away," observed someone.

"See, Stavrogin is getting up too. Stavrogin has not answered the question either," cried the girl-student.

Stavrogin did actually stand up, and at the other end of the table Kirillov rose at the same time.

"Excuse me, Mr. Stavrogin," Madame Virginsky addressed him sharply, "we all answered the question, while you are going away without a word."

"I see no necessity to answer the question which interests you," muttered Stavrogin.

"But we've compromised ourselves and you won't," shouted several voices.

"What business is it of mine if you have compromised yourselves?" laughed Stavrogin, but his eyes flashed.

"What business? What business?" voices exclaimed.

Many people got up from their chairs.

"Allow me, gentlemen, allow me," cried the lame man. "Mr. Verhovensky hasn't answered the question either; he has only asked it."

The remark produced a striking effect. All looked at one another. Stavrogin laughed aloud in the lame man's face and went out; Kirillov followed him; Verhovensky ran after them into the passage.

"What are you doing?" he faltered, seizing Stavrogin's hand and gripping it with all his might in his. Stavrogin pulled away his hand without a word.

"Be at Kirillov's directly, I'll come.... It's absolutely necessary for me to see you!..."

"It isn't necessary for me," Stavrogin cut him short.

"Stavrogin will be there," Kirillov said finally. "Stavrogin, it is necessary for you. I will show you that there."

They went out.

CHAPTER VIII. IVAN THE TSAREVITCH

They had gone. Pyotr Stepanovitch was about to rush back to the meeting to bring order into chaos, but probably reflecting that it wasn't worth bothering about, left everything, and two minutes later was flying after the other two. On the way, he remembered a short cut to Filipov's house. He rushed along it, up to his knees in mud, and did in fact arrive at the very moment when Stavrogin and Kirillov were coming in at the gate.

"You here already?" observed Kirillov. "That's good. Come in."

"How is it you told us you lived alone," asked Stavrogin, passing a boiling samovar in the passage.

"You will see directly who it is I live with," muttered Kirillov. "Go in."

They had hardly entered when Verhovensky at once took out of his pocket the anonymous letter he had taken from Lembke, and laid it before Stavrogin. They all then sat down. Stavrogin read the letter in silence.

"Well?" he asked.

"That scoundrel will do as he writes," Verhovensky explained. "So, as he is under your control, tell me how to act. I assure you he may go to Lembke to-morrow."

"Well, let him go."

"Let him go! And when we can prevent him, too!"

"You are mistaken. He is not dependent on me. Besides, I don't care; he doesn't threaten me in any way; he only threatens you."

"You too."

"I don't think so."

"But there are other people who may not spare you. Surely you understand that? Listen, Stavrogin. This is only playing with words. Surely you don't grudge the money?"

"Why, would it cost money?"

"It certainly would; two thousand or at least fifteen hundred. Give it to me to-morrow or even to-day, and to-morrow evening I'll send him to Petersburg for you. That's just what he wants. If you like, he can take Marya Timofyevna. Note that."

There was something distracted about him. He spoke, as it were, without caution, and he did not reflect on his words. Stavrogin watched him, wondering.

"I've no reason to send Marya Timofyevna away."

"Perhaps you don't even want to," Pyotr Stepanovitch smiled ironically.

"Perhaps I don't."

"In short, will there be the money or not?" he cried with angry impatience, and as it were peremptorily, to Stavrogin. The latter scrutinised him gravely. "There won't be the money."

"Look here, Stavrogin! You know something, or have done something already! You are going it!"

His face worked, the corners of his mouth twitched, and he suddenly laughed an unprovoked and irrelevant laugh.

"But you've had money from your father for the estate," Stavrogin observed calmly. "Maman sent you six or eight thousand for Stepan Trofimovitch. So you can pay the fifteen hundred out of your own money. I don't care to pay for other people. I've given a lot as it is. It annoys me...." He smiled himself at his own words.

"Ah, you are beginning to joke!"

Stavrogin got up from his chair. Verhovensky instantly jumped up too, and mechanically stood with his back to the door as though barring the way to him. Stavrogin had already made a motion to push him aside and go out, when he stopped short.

"I won't give up Shatov to you," he said. Pyotr Stepanovitch started. They looked at one another.

"I told you this evening why you needed Shatov's blood," said Stavrogin, with flashing eyes. "It's the cement you want to bind your groups together with. You drove Shatov away cleverly just now. You knew very well that he wouldn't promise not to inform and he would have thought it mean to lie to you. But what do you want with me? What do you want with me? Ever since we met abroad you won't let me alone. The explanation you've given me so far was simply raving. Meanwhile you are driving at my giving Lebyadkin fifteen hundred roubles, so as to give Fedka an opportunity to murder him. I know that you think I want my wife murdered too. You think to tie my hands by this crime, and have me in your power. That's it, isn't it? What good will that be to you? What the devil do you want with me? Look at me. Once for all, am I the man for you? And let me alone."

"Has Fedka been to you himself?" Verhovensky asked breathlessly.

"Yes, he came. His price is fifteen hundred too.... But here; he'll repeat it himself. There he stands." Stavrogin stretched out his hand.

Pyotr Stepanovitch turned round quickly. A new figure, Fedka, wearing a sheep-skin coat, but without a cap, as though he were at home, stepped out of the darkness in the doorway. He stood there laughing and showing his even white teeth. His black eyes, with yellow whites, darted cautiously about the room watching the gentlemen. There was something he did not understand. He had evidently been just brought in by Kirillov, and his inquiring eyes turned to the latter. He stood in the doorway, but was unwilling to come into the room.

"I suppose you got him ready here to listen to our bargaining, or that he may actually see the money in our hands. Is that it?" asked Stavrogin; and without waiting for an answer he walked out of the house. Verhovensky, almost frantic, overtook him at the gate.

"Stop! Not another step!" he cried, seizing him by the arm. Stavrogin tried to pull away his arm, but did not succeed. He was overcome with fury. Seizing Verhovensky by the hair with his left hand he flung him with all his might on the ground and went out at the gate. But he had not gone thirty paces before Verhovensky overtook him again.

"Let us make it up; let us make it up!" he murmured in a spasmodic whisper.

Stavrogin shrugged his shoulders, but neither answered nor turned round.

"Listen. I will bring you Lizaveta Nikolaevna to-morrow; shall I? No? Why don't you answer? Tell me what you want. I'll do it. Listen. I'll let you have Shatov. Shall I?"

"Then it's true that you meant to kill him?" cried Stavrogin.

"What do you want with Shatov? What is he to you?" Pyotr Stepanovitch went on, gasping, speaking rapidly. He was in a frenzy, and kept running forward and seizing Stavrogin by the elbow, probably unaware of what he was doing. "Listen. I'll let you have him. Let's make it up. Your price is a very great one, but … Let's make it up!"

Stavrogin glanced at him at last, and was amazed. The eyes, the voice, were not the same as always, or as they had been in the room just now. What he saw was almost another face. The intonation of the voice was different. Verhovensky besought, implored. He was a man from whom what was most precious was being taken or had been taken, and who was still stunned by the shock.

"But what's the matter with you?" cried Stavrogin. The other did not answer, but ran after him and gazed at him with the same imploring but yet inflexible expression.

"Let's make it up!" he whispered once more. "Listen. Like Fedka, I have a knife in my boot, but I'll make it up with you!"

"But what do you want with me, damn you?" Stavrogin cried, with intense anger and amazement. "Is there some mystery about it? Am I a sort of talisman for you?"

"Listen. We are going to make a revolution," the other muttered rapidly, and almost in delirium. "You don't believe we shall make a revolution? We are going to make such an upheaval that everything will be uprooted from its foundation. Karmazinov is right that there is nothing to lay hold of. Karmazinov is very intelligent. Another ten such groups in different parts of Russia—and I am safe."

"Groups of fools like that?" broke reluctantly from Stavrogin.

"Oh, don't be so clever, Stavrogin; don't be so clever yourself. And you know you are by no means so intelligent that you need wish others to be. You are afraid, you have no faith. You are frightened at our doing things on such a scale. And why are they fools? They are not such fools. No one has a mind of his own nowadays. There are terribly few original minds nowadays. Virginsky is a pure-hearted man, ten times as pure as you or I; but never mind about him. Liputin is a rogue, but I know one point about him. Every rogue has some point in him.…

Lyamshin is the only one who hasn't, but he is in my hands. A few more groups, and I should have money and passports everywhere; so much at least. Suppose it were only that? And safe places, so that they can search as they like. They might uproot one group but they'd stick at the next. We'll set things in a ferment.... Surely you don't think that we two are not enough?"

"Take Shigalov, and let me alone...."

"Shigalov is a man of genius! Do you know he is a genius like Fourier, but bolder than Fourier; stronger. I'll look after him. He's discovered 'equality'!"

"He is in a fever; he is raving; something very queer has happened to him," thought Stavrogin, looking at him once more. Both walked on without stopping.

"He's written a good thing in that manuscript," Verhovensky went on. "He suggests a system of spying. Every member of the society spies on the others, and it's his duty to inform against them. Every one belongs to all and all to every one. All are slaves and equal in their slavery. In extreme cases he advocates slander and murder, but the great thing about it is equality. To begin with, the level of education, science, and talents is lowered. A high level of education and science is only possible for great intellects, and they are not wanted. The great intellects have always seized the power and been despots. Great intellects cannot help being despots and they've always done more harm than good. They will be banished or put to death. Cicero will have his tongue cut out, Copernicus will have his eyes put out, Shakespeare will be stoned—that's Shigalovism. Slaves are bound to be equal. There has never been either freedom or equality without despotism, but in the herd there is bound to be equality, and that's Shigalovism! Ha ha ha! Do you think it strange? I am for Shigalovism."

Stavrogin tried to quicken his pace, and to reach home as soon as possible. "If this fellow is drunk, where did he manage to get drunk?" crossed his mind. "Can it be the brandy?"

"Listen, Stavrogin. To level the mountains is a fine idea, not an absurd one. I am for Shigalov. Down with culture. We've had enough science! Without science we have material enough to go on for a thousand years, but one must have discipline. The one thing wanting in the world is discipline. The thirst for culture is an aristocratic thirst. The moment you have family ties or love you get the desire for property. We will destroy that desire; we'll make use of drunkenness, slander, spying; we'll make use of incredible corruption; we'll stifle every genius in its infancy. We'll reduce all to a common denominator! Complete equality! 'We've learned a trade, and we are honest men; we need nothing more,' that was an answer given by English working-men recently. Only the necessary is necessary, that's the motto of the whole world henceforward. But it needs a shock. That's for us, the directors, to look after. Slaves must have directors. Absolute submission, absolute loss of individuality, but once in thirty years Shigalov would let them have a shock and they would all suddenly begin eating one another up, to a certain point, simply as a precaution against boredom. Boredom is an aristocratic sensation. The Shigalovians will have no desires. Desire and suffering are our lot, but Shigalovism is for the slaves."

"You exclude yourself?" Stavrogin broke in again.

"You, too. Do you know, I have thought of giving up the world to the Pope. Let him come forth, on foot, and barefoot, and show himself to the rabble, saying, 'See what they have brought me to!' and they will all rush after him, even the troops. The Pope at the head, with us round him, and below us—Shigalovism. All that's needed is that the Internationale should come to an agreement with the Pope; so it will. And the old chap will agree at once. There's nothing else he can do. Remember my words! Ha ha! Is it stupid? Tell me, is it stupid or not?"

"That's enough!" Stavrogin muttered with vexation.

"Enough! Listen. I've given up the Pope! Damn Shigalovism! Damn the Pope! We must have something more everyday. Not Shigalovism, for Shigalovism is a rare specimen of the jeweller's art. It's an ideal; it's in the future. Shigalov is an artist and a fool like every philanthropist. We need coarse work, and Shigalov despises coarse work. Listen. The Pope shall be for the west, and you shall be for us, you shall be for us!"

"Let me alone, you drunken fellow!" muttered Stavrogin, and he quickened his pace.

"Stavrogin, you are beautiful," cried Pyotr Stepanovitch, almost ecstatically. "Do you know that you are beautiful! What's the most precious thing about you is that you sometimes don't know it. Oh, I've studied you! I often watch you on the sly! There's a lot of simpleheartedness and naïveté about you still. Do you know that? There still is, there is! You must be suffering and suffering genuinely from that simple-heartedness. I love beauty. I am a nihilist, but I love beauty. Are nihilists incapable of loving beauty? It's only idols they dislike, but I love an idol. You are my idol! You injure no one, and every one hates you. You treat every one as an equal, and yet every one is afraid of you—that's good. Nobody would slap you on the shoulder. You are an awful aristocrat. An aristocrat is irresistible when he goes in for democracy! To sacrifice life, your own or another's is nothing to you. You are just the man that's needed. It's just such a man as you that I need. I know no one but you. You are the leader, you are the sun and I am your worm."

He suddenly kissed his hand. A shiver ran down Stavrogin's spine, and he pulled away his hand in dismay. They stood still.

"Madman!" whispered Stavrogin.

"Perhaps I am raving; perhaps I am raving," Pyotr Stepanovitch assented, speaking rapidly. "But I've thought of the first step! Shigalov would never have thought of it. There are lots of Shigalovs, but only one man, one man in Russia has hit on the first step and knows how to take it. And I am that man! Why do you look at me? I need you, you; without you I am nothing. Without you I am a fly, a bottled idea; Columbus without America."

Stavrogin stood still and looked intently into his wild eyes.

"Listen. First of all we'll make an upheaval," Verhovensky went on in desperate haste, continually clutching at Stavrogin's left sleeve. "I've already told you. We shall penetrate to the peasantry. Do you know that we are tremendously powerful already? Our party does not consist only of those who commit murder and arson, fire off pistols in the traditional fashion, or bite colonels. They are only a hindrance. I don't accept anything without discipline. I am a scoundrel, of course, and not a socialist. Ha ha! Listen. I've reckoned them all up: a teacher who laughs with children at their God and at their cradle is on our side. The lawyer who defends an educated murderer because he is more cultured than his victims and could not help murdering them to get money is one of us. The schoolboys who murder a peasant for the sake of sensation are ours. The juries who acquit every criminal are ours. The prosecutor who trembles at a trial for fear he should not seem advanced enough is ours, ours. Among officials and literary men we have lots, lots, and they don't know it themselves. On the other hand, the docility of schoolboys and fools has reached an extreme pitch; the schoolmasters are bitter and bilious. On all sides we see vanity puffed up out of all proportion; brutal, monstrous appetites.... Do you know how many we shall catch by little, ready-made ideas? When I left Russia, Littre's dictum that crime is insanity was all the rage; I come back and I find that crime is no longer insanity, but simply common sense, almost a duty; anyway, a gallant protest. 'How can we expect a cultured man not to commit a murder, if he is in need of money.' But these are only the first fruits. The Russian God has already been vanquished by cheap vodka. The peasants are drunk, the mothers are drunk, the children are drunk, the churches are empty, and in the peasant courts one hears, 'Two hundred lashes or stand us a bucket of vodka.' Oh, this generation has only to grow up. It's only a pity we can't afford to wait, or we might have let them get a bit more tipsy! Ah, what a pity there's no proletariat! But there will be, there will be; we are going that way...."

"It's a pity, too, that we've grown greater fools," muttered Stavrogin, moving forward as before.

"Listen. I've seen a child of six years old leading home his drunken mother, whilst she swore at him with foul words. Do you suppose I am glad of that? When it's in our hands, maybe we'll mend things ... if need be, we'll drive them for forty years into the wilderness.... But one or two generations of vice are essential now; monstrous, abject vice by which a man is transformed into a loathsome, cruel, egoistic reptile. That's what we need! And what's more, a little 'fresh blood' that we may get accustomed to it. Why are you laughing? I am not contradicting myself. I am only contradicting the philanthropists and Shigalovism, not myself! I am a scoundrel, not a socialist. Ha ha ha! I'm only sorry there's no time. I promised Karmazinov to begin in May, and to make an end by October. Is that too soon? Ha ha! Do you know what, Stavrogin? Though the Russian people use foul language, there's nothing cynical about them so far. Do you know the serfs had more self-respect than Karmazinov? Though they were beaten they always preserved their gods, which is more than Karmazinov's done."

"Well, Verhovensky, this is the first time I've heard you talk, and I listen with amazement," observed Stavrogin. "So you are really not a socialist, then, but some sort of ... ambitious politician?"

"A scoundrel, a scoundrel! You are wondering what I am. I'll tell you what I am directly, that's what I am leading up to. It was not for nothing that I kissed your hand. But the people must believe that we know what we are after, while the other side do nothing but 'brandish their cudgels and beat their own followers.' Ah, if we only had more time! That's the only trouble, we have no time. We will proclaim destruction.... Why is it, why is it that idea has such a fascination. But we must have a little exercise; we must. We'll set fires going.... We'll set legends going. Every scurvy 'group' will be of use. Out of those very groups I'll pick you out fellows so keen they'll not shrink from shooting, and be grateful for the honour of a job, too. Well, and there will be an upheaval! There's going to be such an upset as the world has never seen before.... Russia will be overwhelmed with darkness, the earth will weep for its old gods.... Well, then we shall bring forward ... whom?"

"Whom?"

"Ivan the Tsarevitch."

"Who-m?"

"Ivan the Tsarevitch. You! You!"

Stavrogin thought a minute.

"A pretender?" he asked suddenly, looking with intense surprise at his frantic companion. "Ah! so that's your plan at last!"

"We shall say that he is 'in hiding,'" Verhovensky said softly, in a sort of tender whisper, as though he really were drunk indeed. "Do you know the magic of that phrase, 'he is in hiding'? But he will appear, he will appear. We'll set a legend going better than the Skoptsis'. He exists, but no one has seen him. Oh, what a legend one can set going! And the great thing is it will be a new force at work! And we need that; that's what they are crying for. What can Socialism do: it's destroyed the old forces but hasn't brought in any new. But in this we have a force, and what a force! Incredible. We only need one lever to lift up the earth. Everything will rise up!"

"Then have you been seriously reckoning on me?" Stavrogin said with a malicious smile.

"Why do you laugh, and so spitefully? Don't frighten me. I am like a little child now. I can be frightened to death by one smile like that. Listen. I'll let no one see you, no one. So it must be. He exists, but no one has seen him; he is in hiding. And do you know, one might show you, to one out of a hundred-thousand, for instance. And the rumour will spread over all the land, 'We've seen him, we've seen him.'

"Ivan Filipovitch the God of Sabaoth,* has been seen, too, when he ascended into heaven in his chariot in the sight of men. They saw him with their own eyes. And you are not an Ivan Filipovitch. You are beautiful and proud as a God; you are seeking nothing for yourself, with the halo of a victim round you, 'in hiding.' The great thing is the legend. You'll conquer them, you'll have only to look, and you will conquer them. He is 'in hiding,' and will come forth bringing a new truth. And, meanwhile, we'll pass two or three judgments as wise as Solomon's. The groups, you know, the quintets—we've no need of newspapers. If out of ten thousand petitions only one is granted, all would come with petitions. In every parish, every peasant will know that there is somewhere a hollow tree where petitions are to be put. And the whole land will resound with the cry, 'A new just law is to come,' and the sea will be troubled and the whole gimcrack show will fall to the ground, and then we shall consider how to build up an edifice of stone. For the first time! We are going to build it, we, and only we!"

** The reference is to the legend current in the sect of*

Flagellants.—Translator's note.

"Madness," said Stavrogin.

"Why, why don't you want it? Are you afraid? That's why I caught at you, because you are afraid of nothing. Is it unreasonable? But you see, so far I am Columbus without America. Would Columbus without America seem reasonable?"

Stavrogin did not speak. Meanwhile they had reached the house and stopped at the entrance.

"Listen," Verhovensky bent down to his ear. "I'll do it for you without the money. I'll settle Marya Timofyevna to-morrow!... Without the money, and to-morrow I'll bring you Liza. Will you have Liza to-morrow?"

"Is he really mad?" Stavrogin wondered smiling. The front door was opened.

"Stavrogin—is America ours?" said Verhovensky, seizing his hand for the last time.

"What for?" said Nikolay Vsyevolodovitch, gravely and sternly.

"You don't care, I knew that!" cried Verhovensky in an access of furious anger. "You are lying, you miserable, profligate, perverted, little aristocrat! I don't believe you, you've the appetite of a wolf!... Understand that you've cost me such a price, I can't give you up now! There's no one on earth but you! I invented you abroad; I invented it all, looking at you. If I hadn't watched you from my corner, nothing of all this would have entered my head!"

Stavrogin went up the steps without answering.

"Stavrogin!" Verhovensky called after him, "I give you a day ... two, then ... three, then; more than three I can't—and then you're to answer!"

CHAPTER IX. A RAID AT STEPAN TROFIMOVITCH'S

Meanwhile an incident had occurred which astounded me and shattered Stepan Trofimovitch. At eight o'clock in the morning, Nastasya ran round to me from him with the news that her master was "raided." At first I could not make out what she meant; I could only gather that the "raid" was carried out by officials, that they had come and taken his papers, and that a soldier had tied them up in a bundle and "wheeled them away in a barrow." It was a fantastic story. I hurried at once to Stepan Trofimovitch.

I found him in a surprising condition: upset and in great agitation, but at the same time unmistakably triumphant. On the table in the middle of the room the samovar was boiling, and there was a glass of tea poured out but untouched and forgotten. Stepan Trofimovitch was wandering round the table and peeping into every corner of the room, unconscious of what he was doing. He was wearing his usual red knitted jacket, but seeing me, he hurriedly put on his coat and waistcoat—a thing he had never done before when any of his intimate friends found him in his jacket. He took me warmly by the hand at once.

"Enfin un ami!" (He heaved a deep sigh.) "Cher, I've sent to you only, and no one knows anything. We must give Nastasya orders to lock the doors and not admit anyone, except, of course them.... Vous comprenez?"

He looked at me uneasily, as though expecting a reply. I made haste, of course, to question him, and from his disconnected and broken sentences, full of unnecessary parentheses, I succeeded in learning that at seven o'clock that morning an official of the province had 'all of a sudden' called on him.

"Pardon, j'ai oublié son nom. Il n'est pas du pays, but I think he came to the town with Lembke, quelque chose de bête et d'Allemand dans la physionomie. Il s'appelle Rosenthal."

"Wasn't it Blum?"

"Yes, that was his name. Vous le connaissez? Quelque chose d'hébété et de très content dans la figure, pourtant très sevère, roide et sérieux. A type of the police, of the submissive subordinates, je m'y connais. I was still asleep, and, would you believe it, he asked to have a look at my books and manuscripts! Oui, je m'en souviens, il a employé ce mot. He did not arrest me, but only the books. Il se tenait à distance, and when he began to explain his visit he looked as though I ... enfin il avait l'air de croire que je tomberai sur lui immédiatement et que je commencerai a le battre comme plâtre. Tous ces gens du bas étage sont comme ça when they have to do with a gentleman. I need hardly say I understood it all at once. Voilà vingt ans que je m'y prépare. I opened all the drawers and handed him all the keys; I gave them myself, I gave him all. J'étais digne et calme. From the books he took the foreign edition of Herzen, the bound volume of The Bell, four copies of my poem, et enfin tout ça. Then he took my letters and my papers et quelques-unes de mes ébauches historiques, critiques et politiques. All that they carried off. Nastasya says that a soldier wheeled them away in a barrow and covered them with an apron; oui, c'est cela, with an apron." It sounded like delirium. Who could make head or tail of it? I pelted him with questions again. Had Blum come alone, or with others? On whose authority? By what right? How had he dared? How did he explain it?

"Il etait seul, bien seul, but there was someone else dans l'antichambre, oui, je m'en souviens, et puis ... Though I believe there was someone else besides, and there was a guard standing in the entry. You must ask Nastasya; she knows all about it better than I do. J'étais surexcité, voyez-vous. Il parlait, il parlait ... un tas de chases; he said very little though, it was I said all that.... I told him the story of my life, simply from that point of view, of course. J'étais surexcité, mais digne, je vous assure.... I am afraid, though, I may have shed tears. They got the barrow from the shop next door."

"Oh, heavens! how could all this have happened? But for mercy's sake, speak more exactly, Stepan Trofimovitch. What you tell me sounds like a dream."

"Cher, I feel as though I were in a dream myself.... Savez-vous! Il a prononcé le nom de Telyatnikof, and I believe that that man was concealed in the entry. Yes, I remember, he suggested calling the prosecutor and Dmitri Dmitritch, I believe ... qui me doit encore quinze roubles I won at cards, soit dit en passant. Enfin, je n'ai pas trop compris. But I got the better of them, and what do I care for Dmitri Dmitritch? I believe I begged him very earnestly to keep it quiet; I begged him particularly, most particularly. I am afraid I demeaned myself, in fact, comment croyez-vous? Enfin il a consenti. Yes, I remember, he suggested that himself—that it would be better to keep it quiet, for he had only come 'to have a look round' et rien de plus, and nothing more, nothing more ... and that if they find nothing, nothing will happen. So that we ended it all en amis, je suis tout à fait content."

"Why, then he suggested the usual course of proceedings in such cases and regular guarantees, and you rejected them yourself," I cried with friendly indignation.

"Yes, it's better without the guarantees. And why make a scandal? Let's keep it en amis so long as we can. You know, in our town, if they get to know it ... mes ennemis, et puis, à quoi bon, le procureur, ce cochon de notre procureur, qui deux fois m'a manqué de politesse et qu'on a rossé à plaisir l'autre année chez cette charmante et belle Natalya Pavlovna quand il se cacha dans son boudoir. Et puis, mon ami, don't make objections and don't depress me, I beg you, for nothing is more unbearable when a man is in trouble than for a hundred friends to point out to him what a fool he has made of himself. Sit down though and have some tea. I must admit I am awfully tired.... Hadn't I better lie down and put vinegar on my head? What do you think?"

"Certainly," I cried, "ice even. You are very much upset. You are pale and your hands are trembling. Lie down, rest, and put off telling me. I'll sit by you and wait."

He hesitated, but I insisted on his lying down. Nastasya brought a cup of vinegar. I wetted a towel and laid it on his head. Then Nastasya stood on a chair and began lighting a lamp before the ikon in the corner. I noticed this with surprise; there had never been a lamp there before and now suddenly it had made its appearance.

"I arranged for that as soon as they had gone away," muttered Stepan Trofimovitch, looking at me slyly. "Quand on a de ces choses-là dans sa chambre et qu'on vient vous arrêter it makes an impression and they are sure to report that they have seen it...."

When she had done the lamp, Nastasya stood in the doorway, leaned her cheek in her right hand, and began gazing at him with a lachrymose air.

"Eloignez-la on some excuse," he nodded to me from the sofa. "I can't endure this Russian sympathy, et puis ça m'embête."

But she went away of herself. I noticed that he kept looking towards the door and listening for sounds in the passage.

"Il faut être prêt, voyez-vous," he said, looking at me significantly, "chaque moment … they may come and take one and, phew!—a man disappears."

"Heavens! who'll come? Who will take you?"

"Voyez-vous, mon cher, I asked straight out when he was going away, what would they do to me now."

"You'd better have asked them where you'd be exiled!" I cried out in the same indignation.

"That's just what I meant when I asked, but he went away without answering. Voyez-vous: as for linen, clothes, warm things especially, that must be as they decide; if they tell me to take them—all right, or they might send me in a soldier's overcoat. But I thrust thirty-five roubles" (he suddenly dropped his voice, looking towards the door by which Nastasya had gone out) "in a slit in my waistcoat pocket, here, feel…. I believe they won't take the waistcoat off, and left seven roubles in my purse to keep up appearances, as though that were all I have. You see, it's in small change and the coppers are on the table, so they won't guess that I've hidden the money, but will suppose that that's all. For God knows where I may have to sleep to-night!"

I bowed my head before such madness. It was obvious that a man could not be arrested and searched in the way he was describing, and he must have mixed things up. It's true it all happened in the days before our present, more recent regulations. It is true, too, that according to his own account they had offered to follow the more regular procedure, but he "got the better of them" and refused…. Of course not long ago a governor might, in extreme cases…. But how could this be an extreme case? That's what baffled me.

"No doubt they had a telegram from Petersburg," Stepan Trofimovitch said suddenly.

"A telegram? About you? Because of the works of Herzen and your poem? Have you taken leave of your senses? What is there in that to arrest you for?"

I was positively angry. He made a grimace and was evidently mortified—not at my exclamation, but at the idea that there was no ground for arrest.

"Who can tell in our day what he may not be arrested for?" he muttered enigmatically.

A wild and nonsensical idea crossed my mind.

"Stepan Trofimovitch, tell me as a friend," I cried, "as a real friend, I will not betray you: do you belong to some secret society or not?"

And on this, to my amazement, he was not quite certain whether he was or was not a member of some secret society.

"That depends, voyez-vous."

"How do you mean 'it depends'?"

"When with one's whole heart one is an adherent of progress and … who can answer it? You may suppose you don't belong, and suddenly it turns out that you do belong to something."

"Now is that possible? It's a case of yes or no."

"Cela date de Pétersburg when she and I were meaning to found a magazine there. That's what's at the root of it. She gave them the slip then, and they forgot us, but now they've remembered. Cher, cher, don't you know me?" he cried hysterically. "And they'll take us, put us in a cart, and march us off to Siberia forever, or forget us in prison."

And he suddenly broke into bitter weeping. His tears positively streamed. He covered his face with his red silk handkerchief and sobbed, sobbed convulsively for five minutes. It wrung my heart. This was the man who had been a prophet among us for twenty years, a leader, a patriarch, the Kukolnik who had borne himself so loftily and majestically before all of us, before whom we bowed down with genuine reverence, feeling proud of doing so—and all of a sudden here he was sobbing, sobbing like a naughty child waiting for the rod which the teacher is fetching for him. I felt fearfully sorry for him. He believed in the reality of that "cart" as he believed that I was sitting by his side, and he expected it that morning, at once, that very minute, and all this on account of his Herzen and some poem! Such complete, absolute ignorance of everyday reality was touching and somehow repulsive.

At last he left off crying, got up from the sofa and began walking about the room again, continuing to talk to me, though he looked out of the window every minute and listened to every sound in the passage. Our conversation was still disconnected. All my assurances and attempts to console him rebounded from him like peas from a wall. He scarcely listened, but yet what he needed was that I should console him and keep on talking with that object. I saw that he could not do without me now, and would not let me go for anything. I remained, and we spent more than two hours together. In conversation, he recalled that Blum had taken with him two manifestoes he had found.

"Manifestoes!" I said, foolishly frightened. "Do you mean to say you …"

"Oh, ten were left here," he answered with vexation (he talked to me at one moment in a vexed and haughty tone and at the next with dreadful plaintiveness and humiliation), "but I had disposed of eight already, and Blum only found two." And he suddenly flushed with indignation. "Vous me mettez avec ces gens-là! Do you suppose I could be working with those scoundrels, those anonymous libellers, with my son Pyotr Stepanovitch, avec ces esprits forts de lâcheté? Oh, heavens!"

"Bah! haven't they mixed you up perhaps?… But it's nonsense, it can't be so," I observed.

"Savez-vous," broke from him suddenly, "I feel at moments que je ferai là-bas quelque esclandre. Oh, don't go away, don't leave me alone! Ma carrière est finie aujourd'hui, je le sens.

Do you know, I might fall on somebody there and bite him, like that lieutenant."

He looked at me with a strange expression—alarmed, and at the same time anxious to alarm me. He certainly was getting more and more exasperated with somebody and about something as time went on and the police-cart did not appear; he was positively wrathful. Suddenly Nastasya, who had come from the kitchen into the passage for some reason, upset a clothes-horse there. Stepan Trofimovitch trembled and turned numb with terror as he sat; but when the noise was explained, he almost shrieked at Nastasya and, stamping, drove her back to the kitchen. A minute later he said, looking at me in despair: "I am ruined! Cher"—he sat down suddenly beside me and looked piteously into my face—"cher, it's not Siberia I am afraid of, I swear. Oh, je vous jure!" (Tears positively stood in his eyes.) "It's something else I fear."

I saw from his expression that he wanted at last to tell me something of great importance which he had till now refrained from telling.

"I am afraid of disgrace," he whispered mysteriously.

"What disgrace? On the contrary! Believe me, Stepan Trofimovitch, that all this will be explained to-day and will end to your advantage...."

"Are you so sure that they will pardon me?"

"Pardon you? What! What a word! What have you done? I assure you you've done nothing."

"Qu'en savez-vous; all my life has been ... cher ... They'll remember everything ... and if they find nothing, it will be worse still," he added all of a sudden, unexpectedly.

"How do you mean it will be worse?"

"It will be worse."

"I don't understand."

"My friend, let it be Siberia, Archangel, loss of rights—if I must perish, let me perish! But ... I am afraid of something else." (Again whispering, a scared face, mystery.)

"But of what? Of what?"

"They'll flog me," he pronounced, looking at me with a face of despair.

"Who'll flog you? What for? Where?" I cried, feeling alarmed that he was going out of his mind.

"Where? Why there ... where 'that's' done."

"But where is it done?"

"Eh, cher," he whispered almost in my ear. "The floor suddenly gives way under you, you drop half through.... Every one knows that."

"Legends!" I cried, guessing what he meant. "Old tales. Can you have believed them till now?" I laughed.

"Tales! But there must be foundation for them; flogged men tell no tales. I've imagined it ten thousand times."

"But you, why you? You've done nothing, you know."

"That makes it worse. They'll find out I've done nothing and flog me for it."

"And you are sure that you'll be taken to Petersburg for that."

"My friend, I've told you already that I regret nothing, ma carrière est finie. From that hour when she said good-bye to me at Skvoreshniki my life has had no value for me ... but disgrace, disgrace, que dira-t-elle if she finds out?"

He looked at me in despair. And the poor fellow flushed all over. I dropped my eyes too.

"She'll find out nothing, for nothing will happen to you. I feel as if I were speaking to you for the first time in my life, Stepan Trofimovitch, you've astonished me so this morning."

"But, my friend, this isn't fear. For even if I am pardoned, even if I am brought here and nothing is done to me—then I am undone. Elle me soupçonnera toute sa vie—me, me, the poet, the thinker, the man whom she has worshipped for twenty-two years!"

"It will never enter her head."

"It will," he whispered with profound conviction. "We've talked of it several times in Petersburg, in Lent, before we came away, when we were both afraid.... Elle me soupçonnera toute sa vie ... and how can I disabuse her? It won't sound likely. And in this wretched town who'd believe it, c'est invraisemblable.... Et puis les femmes, she will be pleased. She will be genuinely grieved like a true friend, but secretly she will be pleased.... I shall give her a weapon against me for the rest of my life. Oh, it's all over with me! Twenty years of such perfect happiness with her ... and now!" He hid his face in his hands.

"Stepan Trofimovitch, oughtn't you to let Varvara Petrovna know at once of what has happened?" I suggested.

"God preserve me!" he cried, shuddering and leaping up from his place. "On no account, never, after what was said at parting at Skvoreshniki—never!"

His eyes flashed.

We went on sitting together another hour or more, I believe, expecting something all the time—the idea had taken such hold of us. He lay down again, even closed his eyes, and lay for twenty minutes without uttering a word, so that I thought he was asleep or unconscious. Suddenly he got up impulsively, pulled the towel off his head, jumped up from the sofa, rushed to the looking-glass, with trembling hands tied his cravat, and in a voice of thunder called to Nastasya, telling her to give him his overcoat, his new hat and his stick.

"I can bear no more," he said in a breaking voice. "I can't, I can't! I am going myself."

"Where?" I cried, jumping up too.

"To Lembke. Cher, I ought, I am obliged. It's my duty. I am a citizen and a man, not a worthless chip. I have rights; I want my rights.... For twenty years I've not insisted on my rights. All my life I've neglected them criminally ... but now I'll demand them. He must tell me everything—everything. He received a telegram. He dare not torture me; if so, let him arrest me, let him arrest me!"

He stamped and vociferated almost with shrieks. "I approve of what you say," I said, speaking as calmly as possible, on purpose, though I was very much afraid for him.

"Certainly it is better than sitting here in such misery, but I can't approve of your state of mind. Just see what you look like and in what a state you are going there! Il faut être digne et calme avec Lembke. You really might rush at someone there and bite him."

"I am giving myself up. I am walking straight into the jaws of the lion...."

"I'll go with you."

"I expected no less of you, I accept your sacrifice, the sacrifice of a true friend; but only as far as the house, only as far as the house. You ought not, you have no right to compromise yourself further by being my confederate. Oh, croyez-moi, je serai calme. I feel that I am at this moment à la hauteur de tout ce que il y a de plus sacré...."

"I may perhaps go into the house with you," I interrupted him. "I had a message from their stupid committee yesterday through Vysotsky that they reckon on me and invite me to the fête to-morrow as one of the stewards or whatever it is ... one of the six young men whose duty it is to look after the trays, wait on the ladies, take the guests to their places, and wear a rosette of crimson and white ribbon on the left shoulder. I meant to refuse, but now why shouldn't I go into the house on the excuse of seeing Yulia Mihailovna herself about it?... So we will go in together."

He listened, nodding, but I think he understood nothing. We stood on the threshold.

"Cher"—he stretched out his arm to the lamp before the ikon—"cher, I have never believed in this, but ... so be it, so be it!" He crossed himself. "Allons!"

"Well, that's better so," I thought as I went out on to the steps with him. "The fresh air will do him good on the way, and we shall calm down, turn back, and go home to bed...."

But I reckoned without my host. On the way an adventure occurred which agitated Stepan Trofimovitch even more, and finally determined him to go on ... so that I should never have expected of our friend so much spirit as he suddenly displayed that morning. Poor friend, kind-hearted friend!

CHAPTER X. FILIBUSTERS. A FATAL MORNING

I

The adventure that befell us on the way was also a surprising one. But I must tell the story in due order. An hour before Stepan Trofimovitch and I came out into the street, a crowd of people, the hands from Shpigulins' factory, seventy or more in number, had been marching through the town, and had been an object of curiosity to many spectators. They walked intentionally in good order and almost in silence. Afterwards it was asserted that these seventy had been elected out of the whole number of factory hands, amounting to about nine hundred, to go to the governor and to try and get from him, in the absence of their employer, a just settlement of their grievances against the manager, who, in closing the factory and dismissing the workmen, had cheated them all in an impudent way—a fact which has since been proved conclusively. Some people still deny that there was any election of delegates, maintaining that seventy was too large a number to elect, and that the crowd simply consisted of those who had been most unfairly treated, and that they only came to ask for help in their own case, so that the general "mutiny" of the factory workers, about which there was such an uproar later on, had never existed at all. Others fiercely maintained that these seventy men were not simple strikers but revolutionists, that is, not merely that they were the most turbulent, but that they must have been worked upon by seditious manifestoes. The fact is, it is still uncertain whether there had been any outside influence or incitement at work or not. My private opinion is that the workmen had not read the seditious manifestoes at all, and if they had read them, would not have understood one word, for one reason because the authors of such literature write very obscurely in spite of the boldness of their style. But as the workmen really were in a difficult plight and the police to whom they appealed would not enter into their grievances, what could be more natural than their idea of going in a body to "the general himself" if possible, with the petition at their head, forming up in an orderly way before his door, and as soon as he showed himself, all falling on their knees and crying out to him as to providence itself? To my mind there is no need to see in this a mutiny or even a deputation, for it's a traditional, historical mode of action; the Russian people have always loved to parley with "the general himself" for the mere satisfaction of doing so, regardless of how the conversation may end.

And so I am quite convinced that, even though Pyotr Stepanovitch, Liputin, and perhaps some others—perhaps even Fedka too—had been flitting about among the workpeople talking to them (and there is fairly good evidence of this), they had only approached two, three, five at the most, trying to sound them, and nothing had come of their conversation. As for the mutiny they advocated, if the factory-workers did understand anything of their propaganda, they would have left off listening to it at once as to something stupid that had nothing to do with them. Fedka was a different matter: he had more success, I believe, than Pyotr Stepanovitch. Two workmen are now known for a fact to have assisted Fedka in causing the fire in the town which occurred three days afterwards, and a month later three men who had worked in the factory were arrested for robbery and arson in the province. But if in these cases Fedka did lure them to direct and immediate action, he could only have succeeded with these five, for we heard of nothing of the sort being done by others.

Be that as it may, the whole crowd of workpeople had at last reached the open space in front of the governor's house and were drawn up there in silence and good order. Then, gaping open-mouthed at the front door, they waited. I am told that as soon as they halted they took off their caps, that is, a good half-hour before the appearance of the governor, who, as ill-luck would have it, was not at home at the moment. The police made their appearance at once, at first individual policemen and then as large a contingent of them as could be gathered together; they began, of course, by being menacing, ordering them to break up. But the workmen remained obstinately, like a flock of sheep at a fence, and replied laconically that they had come to see "the general himself"; it was evident that they were firmly determined. The unnatural shouting of the police ceased, and was quickly succeeded by deliberations, mysterious whispered instructions, and stern, fussy perplexity, which wrinkled the brows of the police officers. The head of the police preferred to await the arrival of the "governor himself." It was not true that he galloped to the spot with three horses at full speed, and began hitting out right and left before he alighted from his carriage. It's true that he used to dash about and was fond of dashing about at full speed in a carriage with a yellow back, and while his trace-horses, who were so trained to carry their heads that they looked "positively perverted," galloped more and more frantically, rousing the enthusiasm of all the shopkeepers in the bazaar, he would rise up in the carriage, stand erect, holding on by a strap which had been fixed on purpose at the side, and with his right arm extended into space like a figure on a monument, survey the town majestically. But in the present case he did not use his fists, and though as he got out of the carriage he could not refrain from a forcible expression, this was simply done to keep up his popularity. There is a still more absurd story that soldiers were brought up with bayonets, and that a telegram was sent for artillery and Cossacks; those are legends which are not believed now even by those who invented them. It's an absurd story, too, that barrels of water were brought from the fire brigade, and that people were drenched with water from them. The simple fact is that Ilya Ilyitch shouted in his heat that he wouldn't let one of them come dry out of the water; probably this was the foundation of the barrel legend which got into the columns of the Petersburg and Moscow newspapers. Probably the most accurate version was that at first all the available police formed a cordon round the crowd, and a messenger was sent for Lembke, a police superintendent, who dashed off in the carriage belonging to the head of the police on the way to Skvoreshniki, knowing that Lembke had gone there in his carriage half an hour before.

But I must confess that I am still unable to answer the question how they could at first sight, from the first moment, have transformed an insignificant, that is to say an ordinary, crowd of petitioners, even though there were several of them, into a rebellion which threatened to shake the foundations of the state. Why did Lembke himself rush at that idea when he arrived twenty minutes after the messenger? I imagine (but again it's only my private opinion) that it was to the interest of Ilya Ilyitch, who was a crony of the factory manager's, to represent the crowd in this light to Lembke, in order to prevent him from going into the case; and Lembke himself had put the idea into his head. In the course of the last two days, he had had two unusual and mysterious conversations with him. It is true they were exceedingly obscure, but Ilya Ilyitch was able to gather from them that the governor had thoroughly made up his mind that there were political manifestoes, and that Shpigulins' factory hands were being incited to a Socialist rising, and that he was so persuaded of it that he would perhaps have regretted it if the story had turned out to be nonsense. "He wants to get distinction in Petersburg," our wily Ilya Ilyitch thought to himself as he left Von Lembke; "well, that just suits me."

But I am convinced that poor Andrey Antonovitch would not have desired a rebellion even for the sake of distinguishing himself. He was a most conscientious official, who had lived in a state of innocence up to the time of his marriage. And was it his fault that, instead of an innocent allowance of wood from the government and an equally innocent Minnchen, a princess of forty summers had raised him to her level? I know almost for certain that the unmistakable symptoms of the mental condition which brought poor Andrey Antonovitch to a well-known establishment in Switzerland, where, I am told, he is now regaining his energies, were first apparent on that fatal morning. But once we admit that unmistakable signs of something were visible that morning, it may well be allowed that similar symptoms may have been evident the day before, though not so clearly. I happen to know from the most private sources (well, you may assume that Yulia Mihailovna later on, not in triumph but almost in remorse—for a woman is incapable of complete remorse—revealed part of it to me herself) that Andrey Antonovitch had gone into his wife's room in the middle of the previous night, past two o'clock in the morning, had waked her up, and had insisted on her listening to his "ultimatum." He demanded it so insistently that she was obliged to get up from her bed in indignation and curl-papers, and, sitting down on a couch, she had to listen, though with sarcastic disdain. Only then she grasped for the first time how far gone her Andrey Antonovitch was, and was secretly horrified. She ought to have thought what she was about and have been softened, but she concealed her horror and was more obstinate than ever. Like every wife she had her own method of treating Andrey Antonovitch, which she had tried more than once already and with it driven him to frenzy. Yulia Mihailovna's method was that of contemptuous silence, for one hour, two, a whole day and almost for three days and nights—silence whatever happened, whatever he said, whatever he did, even if he had clambered up to throw himself out of a three-story window—a method unendurable for a sensitive man! Whether Yulia Mihailovna meant to punish her husband for his blunders of the last few days and the jealous envy he, as the chief authority in the town, felt for her administrative abilities; whether she was indignant at his criticism of her behaviour with the young people and local society generally, and lack of comprehension of her subtle and far-sighted political aims; or was angry with his stupid and senseless jealousy of Pyotr Stepanovitch—however that may have been, she made up her mind not to be softened even now, in spite of its being three o'clock at night, and though Andrey Antonovitch was in a state of emotion such as she had never seen him in before.

Pacing up and down in all directions over the rugs of her boudoir, beside himself, he poured out everything, everything, quite disconnectedly, it's true, but everything that had been rankling in his heart, for—"it was outrageous." He began by saying that he was a laughing-stock to every one and "was being led by the nose."

"Curse the expression," he squealed, at once catching her smile, "let it stand, it's true.... No, madam, the time has come; let me tell you it's not a time for laughter and feminine arts now. We are not in the boudoir of a mincing lady, but like two abstract creatures in a balloon who have met to speak the truth." (He was no doubt confused and could not find the right words for his ideas, however just they were.) "It is you, madam, you who have destroyed my happy past. I took up this post simply for your sake, for the sake of your ambition.... You smile sarcastically? Don't triumph, don't be in a hurry. Let me tell you, madam, let me tell you that I should have been equal to this position, and not only this position but a dozen positions like it, for I have abilities; but with you, madam, with you—it's impossible, for with you here I have no abilities. There cannot be two centres, and you have created two—one of mine and one in your boudoir—two centres of power, madam, but I won't allow it, I won't allow it! In the service, as in marriage, there must be one centre, two are impossible.... How have you repaid me?" he went on. "Our marriage has been nothing but your proving to me all the time, every hour, that I am a nonentity, a fool, and even a rascal, and I have been all the time, every hour, forced in a degrading way to prove to you that I am not a nonentity, not a fool at all, and that I impress every one with my honourable character. Isn't that degrading for both sides?"

At this point he began rapidly stamping with both feet on the carpet, so that Yulia Mihailovna was obliged to get up with stern dignity. He subsided quickly, but passed to being pathetic and began sobbing (yes, sobbing!), beating himself on the breast almost for five minutes, getting more and more frantic at Yulia Mihailovna's profound silence. At last he made a fatal blunder, and let slip that he was jealous of Pyotr Stepanovitch. Realising that he had made an utter fool of himself, he became savagely furious, and shouted that he "would not allow them to deny God" and that he would "send her salon of irresponsible infidels packing," that the governor of a province was bound to believe in God "and so his wife was too," that he wouldn't put up with these young men; that "you, madam, for the sake of your own dignity, ought to have thought of your husband and to have stood up for his intelligence even if he were a man of poor abilities (and I'm by no means a man of poor abilities!), and yet it's your doing that every one here despises me, it was you put them all up to it!" He shouted that he would annihilate the woman question, that he would eradicate every trace of it, that to-morrow he would forbid and break up their silly fête for the benefit of the governesses (damn them!), that the first governess he came across to-morrow morning he would drive out of the province "with a Cossack! I'll make a point of it!" he shrieked. "Do you know," he screamed, "do you know that your rascals are inciting men at the factory, and that I know it? Let me tell you, I know the names of four of these rascals and that I am going out of my mind, hopelessly, hopelessly!..."

But at this point Yulia Mihailovna suddenly broke her silence and sternly announced that she had long been aware of these criminal designs, and that it was all foolishness, and that he had taken it too seriously, and that as for these mischievous fellows, she knew not only those four but all of them (it was a lie); but that she had not the faintest intention of going out of her mind on account of it, but, on the contrary, had all the more confidence in her intelligence and hoped to bring it all to a harmonious conclusion: to encourage the young people, to bring them to reason, to show them suddenly and unexpectedly that their designs were known, and then to point out to them new aims for rational and more noble activity.

Oh, how can I describe the effect of this on Andrey Antonovitch! Hearing that Pyotr Stepanovitch had duped him again and had made a fool of him so coarsely, that he had told her much more than he had told him, and sooner than him, and that perhaps Pyotr Stepanovitch was the chief instigator of all these criminal designs—he flew into a frenzy. "Senseless but malignant woman," he cried, snapping his bonds at one blow, "let me tell you, I shall arrest your worthless lover at once, I shall put him in fetters and send him to the fortress, or—I shall jump out of a window before your eyes this minute!"

Yulia Mihailovna, turning green with anger, greeted this tirade at once with a burst of prolonged, ringing laughter, going off into peals such as one hears at the French theatre when a Parisian actress, imported for a fee of a hundred thousand to play a coquette, laughs in her husband's face for daring to be jealous of her.

Von Lembke rushed to the window, but suddenly stopped as though rooted to the spot, folded his arms across his chest, and, white as a corpse, looked with a sinister gaze at the laughing lady. "Do you know, Yulia, do you know," he said in a gasping and suppliant voice, "do you know that even I can do something?" But at the renewed and even louder laughter that followed his last words he clenched his teeth, groaned, and suddenly rushed, not towards the window, but at his spouse, with his fist raised! He did not bring it down—no, I repeat again and again, no; but it was the last straw. He ran to his own room, not knowing what he was doing, flung himself, dressed as he was, face downwards on his bed, wrapped himself convulsively, head and all, in the sheet, and lay so for two hours—incapable of sleep, incapable of thought, with a load on his heart and blank, immovable despair in his soul. Now and then he shivered all over with an agonising, feverish tremor. Disconnected and irrelevant things kept coming into his mind: at one minute he thought of the old clock which used to hang on his wall fifteen years ago in Petersburg and had lost the minute-hand; at another of the cheerful clerk, Millebois, and how they had once caught a sparrow together in Alexandrovsky Park and had laughed so that they could be heard all over the park, remembering that one of them was already a college assessor. I imagine that about seven in the morning he must have fallen asleep without being aware of it himself, and must have slept with enjoyment, with agreeable dreams.

Waking about ten o'clock, he jumped wildly out of bed remembered everything at once, and slapped himself on the head; he refused his breakfast, and would see neither Blum nor the chief of the police nor the clerk who came to remind him that he was expected to preside over a meeting that morning; he would listen to nothing, and did not want to understand. He ran like one possessed to Yulia Mihailovna's part of the house. There Sofya Antropovna, an old lady of good family who had lived for years with Yulia Mihailovna, explained to him that his wife had set off at ten o'clock that morning with a large company in three carriages to Varvara Petrovna Stavrogin's, to Skvoreshniki, to look over the place with a view to the second fête which was planned for a fortnight later, and that the visit to-day had been arranged with Varvara Petrovna three days before. Overwhelmed with this news, Andrey Antonovitch returned to his study and impulsively ordered the horses. He could hardly wait for them to be got ready. His soul was hungering for Yulia Mihailovna—to look at her, to be near her for five minutes; perhaps she would glance at him, notice him, would smile as before, forgive him ... "O-oh! Aren't the horses ready?" Mechanically he opened a thick book lying on the table. (He sometimes used to try his fortune in this way with a book, opening it at random and reading the three lines at the top of the right-hand page.) What turned up was: "Tout est pour le mieux dans le meilleur des mondes possibles."—Voltaire, Candide. He uttered an ejaculation of contempt and ran to get into the carriage. "Skvoreshniki!"

The coachman said afterwards that his master urged him on all the way, but as soon as they were getting near the mansion he suddenly told him to turn and drive back to the town, bidding him "Drive fast; please drive fast!" Before they reached the town wall "master told me to stop again, got out of the carriage, and went across the road into the field; I thought he felt ill but he stopped and began looking at the flowers, and so he stood for a time. It was strange, really; I began to feel quite uneasy." This was the coachman's testimony. I remember the weather that morning: it was a cold, clear, but windy September day; before Andrey Antonovitch stretched a forbidding landscape of bare fields from which the crop had long been harvested; there were a few dying yellow flowers, pitiful relics blown about by the howling wind. Did he want to compare himself and his fate with those wretched flowers battered by the autumn and the frost? I don't think so; in fact I feel sure it was not so, and that he realised nothing about the flowers in spite of the evidence of the coachman and of the police superintendent, who drove up at that moment and asserted afterwards that he found the governor with a bunch of yellow flowers in his hand. This police superintendent, Flibusterov by name, was an ardent champion of authority who had only recently come to our town but had already distinguished himself and become famous by his inordinate zeal, by a certain vehemence in the execution of his duties, and his inveterate inebriety. Jumping out of the carriage, and not the least disconcerted at the sight of what the governor was doing, he blurted out all in one breath, with a frantic expression, yet with an air of conviction, that "There's an upset in the town."

"Eh? What?" said Andrey Antonovitch, turning to him with a stern face, but without a trace of surprise or any recollection of his carriage and his coachman, as though he had been in his own study.

"Police-superintendent Flibusterov, your Excellency. There's a riot in the town."

"Filibusters?" Andrey Antonovitch said thoughtfully.

"Just so, your Excellency. The Shpigulin men are making a riot."

"The Shpigulin men!..."

The name "Shpigulin" seemed to remind him of something. He started and put his finger to his forehead: "The Shpigulin men!" In silence, and still plunged in thought, he walked without haste to the carriage, took his seat, and told the coachman to drive to the town. The police-superintendent followed in the droshky.

I imagine that he had vague impressions of many interesting things of all sorts on the way, but I doubt whether he had any definite idea or any settled intention as he drove into the open space in front of his house. But no sooner did he see the resolute and orderly ranks of "the rioters," the cordon of police, the helpless (and perhaps purposely helpless) chief of police, and the general expectation of which he was the object, than all the blood rushed to his heart. With a pale face, he stepped out of his carriage.

"Caps off!" he said breathlessly and hardly audibly. "On your knees!" he squealed, to the surprise of every one, to his own surprise too, and perhaps the very unexpectedness of the position was the explanation of what followed. Can a sledge on a switchback at carnival stop short as it flies down the hill? What made it worse, Andrey Antonovitch had been all his life serene in character, and never shouted or stamped at anyone; and such people are always the most dangerous if it once happens that something sets their sledge sliding downhill. Everything was whirling before his eyes.

“Filibusters!” he yelled still more shrilly and absurdly, and his voice broke. He stood, not knowing what he was going to do, but knowing and feeling in his whole being that he certainly would do something directly.

“Lord!” was heard from the crowd. A lad began crossing himself; three or four men actually did try to kneel down, but the whole mass moved three steps forward, and suddenly all began talking at once: “Your Excellency … we were hired for a term … the manager … you mustn’t say,” and so on and so on. It was impossible to distinguish anything.

Alas! Andrey Antonovitch could distinguish nothing: the flowers were still in his hands. The riot was as real to him as the prison carts were to Stepan Trofimovitch. And flitting to and fro in the crowd of “rioters” who gazed open-eyed at him, he seemed to see Pyotr Stepanovitch, who had egged them on—Pyotr Stepanovitch, whom he hated and whose image had never left him since yesterday.

“Rods!” he cried even more unexpectedly. A dead silence followed.

From the facts I have learnt and those I have conjectured, this must have been what happened at the beginning; but I have no such exact information for what followed, nor can I conjecture it so easily. There are some facts, however.

In the first place, rods were brought on the scene with strange rapidity; they had evidently been got ready beforehand in expectation by the intelligent chief of the police. Not more than two, or at most three, were actually flogged, however; that fact I wish to lay stress on. It’s an absolute fabrication to say that the whole crowd of rioters, or at least half of them, were punished. It is a nonsensical story, too, that a poor but respectable lady was caught as she passed by and promptly thrashed; yet I read myself an account of this incident afterwards among the provincial items of a Petersburg newspaper. Many people in the town talked of an old woman called Avdotya Petrovna Tarapygin who lived in the almshouse by the cemetery. She was said, on her way home from visiting a friend, to have forced her way into the crowd of spectators through natural curiosity. Seeing what was going on, she cried out, “What a shame!” and spat on the ground. For this it was said she had been seized and flogged too. This story not only appeared in print, but in our excitement we positively got up a subscription for her benefit. I subscribed twenty kopecks myself. And would you believe it? It appears now that there was no old woman called Tarapygin living in the almshouse at all! I went to inquire at the almshouse by the cemetery myself; they had never heard of anyone called Tarapygin there, and, what’s more, they were quite offended when I told them the story that was going round. I mention this fabulous Avdotya Petrovna because what happened to her (if she really had existed) very nearly happened to Stepan Trofimovitch. Possibly, indeed, his adventure may have been at the bottom of the ridiculous tale about the old woman, that is, as the gossip went on growing he was transformed into this old dame.

What I find most difficult to understand is how he came to slip away from me as soon as he got into the square. As I had a misgiving of something very unpleasant, I wanted to take him round the square straight to the entrance to the governor’s, but my own curiosity was roused, and I stopped only for one minute to question the first person I came across, and suddenly I looked round and found Stepan Trofimovitch no longer at my side. Instinctively I darted off to look for him in the most dangerous place; something made me feel that his sledge, too, was flying downhill. And I did, as a fact, find him in the very centre of things. I remember I seized him by the arm; but he looked quietly and proudly at me with an air of immense authority.

"Cher," he pronounced in a voice which quivered on a breaking note, "if they are dealing with people so unceremoniously before us, in an open square, what is to be expected from that man, for instance … if he happens to act on his own authority?"

And shaking with indignation and with an intense desire to defy them, he pointed a menacing, accusing finger at Flibusterov, who was gazing at us open-eyed two paces away.

"That man!" cried the latter, blind with rage. "What man? And who are you?" He stepped up to him, clenching his fist. "Who are you?" he roared ferociously, hysterically, and desperately. (I must mention that he knew Stepan Trofimovitch perfectly well by sight.) Another moment and he would have certainly seized him by the collar; but luckily, hearing him shout, Lembke turned his head. He gazed intensely but with perplexity at Stepan Trofimovitch, seeming to consider something, and suddenly he shook his hand impatiently. Flibusterov was checked. I drew Stepan Trofimovitch out of the crowd, though perhaps he may have wished to retreat himself.

"Home, home," I insisted; "it was certainly thanks to Lembke that we were not beaten."

"Go, my friend; I am to blame for exposing you to this. You have a future and a career of a sort before you, while I—mon heure est sonnée."

He resolutely mounted the governor's steps. The hall-porter knew me; I said that we both wanted to see Yulia Mihailovna.

We sat down in the waiting-room and waited. I was unwilling to leave my friend, but I thought it unnecessary to say anything more to him. He had the air of a man who had consecrated himself to certain death for the sake of his country. We sat down, not side by side, but in different corners—I nearer to the entrance, he at some distance facing me, with his head bent in thought, leaning lightly on his stick. He held his wide-brimmed hat in his left hand. We sat like that for ten minutes.

II

Lembke suddenly came in with rapid steps, accompanied by the chief of police, looked absent-mindedly at us and, taking no notice of us, was about to pass into his study on the right, but Stepan Trofimovitch stood before him blocking his way. The tall figure of Stepan Trofimovitch, so unlike other people, made an impression. Lembke stopped.

"Who is this?" he muttered, puzzled, as if he were questioning the chief of police, though he did not turn his head towards him, and was all the time gazing at Stepan Trofimovitch.

"Retired college assessor, Stepan Trofimovitch Verhovensky, your Excellency," answered Stepan Trofimovitch, bowing majestically. His Excellency went on staring at him with a very blank expression, however.

"What is it?" And with the curtness of a great official he turned his ear to Stepan

Trofimovitch with disdainful impatience, taking him for an ordinary person with a written petition of some sort.

"I was visited and my house was searched to-day by an official acting in your Excellency's name; therefore I am desirous …"

"Name? Name?" Lembke asked impatiently, seeming suddenly to have an inkling of something. Stepan Trofimovitch repeated his name still more majestically.

"A-a-ah! It's … that hotbed … You have shown yourself, sir, in such a light.… Are you a professor? a professor?"

"I once had the honour of giving some lectures to the young men of the X university."

"The young men!" Lembke seemed to start, though I am ready to bet that he grasped very little of what was going on or even, perhaps, did not know with whom he was talking.

"That, sir, I won't allow," he cried, suddenly getting terribly angry. "I won't allow young men! It's all these manifestoes? It's an assault on society, sir, a piratical attack, filibustering.… What is your request?"

"On the contrary, your wife requested me to read something to-morrow at her fête. I've not come to make a request but to ask for my rights.…"

"At the fête? There'll be no fête. I won't allow your fête. A lecture? A lecture?" he screamed furiously.

"I should be very glad if you would speak to me rather more politely, your Excellency, without stamping or shouting at me as though I were a boy."

"Perhaps you understand whom you are speaking to?" said Lembke, turning crimson.

"Perfectly, your Excellency."

"I am protecting society while you are destroying it!… You … I remember about you, though: you used to be a tutor in the house of Madame Stavrogin?"

"Yes, I was in the position … of tutor … in the house of Madame Stavrogin."

"And have been for twenty years the hotbed of all that has now accumulated … all the fruits.… I believe I saw you just now in the square. You'd better look out, sir, you'd better look out; your way of thinking is well known. You may be sure that I keep my eye on you. I cannot allow your lectures, sir, I cannot. Don't come with such requests to me."

He would have passed on again.

"I repeat that your Excellency is mistaken; it was your wife who asked me to give, not a lecture, but a literary reading at the fête to-morrow. But I decline to do so in any case now. I humbly request that you will explain to me if possible how, why, and for what reason I was subjected to an official search to-day? Some of my books and papers, private letters to me, were taken from me and wheeled through the town in a barrow."

"Who searched you?" said Lembke, starting and returning to full consciousness of the position. He suddenly flushed all over. He turned quickly to the chief of police. At that moment the long, stooping, and awkward figure of Blum appeared in the doorway.

"Why, this official here," said Stepan Trofimovitch, indicating him. Blum came forward with a face that admitted his responsibility but showed no contrition.

"Vous ne faites que des bêtises," Lembke threw at him in a tone of vexation and anger, and suddenly he was transformed and completely himself again.

"Excuse me," he muttered, utterly disconcerted and turning absolutely crimson, "all this … all this was probably a mere blunder, a misunderstanding … nothing but a misunderstanding."

"Your Excellency," observed Stepan Trofimovitch, "once when I was young I saw a characteristic incident. In the corridor of a theatre a man ran up to another and gave him a sounding smack in the face before the whole public. Perceiving at once that his victim was not the person whom he had intended to chastise but someone quite different who only slightly resembled him, he pronounced angrily, with the haste of one whose moments are precious—as your Excellency did just now—'I've made a mistake … excuse me, it was a misunderstanding, nothing but a misunderstanding.' And when the offended man remained resentful and cried out, he observed to him, with extreme annoyance: 'Why, I tell you it was a misunderstanding. What are you crying out about?'"

"That's … that's very amusing, of course"—Lembke gave a wry smile—"but … but can't you see how unhappy I am myself?"

He almost screamed, and seemed about to hide his face in his hands.

This unexpected and piteous exclamation, almost a sob, was almost more than one could bear. It was probably the first moment since the previous day that he had full, vivid consciousness of all that had happened—and it was followed by complete, humiliating despair that could not be disguised—who knows, in another minute he might have sobbed aloud. For the first moment Stepan Trofimovitch looked wildly at him; then he suddenly bowed his head and in a voice pregnant with feeling pronounced:

"Your Excellency, don't trouble yourself with my petulant complaint, and only give orders for my books and letters to be restored to me.… "

He was interrupted. At that very instant Yulia Mihailovna returned and entered noisily with all the party which had accompanied her. But at this point, I should like to tell my story in as much detail as possible.

III

In the first place, the whole company who had filled three carriages crowded into the waiting-room. There was a special entrance to Yulia Mihailovna's apartments on the left as one entered the house; but on this occasion they all went through the waiting-room—and I imagine just because Stepan Trofimovitch was there, and because all that had happened to him as well as the Shpigulin affair had reached Yulia Mihailovna's ears as she drove into the town. Lyamshin, who for some misdemeanour had not been invited to join the party and so knew all that had been happening in the town before anyone else, brought her the news. With spiteful glee he hired a wretched Cossack nag and hastened on the way to Skvoreshniki to meet the returning cavalcade with the diverting intelligence. I fancy that, in spite of her lofty determination, Yulia Mihailovna was a little disconcerted on hearing such surprising news, but probably only for an instant. The political aspect of the affair, for instance, could not cause her uneasiness; Pyotr Stepanovitch had impressed upon her three or four times that the Shpigulin ruffians ought to be flogged, and Pyotr Stepanovitch certainly had for some time past been a great authority in her eyes. "But … anyway, I shall make him pay for it," she doubtless reflected, the "he," of course, referring to her spouse. I must observe in passing that on this occasion, as though purposely, Pyotr Stepanovitch had taken no part in the expedition, and no one had seen him all day. I must mention too, by the way, that Varvara Petrovna had come back to the town with her guests (in the same carriage with Yulia Mihailovna) in order to be present at the last meeting of the committee which was arranging the fête for the next day. She too must have been interested, and perhaps even agitated, by the news about Stepan Trofimovitch communicated by Lyamshin.

The hour of reckoning for Andrey Antonovitch followed at once. Alas! he felt that from the first glance at his admirable wife. With an open air and an enchanting smile she went quickly up to Stepan Trofimovitch, held out her exquisitely gloved hand, and greeted him with a perfect shower of flattering phrases—as though the only thing she cared about that morning was to make haste to be charming to Stepan Trofimovitch because at last she saw him in her house. There was not one hint of the search that morning; it was as though she knew nothing of it. There was not one word to her husband, not one glance in his direction—as though he had not been in the room. What's more, she promptly confiscated Stepan Trofimovitch and carried him off to the drawing-room—as though he had had no interview with Lembke, or as though it was not worth prolonging if he had. I repeat again, I think that in this, Yulia Mihailovna, in spite of her aristocratic tone, made another great mistake. And Karmazinov particularly did much to aggravate this. (He had taken part in the expedition at Yulia Mihailovna's special request, and in that way had, incidentally, paid his visit to Varvara Petrovna, and she was so poor-spirited as to be perfectly delighted at it.) On seeing Stepan Trofimovitch, he called out from the doorway (he came in behind the rest) and pressed forward to embrace him, even interrupting Yulia Mihailovna.

"What years, what ages! At last … excellent ami."

He made as though to kiss him, offering his cheek, of course, and Stepan Trofimovitch was so fluttered that he could not avoid saluting it.

"Cher," he said to me that evening, recalling all the events of that day, "I wondered at that moment which of us was the most contemptible: he, embracing me only to humiliate me, or I, despising him and his face and kissing it on the spot, though I might have turned away.… Foo!"

"Come, tell me about yourself, tell me everything," Karmazinov drawled and lisped, as though it were possible for him on the spur of the moment to give an account of twenty-five years of his life. But this foolish trifling was the height of "chic."

"Remember that the last time we met was at the Granovsky dinner in Moscow, and that twenty-four years have passed since then …" Stepan Trofimovitch began very reasonably (and consequently not at all in the same "chic" style).

"Ce cher homme," Karmazinov interrupted with shrill familiarity, squeezing his shoulder with exaggerated friendliness. "Make haste and take us to your room, Yulia Mihailovna; there he'll sit down and tell us everything."

"And yet I was never at all intimate with that peevish old woman," Stepan Trofimovitch went on complaining to me that same evening, shaking with anger; "we were almost boys, and I'd begun to detest him even then … just as he had me, of course."

Yulia Mihailovna's drawing-room filled up quickly. Varvara Petrovna was particularly excited, though she tried to appear indifferent, but I caught her once or twice glancing with hatred at Karmazinov and with wrath at Stepan Trofimovitch—the wrath of anticipation, the wrath of jealousy and love: if Stepan Trofimovitch had blundered this time and had let Karmazinov make him look small before every one, I believe she would have leapt up and beaten him. I have forgotten to say that Liza too was there, and I had never seen her more radiant, carelessly light-hearted, and happy. Mavriky Nikolaevitch was there too, of course. In the crowd of young ladies and rather vulgar young men who made up Yulia Mihailovna's usual retinue, and among whom this vulgarity was taken for sprightliness, and cheap cynicism for wit, I noticed two or three new faces: a very obsequious Pole who was on a visit in the town; a German doctor, a sturdy old fellow who kept loudly laughing with great zest at his own wit; and lastly, a very young princeling from Petersburg like an automaton figure, with the deportment of a state dignitary and a fearfully high collar. But it was evident that Yulia Mihailovna had a very high opinion of this visitor, and was even a little anxious of the impression her salon was making on him.

"Cher M. Karmazinov," said Stepan Trofimovitch, sitting in a picturesque pose on the sofa and suddenly beginning to lisp as daintily as Karmazinov himself, "cher M. Karmazinov, the life of a man of our time and of certain convictions, even after an interval of twenty-five years, is bound to seem monotonous …"

The German went off into a loud abrupt guffaw like a neigh, evidently imagining that Stepan Trofimovitch had said something exceedingly funny. The latter gazed at him with studied amazement but produced no effect on him whatever. The prince, too, looked at the German, turning head, collar and all, towards him and putting up his pince-nez, though without the slightest curiosity.

"… Is bound to seem monotonous," Stepan Trofimovitch intentionally repeated, drawling each word as deliberately and nonchalantly as possible. "And so my life has been throughout this quarter of a century, et comme on trouve partout plus de moines que de raison, and as I am entirely of this opinion, it has come to pass that throughout this quarter of a century I …"

"C'est charmant, les moines," whispered Yulia Mihailovna, turning to Varvara Petrovna, who was sitting beside her.

Varvara Petrovna responded with a look of pride. But Karmazinov could not stomach the success of the French phrase, and quickly and shrilly interrupted Stepan Trofimovitch.

"As for me, I am quite at rest on that score, and for the past seven years I've been settled at Karlsruhe. And last year, when it was proposed by the town council to lay down a new water-pipe, I felt in my heart that this question of water-pipes in Karlsruhe was dearer and closer to my heart than all the questions of my precious Fatherland ... in this period of so-called reform."

"I can't help sympathising, though it goes against the grain," sighed Stepan Trofimovitch, bowing his head significantly.

Yulia Mihailovna was triumphant: the conversation was becoming profound and taking a political turn.

"A drain-pipe?" the doctor inquired in a loud voice.

"A water-pipe, doctor, a water-pipe, and I positively assisted them in drawing up the plan."

The doctor went off into a deafening guffaw. Many people followed his example, laughing in the face of the doctor, who remained unconscious of it and was highly delighted that every one was laughing.

"You must allow me to differ from you, Karmazinov," Yulia Mihailovna hastened to interpose. "Karlsruhe is all very well, but you are fond of mystifying people, and this time we don't believe you. What Russian writer has presented so many modern types, has brought forward so many contemporary problems, has put his finger on the most vital modern points which make up the type of the modern man of action? You, only you, and no one else. It's no use your assuring us of your coldness towards your own country and your ardent interest in the water-pipes of Karlsruhe. Ha ha!"

"Yes, no doubt," lisped Karmazinov. "I have portrayed in the character of Pogozhev all the failings of the Slavophils and in the character of Nikodimov all the failings of the Westerners...."

"I say, hardly all!" Lyamshin whispered slyly.

"But I do this by the way, simply to while away the tedious hours and to satisfy the persistent demands of my fellow-countrymen."

"You are probably aware, Stepan Trofimovitch," Yulia Mihailovna went on enthusiastically, "that to-morrow we shall have the delight of hearing the charming lines ... one of the last of Semyon Yakovlevitch's exquisite literary inspirations—it's called Merci. He announces in this piece that he will write no more, that nothing in the world will induce him to, if angels from Heaven or, what's more, all the best society were to implore him to change his mind. In fact he is laying down the pen for good, and this graceful Merci is addressed to the public in grateful acknowledgment of the constant enthusiasm with which it has for so many years greeted his unswerving loyalty to true Russian thought."

Yulia Mihailovna was at the acme of bliss.

"Yes, I shall make my farewell; I shall say my Merci and depart and there … in Karlsruhe … I shall close my eyes." Karmazinov was gradually becoming maudlin.

Like many of our great writers (and there are numbers of them amongst us), he could not resist praise, and began to be limp at once, in spite of his penetrating wit. But I consider this is pardonable. They say that one of our Shakespeares positively blurted out in private conversation that "we great men can't do otherwise," and so on, and, what's more, was unaware of it.

"There in Karlsruhe I shall close my eyes. When we have done our duty, all that's left for us great men is to make haste to close our eyes without seeking a reward. I shall do so too."

"Give me the address and I shall come to Karlsruhe to visit your tomb," said the German, laughing immoderately.

"They send corpses by rail nowadays," one of the less important young men said unexpectedly.

Lyamshin positively shrieked with delight. Yulia Mihailovna frowned. Nikolay Stavrogin walked in.

"Why, I was told that you were locked up?" he said aloud, addressing Stepan Trofimovitch before every one else.

"No, it was a case of unlocking," jested Stepan Trofimovitch.

"But I hope that what's happened will have no influence on what I asked you to do," Yulia Mihailovna put in again. "I trust that you will not let this unfortunate annoyance, of which I had no idea, lead you to disappoint our eager expectations and deprive us of the enjoyment of hearing your reading at our literary matinée."

"I don't know, I … now …"

"Really, I am so unlucky, Varvara Petrovna … and only fancy, just when I was so longing to make the personal acquaintance of one of the most remarkable and independent intellects of Russia—and here Stepan Trofimovitch suddenly talks of deserting us."

"Your compliment is uttered so audibly that I ought to pretend not to hear it," Stepan Trofimovitch said neatly, "but I cannot believe that my insignificant presence is so indispensable at your fête to-morrow. However, I …"

"Why, you'll spoil him!" cried Pyotr Stepanovitch, bursting into the room. "I've only just got him in hand—and in one morning he has been searched, arrested, taken by the collar by a policeman, and here ladies are cooing to him in the governor's drawing-room. Every bone in his body is aching with rapture; in his wildest dreams he had never hoped for such good fortune. Now he'll begin informing against the Socialists after this!"

"Impossible, Pyotr Stepanovitch! Socialism is too grand an idea to be unrecognised by Stepan Trofimovitch." Yulia Mihailovna took up the gauntlet with energy.

"It's a great idea but its exponents are not always great men, et brisons-là, mon cher,"

Stepan Trofimovitch ended, addressing his son and rising gracefully from his seat.

But at this point an utterly unexpected circumstance occurred. Von Lembke had been in the room for some time but seemed unnoticed by anyone, though every one had seen him come in. In accordance with her former plan, Yulia Mihailovna went on ignoring him. He took up his position near the door and with a stern face listened gloomily to the conversation. Hearing an allusion to the events of the morning, he began fidgeting uneasily, stared at the prince, obviously struck by his stiffly starched, prominent collar; then suddenly he seemed to start on hearing the voice of Pyotr Stepanovitch and seeing him burst in; and no sooner had Stepan Trofimovitch uttered his phrase about Socialists than Lembke went up to him, pushing against Lyamshin, who at once skipped out of the way with an affected gesture of surprise, rubbing his shoulder and pretending that he had been terribly bruised.

"Enough!" said Von Lembke to Stepan Trofimovitch, vigorously gripping the hand of the dismayed gentleman and squeezing it with all his might in both of his. "Enough! The filibusters of our day are unmasked. Not another word. Measures have been taken...."

He spoke loudly enough to be heard by all the room, and concluded with energy. The impression he produced was poignant. Everybody felt that something was wrong. I saw Yulia Mihailovna turn pale. The effect was heightened by a trivial accident. After announcing that measures had been taken, Lembke turned sharply and walked quickly towards the door, but he had hardly taken two steps when he stumbled over a rug, swerved forward, and almost fell. For a moment he stood still, looked at the rug at which he had stumbled, and, uttering aloud "Change it!" went out of the room. Yulia Mihailovna ran after him. Her exit was followed by an uproar, in which it was difficult to distinguish anything. Some said he was "deranged," others that he was "liable to attacks"; others put their fingers to their forehead; Lyamshin, in the corner, put his two fingers above his forehead. People hinted at some domestic difficulties—in a whisper, of course. No one took up his hat; all were waiting. I don't know what Yulia Mihailovna managed to do, but five minutes later she came back, doing her utmost to appear composed. She replied evasively that Andrey Antonovitch was rather excited, but that it meant nothing, that he had been like that from a child, that she knew "much better," and that the fête next day would certainly cheer him up. Then followed a few flattering words to Stepan Trofimovitch simply from civility, and a loud invitation to the members of the committee to open the meeting now, at once. Only then, all who were not members of the committee prepared to go home; but the painful incidents of this fatal day were not yet over.

I noticed at the moment when Nikolay Stavrogin came in that Liza looked quickly and intently at him and was for a long time unable to take her eyes off him—so much so that at last it attracted attention. I saw Mavriky Nikolaevitch bend over her from behind; he seemed to mean to whisper something to her, but evidently changed his intention and drew himself up quickly, looking round at every one with a guilty air. Nikolay Vsyevolodovitch too excited curiosity; his face was paler than usual and there was a strangely absent-minded look in his eyes. After flinging his question at Stepan Trofimovitch he seemed to forget about him altogether, and I really believe he even forgot to speak to his hostess. He did not once look at Liza—not because he did not want to, but I am certain because he did not notice her either. And suddenly, after the brief silence that followed Yulia Mihailovna's invitation to open the meeting without loss of time, Liza's musical voice, intentionally loud, was heard. She called to

Stavrogin.

"Nikolay Vsyevolodovitch, a captain who calls himself a relation of yours, the brother of your wife, and whose name is Lebyadkin, keeps writing impertinent letters to me, complaining of you and offering to tell me some secrets about you. If he really is a connection of yours, please tell him not to annoy me, and save me from this unpleasantness."

There was a note of desperate challenge in these words—every one realised it. The accusation was unmistakable, though perhaps it was a surprise to herself. She was like a man who shuts his eyes and throws himself from the roof.

But Nikolay Stavrogin's answer was even more astounding.

To begin with, it was strange that he was not in the least surprised and listened to Liza with unruffled attention. There was no trace of either confusion or anger in his face. Simply, firmly, even with an air of perfect readiness, he answered the fatal question:

"Yes, I have the misfortune to be connected with that man. I have been the husband of his sister for nearly five years. You may be sure I will give him your message as soon as possible, and I'll answer for it that he shan't annoy you again."

I shall never forget the horror that was reflected on the face of Varvara Petrovna. With a distracted air she got up from her seat, lifting up her right hand as though to ward off a blow. Nikolay Vsyevolodovitch looked at her, looked at Liza, at the spectators, and suddenly smiled with infinite disdain; he walked deliberately out of the room. Every one saw how Liza leapt up from the sofa as soon as he turned to go and unmistakably made a movement to run after him. But she controlled herself and did not run after him; she went quietly out of the room without saying a word or even looking at anyone, accompanied, of course, by Mavriky Nikolaevitch, who rushed after her.

The uproar and the gossip that night in the town I will not attempt to describe. Varvara Petrovna shut herself up in her town house and Nikolay Vsyevolodovitch, it was said, went straight to Skvoreshniki without seeing his mother. Stepan Trofimovitch sent me that evening to cette chère amie to implore her to allow him to come to her, but she would not see me. He was terribly overwhelmed; he shed tears. "Such a marriage! Such a marriage! Such an awful thing in the family!" he kept repeating. He remembered Karmazinov, however, and abused him terribly. He set to work vigorously to prepare for the reading too and—the artistic temperament!—rehearsed before the looking-glass and went over all the jokes and witticisms uttered in the course of his life which he had written down in a separate notebook, to insert into his reading next day.

"My dear, I do this for the sake of a great idea," he said to me, obviously justifying himself. "Cher ami, I have been stationary for twenty-five years and suddenly I've begun to move—whither, I know not—but I've begun to move...."

PART III

CHAPTER I. THE FETE—FIRST PART

I

The fête took place in spite of all the perplexities of the preceding "Shpigulin" day. I believe that even if Lembke had died the previous night, the fête would still have taken place next morning—so peculiar was the significance Yulia Mihailovna attached to it. Alas! up to the last moment she was blind and had no inkling of the state of public feeling. No one believed at last that the festive day would pass without some tremendous scandal, some "catastrophe" as some people expressed it, rubbing their hands in anticipation. Many people, it is true, tried to assume a frowning and diplomatic countenance; but, speaking generally, every Russian is inordinately delighted at any public scandal and disorder. It is true that we did feel something much more serious than the mere craving for a scandal: there was a general feeling of irritation, a feeling of implacable resentment; every one seemed thoroughly disgusted with everything. A kind of bewildered cynicism, a forced, as it were, strained cynicism was predominant in every one. The only people who were free from bewilderment were the ladies, and they were clear on only one point: their remorseless detestation of Yulia Mihailovna. Ladies of all shades of opinion were agreed in this. And she, poor dear, had no suspicion; up to the last hour she was persuaded that she was "surrounded by followers," and that they were still "fanatically devoted to her."

I have already hinted that some low fellows of different sorts had made their appearance amongst us. In turbulent times of upheaval or transition low characters always come to the front everywhere. I am not speaking now of the so-called "advanced" people who are always in a hurry to be in advance of every one else (their absorbing anxiety) and who always have some more or less definite, though often very stupid, aim. No, I am speaking only of the riff-raff. In every period of transition this riff-raff, which exists in every society, rises to the surface, and is not only without any aim but has not even a symptom of an idea, and merely does its utmost to give expression to uneasiness and impatience. Moreover, this riff-raff almost always falls unconsciously under the control of the little group of "advanced people" who do act with a definite aim, and this little group can direct all this rabble as it pleases, if only it does not itself consist of absolute idiots, which, however, is sometimes the case. It is said among us now that it is all over, that Pyotr Stepanovitch was directed by the Internationale, and Yulia Mihailovna by Pyotr Stepanovitch, while she controlled, under his rule, a rabble of all sorts. The more sober minds amongst us wonder at themselves now, and can't understand how they came to be so foolish at the time.

What constituted the turbulence of our time and what transition it was we were passing through I don't know, nor I think does anyone, unless it were some of those visitors of ours. Yet the most worthless fellows suddenly gained predominant influence, began loudly criticising everything sacred, though till then they had not dared to open their mouths, while the leading people, who had till then so satisfactorily kept the upper hand, began listening to them and holding their peace, some even simpered approval in a most shameless way. People like Lyamshin and Telyatnikov, like Gogol's Tentyotnikov, drivelling home-bred editions of Radishtchev, wretched little Jews with a mournful but haughty smile, guffawing foreigners, poets of advanced tendencies from the capital, poets who made up with peasant coats and tarred boots for the lack of tendencies or talents, majors and colonels who ridiculed the senselessness of the service, and who would have been ready for an extra rouble to unbuckle their swords, and take jobs as railway clerks; generals who had abandoned their duties to become lawyers; advanced mediators, advancing merchants, innumerable divinity students, women who were the embodiment of the woman question—all these suddenly gained complete sway among us and over whom? Over the club, the venerable officials, over generals with wooden legs, over the very strict and inaccessible ladies of our local society. Since even Varvara Petrovna was almost at the beck and call of this rabble, right up to the time of the catastrophe with her son, our other local Minervas may well be pardoned for their temporary aberration. Now all this is attributed, as I have mentioned already, to the Internationale. This idea has taken such root that it is given as the explanation to visitors from other parts. Only lately councillor Kubrikov, a man of sixty-two, with the Stanislav Order on his breast, came forward uninvited and confessed in a voice full of feeling that he had beyond a shadow of doubt been for fully three months under the influence of the Internationale. When with every deference for his years and services he was invited to be more definite, he stuck firmly to his original statement, though he could produce no evidence except that "he had felt it in all his feelings," so that they cross-examined him no further.

I repeat again, there was still even among us a small group who held themselves aloof from the beginning, and even locked themselves up. But what lock can stand against a law of nature? Daughters will grow up even in the most careful families, and it is essential for grown-up daughters to dance.

And so all these people, too, ended by subscribing to the governesses' fund.

The ball was assumed to be an entertainment so brilliant, so unprecedented; marvels were told about it; there were rumours of princes from a distance with lorgnettes; of ten stewards, all young dandies, with rosettes on their left shoulder; of some Petersburg people who were setting the thing going; there was a rumour that Karmazinov had consented to increase the subscriptions to the fund by reading his Merci in the costume of the governesses of the district; that there would be a literary quadrille all in costume, and every costume would symbolise some special line of thought; and finally that "honest Russian thought" would dance in costume—which would certainly be a complete novelty in itself. Who could resist subscribing? Every one subscribed.

II

The programme of the fête was divided into two parts: the literary matinée from midday till four o'clock, and afterwards a ball from ten o'clock onwards through the night. But in this very programme there lay concealed germs of disorder. In the first place, from the very beginning a rumour had gained ground among the public concerning a luncheon immediately after the literary matinée, or even while it was going on, during an interval arranged expressly for it—a free luncheon, of course, which would form part of the programme and be accompanied by champagne. The immense price of the tickets (three roubles) tended to confirm this rumour. "As though one would subscribe for nothing? The fête is arranged for twenty-four hours, so food must be provided. People will get hungry." This was how people reasoned in the town. I must admit that Yulia Mihailovna did much to confirm this disastrous rumour by her own heedlessness. A month earlier, under the first spell of the great project, she would babble about it to anyone she met; and even sent a paragraph to one of the Petersburg papers about the toasts and speeches arranged for her fête. What fascinated her most at that time was the idea of these toasts; she wanted to propose them herself and was continually composing them in anticipation. They were to make clear what was their banner (what was it? I don't mind betting that the poor dear composed nothing after all), they were to get into the Petersburg and Moscow papers, to touch and fascinate the higher powers and then to spread the idea over all the provinces of Russia, rousing people to wonder and imitation.

But for toasts, champagne was essential, and as champagne can't be drunk on an empty stomach, it followed that a lunch was essential too. Afterwards, when by her efforts a committee had been formed and had attacked the subject more seriously, it was proved clearly to her at once that if they were going to dream of banquets there would be very little left for the governesses, however well people subscribed. There were two ways out of the difficulty: either Belshazzar's feast with toasts and speeches, and ninety roubles for the governesses, or a considerable sum of money with the fête only as a matter of form to raise it. The committee, however, only wanted to scare her, and had of course worked out a third course of action, which was reasonable and combined the advantages of both, that is, a very decent fête in every respect only without champagne, and so yielding a very respectable sum, much more than ninety roubles. But Yulia Mihailovna would not agree to it: her proud spirit revolted from paltry compromise. She decided at once that if the original idea could not be carried out they should rush to the opposite extreme, that is, raise an enormous subscription that would be the envy of other provinces. "The public must understand," she said at the end of her flaming speech to the committee, "that the attainment of an object of universal human interest is infinitely loftier than the corporeal enjoyments of the passing moment, that the fête in its essence is only the proclamation of a great idea, and so we ought to be content with the most frugal German ball simply as a symbol, that is, if we can't dispense with this detestable ball altogether," so great was the aversion she suddenly conceived for it. But she was pacified at last. It was then that "the literary quadrille" and the other æsthetic items were invented and proposed as substitutes for the corporeal enjoyments. It was then that Karmazinov finally consented to read Merci (until then he had only tantalised them by his hesitation) and so eradicate the very idea of victuals from the minds of our incontinent public. So the ball was once more to be a magnificent function, though in a different style. And not to be too ethereal it was decided that tea with lemon and round biscuits should be served at the beginning of the ball, and later on "orchade" and lemonade and at the end even ices—but nothing else. For those who always and everywhere are hungry and, still more, thirsty, they might open a buffet in the farthest of the suite of rooms and put it in charge of Prohorovitch, the head cook of the club, who would, subject to the strict supervision of the committee, serve whatever was wanted, at a fixed charge, and a notice should be put up on the door of the hall that refreshments were extra. But on the morning they decided not to open the buffet at all for fear of disturbing the reading, though the buffet would have been five rooms off the White Hall in which Karmazinov had consented to read Merci.

It is remarkable that the committee, and even the most practical people in it, attached enormous consequence to this reading. As for people of poetical tendencies, the marshal's wife, for instance, informed Karmazinov that after the reading she would immediately order a marble slab to be put up in the wall of the White Hall with an inscription in gold letters, that on such a day and year, here, in this place, the great writer of Russia and of Europe had read Merci on laying aside his pen, and so had for the first time taken leave of the Russian public represented by the leading citizens of our town, and that this inscription would be read by all at the ball, that is, only five hours after Merci had been read. I know for a fact that Karmazinov it was who insisted that there should be no buffet in the morning on any account, while he was reading, in spite of some protests from members of the committee that this was rather opposed to our way of doing things.

This was the position of affairs, while in the town people were still reckoning on a Belshazzar feast, that is, on refreshments provided by the committee; they believed in this to the last hour. Even the young ladies were dreaming of masses of sweets and preserves, and something more beyond their imagination. Every one knew that the subscriptions had reached a huge sum, that all the town was struggling to go, that people were driving in from the surrounding districts, and that there were not tickets enough. It was known, too, that there had been some large subscriptions apart from the price paid for tickets: Varvara Petrovna, for instance, had paid three hundred roubles for her ticket and had given almost all the flowers from her conservatory to decorate the room. The marshal's wife, who was a member of the committee, provided the house and the lighting; the club furnished the music, the attendants, and gave up Prohorovitch for the whole day. There were other contributions as well, though lesser ones, so much so indeed that the idea was mooted of cutting down the price of tickets from three roubles to two. Indeed, the committee were afraid at first that three roubles would be too much for young ladies to pay, and suggested that they might have family tickets, so that every family should pay for one daughter only, while the other young ladies of the family, even if there were a dozen specimens, should be admitted free. But all their apprehensions turned out to be groundless: it was just the young ladies who did come. Even the poorest clerks brought their girls, and it was quite evident that if they had had no girls it would never have occurred to them to subscribe for tickets. One insignificant little secretary brought all his seven daughters, to say nothing of his wife and a niece into the bargain, and every one of these persons held in her hand an entrance ticket that cost three roubles.

It may be imagined what an upheaval it made in the town! One has only to remember that as the fête was divided into two parts every lady needed two costumes for the occasion—a morning one for the matinée and a ball dress for the evening. Many middle-class people, as it appeared afterwards, had pawned everything they had for that day, even the family linen, even the sheets, and possibly the mattresses, to the Jews, who had been settling in our town in great numbers during the previous two years and who became more and more numerous as time went on. Almost all the officials had asked for their salary in advance, and some of the landowners sold beasts they could ill spare, and all simply to bring their ladies got up as marchionesses, and to be as good as anybody. The magnificence of dresses on this occasion was something unheard of in our neighbourhood. For a fortnight beforehand the town was overflowing with funny stories which were all brought by our wits to Yulia Mihailovna's court. Caricatures were passed from hand to hand. I have seen some drawings of the sort myself, in Yulia Mihailovna's album. All this reached the ears of the families who were the source of the jokes; I believe this was the cause of the general hatred of Yulia Mihailovna which had grown so strong in the town. People swear and gnash their teeth when they think of it now. But it was evident, even at the time, that if the committee were to displease them in anything, or if anything went wrong at the ball, the outburst of indignation would be something surprising. That's why every one was secretly expecting a scandal; and if it was so confidently expected, how could it fail to come to pass?

The orchestra struck up punctually at midday. Being one of the stewards, that is, one of the twelve "young men with a rosette," I saw with my own eyes how this day of ignominious memory began. It began with an enormous crush at the doors. How was it that everything, including the police, went wrong that day? I don't blame the genuine public: the fathers of families did not crowd, nor did they push against anyone, in spite of their position. On the contrary, I am told that they were disconcerted even in the street, at the sight of the crowd shoving in a way unheard of in our town, besieging the entry and taking it by assault, instead of simply going in. Meanwhile the carriages kept driving up, and at last blocked the street. Now, at the time I write, I have good grounds for affirming that some of the lowest rabble of our town were brought in without tickets by Lyamshin and Liputin, possibly, too, by other people who were stewards like me. Anyway, some complete strangers, who had come from the surrounding districts and elsewhere, were present. As soon as these savages entered the hall they began asking where the buffet was, as though they had been put up to it beforehand, and learning that there was no buffet they began swearing with brutal directness, and an unprecedented insolence; some of them, it is true, were drunk when they came. Some of them were dazed like savages at the splendour of the hall, as they had never seen anything like it, and subsided for a minute gazing at it open-mouthed. This great White Hall really was magnificent, though the building was falling into decay: it was of immense size, with two rows of windows, with an old-fashioned ceiling covered with gilt carving, with a gallery with mirrors on the walls, red and white draperies, marble statues (nondescript but still statues) with heavy old furniture of the Napoleonic period, white and gold, upholstered in red velvet. At the moment I am describing, a high platform had been put up for the literary gentlemen who were to read, and the whole hall was filled with chairs like the parterre of a theatre with wide aisles for the audience.

But after the first moments of surprise the most senseless questions and protests followed. "Perhaps we don't care for a reading.... We've paid our money.... The audience has been impudently swindled.... This is our entertainment, not the Lembkes!" They seemed, in fact, to have been let in for this purpose. I remember specially an encounter in which the princeling with the stand-up collar and the face of a Dutch doll, whom I had met the morning before at Yulia Mihailovna's, distinguished himself. He had, at her urgent request, consented to pin a rosette on his left shoulder and to become one of our stewards. It turned out that this dumb wax figure could act after a fashion of his own, if he could not talk. When a colossal pockmarked captain, supported by a herd of rabble following at his heels, pestered him by asking "which way to the buffet?" he made a sign to a police sergeant. His hint was promptly acted upon, and in spite of the drunken captain's abuse he was dragged out of the hall. Meantime the genuine public began to make its appearance, and stretched in three long files between the chairs. The disorderly elements began to subside, but the public, even the most "respectable" among them, had a dissatisfied and perplexed air; some of the ladies looked positively scared.

At last all were seated; the music ceased. People began blowing their noses and looking about them. They waited with too solemn an air—which is always a bad sign. But nothing was to be seen yet of the Lembkes. Silks, velvets, diamonds glowed and sparkled on every side; whiffs of fragrance filled the air. The men were wearing all their decorations, and the old men were even in uniform. At last the marshal's wife came in with Liza. Liza had never been so dazzlingly charming or so splendidly dressed as that morning. Her hair was done up in curls, her eyes sparkled, a smile beamed on her face. She made an unmistakable sensation: people scrutinised her and whispered about her. They said that she was looking for Stavrogin, but neither Stavrogin nor Varvara Petrovna were there. At the time I did not understand the expression of her face: why was there so much happiness, such joy, such energy and strength in that face? I remembered what had happened the day before and could not make it out.

But still the Lembkes did not come. This was distinctly a blunder. I learned that Yulia Mihailovna waited till the last minute for Pyotr Stepanovitch, without whom she could not stir a step, though she never admitted it to herself. I must mention, in parenthesis, that on the previous day Pyotr Stepanovitch had at the last meeting of the committee declined to wear the rosette of a steward, which had disappointed her dreadfully, even to the point of tears. To her surprise and, later on, her extreme discomfiture (to anticipate things) he vanished for the whole morning and did not make his appearance at the literary matinée at all, so that no one met him till evening. At last the audience began to manifest unmistakable signs of impatience. No one appeared on the platform either. The back rows began applauding, as in a theatre. The elderly gentlemen and the ladies frowned. "The Lembkes are really giving themselves unbearable airs." Even among the better part of the audience an absurd whisper began to gain ground that perhaps there would not be a fête at all, that Lembke perhaps was really unwell, and so on and so on. But, thank God, the Lembkes at last appeared, she was leaning on his arm; I must confess I was in great apprehension myself about their appearance. But the legends were disproved, and the truth was triumphant. The audience seemed relieved. Lembke himself seemed perfectly well. Every one, I remember, was of that opinion, for it can be imagined how many eyes were turned on him. I may mention, as characteristic of our society, that there were very few of the better-class people who saw reason to suppose that there was anything wrong with him; his conduct seemed to them perfectly normal, and so much so that the action he had taken in the square the morning before was accepted and approved.

"That's how it should have been from the first," the higher officials declared. "If a man begins as a philanthropist he has to come to the same thing in the end, though he does not see that it was necessary from the point of view of philanthropy itself"—that, at least, was the opinion at the club. They only blamed him for having lost his temper. "It ought to have been done more coolly, but there, he is a new man," said the authorities.

All eyes turned with equal eagerness to Yulia Mihailovna. Of course no one has the right to expect from me an exact account in regard to one point: that is a mysterious, a feminine question. But I only know one thing: on the evening of the previous day she had gone into Andrey

Antonovitch's study and was there with him till long after midnight. Andrey Antonovitch was comforted and forgiven. The husband and wife came to a complete understanding, everything was forgotten, and when at the end of the interview Lembke went down on his knees, recalling with horror the final incident of the previous night, the exquisite hand, and after it the lips of his wife, checked the fervent flow of penitent phrases of the chivalrously delicate gentleman who was limp with emotion. Every one could see the happiness in her face. She walked in with an open-hearted air, wearing a magnificent dress. She seemed to be at the very pinnacle of her heart's desires, the fête—the goal and crown of her diplomacy—was an accomplished fact. As they walked to their seats in front of the platform, the Lembkes bowed in all directions and responded to greetings. They were at once surrounded. The marshal's wife got up to meet them.

But at that point a horrid misunderstanding occurred; the orchestra, apropos of nothing, struck up a flourish, not a triumphal march of any kind, but a simple flourish such as was played at the club when some one's health was drunk at an official dinner. I know now that Lyamshin, in his capacity of steward, had arranged this, as though in honour of the Lembkes' entrance. Of course he could always excuse it as a blunder or excessive zeal.... Alas! I did not know at the time that they no longer cared even to find excuses, and that all such considerations were from that day a thing of the past. But the flourish was not the end of it: in the midst of the vexatious astonishment and the smiles of the audience there was a sudden "hurrah" from the end of the hall and from the gallery also, apparently in Lembke's honour. The hurrahs were few, but I must confess they lasted for some time. Yulia Mihailovna flushed, her eyes flashed. Lembke stood still at his chair, and turning towards the voices sternly and majestically scanned the audience.... They hastened to make him sit down. I noticed with dismay the same dangerous smile on his face as he had worn the morning before, in his wife's drawing-room, when he stared at Stepan Trofimovitch before going up to him. It seemed to me that now, too, there was an ominous, and, worst of all, a rather comic expression on his countenance, the expression of a man resigned to sacrifice himself to satisfy his wife's lofty aims.... Yulia Mihailovna beckoned to me hurriedly, and whispered to me to run to Karmazinov and entreat him to begin. And no sooner had I turned away than another disgraceful incident, much more unpleasant than the first, took place.

On the platform, the empty platform, on which till that moment all eyes and all expectations were fastened, and where nothing was to be seen but a small table, a chair in front of it, and on the table a glass of water on a silver salver—on the empty platform there suddenly appeared the colossal figure of Captain Lebyadkin wearing a dress-coat and a white tie. I was so astounded I could not believe my eyes. The captain seemed confused and remained standing at the back of the platform. Suddenly there was a shout in the audience, "Lebyadkin! You?" The captain's stupid red face (he was hopelessly drunk) expanded in a broad vacant grin at this greeting. He raised his hand, rubbed his forehead with it, shook his shaggy head and, as though making up his mind to go through with it, took two steps forward and suddenly went off into a series of prolonged, blissful, gurgling, but not loud guffaws, which made him screw up his eyes and set all his bulky person heaving. This spectacle set almost half the audience laughing, twenty people applauded. The serious part of the audience looked at one another gloomily; it all lasted only half a minute, however. Liputin, wearing his steward's rosette, ran on to the platform with two servants; they carefully took the captain by both arms, while Liputin whispered something to him. The captain scowled, muttered "Ah, well, if that's it!" waved his hand, turned his huge back to the public and vanished with his escort. But a minute later Liputin skipped on to the platform again. He was wearing the sweetest of his invariable smiles, which usually suggested vinegar and sugar, and carried in his hands a sheet of note-paper. With tiny but rapid steps he came forward to the edge of the platform.

"Ladies and gentlemen," he said, addressing the public, "through our inadvertency there has arisen a comical misunderstanding which has been removed; but I've hopefully undertaken to do something at the earnest and most respectful request of one of our local poets. Deeply touched by the humane and lofty object … in spite of his appearance … the object which has brought us all together … to wipe away the tears of the poor but well-educated girls of our province … this gentleman, I mean this local poet … although desirous of preserving his incognito, would gladly have heard his poem read at the beginning of the ball … that is, I mean, of the matinée. Though this poem is not in the programme … for it has only been received half an hour ago … yet it has seemed to us"—(Us? Whom did he mean by us? I report his confused and incoherent speech word for word)—"that through its remarkable naïveté of feeling, together with its equally remarkable gaiety, the poem might well be read, that is, not as something serious, but as something appropriate to the occasion, that is to the idea … especially as some lines … And I wanted to ask the kind permission of the audience."

"Read it!" boomed a voice at the back of the hall.

"Then I am to read it?"

"Read it, read it!" cried many voices.

"With the permission of the audience I will read it," Liputin minced again, still with the same sugary smile. He still seemed to hesitate, and I even thought that he was rather excited. These people are sometimes nervous in spite of their impudence. A divinity student would have carried it through without winking, but Liputin did, after all, belong to the last generation.

"I must say, that is, I have the honour to say by way of preface, that it is not precisely an ode such as used to be written for fêtes, but is rather, so to say, a jest, but full of undoubted feeling, together with playful humour, and, so to say, the most realistic truthfulness."

"Read it, read it!"

He unfolded the paper. No one of course was in time to stop him. Besides, he was wearing his steward's badge. In a ringing voice he declaimed:

"To the local governesses of the Fatherland from the poet at the fête:

"Governesses all, good morrow,

Triumph on this festive day.

Retrograde or vowed George-Sander—

Never mind, just frisk away!"

"But that's Lebyadkin's! Lebyadkin's!" cried several voices. There was laughter and even applause, though not from very many.

"Teaching French to wet-nosed children,

You are glad enough to think

You can catch a worn-out sexton—

Even he is worth a wink!"

"Hurrah! hurrah!"

"But in these great days of progress,

Ladies, to your sorrow know,

You can't even catch a sexton,

If you have not got a 'dot'."

"To be sure, to be sure, that's realism. You can't hook a husband without a 'dot'!"

"But, henceforth, since through our feasting

Capital has flowed from all,

And we send you forth to conquest

Dancing, dowried from this hall—

Retrograde or vowed George-Sander,

Never mind, rejoice you may,

You're a governess with a dowry,

Spit on all and frisk away!"

I must confess I could not believe my ears. The insolence of it was so unmistakable that there was no possibility of excusing Liputin on the ground of stupidity. Besides, Liputin was by no means stupid. The intention was obvious, to me, anyway; they seemed in a hurry to create disorder. Some lines in these idiotic verses, for instance the last, were such that no stupidity could have let them pass. Liputin himself seemed to feel that he had undertaken too much; when he had achieved his exploit he was so overcome by his own impudence that he did not even leave the platform but remained standing, as though there were something more he wanted to say. He had probably imagined that it would somehow produce a different effect; but even the group of ruffians who had applauded during the reading suddenly sank into silence, as though they, too, were overcome. What was silliest of all, many of them took the whole episode seriously, that is, did not regard the verses as a lampoon but actually thought it realistic and true as regards the governesses—a poem with a tendency, in fact. But the excessive freedom of the verses struck even them at last; as for the general public they were not only scandalised but obviously offended. I am sure I am not mistaken as to the impression. Yulia Mihailovna said afterwards that in another moment she would have fallen into a swoon. One of the most respectable old gentlemen helped his old wife on to her feet, and they walked out of the hall accompanied by the agitated glances of the audience. Who knows, the example might have infected others if Karmazinov himself, wearing a dress-coat and a white tie and carrying a manuscript, in his hand, had not appeared on the platform at that moment. Yulia Mihailovna turned an ecstatic gaze at him as on her deliverer.... But I was by that time behind the scenes. I was in quest of Liputin.

"You did that on purpose!" I said, seizing him indignantly by the arm.

"I assure you I never thought ..." he began, cringing and lying at once, pretending to be unhappy. "The verses had only just been brought and I thought that as an amusing pleasantry...."

"You did not think anything of the sort. You can't really think that stupid rubbish an amusing pleasantry?"

"Yes, I do."

"You are simply lying, and it wasn't brought to you just now. You helped Lebyadkin to compose it yourself, yesterday very likely, to create a scandal. The last verse must have been yours, the part about the sexton too. Why did he come on in a dress-coat? You must have meant him to read it, too, if he had not been drunk?"

Liputin looked at me coldly and ironically.

"What business is it of yours?" he asked suddenly with strange calm.

"What business is it of mine? You are wearing the steward's badge, too.... Where is Pyotr Stepanovitch?"

"I don't know, somewhere here; why do you ask?"

"Because now I see through it. It's simply a plot against Yulia Mihailovna so as to ruin the day by a scandal...."

Liputin looked at me askance again.

"But what is it to you?" he said, grinning. He shrugged his shoulders and walked away.

It came over me with a rush. All my suspicions were confirmed. Till then, I had been hoping I was mistaken! What was I to do? I was on the point of asking the advice of Stepan Trofimovitch, but he was standing before the looking-glass, trying on different smiles, and continually consulting a piece of paper on which he had notes. He had to go on immediately after Karmazinov, and was not in a fit state for conversation. Should I run to Yulia Mihailovna? But it was too soon to go to her: she needed a much sterner lesson to cure her of her conviction that she had "a following," and that every one was "fanatically devoted" to her. She would not have believed me, and would have thought I was dreaming. Besides, what help could she be? "Eh," I thought, "after all, what business is it of mine? I'll take off my badge and go home when it begins." That was my mental phrase, "when it begins"; I remember it.

But I had to go and listen to Karmazinov. Taking a last look round behind the scenes, I noticed that a good number of outsiders, even women among them, were flitting about, going in and out. "Behind the scenes" was rather a narrow space completely screened from the audience by a curtain and communicating with other rooms by means of a passage. Here our readers were awaiting their turns. But I was struck at that moment by the reader who was to follow Stepan Trofimovitch. He, too, was some sort of professor (I don't know to this day exactly what he was) who had voluntarily left some educational institution after a disturbance among the students, and had arrived in the town only a few days before. He, too, had been recommended to Yulia Mihailovna, and she had received him with reverence. I know now that he had only spent one evening in her company before the reading; he had not spoken all that evening, had listened with an equivocal smile to the jests and the general tone of the company surrounding Yulia Mihailovna, and had made an unpleasant impression on every one by his air of haughtiness, and at the same time almost timorous readiness to take offence. It was Yulia Mihailovna herself who had enlisted his services. Now he was walking from corner to corner, and, like Stepan Trofimovitch, was muttering to himself, though he looked on the ground instead of in the looking-glass. He was not trying on smiles, though he often smiled rapaciously. It was obvious that it was useless to speak to him either. He looked about forty, was short and bald, had a greyish beard, and was decently dressed. But what was most interesting about him was that at every turn he took he threw up his right fist, brandished it above his head and suddenly brought it down again as though crushing an antagonist to atoms. He went through this by-play every moment. It made me uncomfortable. I hastened away to listen to Karmazinov.

III

There was a feeling in the hall that something was wrong again. Let me state to begin with that I have the deepest reverence for genius, but why do our geniuses in the decline of their illustrious years behave sometimes exactly like little boys? What though he was Karmazinov, and came forward with as much dignity as five Kammerherrs rolled into one? How could he expect to keep an audience like ours listening for a whole hour to a single paper? I have observed, in fact, that however big a genius a man may be, he can't monopolise the attention of an audience at a frivolous literary matinée for more than twenty minutes with impunity. The entrance of the great writer was received, indeed, with the utmost respect: even the severest elderly men showed signs of approval and interest, and the ladies even displayed some enthusiasm. The applause was brief, however, and somehow uncertain and not unanimous. Yet there was no unseemly behaviour in the back rows, till Karmazinov began to speak, not that anything very bad followed then, but only a sort of misunderstanding. I have mentioned already that he had rather a shrill voice, almost feminine in fact, and at the same time a genuinely aristocratic lisp. He had hardly articulated a few words when someone had the effrontery to laugh aloud—probably some ignorant simpleton who knew nothing of the world, and was congenitally disposed to laughter. But there was nothing like a hostile demonstration; on the contrary people said "sh-h!" and the offender was crushed. But Mr. Karmazinov, with an affected air and intonation, announced that "at first he had declined absolutely to read." (Much need there was to mention it!) "There are some lines which come so deeply from the heart that it is impossible to utter them aloud, so that these holy things cannot be laid before the public"—(Why lay them then?)—"but as he had been begged to do so, he was doing so, and as he was, moreover, laying down his pen forever, and had sworn to write no more, he had written this last farewell; and as he had sworn never, on any inducement, to read anything in public," and so on, and so on, all in that style.

But all that would not have mattered; every one knows what authors' prefaces are like, though, I may observe, that considering the lack of culture of our audience and the irritability of the back rows, all this may have had an influence. Surely it would have been better to have read a little story, a short tale such as he had written in the past—over-elaborate, that is, and affected, but sometimes witty. It would have saved the situation. No, this was quite another story! It was a regular oration! Good heavens, what wasn't there in it! I am positive that it would have reduced to rigidity even a Petersburg audience, let alone ours. Imagine an article that would have filled some thirty pages of print of the most affected, aimless prattle; and to make matters worse, the gentleman read it with a sort of melancholy condescension as though it were a favour, so that it was almost insulting to the audience. The subject.... Who could make it out? It was a sort of description of certain impressions and reminiscences. But of what? And about what? Though the leading intellects of the province did their utmost during the first half of the reading, they could make nothing of it, and they listened to the second part simply out of politeness. A great deal was said about love, indeed, of the love of the genius for some person, but I must admit it made rather an awkward impression. For the great writer to tell us about his first kiss seemed to my mind a little incongruous with his short and fat little figure ... Another thing that was offensive; these kisses did not occur as they do with the rest of mankind. There had to be a framework of gorse (it had to be gorse or some such plant that one must look up in a flora) and there had to be a tint of purple in the sky, such as no mortal had ever observed before, or if some people had seen it, they had never noticed it, but he seemed to say, "I have seen it and am describing it to you, fools, as if it were a most ordinary thing." The tree under which the interesting couple sat had of course to be of an orange colour. They were sitting somewhere in Germany. Suddenly they see Pompey or Cassius on the eve of a battle, and both are penetrated by a thrill of ecstasy. Some wood-nymph squeaked in the bushes. Gluck played the violin among the reeds. The title of the piece he was playing was given in full, but no one knew it, so that one would have had to look it up in a musical dictionary. Meanwhile a fog came on, such a fog, such a fog, that it was more like a million pillows than a fog. And suddenly everything disappears and the great genius is crossing the frozen Volga in a thaw. Two and a half pages are filled with the crossing, and yet he falls through the ice. The genius is drowning—you imagine he was drowned? Not a bit of it; this was simply in order that when he was drowning and at his last gasp, he might catch sight of a bit of ice, the size of a pea, but pure and crystal "as a frozen tear," and in that tear was reflected Germany, or more accurately the sky of Germany, and its iridescent sparkle recalled to his mind the very tear which "dost thou remember, fell from thine eyes when we were sitting under that emerald tree, and thou didst cry out joyfully: 'There is no crime!' 'No,' I said through my tears, 'but if that is so, there are no righteous either.' We sobbed and parted forever." She went off somewhere to the sea coast, while he went to visit some caves, and then he descends and descends and descends for three years under Suharev Tower in Moscow, and suddenly in the very bowels of the earth, he finds in a cave a lamp, and before the lamp a hermit. The hermit is praying. The genius leans against a little barred window, and suddenly hears a sigh. Do you suppose it was the hermit sighing? Much he cares about the hermit! Not a bit of it, this sigh simply reminds him of her first sigh, thirty-seven years before, "in Germany, when, dost thou remember, we sat under an agate tree and thou didst say to me, 'Why love? See ochra is growing all around and I love thee; but the ochra will cease to grow, and I shall cease to love.'" Then the fog comes on again, Hoffman appears on the scene, the wood-nymph whistles a tune from Chopin, and suddenly out of the fog appears Ancus Marcius over the roofs of Rome, wearing a laurel wreath. "A chill of ecstasy ran down our backs and we parted forever"—and so on and so on.

Perhaps I am not reporting it quite right and don't know how to report it, but the drift of the babble was something of that sort. And after all, how disgraceful this passion of our great intellects for jesting in a superior way really is! The great European philosopher, the great man of science, the inventor, the martyr—all these who labour and are heavy laden, are to the great Russian genius no more than so many cooks in his kitchen. He is the master and they come to him, cap in hand, awaiting orders. It is true he jeers superciliously at Russia too, and there is nothing he likes better than exhibiting the bankruptcy of Russia in every relation before the great minds of Europe, but as regards himself, no, he is at a higher level than all the great minds of Europe; they are only material for his jests. He takes another man's idea, tacks on to it its antithesis, and the epigram is made. There is such a thing as crime, there is no such thing as crime; there is no such thing as justice, there are no just men; atheism, Darwinism, the Moscow bells.... But alas, he no longer believes in the Moscow bells; Rome, laurels.... But he has no belief in laurels even.... We have a conventional attack of Byronic spleen, a grimace from Heine, something of Petchorin—and the machine goes on rolling, whistling, at full speed. "But you may praise me, you may praise me, that I like extremely; it's only in a manner of speaking that I lay down the pen; I shall bore you three hundred times more, you'll grow weary of reading me...."

Of course it did not end without trouble; but the worst of it was that it was his own doing. People had for some time begun shuffling their feet, blowing their noses, coughing, and doing everything that people do when a lecturer, whoever he may be, keeps an audience for longer than twenty minutes at a literary matinée. But the genius noticed nothing of all this. He went on lisping and mumbling, without giving a thought to the audience, so that every one began to wonder. Suddenly in a back row a solitary but loud voice was heard:

"Good Lord, what nonsense!"

The exclamation escaped involuntarily, and I am sure was not intended as a demonstration. The man was simply worn out. But Mr. Karmazinov stopped, looked sarcastically at the audience, and suddenly lisped with the deportment of an aggrieved kammerherr.

"I'm afraid I've been boring you dreadfully, gentlemen?"

That was his blunder, that he was the first to speak; for provoking an answer in this way he gave an opening for the rabble to speak, too, and even legitimately, so to say, while if he had restrained himself, people would have gone on blowing their noses and it would have passed off somehow. Perhaps he expected applause in response to his question, but there was no sound of applause; on the contrary, every one seemed to subside and shrink back in dismay.

"You never did see Ancus Marcius, that's all brag," cried a voice that sounded full of irritation and even nervous exhaustion.

"Just so," another voice agreed at once. "There are no such things as ghosts nowadays, nothing but natural science. Look it up in a scientific book."

"Gentlemen, there was nothing I expected less than such objections," said Karmazinov, extremely surprised. The great genius had completely lost touch with his Fatherland in Karlsruhe.

"Nowadays it's outrageous to say that the world stands on three fishes," a young lady snapped out suddenly. "You can't have gone down to the hermit's cave, Karmazinov. And who talks about hermits nowadays?"

"Gentlemen, what surprises me most of all is that you take it all so seriously. However ... however, you are perfectly right. No one has greater respect for truth and realism than I have...."

Though he smiled ironically he was tremendously overcome. His face seemed to express: "I am not the sort of man you think, I am on your side, only praise me, praise me more, as much as possible, I like it extremely...."

"Gentlemen," he cried, completely mortified at last, "I see that my poor poem is quite out of place here. And, indeed, I am out of place here myself, I think."

"You threw at the crow and you hit the cow," some fool, probably drunk, shouted at the top of his voice, and of course no notice ought to have been taken of him. It is true there was a sound of disrespectful laughter.

"A cow, you say?" Karmazinov caught it up at once, his voice grew shriller and shriller. "As for crows and cows, gentlemen, I will refrain. I've too much respect for any audience to permit myself comparisons, however harmless; but I did think ..."

"You'd better be careful, sir," someone shouted from a back row.

"But I had supposed that laying aside my pen and saying farewell to my readers, I should be heard ..."

"No, no, we want to hear you, we want to," a few voices from the front row plucked up spirit to exclaim at last.

"Read, read!" several enthusiastic ladies' voices chimed in, and at last there was an outburst of applause, sparse and feeble, it is true.

"Believe me, Karmazinov, every one looks on it as an honour ..." the marshal's wife herself could not resist saying.

"Mr. Karmazinov!" cried a fresh young voice in the back of the hall suddenly. It was the voice of a very young teacher from the district school who had only lately come among us, an excellent young man, quiet and gentlemanly. He stood up in his place. "Mr. Karmazinov, if I had the happiness to fall in love as you have described to us, I really shouldn't refer to my love in an article intended for public reading...." He flushed red all over.

"Ladies and gentlemen," cried Karmazinov, "I have finished. I will omit the end and withdraw. Only allow me to read the six last lines:

"Yes, dear reader, farewell!" he began at once from the manuscript without sitting down again in his chair. "Farewell, reader; I do not greatly insist on our parting friends; what need to trouble you, indeed. You may abuse me, abuse me as you will if it affords you any satisfaction. But best of all if we forget one another forever. And if you all, readers, were suddenly so kind as to fall on your knees and begin begging me with tears, 'Write, oh, write for us, Karmazinov—for the sake of Russia, for the sake of posterity, to win laurels,' even then I would answer you, thanking you, of course, with every courtesy, 'No, we've had enough of one another, dear fellow-countrymen, merci! It's time we took our separate ways!' Merci, merci, merci!"

Karmazinov bowed ceremoniously, and, as red as though he had been cooked, retired behind the scenes.

"Nobody would go down on their knees; a wild idea!"

"What conceit!"

"That's only humour," someone more reasonable suggested.

"Spare me your humour."

"I call it impudence, gentlemen!"

"Well, he's finished now, anyway!"

"Ech, what a dull show!"

But all these ignorant exclamations in the back rows (though they were confined to the back rows) were drowned in applause from the other half of the audience. They called for Karmazinov. Several ladies with Yulia Mihailovna and the marshal's wife crowded round the platform. In Yulia Mihailovna's hands was a gorgeous laurel wreath resting on another wreath of living roses on a white velvet cushion.

"Laurels!" Karmazinov pronounced with a subtle and rather sarcastic smile. "I am touched, of course, and accept with real emotion this wreath prepared beforehand, but still fresh and unwithered, but I assure you, mesdames, that I have suddenly become so realistic that I feel laurels would in this age be far more appropriate in the hands of a skilful cook than in mine...."

"Well, a cook is more useful," cried the divinity student, who had been at the "meeting" at Virginsky's.

There was some disorder. In many rows people jumped up to get a better view of the presentation of the laurel wreath.

"I'd give another three roubles for a cook this minute," another voice assented loudly, too loudly; insistently, in fact.

"So would I."

"And I."

"Is it possible there's no buffet?..."

"Gentlemen, it's simply a swindle...."

It must be admitted, however, that all these unbridled gentlemen still stood in awe of our higher officials and of the police superintendent, who was present in the hall. Ten minutes later all had somehow got back into their places, but there was not the same good order as before. And it was into this incipient chaos that poor Stepan Trofimovitch was thrust.

IV

I ran out to him behind the scenes once more, and had time to warn him excitedly that in my opinion the game was up, that he had better not appear at all, but had better go home at once on the excuse of his usual ailment, for instance, and I would take off my badge and come with him. At that instant he was on his way to the platform; he stopped suddenly, and haughtily looking me up and down he pronounced solemnly:

"What grounds have you, sir, for thinking me capable of such baseness?"

I drew back. I was as sure as twice two make four that he would not get off without a catastrophe. Meanwhile, as I stood utterly dejected, I saw moving before me again the figure of the professor, whose turn it was to appear after Stepan Trofimovitch, and who kept lifting up his fist and bringing it down again with a swing. He kept walking up and down, absorbed in himself and muttering something to himself with a diabolical but triumphant smile. I somehow almost unintentionally went up to him. I don't know what induced me to meddle again. "Do you know," I said, "judging from many examples, if a lecturer keeps an audience for more than twenty minutes it won't go on listening. No celebrity is able to hold his own for half an hour."

He stopped short and seemed almost quivering with resentment. Infinite disdain was expressed in his countenance.

"Don't trouble yourself," he muttered contemptuously and walked on. At that moment Stepan Trofimovitch's voice rang out in the hall.

"Oh, hang you all," I thought, and ran to the hall.

Stepan Trofimovitch took his seat in the lecturer's chair in the midst of the still persisting disorder. He was greeted by the first rows with looks which were evidently not over-friendly. (Of late, at the club, people almost seemed not to like him, and treated him with much less respect than formerly.) But it was something to the good that he was not hissed. I had had a strange idea in my head ever since the previous day: I kept fancying that he would be received with hisses as soon as he appeared. They scarcely noticed him, however, in the disorder. What could that man hope for if Karmazinov was treated like this? He was pale; it was ten years since he had appeared before an audience. From his excitement and from all that I knew so well in him, it was clear to me that he, too, regarded his present appearance on the platform as a turning-point of his fate, or something of the kind. That was just what I was afraid of. The man was dear to me. And what were my feelings when he opened his lips and I heard his first phrase?

"Ladies and gentlemen," he pronounced suddenly, as though resolved to venture everything, though in an almost breaking voice. "Ladies and gentlemen! Only this morning there lay before me one of the illegal leaflets that have been distributed here lately, and I asked myself for the hundredth time, 'Wherein lies its secret?'"

The whole hall became instantly still, all looks were turned to him, some with positive alarm. There was no denying, he knew how to secure their interest from the first word. Heads were thrust out from behind the scenes; Liputin and Lyamshin listened greedily. Yulia Mihailovna waved to me again.

"Stop him, whatever happens, stop him," she whispered in agitation. I could only shrug my shoulders: how could one stop a man resolved to venture everything? Alas, I understood what was in Stepan Trofimovitch's mind.

"Ha ha, the manifestoes!" was whispered in the audience; the whole hall was stirred.

"Ladies and gentlemen, I've solved the whole mystery. The whole secret of their effect lies in their stupidity." (His eyes flashed.) "Yes, gentlemen, if this stupidity were intentional, pretended and calculated, oh, that would be a stroke of genius! But we must do them justice: they don't pretend anything. It's the barest, most simple-hearted, most shallow stupidity. C'est la bêtise dans son essence la plus pure, quelque chose comme un simple chimique. If it were expressed ever so little more cleverly, every one would see at once the poverty of this shallow stupidity. But as it is, every one is left wondering: no one can believe that it is such elementary stupidity. 'It's impossible that there's nothing more in it,' every one says to himself and tries to find the secret of it, sees a mystery in it, tries to read between the lines—the effect is attained! Oh, never has stupidity been so solemnly rewarded, though it has so often deserved it.... For, en parenthese, stupidity is of as much service to humanity as the loftiest genius...."

"Epigram of 1840" was commented, in a very modest voice, however, but it was followed by a general outbreak of noise and uproar.

"Ladies and gentlemen, hurrah! I propose a toast to stupidity!" cried Stepan Trofimovitch, defying the audience in a perfect frenzy.

I ran up on the pretext of pouring out some water for him.

"Stepan Trofimovitch, leave off, Yulia Mihailovna entreats you to."

"No, you leave me alone, idle young man," he cried out at me at the top of his voice. I ran away. "Messieurs," he went on, "why this excitement, why the outcries of indignation I hear? I have come forward with an olive branch. I bring you the last word, for in this business I have the last word—and we shall be reconciled."

"Down with him!" shouted some.

"Hush, let him speak, let him have his say!" yelled another section. The young teacher was particularly excited; having once brought himself to speak he seemed now unable to be silent.

"Messieurs, the last word in this business—is forgiveness. I, an old man at the end of my life, I solemnly declare that the spirit of life breathes in us still, and there is still a living strength in the young generation. The enthusiasm of the youth of today is as pure and bright as in our age. All that has happened is a change of aim, the replacing of one beauty by another! The whole difficulty lies in the question which is more beautiful, Shakespeare or boots, Raphael or petroleum?"

"It's treachery!" growled some.

"Compromising questions!"

"Agent provocateur!"

"But I maintain," Stepan Trofimovitch shrilled at the utmost pitch of excitement, "I maintain that Shakespeare and Raphael are more precious than the emancipation of the serfs, more precious than Nationalism, more precious than Socialism, more precious than the young generation, more precious than chemistry, more precious than almost all humanity because they are the fruit, the real fruit of all humanity and perhaps the highest fruit that can be. A form of beauty already attained, but for the attaining of which I would not perhaps consent to live.... Oh, heavens!" he cried, clasping his hands, "ten years ago I said the same thing from the platform in Petersburg, exactly the same thing, in the same words, and in just the same way they did not understand it, they laughed and hissed as now; shallow people, what is lacking in you that you cannot understand? But let me tell you, let me tell you, without the English, life is still possible for humanity, without Germany, life is possible, without the Russians it is only too possible, without science, without bread, life is possible—only without beauty it is impossible, for there will be nothing left in the world. That's the secret at the bottom of everything, that's what history teaches! Even science would not exist a moment without beauty—do you know that, you who laugh—it will sink into bondage, you won't invent a nail even!... I won't yield an inch!" he shouted absurdly in confusion, and with all his might banged his fist on the table.

But all the while that he was shrieking senselessly and incoherently, the disorder in the hall increased. Many people jumped up from their seats, some dashed forward, nearer to the platform. It all happened much more quickly than I describe it, and there was no time to take steps, perhaps no wish to, either.

"It's all right for you, with everything found for you, you pampered creatures!" the same divinity student bellowed at the foot of the platform, grinning with relish at Stepan Trofimovitch, who noticed it and darted to the very edge of the platform.

"Haven't I, haven't I just declared that the enthusiasm of the young generation is as pure and bright as it was, and that it is coming to grief through being deceived only in the forms of beauty! Isn't that enough for you? And if you consider that he who proclaims this is a father crushed and insulted, can one—oh, shallow hearts—can one rise to greater heights of impartiality and fairness?... Ungrateful ... unjust.... Why, why can't you be reconciled!"

And he burst into hysterical sobs. He wiped away his dropping tears with his fingers. His shoulders and breast were heaving with sobs. He was lost to everything in the world.

A perfect panic came over the audience, almost all got up from their seats. Yulia Mihailovna, too, jumped up quickly, seizing her husband by the arm and pulling him up too.... The scene was beyond all belief.

"Stepan Trofimovitch!" the divinity student roared gleefully. "There's Fedka the convict wandering about the town and the neighbourhood, escaped from prison. He is a robber and has recently committed another murder. Allow me to ask you: if you had not sold him as a recruit fifteen years ago to pay a gambling debt, that is, more simply, lost him at cards, tell me, would he have got into prison? Would he have cut men's throats now, in his struggle for existence? What do you say, Mr. Æsthete?"

I decline to describe the scene that followed. To begin with there was a furious volley of applause. The applause did not come from all—probably from some fifth part of the audience—but they applauded furiously. The rest of the public made for the exit, but as the applauding part of the audience kept pressing forward towards the platform, there was a regular block. The ladies screamed, some of the girls began to cry and asked to go home. Lembke, standing up by his chair, kept gazing wildly about him. Yulia Mihailovna completely lost her head—for the first time during her career amongst us. As for Stepan Trofimovitch, for the first moment he seemed literally crushed by the divinity student's words, but he suddenly raised his arms as though holding them out above the public and yelled:

"I shake the dust from off my feet and I curse you.... It's the end, the end...."

And turning, he ran behind the scenes, waving his hands menacingly.

"He has insulted the audience!... Verhovensky!" the angry section roared. They even wanted to rush in pursuit of him. It was impossible to appease them, at the moment, any way, and—a final catastrophe broke like a bomb on the assembly and exploded in its midst: the third reader, the maniac who kept waving his fist behind the scenes, suddenly ran on to the platform. He looked like a perfect madman. With a broad, triumphant smile, full of boundless self-confidence, he looked round at the agitated hall and he seemed to be delighted at the disorder. He was not in the least disconcerted at having to speak in such an uproar, on the contrary, he was obviously delighted. This was so obvious that it attracted attention at once.

"What's this now?" people were heard asking. "Who is this? Sh-h! What does he want to say?"

"Ladies and gentlemen," the maniac shouted with all his might, standing at the very edge of the platform and speaking with almost as shrill, feminine a voice as Karmazinov's, but without the aristocratic lisp. "Ladies and gentlemen! Twenty years ago, on the eve of war with half Europe, Russia was regarded as an ideal country by officials of all ranks! Literature was in the service of the censorship; military drill was all that was taught at the universities; the troops were trained like a ballet, and the peasants paid the taxes and were mute under the lash of serfdom. Patriotism meant the wringing of bribes from the quick and the dead. Those who did not take bribes were looked upon as rebels because they disturbed the general harmony. The birch copses were extirpated in support of discipline. Europe trembled.... But never in the thousand years of its senseless existence had Russia sunk to such ignominy...."

He raised his fist, waved it ecstatically and menacingly over his head and suddenly brought it down furiously, as though pounding an adversary to powder. A frantic yell rose from the whole hall, there was a deafening roar of applause; almost half the audience was applauding: their enthusiasm was excusable. Russia was being put to shame publicly, before every one. Who could fail to roar with delight?

"This is the real thing! Come, this is something like! Hurrah! Yes, this is none of your æsthetics!"

The maniac went on ecstatically:

"Twenty years have passed since then. Universities have been opened and multiplied. Military drill has passed into a legend; officers are too few by thousands, the railways have eaten up all the capital and have covered Russia as with a spider's web, so that in another fifteen years one will perhaps get somewhere. Bridges are rarely on fire, and fires in towns occur only at regular intervals, in turn, at the proper season. In the law courts judgments are as wise as Solomon's, and the jury only take bribes through the struggle for existence, to escape starvation. The serfs are free, and flog one another instead of being flogged by the land-owners. Seas and oceans of vodka are consumed to support the budget, and in Novgorod, opposite the ancient and useless St. Sophia, there has been solemnly put up a colossal bronze globe to celebrate a thousand years of disorder and confusion; Europe scowls and begins to be uneasy again.... Fifteen years of reforms! And yet never even in the most grotesque periods of its madness has Russia sunk ..."

The last words could not be heard in the roar of the crowd. One could see him again raise his arm and bring it down triumphantly again. Enthusiasm was beyond all bounds: people yelled, clapped their hands, even some of the ladies shouted: "Enough, you can't beat that!" Some might have been drunk. The orator scanned them all and seemed revelling in his own triumph. I caught a glimpse of Lembke in indescribable excitement, pointing something out to somebody. Yulia Mihailovna, with a pale face, said something in haste to the prince, who had run up to her. But at that moment a group of six men, officials more or less, burst on to the platform, seized the orator and dragged him behind the scenes. I can't understand how he managed to tear himself away from them, but he did escape, darted up to the edge of the platform again and succeeded in shouting again, at the top of his voice, waving his fist: "But never has Russia sunk ..."

But he was dragged away again. I saw some fifteen men dash behind the scenes to rescue him, not crossing the platform but breaking down the light screen at the side of it.... I saw afterwards, though I could hardly believe my eyes, the girl student (Virginsky's sister) leap on to the platform with the same roll under her arm, dressed as before, as plump and rosy as ever, surrounded by two or three women and two or three men, and accompanied by her mortal enemy, the schoolboy. I even caught the phrase:

"Ladies and gentlemen, I've come to call attention to the sufferings of poor students and to rouse them to a general protest ..."

But I ran away. Hiding my badge in my pocket I made my way from the house into the street by back passages which I knew of. First of all, of course, I went to Stepan Trofimovitch's.

CHAPTER II. THE END OF THE FETE

I

HE WOULD NOT SEE ME. He had shut himself up and was writing. At my repeated knocks and appeals he answered through the door:

"My friend, I have finished everything. Who can ask anything more of me?"

"You haven't finished anything, you've only helped to make a mess of the whole thing. For God's sake, no epigrams, Stepan Trofimovitch! Open the door. We must take steps; they may still come and insult you...."

I thought myself entitled to be particularly severe and even rigorous. I was afraid he might be going to do something still more mad. But to my surprise, I met an extraordinary firmness.

"Don't be the first to insult me then. I thank you for the past, but I repeat I've done with all men, good and bad. I am writing to Darya Pavlovna, whom I've forgotten so unpardonably till now. You may take it to her to-morrow, if you like, now merci."

"Stepan Trofimovitch, I assure you that the matter is more serious than you think. Do you think that you've crushed someone there? You've pulverised no one, but have broken yourself to pieces like an empty bottle." (Oh, I was coarse and discourteous, I remember it with regret.) "You've absolutely no reason to write to Darya Pavlovna ... and what will you do with yourself without me? What do you understand about practical life? I expect you are plotting something else? You'll simply come to grief again if you go plotting something more...."

He rose and came close up to the door.

"You've not been long with them, but you've caught the infection of their tone and language. Dieu vous pardonne, mon ami, et Dieu vous garde. But I've always seen in you the germs of delicate feeling, and you will get over it perhaps—après le temps, of course, like all of us Russians. As for what you say about my impracticability, I'll remind you of a recent idea of mine: a whole mass of people in Russia do nothing whatever but attack other people's impracticability with the utmost fury and with the tiresome persistence of flies in the summer, accusing every one of it except themselves. Cher, remember that I am excited, and don't distress me. Once more merci for everything, and let us part like Karmazinov and the public; that is, let us forget each other with as much generosity as we can. He was posing in begging his former readers so earnestly to forget him; quant à moi, I am not so conceited, and I rest my hopes on the youth of your inexperienced heart. How should you remember a useless old man for long? 'Live more,' my friend, as Nastasya wished me on my last name-day (ces pauvres gens ont quelquefois des mots charmants et pleins de philosophie). I do not wish you much happiness—it will bore you. I do not wish you trouble either, but, following the philosophy of the peasant, I will repeat simply 'live more' and try not to be much bored; this useless wish I add from myself. Well, good-bye, and good-bye for good. Don't stand at my door, I will not open it."

He went away and I could get nothing more out of him. In spite of his "excitement," he spoke smoothly, deliberately, with weight, obviously trying to be impressive. Of course he was rather vexed with me and was avenging himself indirectly, possibly even for the yesterday's "prison carts" and "floors that give way." His tears in public that morning, in spite of a triumph of a sort, had put him, he knew, in rather a comic position, and there never was a man more solicitous of dignity and punctilio in his relations with his friends than Stepan Trofimovitch. Oh, I don't blame him. But this fastidiousness and irony which he preserved in spite of all shocks reassured me at the time. A man who was so little different from his ordinary self was, of course, not in the mood at that moment for anything tragic or extraordinary. So I reasoned at the time, and, heavens, what a mistake I made! I left too much out of my reckoning.

In anticipation of events I will quote the few first lines of the letter to Darya Pavlovna, which she actually received the following day:

"Mon enfant, my hand trembles, but I've done with everything. You were not present at my last struggle: you did not come to that matinée, and you did well to stay away. But you will be told that in our Russia, which has grown so poor in men of character, one man had the courage to stand up and, in spite of deadly menaces showered on him from all sides, to tell the fools the truth, that is, that they are fools. Oh, ce sont—des pauvres petits vauriens et rien de plus, des petits—fools—voilà le mot! The die is cast; I am going from this town forever and I know not whither. Every one I loved has turned from me. But you, you are a pure and naïve creature; you, a gentle being whose life has been all but linked with mine at the will of a capricious and imperious heart; you who looked at me perhaps with contempt when I shed weak tears on the eve of our frustrated marriage; you, who cannot in any case look on me except as a comic figure—for you, for you is the last cry of my heart, for you my last duty, for you alone! I cannot leave you forever thinking of me as an ungrateful fool, a churlish egoist, as probably a cruel and ungrateful heart—whom, alas, I cannot forget—is every day describing me to you...."

And so on and so on, four large pages.

Answering his "I won't open" with three bangs with my fist on the door, and shouting after him that I was sure he would send Nastasya for me three times that day, but I would not come, I gave him up and ran off to Yulia Mihailovna.

II

There I was the witness of a revolting scene: the poor woman was deceived to her face, and I could do nothing. Indeed, what could I say to her? I had had time to reconsider things a little and reflect that I had nothing to go upon but certain feelings and suspicious presentiments. I found her in tears, almost in hysterics, with compresses of eau-de-Cologne and a glass of water. Before her stood Pyotr Stepanovitch, who talked without stopping, and the prince, who held his tongue as though it had been under a lock. With tears and lamentations she reproached Pyotr Stepanovitch for his "desertion." I was struck at once by the fact that she ascribed the whole failure, the whole ignominy of the matinée, everything in fact, to Pyotr Stepanovitch's absence.

In him I observed an important change: he seemed a shade too anxious, almost serious.

As a rule he never seemed serious; he was always laughing, even when he was angry, and he was often angry. Oh, he was angry now! He was speaking coarsely, carelessly, with vexation and impatience. He said that he had been taken ill at Gaganov's lodging, where he had happened to go early in the morning. Alas, the poor woman was so anxious to be deceived again! The chief question which I found being discussed was whether the ball, that is, the whole second half of the fête, should or should not take place. Yulia Mihailovna could not be induced to appear at the ball "after the insults she had received that morning"; in other words, her heart was set on being compelled to do so, and by him, by Pyotr Stepanovitch. She looked upon him as an oracle, and I believe if he had gone away she would have taken to her bed at once. But he did not want to go away; he was desperately anxious that the ball should take place and that Yulia Mihailovna should be present at it.

"Come, what is there to cry about? Are you set on having a scene? On venting your anger on somebody? Well, vent it on me; only make haste about it, for the time is passing and you must make up your mind. We made a mess of it with the matinée; we'll pick up on the ball. Here, the prince thinks as I do. Yes, if it hadn't been for the prince, how would things have ended there?"

The prince had been at first opposed to the ball (that is, opposed to Yulia Mihailovna's appearing at it; the ball was bound to go on in any case), but after two or three such references to his opinion he began little by little to grunt his acquiescence.

I was surprised too at the extraordinary rudeness of Pyotr Stepanovitch's tone. Oh, I scout with indignation the contemptible slander which was spread later of some supposed liaison between Yulia Mihailovna and Pyotr Stepanovitch. There was no such thing, nor could there be. He gained his ascendency over her from the first only by encouraging her in her dreams of influence in society and in the ministry, by entering into her plans, by inventing them for her, and working upon her with the grossest flattery. He had got her completely into his toils and had become as necessary to her as the air she breathed. Seeing me, she cried, with flashing eyes:

"Here, ask him. He kept by my side all the while, just like the prince did. Tell me, isn't it plain that it was all a preconcerted plot, a base, designing plot to damage Andrey Antonovitch and me as much as possible? Oh, they had arranged it beforehand. They had a plan! It's a party, a regular party."

"You are exaggerating as usual. You've always some romantic notion in your head. But I am glad to see Mr.…" (He pretended to have forgotten my name.) "He'll give us his opinion."

"My opinion," I hastened to put in, "is the same as Yulia Mihailovna's. The plot is only too evident. I have brought you these ribbons, Yulia Mihailovna. Whether the ball is to take place or not is not my business, for it's not in my power to decide; but my part as steward is over. Forgive my warmth, but I can't act against the dictates of common sense and my own convictions."

"You hear! You hear!" She clasped her hands.

"I hear, and I tell you this." He turned to me. "I think you must have eaten something which has made you all delirious. To my thinking, nothing has happened, absolutely nothing but what has happened before and is always liable to happen in this town. A plot, indeed! It was an ugly failure, disgracefully stupid. But where's the plot? A plot against Yulia Mihailovna, who has spoiled them and protected them and fondly forgiven them all their schoolboy pranks! Yulia Mihailovna! What have I been hammering into you for the last month continually? What did I warn you? What did you want with all these people—what did you want with them? What induced you to mix yourself up with these fellows? What was the motive, what was the object of it? To unite society? But, mercy on us! will they ever be united?"

"When did you warn me? On the contrary, you approved of it, you even insisted on it.... I confess I am so surprised.... You brought all sorts of strange people to see me yourself."

"On the contrary, I opposed you; I did not approve of it. As for bringing them to see you, I certainly did, but only after they'd got in by dozens and only of late to make up 'the literary quadrille'—we couldn't get on without these rogues. Only I don't mind betting that a dozen or two more of the same sort were let in without tickets to-day."

"Not a doubt of it," I agreed.

"There, you see, you are agreeing already. Think what the tone has been lately here—I mean in this wretched town. It's nothing but insolence, impudence; it's been a crying scandal all the time. And who's been encouraging it? Who's screened it by her authority? Who's upset them all? Who has made all the small fry huffy? All their family secrets are caricatured in your album. Didn't you pat them on the back, your poets and caricaturists? Didn't you let Lyamshin kiss your hand? Didn't a divinity student abuse an actual state councillor in your presence and spoil his daughter's dress with his tarred boots? Now, can you wonder that the public is set against you?"

"But that's all your doing, yours! Oh, my goodness!"

"No, I warned you. We quarrelled. Do you hear, we quarrelled?"

"Why, you are lying to my face!"

"Of course it's easy for you to say that. You need a victim to vent your wrath on. Well, vent it on me as I've said already. I'd better appeal to you, Mr...." (He was still unable to recall my name.) "We'll reckon on our fingers. I maintain that, apart from Liputin, there was nothing preconcerted, nothing! I will prove it, but first let us analyse Liputin. He came forward with that fool Lebyadkin's verses. Do you maintain that that was a plot? But do you know it might simply have struck Liputin as a clever thing to do. Seriously, seriously. He simply came forward with the idea of making every one laugh and entertaining them—his protectress Yulia Mihailovna first of all. That was all. Don't you believe it? Isn't that in keeping with all that has been going on here for the last month? Do you want me to tell the whole truth? I declare that under other circumstances it might have gone off all right. It was a coarse joke—well, a bit strong, perhaps; but it was amusing, you know, wasn't it?"

"What! You think what Liputin did was clever?" Yulia Mihailovna cried in intense indignation. "Such stupidity, such tactlessness, so contemptible, so mean! It was intentional! Oh, you are saying it on purpose! I believe after that you are in the plot with them yourself."

"Of course I was behind the scenes, I was in hiding, I set it all going. But if I were in the plot—understand that, anyway—it wouldn't have ended with Liputin. So according to you I had arranged with my papa too that he should cause such a scene on purpose? Well, whose fault is it that my papa was allowed to read? Who tried only yesterday to prevent you from allowing it, only yesterday?"

"Oh, hier il avait tant d'esprit, I was so reckoning on him; and then he has such manners. I thought with him and Karmazinov ... Only think!"

"Yes, only think. But in spite of tant d'esprit papa has made things worse, and if I'd known beforehand that he'd make such a mess of it, I should certainly not have persuaded you yesterday to keep the goat out of the kitchen garden, should I—since I am taking part in this conspiracy against your fête that you are so positive about? And yet I did try to dissuade you yesterday; I tried to because I foresaw it. To foresee everything was, of course, impossible; he probably did not know himself a minute before what he would fire off—these nervous old men can't be reckoned on like other people. But you can still save the situation: to satisfy the public, send to him to-morrow by administrative order, and with all the ceremonies, two doctors to inquire into his health. Even to-day, in fact, and take him straight to the hospital and apply cold compresses. Every one would laugh, anyway, and see that there was nothing to take offence at. I'll tell people about it in the evening at the ball, as I am his son. Karmazinov is another story. He was a perfect ass and dragged out his article for a whole hour. He certainly must have been in the plot with me! 'I'll make a mess of it too,' he thought, 'to damage Yulia Mihailovna.'"

"Oh, Karmazinov! Quelle honte! I was burning, burning with shame for his audience!"

"Well, I shouldn't have burnt, but have cooked him instead. The audience was right, you know. Who was to blame for Karmazinov, again? Did I foist him upon you? Was I one of his worshippers? Well, hang him! But the third maniac, the political—that's a different matter. That was every one's blunder, not only my plot."

"Ah, don't speak of it! That was awful, awful! That was my fault, entirely my fault!"

"Of course it was, but I don't blame you for that. No one can control them, these candid souls! You can't always be safe from them, even in Petersburg. He was recommended to you, and in what terms too! So you will admit that you are bound to appear at the ball to-night. It's an important business. It was you put him on to the platform. You must make it plain now to the public that you are not in league with him, that the fellow is in the hands of the police, and that you were in some inexplicable way deceived. You ought to declare with indignation that you were the victim of a madman. Because he is a madman and nothing more. That's how you must put it about him. I can't endure these people who bite. I say worse things perhaps, but not from the platform, you know. And they are talking about a senator too."

"What senator? Who's talking?"

"I don't understand it myself, you know. Do you know anything about a senator, Yulia Mihailovna?"

"A senator?"

"You see, they are convinced that a senator has been appointed to be governor here, and that you are being superseded from Petersburg. I've heard it from lots of people."

"I've heard it too," I put in.

"Who said so?" asked Yulia Mihailovna, flushing all over.

"You mean, who said so first? How can I tell? But there it is, people say so. Masses of people are saying so. They were saying so yesterday particularly. They are all very serious about it, though I can't make it out. Of course the more intelligent and competent don't talk, but even some of those listen."

"How mean! And … how stupid!"

"Well, that's just why you must make your appearance, to show these fools."

"I confess I feel myself that it's my duty, but … what if there's another disgrace in store for us? What if people don't come? No one will come, you know, no one!"

"How hot you are! They not come! What about the new clothes? What about the girls' dresses? I give you up as a woman after that! Is that your knowledge of human nature?"

"The marshal's wife won't come, she won't."

"But, after all, what has happened? Why won't they come?" he cried at last with angry impatience.

"Ignominy, disgrace—that's what's happened. I don't know what to call it, but after it I can't face people."

"Why? How are you to blame for it, after all? Why do you take the blame of it on yourself? Isn't it rather the fault of the audience, of your respectable residents, your patresfamilias? They ought to have controlled the roughs and the rowdies—for it was all the work of roughs and rowdies, nothing serious. You can never manage things with the police alone in any society, anywhere. Among us every one asks for a special policeman to protect him wherever he goes. People don't understand that society must protect itself. And what do our patresfamilias, the officials, the wives and daughters, do in such cases? They sit quiet and sulk. In fact there's not enough social initiative to keep the disorderly in check."

"Ah, that's the simple truth! They sit quiet, sulk and … gaze about them."

"And if it's the truth, you ought to say so aloud, proudly, sternly, just to show that you are not defeated, to those respectable residents and mothers of families. Oh, you can do it; you have the gift when your head is clear. You will gather them round you and say it aloud. And then a paragraph in the Voice and the Financial News. Wait a bit, I'll undertake it myself, I'll arrange it all for you. Of course there must be more superintendence: you must look after the buffet; you must ask the prince, you must ask Mr.… You must not desert us, monsieur, just when we have to begin all over again. And finally, you must appear arm-in-arm with Andrey Antonovitch.… How is Andrey Antonovitch?"

"Oh, how unjustly, how untruly, how cruelly you have always judged that angelic man!"

Yulia Mihailovna cried in a sudden, outburst, almost with tears, putting her handkerchief to her eyes.

Pyotr Stepanovitch was positively taken aback for the moment. "Good heavens! I.... What have I said? I've always ..."

"You never have, never! You have never done him justice."

"There's no understanding a woman," grumbled Pyotr Stepanovitch, with a wry smile.

"He is the most sincere, the most delicate, the most angelic of men! The most kind-hearted of men!"

"Well, really, as for kind-heartedness ... I've always done him justice...."

"Never! But let us drop it. I am too awkward in my defence of him. This morning that little Jesuit, the marshal's wife, also dropped some sarcastic hints about what happened yesterday."

"Oh, she has no thoughts to spare for yesterday now, she is full of to-day. And why are you so upset at her not coming to the ball to-night? Of course, she won't come after getting mixed up in such a scandal. Perhaps it's not her fault, but still her reputation ... her hands are soiled."

"What do you mean; I don't understand? Why are her hands soiled?" Yulia Mihailovna looked at him in perplexity.

"I don't vouch for the truth of it, but the town is ringing with the story that it was she brought them together."

"What do you mean? Brought whom together?"

"What, do you mean to say you don't know?" he exclaimed with well-simulated wonder. "Why Stavrogin and Lizaveta Nikolaevna."

"What? How?" we all cried out at once.

"Is it possible you don't know? Phew! Why, it is quite a tragic romance: Lizaveta Nikolaevna was pleased to get out of that lady's carriage and get straight into Stavrogin's carriage, and slipped off with 'the latter' to Skvoreshniki in full daylight. Only an hour ago, hardly an hour."

We were flabbergasted. Of course we fell to questioning him, but to our wonder, although he "happened" to be a witness of the scene himself, he could give us no detailed account of it. The thing seemed to have happened like this: when the marshal's wife was driving Liza and Mavriky Nikolaevitch from the matinée to the house of Praskovya Ivanovna (whose legs were still bad) they saw a carriage waiting a short distance, about twenty-five paces, to one side of the front door. When Liza jumped out, she ran straight to this carriage; the door was flung open and shut again; Liza called to Mavriky Nikolaevitch, "Spare me," and the carriage drove off at full speed to Skvoreshniki. To our hurried questions whether it was by arrangement? Who was in the carriage? Pyotr Stepanovitch answered that he knew nothing about it; no doubt it had been arranged, but that he did not see Stavrogin himself; possibly the old butler, Alexey Yegorytch, might have been in the carriage. To the question "How did he come to be there, and how did he know for a fact that she had driven to Skvoreshniki?" he answered that he happened to be passing and, at seeing Liza, he had run up to the carriage (and yet he could not make out who was in it, an inquisitive man like him!) and that Mavriky Nikolaevitch, far from setting off in pursuit, had not even tried to stop Liza, and had even laid a restraining hand on the marshal's wife, who was shouting at the top of her voice: "She is going to Stavrogin, to Stavrogin." At this point I lost patience, and cried furiously to Pyotr Stepanovitch:

"It's all your doing, you rascal! This was what you were doing this morning. You helped Stavrogin, you came in the carriage, you helped her into it … it was you, you, you! Yulia Mihailovna, he is your enemy; he will be your ruin too! Beware of him!"

And I ran headlong out of the house. I wonder myself and cannot make out to this day how I came to say that to him. But I guessed quite right: it had all happened almost exactly as I said, as appeared later. What struck me most was the obviously artificial way in which he broke the news. He had not told it at once on entering the house as an extraordinary piece of news, but pretended that we knew without his telling us which was impossible in so short a time. And if we had known it, we could not possibly have refrained from mentioning it till he introduced the subject. Besides, he could not have heard yet that the town was "ringing with gossip" about the marshal's wife in so short a time. Besides, he had once or twice given a vulgar, frivolous smile as he told the story, probably considering that we were fools and completely taken in.

But I had no thought to spare for him; the central fact I believed, and ran from Yulia Mihailovna's, beside myself. The catastrophe cut me to the heart. I was wounded almost to tears; perhaps I did shed some indeed. I was at a complete loss what to do. I rushed to Stepan Trofimovitch's, but the vexatious man still refused to open the door. Nastasya informed me, in a reverent whisper, that he had gone to bed, but I did not believe it. At Liza's house, I succeeded in questioning the servants. They confirmed the story of the elopement, but knew nothing themselves. There was great commotion in the house; their mistress had been attacked by fainting fits, and Mavriky Nikolaevitch was with her. I did not feel it possible to ask for Mavriky Nikolaevitch. To my inquiries about Pyotr Stepanovitch they told me that he had been in and out continually of late, sometimes twice in the day. The servants were sad, and showed particular respectfulness in speaking of Liza; they were fond of her. That she was ruined, utterly ruined, I did not doubt; but the psychological aspect of the matter I was utterly unable to understand, especially after her scene with Stavrogin the previous day. To run about the town and inquire at the houses of acquaintances, who would, of course, by now have heard the news and be rejoicing at it, seemed to me revolting, besides being humiliating for Liza. But, strange to say, I ran to see Darya Pavlovna, though I was not admitted (no one had been admitted into the house since the previous morning). I don't know what I could have said to her and what made me run to her. From her I went to her brother's. Shatov listened sullenly and in silence. I may observe that I found him more gloomy than I had ever seen him before; he was awfully preoccupied and seemed only to listen to me with an effort. He said scarcely anything and began walking up and down his cell from corner to corner, treading more noisily than usual. As I was going down the stairs he shouted after me to go to Liputin's: "There you'll hear everything." Yet I did not go to Liputin's, but after I'd gone a good way towards home I turned back to Shatov's again, and, half opening the door without going in, suggested to him laconically and with no kind of explanation, "Won't you go to Marya Timofyevna to-day?" At this Shatov swore at me, and I went away. I note here that I may not forget it that he did purposely go that evening to the other end of the town to see Marya Timofyevna, whom he had not seen for some time. He found her in excellent health and spirits and Lebyadkin dead drunk, asleep on the sofa in the first room. This was at nine o'clock. He told me so himself next day when we met for a moment in the street. Before ten o'clock I made up my mind to go to the ball, but not in the capacity of a steward (besides my rosette had been left at Yulia Mihailovna's). I was tempted by irresistible curiosity to listen, without asking any questions, to what people were saying in the town about all that had happened. I wanted, too, to have a look at Yulia Mihailovna, if only at a distance. I reproached myself greatly that I had left her so abruptly that afternoon.

III

All that night, with its almost grotesque incidents, and the terrible dénouement that followed in the early morning, still seems to me like a hideous nightmare, and is, for me at least, the most painful chapter in my chronicle. I was late for the ball, and it was destined to end so quickly that I arrived not long before it was over. It was eleven o'clock when I reached the entrance of the marshal's house, where the same White Hall in which the matinée had taken place had, in spite of the short interval between, been cleared and made ready to serve as the chief ballroom for the whole town, as we expected, to dance in. But far as I had been that morning from expecting the ball to be a success, I had had no presentiment of the full truth. Not one family of the higher circles appeared; even the subordinate officials of rather more consequence were absent—and this was a very striking fact. As for ladies and girls, Pyotr Stepanovitch's arguments (the duplicity of which was obvious now) turned out to be utterly incorrect: exceedingly few had come; to four men there was scarcely one lady—and what ladies they were! Regimental ladies of a sort, three doctors' wives with their daughters, two or three poor ladies from the country, the seven daughters and the niece of the secretary whom I have mentioned already, some wives of tradesmen, of post-office clerks and other small fry—was this what Yulia Mihailovna expected? Half the tradespeople even were absent. As for the men, in spite of the complete absence of all persons of consequence, there was still a crowd of them, but they made a doubtful and suspicious impression. There were, of course, some quiet and respectful officers with their wives, some of the most docile fathers of families, like that secretary, for instance, the father of his seven daughters. All these humble, insignificant people had come, as one of these gentlemen expressed it, because it was "inevitable." But, on the other hand, the mass of free-and-easy people and the mass too of those whom Pyotr Stepanovitch and I had suspected of coming in without tickets, seemed even bigger than in the afternoon. So far they were all sitting in the refreshment bar, and had gone straight there on arriving, as though it were the meeting-place they had agreed upon. So at least it seemed to me. The refreshment bar had been placed in a large room, the last of several opening out of one another. Here Prohoritch was installed with all the attractions of the club cuisine and with a tempting display of drinks and dainties. I noticed several persons whose coats were almost in rags and whose get-up was altogether suspicious and utterly unsuitable for a ball. They had evidently been with great pains brought to a state of partial sobriety which would not last long; and goodness knows where they had been brought from, they were not local people. I knew, of course, that it was part of Yulia Mihailovna's idea that the ball should be of the most democratic character, and that "even working people and shopmen should not be excluded if any one of that class chanced to pay for a ticket." She could bravely utter such words in her committee with absolute security that none of the working people of our town, who all lived in extreme poverty, would dream of taking a ticket. But in spite of the democratic sentiments of the committee, I could hardly believe that such sinister-looking and shabby people could have been admitted in the regular way. But who could have admitted them, and with what object? Lyamshin and Liputin had already been deprived of their steward's rosettes, though they were present at the ball, as they were taking part in the "literary quadrille." But, to my amazement, Liputin's place was taken by the divinity student, who had caused the greatest scandal at the matinée by his skirmish with Stepan Trofimovitch; and Lyamshin's was taken by Pyotr Stepanovitch himself. What was to be looked for under the circumstances?

I tried to listen to the conversation. I was struck by the wildness of some ideas I heard expressed. It was maintained in one group, for instance, that Yulia Mihailovna had arranged Liza's elopement with Stavrogin and had been paid by the latter for doing so. Even the sum paid was mentioned. It was asserted that she had arranged the whole fête with a view to it, and that that was the reason why half the town had not turned up at the ball, and that Lembke himself was so upset about it that "his mind had given way," and that, crazy as he was, "she had got him in tow." There was a great deal of laughter too, hoarse, wild and significant. Every one was criticising the ball, too, with great severity, and abusing Yulia Mihailovna without ceremony. In fact it was disorderly, incoherent, drunken and excited babble, so it was difficult to put it together and make anything of it. At the same time there were simple-hearted people enjoying themselves at the refreshment-bar; there were even some ladies of the sort who are surprised and frightened at nothing, very genial and festive, chiefly military ladies with their husbands. They made parties at the little tables, were drinking tea, and were very merry. The refreshment-bar made a snug refuge for almost half of the guests. Yet in a little time all this mass of people must stream into the ballroom. It was horrible to think of it!

Meanwhile the prince had succeeded in arranging three skimpy quadrilles in the White Hall. The young ladies were dancing, while their parents were enjoying watching them. But many of these respectable persons had already begun to think how they could, after giving their girls a treat, get off in good time before "the trouble began." Absolutely every one was convinced that it certainly would begin. It would be difficult for me to describe Yulia Mihailovna's state of mind. I did not talk to her though I went close up to her. She did not respond to the bow I made her on entering; she did not notice me (really did not notice). There was a painful look in her face and a contemptuous and haughty though restless and agitated expression in her eyes. She controlled herself with evident suffering—for whose sake, with what object? She certainly ought to have gone away, still more to have got her husband away, and she remained! From her face one could see that her eyes were "fully opened," and that it was useless for her to expect any thing more. She did not even summon Pyotr Stepanovitch (he seemed to avoid her; I saw him in the refreshment-room, he was extremely lively). But she remained at the ball and did not let Andrey Antonovitch leave her side for a moment. Oh, up to the very last moment, even that morning she would have repudiated any hint about his health with genuine indignation. But now her eyes were to be opened on this subject too. As for me, I thought from the first glance that Andrey Antonovitch looked worse than he had done in the morning. He seemed to be plunged into a sort of oblivion and hardly to know where he was. Sometimes he looked about him with unexpected severity—at me, for instance, twice. Once he tried to say something; he began loudly and audibly but did not finish the sentence, throwing a modest old clerk who happened to be near him almost into a panic. But even this humble section of the assembly held sullenly and timidly aloof from Yulia Mihailovna and at the same time turned upon her husband exceedingly strange glances, open and staring, quite out of keeping with their habitually submissive demeanour.

"Yes, that struck me, and I suddenly began to guess about Andrey Antonovitch," Yulia Mihailovna confessed to me afterwards.

Yes, she was to blame again! Probably when after my departure she had settled with Pyotr Stepanovitch that there should be a ball and that she should be present she must have gone again to the study where Andrey Antonovitch was sitting, utterly "shattered" by the matinée; must again have used all her fascinations to persuade him to come with her. But what misery she must have been in now! And yet she did not go away. Whether it was pride or simply she lost her head, I do not know. In spite of her haughtiness, she attempted with smiles and humiliation to enter into conversation with some ladies, but they were confused, confined themselves to distrustful monosyllables, "Yes" and "No," and evidently avoided her.

The only person of undoubted consequence who was present at the ball was that distinguished general whom I have described already, the one who after Stavrogin's duel with Gaganov opened the door to public impatience at the marshal's wife's. He walked with an air of dignity through the rooms, looked about, and listened, and tried to appear as though he had come rather for the sake of observation than for the sake of enjoying himself.... He ended by establishing himself beside Yulia Mihailovna and not moving a step away from her, evidently trying to keep up her spirits, and reassure her. He certainly was a most kind-hearted man, of very high rank, and so old that even compassion from him was not wounding. But to admit to herself that this old gossip was venturing to pity her and almost to protect her, knowing that he was doing her honour by his presence, was very vexatious. The general stayed by her and never ceased chattering.

"They say a town can't go on without seven righteous men ... seven, I think it is, I am not sure of the number fixed.... I don't know how many of these seven, the certified righteous of the town ... have the honour of being present at your ball. Yet in spite of their presence I begin to feel unsafe. Vous me pardonnez, charmante dame, n'est-ce pas? I speak allegorically, but I went into the refreshment-room and I am glad I escaped alive.... Our priceless Prohoritch is not in his place there, and I believe his bar will be destroyed before morning. But I am laughing. I am only waiting to see what the 'literary quadrille' is going to be like, and then home to bed. You must excuse a gouty old fellow. I go early to bed, and I would advise you too to go 'by-by,' as they say aux enfants. I've come, you know, to have a look at the pretty girls ... whom, of course, I could meet nowhere in such profusion as here. They all live beyond the river and I don't drive out so far. There's a wife of an officer ... in the chasseurs I believe he is ... who is distinctly pretty, distinctly, and ... she knows it herself. I've talked to the sly puss; she is a sprightly one ... and the girls too are fresh-looking; but that's all, there's nothing but freshness. Still, it's a pleasure to look at them. There are some rosebuds, but their lips are thick. As a rule there's an irregularity about female beauty in Russia, and … they are a little like buns.… vous me pardonnez, n'est-ce pas? … with good eyes, however, laughing eyes.… These rose buds are charming for two years when they are young … even for three … then they broaden out and are spoilt forever … producing in their husbands that deplorable indifference which does so much to promote the woman movement … that is, if I understand it correctly.… H'm! It's a fine hall; the rooms are not badly decorated. It might be worse. The music might be much worse.… I don't say it ought to have been. What makes a bad impression is that there are so few ladies. I say nothing about the dresses. It's bad that that chap in the grey trousers should dare to dance the cancan so openly. I can forgive him if he does it in the gaiety of his heart, and since he is the local chemist.… Still, eleven o'clock is a bit early even for chemists. There were two fellows fighting in the refreshment-bar and they weren't turned out. At eleven o'clock people ought to be turned out for fighting, whatever the standard of manners.… Three o'clock is a different matter; then one has to make concessions to public opinion—if only this ball survives till three o'clock. Varvara Petrovna has not kept her word, though, and hasn't sent flowers. H'm! She has no thoughts for flowers, pauvre mère! And poor Liza! Have you heard? They say it's a mysterious story … and Stavrogin is to the front again.… H'm! I would have gone home to bed … I can hardly keep my eyes open. But when is this 'literary quadrille' coming on?"

At last the "literary quadrille" began. Whenever of late there had been conversation in the town on the ball it had invariably turned on this literary quadrille, and as no one could imagine what it would be like, it aroused extraordinary curiosity. Nothing could be more unfavourable to its chance of success, and great was the disappointment.

The side doors of the White Hall were thrown open and several masked figures appeared. The public surrounded them eagerly. All the occupants of the refreshment-bar trooped to the last man into the hall. The masked figures took their places for the dance. I succeeded in making my way to the front and installed myself just behind Yulia Mihailovna, Von Lembke, and the general. At this point Pyotr Stepanovitch, who had kept away till that time, skipped up to Yulia Mihailovna.

"I've been in the refreshment-room all this time, watching," he whispered, with the air of a guilty schoolboy, which he, however, assumed on purpose to irritate her even more. She turned crimson with anger.

"You might give up trying to deceive me now at least, insolent man!" broke from her almost aloud, so that it was heard by other people. Pyotr Stepanovitch skipped away extremely well satisfied with himself.

It would be difficult to imagine a more pitiful, vulgar, dull and insipid allegory than this "literary quadrille." Nothing could be imagined less appropriate to our local society. Yet they say it was Karmazinov's idea. It was Liputin indeed who arranged it with the help of the lame teacher who had been at the meeting at Virginsky's. But Karmazinov had given the idea and had, it was said, meant to dress up and to take a special and prominent part in it. The quadrille was made up of six couples of masked figures, who were not in fancy dress exactly, for their clothes were like every one else's. Thus, for instance, one short and elderly gentleman wearing a dress-coat—in fact, dressed like every one else—wore a venerable grey beard, tied on (and this constituted his disguise). As he danced he pounded up and down, taking tiny and rapid steps on the same spot with a stolid expression of countenance. He gave vent to sounds in a subdued but husky bass, and this huskiness was meant to suggest one of the well-known papers. Opposite this figure danced two giants, X and Z, and these letters were pinned on their coats, but what the letters meant remained unexplained. "Honest Russian thought" was represented by a middle-aged gentleman in spectacles, dress-coat and gloves, and wearing fetters (real fetters). Under his arm he had a portfolio containing papers relating to some "case." To convince the sceptical, a letter from abroad testifying to the honesty of "honest Russian thought" peeped out of his pocket. All this was explained by the stewards, as the letter which peeped out of his pocket could not be read. "Honest Russian thought" had his right hand raised and in it held a glass as though he wanted to propose a toast. In a line with him on each side tripped a crop-headed Nihilist girl; while vis-à-vis danced another elderly gentleman in a dress-coat with a heavy cudgel in his hand. He was meant to represent a formidable periodical (not a Petersburg one), and seemed to be saying, "I'll pound you to a jelly." But in spite of his cudgel he could not bear the spectacles of "honest Russian thought" fixed upon him and tried to look away, and when he did the pas de deux, he twisted, turned, and did not know what to do with himself—so terrible, probably, were the stings of his conscience! I don't remember all the absurd tricks they played, however; it was all in the same style, so that I felt at last painfully ashamed. And this same expression, as it were, of shame was reflected in the whole public, even on the most sullen figures that had come out of the refreshment-room. For some time all were silent and gazed with angry perplexity. When a man is ashamed he generally begins to get angry and is disposed to be cynical. By degrees a murmur arose in the audience.

"What's the meaning of it?" a man who had come in from the refreshment-room muttered in one of the groups.

"It's silly."

"It's something literary. It's a criticism of the Voice."

"What's that to me?"

From another group:

"Asses!"

"No, they are not asses; it's we who are the asses."

"Why are you an ass?"

"I am not an ass."

"Well, if you are not, I am certainly not."

From a third group:

"We ought to give them a good smacking and send them flying."

"Pull down the hall!"

From a fourth group:

"I wonder the Lembkes are not ashamed to look on!"

"Why should they be ashamed? You are not."

"Yes, I am ashamed, and he is the governor."

"And you are a pig."

"I've never seen such a commonplace ball in my life," a lady observed viciously, quite close to Yulia Mihailovna, obviously with the intention of being overheard. She was a stout lady of forty with rouge on her cheeks, wearing a bright-coloured silk dress. Almost every one in the town knew her, but no one received her. She was the widow of a civil councillor, who had left her a wooden house and a small pension; but she lived well and kept horses. Two months previously she had called on Yulia Mihailovna, but the latter had not received her.

"That might have been foreseen," she added, looking insolently into Yulia Mihailovna's face.

"If you could foresee it, why did you come?" Yulia Mihailovna could not resist saying.

"Because I was too simple," the sprightly lady answered instantly, up in arms and eager for the fray; but the general intervened.

"Chère dame"—he bent over to Yulia Mihailovna—"you'd really better be going. We are only in their way and they'll enjoy themselves thoroughly without us. You've done your part, you've opened the ball, now leave them in peace. And Andrey Antonovitch doesn't seem to be feeling quite satisfactorily.... To avoid trouble."

But it was too late.

All through the quadrille Andrey Antonovitch gazed at the dancers with a sort of angry perplexity, and when he heard the comments of the audience he began looking about him uneasily. Then for the first time he caught sight of some of the persons who had come from the refreshment-room; there was an expression of extreme wonder in his face. Suddenly there was a loud roar of laughter at a caper that was cut in the quadrille. The editor of the "menacing periodical, not a Petersburg one," who was dancing with the cudgel in his hands, felt utterly unable to endure the spectacled gaze of "honest Russian thought," and not knowing how to escape it, suddenly in the last figure advanced to meet him standing on his head, which was meant, by the way, to typify the continual turning upside down of common sense by the menacing non-Petersburg gazette. As Lyamshin was the only one who could walk standing on his head, he had undertaken to represent the editor with the cudgel. Yulia Mihailovna had had no idea that anyone was going to walk on his head. "They concealed that from me, they concealed it," she repeated to me afterwards in despair and indignation. The laughter from the crowd was, of course, provoked not by the allegory, which interested no one, but simply by a man's walking on his head in a swallow-tail coat. Lembke flew into a rage and shook with fury.

"Rascal!" he cried, pointing to Lyamshin, "take hold of the scoundrel, turn him over ... turn his legs ... his head ... so that his head's up ... up!"

Lyamshin jumped on to his feet. The laughter grew louder.

"Turn out all the scoundrels who are laughing!" Lembke prescribed suddenly.

There was an angry roar and laughter in the crowd.

"You can't do like that, your Excellency."

"You mustn't abuse the public."

"You are a fool yourself!" a voice cried suddenly from a corner.

"Filibusters!" shouted someone from the other end of the room.

Lembke looked round quickly at the shout and turned pale. A vacant smile came on to his lips, as though he suddenly understood and remembered something.

"Gentlemen," said Yulia Mihailovna, addressing the crowd which was pressing round them, as she drew her husband away—"gentlemen, excuse Andrey Antonovitch. Andrey Antonovitch is unwell … excuse … forgive him, gentlemen."

I positively heard her say "forgive him." It all happened very quickly. But I remember for a fact that a section of the public rushed out of the hall immediately after those words of Yulia Mihailovna's as though panic-stricken. I remember one hysterical, tearful feminine shriek:

"Ach, the same thing again!"

And in the retreat of the guests, which was almost becoming a crush, another bomb exploded exactly as in the afternoon.

"Fire! All the riverside quarter is on fire!"

I don't remember where this terrible cry rose first, whether it was first raised in the hall, or whether someone ran upstairs from the entry, but it was followed by such alarm that I can't attempt to describe it. More than half the guests at the ball came from the quarter beyond the river, and were owners or occupiers of wooden houses in that district. They rushed to the windows, pulled back the curtains in a flash, and tore down the blinds. The riverside was in flames. The fire, it is true, was only beginning, but it was in flames in three separate places—and that was what was alarming.

"Arson! The Shpigulin men!" roared the crowd.

I remember some very characteristic exclamations:

"I've had a presentiment in my heart that there'd be arson, I've had a presentiment of it these last few days!"

"The Shpigulin men, the Shpigulin men, no one else!"

"We were all lured here on purpose to set fire to it!"

This last most amazing exclamation came from a woman; it was an unintentional involuntary shriek of a housewife whose goods were burning. Every one rushed for the door. I won't describe the crush in the vestibule over sorting out cloaks, shawls, and pelisses, the shrieks of the frightened women, the weeping of the young ladies. I doubt whether there was any theft, but it was no wonder that in such disorder some went away without their wraps because they were unable to find them, and this grew into a legend with many additions, long preserved in the town. Lembke and Yulia Mihailovna were almost crushed by the crowd at the doors.

"Stop, every one! Don't let anyone out!" yelled Lembke, stretching out his arms menacingly towards the crowding people.

"Every one without exception to be strictly searched at once!"

A storm of violent oaths rose from the crowd.

"Andrey Antonovitch! Andrey Antonovitch!" cried Yulia Mihailovna in complete despair.

"Arrest her first!" shouted her husband, pointing his finger at her threateningly. "Search her first! The ball was arranged with a view to the fire...."

She screamed and fell into a swoon. (Oh, there was no doubt of its being a real one.) The general, the prince, and I rushed to her assistance; there were others, even among the ladies, who helped us at that difficult moment. We carried the unhappy woman out of this hell to her carriage, but she only regained consciousness as she reached the house, and her first utterance was about Andrey Antonovitch again. With the destruction of all her fancies, the only thing left in her mind was Andrey Antonovitch. They sent for a doctor. I remained with her for a whole hour; the prince did so too. The general, in an access of generous feeling (though he had been terribly scared), meant to remain all night "by the bedside of the unhappy lady," but within ten minutes he fell asleep in an arm-chair in the drawing-room while waiting for the doctor, and there we left him.

The chief of the police, who had hurried from the ball to the fire, had succeeded in getting Andrey Antonovitch out of the hall after us, and attempted to put him into Yulia Mihailovna's carriage, trying all he could to persuade his Excellency "to seek repose." But I don't know why he did not insist. Andrey Antonovitch, of course, would not hear of repose, and was set on going to the fire; but that was not a sufficient reason. It ended in his taking him to the fire in his droshky. He told us afterwards that Lembke was gesticulating all the way and "shouting orders that it was impossible to obey owing to their unusualness." It was officially reported later on that his Excellency had at that time been in a delirious condition "owing to a sudden fright."

There is no need to describe how the ball ended. A few dozen rowdy fellows, and with them some ladies, remained in the hall. There were no police present. They would not let the orchestra go, and beat the musicians who attempted to leave. By morning they had pulled all Prohoritch's stall to pieces, had drunk themselves senseless, danced the Kamarinsky in its unexpurgated form, made the rooms in a shocking mess, and only towards daybreak part of this hopelessly drunken rabble reached the scene of the fire to make fresh disturbances there. The other part spent the night in the rooms dead drunk, with disastrous consequences to the velvet sofas and the floor. Next morning, at the earliest possibility, they were dragged out by their legs into the street. So ended the fête for the benefit of the governesses of our province.

IV

The fire frightened the inhabitants of the riverside just because it was evidently a case of arson. It was curious that at the first cry of "fire" another cry was raised that the Shpigulin men had done it. It is now well known that three Shpigulin men really did have a share in setting fire to the town, but that was all; all the other factory hands were completely acquitted, not only officially but also by public opinion. Besides those three rascals (of whom one has been caught and confessed and the other two have so far escaped), Fedka the convict undoubtedly had a hand in the arson. That is all that is known for certain about the fire till now; but when it comes to conjectures it's a very different matter. What had led these three rascals to do it? Had they been instigated by anyone? It is very difficult to answer all these questions even now.

Owing to the strong wind, the fact that the houses at the riverside were almost all wooden, and that they had been set fire to in three places, the fire spread quickly and enveloped the whole quarter with extraordinary rapidity. (The fire burnt, however, only at two ends; at the third spot it was extinguished almost as soon as it began to burn—of which later.) But the Petersburg and Moscow papers exaggerated our calamity. Not more than a quarter, roughly speaking, of the riverside district was burnt down; possibly less indeed. Our fire brigade, though it was hardly adequate to the size and population of the town, worked with great promptitude and devotion. But it would not have been of much avail, even with the zealous co-operation of the inhabitants, if the wind had not suddenly dropped towards morning. When an hour after our flight from the ball I made my way to the riverside, the fire was at its height. A whole street parallel with the river was in flames. It was as light as day. I won't describe the fire; every one in Russia knows what it looks like. The bustle and crush was immense in the lanes adjoining the burning street. The inhabitants, fully expecting the fire to reach their houses, were hauling out their belongings, but had not yet left their dwellings, and were waiting meanwhile sitting on their boxes and feather beds under their windows. Part of the male population were hard at work ruthlessly chopping down fences and even whole huts which were near the fire and on the windward side. None were crying except the children, who had been waked out of their sleep, though the women who had dragged out their chattels were lamenting in sing-song voices. Those who had not finished their task were still silent, busily carrying out their goods. Sparks and embers were carried a long way in all directions. People put them out as best they could. Some helped to put the fire out while others stood about, admiring it. A great fire at night always has a thrilling and exhilarating effect. This is what explains the attraction of fireworks. But in that case, the artistic regularity with which the fire is presented and the complete lack of danger give an impression of lightness and playfulness like the effect of a glass of champagne. A real conflagration is a very different matter. Then the horror and a certain sense of personal danger, together with the exhilarating effect of a fire at night, produce on the spectator (though of course not in the householder whose goods are being burnt) a certain concussion of the brain and, as it were, a challenge to those destructive instincts which, alas, lie hidden in every heart, even that of the mildest and most domestic little clerk.... This sinister sensation is almost always fascinating. "I really don't know whether one can look at a fire without a certain pleasure." This is a word for word what Stepan Trofimovitch said to me one night on returning home after he had happened to witness a fire and was still under the influence of the spectacle. Of course, the very man who enjoys the spectacle will rush into the fire himself to save a child or an old woman; but that is altogether a different matter.

Following in the wake of the crowd of sightseers, I succeeded, without asking questions, in reaching the chief centre of danger, where at last I saw Lembke, whom I was seeking at Yulia

Mihailovna's request. His position was strange and extraordinary. He was standing on the ruins of a fence. Thirty paces to the left of him rose the black skeleton of a two-storied house which had almost burnt out. It had holes instead of windows at each story, its roof had fallen in, and the flames were still here and there creeping among the charred beams. At the farther end of the courtyard, twenty paces away, the lodge, also a two-storied building, was beginning to burn, and the firemen were doing their utmost to save it. On the right the firemen and the people were trying to save a rather large wooden building which was not actually burning, though it had caught fire several times and was inevitably bound to be burnt in the end. Lembke stood facing the lodge, shouting and gesticulating. He was giving orders which no one attempted to carry out. It seemed to me that every one had given him up as hopeless and left him. Anyway, though every one in the vast crowd of all classes, among whom there were gentlemen, and even the cathedral priest, was listening to him with curiosity and wonder, no one spoke to him or tried to get him away. Lembke, with a pale face and glittering eyes, was uttering the most amazing things. To complete the picture, he had lost his hat and was bareheaded.

"It's all incendiarism! It's nihilism! If anything is burning, it's nihilism!" I heard almost with horror; and though there was nothing to be surprised at, yet actual madness, when one sees it, always gives one a shock.

"Your Excellency," said a policeman, coming up to him, "what if you were to try the repose of home?… It's dangerous for your Excellency even to stand here."

This policeman, as I heard afterwards, had been told off by the chief of police to watch over Andrey Antonovitch, to do his utmost to get him home, and in case of danger even to use force—a task evidently beyond the man's power.

"They will wipe away the tears of the people whose houses have been burnt, but they will burn down the town. It's all the work of four scoundrels, four and a half! Arrest the scoundrel! He worms himself into the honour of families. They made use of the governesses to burn down the houses. It's vile, vile! Aie, what's he about?" he shouted, suddenly noticing a fireman at the top of the burning lodge, under whom the roof had almost burnt away and round whom the flames were beginning to flare up. "Pull him down! Pull him down! He will fall, he will catch fire, put him out!… What is he doing there?"

"He is putting the fire out, your Excellency."

"Not likely. The fire is in the minds of men and not in the roofs of houses. Pull him down and give it up! Better give it up, much better! Let it put itself out. Aie, who is crying now? An old woman! It's an old woman shouting. Why have they forgotten the old woman?"

There actually was an old woman crying on the ground floor of the burning lodge. She was an old creature of eighty, a relation of the shopkeeper who owned the house. But she had not been forgotten; she had gone back to the burning house while it was still possible, with the insane idea of rescuing her feather bed from a corner room which was still untouched. Choking with the smoke and screaming with the heat, for the room was on fire by the time she reached it, she was still trying with her decrepit hands to squeeze her feather bed through a broken window pane. Lembke rushed to her assistance. Every one saw him run up to the window, catch hold of one corner of the feather bed and try with all his might to pull it out. As ill luck would have it, a board fell at that moment from the roof and hit the unhappy governor. It did not kill him, it merely grazed him on the neck as it fell, but Andrey Antonovitch's career was over, among us at least; the blow knocked him off his feet and he sank on the ground unconscious.

The day dawned at last, gloomy and sullen. The fire was abating; the wind was followed by a sudden calm, and then a fine drizzling rain fell. I was by that time in another part, some distance from where Lembke had fallen, and here I overheard very strange conversations in the crowd. A strange fact had come to light. On the very outskirts of the quarter, on a piece of waste land beyond the kitchen gardens, not less than fifty paces from any other buildings, there stood a little wooden house which had only lately been built, and this solitary house had been on fire at the very beginning, almost before any other. Even had it burnt down, it was so far from other houses that no other building in the town could have caught fire from it, and, vice versa, if the whole riverside had been burnt to the ground, that house might have remained intact, whatever the wind had been. It followed that it had caught fire separately and independently and therefore not accidentally. But the chief point was that it was not burnt to the ground, and at daybreak strange things were discovered within it. The owner of this new house, who lived in the neighbourhood, rushed up as soon as he saw it in flames and with the help of his neighbours pulled apart a pile of faggots which had been heaped up by the side wall and set fire to. In this way he saved the house. But there were lodgers in the house—the captain, who was well known in the town, his sister, and their elderly servant, and these three persons—the captain, his sister, and their servant—had been murdered and apparently robbed in the night. (It was here that the chief of police had gone while Lembke was rescuing the feather bed.)

By morning the news had spread and an immense crowd of all classes, even the riverside people who had been burnt out had flocked to the waste land where the new house stood. It was difficult to get there, so dense was the crowd. I was told at once that the captain had been found lying dressed on the bench with his throat cut, and that he must have been dead drunk when he was killed, so that he had felt nothing, and he had "bled like a bull"; that his sister Marya Timofeyevna had been "stabbed all over" with a knife and she was lying on the floor in the doorway, so that probably she had been awake and had fought and struggled with the murderer. The servant, who had also probably been awake, had her skull broken. The owner of the house said that the captain had come to see him the morning before, and that in his drunken bragging he had shown him a lot of money, as much as two hundred roubles. The captain's shabby old green pocket-book was found empty on the floor, but Marya Timofeyevna's box had not been touched, and the silver setting of the ikon had not been removed either; the captain's clothes, too, had not been disturbed. It was evident that the thief had been in a hurry and was a man familiar with the captain's circumstances, who had come only for money and knew where it was kept. If the owner of the house had not run up at that moment the burning faggot stack would certainly have set fire to the house and "it would have been difficult to find out from the charred corpses how they had died."

So the story was told. One other fact was added: that the person who had taken this house for the Lebyadkins was no other than Mr. Stavrogin, Nikolay Vsyevolodovitch, the son of Varvara Petrovna. He had come himself to take it and had had much ado to persuade the owner to let it, as the latter had intended to use it as a tavern; but Nikolay Vsyevolodovitch was ready to give any rent he asked and had paid for six months in advance.

"The fire wasn't an accident," I heard said in the crowd.

But the majority said nothing. People's faces were sullen, but I did not see signs of much indignation. People persisted, however, in gossiping about Stavrogin, saying that the murdered woman was his wife; that on the previous day he had "dishonourably" abducted a young lady belonging to the best family in the place, the daughter of Madame Drozdov, and that a complaint was to be lodged against him in Petersburg; and that his wife had been murdered evidently that he might marry the young lady. Skvoreshniki was not more than a mile and a half away, and I remember I wondered whether I should not let them know the position of affairs. I did not notice, however, that there was anyone egging the crowd on and I don't want to accuse people falsely, though I did see and recognised at once in the crowd at the fire two or three of the rowdy lot I had seen in the refreshment-room. I particularly remember one thin, tall fellow, a cabinet-maker, as I found out later, with an emaciated face and a curly head, black as though grimed with soot. He was not drunk, but in contrast to the gloomy passivity of the crowd seemed beside himself with excitement. He kept addressing the people, though I don't remember his words; nothing coherent that he said was longer than "I say, lads, what do you say to this? Are things to go on like this?" and so saying he waved his arms.

CHAPTER III. A ROMANCE ENDED

I

FROM THE LARGE BALLROOM of Skvoreshniki (the room in which the last interview with Varvara Petrovna and Stepan Trofimovitch had taken place) the fire could be plainly seen. At daybreak, soon after five in the morning, Liza was standing at the farthest window on the right looking intently at the fading glow. She was alone in the room. She was wearing the dress she had worn the day before at the matinée—a very smart light green dress covered with lace, but crushed and put on carelessly and with haste. Suddenly noticing that some of the hooks were undone in front she flushed, hurriedly set it right, snatched up from a chair the red shawl she had flung down when she came in the day before, and put it round her neck. Some locks of her luxuriant hair had come loose and showed below the shawl on her right shoulder. Her face looked weary and careworn, but her eyes glowed under her frowning brows. She went up to the window again and pressed her burning forehead against the cold pane. The door opened and Nikolay Vsyevolodovitch came in.

"I've sent a messenger on horseback," he said. "In ten minutes we shall hear all about it, meantime the servants say that part of the riverside quarter has been burnt down, on the right side of the bridge near the quay. It's been burning since eleven o'clock; now the fire is going down."

He did not go near the window, but stood three steps behind her; she did not turn towards him.

"It ought to have been light an hour ago by the calendar, and it's still almost night," she said irritably.

"'Calendars always tell lies,'" he observed with a polite smile, but, a little ashamed; he made haste to add: "It's dull to live by the calendar, Liza."

And he relapsed into silence, vexed at the ineptitude of the second sentence. Liza gave a wry smile.

"You are in such a melancholy mood that you cannot even find words to speak to me. But you need not trouble, there's a point in what you said. I always live by the calendar. Every step I take is regulated by the calendar. Does that surprise you?"

She turned quickly from the window and sat down in a low chair.

"You sit down, too, please. We haven't long to be together and I want to say anything I like.... Why shouldn't you, too, say anything you like?"

Nikolay Vsyevolodovitch sat beside her and softly, almost timidly took her hand.

"What's the meaning of this tone, Liza? Where has it suddenly sprung from? What do you mean by 'we haven't long to be together'? That's the second mysterious phrase since you waked, half an hour ago."

"You are beginning to reckon up my mysterious phrases!" she laughed. "Do you remember I told you I was a dead woman when I came in yesterday? That you thought fit to forget. To forget or not to notice."

"I don't remember, Liza. Why dead? You must live."

"And is that all? You've quite lost your flow of words. I've lived my hour and that's enough. Do you remember Christopher Ivanovitch?"

"No I don't," he answered, frowning.

"Christopher Ivanovitch at Lausanne? He bored you dreadfully. He always used to open the door and say, 'I've come for one minute,' and then stay the whole day. I don't want to be like Christopher Ivanovitch and stay the whole day."

A look of pain came into his face.

"Liza, it grieves me, this unnatural language. This affectation must hurt you, too. What's it for? What's the object of it?"

His eyes glowed.

"Liza," he cried, "I swear I love you now more than yesterday when you came to me!"

"What a strange declaration! Why bring in yesterday and to-day and these comparisons?"

"You won't leave me," he went on, almost with despair; "we will go away together, to-day, won't we? Won't we?"

"Aie, don't squeeze my hand so painfully! Where could we go together to-day? To 'rise again' somewhere? No, we've made experiments enough … and it's too slow for me; and I am not fit for it; it's too exalted for me. If we are to go, let it be to Moscow, to pay visits and entertain—that's my ideal you know; even in Switzerland I didn't disguise from you what I was like. As we can't go to Moscow and pay visits since you are married, it's no use talking of that."

"Liza! What happened yesterday!"

"What happened is over!"

"That's impossible! That's cruel!"

"What if it is cruel? You must bear it if it is cruel."

"You are avenging yourself on me for yesterday's caprice," he muttered with an angry smile. Liza flushed.

"What a mean thought!"

"Why then did you bestow on me … so great a happiness? Have I the right to know?"

"No, you must manage without rights; don't aggravate the meanness of your supposition by stupidity. You are not lucky to-day. By the way, you surely can't be afraid of public opinion and that you will be blamed for this 'great happiness'? If that's it, for God's sake don't alarm yourself. It's not your doing at all and you are not responsible to anyone. When I opened your door yesterday, you didn't even know who was coming in. It was simply my caprice, as you expressed it just now, and nothing more! You can look every one in the face boldly and triumphantly!"

"Your words, that laugh, have been making me feel cold with horror for the last hour. That 'happiness' of which you speak frantically is worth … everything to me. How can I lose you now? I swear I loved you less yesterday. Why are you taking everything from me to-day? Do you know what it has cost me, this new hope? I've paid for it with life."

"Your own life or another's?"

He got up quickly.

"What does that mean?" he brought out, looking at her steadily.

"Have you paid for it with your life or with mine? is what I mean. Or have you lost all power of understanding?" cried Liza, flushing. "Why did you start up so suddenly? Why do you stare at me with such a look? You frighten me. What is it you are afraid of all the time? I noticed some time ago that you were afraid and you are now, this very minute … Good heavens, how pale you are!"

"If you know anything, Liza, I swear I don't … and I wasn't talking of that just now when I said that I had paid for it with life…."

"I don't understand you," she brought out, faltering apprehensively.

At last a slow brooding smile came on to his lips. He slowly sat down, put his elbows on his knees, and covered his face with his hands.

"A bad dream and delirium…. We were talking of two different things."

"I don't know what you were talking about…. Do you mean to say you did not know yesterday that I should leave you to-day, did you know or not? Don't tell a lie, did you or not?"

"I did," he said softly.

"Well then, what would you have? You knew and yet you accepted 'that moment' for yourself. Aren't we quits?"

"Tell me the whole truth," he cried in intense distress. "When you opened my door yesterday, did you know yourself that it was only for one hour?"

She looked at him with hatred.

"Really, the most sensible person can ask most amazing questions. And why are you so uneasy? Can it be vanity that a woman should leave you first instead of your leaving her? Do you know, Nikolay Vsyevolodovitch, since I've been with you I've discovered that you are very generous to me, and it's just that I can't endure from you."

He got up from his seat and took a few steps about the room.

"Very well, perhaps it was bound to end so.... But how can it all have happened?"

"That's a question to worry about! Especially as you know the answer yourself perfectly well, and understand it better than anyone on earth, and were counting on it yourself. I am a young lady, my heart has been trained on the opera, that's how it all began, that's the solution."

"No."

"There is nothing in it to fret your vanity. It is all the absolute truth. It began with a fine moment which was too much for me to bear. The day before yesterday, when I 'insulted' you before every one and you answered me so chivalrously, I went home and guessed at once that you were running away from me because you were married, and not from contempt for me which, as a fashionable young lady, I dreaded more than anything. I understood that it was for my sake, for me, mad as I was, that you ran away. You see how I appreciate your generosity. Then Pyotr Stepanovitch skipped up to me and explained it all to me at once. He revealed to me that you were dominated by a 'great idea,' before which he and I were as nothing, but yet that I was a stumbling-block in your path. He brought himself in, he insisted that we three should work together, and said the most fantastic things about a boat and about maple-wood oars out of some Russian song. I complimented him and told him he was a poet, which he swallowed as the real thing. And as apart from him I had known long before that I had not the strength to do anything for long, I made up my mind on the spot. Well, that's all and quite enough, and please let us have no more explanations. We might quarrel. Don't be afraid of anyone, I take it all on myself. I am horrid and capricious, I was fascinated by that operatic boat, I am a young lady ... but you know I did think that you were dreadfully in love with me. Don't despise the poor fool, and don't laugh at the tear that dropped just now. I am awfully given to crying with self-pity. Come, that's enough, that's enough. I am no good for anything and you are no good for anything; it's as bad for both of us, so let's comfort ourselves with that. Anyway, it eases our vanity."

"Dream and delirium," cried Stavrogin, wringing his hands, and pacing about the room. "Liza, poor child, what have you done to yourself?"

"I've burnt myself in a candle, nothing more. Surely you are not crying, too? You should show less feeling and better breeding...."

"Why, why did you come to me?"

"Don't you understand what a ludicrous position you put yourself in in the eyes of the world by asking such questions?"

"Why have you ruined yourself, so grotesquely and so stupidly, and what's to be done now?"

"And this is Stavrogin, 'the vampire Stavrogin,' as you are called by a lady here who is in love with you! Listen! I have told you already, I've put all my life into one hour and I am at peace. Do the same with yours ... though you've no need to: you have plenty of 'hours' and 'moments' of all sorts before you."

"As many as you; I give you my solemn word, not one hour more than you!"

He was still walking up and down and did not see the rapid penetrating glance she turned upon him, in which there seemed a dawning hope. But the light died away at the same moment.

"If you knew what it costs me that I can't be sincere at this moment, Liza, if I could only tell you ..."

"Tell me? You want to tell me something, to me? God save me from your secrets!" she broke in almost in terror. He stopped and waited uneasily.

"I ought to confess that ever since those days in Switzerland I have had a strong feeling that you have something awful, loathsome, some bloodshed on your conscience ... and yet something that would make you look very ridiculous. Beware of telling me, if it's true: I shall laugh you to scorn. I shall laugh at you for the rest of your life.... Aie, you are turning pale again? I won't, I won't, I'll go at once." She jumped up from her chair with a movement of disgust and contempt.

"Torture me, punish me, vent your spite on me," he cried in despair. "You have the full right. I knew I did not love you and yet I ruined you! Yes, I accepted the moment for my own; I had a hope ... I've had it a long time ... my last hope.... I could not resist the radiance that flooded my heart when you came in to me yesterday, of yourself, alone, of your own accord. I suddenly believed.... Perhaps I have faith in it still."

"I will repay such noble frankness by being as frank. I don't want to be a Sister of Mercy for you. Perhaps I really may become a nurse unless I happen appropriately to die to-day; but if I do I won't be your nurse, though, of course, you need one as much as any crippled creature. I always fancied that you would take me to some place where there was a huge wicked spider, big as a man, and we should spend our lives looking at it and being afraid of it. That's how our love would spend itself. Appeal to Dashenka; she will go with you anywhere you like."

"Can't you help thinking of her even now?"

"Poor little spaniel! Give her my greetings. Does she know that even in Switzerland you had fixed on her for your old age? What prudence! What foresight! Aie, who's that?"

At the farther end of the room a door opened a crack; a head was thrust in and vanished again hurriedly.

"Is that you, Alexey Yegorytch?" asked Stavrogin.

"No, it's only I." Pyotr Stepanovitch thrust himself half in again. "How do you do, Lizaveta Nikolaevna? Good morning, anyway. I guessed I should find you both in this room. I have come for one moment literally, Nikolay Vsyevolodovitch. I was anxious to have a couple of words with you at all costs ... absolutely necessary ... only a few words!"

Stavrogin moved towards him but turned back to Liza at the third step.

"If you hear anything directly, Liza, let me tell you I am to blame for it!"

She started and looked at him in dismay; but he hurriedly went out.

II

The room from which Pyotr Stepanovitch had peeped in was a large oval vestibule. Alexey Yegorytch had been sitting there before Pyotr Stepanovitch came in, but the latter sent him away. Stavrogin closed the door after him and stood expectant. Pyotr Stepanovitch looked rapidly and searchingly at him.

"Well?"

"If you know already," said Pyotr Stepanovitch hurriedly, his eyes looking as though they would dive into Stavrogin's soul, "then, of course, we are none of us to blame, above all not you, for it's such a concatenation … such a coincidence of events … in brief, you can't be legally implicated and I've rushed here to tell you so beforehand."

"Have they been burnt? murdered?"

"Murdered but not burnt, that's the trouble, but I give you my word of honour that it's not been my fault, however much you may suspect me, eh? Do you want the whole truth: you see the idea really did cross my mind—you hinted it yourself, not seriously, but teasing me (for, of course, you would not hint it seriously), but I couldn't bring myself to it, and wouldn't bring myself to it for anything, not for a hundred roubles—and what was there to be gained by it, I mean for me, for me…." (He was in desperate haste and his talk was like the clacking of a rattle.) "But what a coincidence of circumstances: I gave that drunken fool Lebyadkin two hundred and thirty roubles of my own money (do you hear, my own money, there wasn't a rouble of yours and, what's more, you know it yourself) the day before yesterday, in the evening—do you hear, not yesterday after the matinée, but the day before yesterday, make a note of it: it's a very important coincidence for I did not know for certain at that time whether Lizaveta Nikolaevna would come to you or not; I gave my own money simply because you distinguished yourself by taking it into your head to betray your secret to every one. Well, I won't go into that … that's your affair … your chivalry, but I must own I was amazed, it was a knock-down blow. And forasmuch as I was exceeding weary of these tragic stories—and let me tell you, I talk seriously though I do use Biblical language—as it was all upsetting my plans in fact, I made up my mind at any cost, and without your knowledge, to pack the Lebyadkins off to Petersburg, especially as he was set on going himself. I made one mistake: I gave the money in your name;—was it a mistake or not? Perhaps it wasn't a mistake, eh? Listen now, listen how it has all turned out…."

In the heat of his talk he went close up to Stavrogin and took hold of the revers of his coat (really, it may have been on purpose). With a violent movement Stavrogin struck him on the arm.

"Come, what is it … give over … you'll break my arm … what matters is the way things have turned out," he rattled on, not in the least surprised at the blow. "I forked out the money in the evening on condition that his sister and he should set off early next morning; I trusted that rascal Liputin with the job of getting them into the train and seeing them off. But that beast Liputin wanted to play his schoolboy pranks on the public—perhaps you heard? At the matinée? Listen, listen: they both got drunk, made up verses of which half are Liputin's; he rigged Lebyadkin out in a dress-coat, assuring me meanwhile that he had packed him off that morning, but he kept him shut somewhere in a back room, till he thrust him on the platform at the matinée. But Lebyadkin got drunk quickly and unexpectedly. Then came the scandalous scene you know of, and then they got him home more dead than alive, and Liputin filched away the two hundred roubles, leaving him only small change. But it appears unluckily that already that morning Lebyadkin had taken that two hundred roubles out of his pocket, boasted of it and shown it in undesirable quarters. And as that was just what Fedka was expecting, and as he had heard something at Kirillov's (do you remember, your hint?) he made up his mind to take advantage of it. That's the whole truth. I am glad, anyway, that Fedka did not find the money, the rascal was reckoning on a thousand, you know! He was in a hurry and seems to have been frightened by the fire himself.... Would you believe it, that fire came as a thunderbolt for me. Devil only knows what to make of it! It is taking things into their own hands.... You see, as I expect so much of you I will hide nothing from you: I've long been hatching this idea of a fire because it suits the national and popular taste; but I was keeping it for a critical moment, for that precious time when we should all rise up and ... And they suddenly took it into their heads to do it, on their own initiative, without orders, now at the very moment when we ought to be lying low and keeping quiet! Such presumption!... The fact is, I've not got to the bottom of it yet, they talk about two Shpigulin men, but if there are any of our fellows in it, if any one of them has had a hand in it—so much the worse for him! You see what comes of letting people get ever so little out of hand! No, this democratic rabble, with its quintets, is a poor foundation; what we want is one magnificent, despotic will, like an idol, resting on something fundamental and external.... Then the quintets will cringe into obedience and be obsequiously ready on occasion. But, anyway, though, they are all crying out now that Stavrogin wanted his wife to be burnt and that that's what caused the fire in the town, but ..."

"Why, are they all saying that?"

"Well, not yet, and I must confess I have heard nothing of the sort, but what one can do with people, especially when they've been burnt out! Vox populi vox Dei. A stupid rumour is soon set going. But you really have nothing to be afraid of. From the legal point of view you are all right, and with your conscience also. For you didn't want it done, did you? There's no clue, nothing but the coincidence.... The only thing is Fedka may remember what you said that night at Kirillov's (and what made you say it?) but that proves nothing and we shall stop Fedka's mouth. I shall stop it to-day...."

"And weren't the bodies burnt at all?"

"Not a bit; that ruffian could not manage anything properly. But I am glad, anyway, that you are so calm ... for though you are not in any way to blame, even in thought, but all the same.... And you must admit that all this settles your difficulties capitally: you are suddenly free and a widower and can marry a charming girl this minute with a lot of money, who is already yours, into the bargain. See what can be done by crude, simple coincidence—eh?"

"Are you threatening me, you fool?"

"Come, leave off, leave off! Here you are, calling me a fool, and what a tone to use! You ought to be glad, yet you ... I rushed here on purpose to let you know in good time.... Besides, how could I threaten you? As if I cared for what I could get by threats! I want you to help from goodwill and not from fear. You are the light and the sun.... It's I who am terribly afraid of you, not you of me! I am not Mavriky Nikolaevitch.... And only fancy, as I flew here in a racing droshky I saw Mavriky Nikolaevitch by the fence at the farthest corner of your garden ... in his greatcoat, drenched through, he must have been sitting there all night! Queer goings on! How mad people can be!"

"Mavriky Nikolaevitch? Is that true?"

"Yes, yes. He is sitting by the garden fence. About three hundred paces from here, I think. I made haste to pass him, but he saw me. Didn't you know? In that case, I am glad I didn't forget to tell you. A man like that is more dangerous than anyone if he happens to have a revolver about him, and then the night, the sleet, or natural irritability—for after all he is in a nice position, ha ha! What do you think? Why is he sitting there?"

"He is waiting for Lizaveta Nikolaevna, of course."

"Well! Why should she go out to him? And ... in such rain too ... what a fool!"

"She is just going out to him!"

"Eh! That's a piece of news! So then ... But listen, her position is completely changed now. What does she want with Mavriky now? You are free, a widower, and can marry her to-morrow. She doesn't know yet—leave it to me and I'll arrange it all for you. Where is she? We must relieve her mind too."

"Relieve her mind?"

"Rather! Let's go."

"And do you suppose she won't guess what those dead bodies mean?" said Stavrogin, screwing up his eyes in a peculiar way.

"Of course she won't," said Pyotr Stepanovitch with all the confidence of a perfect simpleton, "for legally ... Ech, what a man you are! What if she did guess? Women are so clever at shutting their eyes to such things, you don't understand women! Apart from it's being altogether to her interest to marry you now, because there's no denying she's disgraced herself; apart from that, I talked to her of 'the boat' and I saw that one could affect her by it, so that shows you what the girl is made of. Don't be uneasy, she will step over those dead bodies without turning a hair—especially as you are not to blame for them; not in the least, are you? She will only keep them in reserve to use them against you when you've been married two or three years. Every woman saves up something of the sort out of her husband's past when she gets married, but by that time ... what may not happen in a year? Ha ha!"

"If you've come in a racing droshky, take her to Mavriky Nikolaevitch now. She said just now that she could not endure me and would leave me, and she certainly will not accept my carriage."

"What! Can she really be leaving? How can this have come about?" said Pyotr Stepanovitch, staring stupidly at him.

"She's guessed somehow during this night that I don't love her ... which she knew all along, indeed."

"But don't you love her?" said Pyotr Stepanovitch, with an expression of extreme surprise. "If so, why did you keep her when she came to you yesterday, instead of telling her plainly like an honourable man that you didn't care for her? That was horribly shabby on your part; and how mean you make me look in her eyes!"

Stavrogin suddenly laughed.

"I am laughing at my monkey," he explained at once.

"Ah! You saw that I was putting it on!" cried Pyotr Stepanovitch, laughing too, with great enjoyment. "I did it to amuse you! Only fancy, as soon as you came out to me I guessed from your face that you'd been 'unlucky.' A complete fiasco, perhaps. Eh? There! I'll bet anything," he cried, almost gasping with delight, "that you've been sitting side by side in the drawing-room all night wasting your precious time discussing something lofty and elevated.... There, forgive me, forgive me; it's not my business. I felt sure yesterday that it would all end in foolishness. I brought her to you simply to amuse you, and to show you that you wouldn't have a dull time with me. I shall be of use to you a hundred times in that way. I always like pleasing people. If you don't want her now, which was what I was reckoning on when I came, then ..."

"So you brought her simply for my amusement?"

"Why, what else?"

"Not to make me kill my wife?"

"Come. You've not killed her? What a tragic fellow you are!

"It's just the same; you killed her."

"I didn't kill her! I tell you I had no hand in it.... You are beginning to make me uneasy, though...."

"Go on. You said, 'if you don't want her now, then ... '"

"Then, leave it to me, of course. I can quite easily marry her off to Mavriky Nikolaevitch, though I didn't make him sit down by the fence. Don't take that notion into your head. I am afraid of him, now. You talk about my droshky, but I simply dashed by.... What if he has a revolver? It's a good thing I brought mine. Here it is." He brought a revolver out of his pocket, showed it, and hid it again at once. "I took it as I was coming such a long way.... But I'll arrange all that for you in a twinkling: her little heart is aching at this moment for Mavriky; it should be, anyway.... And, do you know, I am really rather sorry for her? If I take her to Mavriky she will begin about you directly; she will praise you to him and abuse him to his face. You know the heart of woman! There you are, laughing again! I am awfully glad that you are so cheerful now. Come, let's go. I'll begin with Mavriky right away, and about them ... those who've been murdered ... hadn't we better keep quiet now? She'll hear later on, anyway."

"What will she hear? Who's been murdered? What were you saying about Mavriky Nikolaevitch?" said Liza, suddenly opening the door.

"Ah! You've been listening?"

"What were you saying just now about Mavriky Nikolaevitch? Has he been murdered?"

"Ah! Then you didn't hear? Don't distress yourself, Mavriky Nikolaevitch is alive and well, and you can satisfy yourself of it in an instant, for he is here by the wayside, by the garden fence ... and I believe he's been sitting there all night. He is drenched through in his greatcoat! He saw me as I drove past."

"That's not true. You said 'murdered.' ... Who's been murdered?" she insisted with agonising mistrust.

"The only people who have been murdered are my wife, her brother Lebyadkin, and their servant," Stavrogin brought out firmly.

Liza trembled and turned terribly pale.

"A strange brutal outrage, Lizaveta Nikolaevna. A simple case of robbery," Pyotr Stepanovitch rattled off at once "Simply robbery, under cover of the fire. The crime was committed by Fedka the convict, and it was all that fool Lebyadkin's fault for showing every one his money.... I rushed here with the news ... it fell on me like a thunderbolt. Stavrogin could hardly stand when I told him. We were deliberating here whether to tell you at once or not?"

"Nikolay Vsyevolodovitch, is he telling the truth?" Liza articulated faintly.

"No; it's false."

"False?" said Pyotr Stepanovitch, starting. "What do you mean by that?"

"Heavens! I shall go mad!" cried Liza.

"Do you understand, anyway, that he is mad now!" Pyotr Stepanovitch cried at the top of his voice. "After all, his wife has just been murdered. You see how white he is.... Why, he has been with you the whole night. He hasn't left your side a minute. How can you suspect him?"

"Nikolay Vsyevolodovitch, tell me, as before God, are you guilty or not, and I swear I'll believe your word as though it were God's, and I'll follow you to the end of the earth. Yes, I will. I'll follow you like a dog."

"Why are you tormenting her, you fantastic creature?" cried Pyotr Stepanovitch in exasperation. "Lizaveta Nikolaevna, upon my oath, you can crush me into powder, but he is not guilty. On the contrary, it has crushed him, and he is raving, you see that. He is not to blame in any way, not in any way, not even in thought!... It's all the work of robbers who will probably be found within a week and flogged.... It's all the work of Fedka the convict, and some Shpigulin men, all the town is agog with it. That's why I say so too."

"Is that right? Is that right?" Liza waited trembling for her final sentence.

"I did not kill them, and I was against it, but I knew they were going to be killed and I did not stop the murderers. Leave me, Liza," Stavrogin brought out, and he walked into the drawing-room.

Liza hid her face in her hands and walked out of the house. Pyotr Stepanovitch was rushing after her, but at once hurried back and went into the drawing-room.

"So that's your line? That's your line? So there's nothing you are afraid of?" He flew at Stavrogin in an absolute fury, muttering incoherently, scarcely able to find words and foaming at the mouth.

Stavrogin stood in the middle of the room and did not answer a word. He clutched a lock of his hair in his left hand and smiled helplessly. Pyotr Stepanovitch pulled him violently by the sleeve.

"Is it all over with you? So that's the line you are taking? You'll inform against all of us, and go to a monastery yourself, or to the devil.... But I'll do for you, though you are not afraid of me!"

"Ah! That's you chattering!" said Stavrogin, noticing him at last. "Run," he said, coming to himself suddenly, "run after her, order the carriage, don't leave her.... Run, run! Take her home so that no one may know ... and that she mayn't go there ... to the bodies ... to the bodies.... Force her to get into the carriage ... Alexey Yegorytch! Alexey Yegorytch!"

"Stay, don't shout! By now she is in Mavriky's arms.... Mavriky won't put her into your carriage.... Stay! There's something more important than the carriage!"

He seized his revolver again. Stavrogin looked at him gravely.

"Very well, kill me," he said softly, almost conciliatorily.

"Foo. Damn it! What a maze of false sentiment a man can get into!" said Pyotr Stepanovitch, shaking with rage. "Yes, really, you ought to be killed! She ought simply to spit at you! Fine sort of 'magic boat,' you are; you are a broken-down, leaky old hulk!... You ought to pull yourself together if only from spite! Ech! Why, what difference would it make to you since you ask for a bullet through your brains yourself?"

Stavrogin smiled strangely.

"If you were not such a buffoon I might perhaps have said yes now.... If you had only a grain of sense ..."

"I am a buffoon, but I don't want you, my better half, to be one! Do you understand me?"

Stavrogin did understand, though perhaps no one else did. Shatov, for instance, was astonished when Stavrogin told him that Pyotr Stepanovitch had enthusiasm.

"Go to the devil now, and to-morrow perhaps I may wring something out of myself. Come to-morrow."

"Yes? Yes?"

"How can I tell?... Go to hell. Go to hell." And he walked out of the room.

"Perhaps, after all, it may be for the best," Pyotr Stepanovitch muttered to himself as he hid the revolver.

III

He rushed off to overtake Lizaveta Nikolaevna. She had not got far away, only a few steps, from the house. She had been detained by Alexey Yegorytch, who was following a step behind her, in a tail coat, and without a hat; his head was bowed respectfully. He was persistently entreating her to wait for a carriage; the old man was alarmed and almost in tears.

"Go along. Your master is asking for tea, and there's no one to give it to him," said Pyotr Stepanovitch, pushing him away. He took Liza's arm.

She did not pull her arm away, but she seemed hardly to know what she was doing; she was still dazed.

"To begin with, you are going the wrong way," babbled Pyotr Stepanovitch. "We ought to go this way, and not by the garden, and, secondly, walking is impossible in any case. It's over two miles, and you are not properly dressed. If you would wait a second, I came in a droshky; the horse is in the yard. I'll get it instantly, put you in, and get you home so that no one sees you."

"How kind you are," said Liza graciously.

"Oh, not at all. Any humane man in my position would do the same...."

Liza looked at him, and was surprised.

"Good heavens! Why I thought it was that old man here still."

"Listen. I am awfully glad that you take it like this, because it's all such a frightfully stupid convention, and since it's come to that, hadn't I better tell the old man to get the carriage at once. It's only a matter of ten minutes and we'll turn back and wait in the porch, eh?"

"I want first ... where are those murdered people?"

"Ah! What next? That was what I was afraid of.... No, we'd better leave those wretched creatures alone; it's no use your looking at them."

"I know where they are. I know that house."

"Well? What if you do know it? Come; it's raining, and there's a fog. (A nice job this sacred duty I've taken upon myself.) Listen, Lizaveta Nikolaevna! It's one of two alternatives. Either you come with me in the droshky—in that case wait here, and don't take another step, for if we go another twenty steps we must be seen by Mavriky Nikolaevitch."

"Mavriky Nikolaevitch! Where? Where?"

"Well, if you want to go with him, I'll take you a little farther, if you like, and show you where he sits, but I don't care to go up to him just now. No, thank you."

"He is waiting for me. Good God!" she suddenly stopped, and a flush of colour flooded her face.

"Oh! Come now. If he is an unconventional man! You know, Lizaveta Nikolaevna, it's none of my business. I am a complete outsider, and you know that yourself. But, still, I wish you well.... If your 'fairy boat' has failed you, if it has turned out to be nothing more than a rotten old hulk, only fit to be chopped up ..."

"Ah! That's fine, that's lovely," cried Liza.

"Lovely, and yet your tears are falling. You must have spirit. You must be as good as a man in every way. In our age, when woman.... Foo, hang it," Pyotr Stepanovitch was on the point of spitting. "And the chief point is that there is nothing to regret. It may all turn out for the best. Mavriky Nikolaevitch is a man.... In fact, he is a man of feeling though not talkative, but that's a good thing, too, as long as he has no conventional notions, of course...."

"Lovely, lovely!" Liza laughed hysterically.

"Well, hang it all ... Lizaveta Nikolaevna," said Pyotr Stepanovitch suddenly piqued. "I am simply here on your account.... It's nothing to me.... I helped you yesterday when you wanted it yourself. To-day ... well, you can see Mavriky Nikolaevitch from here; there he's sitting; he doesn't see us. I say, Lizaveta Nikolaevna, have you ever read 'Polenka Saxe'?"

"What's that?"

"It's the name of a novel, 'Polenka Saxe.' I read it when I was a student.... In it a very wealthy official of some sort, Saxe, arrested his wife at a summer villa for infidelity.... But, hang it; it's no consequence! You'll see, Mavriky Nikolaevitch will make you an offer before you get home. He doesn't see us yet."

"Ach! Don't let him see us!" Liza cried suddenly, like a mad creature. "Come away, come away! To the woods, to the fields!"

And she ran back.

"Lizaveta Nikolaevna, this is such cowardice," cried Pyotr Stepanovitch, running after her. "And why don't you want him to see you? On the contrary, you must look him straight in the face, with pride.... If it's some feeling about that ... some maidenly ... that's such a prejudice, so out of date ... But where are you going? Where are you going? Ech! she is running! Better go back to Stavrogin's and take my droshky.... Where are you going? That's the way to the fields! There! She's fallen down!..."

He stopped. Liza was flying along like a bird, not conscious where she was going, and Pyotr Stepanovitch was already fifty paces behind her. She stumbled over a mound of earth and fell down. At the same moment there was the sound of a terrible shout from behind. It came from Mavriky Nikolaevitch, who had seen her flight and her fall, and was running to her across the field. In a flash, Pyotr Stepanovitch had retired into Stavrogin's gateway to make haste and get into his droshky.

Mavriky Nikolaevitch was already standing in terrible alarm by Liza, who had risen to her feet; he was bending over her and holding her hands in both of his. All the incredible surroundings of this meeting overwhelmed him, and tears were rolling down his cheeks. He saw the woman for whom he had such reverent devotion running madly across the fields, at such an hour, in such weather, with nothing over her dress, the gay dress she wore the day before now crumpled and muddy from her fall.... He could not utter a word; he took off his greatcoat, and with trembling hands put it round her shoulders. Suddenly he uttered a cry, feeling that she had pressed her lips to his hand.

"Liza," he cried, "I am no good for anything, but don't drive me away from you!"

"Oh, no! Let us make haste away from here. Don't leave me!" and, seizing his hand, she drew him after her. "Mavriky Nikolaevitch," she suddenly dropped her voice timidly, "I kept a bold face there all the time, but now I am afraid of death. I shall die soon, very soon, but I am afraid, I am afraid to die...." she whispered, pressing his hand tight.

"Oh, if there were someone," he looked round in despair. "Some passer-by! You will get your feet wet, you ... will lose your reason!"

"It's all right; it's all right," she tried to reassure him. "That's right. I am not so frightened with you. Hold my hand, lead me.... Where are we going now? Home? No! I want first to see the people who have been murdered. His wife has been murdered they say, and he says he killed her himself. But that's not true, is it? I want to see for myself those three who've been killed ... on my account ... it's because of them his love for me has grown cold since last night.... I shall see and find out everything. Make haste, make haste, I know the house ... there's a fire there.... Mavriky Nikolaevitch, my dear one, don't forgive me in my shame! Why forgive me? Why are you crying? Give me a blow and kill me here in the field, like a dog!"

"No one is your judge now," Mavriky Nikolaevitch pronounced firmly. "God forgive you. I least of all can be your judge."

But it would be strange to describe their conversation. And meanwhile they walked hand in hand quickly, hurrying as though they were crazy. They were going straight towards the fire. Mavriky Nikolaevitch still had hopes of meeting a cart at least, but no one came that way. A mist of fine, drizzling rain enveloped the whole country, swallowing up every ray of light, every gleam of colour, and transforming everything into one smoky, leaden, indistinguishable mass. It had long been daylight, yet it seemed as though it were still night. And suddenly in this cold foggy mist there appeared coming towards them a strange and absurd figure. Picturing it now I think I should not have believed my eyes if I had been in Lizaveta Nikolaevna's place, yet she uttered a cry of joy, and recognised the approaching figure at once. It was Stepan Trofimovitch. How he had gone off, how the insane, impracticable idea of his flight came to be carried out, of that later. I will only mention that he was in a fever that morning, yet even illness did not prevent his starting. He was walking resolutely on the damp ground. It was evident that he had planned the enterprise to the best of his ability, alone with his inexperience and lack of practical sense. He wore "travelling dress," that is, a greatcoat with a wide patent-leather belt, fastened with a buckle and a pair of new high boots pulled over his trousers. Probably he had for some time past pictured a traveller as looking like this, and the belt and the high boots with the shining tops like a hussar's, in which he could hardly walk, had been ready some time before. A broad-brimmed hat, a knitted scarf, twisted close round his neck, a stick in his right hand, and an exceedingly small but extremely tightly packed bag in his left, completed his get-up. He had, besides, in the same right hand, an open umbrella. These three objects—the umbrella, the stick, and the bag—had been very awkward to carry for the first mile, and had begun to be heavy by the second.

"Can it really be you?" cried Liza, looking at him with distressed wonder, after her first rush of instinctive gladness.

"Lise," cried Stepan Trofimovitch, rushing to her almost in delirium too. "Chère, chère.... Can you be out, too ... in such a fog? You see the glow of fire. Vous êtes malheureuse, n'est-ce pas? I see, I see. Don't tell me, but don't question me either. Nous sommes tous malheureux mais il faut les pardonner tous. Pardonnons, Lise, and let us be free forever. To be quit of the world and be completely free. Il faut pardonner, pardonner, et pardonner!"

"But why are you kneeling down?"

"Because, taking leave of the world, I want to take leave of all my past in your person!" He wept and raised both her hands to his tear-stained eyes. "I kneel to all that was beautiful in my life. I kiss and give thanks! Now I've torn myself in half; left behind a mad visionary who dreamed of soaring to the sky. Vingt-deux ans, here. A shattered, frozen old man. A tutor chez ce marchand, s'il existe pourtant ce marchand.... But how drenched you are, Lise!" he cried, jumping on to his feet, feeling that his knees too were soaked by the wet earth. "And how is it possible ... you are in such a dress ... and on foot, and in these fields?... You are crying! Vous êtes malheureuse. Bah, I did hear something.... But where have you come from now?" He asked hurried questions with an uneasy air, looking in extreme bewilderment at Mavriky Nikolaevitch. "Mais savez-vous l'heure qu'il est?"

"Stepan Trofimovitch, have you heard anything about the people who've been murdered?... Is it true? Is it true?"

"These people! I saw the glow of their work all night. They were bound to end in this...." His eyes flashed again. "I am fleeing away from madness, from a delirious dream. I am fleeing away to seek for Russia. Existe-t-elle, la Russie? Bah! C'est vous, cher capitaine! I've never doubted that I should meet you somewhere on some high adventure.... But take my umbrella, and—why must you be on foot? For God's sake, do at least take my umbrella, for I shall hire a carriage somewhere in any case. I am on foot because Stasie (I mean, Nastasya) would have shouted for the benefit of the whole street if she'd found out I was going away. So I slipped away as far as possible incognito. I don't know; in the Voice they write of there being brigands everywhere, but I thought surely I shouldn't meet a brigand the moment I came out on the road. Chère Lise, I thought you said something of someone's being murdered. Oh, mon Dieu! You are ill!"

"Come along, come along!" cried Liza, almost in hysterics, drawing Mavriky Nikolaevitch after her again. "Wait a minute, Stepan Trofimovitch!" she came back suddenly to him. "Stay, poor darling, let me sign you with the cross. Perhaps, it would be better to put you under control, but I'd rather make the sign of the cross over you. You, too, pray for 'poor' Liza—just a little, don't bother too much about it. Mavriky Nikolaevitch, give that baby back his umbrella. You must give it him. That's right.... Come, let us go, let us go!"

They reached the fatal house at the very moment when the huge crowd, which had gathered round it, had already heard a good deal of Stavrogin, and of how much it was to his interest to murder his wife. Yet, I repeat, the immense majority went on listening without moving or uttering a word. The only people who were excited were bawling drunkards and excitable individuals of the same sort as the gesticulatory cabinet-maker. Every one knew the latter as a man really of mild disposition, but he was liable on occasion to get excited and to fly off at a tangent if anything struck him in a certain way. I did not see Liza and Mavriky Nikolaevitch arrive. Petrified with amazement, I first noticed Liza some distance away in the crowd, and I did not at once catch sight of Mavriky Nikolaevitch. I fancy there was a moment when he fell two or three steps behind her or was pressed back by the crush. Liza, forcing her way through the crowd, seeing and noticing nothing round her, like one in a delirium, like a patient escaped from a hospital, attracted attention only too quickly, of course. There arose a hubbub of loud talking and at last sudden shouts. Some one bawled out, "It's Stavrogin's woman!" And on the other side, "It's not enough to murder them, she wants to look at them!" All at once I saw an arm raised above her head from behind and suddenly brought down upon it. Liza fell to the ground. We heard a fearful scream from Mavriky Nikolaevitch as he dashed to her assistance and struck with all his strength the man who stood between him and Liza. But at that instant the same cabinetmaker seized him with both arms from behind. For some minutes nothing could be distinguished in the scrimmage that followed. I believe Liza got up but was knocked down by another blow. Suddenly the crowd parted and a small space was left empty round Liza's prostrate figure, and Mavriky Nikolaevitch, frantic with grief and covered with blood, was standing over her, screaming, weeping, and wringing his hands. I don't remember exactly what followed after; I only remember that they began to carry Liza away. I ran after her. She was still alive and perhaps still conscious. The cabinet-maker and three other men in the crowd were seized. These three still deny having taken any part in the dastardly deed, stubbornly maintaining that they have been arrested by mistake. Perhaps it's the truth. Though the evidence against the cabinet-maker is clear, he is so irrational that he is still unable to explain what happened coherently. I too, as a spectator, though at some distance, had to give evidence at the inquest. I declared that it had all happened entirely accidentally through the action of men perhaps moved by ill-feeling, yet scarcely conscious of what they were doing—drunk and irresponsible. I am of that opinion to this day.

CHAPTER IV. THE LAST RESOLUTION

I

THAT MORNING MANY people saw Pyotr Stepanovitch. All who saw him remembered that he was in a particularly excited state. At two o'clock he went to see Gaganov, who had arrived from the country only the day before, and whose house was full of visitors hotly discussing the events of the previous day. Pyotr Stepanovitch talked more than anyone and made them listen to him. He was always considered among us as a "chatterbox of a student with a screw loose," but now he talked of Yulia Mihailovna, and in the general excitement the theme was an enthralling one. As one who had recently been her intimate and confidential friend, he disclosed many new and unexpected details concerning her; incidentally (and of course unguardedly) he repeated some of her own remarks about persons known to all in the town, and thereby piqued their vanity. He dropped it all in a vague and rambling way, like a man free from guile driven by his sense of honour to the painful necessity of clearing up a perfect mountain of misunderstandings, and so simple-hearted that he hardly knew where to begin and where to leave off. He let slip in a rather unguarded way, too, that Yulia Mihailovna knew the whole secret of Stavrogin and that she had been at the bottom of the whole intrigue. She had taken him in too, for he, Pyotr Stepanovitch, had also been in love with this unhappy Liza, yet he had been so hoodwinked that he had almost taken her to Stavrogin himself in the carriage. "Yes, yes, it's all very well for you to laugh, gentlemen, but if only I'd known, if I'd known how it would end!" he concluded. To various excited inquiries about Stavrogin he bluntly replied that in his opinion the catastrophe to the Lebyadkins was a pure coincidence, and that it was all Lebyadkin's own fault for displaying his money. He explained this particularly well. One of his listeners observed that it was no good his "pretending"; that he had eaten and drunk and almost slept at Yulia Mihailovna's, yet now he was the first to blacken her character, and that this was by no means such a fine thing to do as he supposed. But Pyotr Stepanovitch immediately defended himself.

"I ate and drank there not because I had no money, and it's not my fault that I was invited there. Allow me to judge for myself how far I need to be grateful for that."

The general impression was in his favour. "He may be rather absurd, and of course he is a nonsensical fellow, yet still he is not responsible for Yulia Mihailovna's foolishness. On the contrary, it appears that he tried to stop her."

About two o'clock the news suddenly came that Stavrogin, about whom there was so much talk, had suddenly left for Petersburg by the midday train. This interested people immensely; many of them frowned. Pyotr Stepanovitch was so much struck that I was told he turned quite pale and cried out strangely, "Why, how could they have let him go?" He hurried away from Gaganov's forthwith, yet he was seen in two or three other houses.

Towards dusk he succeeded in getting in to see Yulia Mihailovna though he had the greatest pains to do so, as she had absolutely refused to see him. I heard of this from the lady herself only three weeks afterwards, just before her departure for Petersburg. She gave me no details, but observed with a shudder that "he had on that occasion astounded her beyond all belief." I imagine that all he did was to terrify her by threatening to charge her with being an accomplice if she "said anything." The necessity for this intimidation arose from his plans at the moment, of which she, of course, knew nothing; and only later, five days afterwards, she guessed why he had been so doubtful of her reticence and so afraid of a new outburst of indignation on her part.

Between seven and eight o'clock, when it was dark, all the five members of the quintet met together at Ensign Erkel's lodgings in a little crooked house at the end of the town. The meeting had been fixed by Pyotr Stepanovitch himself, but he was unpardonably late, and the members waited over an hour for him. This Ensign Erkel was that young officer who had sat the whole evening at Virginsky's with a pencil in his hand and a notebook before him. He had not long been in the town; he lodged alone with two old women, sisters, in a secluded by-street and was shortly to leave the town; a meeting at his house was less likely to attract notice than anywhere. This strange boy was distinguished by extreme taciturnity: he was capable of sitting for a dozen evenings in succession in noisy company, with the most extraordinary conversation going on around him, without uttering a word, though he listened with extreme attention, watching the speakers with his childlike eyes. His face was very pretty and even had a certain look of cleverness. He did not belong to the quintet; it was supposed that he had some special job of a purely practical character. It is known now that he had nothing of the sort and probably did not understand his position himself. It was simply that he was filled with hero-worship for Pyotr Stepanovitch, whom he had only lately met. If he had met a monster of iniquity who had incited him to found a band of brigands on the pretext of some romantic and socialistic object, and as a test had bidden him rob and murder the first peasant he met, he would certainly have obeyed and done it. He had an invalid mother to whom he sent half of his scanty pay—and how she must have kissed that poor little flaxen head, how she must have trembled and prayed over it! I go into these details about him because I feel very sorry for him.

"Our fellows" were excited. The events of the previous night had made a great impression on them, and I fancy they were in a panic. The simple disorderliness in which they had so zealously and systematically taken part had ended in a way they had not expected. The fire in the night, the murder of the Lebyadkins, the savage brutality of the crowd with Liza, had been a series of surprises which they had not anticipated in their programme. They hotly accused the hand that had guided them of despotism and duplicity. In fact, while they were waiting for Pyotr Stepanovitch they worked each other up to such a point that they resolved again to ask him for a definite explanation, and if he evaded again, as he had done before, to dissolve the quintet and to found instead a new secret society "for the propaganda of ideas" and on their own initiative on the basis of democracy and equality. Liputin, Shigalov, and the authority on the peasantry supported this plan; Lyamshin said nothing, though he looked approving. Virginsky hesitated and wanted to hear Pyotr Stepanovitch first. It was decided to hear Pyotr Stepanovitch, but still he did not come; such casualness added fuel to the flames. Erkel was absolutely silent and did nothing but order the tea, which he brought from his landladies in glasses on a tray, not bringing in the samovar nor allowing the servant to enter.

Pyotr Stepanovitch did not turn up till half-past eight. With rapid steps he went up to the circular table before the sofa round which the company were seated; he kept his cap in his hand and refused tea. He looked angry, severe, and supercilious. He must have observed at once from their faces that they were "mutinous."

"Before I open my mouth, you've got something hidden; out with it."

Liputin began "in the name of all," and declared in a voice quivering with resentment "that if things were going on like that they might as well blow their brains out." Oh, they were not at all afraid to blow their brains out, they were quite ready to, in fact, but only to serve the common cause (a general movement of approbation). So he must be more open with them so that they might always know beforehand, "or else what would things be coming to?" (Again a stir and some guttural sounds.) To behave like this was humiliating and dangerous. "We don't say so because we are afraid, but if one acts and the rest are only pawns, then one would blunder and all would be lost." (Exclamations. "Yes, yes." General approval.)

"Damn it all, what do you want?"

"What connection is there between the common cause and the petty intrigues of Mr. Stavrogin?" cried Liputin, boiling over. "Suppose he is in some mysterious relation to the centre, if that legendary centre really exists at all, it's no concern of ours. And meantime a murder has been committed, the police have been roused; if they follow the thread they may find what it starts from."

"If Stavrogin and you are caught, we shall be caught too," added the authority on the peasantry.

"And to no good purpose for the common cause," Virginsky concluded despondently.

"What nonsense! The murder is a chance crime; it was committed by Fedka for the sake of robbery."

"H'm! Strange coincidence, though," said Liputin, wriggling.

"And if you will have it, it's all through you."

"Through us?"

"In the first place, you, Liputin, had a share in the intrigue yourself; and the second chief point is, you were ordered to get Lebyadkin away and given money to do it; and what did you do? If you'd got him away nothing would have happened."

"But wasn't it you yourself who suggested the idea that it would be a good thing to set him on to read his verses?"

"An idea is not a command. The command was to get him away."

"Command! Rather a queer word.... On the contrary, your orders were to delay sending him off."

"You made a mistake and showed your foolishness and self-will. The murder was the work of Fedka, and he carried it out alone for the sake of robbery. You heard the gossip and believed it. You were scared. Stavrogin is not such a fool, and the proof of that is he left the town at twelve o'clock after an interview with the vice-governor; if there were anything in it they would not let him go to Petersburg in broad daylight."

"But we are not making out that Mr. Stavrogin committed the murder himself," Liputin rejoined spitefully and unceremoniously. "He may have known nothing about it, like me; and you know very well that I knew nothing about it, though I am mixed up in it like mutton in a hash."

"Whom are you accusing?" said Pyotr Stepanovitch, looking at him darkly.

"Those whose interest it is to burn down towns."

"You make matters worse by wriggling out of it. However, won't you read this and pass it to the others, simply as a fact of interest?"

He pulled out of his pocket Lebyadkin's anonymous letter to Lembke and handed it to Liputin. The latter read it, was evidently surprised, and passed it thoughtfully to his neighbour; the letter quickly went the round.

"Is that really Lebyadkin's handwriting?" observed Shigalov.

"It is," answered Liputin and Tolkatchenko (the authority on the peasantry).

"I simply brought it as a fact of interest and because I knew you were so sentimental over Lebyadkin," repeated Pyotr Stepanovitch, taking the letter back. "So it turns out, gentlemen, that a stray Fedka relieves us quite by chance of a dangerous man. That's what chance does sometimes! It's instructive, isn't it?"

The members exchanged rapid glances.

"And now, gentlemen, it's my turn to ask questions," said Pyotr Stepanovitch, assuming an air of dignity. "Let me know what business you had to set fire to the town without permission."

"What's this! We, we set fire to the town? That is laying the blame on others!" they exclaimed.

"I quite understand that you carried the game too far," Pyotr Stepanovitch persisted stubbornly, "but it's not a matter of petty scandals with Yulia Mihailovna. I've brought you here gentlemen, to explain to you the greatness of the danger you have so stupidly incurred, which is a menace to much besides yourselves."

"Excuse me, we, on the contrary, were intending just now to point out to you the greatness of the despotism and unfairness you have shown in taking such a serious and also strange step without consulting the members," Virginsky, who had been hitherto silent, protested, almost with indignation.

"And so you deny it? But I maintain that you set fire to the town, you and none but you. Gentlemen, don't tell lies! I have good evidence. By your rashness you exposed the common cause to danger. You are only one knot in an endless network of knots—and your duty is blind obedience to the centre. Yet three men of you incited the Shpigulin men to set fire to the town without the least instruction to do so, and the fire has taken place."

"What three? What three of us?"

"The day before yesterday, at three o'clock in the night, you, Tolkatchenko, were inciting Fomka Zavyalov at the 'Forget-me-not.'"

"Upon my word!" cried the latter, jumping up, "I scarcely said a word to him, and what I did say was without intention, simply because he had been flogged that morning. And I dropped it at once; I saw he was too drunk. If you had not referred to it I should not have thought of it again. A word could not set the place on fire."

"You are like a man who should be surprised that a tiny spark could blow a whole powder magazine into the air."

"I spoke in a whisper in his ear, in a corner; how could you have heard of it?"

Tolkatchenko reflected suddenly.

"I was sitting there under the table. Don't disturb yourselves, gentlemen; I know every step you take. You smile sarcastically, Mr. Liputin? But I know, for instance, that you pinched your wife black and blue at midnight, three days ago, in your bedroom as you were going to bed."

Liputin's mouth fell open and he turned pale. (It was afterwards found out that he knew of this exploit of Liputin's from Agafya, Liputin's servant, whom he had paid from the beginning to spy on him; this only came out later.)

"May I state a fact?" said Shigalov, getting up.

"State it."

Shigalov sat down and pulled himself together.

"So far as I understand—and it's impossible not to understand it—you yourself at first and a second time later, drew with great eloquence, but too theoretically, a picture of Russia covered with an endless network of knots. Each of these centres of activity, proselytising and ramifying endlessly, aims by systematic denunciation to injure the prestige of local authority, to reduce the villages to confusion, to spread cynicism and scandals, together with complete disbelief in everything and an eagerness for something better, and finally, by means of fires, as a pre-eminently national method, to reduce the country at a given moment, if need be, to desperation. Are those your words which I tried to remember accurately? Is that the programme you gave us as the authorised representative of the central committee, which is to this day utterly unknown to us and almost like a myth?"

"It's correct, only you are very tedious."

"Every one has a right to express himself in his own way. Giving us to understand that the separate knots of the general network already covering Russia number by now several hundred, and propounding the theory that if every one does his work successfully, all Russia at a given moment, at a signal …"

"Ah, damn it all, I have enough to do without you!" cried Pyotr Stepanovitch, twisting in his chair.

"Very well, I'll cut it short and I'll end simply by asking if we've seen the disorderly scenes, we've seen the discontent of the people, we've seen and taken part in the downfall of local administration, and finally, we've seen with our own eyes the town on fire? What do you find amiss? Isn't that your programme? What can you blame us for?"

"Acting on your own initiative!" Pyotr Stepanovitch cried furiously. "While I am here you ought not to have dared to act without my permission. Enough. We are on the eve of betrayal, and perhaps to-morrow or to-night you'll be seized. So there. I have authentic information."

At this all were agape with astonishment.

"You will be arrested not only as the instigators of the fire, but as a quintet. The traitor knows the whole secret of the network. So you see what a mess you've made of it!"

"Stavrogin, no doubt," cried Liputin.

"What … why Stavrogin?" Pyotr Stepanovitch seemed suddenly taken aback. "Hang it all," he cried, pulling himself together at once, "it's Shatov! I believe you all know now that Shatov in his time was one of the society. I must tell you that, watching him through persons he does not suspect, I found out to my amazement that he knows all about the organisation of the network and … everything, in fact. To save himself from being charged with having formerly belonged, he will give information against all. He has been hesitating up till now and I have spared him. Your fire has decided him: he is shaken and will hesitate no longer. To-morrow we shall be arrested as incendiaries and political offenders."

"Is it true? How does Shatov know?" The excitement was indescribable.

"It's all perfectly true. I have no right to reveal the source from which I learnt it or how I discovered it, but I tell you what I can do for you meanwhile: through one person I can act on Shatov so that without his suspecting it he will put off giving information, but not more than for twenty-four hours." All were silent.

"We really must send him to the devil!" Tolkatchenko was the first to exclaim.

"It ought to have been done long ago," Lyamshin put in malignantly, striking the table with his fist.

"But how is it to be done?" muttered Liputin. Pyotr Stepanovitch at once took up the question and unfolded his plan. The plan was the following day at nightfall to draw Shatov away to a secluded spot to hand over the secret printing press which had been in his keeping and was buried there, and there "to settle things." He went into various essential details which we will omit here, and explained minutely Shatov's present ambiguous attitude to the central society, of which the reader knows already.

"That's all very well," Liputin observed irresolutely, "but since it will be another adventure … of the same sort … it will make too great a sensation."

"No doubt," assented Pyotr Stepanovitch, "but I've provided against that. We have the means of averting suspicion completely."

And with the same minuteness he told them about Kirillov, of his intention to shoot himself, and of his promise to wait for a signal from them and to leave a letter behind him taking on himself anything they dictated to him (all of which the reader knows already).

"His determination to take his own life—a philosophic, or as I should call it, insane decision—has become known there" Pyotr Stepanovitch went on to explain. "There not a thread, not a grain of dust is overlooked; everything is turned to the service of the cause. Foreseeing how useful it might be and satisfying themselves that his intention was quite serious, they had offered him the means to come to Russia (he was set for some reason on dying in Russia), gave him a commission which he promised to carry out (and he had done so), and had, moreover, bound him by a promise, as you already know, to commit suicide only when he was told to. He promised everything. You must note that he belongs to the organisation on a particular footing and is anxious to be of service; more than that I can't tell you. To-morrow, after Shatov's affair, I'll dictate a note to him saying that he is responsible for his death. That will seem very plausible: they were friends and travelled together to America, there they quarrelled; and it will all be explained in the letter … and … and perhaps, if it seems feasible, we might dictate something more to Kirillov—something about the manifestoes, for instance, and even perhaps about the fire. But I'll think about that. You needn't worry yourselves, he has no prejudices; he'll sign anything."

There were expressions of doubt. It sounded a fantastic story. But they had all heard more or less about Kirillov; Liputin more than all.

"He may change his mind and not want to," said Shigalov; "he is a madman anyway, so he is not much to build upon."

"Don't be uneasy, gentlemen, he will want to," Pyotr Stepanovitch snapped out. "I am obliged by our agreement to give him warning the day before, so it must be to-day. I invite Liputin to go with me at once to see him and make certain, and he will tell you, gentlemen, when he comes back—to-day if need be—whether what I say is true. However," he broke off suddenly with intense exasperation, as though he suddenly felt he was doing people like them too much honour by wasting time in persuading them, "however, do as you please. If you don't decide to do it, the union is broken up—but solely through your insubordination and treachery. In that case we are all independent from this moment. But under those circumstances, besides the unpleasantness of Shatov's betrayal and its consequences, you will have brought upon yourselves another little unpleasantness of which you were definitely warned when the union was formed. As far as I am concerned, I am not much afraid of you, gentlemen.… Don't imagine that I am so involved with you.… But that's no matter."

"Yes, we decide to do it," Liputin pronounced.

"There's no other way out of it," muttered Tolkatchenko, "and if only Liputin confirms about Kirillov, then …

"I am against it; with all my soul and strength I protest against such a murderous decision," said Virginsky, standing up.

"But?" asked Pyotr Stepanovitch.…

"But what?"

"You said but … and I am waiting."

"I don't think I did say but … I only meant to say that if you decide to do it, then …"

"Then?"

Virginsky did not answer.

"I think that one is at liberty to neglect danger to one's own life," said Erkel, suddenly opening his mouth, "but if it may injure the cause, then I consider one ought not to dare to neglect danger to one's life.…"

He broke off in confusion, blushing. Absorbed as they all were in their own ideas, they all looked at him in amazement—it was such a surprise that he too could speak.

"I am for the cause," Virginsky pronounced suddenly.

Every one got up. It was decided to communicate once more and make final arrangements at midday on the morrow, though without meeting. The place where the printing press was hidden was announced and each was assigned his part and his duty. Liputin and Pyotr Stepanovitch promptly set off together to Kirillov.

II

All our fellows believed that Shatov was going to betray them; but they also believed that Pyotr Stepanovitch was playing with them like pawns. And yet they knew, too, that in any case they would all meet on the spot next day and that Shatov's fate was sealed. They suddenly felt like flies caught in a web by a huge spider; they were furious, but they were trembling with terror.

Pyotr Stepanovitch, of course, had treated them badly; it might all have gone off far more harmoniously and easily if he had taken the trouble to embellish the facts ever so little. Instead of putting the facts in a decorous light, as an exploit worthy of ancient Rome or something of the sort, he simply appealed to their animal fears and laid stress on the danger to their own skins, which was simply insulting; of course there was a struggle for existence in everything and there was no other principle in nature, they all knew that, but still.…

But Pyotr Stepanovitch had no time to trot out the Romans; he was completely thrown out of his reckoning. Stavrogin's flight had astounded and crushed him. It was a lie when he said that Stavrogin had seen the vice-governor; what worried Pyotr Stepanovitch was that Stavrogin had gone off without seeing anyone, even his mother—and it was certainly strange that he had been allowed to leave without hindrance. (The authorities were called to account for it afterwards.) Pyotr Stepanovitch had been making inquiries all day, but so far had found out nothing, and he had never been so upset. And how could he, how could he give up Stavrogin all at once like this! That was why he could not be very tender with the quintet. Besides, they tied his hands: he had already decided to gallop after Stavrogin at once; and meanwhile he was detained by Shatov; he had to cement the quintet together once for all, in case of emergency. "Pity to waste them, they might be of use." That, I imagine, was his way of reasoning.

As for Shatov, Pyotr Stepanovitch was firmly convinced that he would betray them.

All that he had told the others about it was a lie: he had never seen the document nor heard of it, but he thought it as certain as that twice two makes four. It seemed to him that what had happened—the death of Liza, the death of Marya Timofyevna—would be too much for Shatov, and that he would make up his mind at once. Who knows? perhaps he had grounds for supposing it. It is known, too, that he hated Shatov personally; there had at some time been a quarrel between them, and Pyotr Stepanovitch never forgave an offence. I am convinced, indeed, that this was his leading motive.

We have narrow brick pavements in our town, and in some streets only raised wooden planks instead of a pavement. Pyotr Stepanovitch walked in the middle of the pavement, taking up the whole of it, utterly regardless of Liputin, who had no room to walk beside him and so had to hurry a step behind or run in the muddy road if he wanted to speak to him. Pyotr Stepanovitch suddenly remembered how he had lately splashed through the mud to keep pace with Stavrogin, who had walked, as he was doing now, taking up the whole pavement. He recalled the whole scene, and rage choked him.

But Liputin, too, was choking with resentment. Pyotr Stepanovitch might treat the others as he liked, but him! Why, he knew more than all the rest, was in closer touch with the work and taking more intimate part in it than anyone, and hitherto his services had been continual, though indirect. Oh, he knew that even now Pyotr Stepanovitch might ruin him if it came to the worst. But he had long hated Pyotr Stepanovitch, and not because he was a danger but because of his overbearing manner. Now, when he had to make up his mind to such a deed, he raged inwardly more than all the rest put together. Alas! he knew that next day "like a slave" he would be the first on the spot and would bring the others, and if he could somehow have murdered Pyotr Stepanovitch before the morrow, without ruining himself, of course, he would certainly have murdered him.

Absorbed in his sensations, he trudged dejectedly after his tormentor, who seemed to have forgotten his existence, though he gave him a rude and careless shove with his elbow now and then. Suddenly Pyotr Stepanovitch halted in one of the principal thoroughfares and went into a restaurant.

"What are you doing?" cried Liputin, boiling over. "This is a restaurant."

"I want a beefsteak."

"Upon my word! It is always full of people."

"What if it is?"

"But ... we shall be late. It's ten o'clock already."

"You can't be too late to go there."

"But I shall be late! They are expecting me back."

"Well, let them; but it would be stupid of you to go to them. With all your bobbery I've had no dinner. And the later you go to Kirillov's the more sure you are to find him."

Pyotr Stepanovitch went to a room apart. Liputin sat in an easy chair on one side, angry and resentful, and watched him eating. Half an hour and more passed. Pyotr Stepanovitch did not hurry himself; he ate with relish, rang the bell, asked for a different kind of mustard, then for beer, without saying a word to Liputin. He was pondering deeply. He was capable of doing two things at once—eating with relish and pondering deeply. Liputin loathed him so intensely at last that he could not tear himself away. It was like a nervous obsession. He counted every morsel of beefsteak that Pyotr Stepanovitch put into his mouth; he loathed him for the way he opened it, for the way he chewed, for the way he smacked his lips over the fat morsels, he loathed the steak itself. At last things began to swim before his eyes; he began to feel slightly giddy; he felt hot and cold run down his spine by turns.

"You are doing nothing; read that," said Pyotr Stepanovitch suddenly, throwing him a sheet of paper. Liputin went nearer to the candle. The paper was closely covered with bad handwriting, with corrections in every line. By the time he had mastered it Pyotr Stepanovitch had paid his bill and was ready to go. When they were on the pavement Liputin handed him back the paper.

"Keep it; I'll tell you afterwards.... What do you say to it, though?"

Liputin shuddered all over.

"In my opinion ... such a manifesto ... is nothing but a ridiculous absurdity."

His anger broke out; he felt as though he were being caught up and carried along.

"If we decide to distribute such manifestoes," he said, quivering all over, "we'll make ourselves, contemptible by our stupidity and incompetence."

"H'm! I think differently," said Pyotr Stepanovitch, walking on resolutely.

"So do I; surely it isn't your work?"

"That's not your business."

"I think too that doggerel, 'A Noble Personality,' is the most utter trash possible, and it couldn't have been written by Herzen."

"You are talking nonsense; it's a good poem."

"I am surprised, too, for instance," said Liputin, still dashing along with desperate leaps, "that it is suggested that we should act so as to bring everything to the ground. It's natural in Europe to wish to destroy everything because there's a proletariat there, but we are only amateurs here and in my opinion are only showing off."

"I thought you were a Fourierist."

"Fourier says something quite different, quite different."

"I know it's nonsense."

"No, Fourier isn't nonsense.... Excuse me, I can't believe that there will be a rising in May."

Liputin positively unbuttoned his coat, he was so hot.

"Well, that's enough; but now, that I mayn't forget it," said Pyotr Stepanovitch, passing with extraordinary coolness to another subject, "you will have to print this manifesto with your own hands. We're going to dig up Shatov's printing press, and you will take it to-morrow. As quickly as possible you must print as many copies as you can, and then distribute them all the winter. The means will be provided. You must do as many copies as possible, for you'll be asked for them from other places."

"No, excuse me; I can't undertake such a … I decline."

"You'll take it all the same. I am acting on the instructions of the central committee, and you are bound to obey."

"And I consider that our centres abroad have forgotten what Russia is like and have lost all touch, and that's why they talk such nonsense.… I even think that instead of many hundreds of quintets in Russia, we are the only one that exists, and there is no network at all," Liputin gasped finally.

"The more contemptible of you, then, to run after the cause without believing in it … and you are running after me now like a mean little cur."

"No, I'm not. We have a full right to break off and found a new society."

"Fool!" Pyotr Stepanovitch boomed at him threateningly all of a sudden, with flashing eyes.

They stood facing one another for some time. Pyotr Stepanovitch turned and pursued his way confidently.

The idea flashed through Liputin's mind, "Turn and go back; if I don't turn now I shall never go back." He pondered this for ten steps, but at the eleventh a new and desperate idea flashed into his mind: he did not turn and did not go back.

They were approaching Filipov's house, but before reaching it they turned down a side street, or, to be more accurate, an inconspicuous path under a fence, so that for some time they had to walk along a steep slope above a ditch where they could not keep their footing without holding the fence. At a dark corner in the slanting fence Pyotr Stepanovitch took out a plank, leaving a gap, through which he promptly scrambled. Liputin was surprised, but he crawled through after him; then they replaced the plank after them. This was the secret way by which Fedka used to visit Kirillov.

"Shatov mustn't know that we are here," Pyotr Stepanovitch whispered sternly to Liputin.

III

Kirillov was sitting on his leather sofa drinking tea, as he always was at that hour. He did not get up to meet them, but gave a sort of start and looked at the new-comers anxiously.

"You are not mistaken," said Pyotr Stepanovitch, "it's just that I've come about."

"To-day?"

"No, no, to-morrow … about this time." And he hurriedly sat down at the table, watching Kirillov's agitation with some uneasiness. But the latter had already regained his composure and looked as usual.

"These people still refuse to believe in you. You are not vexed at my bringing Liputin?"

"To-day I am not vexed; to-morrow I want to be alone."

"But not before I come, and therefore in my presence."

"I should prefer not in your presence."

"You remember you promised to write and to sign all I dictated."

"I don't care. And now will you be here long?"

"I have to see one man and to remain half an hour, so whatever you say I shall stay that half-hour."

Kirillov did not speak. Liputin meanwhile sat down on one side under the portrait of the bishop. That last desperate idea gained more and more possession of him. Kirillov scarcely noticed him. Liputin had heard of Kirillov's theory before and always laughed at him; but now he was silent and looked gloomily round him.

"I've no objection to some tea," said Pyotr Stepanovitch, moving up. "I've just had some steak and was reckoning on getting tea with you."

"Drink it. You can have some if you like."

"You used to offer it to me," observed Pyotr Stepanovitch sourly.

"That's no matter. Let Liputin have some too."

"No, I … can't."

"Don't want to or can't?" said Pyotr Stepanovitch, turning quickly to him.

"I am not going to here," Liputin said expressively.

Pyotr Stepanovitch frowned.

"There's a flavour of mysticism about that; goodness knows what to make of you people!"

No one answered; there was a full minute of silence.

"But I know one thing," he added abruptly, "that no superstition will prevent any one of us from doing his duty."

"Has Stavrogin gone?" asked Kirillov.

"Yes."

"He's done well."

Pyotr Stepanovitch's eyes gleamed, but he restrained himself.

"I don't care what you think as long as every one keeps his word."

"I'll keep my word."

"I always knew that you would do your duty like an independent and progressive man."

"You are an absurd fellow."

"That may be; I am very glad to amuse you. I am always glad if I can give people pleasure."

"You are very anxious I should shoot myself and are afraid I might suddenly not?"

"Well, you see, it was your own doing—connecting your plan with our work. Reckoning on your plan we have already done something, so that you couldn't refuse now because you've let us in for it."

"You've no claim at all."

"I understand, I understand; you are perfectly free, and we don't come in so long as your free intention is carried out."

"And am I to take on myself all the nasty things you've done?"

"Listen, Kirillov, are you afraid? If you want to cry off, say so at once."

"I am not afraid."

"I ask because you are making so many inquiries."

"Are you going soon?"

"Asking questions again?"

Kirillov scanned him contemptuously.

"You see," Pyotr Stepanovitch went on, getting angrier and angrier, and unable to take the right tone, "you want me to go away, to be alone, to concentrate yourself, but all that's a bad sign for you—for you above all. You want to think a great deal. To my mind you'd better not think. And really you make me uneasy."

"There's only one thing I hate, that at such a moment I should have a reptile like you beside me."

"Oh, that doesn't matter. I'll go away at the time and stand on the steps if you like. If you are so concerned about trifles when it comes to dying, then … it's all a very bad sign. I'll go out on to the steps and you can imagine I know nothing about it, and that I am a man infinitely below you."

"No, not infinitely; you've got abilities, but there's a lot you don't understand because you are a low man."

"Delighted, delighted. I told you already I am delighted to provide entertainment … at such a moment."

"You don't understand anything."

"That is, I … well, I listen with respect, anyway."

"You can do nothing; even now you can't hide your petty spite, though it's not to your interest to show it. You'll make me cross, and then I may want another six months." Pyotr Stepanovitch looked at his watch. "I never understood your theory, but I know you didn't invent it for our sakes, so I suppose you would carry it out apart from us. And I know too that you haven't mastered the idea but the idea has mastered you, so you won't put it off."

"What? The idea has mastered me?"

"Yes."

"And not I mastered the idea? That's good. You have a little sense. Only you tease me and I am proud."

"That's a good thing, that's a good thing. Just what you need, to be proud."

"Enough. You've drunk your tea; go away."

"Damn it all, I suppose I must"—Pyotr Stepanovitch got up—"though it's early. Listen, Kirillov. Shall I find that man—you know whom I mean—at Myasnitchiha's? Or has she too been lying?"

"You won't find him, because he is here and not there."

"Here! Damn it all, where?"

"Sitting in the kitchen, eating and drinking."

"How dared he?" cried Pyotr Stepanovitch, flushing angrily. "It was his duty to wait … what nonsense! He has no passport, no money!"

"I don't know. He came to say good-bye; he is dressed and ready. He is going away and won't come back. He says you are a scoundrel and he doesn't want to wait for your money."

"Ha ha! He is afraid that I'll … But even now I can … if … Where is he, in the kitchen?"

Kirillov opened a side door into a tiny dark room; from this room three steps led straight to the part of the kitchen where the cook's bed was usually put, behind the partition. Here, in the corner under the ikons, Fedka was sitting now, at a bare deal table. Before him stood a pint bottle, a plate of bread, and some cold beef and potatoes on an earthenware dish. He was eating in a leisurely way and was already half drunk, but he was wearing his sheep-skin coat and was evidently ready for a journey. A samovar was boiling the other side of the screen, but it was not for Fedka, who had every night for a week or more zealously blown it up and got it ready for "Alexey Nilitch, for he's such a habit of drinking tea at nights." I am strongly disposed to believe that, as Kirillov had not a cook, he had cooked the beef and potatoes that morning with his own hands for Fedka.

"What notion is this?" cried Pyotr Stepanovitch, whisking into the room. "Why didn't you wait where you were ordered?"

And swinging his fist, he brought it down heavily on the table.

Fedka assumed an air of dignity.

"You wait a bit, Pyotr Stepanovitch, you wait a bit," he began, with a swaggering emphasis on each word, "it's your first duty to understand here that you are on a polite visit to Mr. Kirillov, Alexey Nilitch, whose boots you might clean any day, because beside you he is a man of culture and you are only—foo!"

And he made a jaunty show of spitting to one side. Haughtiness and determination were evident in his manner, and a certain very threatening assumption of argumentative calm that suggested an outburst to follow. But Pyotr Stepanovitch had no time to realise the danger, and it did not fit in with his preconceived ideas. The incidents and disasters of the day had quite turned his head. Liputin, at the top of the three steps, stared inquisitively down from the little dark room.

"Do you or don't you want a trustworthy passport and good money to go where you've been told? Yes or no?"

"D'you see, Pyotr Stepanovitch, you've been deceiving me from the first, and so you've been a regular scoundrel to me. For all the world like a filthy human louse—that's how I look on you. You've promised me a lot of money for shedding innocent blood and swore it was for Mr. Stavrogin, though it turns out to be nothing but your want of breeding. I didn't get a farthing out of it, let alone fifteen hundred, and Mr. Stavrogin hit you in the face, which has come to our ears. Now you are threatening me again and promising me money—what for, you don't say. And I shouldn't wonder if you are sending me to Petersburg to plot some revenge in your spite against Mr. Stavrogin, Nikolay Vsyevolodovitch, reckoning on my simplicity. And that proves you are the chief murderer. And do you know what you deserve for the very fact that in the depravity of your heart you've given up believing in God Himself, the true Creator? You are no better than an idolater and are on a level with the Tatar and the Mordva. Alexey Nilitch, who is a philosopher, has expounded the true God, the Creator, many a time to you, as well as the creation of the world and the fate that's to come and the transformation of every sort of creature and every sort of beast out of the Apocalypse, but you've persisted like a senseless idol in your deafness and your dumbness and have brought Ensign Erkel to the same, like the veriest evil seducer and so-called atheist...."

"Ah, you drunken dog! He strips the ikons of their setting and then preaches about God!"

"D'you see, Pyotr Stepanovitch, I tell you truly that I have stripped the ikons, but I only took out the pearls; and how do you know? Perhaps my own tear was transformed into a pearl in the furnace of the Most High to make up for my sufferings, seeing I am just that very orphan, having no daily refuge. Do you know from the books that once, in ancient times, a merchant with just such tearful sighs and prayers stole a pearl from the halo of the Mother of God, and afterwards, in the face of all the people, laid the whole price of it at her feet, and the Holy Mother sheltered him with her mantle before all the people, so that it was a miracle, and the command was given through the authorities to write it all down word for word in the

Imperial books. And you let a mouse in, so you insulted the very throne of God. And if you were not my natural master, whom I dandled in my arms when I was a stripling, I would have done for you now, without budging from this place!"

Pyotr Stepanovitch flew into a violent rage.

"Tell me, have you seen Stavrogin to-day?"

"Don't you dare to question me. Mr. Stavrogin is fairly amazed at you, and he had no share in it even in wish, let alone instructions or giving money. You've presumed with me."

"You'll get the money and you'll get another two thousand in Petersburg, when you get there, in a lump sum, and you'll get more."

"You are lying, my fine gentleman, and it makes me laugh to see how easily you are taken in. Mr. Stavrogin stands at the top of the ladder above you, and you yelp at him from below like a silly puppy dog, while he thinks it would be doing you an honour to spit at you."

"But do you know," cried Pyotr Stepanovitch in a rage, "that I won't let you stir a step from here, you scoundrel, and I'll hand you straight over to the police."

Fedka leapt on to his feet and his eyes gleamed with fury. Pyotr Stepanovitch pulled out his revolver. Then followed a rapid and revolting scene: before Pyotr Stepanovitch could take aim, Fedka swung round and in a flash struck him on the cheek with all his might. Then there was the thud of a second blow, a third, then a fourth, all on the cheek. Pyotr Stepanovitch was dazed; with his eyes starting out of his head, he muttered something, and suddenly crashed full length to the ground.

"There you are; take him," shouted Fedka with a triumphant swagger; he instantly took up his cap, his bag from under the bench, and was gone. Pyotr Stepanovitch lay gasping and unconscious. Liputin even imagined that he had been murdered. Kirillov ran headlong into the kitchen.

"Water!" he cried, and ladling some water in an iron dipper from a bucket, he poured it over the injured man's head. Pyotr Stepanovitch stirred, raised his head, sat up, and looked blankly about him.

"Well, how are you?" asked Kirillov. Pyotr Stepanovitch looked at him intently, still not recognising him; but seeing Liputin peeping in from the kitchen, he smiled his hateful smile and suddenly got up, picking up his revolver from the floor.

"If you take it into your head to run away to-morrow like that scoundrel Stavrogin," he cried, pouncing furiously on Kirillov, pale, stammering, and hardly able to articulate his words, "I'll hang you … like a fly … or crush you … if it's at the other end of the world … do you understand!"

And he held the revolver straight at Kirillov's head; but almost at the same minute, coming completely to himself, he drew back his hand, thrust the revolver into his pocket, and without saying another word ran out of the house. Liputin followed him. They clambered through the same gap and again walked along the slope holding to the fence. Pyotr Stepanovitch strode rapidly down the street so that Liputin could scarcely keep up with him. At the first crossing, he suddenly stopped.

"Well?" He turned to Liputin with a challenge.

Liputin remembered the revolver and was still trembling all over after the scene he had witnessed; but the answer seemed to come of itself irresistibly from his tongue:

"I think ... I think that ..."

"Did you see what Fedka was drinking in the kitchen?"

"What he was drinking? He was drinking vodka."

"Well then, let me tell you it's the last time in his life he will drink vodka. I recommend you to remember that and reflect on it. And now go to hell; you are not wanted till to-morrow. But mind now, don't be a fool!"

Liputin rushed home full speed.

IV

He had long had a passport in readiness made out in a false name. It seems a wild idea that this prudent little man, the petty despot of his family, who was, above all things, a sharp man of business and a capitalist, and who was an official too (though he was a Fourierist), should long before have conceived the fantastic project of procuring this passport in case of emergency, that he might escape abroad by means of it if ... he did admit the possibility of this if, though no doubt he was never able himself to formulate what this if might mean.

But now it suddenly formulated itself, and in a most unexpected way. That desperate idea with which he had gone to Kirillov's after that "fool" he had heard from Pyotr Stepanovitch on the pavement, had been to abandon everything at dawn next day and to emigrate abroad. If anyone doubts that such fantastic incidents occur in everyday Russian life, even now, let him look into the biographies of all the Russian exiles abroad. Not one of them escaped with more wisdom or real justification. It has always been the unrestrained domination of phantoms and nothing more.

Running home, he began by locking himself in, getting out his travelling bag, and feverishly beginning to pack. His chief anxiety was the question of money, and how much he could rescue from the impending ruin—and by what means. He thought of it as "rescuing," for it seemed to him that he could not linger an hour, and that by daylight he must be on the high road. He did not know where to take the train either; he vaguely determined to take it at the second or third big station from the town, and to make his way there on foot, if necessary. In that way, instinctively and mechanically he busied himself in his packing with a perfect whirl of ideas in his head—and suddenly stopped short, gave it all up, and with a deep groan stretched himself on the sofa.

He felt clearly, and suddenly realised that he might escape, but that he was by now utterly incapable of deciding whether he ought to make off before or after Shatov's death; that he was simply a lifeless body, a crude inert mass; that he was being moved by an awful outside power;

and that, though he had a passport to go abroad, that though he could run away from Shatov (otherwise what need was there of such haste?), yet he would run away, not from Shatov, not before his murder, but after it, and that that was determined, signed, and sealed.

In insufferable distress, trembling every instant and wondering at himself, alternately groaning aloud and numb with terror, he managed to exist till eleven o'clock next morning locked in and lying on the sofa; then came the shock he was awaiting, and it at once determined him. When he unlocked his door and went out to his household at eleven o'clock they told him that the runaway convict and brigand, Fedka, who was a terror to every one, who had pillaged churches and only lately been guilty of murder and arson, who was being pursued and could not be captured by our police, had been found at daybreak murdered, five miles from the town, at a turning off the high road, and that the whole town was talking of it already. He rushed headlong out of the house at once to find out further details, and learned, to begin with, that Fedka, who had been found with his skull broken, had apparently been robbed and, secondly, that the police already had strong suspicion and even good grounds for believing that the murderer was one of the Shpigulin men called Fomka, the very one who had been his accomplice in murdering the Lebyadkins and setting fire to their house, and that there had been a quarrel between them on the road about a large sum of money stolen from Lebyadkin, which Fedka was supposed to have hidden. Liputin ran to Pyotr Stepanovitch's lodgings and succeeded in learning at the back door, on the sly, that though Pyotr Stepanovitch had not returned home till about one o'clock at night, he had slept there quietly all night till eight o'clock next morning. Of course, there could be no doubt that there was nothing extraordinary about Fedka's death, and that such careers usually have such an ending; but the coincidence of the fatal words that "it was the last time Fedka would drink vodka," with the prompt fulfilment of the prediction, was so remarkable that Liputin no longer hesitated. The shock had been given; it was as though a stone had fallen upon him and crushed him forever. Returning home, he thrust his travelling-bag under the bed without a word, and in the evening at the hour fixed he was the first to appear at the appointed spot to meet Shatov, though it's true he still had his passport in his pocket.

CHAPTER V. A WANDERER

I

THE CATASTROPHE WITH Liza and the death of Marya Timofyevna made an overwhelming impression on Shatov. I have already mentioned that that morning I met him in passing; he seemed to me not himself. He told me among other things that on the evening before at nine o'clock (that is, three hours before the fire had broken out) he had been at Marya Timofyevna's. He went in the morning to look at the corpses, but as far as I know gave no evidence of any sort that morning. Meanwhile, towards the end of the day there was a perfect tempest in his soul, and ... I think I can say with certainty that there was a moment at dusk when he wanted to get up, go out and tell everything. What that everything was, no one but he could say. Of course he would have achieved nothing, and would have simply betrayed himself. He had no proofs whatever with which to convict the perpetrators of the crime, and, indeed, he had nothing but vague conjectures to go upon, though to him they amounted to complete certainty. But he was ready to ruin himself if he could only "crush the scoundrels"—his own words. Pyotr Stepanovitch had guessed fairly correctly at this impulse in him, and he knew himself that he was risking a great deal in putting off the execution of his new awful project till next day. On his side there was, as usual, great self-confidence and contempt for all these "wretched creatures" and for Shatov in particular. He had for years despised Shatov for his "whining idiocy," as he had expressed it in former days abroad, and he was absolutely confident that he could deal with such a guileless creature, that is, keep an eye on him all that day, and put a check on him at the first sign of danger. Yet what saved "the scoundrels" for a short time was something quite unexpected which they had not foreseen....

Towards eight o'clock in the evening (at the very time when the quintet was meeting at Erkel's, and waiting in indignation and excitement for Pyotr Stepanovitch) Shatov was lying in the dark on his bed with a headache and a slight chill; he was tortured by uncertainty, he was angry, he kept making up his mind, and could not make it up finally, and felt, with a curse, that it would all lead to nothing. Gradually he sank into a brief doze and had something like a nightmare. He dreamt that he was lying on his bed, tied up with cords and unable to stir, and meantime he heard a terrible banging that echoed all over the house, a banging on the fence, at the gate, at his door, in Kirillov's lodge, so that the whole house was shaking, and a far-away familiar voice that wrung his heart was calling to him piteously. He suddenly woke and sat up in bed. To his surprise the banging at the gate went on, though not nearly so violent as it had seemed in his dream. The knocks were repeated and persistent, and the strange voice "that wrung his heart" could still be heard below at the gate, though not piteously but angrily and impatiently, alternating with another voice, more restrained and ordinary. He jumped up, opened the casement pane and put his head out.

"Who's there?" he called, literally numb with terror.

"If you are Shatov," the answer came harshly and resolutely from below, "be so good as to tell me straight out and honestly whether you agree to let me in or not?"

It was true: he recognised the voice!

"Marie!… Is it you?"

"Yes, yes, Marya Shatov, and I assure you I can't keep the driver a minute longer."

"This minute … I'll get a candle," Shatov cried faintly. Then he rushed to look for the matches. The matches, as always happens at such moments, could not be found. He dropped the candlestick and the candle on the floor and as soon as he heard the impatient voice from below again, he abandoned the search and dashed down the steep stairs to open the gate.

"Be so good as to hold the bag while I settle with this blockhead," was how Madame Marya Shatov greeted him below, and she thrust into his hands a rather light cheap canvas handbag studded with brass nails, of Dresden manufacture. She attacked the driver with exasperation.

"Allow me to tell you, you are asking too much. If you've been driving me for an extra hour through these filthy streets, that's your fault, because it seems you didn't know where to find this stupid street and imbecile house. Take your thirty kopecks and make up your mind that you'll get nothing more."

"Ech, lady, you told me yourself Voznesensky Street and this is Bogoyavlensky; Voznesensky is ever so far away. You've simply put the horse into a steam."

"Voznesensky, Bogoyavlensky—you ought to know all those stupid names better than I do, as you are an inhabitant; besides, you are unfair, I told you first of all Filipov's house and you declared you knew it. In any case you can have me up to-morrow in the local court, but now I beg you to let me alone."

"Here, here's another five kopecks." With eager haste Shatov pulled a five-kopeck piece out of his pocket and gave it to the driver.

"Do me a favour, I beg you, don't dare to do that!" Madame Shatov flared up, but the driver drove off and Shatov, taking her hand, drew her through the gate.

"Make haste, Marie, make haste … that's no matter, and … you are wet through. Take care, we go up here—how sorry I am there's no light—the stairs are steep, hold tight, hold tight! Well, this is my room. Excuse my having no light … One minute!"

He picked up the candlestick but it was a long time before the matches were found. Madame Shatov stood waiting in the middle of the room, silent and motionless.

"Thank God, here they are at last!" he cried joyfully, lighting up the room. Marya Shatov took a cursory survey of his abode.

"They told me you lived in a poor way, but I didn't expect it to be as bad as this," she pronounced with an air of disgust, and she moved towards the bed.

"Oh, I am tired!" she sat down on the hard bed, with an exhausted air. "Please put down the bag and sit down on the chair yourself. Just as you like though; you are in the way standing there. I have come to you for a time, till I can get work, because I know nothing of this place and I have no money. But if I shall be in your way I beg you again, be so good as to tell me so at once, as you are bound to do if you are an honest man. I could sell something to-morrow and pay for a room at an hotel, but you must take me to the hotel yourself.... Oh, but I am tired!"

Shatov was all of a tremor.

"You mustn't, Marie, you mustn't go to an hotel! An hotel! What for? What for?"

He clasped his hands imploringly....

"Well, if I can get on without the hotel ... I must, any way, explain the position. Remember, Shatov, that we lived in Geneva as man and wife for a fortnight and a few days; it's three years since we parted, without any particular quarrel though. But don't imagine that I've come back to renew any of the foolishness of the past. I've come back to look for work, and that I've come straight to this town is just because it's all the same to me. I've not come to say I am sorry for anything; please don't imagine anything so stupid as that."

"Oh, Marie! This is unnecessary, quite unnecessary," Shatov muttered vaguely.

"If so, if you are so far developed as to be able to understand that, I may allow myself to add, that if I've come straight to you now and am in your lodging, it's partly because I always thought you were far from being a scoundrel and were perhaps much better than other ... blackguards!"

Her eyes flashed. She must have had to bear a great deal at the hands of some "blackguards."

"And please believe me, I wasn't laughing at you just now when I told you-you were good. I spoke plainly, without fine phrases and I can't endure them. But that's all nonsense. I always hoped you would have sense enough not to pester me.... Enough, I am tired."

And she bent on him a long, harassed and weary gaze. Shatov stood facing her at the other end of the room, which was five paces away, and listened to her timidly with a look of new life and unwonted radiance on his face. This strong, rugged man, all bristles on the surface, was suddenly all softness and shining gladness. There was a thrill of extraordinary and unexpected feeling in his soul. Three years of separation, three years of the broken marriage had effaced nothing from his heart. And perhaps every day during those three years he had dreamed of her, of that beloved being who had once said to him, "I love you." Knowing Shatov I can say with certainty that he could never have allowed himself even to dream that a woman might say to him, "I love you." He was savagely modest and chaste, he looked on himself as a perfect monster, detested his own face as well as his character, compared himself to some freak only fit to be exhibited at fairs. Consequently he valued honesty above everything and was fanatically devoted to his convictions; he was gloomy, proud, easily moved to wrath, and sparing of words. But here was the one being who had loved him for a fortnight (that he had never doubted, never!), a being he had always considered immeasurably above him in spite of his perfectly sober understanding of her errors; a being to whom he could forgive everything, everything (of that there could be no question; indeed it was quite the other way, his idea was that he was entirely to blame); this woman, this Marya Shatov, was in his house, in his presence again ... it was almost inconceivable! He was so overcome, there was so much that was terrible and at the same time so much happiness in this event that he could not, perhaps would not—perhaps was afraid to—realise the position. It was a dream. But when she looked at him with that harassed gaze he suddenly understood that this woman he loved so dearly was suffering, perhaps had been wronged. His heart went cold. He looked at her features with anguish: the first bloom of youth had long faded from this exhausted face. It's true that she was still good-looking—in his eyes a beauty, as she had always been. In reality she was a woman of twenty-five, rather strongly built, above the medium height (taller than Shatov), with abundant dark brown hair, a pale oval face, and large dark eyes now glittering with feverish brilliance. But the light-hearted, naïve and good-natured energy he had known so well in the past was replaced now by a sullen irritability and disillusionment, a sort of cynicism which was not yet habitual to her herself, and which weighed upon her. But the chief thing was that she was ill, that he could see clearly. In spite of the awe in which he stood of her he suddenly went up to her and took her by both hands.

"Marie … you know … you are very tired, perhaps, for God's sake, don't be angry.… If you'd consent to have some tea, for instance, eh? Tea picks one up so, doesn't it? If you'd consent!"

"Why talk about consenting! Of course I consent, what a baby you are still. Get me some if you can. How cramped you are here. How cold it is!"

"Oh, I'll get some logs for the fire directly, some logs … I've got logs." Shatov was all astir. "Logs … that is … but I'll get tea directly," he waved his hand as though with desperate determination and snatched up his cap.

"Where are you going? So you've no tea in the house?"

"There shall be, there shall be, there shall be, there shall be everything directly.… I …" he took his revolver from the shelf, "I'll sell this revolver directly … or pawn it.…"

"What foolishness and what a time that will take! Take my money if you've nothing, there's eighty kopecks here, I think; that's all I have. This is like a madhouse."

"I don't want your money, I don't want it I'll be here directly, in one instant. I can manage without the revolver.…"

And he rushed straight to Kirillov's. This was probably two hours before the visit of Pyotr Stepanovitch and Liputin to Kirillov. Though Shatov and Kirillov lived in the same yard they hardly ever saw each other, and when they met they did not nod or speak: they had been too long "lying side by side" in America.…

"Kirillov, you always have tea; have you got tea and a samovar?"

Kirillov, who was walking up and down the room, as he was in the habit of doing all night, stopped and looked intently at his hurried visitor, though without much surprise.

"I've got tea and sugar and a samovar. But there's no need of the samovar, the tea is hot. Sit down and simply drink it."

"Kirillov, we lay side by side in America.… My wife has come to me … I … give me the tea.… I shall want the samovar."

"If your wife is here you want the samovar. But take it later. I've two. And now take the teapot from the table. It's hot, boiling hot. Take everything, take the sugar, all of it. Bread … there's plenty of bread; all of it. There's some veal. I've a rouble."

"Give it me, friend, I'll pay it back to-morrow! Ach, Kirillov!"

"Is it the same wife who was in Switzerland? That's a good thing. And your running in like this, that's a good thing too."

"Kirillov!" cried Shatov, taking the teapot under his arm and carrying the bread and sugar in both hands. "Kirillov, if … if you could get rid of your dreadful fancies and give up your atheistic ravings … oh, what a man you'd be, Kirillov!"

"One can see you love your wife after Switzerland. It's a good thing you do—after Switzerland. When you want tea, come again. You can come all night, I don't sleep at all. There'll be a samovar. Take the rouble, here it is. Go to your wife, I'll stay here and think about you and your wife."

Marya Shatov was unmistakably pleased at her husband's haste and fell upon the tea almost greedily, but there was no need to run for the samovar; she drank only half a cup and swallowed a tiny piece of bread. The veal she refused with disgust and irritation.

"You are ill, Marie, all this is a sign of illness," Shatov remarked timidly as he waited upon her.

"Of course I'm ill, please sit down. Where did you get the tea if you haven't any?"

Shatov told her about Kirillov briefly. She had heard something of him.

"I know he is mad; say no more, please; there are plenty of fools. So you've been in America? I heard, you wrote."

"Yes, I … I wrote to you in Paris."

"Enough, please talk of something else. Are you a Slavophil in your convictions?"

"I … I am not exactly.… Since I cannot be a Russian, I became a Slavophil." He smiled a wry smile with the effort of one who feels he has made a strained and inappropriate jest.

"Why, aren't you a Russian?"

"No, I'm not."

"Well, that's all foolishness. Do sit down, I entreat you. Why are you all over the place? Do you think I am lightheaded? Perhaps I shall be. You say there are only you two in the house."

"Yes.… Downstairs …"

"And both such clever people. What is there downstairs? You said downstairs?"

"No, nothing."

"Why nothing? I want to know."

"I only meant to say that now we are only two in the yard, but that the Lebyadkins used to live downstairs...."

"That woman who was murdered last night?" she started suddenly. "I heard of it. I heard of it as soon as I arrived. There was a fire here, wasn't there?"

"Yes, Marie, yes, and perhaps I am doing a scoundrelly thing this moment in forgiving the scoundrels...." He stood up suddenly and paced about the room, raising his arms as though in a frenzy.

But Marie had not quite understood him. She heard his answers inattentively; she asked questions but did not listen.

"Fine things are being done among you! Oh, how contemptible it all is! What scoundrels men all are! But do sit down, I beg you, oh, how you exasperate me!" and she let her head sink on the pillow, exhausted.

"Marie, I won't.... Perhaps you'll lie down, Marie?" She made no answer and closed her eyes helplessly. Her pale face looked death-like. She fell asleep almost instantly. Shatov looked round, snuffed the candle, looked uneasily at her face once more, pressed his hands tight in front of him and walked on tiptoe out of the room into the passage. At the top of the stairs, he stood in the corner with his face to the wall and remained so for ten minutes without sound or movement. He would have stood there longer, but he suddenly caught the sound of soft cautious steps below. Someone was coming up the stairs. Shatov remembered he had forgotten to fasten the gate.

"Who's there?" he asked in a whisper. The unknown visitor went on slowly mounting the stairs without answering. When he reached the top he stood still; it was impossible to see his face in the dark; suddenly Shatov heard the cautious question:

"Ivan Shatov?"

Shatov said who he was, but at once held out his hand to check his advance. The latter took his hand, and Shatov shuddered as though he had touched some terrible reptile.

"Stand here," he whispered quickly. "Don't go in, I can't receive you just now. My wife has come back. I'll fetch the candle."

When he returned with the candle he found a young officer standing there; he did not know his name but he had seen him before.

"Erkel," said the lad, introducing himself. "You've seen me at Virginsky's."

"I remember; you sat writing. Listen," said Shatov in sudden excitement, going up to him frantically, but still talking in a whisper. "You gave me a sign just now when you took my hand. But you know I can treat all these signals with contempt! I don't acknowledge them.... I don't want them.... I can throw you downstairs this minute, do you know that?"

"No, I know nothing about that and I don't know what you are in such a rage about," the visitor answered without malice and almost ingenuously. "I have only to give you a message, and that's what I've come for, being particularly anxious not to lose time. You have a printing press which does not belong to you, and of which you are bound to give an account, as you know yourself. I have received instructions to request you to give it up to-morrow at seven o'clock in the evening to Liputin. I have been instructed to tell you also that nothing more will be asked of you."

"Nothing?"

"Absolutely nothing. Your request is granted, and you are struck off our list. I was instructed to tell you that positively."

"Who instructed you to tell me?"

"Those who told me the sign."

"Have you come from abroad?"

"I … I think that's no matter to you."

"Oh, hang it! Why didn't you come before if you were told to?"

"I followed certain instructions and was not alone."

"I understand, I understand that you were not alone. Eh … hang it! But why didn't Liputin come himself?"

"So I shall come for you to-morrow at exactly six o'clock in the evening, and we'll go there on foot. There will be no one there but us three."

"Will Verhovensky be there?"

"No, he won't. Verhovensky is leaving the town at eleven o'clock to-morrow morning."

"Just what I thought!" Shatov whispered furiously, and he struck his fist on his hip. "He's run off, the sneak!"

He sank into agitated reflection. Erkel looked intently at him and waited in silence.

"But how will you take it? You can't simply pick it up in your hands and carry it."

"There will be no need to. You'll simply point out the place and we'll just make sure that it really is buried there. We only know whereabouts the place is, we don't know the place itself. And have you pointed the place out to anyone else yet?"

Shatov looked at him.

"You, you, a chit of a boy like you, a silly boy like you, you too have got caught in that net like a sheep? Yes, that's just the young blood they want! Well, go along. E-ech! that scoundrel's taken you all in and run away."

Erkel looked at him serenely and calmly but did not seem to understand.

"Verhovensky, Verhovensky has run away!" Shatov growled fiercely.

"But he is still here, he is not gone away. He is not going till to-morrow," Erkel observed softly and persuasively. "I particularly begged him to be present as a witness; my instructions all referred to him (he explained frankly like a young and inexperienced boy). But I regret to say he did not agree on the ground of his departure, and he really is in a hurry."

Shatov glanced compassionately at the simple youth again, but suddenly gave a gesture of despair as though he thought "they are not worth pitying."

"All right, I'll come," he cut him short. "And now get away, be off."

"So I'll come for you at six o'clock punctually." Erkel made a courteous bow and walked deliberately downstairs.

"Little fool!" Shatov could not help shouting after him from the top.

"What is it?" responded the lad from the bottom.

"Nothing, you can go."

"I thought you said something."

II

Erkel was a "little fool" who was only lacking in the higher form of reason, the ruling power of the intellect; but of the lesser, the subordinate reasoning faculties, he had plenty—even to the point of cunning. Fanatically, childishly devoted to "the cause" or rather in reality to Pyotr Verhovensky, he acted on the instructions given to him when at the meeting of the quintet they had agreed and had distributed the various duties for the next day. When Pyotr Stepanovitch gave him the job of messenger, he succeeded in talking to him aside for ten minutes.

A craving for active service was characteristic of this shallow, unreflecting nature, which was forever yearning to follow the lead of another man's will, of course for the good of "the common" or "the great" cause. Not that that made any difference, for little fanatics like Erkel can never imagine serving a cause except by identifying it with the person who, to their minds, is the expression of it. The sensitive, affectionate and kind-hearted Erkel was perhaps the most callous of Shatov's would-be murderers, and, though he had no personal spite against him, he would have been present at his murder without the quiver of an eyelid. He had been instructed, for instance, to have a good look at Shatov's surroundings while carrying out his commission, and when Shatov, receiving him at the top of the stairs, blurted out to him, probably unaware in the heat of the moment, that his wife had come back to him—Erkel had the instinctive cunning to avoid displaying the slightest curiosity, though the idea flashed through his mind that the fact of his wife's return was of great importance for the success of their undertaking.

And so it was in reality; it was only that fact that saved the "scoundrels" from Shatov's carrying out his intention, and at the same time helped them "to get rid of him." To begin with, it agitated Shatov, threw him out of his regular routine, and deprived him of his usual clear-sightedness and caution. Any idea of his own danger would be the last thing to enter his head at this moment when he was absorbed with such different considerations. On the contrary, he eagerly believed that Pyotr Verhovensky was running away the next day: it fell in exactly with his suspicions! Returning to the room he sat down again in a corner, leaned his elbows on his knees and hid his face in his hands. Bitter thoughts tormented him....

Then he would raise his head again and go on tiptoe to look at her. "Good God! she will be in a fever by to-morrow morning; perhaps it's begun already! She must have caught cold. She is not accustomed to this awful climate, and then a third-class carriage, the storm, the rain, and she has such a thin little pelisse, no wrap at all.... And to leave her like this, to abandon her in her helplessness! Her bag, too, her bag—what a tiny, light thing, all crumpled up, scarcely weighs ten pounds! Poor thing, how worn out she is, how much she's been through! She is proud, that's why she won't complain. But she is irritable, very irritable. It's illness; an angel will grow irritable in illness. What a dry forehead, it must be hot—how dark she is under the eyes, and ... and yet how beautiful the oval of her face is and her rich hair, how ..."

And he made haste to turn away his eyes, to walk away as though he were frightened at the very idea of seeing in her anything but an unhappy, exhausted fellow-creature who needed help—"how could he think of hopes, oh, how mean, how base is man!" And he would go back to his corner, sit down, hide his face in his hands and again sink into dreams and reminiscences ... and again he was haunted by hopes.

"Oh, I am tired, I am tired," he remembered her exclamations, her weak broken voice. "Good God! Abandon her now, and she has only eighty kopecks; she held out her purse, a tiny old thing! She's come to look for a job. What does she know about jobs? What do they know about Russia? Why, they are like naughty children, they've nothing but their own fancies made up by themselves, and she is angry, poor thing, that Russia is not like their foreign dreams! The luckless, innocent creatures!... It's really cold here, though."

He remembered that she had complained, that he had promised to heat the stove. "There are logs here, I can fetch them if only I don't wake her. But I can do it without waking her. But what shall I do about the veal? When she gets up perhaps she will be hungry.... Well, that will do later: Kirillov doesn't go to bed all night. What could I cover her with, she is sleeping so soundly, but she must be cold, ah, she must be cold!" And once more he went to look at her; her dress had worked up a little and her right leg was half uncovered to the knee. He suddenly turned away almost in dismay, took off his warm overcoat, and, remaining in his wretched old jacket, covered it up, trying not to look at it.

A great deal of time was spent in righting the fire, stepping about on tiptoe, looking at the sleeping woman, dreaming in the corner, then looking at her again. Two or three hours had passed. During that time Verhovensky and Liputin had been at Kirillov's. At last he, too, began to doze in the corner. He heard her groan; she waked up and called him; he jumped up like a criminal.

"Marie, I was dropping asleep.... Ah, what a wretch I am, Marie!"

She sat up, looking about her with wonder, seeming not to recognise where she was, and suddenly leapt up in indignation and anger.

"I've taken your bed, I fell asleep so tired I didn't know what I was doing; how dared you not wake me? How could you dare imagine I meant to be a burden to you?"

"How could I wake you, Marie?"

"You could, you ought to have! You've no other bed here, and I've taken yours. You had no business to put me into a false position. Or do you suppose that I've come to take advantage of your charity? Kindly get into your bed at once and I'll lie down in the corner on some chairs."

"Marie, there aren't chairs enough, and there's nothing to put on them."

"Then simply oil the floor. Or you'll have to lie on the floor yourself. I want to lie on the floor at once, at once!"

She stood up, tried to take a step, but suddenly a violent spasm of pain deprived her of all power and all determination, and with a loud groan she fell back on the bed. Shatov ran up, but Marie, hiding her face in the pillow, seized his hand and gripped and squeezed it with all her might. This lasted a minute.

"Marie darling, there's a doctor Frenzel living here, a friend of mine.... I could run for him."

"Nonsense!"

"What do you mean by nonsense? Tell me, Marie, what is it hurting you? For we might try fomentations ... on the stomach for instance.... I can do that without a doctor.... Or else mustard poultices."

"What's this," she asked strangely, raising her head and looking at him in dismay.

"What's what, Marie?" said Shatov, not understanding. "What are you asking about? Good heavens! I am quite bewildered, excuse my not understanding."

"Ach, let me alone; it's not your business to understand. And it would be too absurd ..." she said with a bitter smile. "Talk to me about something. Walk about the room and talk. Don't stand over me and don't look at me, I particularly ask you that for the five-hundredth time!"

Shatov began walking up and down the room, looking at the floor, and doing his utmost not to glance at her.

"There's—don't be angry, Marie, I entreat you—there's some veal here, and there's tea not far off.... You had so little before."

She made an angry gesture of disgust. Shatov bit his tongue in despair.

"Listen, I intend to open a bookbinding business here, on rational co-operative principles. Since you live here what do you think of it, would it be successful?"

"Ech, Marie, people don't read books here, and there are none here at all. And are they likely to begin binding them!"

"Who are they?"

"The local readers and inhabitants generally, Marie."

"Well, then, speak more clearly. They indeed, and one doesn't know who they are. You don't know grammar!"

"It's in the spirit of the language," Shatov muttered.

"Oh, get along with your spirit, you bore me. Why shouldn't the local inhabitant or reader have his books bound?"

"Because reading books and having them bound are two different stages of development, and there's a vast gulf between them. To begin with, a man gradually gets used to reading, in the course of ages of course, but takes no care of his books and throws them about, not thinking them worth attention. But binding implies respect for books, and implies that not only he has grown fond of reading, but that he looks upon it as something of value. That period has not been reached anywhere in Russia yet. In Europe books have been bound for a long while."

"Though that's pedantic, anyway, it's not stupid, and reminds me of the time three years ago; you used to be rather clever sometimes three years ago."

She said this as disdainfully as her other capricious remarks.

"Marie, Marie," said Shatov, turning to her, much moved, "oh, Marie! If you only knew how much has happened in those three years! I heard afterwards that you despised me for changing my convictions. But what are the men I've broken with? The enemies of all true life, out-of-date Liberals who are afraid of their own independence, the flunkeys of thought, the enemies of individuality and freedom, the decrepit advocates of deadness and rottenness! All they have to offer is senility, a glorious mediocrity of the most bourgeois kind, contemptible shallowness, a jealous equality, equality without individual dignity, equality as it's understood by flunkeys or by the French in '93. And the worst of it is there are swarms of scoundrels among them, swarms of scoundrels!"

"Yes, there are a lot of scoundrels," she brought out abruptly with painful effort. She lay stretched out, motionless, as though afraid to move, with her head thrown back on the pillow, rather on one side, staring at the ceiling with exhausted but glowing eyes. Her face was pale, her lips were dry and hot.

"You recognise it, Marie, you recognise it," cried Shatov. She tried to shake her head, and suddenly the same spasm came over her again. Again she hid her face in the pillow, and again for a full minute she squeezed Shatov's hand till it hurt. He had run up, beside himself with alarm.

"Marie, Marie! But it may be very serious, Marie!"

"Be quiet ... I won't have it, I won't have it," she screamed almost furiously, turning her face upwards again. "Don't dare to look at me with your sympathy! Walk about the room, say something, talk...."

Shatov began muttering something again, like one distraught.

"What do you do here?" she asked, interrupting him with contemptuous impatience.

"I work in a merchant's office. I could get a fair amount of money even here if I cared to, Marie."

"So much the better for you…."

"Oh, don't suppose I meant anything, Marie. I said it without thinking."

"And what do you do besides? What are you preaching? You can't exist without preaching, that's your character!"

"I am preaching God, Marie."

"In whom you don't believe yourself. I never could see the idea of that."

"Let's leave that, Marie; we'll talk of that later."

"What sort of person was this Marya Timofyevna here?"

"We'll talk of that later too, Marie."

"Don't dare to say such things to me! Is it true that her death may have been caused by … the wickedness … of these people?"

"Not a doubt of it," growled Shatov.

Marie suddenly raised her head and cried out painfully:

"Don't dare speak of that to me again, don't dare to, never, never!"

And she fell back in bed again, overcome by the same convulsive agony; it was the third time, but this time her groans were louder, in fact she screamed.

"Oh, you insufferable man! Oh, you unbearable man," she cried, tossing about recklessly, and pushing away Shatov as he bent over her.

"Marie, I'll do anything you like…. I'll walk about and talk…."

"Surely you must see that it has begun!"

"What's begun, Marie?"

"How can I tell! Do I know anything about it?… I curse myself! Oh, curse it all from the beginning!"

"Marie, if you'd tell me what's beginning … or else I … if you don't, what am I to make of it?"

"You are a useless, theoretical babbler. Oh, curse everything on earth!"

"Marie, Marie!" He seriously thought that she was beginning to go mad.

"Surely you must see that I am in the agonies of childbirth," she said, sitting up and gazing at him with a terrible, hysterical vindictiveness that distorted her whole face. "I curse him before he is born, this child!"

"Marie," cried Shatov, realising at last what it meant. "Marie … but why didn't you tell me before." He pulled himself together at once and seized his cap with an air of vigorous determination.

"How could I tell when I came in here? Should I have come to you if I'd known? I was told it would be another ten days! Where are you going?… Where are you going? You mustn't dare!"

"To fetch a midwife! I'll sell the revolver. We must get money before anything else now."

"Don't dare to do anything, don't dare to fetch a midwife! Bring a peasant woman, any old woman, I've eighty kopecks in my purse.… Peasant women have babies without midwives.… And if I die, so much the better.…"

"You shall have a midwife and an old woman too. But how am I to leave you alone, Marie!"

But reflecting that it was better to leave her alone now in spite of her desperate state than to leave her without help later, he paid no attention to her groans, nor her angry exclamations, but rushed downstairs, hurrying all he could.

III

First of all he went to Kirillov. It was by now about one o'clock in the night. Kirillov was standing in the middle of the room.

"Kirillov, my wife is in childbirth."

"How do you mean?"

"Childbirth, bearing a child!"

"You … are not mistaken?"

"Oh, no, no, she is in agonies! I want a woman, any old woman, I must have one at once.… Can you get one now? You used to have a lot of old women.…"

"Very sorry that I am no good at childbearing," Kirillov answered thoughtfully; "that is, not at childbearing, but at doing anything for childbearing … or … no, I don't know how to say it."

"You mean you can't assist at a confinement yourself? But that's not what I've come for. An old woman, I want a woman, a nurse, a servant!"

"You shall have an old woman, but not directly, perhaps … If you like I'll come instead.…"

"Oh, impossible; I am running to Madame Virginsky, the midwife, now."

"A horrid woman!"

"Oh, yes, Kirillov, yes, but she is the best of them all. Yes, it'll all be without reverence, without gladness, with contempt, with abuse, with blasphemy in the presence of so great a mystery, the coming of a new creature! Oh, she is cursing it already!"

"If you like I'll ..."

"No, no, but while I'm running (oh, I'll make Madame Virginsky come), will you go to the foot of my staircase and quietly listen? But don't venture to go in, you'll frighten her; don't go in on any account, you must only listen ... in case anything dreadful happens. If anything very bad happens, then run in."

"I understand. I've another rouble. Here it is. I meant to have a fowl to-morrow, but now I don't want to, make haste, run with all your might. There's a samovar all the night."

Kirillov knew nothing of the present design against Shatov, nor had he had any idea in the past of the degree of danger that threatened him. He only knew that Shatov had some old scores with "those people," and although he was to some extent involved with them himself through instructions he had received from abroad (not that these were of much consequence, however, for he had never taken any direct share in anything), yet of late he had given it all up, having left off doing anything especially for the "cause," and devoted himself entirely to a life of contemplation. Although Pyotr Stepanovitch had at the meeting invited Liputin to go with him to Kirillov's to make sure that the latter would take upon himself, at a given moment, the responsibility for the "Shatov business," yet in his interview with Kirillov he had said no word about Shatov nor alluded to him in any way—probably considering it impolitic to do so, and thinking that Kirillov could not be relied upon. He put off speaking about it till next day, when it would be all over and would therefore not matter to Kirillov; such at least was Pyotr Stepanovitch's judgment of him. Liputin, too, was struck by the fact that Shatov was not mentioned in spite of what Pyotr Stepanovitch had promised, but he was too much agitated to protest.

Shatov ran like a hurricane to Virginsky's house, cursing the distance and feeling it endless.

He had to knock a long time at Virginsky's; every one had been asleep a long while. But Shatov did not scruple to bang at the shutters with all his might. The dog chained up in the yard dashed about barking furiously. The dogs caught it up all along the street, and there was a regular babel of barking.

"Why are you knocking and what do you want?" Shatov heard at the window at last Virginsky's gentle voice, betraying none of the resentment appropriate to the "outrage." The shutter was pushed back a little and the casement was opened.

"Who's there, what scoundrel is it?" shrilled a female voice which betrayed all the resentment appropriate to the "outrage." It was the old maid, Virginsky's relation.

"I am Shatov, my wife has come back to me and she is just confined...."

"Well, let her be, get along."

"I've come for Arina Prohorovna; I won't go without Arina Prohorovna!"

"She can't attend to every one. Practice at night is a special line. Take yourself off to

Maksheyev's and don't dare to make that din," rattled the exasperated female voice. He could hear Virginsky checking her; but the old maid pushed him away and would not desist.

"I am not going away!" Shatov cried again.

"Wait a little, wait a little," Virginsky cried at last, overpowering the lady. "I beg you to wait five minutes, Shatov. I'll wake Arina Prohorovna. Please don't knock and don't shout.... Oh, how awful it all is!"

After five endless minutes, Arina Prohorovna made her appearance.

"Has your wife come?" Shatov heard her voice at the window, and to his surprise it was not at all ill-tempered, only as usual peremptory, but Arina Prohorovna could not speak except in a peremptory tone.

"Yes, my wife, and she is in labour."

"Marya Ignatyevna?"

"Yes, Marya Ignatyevna. Of course it's Marya Ignatyevna."

A silence followed. Shatov waited. He heard a whispering in the house.

"Has she been here long?" Madame Virginsky asked again.

"She came this evening at eight o'clock. Please make haste."

Again he heard whispering, as though they were consulting. "Listen, you are not making a mistake? Did she send you for me herself?"

"No, she didn't send for you, she wants a peasant woman, so as not to burden me with expense, but don't be afraid, I'll pay you."

"Very good, I'll come, whether you pay or not. I always thought highly of Marya Ignatyevna for the independence of her sentiments, though perhaps she won't remember me. Have you got the most necessary things?"

"I've nothing, but I'll get everything, everything."

"There is something generous even in these people," Shatov reflected, as he set off to Lyamshin's. "The convictions and the man are two very different things, very likely I've been very unfair to them!... We are all to blame, we are all to blame ... and if only all were convinced of it!"

He had not to knock long at Lyamshin's; the latter, to Shatov's surprise, opened his casement at once, jumping out of bed, barefoot and in his night-clothes at the risk of catching cold; and he was hypochondriacal and always anxious about his health. But there was a special cause for such alertness and haste: Lyamshin had been in a tremor all the evening, and had not been able to sleep for excitement after the meeting of the quintet; he was haunted by the dread of uninvited and undesired visitors. The news of Shatov's giving information tormented him more than anything.... And suddenly there was this terrible loud knocking at the window as though to justify his fears.

He was so frightened at seeing Shatov that he at once slammed the casement and jumped back into bed. Shatov began furiously knocking and shouting.

"How dare you knock like that in the middle of the night?" shouted Lyamshin, in a threatening voice, though he was numb with fear, when at least two minutes later he ventured to open the casement again, and was at last convinced that Shatov had come alone.

"Here's your revolver for you; take it back, give me fifteen roubles."

"What's the matter, are you drunk? This is outrageous, I shall simply catch cold. Wait a minute, I'll just throw my rug over me."

"Give me fifteen roubles at once. If you don't give it me, I'll knock and shout till daybreak; I'll break your window-frame."

"And I'll shout police and you'll be taken to the lock-up."

"And am I dumb? Can't I shout 'police' too? Which of us has most reason to be afraid of the police, you or I?"

"And you can hold such contemptible opinions! I know what you are hinting at.... Stop, stop, for God's sake don't go on knocking! Upon my word, who has money at night? What do you want money for, unless you are drunk?"

"My wife has come back. I've taken ten roubles off the price, I haven't fired it once; take the revolver, take it this minute!"

Lyamshin mechanically put his hand out of the casement and took the revolver; he waited a little, and suddenly thrusting his head out of the casement, and with a shiver running down his spine, faltered as though he were beside himself.

"You are lying, your wife hasn't come back to you.... It's ... it's simply that you want to run away."

"You are a fool. Where should I run to? It's for your Pyotr Verhovensky to run away, not for me. I've just been to the midwife, Madame Virginsky, and she consented at once to come to me. You can ask them. My wife is in agony; I need the money; give it me!"

A swarm of ideas flared up in Lyamshin's crafty mind like a shower of fireworks. It all suddenly took a different colour, though still panic prevented him from reflecting.

"But how ... you are not living with your wife?"

"I'll break your skull for questions like that."

"Oh dear, I understand, forgive me, I was struck all of a heap.... But I understand, I understand ... is Arina Prohorovna really coming? You said just now that she had gone? You know, that's not true. You see, you see, you see what lies you tell at every step."

"By now, she must be with my wife ... don't keep me ... it's not my fault you are a fool."

"That's a lie, I am not a fool. Excuse me, I really can't ..."

And utterly distraught he began shutting the casement again for the third time, but Shatov gave such a yell that he put his head out again.

"But this is simply an unprovoked assault! What do you want of me, what is it, what is it, formulate it? And think, only think, it's the middle of the night!"

"I want fifteen roubles, you sheep's-head!"

"But perhaps I don't care to take back the revolver. You have no right to force me. You bought the thing and the matter is settled, and you've no right.... I can't give you a sum like that in the night, anyhow. Where am I to get a sum like that?"

"You always have money. I've taken ten roubles off the price, but every one knows you are a skinflint."

"Come the day after to-morrow, do you hear, the day after to-morrow at twelve o'clock, and I'll give you the whole of it, that will do, won't it?"

Shatov knocked furiously at the window-frame for the third time.

"Give me ten roubles, and to-morrow early the other five."

"No, the day after to-morrow the other five, to-morrow I swear I shan't have it. You'd better not come, you'd better not come."

"Give me ten, you scoundrel!"

"Why are you so abusive. Wait a minute, I must light a candle; you've broken the window.... Nobody swears like that at night. Here you are!" He held a note to him out of the window.

Shatov seized it—it was a note for five roubles.

"On my honour I can't do more, if you were to murder me, I couldn't; the day after to-morrow I can give you it all, but now I can do nothing."

"I am not going away!" roared Shatov.

"Very well, take it, here's some more, see, here's some more, and I won't give more. You can shout at the top of your voice, but I won't give more, I won't, whatever happens, I won't, I won't."

He was in a perfect frenzy, desperate and perspiring. The two notes he had just given him were each for a rouble. Shatov had seven roubles altogether now.

"Well, damn you, then, I'll come to-morrow. I'll thrash you, Lyamshin, if you don't give me the other eight."

"You won't find me at home, you fool!" Lyamshin reflected quickly.

"Stay, stay!" he shouted frantically after Shatov, who was already running off. "Stay, come back. Tell me please, is it true what you said that your wife has come back?"

"Fool!" cried Shatov, with a gesture of disgust, and ran home as hard as he could.

IV

I may mention that Anna Prohorovna knew nothing of the resolutions that had been taken at the meeting the day before. On returning home overwhelmed and exhausted, Virginsky had not ventured to tell her of the decision that had been taken, yet he could not refrain from telling her half—that is, all that Verhovensky had told them of the certainty of Shatov's intention to betray them; but he added at the same time that he did not quite believe it. Arina Prohorovna was terribly alarmed. This was why she decided at once to go when Shatov came to fetch her, though she was tired out, as she had been hard at work at a confinement all the night before. She had always been convinced that "a wretched creature like Shatov was capable of any political baseness," but the arrival of Marya Ignatyevna put things in a different light. Shatov's alarm, the despairing tone of his entreaties, the way he begged for help, clearly showed a complete change of feeling in the traitor: a man who was ready to betray himself merely for the sake of ruining others would, she thought, have had a different air and tone. In short, Arina Prohorovna resolved to look into the matter for herself, with her own eyes. Virginsky was very glad of her decision, he felt as though a hundredweight had been lifted off him! He even began to feel hopeful: Shatov's appearance seemed to him utterly incompatible with Verhovensky's supposition.

Shatov was not mistaken: on getting home he found Arina Prohorovna already with Marie. She had just arrived, had contemptuously dismissed Kirillov, whom she found hanging about the foot of the stairs, had hastily introduced herself to Marie, who had not recognised her as her former acquaintance, found her in "a very bad way," that is ill-tempered, irritable and in "a state of cowardly despair," and within five minutes had completely silenced all her protests.

"Why do you keep on that you don't want an expensive midwife?" she was saying at the moment when Shatov came in. "That's perfect nonsense, it's a false idea arising from the abnormality of your condition. In the hands of some ordinary old woman, some peasant midwife, you'd have fifty chances of going wrong and then you'd have more bother and expense than with a regular midwife. How do you know I am an expensive midwife? You can pay afterwards; I won't charge you much and I answer for my success; you won't die in my hands, I've seen worse cases than yours. And I can send the baby to a foundling asylum to-morrow, if you like, and then to be brought up in the country, and that's all it will mean. And meantime you'll grow strong again, take up some rational work, and in a very short time you'll repay Shatov for sheltering you and for the expense, which will not be so great."

"It's not that … I've no right to be a burden…."

"Rational feelings and worthy of a citizen, but you can take my word for it, Shatov will spend scarcely anything, if he is willing to become ever so little a man of sound ideas instead of the fantastic person he is. He has only not to do anything stupid, not to raise an alarm, not to run about the town with his tongue out. If we don't restrain him he will be knocking up all the doctors of the town before the morning; he waked all the dogs in my street. There's no need of doctors I've said already. I'll answer for everything. You can hire an old woman if you like to wait on you, that won't cost much. Though he too can do something besides the silly things he's been doing. He's got hands and feet, he can run to the chemist's without offending your feelings by being too benevolent. As though it were a case of benevolence! Hasn't he brought you into this position? Didn't he make you break with the family in which you were a governess, with the egoistic object of marrying you? We heard of it, you know … though he did run for me like one possessed and yell so all the street could hear. I won't force myself upon anyone and have come only for your sake, on the principle that all of us are bound to hold together! And I told him so before I left the house. If you think I am in the way, good-bye, I only hope you won't have trouble which might so easily be averted."

And she positively got up from the chair. Marie was so helpless, in such pain, and—the truth must be confessed—so frightened of what was before her that she dared not let her go. But this woman was suddenly hateful to her, what she said was not what she wanted, there was something quite different in Marie's soul. Yet the prediction that she might possibly die in the hands of an inexperienced peasant woman overcame her aversion. But she made up for it by being more exacting and more ruthless than ever with Shatov. She ended by forbidding him not only to look at her but even to stand facing her. Her pains became more violent. Her curses, her abuse became more and more frantic.

"Ech, we'll send him away," Arina Prohorovna rapped out. "I don't know what he looks like, he is simply frightening you; he is as white as a corpse! What is it to you, tell me please, you absurd fellow? What a farce!"

Shatov made no reply, he made up his mind to say nothing. "I've seen many a foolish father, half crazy in such cases. But they, at any rate …"

"Be quiet or leave me to die! Don't say another word! I won't have it, I won't have it!" screamed Marie.

"It's impossible not to say another word, if you are not out of your mind, as I think you are in your condition. We must talk of what we want, anyway: tell me, have you anything ready? You answer, Shatov, she is incapable."

"Tell me what's needed?"

"That means you've nothing ready." She reckoned up all that was quite necessary, and one must do her the justice to say she only asked for what was absolutely indispensable, the barest necessaries. Some things Shatov had. Marie took out her key and held it out to him, for him to look in her bag. As his hands shook he was longer than he should have been opening the unfamiliar lock. Marie flew into a rage, but when Arina Prohorovna rushed up to take the key from him, she would not allow her on any account to look into her bag and with peevish cries and tears insisted that no one should open the bag but Shatov.

Some things he had to fetch from Kirillov's. No sooner had Shatov turned to go for them than she began frantically calling him back and was only quieted when Shatov had rushed impetuously back from the stairs, and explained that he should only be gone a minute to fetch something indispensable and would be back at once.

"Well, my lady, it's hard to please you," laughed Arina Prohorovna, "one minute he must stand with his face to the wall and not dare to look at you, and the next he mustn't be gone for a minute, or you begin crying. He may begin to imagine something. Come, come, don't be silly, don't blubber, I was laughing, you know."

"He won't dare to imagine anything."

"Tut, tut, tut, if he didn't love you like a sheep he wouldn't run about the streets with his tongue out and wouldn't have roused all the dogs in the town. He broke my window-frame."

V

He found Kirillov still pacing up and down his room so preoccupied that he had forgotten the arrival of Shatov's wife, and heard what he said without understanding him.

"Oh, yes!" he recollected suddenly, as though tearing himself with an effort and only for an instant from some absorbing idea, "yes … an old woman.… A wife or an old woman? Stay a minute: a wife and an old woman, is that it? I remember. I've been, the old woman will come, only not just now. Take the pillow. Is there anything else? Yes.… Stay, do you have moments of the eternal harmony, Shatov?"

"You know, Kirillov, you mustn't go on staying up every night."

Kirillov came out of his reverie and, strange to say, spoke far more coherently than he usually did; it was clear that he had formulated it long ago and perhaps written it down.

"There are seconds—they come five or six at a time—when you suddenly feel the presence of the eternal harmony perfectly attained. It's something not earthly—I don't mean in the sense that it's heavenly—but in that sense that man cannot endure it in his earthly aspect. He must be physically changed or die. This feeling is clear and unmistakable; it's as though you apprehend all nature and suddenly say, 'Yes, that's right.' God, when He created the world, said at the end of each day of creation, 'Yes, it's right, it's good.' It … it's not being deeply moved, but simply joy. You don't forgive anything because there is no more need of forgiveness. It's not that you love—oh, there's something in it higher than love—what's most awful is that it's terribly clear and such joy. If it lasted more than five seconds, the soul could not endure it and must perish. In those five seconds I live through a lifetime, and I'd give my whole life for them, because they are worth it. To endure ten seconds one must be physically changed. I think man ought to give up having children—what's the use of children, what's the use of evolution when the goal has been attained? In the gospel it is written that there will be no child-bearing in the resurrection, but that men will be like the angels of the Lord. That's a hint. Is your wife bearing a child?"

"Kirillov, does this often happen?"

"Once in three days, or once a week."

"Don't you have fits, perhaps?"

"No."

"Well, you will. Be careful, Kirillov. I've heard that's just how fits begin. An epileptic described exactly that sensation before a fit, word for word as you've done. He mentioned five seconds, too, and said that more could not be endured. Remember Mahomet's pitcher from which no drop of water was spilt while he circled Paradise on his horse. That was a case of five seconds too; that's too much like your eternal harmony, and Mahomet was an epileptic. Be careful, Kirillov, it's epilepsy!"

"It won't have time," Kirillov smiled gently.

VI

The night was passing. Shatov was sent hither and thither, abused, called back. Marie was reduced to the most abject terror for life. She screamed that she wanted to live, that "she must, she must," and was afraid to die. "I don't want to, I don't want to!" she repeated. If Arina Prohorovna had not been there, things would have gone very badly. By degrees she gained complete control of the patient—who began to obey every word, every order from her like a child. Arina Prohorovna ruled by sternness not by kindness, but she was first-rate at her work. It began to get light ... Arina Prohorovna suddenly imagined that Shatov had just run out on to the stairs to say his prayers and began laughing. Marie laughed too, spitefully, malignantly, as though such laughter relieved her. At last they drove Shatov away altogether. A damp, cold morning dawned. He pressed his face to the wall in the corner just as he had done the evening before when Erkel came. He was trembling like a leaf, afraid to think, but his mind caught at every thought as it does in dreams.

He was continually being carried away by day-dreams, which snapped off short like a rotten thread. From the room came no longer groans but awful animal cries, unendurable, incredible. He tried to stop up his ears, but could not, and he fell on his knees, repeating unconsciously, "Marie, Marie!" Then suddenly he heard a cry, a new cry, which made Shatov start and jump up from his knees, the cry of a baby, a weak discordant cry. He crossed himself and rushed into the room. Arina Prohorovna held in her hands a little red wrinkled creature, screaming, and moving its little arms and legs, fearfully helpless, and looking as though it could be blown away by a puff of wind, but screaming and seeming to assert its full right to live. Marie was lying as though insensible, but a minute later she opened her eyes, and bent a strange, strange look on Shatov: it was something quite new, that look. What it meant exactly he was not able to understand yet, but he had never known such a look on her face before.

"Is it a boy? Is it a boy?" she asked Arina Prohorovna in an exhausted voice.

"It is a boy," the latter shouted in reply, as she bound up the child.

When she had bound him up and was about to lay him across the bed between the two pillows, she gave him to Shatov for a minute to hold. Marie signed to him on the sly as though afraid of Arina Prohorovna. He understood at once and brought the baby to show her.

"How ... pretty he is," she whispered weakly with a smile.

"Foo, what does he look like," Arina Prohorovna laughed gaily in triumph, glancing at Shatov's face. "What a funny face!"

"You may be merry, Arina Prohorovna.... It's a great joy," Shatov faltered with an expression of idiotic bliss, radiant at the phrase Marie had uttered about the child.

"Where does the great joy come in?" said Arina Prohorovna good-humouredly, bustling about, clearing up, and working like a convict.

"The mysterious coming of a new creature, a great and inexplicable mystery; and what a pity it is, Arina Prohorovna, that you don't understand it."

Shatov spoke in an incoherent, stupefied and ecstatic way. Something seemed to be tottering in his head and welling up from his soul apart from his own will.

"There were two and now there's a third human being, a new spirit, finished and complete, unlike the handiwork of man; a new thought and a new love ... it's positively frightening.... And there's nothing grander in the world."

"Ech, what nonsense he talks! It's simply a further development of the organism, and there's nothing else in it, no mystery," said Arina Prohorovna with genuine and good-humoured laughter. "If you talk like that, every fly is a mystery. But I tell you what: superfluous people ought not to be born. We must first remould everything so that they won't be superfluous and then bring them into the world. As it is, we shall have to take him to the Foundling, the day after to-morrow.... Though that's as it should be."

"I will never let him go to the Foundling," Shatov pronounced resolutely, staring at the floor.

"You adopt him as your son?"

"He is my son."

"Of course he is a Shatov, legally he is a Shatov, and there's no need for you to pose as a humanitarian. Men can't get on without fine words. There, there, it's all right, but look here, my friends," she added, having finished clearing up at last, "it's time for me to go. I'll come again this morning, and again in the evening if necessary, but now, since everything has gone off so well, I must run off to my other patients, they've been expecting me long ago. I believe you got an old woman somewhere, Shatov; an old woman is all very well, but don't you, her tender husband, desert her; sit beside her, you may be of use; Marya Ignatyevna won't drive you away, I fancy.... There, there, I was only laughing."

At the gate, to which Shatov accompanied her, she added to him alone.

"You've given me something to laugh at for the rest of my life; I shan't charge you anything; I shall laugh at you in my sleep! I have never seen anything funnier than you last night."

She went off very well satisfied. Shatov's appearance and conversation made it as clear as daylight that this man "was going in for being a father and was a ninny." She ran home on purpose to tell Virginsky about it, though it was shorter and more direct to go to another patient.

"Marie, she told you not to go to sleep for a little time, though, I see, it's very hard for you," Shatov began timidly. "I'll sit here by the window and take care of you, shall I?"

And he sat down, by the window behind the sofa so that she could not see him. But before a minute had passed she called him and fretfully asked him to arrange the pillow. He began arranging it. She looked angrily at the wall.

"That's not right, that's not right.... What hands!"

Shatov did it again.

"Stoop down to me," she said wildly, trying hard not to look at him.

He started but stooped down.

"More ... not so ... nearer," and suddenly her left arm was impulsively thrown round his neck and he felt her warm moist kiss on his forehead.

"Marie!"

Her lips were quivering, she was struggling with herself, but suddenly she raised herself and said with flashing eyes:

"Nikolay Stavrogin is a scoundrel!" And she fell back helplessly with her face in the pillow, sobbing hysterically, and tightly squeezing Shatov's hand in hers.

From that moment she would not let him leave her; she insisted on his sitting by her pillow. She could not talk much but she kept gazing at him and smiling blissfully. She seemed suddenly to have become a silly girl. Everything seemed transformed. Shatov cried like a boy, then talked of God knows what, wildly, crazily, with inspiration, kissed her hands; she listened entranced, perhaps not understanding him, but caressingly ruffling his hair with her weak hand, smoothing it and admiring it. He talked about Kirillov, of how they would now begin "a new life" for good, of the existence of God, of the goodness of all men.... She took out the child again to gaze at it rapturously.

"Marie," he cried, as he held the child in his arms, "all the old madness, shame, and deadness is over, isn't it? Let us work hard and begin a new life, the three of us, yes, yes!... Oh, by the way, what shall we call him, Marie?"

"What shall we call him?" she repeated with surprise, and there was a sudden look of terrible grief in her face.

She clasped her hands, looked reproachfully at Shatov and hid her face in the pillow.

"Marie, what is it?" he cried with painful alarm.

"How could you, how could you ... Oh, you ungrateful man!"

"Marie, forgive me, Marie ... I only asked you what his name should be. I don't know...."

"Ivan, Ivan." She raised her flushed and tear-stained face. "How could you suppose we should call him by another horrible name?"

"Marie, calm yourself; oh, what a nervous state you are in!"

"That's rude again, putting it down to my nerves. I bet that if I'd said his name was to be that other ... horrible name, you'd have agreed at once and not have noticed it even! Oh, men, the mean ungrateful creatures, they are all alike!"

A minute later, of course, they were reconciled. Shatov persuaded her to have a nap. She fell asleep but still kept his hand in hers; she waked up frequently, looked at him, as though afraid he would go away, and dropped asleep again.

Kirillov sent an old woman "to congratulate them," as well as some hot tea, some freshly cooked cutlets, and some broth and white bread for Marya Ignatyevna. The patient sipped the broth greedily, the old woman undid the baby's wrappings and swaddled it afresh, Marie made Shatov have a cutlet too.

Time was passing. Shatov, exhausted, fell asleep himself in his chair, with his head on Marie's pillow. So they were found by Arina Prohorovna, who kept her word. She waked them up gaily, asked Marie some necessary questions, examined the baby, and again forbade Shatov to leave her. Then, jesting at the "happy couple," with a shade of contempt and superciliousness she went away as well satisfied as before.

It was quite dark when Shatov waked up. He made haste to light the candle and ran for the old woman; but he had hardly begun to go down the stairs when he was struck by the sound of the soft, deliberate steps of someone coming up towards him. Erkel came in.

"Don't come in," whispered Shatov, and impulsively seizing him by the hand he drew him back towards the gate. "Wait here, I'll come directly, I'd completely forgotten you, completely! Oh, how you brought it back!"

He was in such haste that he did not even run in to Kirillov's, but only called the old woman. Marie was in despair and indignation that "he could dream of leaving her alone."

"But," he cried ecstatically, "this is the very last step! And then for a new life and we'll never, never think of the old horrors again!"

He somehow appeased her and promised to be back at nine o'clock; he kissed her warmly, kissed the baby and ran down quickly to Erkel.

They set off together to Stavrogin's park at Skvoreshniki, where, in a secluded place at the very edge of the park where it adjoined the pine wood, he had, eighteen months before, buried the printing press which had been entrusted to him. It was a wild and deserted place, quite hidden and at some distance from the Stavrogins' house. It was two or perhaps three miles from Filipov's house.

"Are we going to walk all the way? I'll take a cab."

"I particularly beg you not to," replied Erkel.

They insisted on that. A cabman would be a witness.

"Well … bother! I don't care, only to make an end of it."

They walked very fast.

"Erkel, you little boy," cried Shatov, "have you ever been happy?"

"You seem to be very happy just now," observed Erkel with curiosity.

CHAPTER VI. A BUSY NIGHT

I

During that day Virginsky had spent two hours in running round to see the members of the quintet and to inform them that Shatov would certainly not give information, because his wife had come back and given birth to a child, and no one "who knew anything of human nature" could suppose that Shatov could be a danger at this moment. But to his discomfiture he found none of them at home except Erkel and Lyamshin. Erkel listened in silence, looking candidly into his eyes, and in answer to the direct question "Would he go at six o'clock or not?" he replied with the brightest of smiles that "of course he would go."

Lyamshin was in bed, seriously ill, as it seemed, with his head covered with a quilt. He was alarmed at Virginsky's coming in, and as soon as the latter began speaking he waved him off from under the bedclothes, entreating him to let him alone. He listened to all he said about Shatov, however, and seemed for some reason extremely struck by the news that Virginsky had found no one at home. It seemed that Lyamshin knew already (through Liputin) of Fedka's death, and hurriedly and incoherently told Virginsky about it, at which the latter seemed struck in his turn. To Virginsky's direct question, "Should they go or not?" he began suddenly waving his hands again, entreating him to let him alone, and saying that it was not his business, and that he knew nothing about it.

Virginsky returned home dejected and greatly alarmed. It weighed upon him that he had to hide it from his family; he was accustomed to tell his wife everything; and if his feverish brain had not hatched a new idea at that moment, a new plan of conciliation for further action, he might have taken to his bed like Lyamshin. But this new idea sustained him; what's more, he began impatiently awaiting the hour fixed, and set off for the appointed spot earlier than was necessary. It was a very gloomy place at the end of the huge park. I went there afterwards on purpose to look at it. How sinister it must have looked on that chill autumn evening! It was at the edge of an old wood belonging to the Crown. Huge ancient pines stood out as vague sombre blurs in the darkness. It was so dark that they could hardly see each other two paces off, but Pyotr Stepanovitch, Liputin, and afterwards Erkel, brought lanterns with them. At some unrecorded date in the past a rather absurd-looking grotto had for some reason been built here of rough unhewn stones. The table and benches in the grotto had long ago decayed and fallen. Two hundred paces to the right was the bank of the third pond of the park. These three ponds stretched one after another for a mile from the house to the very end of the park. One could scarcely imagine that any noise, a scream, or even a shot, could reach the inhabitants of the Stavrogins' deserted house. Nikolay Vsyevolodovitch's departure the previous day and Alexey Yegorytch's absence left only five or six people in the house, all more or less invalided, so to speak. In any case it might be assumed with perfect confidence that if cries or shouts for help were heard by any of the inhabitants of the isolated house they would only have excited terror; no one would have moved from his warm stove or snug shelf to give assistance.

By twenty past six almost all of them except Erkel, who had been told off to fetch Shatov, had turned up at the trysting-place. This time Pyotr Stepanovitch was not late; he came with

Tolkatchenko. Tolkatchenko looked frowning and anxious; all his assumed determination and insolent bravado had vanished. He scarcely left Pyotr Stepanovitch's side, and seemed to have become all at once immensely devoted to him. He was continually thrusting himself forward to whisper fussily to him, but the latter scarcely answered him, or muttered something irritably to get rid of him.

Shigalov and Virginsky had arrived rather before Pyotr Stepanovitch, and as soon as he came they drew a little apart in profound and obviously intentional silence. Pyotr Stepanovitch raised his lantern and examined them with unceremonious and insulting minuteness. "They mean to speak," flashed through his mind.

"Isn't Lyamshin here?" he asked Virginsky. "Who said he was ill?"

"I am here," responded Lyamshin, suddenly coming from behind a tree. He was in a warm greatcoat and thickly muffled in a rug, so that it was difficult to make out his face even with a lantern.

"So Liputin is the only one not here?"

Liputin too came out of the grotto without speaking. Pyotr Stepanovitch raised the lantern again.

"Why were you hiding in there? Why didn't you come out?"

"I imagine we still keep the right of freedom … of our actions," Liputin muttered, though probably he hardly knew what he wanted to express.

"Gentlemen," said Pyotr Stepanovitch, raising his voice for the first time above a whisper, which produced an effect, "I think you fully understand that it's useless to go over things again. Everything was said and fully thrashed out yesterday, openly and directly. But perhaps—as I see from your faces—someone wants to make some statement; in that case I beg you to make haste. Damn it all! there's not much time, and Erkel may bring him in a minute…."

"He is sure to bring him," Tolkatchenko put in for some reason.

"If I am not mistaken, the printing press will be handed over, to begin with?" inquired Liputin, though again he seemed hardly to understand why he asked the question.

"Of course. Why should we lose it?" said Pyotr Stepanovitch, lifting the lantern to his face. "But, you see, we all agreed yesterday that it was not really necessary to take it. He need only show you the exact spot where it's buried; we can dig it up afterwards for ourselves. I know that it's somewhere ten paces from a corner of this grotto. But, damn it all! how could you have forgotten, Liputin? It was agreed that you should meet him alone and that we should come out afterwards…. It's strange that you should ask—or didn't you mean what you said?"

Liputin kept gloomily silent. All were silent. The wind shook the tops of the pine-trees.

"I trust, however, gentlemen, that every one will do his duty," Pyotr Stepanovitch rapped out impatiently.

"I know that Shatov's wife has come back and has given birth to a child," Virginsky said suddenly, excited and gesticulating and scarcely able to speak distinctly. "Knowing what human nature is, we can be sure that now he won't give information … because he is happy.… So I went to every one this morning and found no one at home, so perhaps now nothing need be done.…"

He stopped short with a catch in his breath.

"If you suddenly became happy, Mr. Virginsky," said Pyotr Stepanovitch, stepping up to him, "would you abandon—not giving information; there's no question of that—but any perilous public action which you had planned before you were happy and which you regarded as a duty and obligation in spite of the risk and loss of happiness?"

"No, I wouldn't abandon it! I wouldn't on any account!" said Virginsky with absurd warmth, twitching all over.

"You would rather be unhappy again than be a scoundrel?"

"Yes, yes.… Quite the contrary.… I'd rather be a complete scoundrel … that is no … not a scoundrel at all, but on the contrary completely unhappy rather than a scoundrel."

"Well then, let me tell you that Shatov looks on this betrayal as a public duty. It's his most cherished conviction, and the proof of it is that he runs some risk himself; though, of course, they will pardon him a great deal for giving information. A man like that will never give up the idea. No sort of happiness would overcome him. In another day he'll go back on it, reproach himself, and will go straight to the police. What's more, I don't see any happiness in the fact that his wife has come back after three years' absence to bear him a child of Stavrogin's."

"But no one has seen Shatov's letter," Shigalov brought out all at once, emphatically.

"I've seen it," cried Pyotr Stepanovitch. "It exists, and all this is awfully stupid, gentlemen."

"And I protest …" Virginsky cried, boiling over suddenly: "I protest with all my might.… I want … this is what I want. I suggest that when he arrives we all come out and question him, and if it's true, we induce him to repent of it; and if he gives us his word of honour, let him go. In any case we must have a trial; it must be done after trial. We mustn't lie in wait for him and then fall upon him."

"Risk the cause on his word of honour—that's the acme of stupidity! Damnation, how stupid it all is now, gentlemen! And a pretty part you are choosing to play at the moment of danger!"

"I protest, I protest!" Virginsky persisted.

"Don't bawl, anyway; we shan't hear the signal. Shatov, gentlemen.… (Damnation, how stupid this is now!) I've told you already that Shatov is a Slavophil, that is, one of the stupidest set of people.… But, damn it all, never mind, that's no matter! You put me out!… Shatov is an embittered man, gentlemen, and since he has belonged to the party, anyway, whether he wanted to or no, I had hoped till the last minute that he might have been of service to the cause and might have been made use of as an embittered man. I spared him and was keeping him in reserve, in spite of most exact instructions.… I've spared him a hundred times more than he deserved! But he's ended by betraying us.... But, hang it all, I don't care! You'd better try running away now, any of you! No one of you has the right to give up the job! You can kiss him if you like, but you haven't the right to stake the cause on his word of honour! That's acting like swine and spies in government pay!"

"Who's a spy in government pay here?" Liputin filtered out.

"You, perhaps. You'd better hold your tongue, Liputin; you talk for the sake of talking, as you always do. All men are spies, gentlemen, who funk their duty at the moment of danger. There will always be some fools who'll run in a panic at the last moment and cry out, 'Aie, forgive me, and I'll give them all away!' But let me tell you, gentlemen, no betrayal would win you a pardon now. Even if your sentence were mitigated it would mean Siberia; and, what's more, there's no escaping the weapons of the other side—and their weapons are sharper than the government's."

Pyotr Stepanovitch was furious and said more than he meant to. With a resolute air Shigalov took three steps towards him. "Since yesterday evening I've thought over the question," he began, speaking with his usual pedantry and assurance. (I believe that if the earth had given way under his feet he would not have raised his voice nor have varied one tone in his methodical exposition.) "Thinking the matter over, I've come to the conclusion that the projected murder is not merely a waste of precious time which might be employed in a more suitable and befitting manner, but presents, moreover, that deplorable deviation from the normal method which has always been most prejudicial to the cause and has delayed its triumph for scores of years, under the guidance of shallow thinkers and pre-eminently of men of political instead of purely socialistic leanings. I have come here solely to protest against the projected enterprise, for the general edification, intending then to withdraw at the actual moment, which you, for some reason I don't understand, speak of as a moment of danger to you. I am going—not from fear of that danger nor from a sentimental feeling for Shatov, whom I have no inclination to kiss, but solely because all this business from beginning to end is in direct contradiction to my programme. As for my betraying you and my being in the pay of the government, you can set your mind completely at rest. I shall not betray you."

He turned and walked away.

"Damn it all, he'll meet them and warn Shatov!" cried Pyotr Stepanovitch, pulling out his revolver. They heard the click of the trigger.

"You may be confident," said Shigalov, turning once more, "that if I meet Shatov on the way I may bow to him, but I shall not warn him."

"But do you know, you may have to pay for this, Mr. Fourier?"

"I beg you to observe that I am not Fourier. If you mix me up with that mawkish theoretical twaddler you simply prove that you know nothing of my manuscript, though it has been in your hands. As for your vengeance, let me tell you that it's a mistake to cock your pistol: that's absolutely against your interests at the present moment. But if you threaten to shoot me to-morrow, or the day after, you'll gain nothing by it but unnecessary trouble. You may kill me, but sooner or later you'll come to my system all the same. Good-bye."

At that instant a whistle was heard in the park, two hundred paces away from the direction of the pond. Liputin at once answered, whistling also as had been agreed the evening before. (As he had lost several teeth and distrusted his own powers, he had this morning bought for a farthing in the market a child's clay whistle for the purpose.) Erkel had warned Shatov on the way that they would whistle as a signal, so that the latter felt no uneasiness.

"Don't be uneasy, I'll avoid them and they won't notice me at all," Shigalov declared in an impressive whisper; and thereupon deliberately and without haste he walked home through the dark park.

Everything, to the smallest detail of this terrible affair, is now fully known. To begin with, Liputin met Erkel and Shatov at the entrance to the grotto. Shatov did not bow or offer him his hand, but at once pronounced hurriedly in a loud voice:

"Well, where have you put the spade, and haven't you another lantern? You needn't be afraid, there's absolutely no one here, and they wouldn't hear at Skvoreshniki now if we fired a cannon here. This is the place, here this very spot."

And he stamped with his foot ten paces from the end of the grotto towards the wood. At that moment Tolkatchenko rushed out from behind a tree and sprang at him from behind, while Erkel seized him by the elbows. Liputin attacked him from the front. The three of them at once knocked him down and pinned him to the ground. At this point Pyotr Stepanovitch darted up with his revolver. It is said that Shatov had time to turn his head and was able to see and recognise him. Three lanterns lighted up the scene. Shatov suddenly uttered a short and desperate scream. But they did not let him go on screaming. Pyotr Stepanovitch firmly and accurately put his revolver to Shatov's forehead, pressed it to it, and pulled the trigger. The shot seems not to have been loud; nothing was heard at Skvoreshniki, anyway. Shigalov, who was scarcely three paces away, of course heard it—he heard the shout and the shot, but, as he testified afterwards, he did not turn nor even stop. Death was almost instantaneous. Pyotr Stepanovitch was the only one who preserved all his faculties, but I don't think he was quite cool. Squatting on his heels, he searched the murdered man's pockets hastily, though with steady hand. No money was found (his purse had been left under Marya Ignatyevna's pillow). Two or three scraps of paper of no importance were found: a note from his office, the title of some book, and an old bill from a restaurant abroad which had been preserved, goodness knows why, for two years in his pocket. Pyotr Stepanovitch transferred these scraps of paper to his own pocket, and suddenly noticing that they had all gathered round, were gazing at the corpse and doing nothing, he began rudely and angrily abusing them and urging them on. Tolkatchenko and Erkel recovered themselves, and running to the grotto brought instantly from it two stones which they had got ready there that morning. These stones, which weighed about twenty pounds each, were securely tied with cord. As they intended to throw the body in the nearest of the three ponds, they proceeded to tie the stones to the head and feet respectively. Pyotr Stepanovitch fastened the stones while Tolkatchenko and Erkel only held and passed them. Erkel was foremost, and while Pyotr Stepanovitch, grumbling and swearing, tied the dead man's feet together with the cord and fastened the stone to them—a rather lengthy operation—Tolkatchenko stood holding the other stone at arm's-length, his whole person bending forward, as it were, deferentially, to be in readiness to hand it without delay. It never once occurred to him to lay his burden on the ground in the interval. When at last both stones were tied on and Pyotr Stepanovitch got up from the ground to scrutinise the faces of his companions, something strange happened, utterly unexpected and surprising to almost every one.

As I have said already, all except perhaps Tolkatchenko and Erkel were standing still doing nothing. Though Virginsky had rushed up to Shatov with the others he had not seized him or helped to hold him. Lyamshin had joined the group after the shot had been fired. Afterwards, while Pyotr Stepanovitch was busy with the corpse—for perhaps ten minutes—none of them seemed to have been fully conscious. They grouped themselves around and seemed to have felt amazement rather than anxiety or alarm. Liputin stood foremost, close to the corpse. Virginsky stood behind him, peeping over his shoulder with a peculiar, as it were unconcerned, curiosity; he even stood on tiptoe to get a better view. Lyamshin hid behind Virginsky. He took an apprehensive peep from time to time and slipped behind him again at once. When the stones had been tied on and Pyotr Stepanovitch had risen to his feet, Virginsky began faintly shuddering all over, clasped his hands, and cried out bitterly at the top of his voice:

"It's not the right thing, it's not, it's not at all!" He would perhaps have added something more to his belated exclamation, but Lyamshin did not let him finish: he suddenly seized him from behind and squeezed him with all his might, uttering an unnatural shriek. There are moments of violent emotion, of terror, for instance, when a man will cry out in a voice not his own, unlike anything one could have anticipated from him, and this has sometimes a very terrible effect. Lyamshin gave vent to a scream more animal than human. Squeezing Virginsky from behind more and more tightly and convulsively, he went on shrieking without a pause, his mouth wide open and his eyes starting out of his head, keeping up a continual patter with his feet, as though he were beating a drum. Virginsky was so scared that he too screamed out like a madman, and with a ferocity, a vindictiveness that one could never have expected of Virginsky. He tried to pull himself away from Lyamshin, scratching and punching him as far as he could with his arms behind him. Erkel at last helped to pull Lyamshin away. But when, in his terror, Virginsky had skipped ten paces away from him, Lyamshin, catching sight of Pyotr Stepanovitch, began yelling again and flew at him. Stumbling over the corpse, he fell upon Pyotr Stepanovitch, pressing his head to the latter's chest and gripping him so tightly in his arms that Pyotr Stepanovitch, Tolkatchenko, and Liputin could all of them do nothing at the first moment. Pyotr Stepanovitch shouted, swore, beat him on the head with his fists. At last, wrenching himself away, he drew his revolver and put it in the open mouth of Lyamshin, who was still yelling and was by now tightly held by Tolkatchenko, Erkel, and Liputin. But Lyamshin went on shrieking in spite of the revolver. At last Erkel, crushing his silk handkerchief into a ball, deftly thrust it into his mouth and the shriek ceased. Meantime Tolkatchenko tied his hands with what was left of the rope.

"It's very strange," said Pyotr Stepanovitch, scrutinising the madman with uneasy wonder. He was evidently struck. "I expected something very different from him," he added thoughtfully.

They left Erkel in charge of him for a time. They had to make haste to get rid of the corpse: there had been so much noise that someone might have heard. Tolkatchenko and Pyotr Stepanovitch took up the lanterns and lifted the corpse by the head, while Liputin and Virginsky took the feet, and so they carried it away. With the two stones it was a heavy burden, and the distance was more than two hundred paces. Tolkatchenko was the strongest of them. He advised them to keep in step, but no one answered him and they all walked anyhow. Pyotr Stepanovitch walked on the right and, bending forward, carried the dead man's head on his shoulder while with the left hand he supported the stone. As Tolkatchenko walked more than half the way without thinking of helping him with the stone, Pyotr Stepanovitch at last shouted at him with an oath. It was a single, sudden shout. They all went on carrying the body in silence, and it was only when they reached the pond that Virginsky, stooping under his burden and seeming to be exhausted by the weight of it, cried out again in the same loud and wailing voice:

"It's not the right thing, no, no, it's not the right thing!"

The place to which they carried the dead man at the extreme end of the rather large pond, which was the farthest of the three from the house, was one of the most solitary and unfrequented spots in the park, especially at this late season of the year. At that end the pond was overgrown with weeds by the banks. They put down the lantern, swung the corpse and threw it into the pond. They heard a muffled and prolonged splash. Pyotr Stepanovitch raised the lantern and every one followed his example, peering curiously to see the body sink, but nothing could be seen: weighted with the two stones, the body sank at once. The big ripples spread over the surface of the water and quickly passed away. It was over.

Virginsky went off with Erkel, who before giving up Lyamshin to Tolkatchenko brought him to Pyotr Stepanovitch, reporting to the latter that Lyamshin had come to his senses, was penitent and begged forgiveness, and indeed had no recollection of what had happened to him. Pyotr Stepanovitch walked off alone, going round by the farther side of the pond, skirting the park. This was the longest way. To his surprise Liputin overtook him before he got half-way home.

"Pyotr Stepanovitch! Pyotr Stepanovitch! Lyamshin will give information!"

"No, he will come to his senses and realise that he will be the first to go to Siberia if he did. No one will betray us now. Even you won't."

"What about you?"

"No fear! I'll get you all out of the way the minute you attempt to turn traitors, and you know that. But you won't turn traitors. Have you run a mile and a half to tell me that?"

"Pyotr Stepanovitch, Pyotr Stepanovitch, perhaps we shall never meet again!"

"What's put that into your head?"

"Only tell me one thing."

"Well, what? Though I want you to take yourself off."

"One question, but answer it truly: are we the only quintet in the world, or is it true that there are hundreds of others? It's a question of the utmost importance to me, Pyotr Stepanovitch."

"I see that from the frantic state you are in. But do you know, Liputin, you are more dangerous than Lyamshin?"

"I know, I know; but the answer, your answer!"

"You are a stupid fellow! I should have thought it could make no difference to you now whether it's the only quintet or one of a thousand."

"That means it's the only one! I was sure of it ..." cried Liputin. "I always knew it was the only one, I knew it all along." And without waiting for any reply he turned and quickly vanished into the darkness.

Pyotr Stepanovitch pondered a little.

"No, no one will turn traitor," he concluded with decision, "but the group must remain a group and obey, or I'll ... What a wretched set they are though!"

II

He first went home, and carefully, without haste, packed his trunk. At six o'clock in the morning there was a special train from the town. This early morning express only ran once a week, and was only a recent experiment. Though Pyotr Stepanovitch had told the members of the quintet that he was only going to be away for a short time in the neighbourhood, his intentions, as appeared later, were in reality very different. Having finished packing, he settled accounts with his landlady to whom he had previously given notice of his departure, and drove in a cab to Erkel's lodgings, near the station. And then just upon one o'clock at night he walked to Kirillov's, approaching as before by Fedka's secret way.

Pyotr Stepanovitch was in a painful state of mind. Apart from other extremely grave reasons for dissatisfaction (he was still unable to learn anything of Stavrogin), he had, it seems—for I cannot assert it for a fact—received in the course of that day, probably from Petersburg, secret information of a danger awaiting him in the immediate future. There are, of course, many legends in the town relating to this period; but if any facts were known, it was only to those immediately concerned. I can only surmise as my own conjecture that Pyotr Stepanovitch may well have had affairs going on in other neighbourhoods as well as in our town, so that he really may have received such a warning. I am convinced, indeed, in spite of Liputin's cynical and despairing doubts, that he really had two or three other quintets; for instance, in Petersburg and Moscow, and if not quintets at least colleagues and correspondents, and possibly was in very curious relations with them. Not more than three days after his departure an order for his immediate arrest arrived from Petersburg—whether in connection with what had happened among us, or elsewhere, I don't know. This order only served to increase the overwhelming, almost panic terror which suddenly came upon our local authorities and the society of the town, till then so persistently frivolous in its attitude, on the discovery of the mysterious and portentous murder of the student Shatov—the climax of the long series of senseless actions in our midst—as well as the extremely mysterious circumstances that accompanied that murder. But the order came too late: Pyotr Stepanovitch was already in Petersburg, living under another name, and, learning what was going on, he made haste to make his escape abroad.... But I am anticipating in a shocking way.

He went in to Kirillov, looking ill-humoured and quarrelsome. Apart from the real task before him, he felt, as it were, tempted to satisfy some personal grudge, to avenge himself on Kirillov for something. Kirillov seemed pleased to see him; he had evidently been expecting him a long time with painful impatience. His face was paler than usual; there was a fixed and heavy look in his black eyes.

"I thought you weren't coming," he brought out drearily from his corner of the sofa, from which he had not, however, moved to greet him.

Pyotr Stepanovitch stood before him and, before uttering a word, looked intently at his face.

"Everything is in order, then, and we are not drawing back from our resolution. Bravo!" He smiled an offensively patronising smile. "But, after all," he added with unpleasant jocosity, "if I am behind my time, it's not for you to complain: I made you a present of three hours."

"I don't want extra hours as a present from you, and you can't make me a present … you fool!"

"What?" Pyotr Stepanovitch was startled, but instantly controlled himself. "What huffiness! So we are in a savage temper?" he rapped out, still with the same offensive superciliousness. "At such a moment composure is what you need. The best thing you can do is to consider yourself a Columbus and me a mouse, and not to take offence at anything I say. I gave you that advice yesterday."

"I don't want to look upon you as a mouse."

"What's that, a compliment? But the tea is cold—and that shows that everything is topsy-turvy. Bah! But I see something in the window, on a plate." He went to the window. "Oh oh, boiled chicken and rice!… But why haven't you begun upon it yet? So we are in such a state of mind that even chicken …"

"I've dined, and it's not your business. Hold your tongue!"

"Oh, of course; besides, it's no consequence—though for me at the moment it is of consequence. Only fancy, I scarcely had any dinner, and so if, as I suppose, that chicken is not wanted now … eh?"

"Eat it if you can."

"Thank you, and then I'll have tea."

He instantly settled himself at the other end of the sofa and fell upon the chicken with extraordinary greediness; at the same time he kept a constant watch on his victim. Kirillov looked at him fixedly with angry aversion, as though unable to tear himself away.

"I say, though," Pyotr Stepanovitch fired off suddenly, while he still went on eating, "what about our business? We are not crying off, are we? How about that document?"

"I've decided in the night that it's nothing to me. I'll write it. About the manifestoes?"

"Yes, about the manifestoes too. But I'll dictate it. Of course, that's nothing to you. Can you possibly mind what's in the letter at such a moment?"

"That's not your business."

"It's not mine, of course. It need only be a few lines, though: that you and Shatov distributed the manifestoes and with the help of Fedka, who hid in your lodgings. This last point about Fedka and your lodgings is very important—the most important of all, indeed. You see, I am talking to you quite openly."

"Shatov? Why Shatov? I won't mention Shatov for anything."

"What next! What is it to you? You can't hurt him now."

"His wife has come back to him. She has waked up and has sent to ask me where he is."

"She has sent to ask you where he is? H'm … that's unfortunate. She may send again; no one ought to know I am here."

Pyotr Stepanovitch was uneasy.

"She won't know, she's gone to sleep again. There's a midwife with her, Arina Virginsky."

"So that's how it was.… She won't overhear, I suppose? I say, you'd better shut the front door."

"She won't overhear anything. And if Shatov comes I'll hide you in another room."

"Shatov won't come; and you must write that you quarrelled with him because he turned traitor and informed the police … this evening … and caused his death."

"He is dead!" cried Kirillov, jumping up from the sofa.

"He died at seven o'clock this evening, or rather, at seven o'clock yesterday evening, and now it's one o'clock."

"You have killed him!… And I foresaw it yesterday!"

"No doubt you did! With this revolver here." (He drew out his revolver as though to show it, but did not put it back again and still held it in his right hand as though in readiness.) "You are a strange man, though, Kirillov; you knew yourself that the stupid fellow was bound to end like this. What was there to foresee in that? I made that as plain as possible over and over again. Shatov was meaning to betray us; I was watching him, and it could not be left like that. And you too had instructions to watch him; you told me so yourself three weeks ago.…"

"Hold your tongue! You've done this because he spat in your face in Geneva!"

"For that and for other things too—for many other things; not from spite, however. Why do you jump up? Why look like that? Oh oh, so that's it, is it?"

He jumped up and held out his revolver before him. Kirillov had suddenly snatched up from the window his revolver, which had been loaded and put ready since the morning. Pyotr Stepanovitch took up his position and aimed his weapon at Kirillov. The latter laughed angrily.

"Confess, you scoundrel, that you brought your revolver because I might shoot you.... But I shan't shoot you ... though ... though ..."

And again he turned his revolver upon Pyotr Stepanovitch, as it were rehearsing, as though unable to deny himself the pleasure of imagining how he would shoot him. Pyotr Stepanovitch, holding his ground, waited for him, waited for him till the last minute without pulling the trigger, at the risk of being the first to get a bullet in his head: it might well be expected of "the maniac." But at last "the maniac" dropped his hand, gasping and trembling and unable to speak.

"You've played your little game and that's enough." Pyotr Stepanovitch, too, dropped his weapon. "I knew it was only a game; only you ran a risk, let me tell you: I might have fired."

And he sat down on the sofa with a fair show of composure and poured himself out some tea, though his hand trembled a little. Kirillov laid his revolver on the table and began walking up and down.

"I won't write that I killed Shatov ... and I won't write anything now. You won't have a document!"

"I shan't?"

"No, you won't."

"What meanness and what stupidity!" Pyotr Stepanovitch turned green with resentment. "I foresaw it, though. You've not taken me by surprise, let me tell you. As you please, however. If I could make you do it by force, I would. You are a scoundrel, though." Pyotr Stepanovitch was more and more carried away and unable to restrain himself. "You asked us for money out there and promised us no end of things.... I won't go away with nothing, however: I'll see you put the bullet through your brains first, anyway."

"I want you to go away at once." Kirillov stood firmly before him.

"No, that's impossible." Pyotr Stepanovitch took up his revolver again. "Now in your spite and cowardice you may think fit to put it off and to turn traitor to-morrow, so as to get money again; they'll pay you for that, of course. Damn it all, fellows like you are capable of anything! Only don't trouble yourself; I've provided for all contingencies: I am not going till I've dashed your brains out with this revolver, as I did to that scoundrel Shatov, if you are afraid to do it yourself and put off your intention, damn you!"

"You are set on seeing my blood, too?"

"I am not acting from spite; let me tell you, it's nothing to me. I am doing it to be at ease about the cause. One can't rely on men; you see that for yourself. I don't understand what fancy possesses you to put yourself to death. It wasn't my idea; you thought of it yourself before I appeared, and talked of your intention to the committee abroad before you said anything to me. And you know, no one has forced it out of you; no one of them knew you, but you came to confide in them yourself, from sentimentalism. And what's to be done if a plan of action here, which can't be altered now, was founded upon that with your consent and upon your suggestion?... your suggestion, mind that! You have put yourself in a position in which you know too much. If you are an ass and go off to-morrow to inform the police, that would be rather a disadvantage to us; what do you think about it? Yes, you've bound yourself; you've given your word, you've taken money. That you can't deny...."

Pyotr Stepanovitch was much excited, but for some time past Kirillov had not been listening. He paced up and down the room, lost in thought again.

"I am sorry for Shatov," he said, stopping before Pyotr Stepanovitch again.

"Why so? I am sorry, if that's all, and do you suppose ..."

"Hold your tongue, you scoundrel," roared Kirillov, making an alarming and unmistakable movement; "I'll kill you."

"There, there, there! I told a lie, I admit it; I am not sorry at all. Come, that's enough, that's enough." Pyotr Stepanovitch started up apprehensively, putting out his hand.

Kirillov subsided and began walking up and down again.

"I won't put it off; I want to kill myself now: all are scoundrels."

"Well, that's an idea; of course all are scoundrels; and since life is a beastly thing for a decent man ..."

"Fool, I am just such a scoundrel as you, as all, not a decent man. There's never been a decent man anywhere."

"He's guessed the truth at last! Can you, Kirillov, with your sense, have failed to see till now that all men are alike, that there are none better or worse, only some are stupider, than others, and that if all are scoundrels (which is nonsense, though) there oughtn't to be any people that are not?"

"Ah! Why, you are really in earnest?" Kirillov looked at him with some wonder. "You speak with heat and simply.... Can it be that even fellows like you have convictions?"

"Kirillov, I've never been able to understand why you mean to kill yourself. I only know it's from conviction ... strong conviction. But if you feel a yearning to express yourself, so to say, I am at your service.... Only you must think of the time."

"What time is it?"

"Oh oh, just two." Pyotr Stepanovitch looked at his watch and lighted a cigarette.

"It seems we can come to terms after all," he reflected.

"I've nothing to say to you," muttered Kirillov.

"I remember that something about God comes into it ... you explained it to me once—twice, in fact. If you stopped yourself, you become God; that's it, isn't it?"

"Yes, I become God."

Pyotr Stepanovitch did not even smile; he waited. Kirillov looked at him subtly.

"You are a political impostor and intriguer. You want to lead me on into philosophy and enthusiasm and to bring about a reconciliation so as to disperse my anger, and then, when I am reconciled with you, beg from me a note to say I killed Shatov."

Pyotr Stepanovitch answered with almost natural frankness.

"Well, supposing I am such a scoundrel. But at the last moments does that matter to you, Kirillov? What are we quarrelling about? Tell me, please. You are one sort of man and I am another—what of it? And what's more, we are both of us ..."

"Scoundrels."

"Yes, scoundrels if you like. But you know that that's only words."

"All my life I wanted it not to be only words. I lived because I did not want it to be. Even now every day I want it to be not words."

"Well, every one seeks to be where he is best off. The fish ... that is, every one seeks his own comfort, that's all. That's been a commonplace for ages and ages."

"Comfort, do you say?"

"Oh, it's not worth while quarrelling over words."

"No, you were right in what you said; let it be comfort. God is necessary and so must exist."

"Well, that's all right, then."

"But I know He doesn't and can't."

"That's more likely."

"Surely you must understand that a man with two such ideas can't go on living?"

"Must shoot himself, you mean?"

"Surely you must understand that one might shoot oneself for that alone? You don't understand that there may be a man, one man out of your thousands of millions, one man who won't bear it and does not want to."

"All I understand is that you seem to be hesitating.... That's very bad."

"Stavrogin, too, is consumed by an idea," Kirillov said gloomily, pacing up and down the room. He had not noticed the previous remark.

"What?" Pyotr Stepanovitch pricked up his ears. "What idea? Did he tell you something himself?"

"No, I guessed it myself: if Stavrogin has faith, he does not believe that he has faith. If he hasn't faith, he does not believe that he hasn't."

"Well, Stavrogin has got something else worse than that in his head," Pyotr Stepanovitch muttered peevishly, uneasily watching the turn the conversation had taken and the pallor of Kirillov.

"Damn it all, he won't shoot himself!" he was thinking. "I always suspected it; it's a maggot in the brain and nothing more; what a rotten lot of people!"

"You are the last to be with me; I shouldn't like to part on bad terms with you," Kirillov vouchsafed suddenly.

Pyotr Stepanovitch did not answer at once. "Damn it all, what is it now?" he thought again.

"I assure you, Kirillov, I have nothing against you personally as a man, and always …"

"You are a scoundrel and a false intellect. But I am just the same as you are, and I will shoot myself while you will remain living."

"You mean to say, I am so abject that I want to go on living."

He could not make up his mind whether it was judicious to keep up such a conversation at such a moment or not, and resolved "to be guided by circumstances." But the tone of superiority and of contempt for him, which Kirillov had never disguised, had always irritated him, and now for some reason it irritated him more than ever—possibly because Kirillov, who was to die within an hour or so (Pyotr Stepanovitch still reckoned upon this), seemed to him, as it were, already only half a man, some creature whom he could not allow to be haughty.

"You seem to be boasting to me of your shooting yourself."

"I've always been surprised at every one's going on living," said Kirillov, not hearing his remark.

"H'm! Admitting that's an idea, but …"

"You ape, you assent to get the better of me. Hold your tongue; you won't understand anything. If there is no God, then I am God."

"There, I could never understand that point of yours: why are you God?"

"If God exists, all is His will and from His will I cannot escape. If not, it's all my will and I am bound to show self-will."

"Self-will? But why are you bound?"

"Because all will has become mine. Can it be that no one in the whole planet, after making an end of God and believing in his own will, will dare to express his self-will on the most vital point? It's like a beggar inheriting a fortune and being afraid of it and not daring to approach the bag of gold, thinking himself too weak to own it. I want to manifest my self-will. I may be the only one, but I'll do it."

"Do it by all means."

"I am bound to shoot myself because the highest point of my self-will is to kill myself with my own hands."

"But you won't be the only one to kill yourself; there are lots of suicides."

"With good cause. But to do it without any cause at all, simply for self-will, I am the only one."

"He won't shoot himself," flashed across Pyotr Stepanovitch's mind again.

"Do you know," he observed irritably, "if I were in your place I should kill someone else to show my self-will, not myself. You might be of use. I'll tell you whom, if you are not afraid. Then you needn't shoot yourself to-day, perhaps. We may come to terms."

"To kill someone would be the lowest point of self-will, and you show your whole soul in that. I am not you: I want the highest point and I'll kill myself."

"He's come to it of himself," Pyotr Stepanovitch muttered malignantly.

"I am bound to show my unbelief," said Kirillov, walking about the room. "I have no higher idea than disbelief in God. I have all the history of mankind on my side. Man has done nothing but invent God so as to go on living, and not kill himself; that's the whole of universal history up till now. I am the first one in the whole history of mankind who would not invent God. Let them know it once for all."

"He won't shoot himself," Pyotr Stepanovitch thought anxiously.

"Let whom know it?" he said, egging him on. "It's only you and me here; you mean Liputin?"

"Let every one know; all will know. There is nothing secret that will not be made known. He said so."

And he pointed with feverish enthusiasm to the image of the Saviour, before which a lamp was burning. Pyotr Stepanovitch lost his temper completely.

"So you still believe in Him, and you've lighted the lamp; 'to be on the safe side,' I suppose?"

The other did not speak.

"Do you know, to my thinking, you believe perhaps more thoroughly than any priest."

"Believe in whom? In Him? Listen." Kirillov stood still, gazing before him with fixed and ecstatic look. "Listen to a great idea: there was a day on earth, and in the midst of the earth there stood three crosses. One on the Cross had such faith that he said to another, 'To-day thou shalt be with me in Paradise.' The day ended; both died and passed away and found neither Paradise nor resurrection. His words did not come true. Listen: that Man was the loftiest of all on earth, He was that which gave meaning to life. The whole planet, with everything on it, is mere madness without that Man. There has never been any like Him before or since, never, up to a miracle. For that is the miracle, that there never was or never will be another like Him.

And if that is so, if the laws of nature did not spare even Him, have not spared even their miracle and made even Him live in a lie and die for a lie, then all the planet is a lie and rests on a lie and on mockery. So then, the very laws of the planet are a lie and the vaudeville of devils. What is there to live for? Answer, if you are a man."

"That's a different matter. It seems to me you've mixed up two different causes, and that's a very unsafe thing to do. But excuse me, if you are God? If the lie were ended and if you realised that all the falsity comes from the belief in that former God?"

"So at last you understand!" cried Kirillov rapturously. "So it can be understood if even a fellow like you understands. Do you understand now that the salvation for all consists in proving this idea to every one? Who will prove it? I! I can't understand how an atheist could know that there is no God and not kill himself on the spot. To recognise that there is no God and not to recognise at the same instant that one is God oneself is an absurdity, else one would certainly kill oneself. If you recognise it you are sovereign, and then you won't kill yourself but will live in the greatest glory. But one, the first, must kill himself, for else who will begin and prove it? So I must certainly kill myself, to begin and prove it. Now I am only a god against my will and I am unhappy, because I am bound to assert my will. All are unhappy because all are afraid to express their will. Man has hitherto been so unhappy and so poor because he has been afraid to assert his will in the highest point and has shown his self-will only in little things, like a schoolboy. I am awfully unhappy, for I'm awfully afraid. Terror is the curse of man.... But I will assert my will, I am bound to believe that I don't believe. I will begin and will make an end of it and open the door, and will save. That's the only thing that will save mankind and will re-create the next generation physically; for with his present physical nature man can't get on without his former God, I believe. For three years I've been seeking for the attribute of my godhead and I've found it; the attribute of my godhead is self-will! That's all I can do to prove in the highest point my independence and my new terrible freedom. For it is very terrible. I am killing myself to prove my independence and my new terrible freedom."

His face was unnaturally pale, and there was a terribly heavy look in his eyes. He was like a man in delirium. Pyotr Stepanovitch thought he would drop on to the floor.

"Give me the pen!" Kirillov cried suddenly, quite unexpectedly, in a positive frenzy. "Dictate; I'll sign anything. I'll sign that I killed Shatov even. Dictate while it amuses me. I am not afraid of what the haughty slaves will think! You will see for yourself that all that is secret shall be made manifest! And you will be crushed.... I believe, I believe!"

Pyotr Stepanovitch jumped up from his seat and instantly handed him an inkstand and paper, and began dictating, seizing the moment, quivering with anxiety.

"I, Alexey Kirillov, declare ..."

"Stay; I won't! To whom am I declaring it?"

Kirillov was shaking as though he were in a fever. This declaration and the sudden strange idea of it seemed to absorb him entirely, as though it were a means of escape by which his tortured spirit strove for a moment's relief.

"To whom am I declaring it? I want to know to whom?"

"To no one, every one, the first person who reads it. Why define it? The whole world!"

"The whole world! Bravo! And I won't have any repentance. I don't want penitence and I don't want it for the police!"

"No, of course, there's no need of it, damn the police! Write, if you are in earnest!" Pyotr Stepanovitch cried hysterically.

"Stay! I want to put at the top a face with the tongue out."

"Ech, what nonsense," cried Pyotr Stepanovitch crossly, "you can express all that without the drawing, by—the tone."

"By the tone? That's true. Yes, by the tone, by the tone of it. Dictate, the tone."

"I, Alexey Kirillov," Pyotr Stepanovitch dictated firmly and peremptorily, bending over Kirillov's shoulder and following every letter which the latter formed with a hand trembling with excitement, "I, Kirillov, declare that to-day, the —th October, at about eight o'clock in the evening, I killed the student Shatov in the park for turning traitor and giving information of the manifestoes and of Fedka, who has been lodging with us for ten days in Filipov's house. I am shooting myself to-day with my revolver, not because I repent and am afraid of you, but because when I was abroad I made up my mind to put an end to my life."

"Is that all?" cried Kirillov with surprise and indignation.

"Not another word," cried Pyotr Stepanovitch, waving his hand, attempting to snatch the document from him.

"Stay." Kirillov put his hand firmly on the paper. "Stay, it's nonsense! I want to say with whom I killed him. Why Fedka? And what about the fire? I want it all and I want to be abusive in tone, too, in tone!"

"Enough, Kirillov, I assure you it's enough," cried Pyotr Stepanovitch almost imploringly, trembling lest he should tear up the paper; "that they may believe you, you must say it as obscurely as possible, just like that, simply in hints. You must only give them a peep of the truth, just enough to tantalise them. They'll tell a story better than ours, and of course they'll believe themselves more than they would us; and you know, it's better than anything—better than anything! Let me have it, it's splendid as it is; give it to me, give it to me!"

And he kept trying to snatch the paper. Kirillov listened open-eyed and appeared to be trying to reflect, but he seemed beyond understanding now.

"Damn it all," Pyotr Stepanovitch cried all at once, ill-humouredly, "he hasn't signed it! Why are you staring like that? Sign!"

"I want to abuse them," muttered Kirillov. He took the pen, however, and signed. "I want to abuse them."

"Write 'Vive la république,' and that will be enough."

"Bravo!" Kirillov almost bellowed with delight. "'Vive la république démocratique sociale et universelle ou la mort!' No, no, that's not it. 'Liberté, égalité, fraternité ou la mort.' There, that's better, that's better." He wrote it gleefully under his signature.

"Enough, enough," repeated Pyotr Stepanovitch.

"Stay, a little more. I'll sign it again in French, you know. 'De Kirillov, gentilhomme russe et citoyen du monde.' Ha ha!" He went off in a peal of laughter. "No, no, no; stay. I've found something better than all. Eureka! 'Gentilhomme, séminariste russe et citoyen du monde civilisé!' That's better than any...." He jumped up from the sofa and suddenly, with a rapid gesture, snatched up the revolver from the window, ran with it into the next room, and closed the door behind him.

Pyotr Stepanovitch stood for a moment, pondering and gazing at the door.

"If he does it at once, perhaps he'll do it, but if he begins thinking, nothing will come of it."

Meanwhile he took up the paper, sat down, and looked at it again. The wording of the document pleased him again.

"What's needed for the moment? What's wanted is to throw them all off the scent and keep them busy for a time. The park? There's no park in the town and they'll guess its Skvoreshniki of themselves. But while they are arriving at that, time will be passing; then the search will take time too; then when they find the body it will prove that the story is true, and it will follow that's it all true, that it's true about Fedka too. And Fedka explains the fire, the Lebyadkins; so that it was all being hatched here, at Filipov's, while they overlooked it and saw nothing—that will quite turn their heads! They will never think of the quintet; Shatov and Kirillov and Fedka and Lebyadkin, and why they killed each other—that will be another question for them. Oh, damn it all, I don't hear the shot!"

Though he had been reading and admiring the wording of it, he had been listening anxiously all the time, and he suddenly flew into a rage. He looked anxiously at his watch; it was getting late and it was fully ten minutes since Kirillov had gone out.... Snatching up the candle, he went to the door of the room where Kirillov had shut himself up. He was just at the door when the thought struck him that the candle had burnt out, that it would not last another twenty minutes, and that there was no other in the room. He took hold of the handle and listened warily; he did not hear the slightest sound. He suddenly opened the door and lifted up the candle: something uttered a roar and rushed at him. He slammed the door with all his might and pressed his weight against it; but all sounds died away and again there was deathlike stillness.

He stood for a long while irresolute, with the candle in his hand. He had been able to see very little in the second he held the door open, but he had caught a glimpse of the face of Kirillov standing at the other end of the room by the window, and the savage fury with which the latter had rushed upon him. Pyotr Stepanovitch started, rapidly set the candle on the table, made ready his revolver, and retreated on tiptoe to the farthest corner of the room, so that if Kirillov opened the door and rushed up to the table with the revolver he would still have time to be the first to aim and fire.

Pyotr Stepanovitch had by now lost all faith in the suicide. "He was standing in the middle of the room, thinking," flashed like a whirlwind through Pyotr Stepanovitch's mind, "and the room was dark and horrible too.... He roared and rushed at me. There are two possibilities: either I interrupted him at the very second when he was pulling the trigger or ... or he was standing planning how to kill me. Yes, that's it, he was planning it.... He knows I won't go away without killing him if he funks it himself—so that he would have to kill me first to prevent my killing him.... And again, again there is silence. I am really frightened: he may open the door all of a sudden.... The nuisance of it is that he believes in God like any priest.... He won't shoot himself for anything! There are lots of these people nowadays 'who've come to it of themselves.' A rotten lot! Oh, damn it, the candle, the candle! It'll go out within a quarter of an hour for certain.... I must put a stop to it; come what may, I must put a stop to it.... Now I can kill him.... With that document here no one would think of my killing him. I can put him in such an attitude on the floor with an unloaded revolver in his hand that they'd be certain he'd done it himself.... Ach, damn it! how is one to kill him? If I open the door he'll rush out again and shoot me first. Damn it all, he'll be sure to miss!"

He was in agonies, trembling at the necessity of action and his own indecision. At last he took up the candle and again approached the door with the revolver held up in readiness; he put his left hand, in which he held the candle, on the doorhandle. But he managed awkwardly: the handle clanked, there was a rattle and a creak. "He will fire straightway," flashed through Pyotr Stepanovitch's mind. With his foot he flung the door open violently, raised the candle, and held out the revolver; but no shot nor cry came from within.... There was no one in the room.

He started. The room led nowhere. There was no exit, no means of escape from it. He lifted the candle higher and looked about him more attentively: there was certainly no one. He called Kirillov's name in a low voice, then again louder; no one answered.

"Can he have got out by the window?" The casement in one window was, in fact, open. "Absurd! He couldn't have got away through the casement." Pyotr Stepanovitch crossed the room and went up to the window. "He couldn't possibly." All at once he turned round quickly and was aghast at something extraordinary.

Against the wall facing the windows on the right of the door stood a cupboard. On the right side of this cupboard, in the corner formed by the cupboard and the wall, stood Kirillov, and he was standing in a very strange way; motionless, perfectly erect, with his arms held stiffly at his sides, his head raised and pressed tightly back against the wall in the very corner, he seemed to be trying to conceal and efface himself. Everything seemed to show that he was hiding, yet somehow it was not easy to believe it. Pyotr Stepanovitch was standing a little sideways to the corner, and could only see the projecting parts of the figure. He could not bring himself to move to the left to get a full view of Kirillov and solve the mystery. His heart began beating violently, and he felt a sudden rush of blind fury: he started from where he stood, and, shouting and stamping with his feet, he rushed to the horrible place.

But when he reached Kirillov he stopped short again, still more overcome, horror-stricken. What struck him most was that, in spite of his shout and his furious rush, the figure did not stir, did not move in a single limb—as though it were of stone or of wax. The pallor of the face was unnatural, the black eyes were quite unmoving and were staring away at a point in the distance. Pyotr Stepanovitch lowered the candle and raised it again, lighting up the figure from all points of view and scrutinising it. He suddenly noticed that, although Kirillov was looking straight before him, he could see him and was perhaps watching him out of the corner of his eye. Then the idea occurred to him to hold the candle right up to the wretch's face, to scorch him and see what he would do. He suddenly fancied that Kirillov's chin twitched and that something like a mocking smile passed over his lips—as though he had guessed Pyotr Stepanovitch's thought. He shuddered and, beside himself, clutched violently at Kirillov's shoulder.

Then something happened so hideous and so soon over that Pyotr Stepanovitch could never afterwards recover a coherent impression of it. He had hardly touched Kirillov when the latter bent down quickly and with his head knocked the candle out of Pyotr Stepanovitch's hand; the candlestick fell with a clang on the ground and the candle went out. At the same moment he was conscious of a fearful pain in the little finger of his left hand. He cried out, and all that he could remember was that, beside himself, he hit out with all his might and struck three blows with the revolver on the head of Kirillov, who had bent down to him and had bitten his finger. At last he tore away his finger and rushed headlong to get out of the house, feeling his way in the dark. He was pursued by terrible shouts from the room.

"Directly, directly, directly, directly." Ten times. But he still ran on, and was running into the porch when he suddenly heard a loud shot. Then he stopped short in the dark porch and stood deliberating for five minutes; at last he made his way back into the house. But he had to get the candle. He had only to feel on the floor on the right of the cupboard for the candlestick; but how was he to light the candle? There suddenly came into his mind a vague recollection: he recalled that when he had run into the kitchen the day before to attack Fedka he had noticed in passing a large red box of matches in a corner on a shelf. Feeling with his hands, he made his way to the door on the left leading to the kitchen, found it, crossed the passage, and went down the steps. On the shelf, on the very spot where he had just recalled seeing it, he felt in the dark a full unopened box of matches. He hurriedly went up the steps again without striking a light, and it was only when he was near the cupboard, at the spot where he had struck Kirillov with the revolver and been bitten by him, that he remembered his bitten finger, and at the same instant was conscious that it was unbearably painful. Clenching his teeth, he managed somehow to light the candle-end, set it in the candlestick again, and looked about him: near the open casement, with his feet towards the right-hand corner, lay the dead body of Kirillov. The shot had been fired at the right temple and the bullet had come out at the top on the left, shattering the skull. There were splashes of blood and brains. The revolver was still in the suicide's hand on the floor. Death must have been instantaneous. After a careful look round, Pyotr Stepanovitch got up and went out on tiptoe, closed the door, left the candle on the table in the outer room, thought a moment, and resolved not to put it out, reflecting that it could not possibly set fire to anything. Looking once more at the document left on the table, he smiled mechanically and then went out of the house, still for some reason walking on tiptoe. He crept through Fedka's hole again and carefully replaced the posts after him.

III

Precisely at ten minutes to six Pyotr Stepanovitch and Erkel were walking up and down the platform at the railway-station beside a rather long train. Pyotr Stepanovitch was setting off and Erkel was saying good-bye to him. The luggage was in, and his bag was in the seat he had taken in a second-class carriage. The first bell had rung already; they were waiting for the second. Pyotr Stepanovitch looked about him, openly watching the passengers as they got into the train. But he did not meet anyone he knew well; only twice he nodded to acquaintances—a merchant whom he knew slightly, and then a young village priest who was going to his parish two stations away. Erkel evidently wanted to speak of something of importance in the last moments, though possibly he did not himself know exactly of what, but he could not bring himself to begin! He kept fancying that Pyotr Stepanovitch seemed anxious to get rid of him and was impatient for the last bell.

"You look at every one so openly," he observed with some timidity, as though he would have warned him.

"Why not? It would not do for me to conceal myself at present. It's too soon. Don't be uneasy. All I am afraid of is that the devil might send Liputin this way; he might scent me out and race off here."

"Pyotr Stepanovitch, they are not to be trusted," Erkel brought out resolutely.

"Liputin?"

"None of them, Pyotr Stepanovitch."

"Nonsense! they are all bound by what happened yesterday. There isn't one who would turn traitor. People won't go to certain destruction unless they've lost their reason."

"Pyotr Stepanovitch, but they will lose their reason." Evidently that idea had already occurred to Pyotr Stepanovitch too, and so Erkel's observation irritated him the more.

"You are not in a funk too, are you, Erkel? I rely on you more than on any of them. I've seen now what each of them is worth. Tell them to-day all I've told you. I leave them in your charge. Go round to each of them this morning. Read them my written instructions to-morrow, or the day after, when you are all together and they are capable of listening again … and believe me, they will be by to-morrow, for they'll be in an awful funk, and that will make them as soft as wax.… The great thing is that you shouldn't be downhearted."

"Ach, Pyotr Stepanovitch, it would be better if you weren't going away."

"But I am only going for a few days; I shall be back in no time."

"Pyotr Stepanovitch," Erkel brought out warily but resolutely, "what if you were going to Petersburg? Of course, I understand that you are only doing what's necessary for the cause."

"I expected as much from you, Erkel. If you have guessed that I am going to Petersburg you can realise that I couldn't tell them yesterday, at that moment, that I was going so far for fear of frightening them. You saw for yourself what a state they were in. But you understand that I am going for the cause, for work of the first importance, for the common cause, and not to save my skin, as Liputin imagines."

"Pyotr Stepanovitch, what if you were going abroad? I should understand … I should understand that you must be careful of yourself because you are everything and we are nothing. I shall understand, Pyotr Stepanovitch." The poor boy's voice actually quivered.

"Thank you, Erkel.... Aie, you've touched my bad finger." (Erkel had pressed his hand awkwardly; the bad finger was discreetly bound up in black silk.) "But I tell you positively again that I am going to Petersburg only to sniff round, and perhaps shall only be there for twenty-four hours and then back here again at once. When I come back I shall stay at Gaganov's country place for the sake of appearances. If there is any notion of danger, I should be the first to take the lead and share it. If I stay longer in Petersburg I'll let you know at once ... in the way we've arranged, and you'll tell them." The second bell rang.

"Ah, then there's only five minutes before the train starts. I don't want the group here to break up, you know. I am not afraid; don't be anxious about me. I have plenty of such centres, and it's not much consequence; but there's no harm in having as many centres as possible. But I am quite at ease about you, though I am leaving you almost alone with those idiots. Don't be uneasy; they won't turn traitor, they won't have the pluck.... Ha ha, you going to-day too?" he cried suddenly in a quite different, cheerful voice to a very young man, who came up gaily to greet him. "I didn't know you were going by the express too. Where are you off to ... your mother's?"

The mother of the young man was a very wealthy landowner in a neighbouring province, and the young man was a distant relation of Yulia Mihailovna's and had been staying about a fortnight in our town.

"No, I am going farther, to R——. I've eight hours to live through in the train. Off to Petersburg?" laughed the young man.

"What makes you suppose I must be going to Petersburg?" said Pyotr Stepanovitch, laughing even more openly.

The young man shook his gloved finger at him.

"Well, you've guessed right," Pyotr Stepanovitch whispered to him mysteriously. "I am going with letters from Yulia Mihailovna and have to call on three or four personages, as you can imagine—bother them all, to speak candidly. It's a beastly job!"

"But why is she in such a panic? Tell me," the young man whispered too. "She wouldn't see even me yesterday. I don't think she has anything to fear for her husband, quite the contrary; he fell down so creditably at the fire—ready to sacrifice his life, so to speak."

"Well, there it is," laughed Pyotr Stepanovitch. "You see, she is afraid that people may have written from here already ... that is, some gentlemen.... The fact is, Stavrogin is at the bottom of it, or rather Prince K.... Ech, it's a long story; I'll tell you something about it on the journey if you like—as far as my chivalrous feelings will allow me, at least.... This is my relation, Lieutenant Erkel, who lives down here."

The young man, who had been stealthily glancing at Erkel, touched his hat; Erkel made a bow.

"But I say, Verhovensky, eight hours in the train is an awful ordeal. Berestov, the colonel, an awfully funny fellow, is travelling with me in the first class. He is a neighbour of ours in the country, and his wife is a Garin (née de Garine), and you know he is a very decent fellow. He's got ideas too. He's only been here a couple of days. He's passionately fond of whist; couldn't we get up a game, eh? I've already fixed on a fourth—Pripuhlov, our merchant from T——with a beard, a millionaire—I mean it, a real millionaire; you can take my word for it.... I'll introduce you; he is a very interesting money-bag. We shall have a laugh."

"I shall be delighted, and I am awfully fond of cards in the train, but I am going second class."

"Nonsense, that's no matter. Get in with us. I'll tell them directly to move you to the first class. The chief guard would do anything I tell him. What have you got?... a bag? a rug?"

"First-rate. Come along!"

Pyotr Stepanovitch took his bag, his rug, and his book, and at once and with alacrity transferred himself to the first class. Erkel helped him. The third bell rang.

"Well, Erkel." Hurriedly, and with a preoccupied air, Pyotr Stepanovitch held out his hand from the window for the last time. "You see, I am sitting down to cards with them."

"Why explain, Pyotr Stepanovitch? I understand, I understand it all!"

"Well, au revoir," Pyotr Stepanovitch turned away suddenly on his name being called by the young man, who wanted to introduce him to his partners. And Erkel saw nothing more of Pyotr Stepanovitch.

He returned home very sad. Not that he was alarmed at Pyotr Stepanovitch's leaving them so suddenly, but ... he had turned away from him so quickly when that young swell had called to him and ... he might have said something different to him, not "Au revoir," or ... or at least have pressed his hand more warmly. That last was bitterest of all. Something else was beginning to gnaw in his poor little heart, something which he could not understand himself yet, something connected with the evening before.

CHAPTER VII. STEPAN TROFIMOVITCH'S LAST WANDERING

I

I am persuaded that Stepan Trofimovitch was terribly frightened as he felt the time fixed for his insane enterprise drawing near. I am convinced that he suffered dreadfully from terror, especially on the night before he started—that awful night. Nastasya mentioned afterwards that he had gone to bed late and fallen asleep. But that proves nothing; men sentenced to death sleep very soundly, they say, even the night before their execution. Though he set off by daylight, when a nervous man is always a little more confident (and the major, Virginsky's relative, used to give up believing in God every morning when the night was over), yet I am convinced he could never, without horror, have imagined himself alone on the high road in such a position. No doubt a certain desperation in his feelings softened at first the terrible sensation of sudden solitude in which he at once found himself as soon as he had left Nastasya, and the corner in which he had been warm and snug for twenty years. But it made no difference; even with the clearest recognition of all the horrors awaiting him he would have gone out to the high road and walked along it! There was something proud in the undertaking which allured him in spite of everything. Oh, he might have accepted Varvara Petrovna's luxurious provision and have remained living on her charity, "comme un humble dependent." But he had not accepted her charity and was not remaining! And here he was leaving her of himself, and holding aloft the "standard of a great idea, and going to die for it on the open road." That is how he must have been feeling; that's how his action must have appeared to him.

Another question presented itself to me more than once. Why did he run away, that is, literally run away on foot, rather than simply drive away? I put it down at first to the impracticability of fifty years and the fantastic bent of his mind under the influence of strong emotion. I imagined that the thought of posting tickets and horses (even if they had bells) would have seemed too simple and prosaic to him; a pilgrimage, on the other hand, even under an umbrella, was ever so much more picturesque and in character with love and resentment. But now that everything is over, I am inclined to think that it all came about in a much simpler way. To begin with, he was afraid to hire horses because Varvara Petrovna might have heard of it and prevented him from going by force; which she certainly would have done, and he certainly would have given in, and then farewell to the great idea forever. Besides, to take tickets for anywhere he must have known at least where he was going. But to think about that was the greatest agony to him at that moment; he was utterly unable to fix upon a place. For if he had to fix on any particular town his enterprise would at once have seemed in his own eyes absurd and impossible; he felt that very strongly. What should he do in that particular town rather than in any other? Look out for ce marchand? But what marchand? At that point his second and most terrible question cropped up. In reality there was nothing he dreaded more than ce marchand, whom he had rushed off to seek so recklessly, though, of course, he was terribly afraid of finding him. No, better simply the high road, better simply to set off for it, and walk along it and to think of nothing so long as he could put off thinking. The high road is something very very long, of which one cannot see the end—like human life, like human dreams. There is an idea in the open road, but what sort of idea is there in travelling with posting tickets? Posting tickets mean an end to ideas. Vive la grande route and then as God wills.

After the sudden and unexpected interview with Liza which I have described, he rushed on, more lost in forgetfulness than ever. The high road passed half a mile from Skvoreshniki and, strange to say, he was not at first aware that he was on it. Logical reasoning or even distinct consciousness was unbearable to him at this moment. A fine rain kept drizzling, ceasing, and drizzling again; but he did not even notice the rain. He did not even notice either how he threw his bag over his shoulder, nor how much more comfortably he walked with it so. He must have walked like that for nearly a mile or so when he suddenly stood still and looked round. The old road, black, marked with wheel-ruts and planted with willows on each side, ran before him like an endless thread; on the right hand were bare plains from which the harvest had long ago been carried; on the left there were bushes and in the distance beyond them a copse.

And far, far away a scarcely perceptible line of the railway, running aslant, and on it the smoke of a train, but no sound was heard. Stepan Trofimovitch felt a little timid, but only for a moment. He heaved a vague sigh, put down his bag beside a willow, and sat down to rest. As he moved to sit down he was conscious of being chilly and wrapped himself in his rug; noticing at the same time that it was raining, he put up his umbrella. He sat like that for some time, moving his lips from time to time and firmly grasping the umbrella handle. Images of all sorts passed in feverish procession before him, rapidly succeeding one another in his mind.

"Lise, Lise," he thought, "and with her ce Maurice.... Strange people.... But what was the strange fire, and what were they talking about, and who were murdered? I fancy Nastasya has not found out yet and is still waiting for me with my coffee ... cards? Did I really lose men at cards? H'm! Among us in Russia in the times of serfdom, so called.... My God, yes—Fedka!"

He started all over with terror and looked about him. "What if that Fedka is in hiding somewhere behind the bushes? They say he has a regular band of robbers here on the high road. Oh, mercy, I ... I'll tell him the whole truth then, that I was to blame ... and that I've been miserable about him for ten years. More miserable than he was as a soldier, and ... I'll give him my purse. H'm! J'ai en tout quarante roubles; il prendra les roubles et il me tuera tout de même."

In his panic he for some reason shut up the umbrella and laid it down beside him. A cart came into sight on the high road in the distance coming from the town.

"Grace à Dieu, that's a cart and it's coming at a walking pace; that can't be dangerous. The wretched little horses here ... I always said that breed ... It was Pyotr Ilyitch though, he talked at the club about horse-breeding and I trumped him, et puis ... but what's that behind?... I believe there's a woman in the cart. A peasant and a woman, cela commence à être rassurant. The woman behind and the man in front— c'est très rassurant. There's a cow behind the cart tied by the horns, c'est rassurant au plus haut degré."

The cart reached him; it was a fairly solid peasant cart. The woman was sitting on a tightly stuffed sack and the man on the front of the cart with his legs hanging over towards Stepan Trofimovitch. A red cow was, in fact, shambling behind, tied by the horns to the cart. The man and the woman gazed open-eyed at Stepan Trofimovitch, and Stepan Trofimovitch gazed back at them with equal wonder, but after he had let them pass twenty paces, he got up hurriedly all of a sudden and walked after them. In the proximity of the cart it was natural that he should feel safer, but when he had overtaken it he became oblivious of everything again and sank back into his disconnected thoughts and fancies. He stepped along with no suspicion, of course, that for the two peasants he was at that instant the most mysterious and interesting object that one could meet on the high road.

"What sort may you be, pray, if it's not uncivil to ask?" the woman could not resist asking at last when Stepan Trofimovitch glanced absent-mindedly at her. She was a woman of about seven and twenty, sturdily built, with black eyebrows, rosy cheeks, and a friendly smile on her red lips, between which gleamed white even teeth.

"You … you are addressing me?" muttered Stepan Trofimovitch with mournful wonder.

"A merchant, for sure," the peasant observed confidently. He was a well-grown man of forty with a broad and intelligent face, framed in a reddish beard.

"No, I am not exactly a merchant, I … I … moi c'est autre chose." Stepan Trofimovitch parried the question somehow, and to be on the safe side he dropped back a little from the cart, so that he was walking on a level with the cow.

"Must be a gentleman," the man decided, hearing words not Russian, and he gave a tug at the horse.

"That's what set us wondering. You are out for a walk seemingly?" the woman asked inquisitively again.

"You … you ask me?"

"Foreigners come from other parts sometimes by the train; your boots don't seem to be from hereabouts.…"

"They are army boots," the man put in complacently and significantly.

"No, I am not precisely in the army, I …"

"What an inquisitive woman!" Stepan Trofimovitch mused with vexation. "And how they stare at me … mais enfin. In fact, it's strange that I feel, as it were, conscience-stricken before them, and yet I've done them no harm."

The woman was whispering to the man.

"If it's no offence, we'd give you a lift if so be it's agreeable."

Stepan Trofimovitch suddenly roused himself.

"Yes, yes, my friends, I accept it with pleasure, for I'm very tired; but how am I to get in?"

"How wonderful it is," he thought to himself, "that I've been walking so long beside that cow and it never entered my head to ask them for a lift. This 'real life' has something very original about it."

But the peasant had not, however, pulled up the horse.

"But where are you bound for?" he asked with some mistrustfulness.

Stepan Trofimovitch did not understand him at once.

"To Hatovo, I suppose?"

"Hatov? No, not to Hatov's exactly … And I don't know him though I've heard of him."

"The village of Hatovo, the village, seven miles from here."

"A village? C'est charmant, to be sure I've heard of it…."

Stepan Trofimovitch was still walking, they had not yet taken him into the cart. A guess that was a stroke of genius flashed through his mind.

"You think perhaps that I am … I've got a passport and I am a professor, that is, if you like, a teacher … but a head teacher. I am a head teacher. Oui, c'est comme ça qu'on peut traduire. I should be very glad of a lift and I'll buy you … I'll buy you a quart of vodka for it."

"It'll be half a rouble, sir; it's a bad road."

"Or it wouldn't be fair to ourselves," put in the woman.

"Half a rouble? Very good then, half a rouble. C'est encore mieux; j'ai en tout quarante roubles mais …"

The peasant stopped the horse and by their united efforts Stepan Trofimovitch was dragged into the cart, and seated on the sack by the woman. He was still pursued by the same whirl of ideas. Sometimes he was aware himself that he was terribly absent-minded, and that he was not thinking of what he ought to be thinking of and wondered at it. This consciousness of abnormal weakness of mind became at moments very painful and even humiliating to him.

"How … how is this you've got a cow behind?" he suddenly asked the woman.

"What do you mean, sir, as though you'd never seen one," laughed the woman.

"We bought it in the town," the peasant put in. "Our cattle died last spring … the plague. All the beasts have died round us, all of them. There aren't half of them left, it's heartbreaking."

And again he lashed the horse, which had got stuck in a rut.

"Yes, that does happen among you in Russia … in general we Russians … Well, yes, it happens," Stepan Trofimovitch broke off.

"If you are a teacher, what are you going to Hatovo for? Maybe you are going on farther."

"I … I'm not going farther precisely…. C'est-à-dire, I'm going to a merchant's."

"To Spasov, I suppose?"

"Yes, yes, to Spasov. But that's no matter."

"If you are going to Spasov and on foot, it will take you a week in your boots," laughed the woman.

"I dare say, I dare say, no matter, mes amis, no matter." Stepan Trofimovitch cut her short impatiently.

"Awfully inquisitive people; but the woman speaks better than he does, and I notice that since February 19,* their language has altered a little, and ... and what business is it of mine whether I'm going to Spasov or not? Besides, I'll pay them, so why do they pester me."

**February 19, 1861, the day of the Emancipation of the Serfs, is*

meant.—Translator's note.

"If you are going to Spasov, you must take the steamer," the peasant persisted.

"That's true indeed," the woman put in with animation, "for if you drive along the bank it's twenty-five miles out of the way."

"Thirty-five."

"You'll just catch the steamer at Ustyevo at two o'clock tomorrow," the woman decided finally. But Stepan Trofimovitch was obstinately silent. His questioners, too, sank into silence. The peasant tugged at his horse at rare intervals; the peasant woman exchanged brief remarks with him. Stepan Trofimovitch fell into a doze. He was tremendously surprised when the woman, laughing, gave him a poke and he found himself in a rather large village at the door of a cottage with three windows.

"You've had a nap, sir?"

"What is it? Where am I? Ah, yes! Well ... never mind," sighed Stepan Trofimovitch, and he got out of the cart.

He looked about him mournfully; the village scene seemed strange to him and somehow terribly remote.

"And the half-rouble, I was forgetting it!" he said to the peasant, turning to him with an excessively hurried gesture; he was evidently by now afraid to part from them.

"We'll settle indoors, walk in," the peasant invited him.

"It's comfortable inside," the woman said reassuringly.

Stepan Trofimovitch mounted the shaky steps. "How can it be?" he murmured in profound and apprehensive perplexity. He went into the cottage, however. "Elle l'a voulu" he felt a stab at his heart and again he became oblivious of everything, even of the fact that he had gone into the cottage.

It was a light and fairly clean peasant's cottage, with three windows and two rooms; not exactly an inn, but a cottage at which people who knew the place were accustomed to stop on their way through the village. Stepan Trofimovitch, quite unembarrassed, went to the foremost corner; forgot to greet anyone, sat down and sank into thought. Meanwhile a sensation of warmth, extremely agreeable after three hours of travelling in the damp, was suddenly diffused throughout his person. Even the slight shivers that spasmodically ran down his spine—such as always occur in particularly nervous people when they are feverish and have suddenly come into a warm room from the cold—became all at once strangely agreeable. He raised his head and the delicious fragrance of the hot pancakes with which the woman of the house was busy at the stove tickled his nostrils. With a childlike smile he leaned towards the woman and suddenly said:

"What's that? Are they pancakes? Mais … c'est charmant."

"Would you like some, sir?" the woman politely offered him at once.

"I should like some, I certainly should, and … may I ask you for some tea too," said Stepan Trofimovitch, reviving.

"Get the samovar? With the greatest pleasure."

On a large plate with a big blue pattern on it were served the pancakes—regular peasant pancakes, thin, made half of wheat, covered with fresh hot butter, most delicious pancakes. Stepan Trofimovitch tasted them with relish.

"How rich they are and how good! And if one could only have un doigt d'eau de vie."

"It's a drop of vodka you would like, sir, isn't it?"

"Just so, just so, a little, un tout petit rien."

"Five farthings' worth, I suppose?"

"Five, yes, five, five, five, un tout petit rien," Stepan Trofimovitch assented with a blissful smile.

Ask a peasant to do anything for you, and if he can, and will, he will serve you with care and friendliness; but ask him to fetch you vodka—and his habitual serenity and friendliness will pass at once into a sort of joyful haste and alacrity; he will be as keen in your interest as though you were one of his family. The peasant who fetches vodka—even though you are going to drink it and not he and he knows that beforehand—seems, as it were, to be enjoying part of your future gratification. Within three minutes (the tavern was only two paces away), a bottle and a large greenish wineglass were set on the table before Stepan Trofimovitch.

"Is that all for me!" He was extremely surprised. "I've always had vodka but I never knew you could get so much for five farthings."

He filled the wineglass, got up and with a certain solemnity crossed the room to the other corner where his fellow-traveller, the black-browed peasant woman, who had shared the sack with him and bothered him with her questions, had ensconced herself. The woman was taken aback, and began to decline, but after having said all that was prescribed by politeness, she stood up and drank it decorously in three sips, as women do, and, with an expression of intense suffering on her face, gave back the wineglass and bowed to Stepan Trofimovitch. He returned the bow with dignity and returned to the table with an expression of positive pride on his countenance.

All this was done on the inspiration of the moment: a second before he had no idea that he would go and treat the peasant woman.

"I know how to get on with peasants to perfection, to perfection, and I've always told them so," he thought complacently, pouring out the rest of the vodka; though there was less than a glass left, it warmed and revived him, and even went a little to his head.

"Je suis malade tout à fait, mais ce n'est pas trop mauvais d'être malade."

"Would you care to purchase?" a gentle feminine voice asked close by him.

He raised his eyes and to his surprise saw a lady—une dame et elle en avait l'air, somewhat over thirty, very modest in appearance, dressed not like a peasant, in a dark gown with a grey shawl on her shoulders. There was something very kindly in her face which attracted Stepan Trofimovitch immediately. She had only just come back to the cottage, where her things had been left on a bench close by the place where Stepan Trofimovitch had seated himself. Among them was a portfolio, at which he remembered he had looked with curiosity on going in, and a pack, not very large, of American leather. From this pack she took out two nicely bound books with a cross engraved on the cover, and offered them to Stepan Trofimovitch.

"Et … mais je crois que c'est l'Evangile … with the greatest pleasure.… Ah, now I understand.… Vous êtes ce qu'on appelle a gospel-woman; I've read more than once.… Half a rouble?"

"Thirty-five kopecks," answered the gospel-woman. "With the greatest pleasure. Je n'ai rien contre l'Evangile, and I've been wanting to re-read it for a long time.…"

The idea occurred to him at the moment that he had not read the gospel for thirty years at least, and at most had recalled some passages of it, seven years before, when reading Renan's "Vie de Jésus." As he had no small change he pulled out his four ten-rouble notes—all that he had. The woman of the house undertook to get change, and only then he noticed, looking round, that a good many people had come into the cottage, and that they had all been watching him for some time past, and seemed to be talking about him. They were talking too of the fire in the town, especially the owner of the cart who had only just returned from the town with the cow. They talked of arson, of the Shpigulin men.

"He said nothing to me about the fire when he brought me along, although he talked of everything," struck Stepan Trofimovitch for some reason.

"Master, Stepan Trofimovitch, sir, is it you I see? Well, I never should have thought it!… Don't you know me?" exclaimed a middle-aged man who looked like an old-fashioned house-serf, wearing no beard and dressed in an overcoat with a wide turn-down collar. Stepan Trofimovitch was alarmed at hearing his own name.

"Excuse me," he muttered, "I don't quite remember you."

"You don't remember me. I am Anisim, Anisim Ivanov. I used to be in the service of the late Mr. Gaganov, and many's the time I've seen you, sir, with Varvara Petrovna at the late Avdotya Sergyevna's. I used to go to you with books from her, and twice I brought you Petersburg sweets from her...."

"Why, yes, I remember you, Anisim," said Stepan Trofimovitch, smiling. "Do you live here?"

"I live near Spasov, close to the V—— Monastery, in the service of Marta Sergyevna, Avdotya Sergyevna's sister. Perhaps your honour remembers her; she broke her leg falling out of her carriage on her way to a ball. Now her honour lives near the monastery, and I am in her service. And now as your honour sees, I am on my way to the town to see my kinsfolk."

"Quite so, quite so."

"I felt so pleased when I saw you, you used to be so kind to me," Anisim smiled delightedly. "But where are you travelling to, sir, all by yourself as it seems.... You've never been a journey alone, I fancy?"

Stepan Trofimovitch looked at him in alarm.

"You are going, maybe, to our parts, to Spasov?"

"Yes, I am going to Spasov. Il me semble que tout le monde va à Spassof."

"You don't say it's to Fyodor Matveyevitch's? They will be pleased to see you. He had such a respect for you in old days; he often speaks of you now."

"Yes, yes, to Fyodor Matveyevitch's."

"To be sure, to be sure. The peasants here are wondering; they make out they met you, sir, walking on the high road. They are a foolish lot."

"I ... I ... Yes, you know, Anisim, I made a wager, you know, like an Englishman, that I would go on foot and I ..."

The perspiration came out on his forehead.

"To be sure, to be sure." Anisim listened with merciless curiosity. But Stepan Trofimovitch could bear it no longer. He was so disconcerted that he was on the point of getting up and going out of the cottage. But the samovar was brought in, and at the same moment the gospel-woman, who had been out of the room, returned. With the air of a man clutching at a straw he turned to her and offered her tea. Anisim submitted and walked away.

The peasants certainly had begun to feel perplexed: "What sort of person is he? He was found walking on the high road, he says he is a teacher, he is dressed like a foreigner, and has no more sense than a little child; he answers queerly as though he had run away from someone, and he's got money!" An idea was beginning to gain ground that information must be given to the authorities, "especially as things weren't quite right in the town." But Anisim set all that right in a minute. Going into the passage he explained to every one who cared to listen that Stepan Trofimovitch was not exactly a teacher but "a very learned man and busy with very learned studies, and was a landowner of the district himself, and had been living for twenty-two years with her excellency, the general's widow, the stout Madame Stavrogin, and was by way of being the most important person in her house, and was held in the greatest respect by every one in the town. He used to lose by fifties and hundreds in an evening at the club of the nobility, and in rank he was a councillor, which was equal to a lieutenant-colonel in the army, which was next door to being a colonel. As for his having money, he had so much from the stout Madame Stavrogin that there was no reckoning it"—and so on and so on.

"Mais c'est une dame et très comme il faut," thought Stepan Trofimovitch, as he recovered from Anisim's attack, gazing with agreeable curiosity at his neighbour, the gospel pedlar, who was, however, drinking the tea from a saucer and nibbling at a piece of sugar. "Ce petit morceau de sucre, ce n'est rien.... There is something noble and independent about her, and at the same time—gentle. Le comme il faut tout pur, but rather in a different style."

He soon learned from her that her name was Sofya Matveyevna Ulitin and she lived at K——, that she had a sister there, a widow; that she was a widow too, and that her husband, who was a sub-lieutenant risen from the ranks, had been killed at Sevastopol.

"But you are still so young, vous n'avez pas trente ans."

"Thirty-four," said Sofya Matveyevna, smiling.

"What, you understand French?"

"A little. I lived for four years after that in a gentleman's family, and there I picked it up from the children."

She told him that being left a widow at eighteen she was for some time in Sevastopol as a nurse, and had afterwards lived in various places, and now she travelled about selling the gospel.

"Mais, mon Dieu, wasn't it you who had a strange adventure in our town, a very strange adventure?"

She flushed; it turned out that it had been she.

"Ces vauriens, ces malheureux," he began in a voice quivering with indignation; miserable and hateful recollections stirred painfully in his heart. For a minute he seemed to sink into oblivion.

"Bah, but she's gone away again," he thought, with a start, noticing that she was not by his side. "She keeps going out and is busy about something; I notice that she seems upset too.... Bah, je deviens egoiste!"

He raised his eyes and saw Anisim again, but this time in the most menacing surroundings. The whole cottage was full of peasants, and it was evidently Anisim who had brought them all in. Among them were the master of the house, and the peasant with the cow, two other peasants (they turned out to be cab-drivers), another little man, half drunk, dressed like a peasant but clean-shaven, who seemed like a townsman ruined by drink and talked more than any of them. And they were all discussing him, Stepan Trofimovitch. The peasant with the cow insisted on his point that to go round by the lake would be thirty-five miles out of the way, and that he certainly must go by steamer. The half-drunken man and the man of the house warmly retorted:

"Seeing that, though of course it will be nearer for his honour on the steamer over the lake; that's true enough, but maybe according to present arrangements the steamer doesn't go there, brother."

"It does go, it does, it will go for another week," cried Anisim, more excited than any of them.

"That's true enough, but it doesn't arrive punctually, seeing it's late in the season, and sometimes it'll stay three days together at Ustyevo."

"It'll be there to-morrow at two o'clock punctually. You'll be at Spasov punctually by the evening," cried Anisim, eager to do his best for Stepan Trofimovitch.

"Mais qu'est-ce qu'il a cet homme," thought Stepan Trofimovitch, trembling and waiting in terror for what was in store for him.

The cab-drivers, too, came forward and began bargaining with him; they asked three roubles to Ustyevo. The others shouted that that was not too much, that that was the fare, and that they had been driving from here to Ustyevo all the summer for that fare.

"But ... it's nice here too.... And I don't want ..." Stepan Trofimovitch mumbled in protest.

"Nice it is, sir, you are right there, it's wonderfully nice at Spasov now and Fyodor Matveyevitch will be so pleased to see you."

"Mon Dieu, mes amis, all this is such a surprise to me."

At last Sofya Matveyevna came back. But she sat down on the bench looking dejected and mournful.

"I can't get to Spasov!" she said to the woman of the cottage.

"Why, you are bound to Spasov, too, then?" cried Stepan Trofimovitch, starting.

It appeared that a lady had the day before told her to wait at Hatovo and had promised to take her to Spasov, and now this lady had not turned up after all.

"What am I to do now?" repeated Sofya Matveyevna.

"Mais, ma chère et nouvelle amie, I can take you just as well as the lady to that village, whatever it is, to which I've hired horses, and to-morrow—well, to-morrow, we'll go on together to Spasov."

"Why, are you going to Spasov too?"

"Mais que faire, et je suis enchanté! I shall take you with the greatest pleasure; you see they want to take me, I've engaged them already. Which of you did I engage?" Stepan Trofimovitch suddenly felt an intense desire to go to Spasov.

Within a quarter of an hour they were getting into a covered trap, he very lively and quite satisfied, she with her pack beside him, with a grateful smile on her face. Anisim helped them in.

"A good journey to you, sir," said he, bustling officiously round the trap, "it has been a treat to see you."

"Good-bye, good-bye, my friend, good-bye."

"You'll see Fyodor Matveyevitch, sir …"

"Yes, my friend, yes … Fyodor Petrovitch … only good-bye."

II

"You see, my friend … you'll allow me to call myself your friend, n'est-ce pas?" Stepan Trofimovitch began hurriedly as soon as the trap started. "You see I … J'aime le peuple, c'est indispensable, mais il me semble que je ne m'avais jamais vu de près. Stasie … cela va sans dire qu'elle est aussi du peuple, mais le vrai peuple, that is, the real ones, who are on the high road, it seems to me they care for nothing, but where exactly I am going … But let bygones be bygones. I fancy I am talking at random, but I believe it's from being flustered."

"You don't seem quite well." Sofya Matveyevna watched him keenly though respectfully.

"No, no, I must only wrap myself up, besides there's a fresh wind, very fresh in fact, but … let us forget that. That's not what I really meant to say. Chère et incomparable amie, I feel that I am almost happy, and it's your doing. Happiness is not good for me for it makes me rush to forgive all my enemies at once.…"

"Why, that's a very good thing, sir."

"Not always, chère innocente. L'Evangile … voyez-vous, désormais nous prêcherons ensemble and I will gladly sell your beautiful little books. Yes, I feel that that perhaps is an idea, quelque chose de très nouveau dans ce genre. The peasants are religious, c'est admis, but they don't yet know the gospel. I will expound it to them.… By verbal explanation one might correct the mistakes in that remarkable book, which I am of course prepared to treat with the utmost respect. I will be of service even on the high road. I've always been of use, I always told them so et à cette chère ingrate.… Oh, we will forgive, we will forgive, first of all we will forgive all and always.… We will hope that we too shall be forgiven. Yes, for all, every one of us, have wronged one another, all are guilty!"

"That's a very good saying, I think, sir."

"Yes, yes.… I feel that I am speaking well. I shall speak to them very well, but what was the chief thing I meant to say? I keep losing the thread and forgetting.… Will you allow me to remain with you? I feel that the look in your eyes and … I am surprised in fact at your manners. You are simple-hearted, you call me 'sir,' and turn your cup upside down on your saucer … and that horrid lump of sugar; but there's something charming about you, and I see from your features.… Oh, don't blush and don't be afraid of me as a man. Chère et incomparable, pour moi une femme c'est tout. I can't live without a woman, but only at her side, only at her side … I am awfully muddled, awfully. I can't remember what I meant to say. Oh, blessed is he to whom God always sends a woman and … and I fancy, indeed, that I am in a sort of ecstasy. There's a lofty idea in the open road too! That's what I meant to say, that's it—about the idea. Now I've remembered it, but I kept losing it before. And why have they taken us farther. It was nice there too, but here—cela devien trop froid. A propos, j'ai en tout quarante roubles et voilà cet argent, take it, take it, I can't take care of it, I shall lose it or it will be taken away from me.… I seem to be sleepy, I've a giddiness in my head. Yes, I am giddy, I am giddy, I am giddy. Oh, how kind you are, what's that you are wrapping me up in?"

"You are certainly in a regular fever and I've covered you with my rug; only about the money, I'd rather."

"Oh, for God's sake, n'en parlons plus parce que cela me fait mal. Oh, how kind you are!"

He ceased speaking, and with strange suddenness dropped into a feverish shivery sleep. The road by which they drove the twelve miles was not a smooth one, and their carriage jolted cruelly. Stepan Trofimovitch woke up frequently, quickly raised his head from the little pillow which Sofya Matveyevna had slipped under it, clutched her by the hand and asked "Are you here?" as though he were afraid she had left him. He told her, too, that he had dreamed of gaping jaws full of teeth, and that he had very much disliked it. Sofya Matveyevna was in great anxiety about him.

They were driven straight up to a large cottage with a frontage of four windows and other rooms in the yard. Stepan Trofimovitch waked up, hurriedly went in and walked straight into the second room, which was the largest and best in the house. An expression of fussiness came into his sleepy face. He spoke at once to the landlady, a tall, thick-set woman of forty with very dark hair and a slight moustache, and explained that he required the whole room for himself, and that the door was to be shut and no one else was to be admitted, "parce que nous avons à parler. Oui, j'ai beaucoup à vous dire, chère amie. I'll pay you, I'll pay you," he said with a wave of dismissal to the landlady.

Though he was in a hurry, he seemed to articulate with difficulty. The landlady listened grimly, and was silent in token of consent, but there was a feeling of something menacing about her silence. He did not notice this, and hurriedly (he was in a terrible hurry) insisted on her going away and bringing them their dinner as quickly as possible, without a moment's delay.

At that point the moustached woman could contain herself no longer.

"This is not an inn, sir; we don't provide dinners for travellers. We can boil you some crayfish or set the samovar, but we've nothing more. There won't be fresh fish till to-morrow."

But Stepan Trofimovitch waved his hands, repeating with wrathful impatience: "I'll pay, only make haste, make haste."

They settled on fish, soup, and roast fowl; the landlady declared that fowl was not to be procured in the whole village; she agreed, however, to go in search of one, but with the air of doing him an immense favour.

As soon as she had gone Stepan Trofimovitch instantly sat down on the sofa and made

Sofya Matveyevna sit down beside him. There were several arm-chairs as well as a sofa in the room, but they were of a most uninviting appearance. The room was rather a large one, with a corner, in which there was a bed, partitioned off. It was covered with old and tattered yellow paper, and had horrible lithographs of mythological subjects on the walls; in the corner facing the door there was a long row of painted ikons and several sets of brass ones. The whole room with its strangely ill-assorted furniture was an unattractive mixture of the town element and of peasant traditions. But he did not even glance at it all, nor look out of the window at the vast lake, the edge of which was only seventy feet from the cottage.

"At last we are by ourselves and we will admit no one! I want to tell you everything, everything from the very beginning."

Sofya Matveyevna checked him with great uneasiness.

"Are you aware, Stepan Trofimovitch?…"

"Comment, vous savez déjà mon nom?" He smiled with delight.

"I heard it this morning from Anisim Ivanovitch when you were talking to him. But I venture to tell you for my part …"

And she whispered hurriedly to him, looking nervously at the closed door for fear anyone should overhear—that here in this village, it was dreadful. That though all the peasants were fishermen, they made their living chiefly by charging travellers every summer whatever they thought fit. The village was not on the high road but an out-of-the-way one, and people only called there because the steamers stopped there, and that when the steamer did not call—and if the weather was in the least unfavourable, it would not—then numbers of travellers would be waiting there for several days, and all the cottages in the village would be occupied, and that was just the villagers' opportunity, for they charged three times its value for everything—and their landlord here was proud and stuck up because he was, for these parts, very rich; he had a net which had cost a thousand roubles.

Stepan Trofimovitch looked almost reproachfully at Sofya Matveyevna's extremely excited face, and several times he made a motion to stop her. But she persisted and said all she had to say: she said she had been there before already in the summer "with a very genteel lady from the town," and stayed there too for two whole days till the steamer came, and what they had to put up with did not bear thinking of. "Here, Stepan Trofimovitch, you've been pleased to ask for this room for yourself alone.… I only speak to warn you.… In the other room there are travellers already. An elderly man and a young man and a lady with children, and by to-morrow before two o'clock the whole house will be filled up, for since the steamer hasn't been here for two days it will be sure to come to-morrow. So for a room apart and for ordering dinner, and for putting out the other travellers, they'll charge you a price unheard of even in the capital.…"

But he was in distress, in real distress. "Assez, mon enfant, I beseech you, nous avons notre argent—et après, le bon Dieu. And I am surprised that, with the loftiness of your ideas, you … Assez, assez, vous me tourmentez," he articulated hysterically, "we have all our future before us, and you … you fill me with alarm for the future."

He proceeded at once to unfold his whole story with such haste that at first it was difficult to understand him. It went on for a long time. The soup was served, the fowl was brought in, followed at last by the samovar, and still he talked on. He told it somewhat strangely and hysterically, and indeed he was ill. It was a sudden, extreme effort of his intellectual faculties, which was bound in his overstrained condition, of course—Sofya Matveyevna foresaw it with distress all the time he was talking—to result immediately afterwards in extreme exhaustion. He began his story almost with his childhood, when, "with fresh heart, he ran about the meadows; it was an hour before he reached his two marriages and his life in Berlin. I dare not laugh, however. It really was for him a matter of the utmost importance, and to adopt the modern jargon, almost a question of struggling for existence." He saw before him the woman whom he had already elected to share his new life, and was in haste to consecrate her, so to speak. His genius must not be hidden from her.... Perhaps he had formed a very exaggerated estimate of Sofya Matveyevna, but he had already chosen her. He could not exist without a woman. He saw clearly from her face that she hardly understood him, and could not grasp even the most essential part. "Ce n'est rien, nous attendrons, and meanwhile she can feel it intuitively.... My friend, I need nothing but your heart!" he exclaimed, interrupting his narrative, "and that sweet enchanting look with which you are gazing at me now. Oh, don't blush! I've told you already ..." The poor woman who had fallen into his hands found much that was obscure, especially when his autobiography almost passed into a complete dissertation on the fact that no one had been ever able to understand Stepan Trofimovitch, and that "men of genius are wasted in Russia." It was all "so very intellectual," she reported afterwards dejectedly. She listened in evident misery, rather round-eyed. When Stepan Trofimovitch fell into a humorous vein and threw off witty sarcasms at the expense of our advanced and governing classes, she twice made grievous efforts to laugh in response to his laughter, but the result was worse than tears, so that Stepan Trofimovitch was at last embarrassed by it himself and attacked "the nihilists and modern people" with all the greater wrath and zest. At this point he simply alarmed her, and it was not until he began upon the romance of his life that she felt some slight relief, though that too was deceptive. A woman is always a woman even if she is a nun. She smiled, shook her head and then blushed crimson and dropped her eyes, which roused Stepan Trofimovitch to absolute ecstasy and inspiration so much that he began fibbing freely. Varvara Petrovna appeared in his story as an enchanting brunette (who had been the rage of Petersburg and many European capitals) and her husband "had been struck down on the field of Sevastopol" simply because he had felt unworthy of her love, and had yielded her to his rival, that is, Stepan Trofimovitch.... "Don't be shocked, my gentle one, my Christian," he exclaimed to Sofya Matveyevna, almost believing himself in all that he was telling, "it was something so lofty, so subtle, that we never spoke of it to one another all our lives." As the story went on, the cause of this position of affairs appeared to be a blonde lady (if not Darya Pavlovna I don't know of whom Stepan Trofimovitch could have been thinking), this blonde owed everything to the brunette, and had grown up in her house, being a distant relation. The brunette observing at last the love of the blonde girl to Stepan Trofimovitch, kept her feelings locked up in her heart. The blonde girl, noticing on her part the love of the brunette to Stepan Trofimovitch, also locked her feelings in her own heart. And all three, pining with mutual magnanimity, kept silent in this way for twenty years, locking their feelings in their hearts. "Oh, what a passion that was, what a passion that was!" he exclaimed with a stifled sob of genuine ecstasy. "I saw the full blooming of her beauty" (of the brunette's, that is), "I saw daily with an ache in my heart how she passed by me as though ashamed she was so fair" (once he said "ashamed she was so fat"). At last he had run away, casting off all this feverish dream of twenty years—vingt ans—and now here he was on the high road....

Then in a sort of delirium be began explaining to Sofya Matveyevna the significance of their meeting that day, "so chance an encounter and so fateful for all eternity." Sofya Matveyevna got up from the sofa in terrible confusion at last. He had positively made an attempt to drop on his knees before her, which made her cry. It was beginning to get dark. They had been for some hours shut up in the room....

"No, you'd better let me go into the other room," she faltered, "or else there's no knowing what people may think...."

She tore herself away at last; he let her go, promising her to go to bed at once. As they parted he complained that he had a bad headache. Sofya Matveyevna had on entering the cottage left her bag and things in the first room, meaning to spend the night with the people of the house; but she got no rest.

In the night Stepan Trofimovitch was attacked by the malady with which I and all his friends were so familiar—the summer cholera, which was always the outcome of any nervous strain or moral shock with him. Poor Sofya Matveyevna did not sleep all night. As in waiting on the invalid she was obliged pretty often to go in and out of the cottage through the landlady's room, the latter, as well as the travellers who were sleeping there, grumbled and even began swearing when towards morning she set about preparing the samovar. Stepan Trofimovitch was half unconscious all through the attack; at times he had a vision of the samovar being set, of someone giving him something to drink (raspberry tea), and putting something warm to his stomach and his chest. But he felt almost every instant that she was here, beside him; that it was she going out and coming in, lifting him off the bed and settling him in it again. Towards three o'clock in the morning he began to be easier; he sat up, put his legs out of bed and thinking of nothing he fell on the floor at her feet. This was a very different matter from the kneeling of the evening; he simply bowed down at her feet and kissed the hem of her dress.

"Don't, sir, I am not worth it," she faltered, trying to get him back on to the bed.

"My saviour," he cried, clasping his hands reverently before her. "Vous êtes noble comme une marquise! I—I am a wretch. Oh, I've been dishonest all my life...."

"Calm yourself!" Sofya Matveyevna implored him.

"It was all lies that I told you this evening—to glorify myself, to make it splendid, from pure wantonness—all, all, every word, oh, I am a wretch, I am a wretch!"

The first attack was succeeded in this way by a second—an attack of hysterical remorse. I have mentioned these attacks already when I described his letters to Varvara Petrovna. He suddenly recalled Lise and their meeting the previous morning. "It was so awful, and there must have been some disaster and I didn't ask, didn't find out! I thought only of myself. Oh, what's the matter with her? Do you know what's the matter with her?" he besought Sofya Matveyevna.

Then he swore that "he would never change," that he would go back to her (that is,

Varvara Petrovna). "We" (that is, he and Sofya Matveyevna) "will go to her steps every day when she is getting into her carriage for her morning drive, and we will watch her in secret.... Oh, I wish her to smite me on the other cheek; it's a joy to wish it! I shall turn her my other cheek comme dans votre livre! Only now for the first time, I understand what is meant by ... turning the other cheek. I never understood before!"

The two days that followed were among the most terrible in Sofya Matveyevna's life; she remembers them with a shudder to this day. Stepan Trofimovitch became so seriously ill that he could not go on board the steamer, which on this occasion arrived punctually at two o'clock in the afternoon. She could not bring herself to leave him alone, so she did not leave for Spasov either. From her account he was positively delighted at the steamer's going without him.

"Well, that's a good thing, that's capital!" he muttered in his bed. "I've been afraid all the time that we should go. Here it's so nice, better than anywhere.... You won't leave me? Oh, you have not left me!"

It was by no means so nice "here", however. He did not care to hear of her difficulties; his head was full of fancies and nothing else. He looked upon his illness as something transitory, a trifling ailment, and did not think about it at all; he thought of nothing but how they would go and sell "these books." He asked her to read him the gospel.

"I haven't read it for a long time ... in the original. Some one may ask me about it and I shall make a mistake; I ought to prepare myself after all."

She sat down beside him and opened the book.

"You read beautifully," he interrupted her after the first line. "I see, I see I was not mistaken," he added obscurely but ecstatically. He was, in fact, in a continual state of enthusiasm. She read the Sermon on the Mount.

"Assez, assez, mon enfant, enough.... Don't you think that that is enough?"

And he closed his eyes helplessly. He was very weak, but had not yet lost consciousness. Sofya Matveyevna was getting up, thinking that he wanted to sleep. But he stopped her.

"My friend, I've been telling lies all my life. Even when I told the truth I never spoke for the sake of the truth, but always for my own sake. I knew it before, but I only see it now.... Oh, where are those friends whom I have insulted with my friendship all my life? And all, all! Savez-vous ... perhaps I am telling lies now; no doubt I am telling lies now. The worst of it is that I believe myself when I am lying. The hardest thing in life is to live without telling lies ... and without believing in one's lies. Yes, yes, that's just it.... But wait a bit, that can all come afterwards.... We'll be together, together," he added enthusiastically.

"Stepan Trofimovitch," Sofya Matveyevna asked timidly, "hadn't I better send to the town for the doctor?"

He was tremendously taken aback.

"What for? Est-ce que je suis si malade? Mais rien de sérieux. What need have we of outsiders? They may find, besides—and what will happen then? No, no, no outsiders and we'll be together."

"Do you know," he said after a pause, "read me something more, just the first thing you come across."

Sofya Matveyevna opened the Testament and began reading.

"Wherever it opens, wherever it happens to open," he repeated.

"'And unto the angel of the church of the Laodiceans …'"

"What's that? What is it? Where is that from?"

"It's from the Revelation."

"Oh, je m'en souviens, oui, l'Apocalypse. Lisez, lisez, I am trying our future fortunes by the book. I want to know what has turned up. Read on from there…."

"'And unto the angel of the church of the Laodiceans write: These things saith the Amen, the faithful and true witness, the beginning of the creation of God;

"'I know thy works, that thou art neither cold nor hot; I would thou wert cold or hot.

"'So then because thou art lukewarm, and neither cold nor hot, I will spue thee out of my mouth.

"'Because thou sayest, I am rich and increased with goods, and have need of nothing: and thou knowest not that thou art wretched, and miserable, and poor, and blind, and naked.'"

"That too … and that's in your book too!" he exclaimed, with flashing eyes and raising his head from the pillow. "I never knew that grand passage! You hear, better be cold, better be cold than lukewarm, than only lukewarm. Oh, I'll prove it! Only don't leave me, don't leave me alone! We'll prove it, we'll prove it!"

"I won't leave you, Stepan Trofimovitch. I'll never leave you!" She took his hand, pressed it in both of hers, and laid it against her heart, looking at him with tears in her eyes. ("I felt very sorry for him at that moment," she said, describing it afterwards.)

His lips twitched convulsively.

"But, Stepan Trofimovitch, what are we to do though? Oughtn't we to let some of your friends know, or perhaps your relations?"

But at that he was so dismayed that she was very sorry that she had spoken of it again. Trembling and shaking, he besought her to fetch no one, not to do anything. He kept insisting, "No one, no one! We'll be alone, by ourselves, alone, nous partirons ensemble."

Another difficulty was that the people of the house too began to be uneasy; they grumbled, and kept pestering Sofya Matveyevna. She paid them and managed to let them see her money. This softened them for the time, but the man insisted on seeing Stepan Trofimovitch's "papers." The invalid pointed with a supercilious smile to his little bag. Sofya Matveyevna found in it the certificate of his having resigned his post at the university, or something of the kind, which had served him as a passport all his life. The man persisted, and said that "he must be taken somewhere, because their house wasn't a hospital, and if he were to die there might be a bother. We should have no end of trouble." Sofya Matveyevna tried to speak to him of the doctor, but it appeared that sending to the town would cost so much that she had to give up all idea of the doctor. She returned in distress to her invalid. Stepan Trofimovitch was getting weaker and weaker.

"Now read me another passage.... About the pigs," he said suddenly.

"What?" asked Sofya Matveyevna, very much alarmed.

"About the pigs ... that's there too ... ces cochons. I remember the devils entered into swine and they all were drowned. You must read me that; I'll tell you why afterwards. I want to remember it word for word. I want it word for word."

Sofya Matveyevna knew the gospel well and at once found the passage in St. Luke which I have chosen as the motto of my record. I quote it here again:

"'And there was there one herd of many swine feeding on the mountain; and they besought him that he would suffer them to enter into them. And he suffered them.

"'Then went the devils out of the man and entered into the swine; and the herd ran violently down a steep place into the lake, and were choked.

"'When they that fed them saw what was done, they fled, and went and told it in the city and in the country.

"'Then they went out to see what was done; and came to Jesus and found the man, out of whom the devils were departed, sitting at the feet of Jesus, clothed, and in his right mind; and they were afraid.'"

"My friend," said Stepan Trofimovitch in great excitement "savez-vous, that wonderful and ... extraordinary passage has been a stumbling-block to me all my life ... dans ce livre.... so much so that I remembered those verses from childhood. Now an idea has occurred to me; une comparaison. A great number of ideas keep coming into my mind now. You see, that's exactly like our Russia, those devils that come out of the sick man and enter into the swine. They are all the sores, all the foul contagions, all the impurities, all the devils great and small that have multiplied in that great invalid, our beloved Russia, in the course of ages and ages. Oui, cette Russie que j'aimais toujours. But a great idea and a great Will will encompass it from on high, as with that lunatic possessed of devils ... and all those devils will come forth, all the impurity, all the rottenness that was putrefying on the surface ... and they will beg of themselves to enter into swine; and indeed maybe they have entered into them already! They are we, we and those ... and Petrusha and les autres avec lui ... and I perhaps at the head of them, and we shall cast ourselves down, possessed and raving, from the rocks into the sea, and we shall all be drowned—and a good thing too, for that is all we are fit for. But the sick man will be healed and 'will sit at the feet of Jesus,' and all will look upon him with astonishment.... My dear, vous comprendrez après, but now it excites me very much.... Vous comprendrez après. Nous comprendrons ensemble."

He sank into delirium and at last lost consciousness. So it went on all the following day.

Sofya Matveyevna sat beside him, crying. She scarcely slept at all for three nights, and avoided seeing the people of the house, who were, she felt, beginning to take some steps. Deliverance only came on the third day. In the morning Stepan Trofimovitch returned to consciousness, recognised her, and held out his hand to her. She crossed herself hopefully. He wanted to look out of the window. "Tiens, un lac!" he said. "Good heavens, I had not seen it before!..." At that moment there was the rumble of a carriage at the cottage door and a great hubbub in the house followed.

III

It was Varvara Petrovna herself. She had arrived, with Darya Pavlovna, in a closed carriage drawn by four horses, with two footmen. The marvel had happened in the simplest way: Anisim, dying of curiosity, went to Varvara Petrovna's the day after he reached the town and gossiped to the servants, telling them he had met Stepan Trofimovitch alone in a village, that the latter had been seen by peasants walking by himself on the high road, and that he had set off for Spasov by way of Ustyevo accompanied by Sofya Matveyevna. As Varvara Petrovna was, for her part, in terrible anxiety and had done everything she could to find her fugitive friend, she was at once told about Anisim. When she had heard his story, especially the details of the departure for Ustyevo in a cart in the company of some Sofya Matveyevna, she instantly got ready and set off post-haste for Ustyevo herself.

Her stern and peremptory voice resounded through the cottage; even the landlord and his wife were intimidated. She had only stopped to question them and make inquiries, being persuaded that Stepan Trofimovitch must have reached Spasov long before. Learning that he was still here and ill, she entered the cottage in great agitation.

"Well, where is he? Ah, that's you!" she cried, seeing Sofya Matveyevna, who appeared at that very instant in the doorway of the next room. "I can guess from your shameless face that it's you. Go away, you vile hussy! Don't let me find a trace of her in the house! Turn her out, or else, my girl, I'll get you locked up for good. Keep her safe for a time in another house. She's been in prison once already in the town; she can go back there again. And you, my good man, don't dare to let anyone in while I am here, I beg of you. I am Madame Stavrogin, and I'll take the whole house. As for you, my dear, you'll have to give me a full account of it all."

The familiar sounds overwhelmed Stepan Trofimovitch. He began to tremble. But she had already stepped behind the screen. With flashing eyes she drew up a chair with her foot, and, sinking back in it, she shouted to Dasha:

"Go away for a time! Stay in the other room. Why are you so inquisitive? And shut the door properly after you."

For some time she gazed in silence with a sort of predatory look into his frightened face.

"Well, how are you getting on, Stepan Trofimovitch? So you've been enjoying yourself?" broke from her with ferocious irony.

"Chère," Stepan Trofimovitch faltered, not knowing what he was saying, "I've learnt to know real life in Russia ... et je prêcherai l'Evangile."

"Oh, shameless, ungrateful man!" she wailed suddenly, clasping her hands. "As though you had not disgraced me enough, you've taken up with … oh, you shameless old reprobate!"

"Chère …" His voice failed him and he could not articulate a syllable but simply gazed with eyes wide with horror.

"Who is she?"

"C'est un ange; c'était plus qu'un ange pour moi. She's been all night … Oh, don't shout, don't frighten her, chère, chère …"

With a loud noise, Varvara Petrovna pushed back her chair, uttering a loud cry of alarm.

"Water, water!"

Though he returned to consciousness, she was still shaking with terror, and, with pale cheeks, looked at his distorted face. It was only then, for the first time, that she guessed the seriousness of his illness.

"Darya," she whispered suddenly to Darya Pavlovna, "send at once for the doctor, for Salzfish; let Yegorytch go at once. Let him hire horses here and get another carriage from the town. He must be here by night."

Dasha flew to do her bidding. Stepan Trofimovitch still gazed at her with the same wide-open, frightened eyes; his blanched lips quivered.

"Wait a bit, Stepan Trofimovitch, wait a bit, my dear!" she said, coaxing him like a child. "There, there, wait a bit! Darya will come back and … My goodness, the landlady, the landlady, you come, anyway, my good woman!"

In her impatience she ran herself to the landlady.

"Fetch that woman back at once, this minute. Bring her back, bring her back!"

Fortunately Sofya Matveyevna had not yet had time to get away and was only just going out of the gate with her pack and her bag. She was brought back. She was so panic-stricken that she was trembling in every limb. Varvara Petrovna pounced on her like a hawk on a chicken, seized her by the hand and dragged her impulsively to Stepan Trofimovitch.

"Here, here she is, then. I've not eaten her. You thought I'd eaten her."

Stepan Trofimovitch clutched Varvara Petrovna's hand, raised it to his eyes, and burst into tears, sobbing violently and convulsively.

"There, calm yourself, there, there, my dear, there, poor dear man! Ach, mercy on us! Calm yourself, will you?" she shouted frantically. "Oh, you bane of my life!"

"My dear," Stepan Trofimovitch murmured at last, addressing Sofya Matveyevna, "stay out there, my dear, I want to say something here…."

Sofya Matveyevna hurried out at once.

"Chérie … chérie …" he gasped.

"Don't talk for a bit, Stepan Trofimovitch, wait a little till you've rested. Here's some water. Do wait, will you!"

She sat down on the chair again. Stepan Trofimovitch held her hand tight. For a long while she would not allow him to speak. He raised her hand to his lips and fell to kissing it. She set her teeth and looked away into the corner of the room.

"Je vous aimais," broke from him at last. She had never heard such words from him, uttered in such a voice.

"H'm!" she growled in response.

"Je vous aimais toute ma vie … vingt ans!"

She remained silent for two or three minutes.

"And when you were getting yourself up for Dasha you sprinkled yourself with scent," she said suddenly, in a terrible whisper.

Stepan Trofimovitch was dumbfounded.

"You put on a new tie …"

Again silence for two minutes.

"Do you remember the cigar?"

"My friend," he faltered, overcome with horror.

"That cigar at the window in the evening … the moon was shining … after the arbour … at Skvoreshniki? Do you remember, do you remember?" She jumped up from her place, seized his pillow by the corners and shook it with his head on it. "Do you remember, you worthless, worthless, ignoble, cowardly, worthless man, always worthless!" she hissed in her furious whisper, restraining herself from speaking loudly. At last she left him and sank on the chair, covering her face with her hands. "Enough!" she snapped out, drawing herself up. "Twenty years have passed, there's no calling them back. I am a fool too."

"Je vous aimais." He clasped his hands again.

"Why do you keep on with your aimais and aimais? Enough!" she cried, leaping up again. "And if you don't go to sleep at once I'll … You need rest; go to sleep, go to sleep at once, shut your eyes. Ach, mercy on us, perhaps he wants some lunch! What do you eat? What does he eat? Ach, mercy on us! Where is that woman? Where is she?"

There was a general bustle again. But Stepan Trofimovitch faltered in a weak voice that he really would like to go to sleep une heure, and then un bouillon, un thé.... enfin il est si heureux. He lay back and really did seem to go to sleep (he probably pretended to). Varvara Petrovna waited a little, and stole out on tiptoe from behind the partition.

She settled herself in the landlady's room, turned out the landlady and her husband, and told Dasha to bring her that woman. There followed an examination in earnest.

"Tell me all about it, my good girl. Sit down beside me; that's right. Well?"

"I met Stepan Trofimovitch ..."

"Stay, hold your tongue! I warn you that if you tell lies or conceal anything, I'll ferret it out. Well?"

"Stepan Trofimovitch and I ... as soon as I came to Hatovo ..." Sofya Matveyevna began almost breathlessly.

"Stay, hold your tongue, wait a bit! Why do you gabble like that? To begin with, what sort of creature are you?"

Sofya Matveyevna told her after a fashion, giving a very brief account of herself, however, beginning with Sevastopol. Varvara Petrovna listened in silence, sitting up erect in her chair, looking sternly straight into the speaker's eyes.

"Why are you so frightened? Why do you look at the ground? I like people who look me straight in the face and hold their own with me. Go on."

She told of their meeting, of her books, of how Stepan Trofimovitch had regaled the peasant woman with vodka ... "That's right, that's right, don't leave out the slightest detail," Varvara Petrovna encouraged her.

At last she described how they had set off, and how Stepan Trofimovitch had gone on talking, "really ill by that time," and here had given an account of his life from the very beginning, talking for some hours. "Tell me about his life."

Sofya Matveyevna suddenly stopped and was completely nonplussed.

"I can't tell you anything about that, madam," she brought out, almost crying; "besides, I could hardly understand a word of it."

"Nonsense! You must have understood something."

"He told a long time about a distinguished lady with black hair." Sofya Matveyevna flushed terribly though she noticed Varvara Petrovna's fair hair and her complete dissimilarity with the "brunette" of the story.

"Black-haired? What exactly? Come, speak!"

"How this grand lady was deeply in love with his honour all her life long and for twenty years, but never dared to speak, and was shamefaced before him because she was a very stout lady...."

"The fool!" Varvara Petrovna rapped out thoughtfully but resolutely.

Sofya Matveyevna was in tears by now.

"I don't know how to tell any of it properly, madam, because I was in a great fright over his honour; and I couldn't understand, as he is such an intellectual gentleman."

"It's not for a goose like you to judge of his intellect. Did he offer you his hand?"

The speaker trembled.

"Did he fall in love with you? Speak! Did he offer you his hand?" Varvara Petrovna shouted peremptorily.

"That was pretty much how it was," she murmured tearfully. "But I took it all to mean nothing, because of his illness," she added firmly, raising her eyes.

"What is your name?"

"Sofya Matveyevna, madam."

"Well, then, let me tell you, Sofya Matveyevna, that he is a wretched and worthless little man.... Good Lord! Do you look upon me as a wicked woman?"

Sofya Matveyevna gazed open-eyed.

"A wicked woman, a tyrant? Who has ruined his life?"

"How can that be when you are crying yourself, madam?"

Varvara Petrovna actually had tears in her eyes.

"Well, sit down, sit down, don't be frightened. Look me straight in the face again. Why are you blushing? Dasha, come here. Look at her. What do you think of her? Her heart is pure...."

And to the amazement and perhaps still greater alarm of Sofya Matveyevna, she suddenly patted her on the cheek.

"It's only a pity she is a fool. Too great a fool for her age. That's all right, my dear, I'll look after you. I see that it's all nonsense. Stay near here for the time. A room shall be taken for you and you shall have food and everything else from me ... till I ask for you."

Sofya Matveyevna stammered in alarm that she must hurry on.

"You've no need to hurry. I'll buy all your books, and meantime you stay here. Hold your tongue; don't make excuses. If I hadn't come you would have stayed with him all the same, wouldn't you?"

"I wouldn't have left him on any account," Sofya Matveyevna brought out softly and firmly, wiping her tears.

It was late at night when Doctor Salzfish was brought. He was a very respectable old man and a practitioner of fairly wide experience who had recently lost his post in the service in consequence of some quarrel on a point of honour with his superiors. Varvara Petrovna instantly and actively took him under her protection. He examined the patient attentively, questioned him, and cautiously pronounced to Varvara Petrovna that "the sufferer's" condition was highly dubious in consequence of complications, and that they must be prepared "even for the worst." Varvara Petrovna, who had during twenty years got accustomed to expecting nothing serious or decisive to come from Stepan Trofimovitch, was deeply moved and even turned pale. "Is there really no hope?"

"Can there ever be said to be absolutely no hope? But …" She did not go to bed all night, and felt that the morning would never come. As soon as the patient opened his eyes and returned to consciousness (he was conscious all the time, however, though he was growing weaker every hour), she went up to him with a very resolute air.

"Stepan Trofimovitch, one must be prepared for anything. I've sent for a priest. You must do what is right.…"

Knowing his convictions, she was terribly afraid of his refusing. He looked at her with surprise.

"Nonsense, nonsense!" she vociferated, thinking he was already refusing. "This is no time for whims. You have played the fool enough."

"But … am I really so ill, then?"

He agreed thoughtfully. And indeed I was much surprised to learn from Varvara Petrovna afterwards that he showed no fear of death at all. Possibly it was that he simply did not believe it, and still looked upon his illness as a trifling one.

He confessed and took the sacrament very readily. Every one, Sofya Matveyevna, and even the servants, came to congratulate him on taking the sacrament. They were all moved to tears looking at his sunken and exhausted face and his blanched and quivering lips.

"Oui, mes amis, and I only wonder that you … take so much trouble. I shall most likely get up to-morrow, and we will … set off.… Toute cette cérémonie … for which, of course, I feel every proper respect … was …"

"I beg you, father, to remain with the invalid," said Varvara Petrovna hurriedly, stopping the priest, who had already taken off his vestments. "As soon as tea has been handed, I beg you to begin to speak of religion, to support his faith."

The priest spoke; every one was standing or sitting round the sick-bed.

"In our sinful days," the priest began smoothly, with a cup of tea in his hand, "faith in the Most High is the sole refuge of the race of man in all the trials and tribulations of life, as well as its hope for that eternal bliss promised to the righteous."

Stepan Trofimovitch seemed to revive, a subtle smile strayed on his lips.

"Mon père, je vous remercie et vous êtes bien bon, mais …"

"No mais about it, no mais at all!" exclaimed Varvara Petrovna, bounding up from her chair. "Father," she said, addressing the priest, "he is a man who … he is a man who … You will have to confess him again in another hour! That's the sort of man he is."

Stepan Trofimovitch smiled faintly.

"My friends," he said, "God is necessary to me, if only because He is the only being whom one can love eternally."

Whether he was really converted, or whether the stately ceremony of the administration of the sacrament had impressed him and stirred the artistic responsiveness of his temperament or not, he firmly and, I am told, with great feeling uttered some words which were in flat contradiction with many of his former convictions.

"My immortality is necessary if only because God will not be guilty of injustice and extinguish altogether the flame of love for Him once kindled in my heart. And what is more precious than love? Love is higher than existence, love is the crown of existence; and how is it possible that existence should not be under its dominance? If I have once loved Him and rejoiced in my love, is it possible that He should extinguish me and my joy and bring me to nothingness again? If there is a God, then I am immortal. Voilà ma profession de foi."

"There is a God, Stepan Trofimovitch, I assure you there is," Varvara Petrovna implored him. "Give it up, drop all your foolishness for once in your life!" (I think she had not quite understood his profession de foi.)

"My friend," he said, growing more and more animated, though his voice broke frequently, "as soon as I understood … that turning of the cheek, I … understood something else as well. J'ai menti toute ma vie, all my life, all! I should like … but that will do to-morrow.… To-morrow we will all set out."

Varvara Petrovna burst into tears. He was looking about for someone.

"Here she is, she is here!" She seized Sofya Matveyevna by the hand and led her to him. He smiled tenderly.

"Oh, I should dearly like to live again!" he exclaimed with an extraordinary rush of energy. "Every minute, every instant of life ought to be a blessing to man … they ought to be, they certainly ought to be! It's the duty of man to make it so; that's the law of his nature, which always exists even if hidden.… Oh, I wish I could see Petrusha … and all of them … Shatov …"

I may remark that as yet no one had heard of Shatov's fate—not Varvara Petrovna nor Darya Pavlovna, nor even Salzfish, who was the last to come from the town.

Stepan Trofimovitch became more and more excited, feverishly so, beyond his strength.

"The mere fact of the ever present idea that there exists something infinitely more just and more happy than I am fills me through and through with tender ecstasy—and glorifies me—oh, whoever I may be, whatever I have done! What is far more essential for man than personal happiness is to know and to believe at every instant that there is somewhere a perfect and serene happiness for all men and for everything.… The one essential condition of human existence is that man should always be able to bow down before something infinitely great. If men are deprived of the infinitely great they will not go on living and will die of despair. The Infinite and the Eternal are as essential for man as the little planet on which he dwells. My friends, all, all: hail to the Great Idea! The Eternal, Infinite Idea! It is essential to every man, whoever he may be, to bow down before what is the Great Idea. Even the stupidest man needs something great. Petrusha ... oh, how I want to see them all again! They don't know, they don't know that that same Eternal, Grand Idea lies in them all!"

Doctor Salzfish was not present at the ceremony. Coming in suddenly, he was horrified, and cleared the room, insisting that the patient must not be excited.

Stepan Trofimovitch died three days later, but by that time he was completely unconscious. He quietly went out like a candle that is burnt down. After having the funeral service performed, Varvara Petrovna took the body of her poor friend to Skvoreshniki. His grave is in the precincts of the church and is already covered with a marble slab. The inscription and the railing will be added in the spring.

Varvara Petrovna's absence from town had lasted eight days. Sofya Matveyevna arrived in the carriage with her and seems to have settled with her for good. I may mention that as soon as Stepan Trofimovitch lost consciousness (the morning that he received the sacrament) Varvara Petrovna promptly asked Sofya Matveyevna to leave the cottage again, and waited on the invalid herself unassisted to the end, but she sent for her at once when he had breathed his last. Sofya Matveyevna was terribly alarmed by Varvara Petrovna's proposition, or rather command, that she should settle for good at Skvoreshniki, but the latter refused to listen to her protests.

"That's all nonsense! I will go with you to sell the gospel. I have no one in the world now."

"You have a son, however," Salzfish observed.

"I have no son!" Varvara Petrovna snapped out—and it was like a prophecy.

CHAPTER VIII. CONCLUSION

ALL THE CRIMES AND VILLAINIES THAT had been perpetrated were discovered with extraordinary rapidity, much more quickly than Pyotr Stepanovitch had expected. To begin with, the luckless Marya Ignatyevna waked up before daybreak on the night of her husband's murder, missed him and flew into indescribable agitation, not seeing him beside her. The woman who had been hired by Anna Prohorovna, and was there for the night, could not succeed in calming her, and as soon as it was daylight ran to fetch Arina Prohorovna herself, assuring the invalid that the latter knew where her husband was, and when he would be back. Meantime Arina Prohorovna was in some anxiety too; she had already heard from her husband of the deed perpetrated that night at Skvoreshniki. He had returned home about eleven o'clock in a terrible state of mind and body; wringing his hands, he flung himself face downwards on his bed and shaking with convulsive sobs kept repeating, "It's not right, it's not right, it's not right at all!" He ended, of course, by confessing it all to Arina Prohorovna—but to no one else in the house. She left him on his bed, sternly impressing upon him that "if he must blubber he must do it in his pillow so as not to be overheard, and that he would be a fool if he showed any traces of it next day." She felt somewhat anxious, however, and began at once to clear things up in case of emergency; she succeeded in hiding or completely destroying all suspicious papers, books, manifestoes perhaps. At the same time she reflected that she, her sister, her aunt, her sister-in-law the student, and perhaps even her long-eared brother had really nothing much to be afraid of. When the nurse ran to her in the morning she went without a second thought to Marya Ignatyevna's. She was desperately anxious, moreover, to find out whether what her husband had told her that night in a terrified and frantic whisper, that was almost like delirium, was true—that is, whether Pyotr Stepanovitch had been right in his reckoning that Kirillov would sacrifice himself for the general benefit.

But she arrived at Marya Ignatyevna's too late: when the latter had sent off the woman and was left alone, she was unable to bear the suspense; she got out of bed, and throwing round her the first garment she could find, something very light and unsuitable for the weather, I believe, she ran down to Kirillov's lodge herself, thinking that he perhaps would be better able than anyone to tell her something about her husband. The terrible effect on her of what she saw there may well be imagined. It is remarkable that she did not read Kirillov's last letter, which lay conspicuously on the table, overlooking it, of course, in her fright. She ran back to her room, snatched up her baby, and went with it out of the house into the street. It was a damp morning, there was a fog. She met no passers-by in such an out-of-the-way street. She ran on breathless through the wet, cold mud, and at last began knocking at the doors of the houses. In the first house no one came to the door, in the second they were so long in coming that she gave it up impatiently and began knocking at a third door. This was the house of a merchant called Titov. Here she wailed and kept declaring incoherently that her husband was murdered, causing a great flutter in the house. Something was known about Shatov and his story in the Titov household; they were horror-stricken that she should be running about the streets in such attire and in such cold with the baby scarcely covered in her arms, when, according to her story, she had only been confined the day before. They thought at first that she was delirious, especially as they could not make out whether it was Kirillov who was murdered or her husband. Seeing that they did not believe her she would have run on farther, but they kept her by force, and I am told she screamed and struggled terribly. They went to Filipov's, and within two hours Kirillov's suicide and the letter he had left were known to the whole town. The police came to question Marya Ignatyevna, who was still conscious, and it appeared at once that she had not read Kirillov's letter, and they could not find out from her what had led her to conclude that her husband had been murdered. She only screamed that if Kirillov was murdered, then her husband was murdered, they were together. Towards midday she sank into a state of unconsciousness from which she never recovered, and she died three days later. The baby had caught cold and died before her.

Arina Prohorovna not finding Marya Ignatyevna and the baby, and guessing something was wrong, was about to run home, but she checked herself at the gate and sent the nurse to inquire of the gentleman at the lodge whether Marya Ignatyevna was not there and whether he knew anything about her. The woman came back screaming frantically. Persuading her not to scream and not to tell anyone by the time-honoured argument that "she would get into trouble," she stole out of the yard.

It goes without saying that she was questioned the same morning as having acted as midwife to Marya Ignatyevna; but they did not get much out of her. She gave a very cool and sensible account of all she had herself heard and seen at Shatov's, but as to what had happened she declared that she knew nothing, and could not understand it.

It may well be imagined what an uproar there was in the town. A new "sensation," another murder! But there was another element in this case: it was clear that a secret society of murderers, incendiaries, and revolutionists did exist, did actually exist. Liza's terrible death, the murder of Stavrogin's wife, Stavrogin himself, the fire, the ball for the benefit of the governesses, the laxity of manners and morals in Yulia Mihailovna's circle.... Even in the disappearance of Stepan Trofimovitch people insisted on scenting a mystery. All sorts of things were whispered about Nikolay Vsyevolodovitch. By the end of the day people knew of Pyotr Stepanovitch's absence too, and, strange to say, less was said of him than of anyone. What was talked of most all that day was "the senator." There was a crowd almost all day at Filipov's house. The police certainly were led astray by Kirillov's letter. They believed that Kirillov had murdered Shatov and had himself committed suicide. Yet, though the authorities were thrown into perplexity, they were not altogether hoodwinked. The word "park," for instance, so vaguely inserted in Kirillov's letter, did not puzzle anyone as Pyotr Stepanovitch had expected it would. The police at once made a rush for Skvoreshniki, not simply because it was the only park in the neighbourhood but also led thither by a sort of instinct because all the horrors of the last few days were connected directly or indirectly with Skvoreshniki. That at least is my theory. (I may remark that Varvara Petrovna had driven off early that morning in chase of Stepan Trofimovitch, and knew nothing of what had happened in the town.)

The body was found in the pond that evening. What led to the discovery of it was the finding of Shatov's cap at the scene of the murder, where it had been with extraordinary carelessness overlooked by the murderers. The appearance of the body, the medical examination and certain deductions from it roused immediate suspicions that Kirillov must have had accomplices. It became evident that a secret society really did exist of which Shatov and Kirillov were members and which was connected with the manifestoes. Who were these accomplices?

No one even thought of any member of the quintet that day. It was ascertained that Kirillov had lived like a hermit, and in so complete a seclusion that it had been possible, as stated in the letter, for Fedka to lodge with him for so many days, even while an active search was being made for him. The chief thing that worried every one was the impossibility of discovering a connecting-link in this chaos.

There is no saying what conclusions and what disconnected theories our panic-stricken townspeople would have reached, if the whole mystery had not been suddenly solved next day, thanks to Lyamshin.

He broke down. He behaved as even Pyotr Stepanovitch had towards the end begun to fear he would. Left in charge of Tolkatchenko, and afterwards of Erkel, he spent all the following day lying in his bed with his face turned to the wall, apparently calm, not uttering a word, and scarcely answering when he was spoken to. This is how it was that he heard nothing all day of what was happening in the town. But Tolkatchenko, who was very well informed about everything, took into his head by the evening to throw up the task of watching Lyamshin which Pyotr Stepanovitch had laid upon him, and left the town, that is, to put it plainly, made his escape; the fact is, they lost their heads as Erkel had predicted they would. I may mention, by the way, that Liputin had disappeared the same day before twelve o'clock. But things fell out so that his disappearance did not become known to the authorities till the evening of the following day, when, the police went to question his family, who were panic-stricken at his absence but kept quiet from fear of consequences. But to return to Lyamshin: as soon as he was left alone (Erkel had gone home earlier, relying on Tolkatchenko) he ran out of his house, and, of course, very soon learned the position of affairs. Without even returning home he too tried to run away without knowing where he was going. But the night was so dark and to escape was so terrible and difficult, that after going through two or three streets, he returned home and locked himself up for the whole night. I believe that towards morning he attempted to commit suicide but did not succeed. He remained locked up till midday—and then suddenly he ran to the authorities. He is said to have crawled on his knees, to have sobbed and shrieked, to have kissed the floor crying out that he was not worthy to kiss the boots of the officials standing before him. They soothed him, were positively affable to him. His examination lasted, I am told, for three hours. He confessed everything, everything, told every detail, everything he knew, every point, anticipating their questions, hurried to make a clean breast of it all, volunteering unnecessary information without being asked. It turned out that he knew enough, and presented things in a fairly true light: the tragedy of Shatov and Kirillov, the fire, the death of the Lebyadkins, and the rest of it were relegated to the background. Pyotr Stepanovitch, the secret society, the organisation, and the network were put in the first place. When asked what was the object of so many murders and scandals and dastardly outrages, he answered with feverish haste that "it was with the idea of systematically undermining the foundations, systematically destroying society and all principles; with the idea of nonplussing every one and making hay of everything, and then, when society was tottering, sick and out of joint, cynical and sceptical though filled with an intense eagerness for self-preservation and for some guiding idea, suddenly to seize it in their hands, raising the standard of revolt and relying on a complete network of quintets, which were actively, meanwhile, gathering recruits and seeking out the weak spots which could be attacked." In conclusion, he said that here in our town Pyotr Stepanovitch had organised only the first experiment in such systematic disorder, so to speak, as a programme for further activity, and for all the quintets—and that this was his own (Lyamshin's) idea, his own theory, "and that he hoped they would remember it and bear in mind how openly and properly he had given his information, and therefore might be of use hereafter." Being asked definitely how many quintets there were, he answered that there were immense numbers of them, that all Russia was overspread with a network, and although he brought forward no proofs, I believe his answer was perfectly sincere. He produced only the programme of the society, printed abroad, and the plan for developing a system of future activity roughly sketched in Pyotr Stepanovitch's own handwriting. It appeared that Lyamshin had quoted the phrase about "undermining the foundation," word for word from this document, not omitting a single stop or comma, though he had declared that it was all his own theory. Of Yulia Mihailovna he very funnily and quite without provocation volunteered the remark, that "she was innocent and had been made a fool of." But, strange to say, he exonerated Nikolay Stavrogin from all share in the secret society, from any collaboration with Pyotr Stepanovitch. (Lyamshin had no conception of the secret and very absurd hopes that Pyotr Stepanovitch was resting on Stavrogin.) According to his story Nikolay Stavrogin had nothing whatever to do with the death of the Lebyadkins, which had been planned by Pyotr Stepanovitch alone and with the subtle aim of implicating the former in the crime, and therefore making him dependent on Pyotr Stepanovitch; but instead of the gratitude on which Pyotr Stepanovitch had reckoned with shallow confidence, he had roused nothing but indignation and even despair in "the generous heart of Nikolay Vsyevolodovitch." He wound up, by a hint, evidently intentional, volunteered hastily, that Stavrogin was perhaps a very important personage, but that there was some secret about that, that he had been living among us, so to say, incognito, that he had some commission, and that very possibly he would come back to us again from Petersburg. (Lyamshin was convinced that Stavrogin had gone to Petersburg), but in quite a different capacity and in different surroundings, in the suite of persons of whom perhaps we should soon hear, and that all this he had heard from Pyotr Stepanovitch, "Nikolay Vsyevolodovitch's secret enemy."

Here I will note that two months later, Lyamshin admitted that he had exonerated Stavrogin on purpose, hoping that he would protect him and would obtain for him a mitigation in the second degree of his sentence, and that he would provide him with money and letters of introduction in Siberia. From this confession, it is evident that he had an extraordinarily exaggerated conception of Stavrogin's powers.

On the same day, of course, the police arrested Virginsky and in their zeal took his whole family too. (Arina Prohorovna, her sister, aunt, and even the girl student were released long ago; they say that Shigalov too will be set free very shortly because he cannot be classed with any of the other prisoners. But all that is so far only gossip.) Virginsky at once pleaded guilty. He was lying ill with fever when he was arrested. I am told that he seemed almost relieved; "it was a load off his heart," he is reported to have said. It is rumoured that he is giving his evidence without reservation, but with a certain dignity, and has not given up any of his "bright hopes," though at the same time he curses the political method (as opposed to the Socialist one), in which he had been unwittingly and heedlessly carried "by the vortex of combined circumstances." His conduct at the time of the murder has been put in a favourable light, and I imagine that he too may reckon on some mitigation of his sentence. That at least is what is asserted in the town.

But I doubt whether there is any hope for mercy in Erkel's case. Ever since his arrest he has been obstinately silent, or has misrepresented the facts as far as he could. Not one word of regret has been wrung from him so far. Yet even the sternest of the judges trying him has been moved to some compassion by his youth, by his helplessness, by the unmistakable evidence that he is nothing but a fanatical victim of a political impostor, and, most of all, by his conduct to his mother, to whom, as it appears, he used to send almost the half of his small salary. His mother is now in the town; she is a delicate and ailing woman, aged beyond her years; she weeps and positively grovels on the ground imploring mercy for her son. Whatever may happen, many among us feel sorry for Erkel.

Liputin was arrested in Petersburg, where he had been living for a fortnight. His conduct there sounds almost incredible and is difficult to explain. He is said to have had a passport in a forged name and quite a large sum of money upon him, and had every possibility of escaping abroad, yet instead of going he remained in Petersburg. He spent some time hunting for Stavrogin and Pyotr Stepanovitch. Suddenly he took to drinking and gave himself up to a debauchery that exceeded all bounds, like a man who had lost all reason and understanding of his position. He was arrested in Petersburg drunk in a brothel. There is a rumour that he has not by any means lost heart, that he tells lies in his evidence and is preparing for the approaching trial hopefully (?) and, as it were, triumphantly. He even intends to make a speech at the trial. Tolkatchenko, who was arrested in the neighbourhood ten days after his flight, behaves with incomparably more decorum; he does not shuffle or tell lies, he tells all he knows, does not justify himself, blames himself with all modesty, though he, too, has a weakness for rhetoric; he tells readily what he knows, and when knowledge of the peasantry and the revolutionary elements among them is touched upon, he positively attitudinises and is eager to produce an effect. He, too, is meaning, I am told, to make a speech at the trial. Neither he nor Liputin seem very much afraid, curious as it seems.

I repeat that the case is not yet over. Now, three months afterwards, local society has had time to rest, has recovered, has got over it, has an opinion of its own, so much so that some people positively look upon Pyotr Stepanovitch as a genius or at least as possessed of "some characteristics of a genius." "Organisation!" they say at the club, holding up a finger. But all this is very innocent and there are not many people who talk like that. Others, on the other hand, do not deny his acuteness, but point out that he was utterly ignorant of real life, that he was terribly theoretical, grotesquely and stupidly one-sided, and consequently shallow in the extreme. As for his moral qualities all are agreed; about that there are no two opinions.

I do not know whom to mention next so as not to forget anyone. Mavriky Nikolaevitch has gone away for good, I don't know where. Old Madame Drozdov has sunk into dotage.... I have still one very gloomy story to tell, however. I will confine myself to the bare facts.

On her return from Ustyevo, Varvara Petrovna stayed at her town house. All the accumulated news broke upon her at once and gave her a terrible shock. She shut herself up alone. It was evening; every one was tired and went to bed early.

In the morning a maid with a mysterious air handed a note to Darya Pavlovna. The note had, so she said, arrived the evening before, but late, when all had gone to bed, so that she had not ventured to wake her. It had not come by post, but had been put in Alexey Yegorytch's hand in Skvoreshniki by some unknown person. And Alexey Yegorytch had immediately set off and put it into her hands himself and had then returned to Skvoreshniki.

For a long while Darya Pavlovna gazed at the letter with a beating heart, and dared not open it. She knew from whom it came: the writer was Nikolay Stavrogin. She read what was written on the envelope: "To Alexey Yegorytch, to be given secretly to Darya Pavlovna."

Here is the letter word for word, without the slightest correction of the defects in style of a Russian aristocrat who had never mastered the Russian grammar in spite of his European education.

"Dear Darya Pavlovna,—At one time you expressed a wish to be my nurse and made me promise to send for you when I wanted you. I am going away in two days and shall not come back. Will you go with me?

"Last year, like Herzen, I was naturalised as a citizen of the canton of Uri, and that nobody knows. There I've already bought a little house. I've still twelve thousand roubles left; we'll go and live there for ever. I don't want to go anywhere else ever.

"It's a very dull place, a narrow valley, the mountains restrict both vision and thought. It's very gloomy. I chose the place because there was a little house to be sold. If you don't like it I'll sell it and buy another in some other place.

"I am not well, but I hope to get rid of hallucinations in that air. It's physical, and as for the moral you know everything; but do you know all?

"I've told you a great deal of my life, but not all. Even to you! Not all. By the way, I repeat that in my conscience I feel myself responsible for my wife's death. I haven't seen you since then, that's why I repeat it. I feel guilty about Lizaveta Nikolaevna too; but you know about that; you foretold almost all that.

"Better not come to me. My asking you to is a horrible meanness. And why should you bury your life with me? You are dear to me, and when I was miserable it was good to be beside you; only with you I could speak of myself aloud. But that proves nothing. You defined it yourself, 'a nurse'—it's your own expression; why sacrifice so much? Grasp this, too, that I have no pity for you since I ask you, and no respect for you since I reckon on you. And yet I ask you and I reckon on you. In any case I need your answer for I must set off very soon. In that case I shall go alone.

"I expect nothing of Uri; I am simply going. I have not chosen a gloomy place on purpose. I have no ties in Russia—everything is as alien to me there as everywhere. It's true that I dislike living there more than anywhere; but I can't hate anything even there!

"I've tried my strength everywhere. You advised me to do this 'that I might learn to know myself.' As long as I was experimenting for myself and for others it seemed infinite, as it has all my life. Before your eyes I endured a blow from your brother; I acknowledged my marriage in public. But to what to apply my strength, that is what I've never seen, and do not see now in spite of all your praises in Switzerland, which I believed in. I am still capable, as I always was, of desiring to do something good, and of feeling pleasure from it; at the same time I desire evil and feel pleasure from that too. But both feelings are always too petty, and are never very strong. My desires are too weak; they are not enough to guide me. On a log one may cross a river but not on a chip. I say this that you may not believe that I am going to Uri with hopes of any sort.

"As always I blame no one. I've tried the depths of debauchery and wasted my strength over it. But I don't like vice and I didn't want it. You have been watching me of late. Do you know that I looked upon our iconoclasts with spite, from envy of their hopes? But you had no need to be afraid. I could not have been one of them for I never shared anything with them. And to do it for fun, from spite I could not either, not because I am afraid of the ridiculous—I cannot be afraid of the ridiculous—but because I have, after all, the habits of a gentleman and it disgusted me. But if I had felt more spite and envy of them I might perhaps have joined them. You can judge how hard it has been for me, and how I've struggled from one thing to another.

"Dear friend! Great and tender heart which I divined! Perhaps you dream of giving me so much love and lavishing on me so much that is beautiful from your beautiful soul, that you hope to set up some aim for me at last by it? No, it's better for you to be more cautious, my love will be as petty as I am myself and you will be unhappy. Your brother told me that the man who loses connection with his country loses his gods, that is, all his aims. One may argue about everything endlessly, but from me nothing has come but negation, with no greatness of soul, no force. Even negation has not come from me. Everything has always been petty and spiritless. Kirillov, in the greatness of his soul, could not compromise with an idea, and shot himself; but I see, of course, that he was great-souled because he had lost his reason. I can never lose my reason, and I can never believe in an idea to such a degree as he did. I cannot even be interested in an idea to such a degree. I can never, never shoot myself.

"I know I ought to kill myself, to brush myself off the earth like a nasty insect; but I am afraid of suicide, for I am afraid of showing greatness of soul. I know that it will be another sham again—the last deception in an endless series of deceptions. What good is there in deceiving oneself? Simply to play at greatness of soul? Indignation and shame I can never feel, therefore not despair.

"Forgive me for writing so much. I wrote without noticing. A hundred pages would be too little and ten lines would be enough. Ten lines would be enough to ask you to be a nurse. Since I left Skvoreshniki I've been living at the sixth station on the line, at the stationmaster's. I got to know him in the time of debauchery five years ago in Petersburg. No one knows I am living there. Write to him. I enclose the address.

"Nikolay Stavrogin."

Darya Pavlovna went at once and showed the letter to Varvara Petrovna. She read it and asked Dasha to go out of the room so that she might read it again alone; but she called her back very quickly.

"Are you going?" she asked almost timidly.

"I am going," answered Dasha.

"Get ready! We'll go together."

Dasha looked at her inquiringly.

"What is there left for me to do here? What difficulty will it make? I'll be naturalised in Uri, too, and live in the valley.... Don't be uneasy, I won't be in the way."

They began packing quickly to be in time to catch the midday train. But in less than half an hour's time Alexey Yegorytch arrived from Skvoreshniki. He announced that Nikolay Vsyevolodovitch had suddenly arrived that morning by the early train, and was now at Skvoreshniki but "in such a state that his honour did not answer any questions, walked through all the rooms and shut himself up in his own wing...."

"Though I received no orders I thought it best to come and inform you," Alexey Yegorytch concluded with a very significant expression.

Varvara Petrovna looked at him searchingly and did not question him. The carriage was got ready instantly. Varvara Petrovna set off with Dasha. They say that she kept crossing herself on the journey.

In Nikolay Vsyevolodovitch's wing of the house all the doors were open and he was nowhere to be seen.

"Wouldn't he be upstairs?" Fomushka ventured.

It was remarkable that several servants followed Varvara Petrovna while the others all stood waiting in the drawing-room. They would never have dared to commit such a breach of etiquette before. Varvara Petrovna saw it and said nothing.

They went upstairs. There there were three rooms; but they found no one there.

"Wouldn't his honour have gone up there?" someone suggested, pointing to the door of the loft. And in fact, the door of the loft which was always closed had been opened and was standing ajar. The loft was right under the roof and was reached by a long, very steep and narrow wooden ladder. There was a sort of little room up there too.

"I am not going up there. Why should he go up there?" said Varvara Petrovna, turning terribly pale as she looked at the servants. They gazed back at her and said nothing. Dasha was trembling.

Varvara Petrovna rushed up the ladder; Dasha followed, but she had hardly entered the loft when she uttered a scream and fell senseless.

The citizen of the canton of Uri was hanging there behind the door. On the table lay a piece of paper with the words in pencil: "No one is to blame, I did it myself." Beside it on the table lay a hammer, a piece of soap, and a large nail—obviously an extra one in case of need. The strong silk cord upon which Nikolay Vsyevolodovitch had hanged himself had evidently been chosen and prepared beforehand and was thickly smeared with soap. Everything proved that there had been premeditation and consciousness up to the last moment.

At the inquest our doctors absolutely and emphatically rejected all idea of insanity.

THE END

About Author

After graduating, he worked as an engineer and briefly enjoyed a lavish lifestyle, translating books to earn extra money. In the mid-1840s he wrote his first novel, Poor Folk, which gained him entry into St. Petersburg's literary circles. Arrested in 1849 for belonging to a literary group that discussed banned books critical of Tsarist Russia, he was sentenced to death but the sentence was commuted at the last moment. He spent four years in a Siberian prison camp, followed by six years of compulsory military service in exile. In the following years, Dostoevsky worked as a journalist, publishing and editing several magazines of his own and later A Writer's Diary, a collection of his writings. He began to travel around western Europe and developed a gambling addiction, which led to financial hardship. For a time, he had to beg for money, but he eventually became one of the most widely read and highly regarded Russian writers.

Dostoevsky was influenced by a wide variety of philosophers and authors including Pushkin, Gogol, Augustine, Shakespeare, Dickens, Balzac, Lermontov, Hugo, Poe, Plato, Cervantes, Herzen, Kant, Belinsky, Hegel, Schiller, Solovyov, Bakunin, Sand, Hoffmann, and Mickiewicz. His writings were widely read both within and beyond his native Russia and influenced an equally great number of later writers including Russians like Aleksandr Solzhenitsyn and Anton Chekhov as well as philosophers such as Friedrich Nietzsche and Jean-Paul Sartre. His books have been translated into more than 170 languages.

Ancestry

Dostoevsky's parents were part of a multi-ethnic and multi-denominational noble family, its branches including Russian Orthodox Christians, Polish Roman Catholics and Ukrainian Eastern Catholics. The family traced its roots back to a Tatar, Aslan Chelebi-Murza, who in 1389 defected from the Golden Horde and joined the forces of Dmitry Donskoy, the first prince of Muscovy to openly challenge the Mongol authority in the region, and whose descendant, Danilo Irtishch, was ennobled and given lands in the Pinsk region (for centuries part of the Grand Duchy of Lithuania, now in modern-day Belarus) in 1509 for his services under a local prince, his progeny then taking the name "Dostoevsky" based on a village there called Dostoïevo.

Dostoevsky's immediate ancestors on his mother's side were merchants; the male line on his father's side were priests. His father, Mikhail Andreevich, was expected to join the clergy but instead ran away from home and broke with the family permanently.

In 1809, the 20-year-old Mikhail Andreevich Dostoevsky enrolled in Moscow's Imperial Medical-Surgical Academy. From there he was assigned to a Moscow hospital, where he served as military doctor, and in 1818, he was appointed a senior physician. In 1819 he married Maria Nechayeva. The following year, he took up a post at the Mariinsky Hospital for the poor. In 1828, when his two sons, Mikhail and Fyodor, were eight and seven respectively, he was promoted to collegiate assessor, a position which raised his legal status to that of the nobility and enabled him to acquire a small estate in Darovoye, a town about 150 km (100 miles) from Moscow, where the family usually spent the summers. Dostoevsky's parents subsequently had six more children: Varvara (1822–1892), Andrei (1825–1897), Lyubov (born and died 1829), Vera (1829–1896), Nikolai (1831–1883) and Aleksandra (1835–1889).

Childhood (1821–1835)

Fyodor Dostoevsky, born on 11 November [O.S. 30 October] 1821, was the second child of Dr. Mikhail Dostoevsky and Maria Dostoevskaya (born Nechayeva). He was raised in the family home in the grounds of the Mariinsky Hospital for the Poor, which was in a lower class district on the edges of Moscow. Dostoevsky encountered the patients, who were at the lower end of the Russian social scale, when playing in the hospital gardens.

Dostoevsky was introduced to literature at an early age. From the age of three, he was read heroic sagas, fairy tales and legends by his nanny, Alena Frolovna, an especially influential figure in his upbringing and love for fictional stories. When he was four his mother used the Bible to teach him to read and write. His parents introduced him to a wide range of literature, including Russian writers Karamzin, Pushkin and Derzhavin; Gothic fiction such as Ann Radcliffe; romantic works by Schiller and Goethe; heroic tales by Cervantes and Walter Scott; and Homer's epics. Although his father's approach to education has been described as strict and harsh, Dostoevsky himself reports that his imagination was brought alive by nightly readings by his parents.

Some of his childhood experiences found their way into his writings. When a nine-year-old girl had been raped by a drunk, he was asked to fetch his father to attend to her. The incident haunted him, and the theme of the desire of a mature man for a young girl appears in The Devils, The Brothers Karamazov, Crime and Punishment, and other writings. An incident involving a family servant, or serf, in the estate in Darovoye, is described in "The Peasant Marey": when the young Dostoevsky imagines hearing a wolf in the forest, Marey, who is working nearby, comforts him.

Although Dostoevsky had a delicate physical constitution, his parents described him as hot-headed, stubborn and cheeky. In 1833, Dostoevsky's father, who was profoundly religious, sent him to a French boarding school and then to the Chermak boarding school. He was described as a pale, introverted dreamer and an over-excitable romantic. To pay the school fees, his father borrowed money and extended his private medical practice. Dostoevsky felt out of place among his aristocratic classmates at the Moscow school, and the experience was later reflected in some of his works, notably The Adolescent.

Youth (1836–1843)

On 27 September 1837 Dostoevsky's mother died of tuberculosis. The previous May, his parents had sent Dostoevsky and his brother Mikhail to St Petersburg to attend the free Nikolayev Military Engineering Institute, forcing the brothers to abandon their academic studies for military careers. Dostoevsky entered the academy in January 1838, but only with the help of family members. Mikhail was refused admission on health grounds and was sent to the Academy in Reval, Estonia.

Dostoevsky disliked the academy, primarily because of his lack of interest in science, mathematics and military engineering and his preference for drawing and architecture. As his friend Konstantin Trutovsky once said, "There was no student in the entire institution with less of a military bearing than F.M. Dostoevsky. He moved clumsily and jerkily; his uniform hung awkwardly on him; and his knapsack, shako and rifle all looked like some sort of fetter he had been forced to wear for a time and which lay heavily on him." Dostoevsky's character and interests made him an outsider among his 120 classmates: he showed bravery and a strong sense of justice, protected newcomers, aligned himself with teachers, criticised corruption among officers and helped poor farmers. Although he was solitary and inhabited his own literary world, he was respected by his classmates. His reclusiveness and interest in religion earned him the nickname "Monk Photius".

Signs of Dostoevsky's epilepsy may have first appeared on learning of the death of his father on 16 June 1839, although the reports of a seizure originated from accounts written by his daughter (later expanded by Sigmund Freud.) which are now considered to be unreliable. His father's official cause of death was an apoplectic stroke, but a neighbour, Pavel Khotiaintsev, accused the father's serfs of murder. Had the serfs been found guilty and sent to Siberia, Khotiaintsev would have been in a position to buy the vacated land. The serfs were acquitted in a trial in Tula, but Dostoevsky's brother Andrei perpetuated the story. After his father's death, Dostoevsky continued his studies, passed his exams and obtained the rank of engineer cadet, entitling him to live away from the academy. He visited Mikhail in Reval, and frequently attended concerts, operas, plays and ballets. During this time, two of his friends introduced him to gambling.

On 12 August 1843 Dostoevsky took a job as a lieutenant engineer and lived with Adolph Totleben in an apartment owned by Dr. Rizenkampf, a friend of Mikhail. Rizenkampf characterised him as "no less good-natured and no less courteous than his brother, but when not in a good mood he often looked at everything through dark glasses, became vexed, forgot good manners, and sometimes was carried away to the point of abusiveness and loss of self-awareness". Dostoevsky's first completed literary work, a translation of Honoré de Balzac's novel Eugénie Grandet, was published in June and July 1843 in the 6th and 7th volume of the journal Repertoire and Pantheon, followed by several other translations. None were successful, and his financial difficulties led him to write a novel.

Career

Early career (1844–1849)

Dostoevsky completed his first novel, Poor Folk, in May 1845. His friend Dmitry Grigorovich, with whom he was sharing an apartment at the time, took the manuscript to the poet Nikolay Nekrasov, who in turn showed it to the renowned and influential literary critic Vissarion Belinsky. Belinsky described it as Russia's first "social novel". Poor Folk was released on 15 January 1846 in the St Petersburg Collection almanac and became a commercial success.

Dostoevsky felt that his military career would endanger his now flourishing literary career, so he wrote a letter asking to resign his post. Shortly thereafter, he wrote his second novel, The Double, which appeared in the journal Notes of the Fatherland on 30 January 1846, before being published in February. Around the same time, Dostoevsky discovered socialism through the writings of French thinkers Fourier, Cabet, Proudhon and Saint-Simon. Through his relationship with Belinsky he expanded his knowledge of the philosophy of socialism. He was attracted to its logic, its sense of justice and its preoccupation with the destitute and the disadvantaged. However, his relationship with Belinsky became increasingly strained as Belinsky's atheism and dislike of religion clashed with Dostoevsky's Russian Orthodox beliefs. Dostoevsky eventually parted with him and his associates.

After The Double received negative reviews, Dostoevsky's health declined and he had more frequent seizures, but he continued writing. From 1846 to 1848 he released several short stories in the magazine Annals of the Fatherland, including "Mr. Prokharchin", "The Landlady", "A Weak Heart", and "White Nights". These stories were unsuccessful, leaving Dostoevsky once more in financial trouble, so he joined the utopian socialist Betekov circle, a tightly knit community which helped him to survive. When the circle dissolved, Dostoevsky befriended Apollon Maykov and his brother Valerian. In 1846, on the recommendation of the poet Aleksey Pleshcheyev, he joined the Petrashevsky Circle, founded by Mikhail Petrashevsky, who had proposed social reforms in Russia. Mikhail Bakunin once wrote to Alexander Herzen that the group was "the most innocent and harmless company" and its members were "systematic opponents of all revolutionary goals and means". Dostoevsky used the circle's library on Saturdays and Sundays and occasionally participated in their discussions on freedom from censorship and the abolition of serfdom.

In 1849, the first parts of Netochka Nezvanova, a novel Dostoevsky had been planning since 1846, were published in Annals of the Fatherland, but his banishment ended the project. Dostoevsky never attempted to complete it.

Siberian exile (1849–1854)

The members of the Petrashevsky Circle were denounced to Liprandi, an official at the Ministry of Internal Affairs. Dostoevsky was accused of reading works by Belinsky, including the banned Letter to Gogol, and of circulating copies of these and other works. Antonelli, the government agent who had reported the group, wrote in his statement that at least one of the papers criticised Russian politics and religion. Dostoevsky responded to these charges by declaring that he had read the essays only "as a literary monument, neither more nor less"; he spoke of "personality and human egoism" rather than of politics. Even so, he and his fellow "conspirators" were arrested on 23 April 1849 at the request of Count A. Orlov and Tsar Nicolas I, who feared a revolution like the Decembrist revolt of 1825 in Russia and the Revolutions of 1848 in Europe. The members were held in the well-defended Peter and Paul Fortress, which housed the most dangerous convicts.

The case was discussed for four months by an investigative commission headed by the Tsar, with Adjutant General Ivan Nabokov, senator Prince Pavel Gagarin, Prince Vasili Dolgorukov, General Yakov Rostovtsev and General Leonty Dubelt, head of the secret police. They sentenced the members of the circle to death by firing squad, and the prisoners were taken to Semyonov Place in St Petersburg on 23 December 1849 where they were split into three-man groups. Dostoevsky was the third in the second row; next to him stood Pleshcheyev and Durov. The execution was stayed when a cart delivered a letter from the Tsar commuting the sentence.

Dostoevsky served four years of exile with hard labour at a katorga prison camp in Omsk, Siberia, followed by a term of compulsory military service. After a fourteen-day sleigh ride, the prisoners reached Tobolsk, a prisoner way station. Despite the circumstances, Dostoevsky consoled the other prisoners, such as the Petrashevist Ivan Yastrzhembsky, who was surprised by Dostoevsky's kindness and eventually abandoned his decision to commit suicide. In Tobolsk, the members received food and clothes from the Decembrist women, as well as several copies of the New Testament with a ten-ruble banknote inside each copy. Eleven days later, Dostoevsky reached Omsk together with just one other member of the Petrashevsky Circle, the poet Sergei

Durov. Dostoevsky described his barracks:

> In summer, intolerable closeness; in winter, unendurable cold. All the floors were rotten. Filth on the floors an inch thick; one could slip and fall ... We were packed like herrings in a barrel ... There was no room to turn around. From dusk to dawn it was impossible not to behave like pigs ... Fleas, lice, and black beetles by the bushel ...

Classified as "one of the most dangerous convicts", Dostoevsky had his hands and feet shackled until his release. He was only permitted to read his New Testament Bible. In addition to his seizures, he had haemorrhoids, lost weight and was "burned by some fever, trembling and feeling too hot or too cold every night". The smell of the privy pervaded the entire building, and the small bathroom had to suffice for more than 200 people. Dostoevsky was occasionally sent to the military hospital, where he read newspapers and Dickens novels. He was respected by most of the other prisoners, and despised by some because of his xenophobic statements.

Release from prison and first marriage (1854–1866)

After his release on 14 February 1854, Dostoevsky asked Mikhail to help him financially and to send him books by Vico, Guizot, Ranke, Hegel and Kant. The House of the Dead, based on his experience in prison, was published in 1861 in the journal Vremya ("Time") – it was the first published novel about Russian prisons. Before moving in mid-March to Semipalatinsk, where he was forced to serve in the Siberian Army Corps of the Seventh Line Battalion, Dostoevsky met geographer Pyotr Semyonov and ethnographer Shokan Walikhanuli. Around November 1854, he met Baron Alexander Egorovich Wrangel, an admirer of his books, who had attended the aborted execution. They both rented houses in the Cossack Garden outside Semipalatinsk. Wrangel remarked that Dostoevsky "looked morose. His sickly, pale face was covered with freckles, and his blond hair was cut short. He was a little over average height and looked at me intensely with his sharp, grey-blue eyes. It was as if he were trying to look into my soul and discover what kind of man I was."

In Semipalatinsk, Dostoevsky tutored several schoolchildren and came into contact with upper-class families, including that of Lieutenant-Colonel Belikhov, who used to invite him to read passages from newspapers and magazines. During a visit to Belikhov, Dostoevsky met the family of Alexander Ivanovich Isaev and Maria Dmitrievna Isaeva and fell in love with the latter. Alexander Isaev took a new post in Kuznetsk, where he died in August 1855. Maria and her son then moved with Dostoevsky to Barnaul. In 1856 Dostoevsky sent a letter through Wrangel to General Eduard Totleben, apologising for his activity in several utopian circles. As a result, he obtained the right to publish books and to marry, although he remained under police surveillance for the rest of his life. Maria married Dostoevsky in Semipalatinsk on 7 February 1857, even though she had initially refused his marriage proposal, stating that they were not meant for each other and that his poor financial situation precluded marriage. Their family life was unhappy and she found it difficult to cope with his seizures. Describing their relationship, he wrote: "Because of her strange, suspicious and fantastic character, we were definitely not happy together, but we could not stop loving each other; and the more unhappy we were, the more attached to each other we became". They mostly lived apart. In 1859 he was released from military service because of deteriorating health and was granted permission to return to Russia, first to Tver, where he met his brother for the first time in ten years, and then to St Petersburg.

"A Little Hero" (Dostoevsky's only work completed in prison) appeared in a journal, but "Uncle's Dream" and "The Village of Stepanchikovo" were not published until 1860. Notes from the House of the Dead was released in Russky Mir (Russian World) in September 1860. "The Insulted and the Injured" was published in the new Vremya magazine, which had been created with the help of funds from his brother's cigarette factory.

Dostoevsky travelled to western Europe for the first time on 7 June 1862, visiting Cologne, Berlin, Dresden, Wiesbaden, Belgium, and Paris. In London, he met Herzen and visited the Crystal Palace. He travelled with Nikolay Strakhov through Switzerland and several North Italian cities, including Turin, Livorno, and Florence. He recorded his impressions of those trips in Winter Notes on Summer Impressions, in which he criticised capitalism, social modernisation, materialism, Catholicism and Protestantism.

From August to October 1863, Dostoevsky made another trip to western Europe. He met his second love, Polina Suslova, in Paris and lost nearly all his money gambling in Wiesbaden and Baden-Baden. In 1864 his wife Maria and brother Mikhail died, and Dostoevsky became the lone parent of his stepson Pasha and the sole supporter of his brother's family. The failure of Epoch, the magazine he had founded with Mikhail after the suppression of Vremya, worsened his financial situation, although the continued help of his relatives and friends averted bankruptcy.

Second marriage and honeymoon (1866–1871)

The first two parts of Crime and Punishment were published in January and February 1866 in the periodical The Russian Messenger, attracting at least 500 new subscribers to the magazine.

Dostoevsky returned to Saint Petersburg in mid-September and promised his editor, Fyodor Stellovsky, that he would complete The Gambler, a short novel focused on gambling addiction, by November, although he had not yet begun writing it. One of Dostoevsky's friends, Milyukov, advised him to hire a secretary. Dostoevsky contacted stenographer Pavel Olkhin from Saint Petersburg, who recommended his pupil, the twenty-year-old Anna Grigoryevna Snitkina. Her shorthand helped Dostoevsky to complete The Gambler on 30 October, after 26 days' work. She remarked that Dostoevsky was of average height but always tried to carry himself erect. "He had light brown, slightly reddish hair, he used some hair conditioner, and he combed his hair in a diligent way ... his eyes, they were different: one was dark brown; in the other, the pupil was so big that you could not see its color, [this was caused by an injury]. The strangeness of his eyes gave Dostoyevsky some mysterious appearance. His face was pale, and it looked unhealthy."

On 15 February 1867 Dostoevsky married Snitkina in Trinity Cathedral, Saint Petersburg. The 7,000 rubles he had earned from Crime and Punishment did not cover their debts, forcing Anna to sell her valuables. On 14 April 1867, they began a delayed honeymoon in Germany with the money gained from the sale. They stayed in Berlin and visited the Gemäldegalerie Alte Meister in Dresden, where he sought inspiration for his writing. They continued their trip through Germany, visiting Frankfurt, Darmstadt, Heidelberg and Karlsruhe. They spent five weeks in Baden-Baden, where Dostoevsky had a quarrel with Turgenev and again lost much money at the roulette table. The couple travelled on to Geneva.

In September 1867, Dostoevsky began work on The Idiot, and after a prolonged planning process that bore little resemblance to the published novel, he eventually managed to write the first 100 pages in only 23 days; the serialisation began in The Russian Messenger in January 1868.

Their first child, Sonya, had been conceived in Baden-Baden, and was born in Geneva on 5 March 1868. The baby died of pneumonia three months later, and Anna recalled how Dostoevsky "wept and sobbed like a woman in despair". The couple moved from Geneva to Vevey and then to Milan, before continuing to Florence. The Idiot was completed there in January 1869, the final part appearing in The Russian Messenger in February 1869. Anna gave birth to their second daughter, Lyubov, on 26 September 1869 in Dresden. In April 1871, Dostoevsky made a final visit to a gambling hall in Wiesbaden. Anna claimed that he stopped gambling after the birth of their second daughter, but this is a subject of debate.

After hearing news that the socialist revolutionary group "People's Vengeance" had murdered one of its own members, Ivan Ivanov, on 21 November 1869, Dostoevsky began writing Demons. In 1871, Dostoevsky and Anna travelled by train to Berlin. During the trip, he burnt several manuscripts, including those of The Idiot, because he was concerned about potential problems with customs. The family arrived in Saint Petersburg on 8 July, marking the end of a honeymoon (originally planned for three months) that had lasted over four years.

Back in Russia (1871–1875)

Back in Russia in July 1871, the family was again in financial trouble and had to sell their remaining possessions. Their son Fyodor was born on 16 July, and they moved to an apartment near the Institute of Technology soon after. They hoped to cancel their large debts by selling their rental house in Peski, but difficulties with the tenant resulted in a relatively low selling price, and disputes with their creditors continued. Anna proposed that they raise money on her husband's copyrights and negotiate with the creditors to pay off their debts in installments.

Dostoevsky revived his friendships with Maykov and Strakhov and made new acquaintances, including church politician Terty Filipov and the brothers Vsevolod and Vladimir Solovyov. Konstantin Pobedonostsev, future Imperial High Commissioner of the Most Holy Synod, influenced Dostoevsky's political progression to conservatism. Around early 1872 the family spent several months in Staraya Russa, a town known for its mineral spa. Dostoevsky's work was delayed when Anna's sister Maria Svatkovskaya died on 1 May 1872, either from typhus or malaria, and Anna developed an abscess on her throat.

The family returned to St Petersburg in September. Demons was finished on 26 November and released in January 1873 by the "Dostoevsky Publishing Company", which was founded by Dostoevsky and his wife. Although they only accepted cash payments and the bookshop was in their own apartment, the business was successful, and they sold around 3,000 copies of Demons. Anna managed the finances. Dostoevsky proposed that they establish a new periodical, which would be called A Writer's Diary and would include a collection of essays, but funds were lacking, and the Diary was published in Vladimir Meshchersky's The Citizen, beginning on 1 January, in return for a salary of 3,000 rubles per year. In the summer of 1873, Anna returned to Staraya Russa with the children, while Dostoevsky stayed in St Petersburg to continue with his Diary.

In March 1874, Dostoevsky left The Citizen because of the stressful work and interference from the Russian bureaucracy. In his fifteen months with The Citizen, he had been taken to court twice: on 11 June 1873 for citing the words of Prince Meshchersky without permission, and again on 23 March 1874. Dostoevsky offered to sell a new novel he had not yet begun to write to The Russian Messenger, but the magazine refused. Nikolay Nekrasov suggested that he publish A Writer's Diary in Notes of the Fatherland; he would receive 250 rubles for each printer's sheet – 100 more than the text's publication in The Russian Messenger would have earned. Dostoevsky accepted. As his health began to decline, he consulted several doctors in St Petersburg and was advised to take a cure outside Russia. Around July, he reached Ems and consulted a physician, who diagnosed him with acute catarrh. During his stay he began The Adolescent. He returned to Saint Petersburg in late July.

Anna proposed that they spend the winter in Staraya Russa to allow Dostoevsky to rest, although doctors had suggested a second visit to Ems because his health had previously improved there. On 10 August 1875 his son Alexey was born in Staraya Russa, and in mid-September the family returned to Saint Petersburg. Dostoevsky finished The Adolescent at the end of 1875, although passages of it had been serialised in Notes of the Fatherland since January. The Adolescent chronicles the life of Arkady Dolgoruky, the illegitimate child of the landowner Versilov and a peasant mother. It deals primarily with the relationship between father and son, which became a frequent theme in Dostoevsky's subsequent works.

Last years (1876–1881)

In early 1876, Dostoevsky continued work on his Diary. The book includes numerous essays and a few short stories about society, religion, politics and ethics. The collection sold more than twice as many copies as his previous books. Dostoevsky received more letters from readers than ever before, and people of all ages and occupations visited him. With assistance from Anna's brother, the family bought a dacha in Staraya Russa. In the summer of 1876, Dostoevsky began experiencing shortness of breath again. He visited Ems for the third time and was told that he might live for another 15 years if he moved to a healthier climate. When he returned to Russia, Tsar Alexander II ordered Dostoevsky to visit his palace to present the Diary to him, and he asked him to educate his sons, Sergey and Paul. This visit further increased Dosteyevsky's circle of acquaintances. He was a frequent guest in several salons in Saint Petersburg and met many famous people, including Princess Sophia Tolstaya, Yakov Polonsky, Sergei Witte, Alexey Suvorin, Anton Rubinstein and Ilya Repin.

Dostoevsky's health declined further, and in March 1877 he had four epileptic seizures. Rather than returning to Ems, he visited Maly Prikol, a manor near Kursk. While returning to St Petersburg to finalise his Diary, he visited Darovoye, where he had spent much of his childhood. In December he attended Nekrasov's funeral and gave a speech. He was appointed an honorary member of the Russian Academy of Sciences, from which he received an honorary certificate in February 1879. He declined an invitation to an international congress on copyright in Paris after his son Alyosha had a severe epileptic seizure and died on 16 May. The family later moved to the apartment where Dostoevsky had written his first works. Around this time, he was elected to the board of directors of the Slavic Benevolent Society in Saint Petersburg. That summer, he was elected to the honorary committee of the Association Littéraire et Artistique Internationale, whose members included Victor Hugo, Ivan Turgenev, Paul Heyse, Alfred Tennyson, Anthony Trollope, Henry Longfellow, Ralph Waldo Emerson and Leo Tolstoy. Dostoevsky made his fourth and final visit to Ems in early August 1879. He was diagnosed with early-stage pulmonary emphysema, which his doctor believed could be successfully managed, but not cured.

On 3 February 1880 Dostoevsky was elected vice-president of the Slavic Benevolent Society, and he was invited to speak at the unveiling of the Pushkin memorial in Moscow. On 8 June he delivered his speech, giving an impressive performance that had a significant emotional impact on his audience. His speech was met with thunderous applause, and even his long-time rival Turgenev embraced him. Konstantin Staniukovich praised the speech in his essay "The Pushkin Anniversary and Dostoevsky's Speech" in The Business, writing that "the language of Dostoevsky's [Pushkin Speech] really looks like a sermon. He speaks with the tone of a prophet. He makes a sermon like a pastor; it is very deep, sincere, and we understand that he wants to impress the emotions of his listeners." The speech was criticised later by liberal political scientist Alexander Gradovsky, who thought that Dostoevsky idolised "the people", and by conservative thinker Konstantin Leontiev, who, in his essay "On Universal Love", compared the speech to French utopian socialism. The attacks led to a further deterioration in his health.

Death

On 25 January 1881, while searching for members of the terrorist organisation Narodnaya Volya ("The People's Will") who would soon assassinate Tsar Alexander II, the Tsar's secret police executed a search warrant in the apartment of one of Dostoevsky's neighbours. On the following day, Dostoevsky suffered a pulmonary haemorrhage. Anna denied that the search had caused it, saying that the haemorrhage had occurred after her husband had been looking for a dropped pen holder. After another haemorrhage, Anna called the doctors, who gave a poor prognosis. A third haemorrhage followed shortly afterwards. While seeing his children before dying, Dostoevsky requested that the parable of the Prodigal Son be read to his children. The profound meaning of this request is pointed out by Frank:

It was this parable of transgression, repentance, and forgiveness that he wished to leave as a last heritage to his children, and it may well be seen as his own ultimate understanding of the meaning of his life and the message of his work.

Among Dostoevsky's last words was his quotation of Matthew 3:14–15: "But John forbad him, saying, I have a need to be baptised of thee, and comest thou to me? And Jesus answering said unto him, Suffer it to be so now: for thus it becometh us to fulfil all righteousness", and he finished with "Hear now—permit it. Do not restrain me!" When he died, his body was placed on a table, following Russian custom. He was interred in the Tikhvin Cemetery at the Alexander Nevsky Convent, near his favourite poets, Nikolay Karamzin and Vasily Zhukovsky. It is unclear how many attended his funeral. According to one reporter, more than 100,000 mourners were present, while others describe attendance between 40,000 and 50,000. His tombstone is inscribed with lines from the New Testament:

Verily, verily, I say unto you, Except a corn of wheat fall into the ground and die, it abideth alone: but if it dies, it bringeth forth much fruit.

—John 12:24

Personal life

Extramarital affairs

Dostoevsky had his first known affair with Avdotya Yakovlevna, whom he met in the

Panayev circle in the early 1840s. He described her as educated, interested in literature, and a femme fatale. He admitted later that he was uncertain about their relationship. According to Anna Dostoevskaya's memoirs, Dostoevsky once asked his sister's sister-in-law, Yelena Ivanova, whether she would marry him, hoping to replace her mortally ill husband after he died, but she rejected his proposal.

Dostoevsky and Apollonia (Polina) Suslova had a short but intimate affair, which peaked in the winter of 1862–1863. Suslova's dalliance with a Spaniard in late spring and Dostoevsky's gambling addiction and age ended their relationship. He later described her in a letter to Nadezhda Suslova as a "great egoist. Her egoism and her vanity are colossal. She demands everything of other people, all the perfections, and does not pardon the slightest imperfection in the light of other qualities that one may possess", and later stated "I still love her, but I do not want to love her any more. She doesn't deserve this love ..." In 1858 Dostoevsky had a romance with comic actress Aleksandra Ivanovna Schubert. Although she divorced Dostoevsky's friend Stepan Yanovsky, she would not live with him. Dostoevsky did not love her either, but they were probably good friends. She wrote that he "became very attracted to me".

Through a worker in Epoch, Dostoevsky learned of the Russian-born Martha Brown (née Elizaveta Andreyevna Chlebnikova), who had had affairs with several westerners. Her relationship with Dostoevsky is known only through letters written between November 1864 and January 1865. In 1865, Dostoevsky met Anna Korvin-Krukovskaya. Their relationship is not verified; Anna Dostoevskaya spoke of a good affair, but Korvin-Krukovskaya's sister, the mathematician Sofia Kovalevskaya, thought that Korvin-Krukovskaya had rejected him.

Political beliefs

In his youth, Dostoevsky enjoyed reading Nikolai Karamzin's History of the Russian State, which praised conservatism and Russian independence, ideas that Dostoevsky would embrace later in life. Before his arrest for participating in the Petrashevsky Circle in 1849, Dostoevsky remarked, "As far as I am concerned, nothing was ever more ridiculous than the idea of a republican government in Russia." In an 1881 edition of his Diaries, Dostoevsky stated that the Tsar and the people should form a unity: "For the people, the tsar is not an external power, not the power of some conqueror ... but a power of all the people, an all-unifying power the people themselves desired."

While critical of serfdom, Dostoevsky was skeptical about the creation of a constitution, a concept he viewed as unrelated to Russia's history. He described it as a mere "gentleman's rule" and believed that "a constitution would simply enslave the people". He advocated social change instead, for example removal of the feudal system and a weakening of the divisions between the peasantry and the affluent classes. His ideal was a utopian, Christianized Russia where "if everyone were actively Christian, not a single social question would come up ... If they were Christians they would settle everything". He thought democracy and oligarchy were poor systems; of France he wrote, "the oligarchs are only concerned with the interest of the wealthy; the democrats, only with the interest of the poor; but the interests of society, the interest of all and the future of France as a whole—no one there bothers about these things." He maintained that political parties ultimately led to social discord. In the 1860s, he discovered Pochvennichestvo, a movement similar to Slavophilism in that it rejected Europe's culture and contemporary philosophical movements, such as nihilism and materialism. Pochvennichestvo differed from Slavophilism in aiming to establish, not an isolated Russia, but a more open state modelled on the Russia of Peter the Great.

In his incomplete article "Socialism and Christianity", Dostoevsky claimed that civilisation ("the second stage in human history") had become degraded, and that it was moving towards liberalism and losing its faith in God. He asserted that the traditional concept of Christianity should be recovered. He thought that contemporary western Europe had "rejected the single formula for their salvation that came from God and was proclaimed through revelation, 'Thou shalt love thy neighbour as thyself', and replaced it with practical conclusions such as, 'Chacun pour soi et Dieu pour tous' [Every man for himself and God for all], or "scientific" slogans like 'the struggle for survival'". He considered this crisis to be the consequence of the collision between communal and individual interests, brought about by a decline in religious and moral principles.

Dostoevsky distinguished three "enormous world ideas" prevalent in his time: Roman Catholicism, Protestantism and Russian Orthodoxy. He claimed that Catholicism had continued the tradition of Imperial Rome and had thus become anti-Christian and proto-socialist, inasmuch as the Church's interest in political and mundane affairs led it to abandon the idea of Christ. For Dostoevsky, socialism was "the latest incarnation of the Catholic idea" and its "natural ally". He found Protestantism self-contradictory and claimed that it would ultimately lose power and spirituality. He deemed Russian Orthodoxy to be the ideal form of Christianity.

For all that, to place politically Dostoevsky is not that simple, but: as a Christian, he rejected the atheistic socialism; as a traditionalist, he rejected the destruction of the institutions and, as a pacifist, any violent method or upheaval led by both progressives or reactionaries.

During the Russo-Turkish War, Dostoevsky asserted that war might be necessary if salvation were to be granted. He wanted the Muslim Ottoman Empire eliminated and the Christian Byzantine Empire restored, and he hoped for the liberation of Balkan Slavs and their unification with the Russian Empire.

Racial beliefs

Jewish characters in Dostoevsky's works have been described as displaying negative stereotypes. In a letter to Arkady Kovner from 1877, a Jew who had accused Dostoevsky of antisemitism, he replied with the following:

"I am not an enemy of the Jews at all and never have been. But as you say, its 40-century existence proves that this tribe has exceptional vitality, which would not help, during the course of its history, taking the form of various Status in Statu .... how can they fail to find themselves, even if only partially, at variance with the indigenuous population – the Russian tribe?"

Dostoevsky held negative views of the Ottoman Turks, dedicating multiple pages to them in his "Writer's Diary", professing the need to have no pity for Turks at war, no regrets in killing Turks and depopulating Istanbul of the Turkish population and shipping it off to Asia.

Religious beliefs

Dostoevsky was an Orthodox Christian, was raised in a religious family and knew the Gospel from a very young age. He was influenced by the Russian translation of Johannes Hübner's One Hundred and Four Sacred Stories from the Old and New Testaments Selected for Children (partly a German bible for children and partly a catechism). He attended Sunday liturgies from an early age and took part in annual pilgrimages to the St. Sergius Trinity Monastery. A deacon at the hospital gave him religious instruction. Among his most cherished childhood memories were the prayers he used to recite in front of guests and a reading from the Book of Job that impressed him while "still almost a child."

According to an officer at the military academy, Dostoevsky was profoundly religious, followed Orthodox practice, and regularly read the Gospels and Heinrich Zschokke's Die Stunden der Andacht ("Hours of Devotion"), which "preached a sentimental version of Christianity entirely free from dogmatic content and with a strong emphasis on giving Christian love a social application." This book may have prompted his later interest in Christian socialism. Through the literature of Hoffmann, Balzac, Eugène Sue and Goethe, Dostoevsky created his own belief system, similar to Russian sectarianism and the Old Belief. After his arrest, aborted execution and subsequent imprisonment, he focused intensely on the figure of Christ and on the New Testament, the only book allowed in prison. In a January 1854 letter to the woman who had sent him the New Testament, Dostoevsky wrote that he was a "child of unbelief and doubt up to this moment, and I am certain that I shall remain so to the grave." He also wrote that "even if someone were to prove to me that the truth lay outside Christ, I should choose to remain with Christ rather than with the truth."

In Semipalatinsk, Dostoevsky revived his faith by looking frequently at the stars. Wrangel said that he was "rather pious, but did not often go to church, and disliked priests, especially the Siberian ones. But he spoke about Christ ecstatically." Both planned to translate Hegel's works and Carus' Psyche. Two pilgrimages and two works by Dmitri Rostovsky, an archbishop who influenced Ukrainian and Russian literature by composing groundbreaking religious plays, strengthened his beliefs. Through his visits to western Europe and discussions with Herzen, Grigoriev, and Strakhov, Dostoevsky discovered the Pochvennichestvo movement and the theory that the Catholic Church had adopted the principles of rationalism, legalism, materialism, and individualism from ancient Rome and had passed on its philosophy to Protestantism and consequently to atheistic socialism.

Themes and style

Dostoevsky's canon includes novels, novellas, novelettes, short stories, essays, pamphlets, limericks, epigrams and poems. He wrote more than 700 letters, a dozen of which are lost.

Dostoevsky expressed religious, psychological and philosophical ideas in his writings. His works explore such themes as suicide, poverty, human manipulation, and morality. Psychological themes include dreaming, first seen in "White Nights", and the father-son relationship, beginning in The Adolescent. Most of his works demonstrate a vision of the chaotic sociopolitical structure of contemporary Russia. His early works viewed society (for example, the differences between poor and rich) through the lens of literary realism and naturalism. The influences of other writers, particularly evident in his early works, led to accusations of plagiarism, but his style gradually became more individual. After his release from prison, Dostoevsky incorporated religious themes, especially those of Russian Orthodoxy, into his writing. Elements of gothic fiction, romanticism, and satire are observable in some of his books. He frequently used autobiographical or semi-autobiographical details.

Dostoevsky's works were often called "philosophical", although he described himself as "weak in philosophy". "Fyodor Mikhailovich loved these questions about the essence of things and the limits of knowledge", wrote Strakhov. Although theologian George Florovsky described Dostoevsky as a "philosophical problem", because it is unknown whether Dostoevsky believed in what he wrote, many philosophical ideas are found in books such as A Writer's Diary and The Brothers Karamazov. He may have been critical of rational and logical thinking because he was "more a sage and an artist than a strictly logical, consistent thinker". His irrationalism is mentioned in William Barrett's Irrational Man: A Study in Existential Philosophy and in Walter Kaufmann's Existentialism from Dostoevsky to Sartre.

An important stylistic element in Dostoevsky's writing is polyphony, the simultaneous presence of multiple narrative voices and perspectives. Polyphony is a literary concept, analogous with musical polyphony, developed by Mikhail Bakhtin on the basis of his analyses of Dostoevsky's works.

Legacy

Reception and influence

Dostoevsky is regarded as one of the greatest and most influential novelists of the Golden Age of Russian literature. Albert Einstein put him above the mathematician Carl Friedrich Gauss, calling him a "great religious writer" who explores "the mystery of spiritual existence". Friedrich Nietzsche at one point called Dostoevsky "the only psychologist ... from whom I had something to learn; he ranks among the most beautiful strokes of fortune in my life", although the mature Nietzsche later turned against Dostoevsky likening him to Jesus and calling him decadent. Hermann Hesse enjoyed Dostoevsky's work and cautioned that to read him is like a "glimpse into the havoc". The Norwegian novelist Knut Hamsun wrote that "no one has analyzed the complicated human structure as Dostoyevsky. His psychologic sense is overwhelming and visionary." The Russian literary theorist Mikhail Bakhtin's analysis of Dostoevsky came to be at the foundation of his theory of the novel. Bakhtin argued that Dostoevsky's use of multiple voices was a major advancement in the development of the novel as a genre.

In his posthumous collection of sketches A Moveable Feast, Ernest Hemingway stated that in Dostoevsky "there were things believable and not to be believed, but some so true that they changed you as you read them; frailty and madness, wickedness and saintliness, and the insanity of gambling were there to know". James Joyce praised Dostoevsky's prose: "... he is the man more than any other who has created modern prose, and intensified it to its present-day pitch. It was his explosive power which shattered the Victorian novel with its simpering maidens and ordered commonplaces; books which were without imagination or violence." In her essay The Russian Point of View, Virginia Woolf said, "Out of Shakespeare there is no more exciting reading". Franz Kafka called Dostoevsky his "blood-relative" and was heavily influenced by his works, particularly The Brothers Karamazov and Crime and Punishment, both of which profoundly influenced The Trial. Sigmund Freud called The Brothers Karamazov "the most magnificent novel ever written". Modern cultural movements such as the surrealists, the existentialists and the Beats cite Dostoevsky as an influence, and he is cited as the forerunner of Russian symbolism, existentialism, expressionism and psychoanalysis. In her essay, What Is Romanticism?, Russian-American author Ayn Rand wrote that Dostoevsky was one of the two greatest novelists (the other being Victor Hugo).

Honours

In 1956 an olive-green postage stamp dedicated to Dostoevsky was released in the Soviet Union, with a print run of 1,000 copies. A Dostoevsky Museum was opened on 12 November 1971 in the apartment where he wrote his first and final novels. A crater on Mercury was named after him in 1979, and a minor planet discovered in 1981 by Lyudmila Karachkina was named 3453 Dostoevsky. Music critic and broadcaster Artemy Troitsky has hosted the radio show (FM Dostoevsky) since 1997. J.M. Coetzee featured Dostoevsky as the protagonist in his 1997 novel The Master of Petersburg. The famous Malayalam novel Oru Sankeerthanam Pole by Perumbadavam Sreedharan deals with the life of Dostoevsky and his love affair with Anna. Viewers of the TV show Name of Russia voted him the ninth greatest Russian of all time, behind chemist Dmitry Mendeleev and ahead of ruler Ivan IV. An Eagle Award-winning TV series directed by Vladimir Khotinenko about Dostoevsky's life was screened in 2011.

Numerous memorials were inaugurated in cities and regions such as Moscow, Saint Petersburg, Novosibirsk, Omsk, Semipalatinsk, Kusnetsk, Darovoye, Staraya Russa, Lyublino, Tallinn, Dresden, Baden-Baden and Wiesbaden. The Dostoyevskaya metro station in Saint Petersburg was opened on 30 December 1991, and the station of the same name in Moscow was opened on 19 June 2010, the 75th anniversary of the Moscow Metro. The Moscow station is decorated with murals by artist Ivan Nikolaev depicting scenes from Dostoevsky's works, such as controversial suicides.

Criticism

Dostoevsky's work did not always gain a positive reception. Several critics, such as Nikolay Dobrolyubov, Ivan Bunin and Vladimir Nabokov, viewed his writing as excessively psychological and philosophical rather than artistic. Others found fault with chaotic and disorganised plots, and others, like Turgenev, objected to "excessive psychologising" and too-detailed naturalism. His style was deemed "prolix, repetitious and lacking in polish, balance, restraint and good taste". Saltykov-Shchedrin, Tolstoy, Nikolay Mikhaylovsky and others criticised his puppet-like characters, most prominently in The Idiot, Demons (The Possessed, The Devils) and The Brothers Karamazov. These characters were compared to those of Hoffmann, an author whom Dostoevsky admired.

Basing his estimation on stated criteria of enduring art and individual genius, Nabokov judges Dostoevsky "not a great writer, but rather a mediocre one—with flashes of excellent humour but, alas, with wastelands of literary platitudes in between". Nabokov complains that the novels are peopled by "neurotics and lunatics" and states that Dostoevsky's characters do not develop: "We get them all complete at the beginning of the tale and so they remain." He finds the novels full of contrived "surprises and complications of plot", which are effective when first read, but on second reading, without the shock and benefit of these surprises, appear loaded with "glorified cliché".

Reputation

Dostoevsky's books have been translated into more than 170 languages. The German translator Wilhelm Wolfsohn published one of the first translations, parts of Poor Folk, in an 1846–1847 magazine, and a French translation followed. French, German and Italian translations usually came directly from the original, while English translations were second-hand and of poor quality. The first English translations were by Marie von Thilo in 1881, but the first highly regarded ones were produced between 1912 and 1920 by Constance Garnett.

Her flowing and easy translations helped popularise Dostoevsky's novels in anglophone countries, and Bakthin's Problems of Dostoevsky's Creative Art (1929) (republished and revised as Problems of Dostoevsky's Poetics in 1963) provided further understanding of his style.

Dostoevsky's works were interpreted in film and on stage in many different countries. Princess Varvara Dmitrevna Obolenskaya was among the first to propose staging Crime and Punishment. Dostoevsky did not refuse permission, but he advised against it, as he believed that "each art corresponds to a series of poetic thoughts, so that one idea cannot be expressed in another non-corresponding form". His extensive explanations in opposition to the transposition of his works into other media were groundbreaking in fidelity criticism. He thought that just one episode should be dramatised, or an idea should be taken and incorporated into a separate plot. According to critic Alexander Burry, some of the most effective adaptions are Sergei Prokofiev's opera The Gambler, Leoš Janáček's opera From the House of the Dead, Akira Kurosawa's film The Idiot and Andrzej Wajda's film The Possessed.

In later years, director Janek Ambros adapted "The Grand Inquisitor" into Nazi Croatia (the Ustasa regime) during World War II and the television detective character of Columbo was partially inspired by Crime and Punishment character Porfiry Petrovich.

After the 1917 Russian Revolution, passages of Dostoevsky books were sometimes shortened, although only two books were censored: Demons and Diary of a Writer. His philosophy, particularly in Demons, was deemed anti-capitalist but also anti-Communist and reactionary. Despite his works being censored, the writer was very popular and well received in the Soviet Union, his books selling over 34.4 million copies from 1917 to 1981, around 540 thousand copies per year. According to historian Boris Ilizarov, Stalin read Dostoevsky's The Brothers Karamazov several times.

Works

Dostoevsky's works of fiction include 15 novels and novellas, 17 short stories, and 5 translations. Many of his longer novels were first published in serialised form in literary magazines and journals. The years given below indicate the year in which the novel's final part or first complete book edition was published. In English many of his novels and stories are known by different titles.

Major works

Poor Folk

Poor Folk is an epistolary novel that describes the relationship between the small, elderly official Makar Devushkin and the young seamstress Varvara Dobroselova, remote relatives who write letters to each other. Makar's tender, sentimental adoration for Varvara and her confident, warm friendship for him explain their evident preference for a simple life, although it keeps them in humiliating poverty. An unscrupulous merchant finds the inexperienced girl and hires her as his housewife and guarantor. He sends her to a manor somewhere on a steppe, while Makar alleviates his misery and pain with alcohol.

The story focuses on poor people who struggle with their lack of self-esteem. Their misery leads to the loss of their inner freedom, to dependence on the social authorities, and to the extinction of their individuality. Dostoevsky shows how poverty and dependence are indissolubly aligned with deflection and deformation of self-esteem, combining inward and outerward suffering.

Notes from Underground

Notes from Underground is split into two stylistically different parts, the first essay-like, the second in narrative style. The protagonist and first-person narrator is an unnamed 40-year-old civil servant known as The Underground Man. The only known facts about his situation are that he has quit the service, lives in a basement flat on the outskirts of Saint Petersburg and finances his livelihood from a modest inheritance.

The first part is a record of his thoughts about society and his character. He describes himself as vicious, squalid and ugly; the chief focuses of his polemic are the "modern human" and his vision of the world, which he attacks severely and cynically, and towards which he develops aggression and vengefulness. He considers his own decline natural and necessary. Although he emphasises that he does not intend to publish his notes for the public, the narrator appeals repeatedly to an ill-described audience, whose questions he tries to address.

In the second part he describes scenes from his life that are responsible for his failure in personal and professional life and in his love life. He tells of meeting old school friends, who are in secure positions and treat him with condescension. His aggression turns inward on to himself and he tries to humiliate himself further. He presents himself as a possible saviour to the poor prostitute Lisa, advising her to reject self-reproach when she looks to him for hope. Dostoevsky added a short commentary saying that although the storyline and characters are fictional, such things were inevitable in contemporary society.

The Underground Man was very influential on philosophers. His alienated existence from the mainstream influenced modernist literature.

Crime and Punishment

Crime and Punishment describes Rodion Raskolnikov's life, from the murder of a pawnbroker and her sister, through spiritual regeneration with the help of Sonya (a "hooker with a heart of gold"), to his sentence in Siberia. Strakhov liked the novel, remarking that "Only Crime and Punishment was read in 1866" and that Dostoevsky had managed to portray a Russian person aptly and realistically. Otherwise, it received a mixed reception from critics, with most of the negative responses coming from nihilists. Grigory Eliseev of the radical magazine The Contemporary called the novel a "fantasy according to which the entire student body is accused without exception of attempting murder and robbery".

The Idiot

The novel's protagonist, the 26-year-old Prince Myshkin, returns to Russia after several years at a Swiss sanatorium. Scorned by Saint Petersburg society for his trusting nature and naivety, he finds himself at the center of a struggle between a beautiful kept woman, Nastasya, and a jealous but pretty young girl, Aglaya, both of whom win his affection. Unfortunately, Myshkin's goodness precipitates disaster, leaving the impression that, in a world obsessed with money, power and sexual conquest, a sanatorium may be the only place for a saint. Myshkin is the personification of a "relatively beautiful man", namely Christ. Coming "from above" (the Swiss mountains), he physically resembles common depictions of Jesus Christ: slightly larger than average, with thick, blond hair, sunken cheeks and a thin, almost entirely white goatee. Like Christ, Myshkin is a teacher, confessor and mysterious outsider. Passions such as greed and jealousy are alien to him. In contrast to those around him, he puts no value on money and power. He feels compassion and love, sincerely, without judgment. His relationship with the immoral Nastasya is obviously inspired by Christ's relationship with Mary Magdalene. He is called "Idiot" because of such differences.

Demons

The story of Demons (sometimes also titled The Possessed or The Devils) is based largely on the murder of Ivan Ivanov by "People's Vengeance" members in 1869. It was influenced by the Book of Revelation. The secondary characters, Pyotr and Stepan Verkhovensky, are based on Sergei Nechayev and Timofey Granovsky respectively. The novel takes place in a provincial Russian setting, primarily on the estates of Stepan Verkhovensky and Varvara Stavrogina. Stepan's son Pyotr is an aspiring revolutionary conspirator who attempts to organise revolutionaries in the area. He considers Varvara's son Nikolai central to his plot, because he thinks that Nikolai lacks sympathy for mankind. Pyotr gathers conspirators such as the philosophising Shigalyov, the suicidal Kirillov and the former military man Virginsky. He schemes to consolidate their loyalty to him and each other by murdering Ivan Shatov, a fellow conspirator. Pyotr plans to have Kirillov, who is committed to killing himself, take credit for the murder in his suicide note. Kirillov complies and Pyotr murders Shatov, but his scheme goes awry. Pyotr escapes, but the remainder of his aspiring revolutionary crew is arrested. In the denouement, Nikolai kills himself, tortured by his own misdeeds.

The Brothers Karamazov

At nearly 800 pages, The Brothers Karamazov is Dostoevsky's largest work. It received both critical and popular acclaim and is often cited as his magnum opus. Composed of 12 "books", the novel tells the story of the novice Alyosha Karamazov, the non-believer Ivan Karamazov and the soldier Dmitri Karamazov. The first books introduce the Karamazovs. The main plot is the death of their father Fyodor, while other parts are philosophical and religious arguments by Father Zosima to Alyosha.

The most famous chapter is "The Grand Inquisitor", a parable told by Ivan to Alyosha about Christ's Second Coming in Seville, Spain, in which Christ is imprisoned by a ninety-year-old Catholic Grand Inquisitor. Instead of answering him, Christ gives him a kiss, and the Inquisitor subsequently releases him, telling him not to return. The tale was misunderstood as a defence of the Inquisitor, but some, such as Romano Guardini, have argued that the Christ of the parable was Ivan's own interpretation of Christ, "the idealistic product of the unbelief". Ivan, however, has stated that he is against Christ. Most contemporary critics and scholars agree that Dostoevsky is attacking Roman Catholicism and socialist atheism, both represented by the Inquisitor. He warns the readers against a terrible revelation in the future, referring to the Donation of Pepin around 750 and the Spanish Inquisition in the 16th century, which in his view corrupted true Christianity. (Source: Wikipedia)